RITERS

ROY HARRIS

This book was written in part with grants from the Gilmore Foundation and the Greater Kalamazoo Council of the Arts.

Cover painting by Sarah Lynn Meyers

Library of Congress Control Number: 2021906786

ISBN: 979-8-89031-667-7 (sc)
ISBN: 979-8-89031-668-4 (hc)
ISBN: 979-8-89031-669-1 (e)

THE EWINGS
PUBLISHING

One Galleria Blvd., Suite 1900, Metairie, LA 70001
(504) 702-6708

The lieutenant realized in that moment, what few people ever come to know . . . that not only was he a victim of outrageous fortune, he was also one of her most ruthless perpetrators.

—Kurt Vonnegut,
The Sirens of Titan

Motive is everything.

—Sir Arthur Conan Doyle,
The Adventures of Sherlock Holmes

*For Sarah
and our girls*

FORWARD

That good looking fellow in the adjacent photograph is me at forty four years old. When I look at that picture I see in my faint smile, someone who still has in him a sense of wonder. Now, twenty nine years later, I don't think that would still be discernable in my old man's face. But I do know that despite the ravages of time and the chaos of living…it is still there. Over the years I have seen thousands of faces in which that glint has faded, erased by various applications of entropy's philosophical 'proof'—"defecate in one hand and wish in the other, and see which fills up faster." My purpose in writing this book was to rejuvenate that sense of wonder in those who still possess it, and bring it back from

the dead for those who don't. In order for this revival to be convincing
I would need to wade into the heart of mayhem and what better way
than in a dystopian tale of the future. I've always been a big fan of
science fiction. But, I also realized that the only way to navigate the
madness humanity is prone to and have any hope of keeping all hands
on deck during the sex, drugs, and rock and roll of violence, would
be to employ the perspective of farce and the bizarre humor it fosters.
In full disclosure, I need to let you know this is not an "easy" book to
read. There is a good deal of "future jargon" which is designed to make
you feel like an alien in an alien world. Uncertainty is prerequisite to
seeing things differently. I make a point of defining all these various
terms in context, at least twice on the page they are introduced. So, it's
not that hard to pick up the lingo if you pay attention. I just want your
attention. Right now, you are probably asking yourself, who does this
guy think he is? For the purposes of this book, I'm the one who wants
to reignite that sense of wonder.

PROLOGUE

September 16, 2197

C-power hum was audible in the belly of the ship as Splatter slowly negotiated the ramp to the podium. Shuta, kneeling at its base, took the opportunity to discreetly raise his head and glance across to where the assembly sat. He was hoping to spot Dysan's personal sash. Larger than most, it would stand out. They'd drawn from the entire color spectrum, choosing a jump to wear for the centennial celebration, though some had stayed to either end of the palate to ensure a semblance of decorum at the long-awaited rite. They all thought Shuta was insane, using a Musashi match to declare himself for Dysan's consideration—and on such an important day for her house. But it was the only way he could make his formal request. Her house had to be present at the assembly, and so would be forced to acknowledge him—if he won. To say they wouldn't give him the time of day otherwise was putting it mildly.

He finally spotted her buoyant mane, shining blacker than the raven jump she wore. She was moving higher up. On his periphery, Splatter's ebony arms grasped the podium, and Shuta quickly lowered his head. The old man's guttural rasp rumbled through the chamber, invoking their fromness with the ritual G. Harrison verse: "A time will come when you'll see we're all one, and life goes on within you and without you." The last three words were delivered in a tone intended especially for Shuta. He could feel Splatter's eyes boring into his cranial stem.

"Today, on the hundredth anniversary of the beginning of our journey, we will have all our questions answered concerning the mysterious events that made it possible—revealed by the house sworn to silence for a hundred years! Today, we will finally know the opening chapter."

But first, the old man was going to make them sweat through what little they already knew.

"An astronaut training for a prolonged galaxy probe was being tested for communication deprivation. During the thousands of minutes without any screens, a remarkable thing happened. He remembered a purple room and being held by a woman. He'd never before recalled anything so far back in his life. After being released from his chamber, he soon forgot the woman and being held, but he did remember remembering. And he wondered why he couldn't remember anything past the day before yesterday. As a sort of game, he started holding bytes in his mind, not sharing them with the screens. His name was Harrison, Jack. 'Harrison, Jack, who never looks back,' he muttered the rhyme in the odd moments between screens to prod his embryonic memory."

A spacecase hero called Harrison, Jack. Shuta didn't think he would ever stand outside his shadow, not in Dysan's eyes at any rate. Putting himself forward for consideration by her (especially today) was even more stupid than falling in love with Harrison's great-granddaughter. Now on his knees, neck stretched, Shuta listened as Splatter droned on about "grandpa's" abilities.

"He was String trained, a spacecase! If Harrison wanted to, he could suck up bytes the way a dead star eats up space. But he didn't think to bother. Appropriate-recall was online. Why waste the energy except for a game? As time passed, he felt the urge to play his knowing game more and more until finally it became as fascinating as his Screx."

Shuta suppressed a snicker. Screx! What a debauched bunch of zombies they were, floating in their "Barka Buckers" at the end of the day. Being thoroughly immersed in the reality of your choice—anything, do or be done unto you—all in the privacy of your own mode. At the beginning of the twenty-first, screens converted to digital with over 1,200 lines of resolution in "high definition" and 3-D. Colors glowed with a hot richness; so inundating retinas that overloaded optic nerves were buzzing every pleasure center in the brain. *Hyperreality* had arrived.

Add the multitude of chem enhancers around—*drugs*, as they were affectionately known—with personal fiber-feeds providing very personal services, and you had one hell of a sensational life! But a quest for the total tactile experience drove them to the breakthrough christened *Screx*. Introduced in 2059, the premiere Fuji Topgridder looked like a golden sun hovering over a rectangular black slab. Suspended in the magic ball, you could fuck your favorite Screenrage, saw off an offending clonie's balls with a rusty butter knife, and be crowned god of the universe by adoring billions—all in under an hour.

It was everything the first Maytags in Levittown promised it would be: Screx was the end of the line.

Screx technology was configured to perform a very different function now, one that Shuta longed to share with Dysan. The image of their glistening bodies locked in Lotus, heads on each other's shoulders, holding on for dear life, as imagination rides the waves of a lover's unconscious—spinning through a million traces, searching past a thousand lies, finally tasting grail—everything shared in their shuddering bodies. That was the stuff dreams got made of, and nothing was denied. Denial was no longer a necessity of life. Splatter's ceaseless growl pulled him back to his present plight.

"Having accumulated a quarter cycle of off-line time, Harrison applied for a mode transport to Cincinnati retrieval, an archaic computer bank located in the waste fill outside of Big New. Once there, he used the String to quickly run through all the bytes from the past. Then he did it again and again and again, until eventually the idea of a tracked time continuum registered in his brain, growing quickly into a concept of history—human history—in which he was the first Topgridder in over a decade to comprehend. And just as this amazing discovery was being tentatively reined in, he encountered something far different from all the screen-induced sensations he'd ever known, his first individual feeling—empathy for the ones behind. Harrison felt the fromness in him."

Under respectfully lowered lashes, Shuta watched the crowd "feel" for their hero. Conversely, he felt no empathy for Harrison or his contemporaries, using screens to fuel their isolated fanaticizing, incorporating personal images into themes of self-aggrandizement, making their somnambulant amble in numbed mortal coils—all while screens tickled screens around the globe, providing ever brighter orgasmic displays. The machine hummed along while they all nodded off and eventually went on to organize everybody's day. Not quite inured to the luxury of their electronic attendants, they made an entertainment out of their anxieties concerning the computers developing a consciousness and taking over. A preoccupation that became their "sci-fi cliché." It never occurred to the dolts. The machines didn't have to wake up to put them all to sleep. Gradually, they turned their lives over to an automatic pilot that, with pathetic irony, was called Appropriate-recall. The medium, already the message, became the messenger as well. They were morons.

And furthermore, may I point out to your prattling "pompitus," before that, they tried to obliterate the entire planet in 3TC, "Third time's a charm!" which proved one thing: electronic data systems could at least perform their survival function. It also proved that, under enough stress, all forms of government fail. Over the entire planet, a reversion to regionalism and local councils prevailed.

Crawling from under the rubble, the "movers and shakers" used their stored data to put it all back together. They incorporated sweeping changes in transportation based on breakthroughs made in electromagnetic superconductivity just before everything was blown to hell. Pulse-grid systems based on these new electronic capabilities made it possible to create "E-Mag" highways for levitated vehicles to travel on. They finally freed themselves of fossil fuels. Advancements in lightweight materials with extremely high tensile strength allowed them to create interlocking modular units with plumbing and electrical capabilities built right in, revolutionizing construction. Thrown to the very edge of their prehistoric beginnings, they wanted only to rebuild and rebuild faster and better now.

Fortunately, they no longer had an overpopulation problem. Unfortunately, the planet had been used up at a furious rate. 3TC left innumerable "hot spots" with global wind currents carrying the deadly particles, hither and yon.

Then too the oceans were poisoned, and the entire ozone layer was gone. They realized they were not long for this world. Shuta found it hard, never having set foot on a planet, not to loathe the dumb fucks. So the Seven Cartels (7, as they came to be known, comprised of the elite 1 percent) put their heads together to find some way to get off the old dirt ball and still survive. The pressure of diminished time spawned a breakthrough in producing lower subzero temperatures, which led to the development of more powerful electromagnetic generators. That made it possible to design high-intensity microscopic lasers, and that perfected fusion drive. With uncharacteristic simplicity, the scientific community dubbed these combined energies *C-power*.

They built castles in the sky, then satellite cities ("Satcits") spinning around the Earth like tiny moons. Eventually, only Sackers, along with techies and the inhabitants of Bellytown, remained permanently on its surface. Still, two great cities hovered above that surface. Sanatan, their final attempt at resort heaven, was located near the North Pole, where monolithic subzero units were submerged to recreate the arctic ice. With a mean temperature of thirty-four degrees and powdery beaches, Sanatan did a booming business with the new order. Topgridders, they were called. They visited Sanatan for cool fun, gambling, and any medical needs that arose. The other urban wonder was Big New, where spacious modes were kept to escape the close quarters of Satcits and oversee the final extraction of their inheritance.

Originally built by 7 as the testing ground for their new technologies, Big New was the place for visionary entrepreneurs from each cartel to come together. It was the megatropolis where street level began, two grids above the charred skeleton of the Freedom Tower. Shuta had seen holos of the great burg. Super E-Mags made it possible to use the steel from all the burnt-out scrapers (fire-bombed instead of nuked, presumably for the real estate), connecting all their blackened hulls and energizing the whole mass to a positive polarity, creating a gigantic electromagnet. Then they positioned a sealed "Valhalla," its foundation plate coated with strontium-yttrium (also energized to positive polarity) over the remains. This created the Meissner effect, and the monstrous burg hung perpetually suspended over old New York and all her five boroughs. Below, the dark old city refused to die and, in fact, grew. Composed of virus-carrying slime called bellygridders, they scrambled in a cindered ruin called Bellytown. Beneath them lived the final hope of mankind.

Vague contempt was all Shuta could "feel" for Topgridder Harrison, Jack. It wasn't a topic he brought up with Dysan. Frankly, he was hoping her long-awaited account would provide him with insights that might change his opinion. Thank God, Splatter was finally reaching his crescendo.

"On his last night in the bowels of Cincinnati retrieval, Harrison sat scanning rapidly through the earliest disks, looking for some direction from the ones left behind. Suddenly, slipping silently past his eyes, the screen briefly displayed ten words—"A life unexamined is not worth the living." Source: Socrates. Something about the exotic name of the author and the godlike accountability in the statement staggered him. The painful irony of a passionate commitment to personal awareness, coupled with the certainty that the author was ancient dust, produced the second personal emotion Harrison ever felt . . . compassion. Now he understood the purpose of his knowing game. He wanted to leave something behind, some personal insight for some unknown searcher in the march of time.

"His first day back in Big New, Harrison stole a micro-thought-recorder. That night in his mode, after tapping his screens off-line, he took a small survival disk and preformed a crude implant on the left side of his head, just behind the temple and above the ear, near the language center of his brain. Touching the spot, he heard a familiar voice repeating his thoughts, *Shit! That hurts.*

"It took thirteen hours from the discovery of the theft for relevant machines to do an information interface of the data and create a demographic previewing Harrison as primary on the scene. It took Sackers less than three minutes to rip the thought recorder out of his skull, and another twenty-two minutes in surgery to remove his Appro-recall Ident. Fortunately, because of a glitch at 7, he was still listed off-line, not on active spacecase records. That meant his wave amp remained in place. It took four more days to ship him to the mines. So began the journey of our very first Riter."

And today, a hundred years after they set foot on *Protostar*, while Dysan wrestled with the archaic "ballpoint and paper," revealing secrets passed down by four generations of her house, Shuta was going to try keeping his head on his shoulders, playing the "String game."

CHAPTER

Alaska

Late September 2096

His legs were badly cramped. He worried he wouldn't be able to stand when they were finally released. From time to time, holes permeating the container produced pin shafts of light supplying flickering glimpses of dazed, despairing faces. They'd all taken the tranqs. Food tabs were used up, as were elimination blockers. Not more than a couple of hours before they'd be up to their necks in diarrhea. Long gone was the bracing filtered air of Big New. When the transport landed and their containers were transferred, it was in the combustive, rotting odor of the waste fill. On this final leg of the journey, their container was being carried by a ground vehicle, and the constant jolting had taken its toll. Tranq vomit was the predominant odor now. He'd never ridden in a ground vehicle before, except on the C-power trains that zipped around Sanatan. But they didn't actually touch the ground. Travel must've been endless hell back when they used these crates. He remembered seeing screens of the lumbering machines at Cincinnati retrieval. Briefly ignoring his misery and terror, he smiled. He hadn't run his bytes in days, not since being bagged.

Suddenly they lurched to a stop. The container's lid started to whine, open, and he was blinded by a searing light. The naked sun knifed through the growing fissure as the huge container began upending. Everybody was screaming. Harrison grabbed an edge and tried to hold on. Another desperate coke grabbed his legs and soon he was falling. He landed on a tangle of bodies just before someone landed on him. Clawing through the writhing torsos, he fought to escape being crushed. Squirming frantically toward the light, he finally burst from the human roil and fell a couple centigrid to the ground.

Feeling the dirt with his fingers, he realized this must be real ground, just as a Topgrid gourmand spurted from the mound, landing three hundred kilos beside him. He was thanking his lucky stars for the near miss when the gourmand unexpectedly rolled over on top of him. When he eventually managed to poke his head out from under the blubber, the sun was still burning. He worried he didn't have an image on. *The sun will irradiate me*, he thought and was surprised by his own burst of laughter. *What's a little radiation when you're being fried?*

Frying was in progress. He could hear the truncated screams above the grating buzz and smell the burning flesh. A boot like a piston blew the gourmand off him, and Harrison looked up to see the black-plated form of a Sacker slide into view. Just when he was sure his luck had run out, a magnificent coke appeared behind the Sacker, yelling at him. With chiseled features and muscles bulging in perfect symmetry beneath his khaki jump, Harrison was shocked to realize he'd seen this blond giant somewhere before.

The two were arguing furiously. About what, he had no idea. Being Topgrid all his life, he'd never bothered to learn Amerab. The blond ended the altercation by bending down, scooping him up, and walking away.

"Waiting to fry under some clonie and you laugh, evil cap!" The blond let out a mirthful roar. Dazed and dangling in the giant's grasp, he was again surprised. This coke spoke English, as well as Amerab, and with the fosh from Big New at that.

His eyes were adjusting to the light now, and in the giant's arms, he had an excellent vantage point to see where he was. Where he was, was a great earthen pit that measured at least ten grid square, entirely surrounded by snowcapped purple mountains jutting up into infinite blue. Sackers were still frying the cokes, too injured to stand. Their screams filled his ears, but for a moment, all savagery was diminished to a dark disturbance in the lower frame as Harrison took in the splendor of the place. Nothing in the screens could touch it.

Ahead, what had to be another ground vehicle waited, a rectangular cube perched on metal treads with a ramp leading into the interior. The giant carried him up the ramp, and they were swallowed by darkness. He felt himself being gently lowered onto a shelf. The bladelike pain of broken ribs stabbed him in both sides. He heard what he assumed was the sound of the ramp retracting. The vehicle started to move, and Harrison realized how much he was dreading another land ride. With the second jolt, he blacked out.

He woke from the itching sensation created by the heat-tape wrapped around his ribs. He was desperately trying to scratch its plastic surface when he opened his eyes and took in his surroundings. Now he was in a concrete room with one wall of bars. He was lying on a metal shelf. The lock in the wall of bars stood open. Cradling the soreness in his torso, he cautiously raised himself up and swung his legs down. As if on cue, the blond giant reappeared, standing in the lockway.

"Up? Good. You slept well." He pointed to the tape around Harrison's ribs. "Probably a three-day mend. You keep sleeping like that!" He ventured a step through the lockway.

Tensing, Harrison remained seated, taking him in. Technically, he wasn't really a giant, but he was well over two centigrid. Very big and, as noted earlier, powerfully muscled for speed and balance. He would pass for a giant till one came along. He remembered now where he'd seen the golden mane, crystal blue eyes, hammered jaw, and winsome smile. He was Screenrage. Harrison used him in Screx orgies.

His memory was hazy, but he was pretty sure he'd fucked him several times. Those crystal eyes suddenly grew wider. He was quick.

"You recognize me, don't you?" The blond's lubricious roar echoed off the concrete walls. "Well, I'll be damned." He bent down, bringing the big grin closer. "Not to worry, I wasn't really there, was I?" Again, he burst out with his deafening laugh, thrusting forward his right fist and extending the middle finger.

"Larkill, Han. What's your ID?"

Harrison stared at the overly familiar gesture a moment before finally extending his fist in the same manner, touching Larkill's finger with his own. "Harrison, Jack."

"Cliqued." Larkill quickly snatched the hand away. "I knew you were pure Topgrid the moment I laid eyes on you. That Sacker wanted to fry you anyway. I think it pissed him off, you laughing."

"So why save me?"

"Looking for the vector, eh, Topgrid? I'm going to use you. That's why."

It was very bizarre, hearing this coke talk to him like some mutant scab. Instantly, all the repressed anger at his recent misfortunes came percolating to the surface. Despite the shooting pain in both sides, Harrison stood and began visualizing his pattern. This "Larkill" might be big and quick, but the "Fiber Fool" was in for a nasty surprise if he thought he could make a spacecase his personal slave.

As the Screenrage watched the air around him vibrate into a bluish haze, his cocky sneer shattered in a mosaic of terror. Slowly, he backed outside the lockway, great jaw sagging, blue eyes big as platters. Eventually, he managed a whisper, "You're a spacecase. Holy motherduffer, you're a fucking spacecase."

"I've been up." Harrison couldn't suppress a smile, letting his pattern go.

Larkill continued to gawk, watching the blue fog dissipate. Finally, he spoke again, still in the hushed voice, "Well, I'm a very lucky coke." Making a tentative reach through the bars, he pointed to a small black box above the lock inside his cell.

"Boot up! Enjoy your recovery time. Then we'll talk." Still incredulous, Larkill slowly backed down the corridor a few paces, then turned and hurried away.

Now it was Harrison's turn to be incredulous. When the giant challenged him, he'd just snapped to his pattern. In the moment, he forgot that he'd been bagged. *He forgot his operation!* If they'd taken out his wave amp, along with his Appro-recall, he wouldn't be able to jump the String. But he had . . . well, almost. If he could get to the fourth, he could get to the fifth. The only explanation was, they screwed up. *They hadn't taken out his wave amp!* This was an unbelievable zap. It was a reprieve beyond his wildest dreams, almost more than he could take in. He fixed on the black box again, trying to wrap his head around his extraordinary good fortune. It had a small screen with two knobs beneath it—one large and one small. He turned the small one. The screen sputtered on. Two ghostly figures in shades of gray frantically ran around inside it. He turned the larger knob.

"LUUUUCY . . . YOU GOT SOME 'SPLAININ' TO DO!"

"BUT, RICKY! WAAAAAAA! WAAAAAAAAA! WAAAAAAAAAAA!"

Quickly turning the knobs back, he watched the anemic glow die in the glass. So this was hell. Well, now he could escape. It would be tube-play once he reconned the place. He'd live up in those purple mountains, if that's what it took to alter this miserable fate. First, he'd need to get some things: a small levi-loader stacked with provisions, Sacker body armor, and a frybar—things he could acquire effortlessly on the String. It was unfortunate he had to lose his temper in front of the Screenrage to realize he still had his spacecase abilities. If Sackers found out, he was dead. But he'd seen those Screenrage "wheels" start spinning. Larkill would keep it to himself while he figured out some scheme to use him, and he'd play along until he was ready to make his move.

Glancing around the rest of the cell, he remembered the balcony of his mode in Big New: the cool breeze that always blew, the distant glow of the smoldering waste fill at night. Who knows, maybe a new paradise waited in the purple mountains. Whatever waited would be better than the gray barrenness he was presently forced to call mode.

In the weeks that followed, he learned his original assessment wasn't far off. They all had to adjust to the reduced quality of life that came with their new nonstatus. That consisted of being locked in an ancient penal colony, working fourteen- to sixteen-hour days, having two hours at night to watch their black boxes and view decrepit vids, around 150 cycles old. Most cokes were assigned to the fabrication factories, but he and a lucky few were selected for deep-dig training. Much to his surprise, he found himself becoming fascinated with the leviathan machines that burrowed far beneath the planet's surface, hunting basic metals, precious metals, and the real mother lode for 7, the rare Earth metals so necessary for their machines. He'd never even heard of a "Screwhog" before coming here. They did their training on mockups as the real Hogs were based beneath the surface at underground foundries. He was so intrigued to actually see one he decided to postpone his escape until after he'd gone on his first dig.

It turned out, Han Larkill was a Screwhog pilot, which made him a valuable slave. He was allowed to go out with "greeting parties" for the purpose of finding worthy candidates for deep-dig. Luckily for Harrison, he'd spotted the port for a C-comp receptor on the side of his head and threatened to report the Sacker who wanted to fry him. That receptor proved he could run a C-power rig, which meant he could handle the subzero units in a Screwhog. That was his salvation.

He'd seen the blond several times when returning from his training sessions. They'd talked briefly, nothing of consequence, just exchanging "pleasantries." It wasn't until the night before he was going on his first dig that their discussions took a serious turn. He was out on the walled grid, an area they could walk in for an hour in the evening if they didn't care to watch the vids. The last slice of sun was just a golden bar on the rim of one wall as Larkill approached him. It made a radiant halo above the giant's curls. He stopped a centigrid away from Harrison.

"Not watchin' your screen? Not quite, Topgrid, hm?"

"Not quite."

"You must have been a big user. Probably had the full Fuji rig . . . yeah, sure you did. You made me. You had to be a serious juicer, right?"

"I did a bit."

"A bit, shit! You probably humped every hole in the universe. That's what they bagged you for . . . getting hung up in your Screx?"

Harrison ignored the question, and after a pause, Larkill took a step closer. "No offense, spacecase. I just know how Topgrid like their Screx. That was my line of work, after all." Larkill gave him a sly grin.

"What's the cap, Han?"

"Thought I'd let you know, I cut a piece for you. You're gonna be the new drive-assist on my Screw."

Of course, he should have seen it coming. "Do I get a decoder ring too?"

Larkill stared back at him, uncomprehending.

"Private joke, old mold."

Fury lit those big blue eyes, and for the moment, it was clear. He'd forgotten his fear. "I had a grid badge, spacecase! I was top plenty of times. Just like you, 'an apple for sore eyes in Big New'. I had one hellashious bellymode. Put your crumby Topgrid dump to shame. Had enough graft to snag a Fuji implant, didn't I? A bit longer with an ID, and I'd have been pure Topgrid! So don't give me any of your better-than-best screenshit."

Harrison watched Larkill fume, reminding himself it was in his best interest not to piss the Screenrage off too much. Besides, he'd just learned something very interesting. This coke had been a bellygrid. He was obviously from a top lab, maybe even Ruger. That meant he'd been snagged by a Bellytown kingpin. Harrison was curious to hear his tale, but not until he calmed down. He waited, watching the sun slip completely behind the wall before making his innocuous query. "So what happened?"

Larkill grinned. "You show me yours, and I'll show you mine."

Why not? He already knew he was spacecase. "I tried to make a personal record. I stole a thought recorder."

"You, Topgrid motherduffer! A personal record?" Han cut loose with the jocular roar. "Just wanted to fuck your own terminal, huh?"

Put like that, he did feel a little foolish. Making a personal record was in a way sucking your own jerk. It took him a moment to come up with a suitable retort. "So what happened to you? You finally stick it in live bait?"

Larkill stopped laughing so quickly Harrison thought he might have gone too far. But slowly an evil grin split the entire expanse of the giant's face. "Exactly . . . that's exactly what I did. I had an urge for the real thing . . . and I had it."

"You're lying."

"Am I, spacecase?" The wicked smile stayed in place.

Harrison was dumbfounded. Oh, he'd heard of pitiful bellygrid mixing their juices in the dark spindled towers of Bellytown, performing lewd vids for other bellygrid to watch on their ancient screens. But to think he'd actually cliqued with a coke who'd done a live sheed—was it a sheed?

"With a sheed?" he finally croaked. The grin still unchanged, Larkill coyly nodded and Harrison saw he really wasn't lying. Here stood a coke who'd done a live sheed. Insane! Myth was just to hook screens. Cokes spent lifetimes sifting through personal fiber-feeds, toying with the idea of linking up, becoming some clone's Screx-mate. Downloading personal profiles was as close as they ever got. Screx-mates were mostly comp-gen, except for Screenrage. Screenrage survived: the throwback to ancient "Hollywood." For those who could afford the special thrill of knowing real flesh was behind the image you were humping. And really, you could feel the difference. But Screenrage, like everyone else, avoided all secretive contact "LIKE THE PLAGUE?" as the zap campaign put it. What with HIV making a comeback after 3TC, when their pharmaceutical factories were destroyed and their drug-resistant superbugs (NDM-1 and KPC) thriving in the ruins, combined with the plethora of inherent diseases they carried in their genes, it was clear: lab conception was the only course. With the species soon to embark on a search for another planet, they were careful to avoid fluid discharge of any kind. Only the pure would be allowed to travel, almost entirely Topgrid. And any lowly bellygridder lucky enough to be free of disease and genetic defects who had the *pull* to stand on the moving walks of Big New did the same.

Yet here stood a lunatic who'd risked his entire future, one far brighter than most bellygrid ever dreamed of, for some slimy prehistoric act. A wave of nausea overwhelmed Harrison, appalled that his quest for a personal identity had brought him here, face-to-face with unconscionable depravity. He longed even more for those purple mountains and a final sacrifice of all things sensual. But Larkill wasn't finished, giving the knife in his gut a final twist.

"You'll clique four healthy sheed in our crew."

———•◆◆•———

The machine that earned the moniker Screwhog was a fascinating application of C-power and the most voracious mining tool ever conceived. As the ID implied, it was a silo-sized segmented niobium-titanium cylinder, fifty-centigrid long. It had a massive drill head that pulverized any material it bored into. It was comprised of an outer and inner hull. The inner hull was where the fusion core, subzero units, C-power generators, and crew resided. The outer hull contained the slag scoops, elemental separation diverters, kiln coils, kiln canals, storage tanks, heat exhaust, and baffles. The phenomenal amount of electrical energy created in a Screwhog not only powered the subzero units but also powered the massive kiln coils that melted the various metals and held them, liquefied, in ceramic storage tanks at the rear of the ship, encircled by the heat exhausts.

Any debris that remained was simultaneously crushed, heated, and pushed back until at the consistency of putty; it was pounded into glazed earthen walls by the baffling on the heat exhausts. Once cooled, it left a relatively smooth slag tunnel behind. When the cargo tanks were filled, scoops behind the drilling head were repositioned to lock into exhaust nozzles on four solid-fuel rocket engines (based on twentieth designs for launching cokes into space) located around the subzero units of the inner hull. These "surface thrusters," as the rockets were called, blasted the Hog back up to the robo kilns once they returned to their entry tunnel. In an emergency, their nozzles could also be connected to the heat exhausts. In the event the drilling head froze up or got stuck in whatever they were digging into, brief bursts from these thrusters would ram the Hog loose.

Harrison's job was second engineer. He was responsible for monitoring the subzero units while the first engineer was running the electromagnetic generators. Riding down with the rest of the crew in one of the central shaft's levitators, he was a little concerned that First Engineer Zim might not be much help on his maiden voyage. Zim, thin and angular with bright-pink hair, stood beside him, nervously wiping his view plate and running his tongue over glistening lips. Obvious Topgridder gone completely sensate, probably had to blow the lid off his Screx to get him out.

Besides Zim and Larkill, there were two other cokes—a short hairy one called Tooco, without a doubt a low-grade bellygridder; and a tall black called Baylor. Broad-shouldered and very muscular with a face like chipped obsidian, he was almost as imposing as Larkill, probably ex-Sacker.

Behind the cokes were the sheed Larkill mentioned, four of them. There was something about the way they moved, a kind of looseness to their gestures that made Harrison uneasy. For their part, they completely ignored him, giving only slight nods when introduced by their Screenrage captain. He couldn't remember any of their IDs. He'd only glanced at their view plates during the introductions. Harrison could tell they'd all been informed of his little secret. Clones usually kept a superstitious distance from a spacecase.

A level indicator blinked by proclaiming level 56. The Hogs were at 80. He watched as a huge stack of sheet metal passed by on a freight levitator, heading for the surface. The scent of smoldering ore was becoming overwhelming. The others darkened their view plates and tapped up oxygen. Harrison did likewise. Another indicator flashed level 72 as the red haze of the foundry fires began glowing from below. Slowly, a mammoth circular cavern at least eight grid in diameter came into view. There was more than enough room for the robo foundry at its center with ten Hog ports, spaced evenly around the circumference, all with feeder lines running directly to the kilns.

He could just make out two Sackers, both armed with frybars, and roughly a dozen techies monitoring operations. Apparently, many of the techies working in the mines were slimed. Even slimed, they could look forward to two weeks in Sanatan every cycle as long as they confined themselves to the techie quarter. If they managed to survive twenty cycles of service, they also enjoyed a brief retirement on Sunsat. Harrison had been to the agrarian satellite during an emergency repair on its rotational mechanism. One of its hundreds of levels of hydroponic soybean fields was set aside for their senescent retreat.

The levitator settled on level 80 with the crackling sounds of sudden reversed polarity. Larkill stepped out, and the crew followed, two abreast, under the watchful eye of the Sackers. Harrison paired up with Tooco at the end of the troop. Walking beside him, he realized just how short the bellygridder was. He was lucky if he made one and a half centigrid. Harrison measured a little under two centigrid, thanks to filtered air and healthy food. "Under the cool crystal dome, riding the quicksilver walks, talking that Topgridder fosh, an apple for sore eyes in Big New, Big, Big New!"

He could only imagine the strange path Tooco traveled to ultimately march beside him—the shrunken bellygridder "emerging from the flesh" far below, probably at the very base of the Great Grid Pillars. Under wane incandescent light, another scrambling predator clawing his way up, finally cutting a piece for a hit on some Big New replicator shop and getting bagged the "micro" his boot touched Topgrid. He couldn't help smiling at the thought. Still, he had to admit the runt must have been very tenacious to make it this far. No doubt, even here, life was appreciably better than in the bowels of Bellytown. He would've loved to hear the details of his subterranean heritage, but Tooco spoke only Amerab—poor Tooco.

Moments later, filing into a streamlined silver transporter, he was reminded of the "roller coasters" he'd viewed at retrieval. Riding out to the Hog, he pondered this newfound tool of perception: memory, correlating past with present. It was a process he discovered only after his Appro-recall ident was removed. He'd first become aware of it in his training sessions when associations popped into his head that were tangential to his lessons. Part of Appro-recall's function was to filter out associations between memory and the present, except where 7 tasks were concerned. Back in the container, when he realized he hadn't run his bytes in days, that was the reignition point of his memory. The random bytes from Cincinnati retrieval emerged in the training sessions because the firewall was no longer in place. Who knows what memories he could dredge up now; he knew they were there. Unfortunately, without the thought recorder, he couldn't actively reference them. If he thought about something, then related retrieval facts *might* pop in his head.

The Screwhog loomed suddenly in front of them. A pink-hued gunmetal jerk suspended inside a soaring steel tower, a bullet poised to plunge into the planet. Busy robos scoured outer-blade edges while their smaller brethren scrubbed the hundreds of minidrills embedded in the massive head. Still, other robo units moved up and down the tower, spraying coolant on the outer hull and heat exhausts. That pinkish tint was from the heat, still warm enough to make niobium-titanium blush. Ceramic nozzles from the robo kilns were disconnecting, retracting into the support tower as the transport pulled to a stop at the Hog's boarding platform. Disembarking into its levitator, they rode up to the entry cylinder. Upon stepping into the slate-blue capsule, each of them sealed their body plates and punched up internal thermostat. The Hog's internal temperature was probably fine, but this was a safety protocol initiated when a new crew entered a ship. The cylinder immediately moved forward, injecting itself into the Hog through aligned entry ports in the ship's double hull.

When the capsule slid open, Harrison viewed the inside of his first real Hog. Training mockups didn't do justice to the gleaming blackness of its strontium-yttrium interior. The entire inner hull was coated with the magical superconductor. The old way of channeling electrical energy crumbled with discoveries pioneered by electromagnetic superconductivity. It was a far scream from the ancient pathways of printed circuitry. On a strontium-yttrium frame, you could run an application with a specific series of taps (something like ancient Morse code), and with the appropriate hand unit, you could "tap" at any point for information or power. Developing ever more sophisticated "taps" was what technocrats busied themselves with nowadays.

The entry port into the Hog's inner hull was in the elemental separation chamber. The multitude of taps located on every surface was impressive. This was where Tooco performed. Maybe he'd been too short with the bellygridder. Harrison had to admit, he had an impressive command center—a gyro couch that was attached to a rotating arm, locked into an elaborate track system. Crouched in his couch, he could move anywhere in the chamber simply by manipulating the joystick between his knees.

One sheed worked in a gyro couch locked to one wall. She opened the kiln canals inside the outer hull, channeling every elemental grouping Tooco made. Harrison got a better look at her face when she jumped into her couch and cleared her view plate. It was a soft oval with deep-set black eyes that angled slightly upward at the corners. Her nose was broad but flat with flaring nostrils. Her mouth was small but full. The raven hair framing her features shined like the strontium-yttrium surface she faced. He caught himself wishing she were comp-gen.

"Okada!" Tooco barked her ID as he slipped into his couch. "Poppit."

She punched several taps, and the interior lit up like an X-mas tube. Tooco proceeded to take a spin around the chamber, performing lightning aerial feats before finally whipping in for a landing and drumming off his taps. "Doken." He climbed out while Okada closed the taps and unstrapped.

They followed Larkill into a clear plexi canister that was the ship's cramped levitator, heading to the C-power control center and, from there, to the ship's bridge. Runners of dark-gray electromagnetic carpet covered many areas of the glossy black interior as they continued down. That was so the crew could move around in the ship no matter what direction the Hog was pointed in. It entailed a kind of "forearms and knees" scuttle. You simply activated your jump and crawled your way along, even upside down.

The C-power control center was much less cluttered than the elemental separation chamber. All surfaces were covered by the ubiquitous gray carpet, except for the wall screens surrounding two gyro couches locked onto a circular track at the center of the mode. One of these couches would be Harrison's workstation. For their launch, he'd be on the bridge. After checking the chamber's oxygen content, Zim snapped off his helmet and brushed past the others. He hopped into the couch on his right, parting his spiny pink stalks at the temple then plugging a red cord into his head. Suddenly the screens lit up with bright displays of various diagnostic readouts. Zim looked up to make sure Harrison was watching before he punched out an elaborate percussion of taps. C-power hum kicked in as a huge surge of power bolted from the electromagnets. Apparently, Zim was skeptical of the vaunted powers of retention that spacecases possessed, watching Harrison's face for any sign of a quizzical expression. But the sequence was tube play.

"Just like your training vids." Zim's voice was much deeper than Harrison expected. "You can fire it up from now on." A snide smile slid over his elongated face. Both Larkill and Baylor started chuckling. Over his helmet's intercom, Harrison could hear the sheed joining in. He failed to get the cap. Tooco, it seems, was unhappy with his lack of agitation at being baited. Flipping up his view plate, he mock-spat in the direction of Harrison's boots to drive home their obscure taunt.

The edge of Larkill's hand cut an arc across the bellygridder's helmet. "Play nice." There was a brief silence as Larkill waited for any response, but Tooco only bowed his head, staring at the carpet. The Screenrage motioned them back to the Levitator, turning to address Zim. "Come up for launch."

Next, they rode down through crew quarters. From a brief glimpse, he realized everything was on a more spacious scale than he'd originally imagined.

Every crew member had a small personal niche with their ID on the lock. Life in a Hog wouldn't be so bad for the one trip he planned to take. When they reached the bridge, the levitator settled on the top ring of a series of four concentric rings. The bottom ring was no more than three centigrid in diameter. It contained Larkill's command couch, with a joystick on the left arm and command tap pad on the right. On the largest ring, where they stood, wraparound screens surrounded the entire circumference just above a carpeted wall. Once they reached the bottom of their entry tunnel, these screens would register strata patterns and formations up to two thousand grid from the ship. On the ring just below them, smaller screens were stacked four high. Beneath these screens was a circular tap pad, defining the ring's circumference. It was where the other three sheed sat in gyro couches locked on a circular track, monitoring all the internal systems of the Hog. The last ring before Han's was where Baylor spun 'round, constantly scanning everything and comparing the big screens on the top ring with the planned route projected on the bridge ceiling, trying to keep two things from happening—hitting an oil deposit or running into a magma flow.

Larkill climbed down the chrome step ladder that descended through the center of the rings. At the bottom, he slid into his couch and began tapping up the army of drills he commanded, making sure they were all online. Next, he pulled up the outer hull's temperature readings. Firing up a Hog was a delicate process, engaging the subzero units to keep the inner hull cool while simultaneously bringing up the temperature in the outer hull for the smelting process. You never let the kiln coils cool off completely because it took too long to get them back up. Larkill had to make sure the hulls' temperatures were diverging away from each other at the proper intervals. Zim would be monitoring the same thing in C-power control. It was a process to be closely watched. If a Hog was going to explode, this was when it blew. Satisfied things were progressing safely, he called up to the rest of the crew, "Strap up."

Baylor and the three sheed climbed down into their designated couches.

Harrison strapped into one of four, located near the Levitator entrance to the bridge. Okada and Tooco claimed the two on his right. Larkill punched off internal-thermostat and oxygen in his jump, then flipped up his face plate. The rest of the crew followed suit.

Now Harrison tried to get a good look at the sheed's faces as they zipped back and forth below him, busy activating numerous screens and taps. The tallest one spun around to face him first. Almost as big as Larkill, she too was obviously bred for Screenrage. Pale blonde hair framed the soft features of her face. From where he sat, looking down at a steep angle, her childlike expression was a stimulating paradox to her voluptuous frame. He tried to remember her ID. He was sorry he hadn't paid more attention when they cliqued. Maybe somewhere in his reawakened mind, hanging on a neuron at some obscure synapse, was a memory of the moment. Waiting for the levitator, Larkill introduced her first. He remembered her towering over him, her chestplate almost in his face. "Sunsue!"

"Yeah?" She stared up at him with wondrous cobalt eyes.

Harrison, realizing he'd just blurted out her ID, stared back, mute, amazed at this little magic in his head. Maybe the shine on her chestplate linked to her ID, under the general category of light? Sunsue grinned up at him.

"Stick to your Screx, Topgridder." She spun away on her track.

Next, the smallest one swung into view. Not much bigger than Tooco, curly red hair crowding the edges of her helmet, she was all business, staring at the screens with intense little eyes—Ryka. He had no idea how he'd come up with this ID but managed to keep it to himself this time. This was getting interesting.

The final sheed swung around beside Ryka. She was the last one Larkill cliqued as the levitator arrived. Concerned with boarding at the time, Harrison hadn't even bothered to look in her direction. Now he was riveted by her bizarre perfection. She was a Rebino, an ultraprincess from the upper reaches of Topgrid society. Genetically engineered to block the sun's ultraviolet rays without the aid of an image, every exterior cell of her body, with the exception of her jet-black mane, was an opaque marble white. The gleam of her porcelain lips and the glistening wetness of her ivory eyes were the only features that stood out in her statuesque patina. He couldn't begin to imagine what she'd done to end up here. He couldn't remember her ID either.

Zim emerged from the levitator and strapped into the last available couch on his left. Noting his arrival, Han gave the command, "Prepare to launch." He drummed the final tap, beating out a familiar syncopation to any pilot's ears. Harrison guessed the Screenrage could probably handle the console of a Satcruiser without much trouble. The *Protostar* would be another matter. The high whine of the drive reverberated through the front of the ship, and Harrison felt a slight tingling in the balls of his feet.

He pictured their imminent ride, looking something like retrieval vids of crude sleds barreling down icy runs. The big difference here was, this run would be on a 360-degree surface, and they'd reach speeds of 3,200 grid an hour—more like riding a runaway levi cycle straight to hell. He smiled, remembering a coke he'd watched "lose it" in Big New when the E-Mags on his levi cycle kept switching polarities on each other. There was nothing left but the goo in his boots when he finished bouncing off the scrapers he was flying through.

The screeching of runner blades partially rising out of the drill head joined the C-power hum. Functioning both as brake and guide rails on the trip down when fully extended, they enabled the Hog to turn and follow promising metallurgical veins.

"Launch."

The pit of Harrison's stomach hit the roof of his mouth as the massive ship hurled straight down, a monolith dropping at ten centigrid per second exponentially—ten seconds welded his helmet to the couch. At 15 G's, they suddenly banked thirty-two degrees right, wrenching him between concurrent g-forces, snapping his head to the left and prying open his mouth. He shook there for an eternity until his entire body convulsed. He briefly spied his half-digested soya disks spewing in the direction of Zim's couch. The last thing he heard was the "Toon voice" from a prison vid squawking in his head, "That's all, cokes!"

Han relished the sharp edges of Darl's nails cutting microscopic tracks along his spine, the gurgling laughter announcing her jungle cat. She loved to challenge on the mat, thrilled by her own boldness and the certain vanquishing to come. He'd seen the way "Jack" looked at her just before they launched, taking in her flawless white; far from his beloved Screx, thinking new thoughts in his musty Topgrid brain, having urges he hadn't dared dream of—to dip it in the real shy. Pathetic Screxhead.

They were all alike, although this one was slightly off. A personal record! *What could you possibly put in it, screen brain? You've never lived. It's all been in your fucking Screx!*

His father had loathed them too, but for a different reason. He was jealous of their effortless birthright, privy by selection to the perfect life. Yet his father had been wiser, quicker, and far tougher than any Topgrid clone he'd ever met. He'd forged an empire in the cloistered heavens of Bellytown, harnessing the electromagnetic storm under the grid plate. He was the magician who brought electric power to illuminate their night.

She bit his shoulder, growling as he forced her down, his knees spreading and pinning her thighs high and wide, like a butterfly in his father's study. He'd picked him from an observation room filled with dozens of Ruger toddlers. It was the first of their many miscommunications. Han was just beginning to enjoy the newfound superiority of standing when this other screenbait, apparently threatened by his joining their bipod ranks, came over and began beating him in the face with his pudgy little fists. Han let him go on for quite a while, blood finally trickling from his nose. Even as a tube-born, he had a strong presentiment of his power, standing there, genuinely amazed at the lack of temerity this foolish creature was displaying. The next thing he knew, his father was lifting him up in his arms, saying over and over, "There's my little angel."

Here's my little angel surrendering fnally, a changeling softness suffusing her body. Brushing his fingers down her porcelain belly, parting gossamer petals, he nuzzled the head of his elegant jerk into her glistening shy.

His father was one of those conundrums that survive and prosper because of their proficiency with various weapons, both physical and psychological, who then feel compelled to instill in their offspring a high and holy regard for all things genteel and civilized, believing an enlightened education consisted of extracting your progeny's canines! Han honored him, though, learning to mimic his appreciation for the tepid civilities of cokekind. To please him, he applied to become a Screenrage at the age of eleven and was allowed to begin his studies in Big New, a precious Topgrid for two hours a day. He'd observed them up close then.

Moaning her mantra, she began cooing, "Uh-huh," chanting over and over, a mindless affirmation of her sensual abandon when coming to a boil. He loved seeing that statuesque purity dissolve in the carnal mire, rivulets of passion rippling from her marble cleft. He loved secretions most of all. Sinking himself into blossoming pink, he felt her nectar soothe his aching shaft.

Han spent a little of his Topgrid time playing in their Screx, enough to know it was exactly what you wanted. Evil cap! There was no real risk, no real adventure, no discoveries—just you and your wildest fantasies alone together.

It was in their eyes. It was over before it started. They were record before they ever took a step. Disked and docked, and that was fine by them. They were safe, and they were comfortable. They had all the pleasure they could handle, any illusion they desired. As an added bonus, they didn't even have to remember where they left their minds— "Appro-recall's got you covered! What you wanna know?"

He would've joined the Yakuza in Bellytown and become a terrorist if there'd been anything left to take back. But it was all gone, used up on a grand scheme to send them out into the universe. It pained him that his father never saw them for what they were—pathetic, asleep at the stick, twits. Well, they'd let their spacecase sleep awhile longer and recover from gravity sickness and an ample cup of Booz. Soon enough, he'd learn what a surprise they had in store for him. Urgent now, Han submerged himself in her overflowing bliss.

⚬━◆━⚬

Something was very weird. Harrison remembered throwing up. He remembered passing out, remembered regaining consciousness and being helped back to his mode, Zim telling him to rest, giving him something to drink. It was the infernal screeching of the runner blades that finally woke him from his stupor. They were boring a wider chamber for the Hog to turn in a new direction. He should be at his station in C-power control. He sat up and began pulling on his boots, listening to transmissions on the intercom speaker just above his mat. It was Larkill and the techie back at the Hog port, monitoring their operations. The techie sounded mad. He was demanding Han transmit seismic readouts of their present location before authorizing any deviation from their predetermined course. Larkill's contempt dripped from the speaker as he shouted there wasn't time! He was busy turning the Hog to avoid an underground magma flow erupting into their projected path. Han screamed at the techie. He'd have to wait until they weren't so preoccupied with trying to stay alive.

Harrison finished with his boots, grabbed his helmet, and slapped the lock open. He ran to the levitator, slapped it open, and leapt inside. He hit the press plate marked "C-power control" and felt his knees buckle as the levitator lifted off. He was still a little woozy. The Screwhog was finally making the turn, and both the inner and outer hull began to rotate from the torque. He could feel the shuddering as the segments unlocked to allow for the turn. By the time the levitator opened, Harrison was already on all fours. Punching up his jump's electromagnetic field, he began scuttling over the gray padding toward his station. Boring a path for their escape, the drill head's accelerated speed was deafening now. The Hog continued to torque clockwise as the first two segments behind the drill head began turning to the right.

When he slapped open the lock, it revealed Zim in his gyro couch, completely upside down.

"Well, well, welcome to crisis central. Didn't think, I'd see you for a while. Might as well crawl over to your couch and plug up. Just get comfortable, and I'll interpret data as it arrives."

Supercool from this freak was the last thing Harrison expected. He crawled across the ceiling and pulled himself into his couch. He found the red cord on his right armrest and plugged it in his head.

"You know, you're a little clumsy for a spacecase. By the way, I believe I owe you a meal." Zim's soprano giggle was a bizarre contrast to his low-timbered speaking voice.

"How close is the flow?" Harrison was getting annoyed at this pink-haired clone, but before Zim could reply to his query, Larkill was back on the intercom, answering for him.

"Estimate three minutes to contact. We may just have time to complete the turn and get out of its path."

Zim yawned, and Harrison considered crawling over and strangling him.

"Wake up, you Screx-fried piece of shit! We're about to die!"

"Is this an example of the 'nerves of titanium' we're led to believe our spacecase possess?"

Suddenly Harrison knew it was all a setup, something they'd concocted to make him look the fool on his first voyage under—some sophomoric initiation ritual—power games in their little kingdom a hundred grid beneath the planet's crust. The warning siren to punch up internal-thermostat and oxygen began to wail. The fact Zim made no move to put on his helmet and seal up his jump confirmed his suspicions.

Harrison gave the creep a withering glance. "So what now? We die?"

"Exactly! Listen." Zim cocked his head expectantly. The thought occurred to Harrison, he wasn't the butt of their joke.

The techie broke in again, "Give me precise coordinates, deep dig 5, *precise coordinates*!"

The techie—this was all for the techie.

There was a horrific tearing sound. Harrison felt no jarring or vibrations, but the noise grew until it was maddening. Various warning sirens were signaling breeches in the hull. He looked up to see Zim spinning in his gyro couch and giggling hysterically. The hog completed its turn, and the hull began to rotate counterclockwise, realigning the ship to the center of gravity. Zim stopped his spinning and made a quick double tap on his control console. Immediately, there was a loud explosion behind the ship, and this time, Harrison felt the vibrations!

"What in Dog's ID was that?"

Zim unstrapped from his couch, unplugged from the console, and started for the lock. "That was it! The end. Let's eat. I'm starved."

Harrison was quick enough to reach him before he made it to the lock. He grabbed one gangly arm. "What's going on?"

"Oooh, gonna get rough? I like it rough."

Harrison increased the pressure of his grip, but Zim's contemptuous expression only hardened. "What are you gonna do, kill me then take off on your String? I know a little bit about your *supposed* powers. You'd have to eat a lot of rock to get back to the surface. You'd be merged with heavy-density matter for a long time before you saw the sky. I bet you wouldn't even have two days of core left if you snagged your big String now." He released the scrawny wacko's arm.

"Or I could go back up the tunnel we dug to get down here, genius. Just tell me what's going on."

Zim's chagrin was apparent behind his still-dismissive sneer. "All right, have you been watching your old vids? You've just joined a 'prison break'. We were going to surprise you, but I guess your medication wore off a tad early. We wanted to spare you all the commotion. We're escaping!"

That's why Harrison felt so strange. It wasn't just the g-forces; he'd been drugged. "Escaping where?"

Zim slipped past him through the lock. "Han will explain everything. You're a very lucky clone."

The party was in full swing by the time Harrison and Zim stepped into the food center. Larkill was merrily holding court over by the food replicator, a large flask in one hand, pouring drinks into plastic cups being thrust in front of him by members of the crew.

"Ah, here he is, back from the dead, Harrison! Welcome to the first real freedom."

"I told him, he was a lucky clone!" Zim rushed to get a cup and have it filled.

"Some pruno, Harrison?" Larkill held out the flask.

Harrison had heard of the bellygrid brew but never seen or tasted it. The Screenrage waved the flask back and forth, beckoning him. A fecund aroma wafted over the mode. It smelled like the drink, Zim gave him.

"It's safe, made by techies." The remark produced an explosion of mirth, Tooco spraying the front of his jump with the reeking fluid.

"To techies, everywhere!" Larkill raised his cup, and the others did likewise. He locked eyes with Harrison, who hadn't moved since entering the center.

"What's the matter, Topgrid? Don't you want to share our common brew?"

Harrison gave Zim another withering glance. "No, thanks. I've already tried it." His eyes went back to the Screenrage. "Where are we going, Han?"

Baylor, whose back was to Harrison, turned and eyed him with a look of total hatred. "What the fuck gave you the idea we have to answer to you?" He took a step toward Harrison. "You pathetic piece of spaceshit."

"Better watch out, Jack. You're dealing with an ex-Sacker." This from an already-elated Zim.

Baylor took another step in his direction. "I'm not afraid of your String. I'll wrap your String around your fucking neck!"

"Bay! You know you're a mean drunk." Larkill stepped between them, turning to Harrison. "We're going to Sanatan for a little R & R, and that's where you come in, Jack. You made all this possible."

Han raised his cup again. "To Harrison!" The others followed suit with the exception of Baylor. "Your String will get us all the graft we need to make it back to Bellytown."

"Back to Bellytown?"

"Well, I suppose once we get there, you could always choose to go, Topgrid, if you like." There was another boisterous roar, but Larkill rose above it. "What? You wanted to stay in that hellhole and dig for rocks till you died? We've escaped! Those techies think we were swallowed by molten lava. They heard our drive explode. And Zim here put a spare recharge rod in that big bang we just set off! The only thing they're gonna pick up from the hole we went down is radiation. And they'll seal it over and dock us, fried. We're *free*, coke! Don't you get it?"

"They're not going to let go of a Screwhog that easy. You should know that. They'll come down and take a very close look just to make sure. And when they don't find significant thermal traces or hardened lava, they'll come looking for you"

Larkill turned back to the crew. "You see, he is different. He does think."

With their cups close to empty now, Zim and Tooco almost fell over laughing. When their latest outburst finally abated, Larkill returned his attention to Harrison. "There will be residual heat from that explosion. And I know this is going to come as somewhat of a shock to someone who has absolutely no idea where they are . . . but, in fact, at this very moment, we are nestled in a channel of hardened lava from a fairly recent magma flow, recent enough that we probably shouldn't hang around too long." The Screenrage slowly reached out a hand and gently brought it down on Harrison's shoulder. For some reason, he let it stay there.

"Join us. Help us. It's better than rotting in their rotten world. You can have a personal record . . . and you can have something to put in it."

Zim started to snicker, but Han cut him off with a look. "We can't do it without you. We need your unique abilities. Help us."

"Help yourself!"

Harrison was startled by Okada's urgent rejoinder. "Do I really have a choice?"

Han beamed back at him. "You could always go back and let them fry you." The hand gently squeezed Harrison's shoulder. "Let's eat while I explain our plans a little further. Then we'll take a short rest and be on our way . . . to *Sanatan*!" Han led him over to the food replicator, where Tooco was already grabbing red soya disks as they popped out. "Believe me, we've thought this through very thoroughly."

So this is it. *Din'e time.*" He was secretly shocked sitting on one of the stools positioned around the replicator, shocked but very pleased that at a moment of unexpected upheaval, his mind (all on its own) was conjuring up a play on words with data scanned in retrieval. Even if it was a bit of a stretch: *dinner*, from 1400's English, meaning "evening meal"; *din'e*, from Navaho, much earlier, meaning "the people." He picked up one of the red disks and took a bite, certain he was only sharing dinner with the wackos.

"How do you plan to get us into Sanatan?" He was savoring the faint chili flavor.

"Leave that to me." Baylor's threatening glare was unchanged, but in his tone, there was a guarded offer of armistice.

"Bay's got some friends in Sanatan," Zim chimed in. "Good friends."

"Stumufu," a munching Tooco joined the conversation.

"What did he just say?" Harrison was pretty sure he got the gist of it. He just wanted to put the little troll on notice.

"Hesa welco, spashee!" The grinning Rebino princess reached across the replicator counter, plucking a half-eaten disk from his hand. "Hi, I'm Darl."

Darl then popped his disk in her mouth and began chewing. He wasn't sure whether she was making fun of him or the little bellygridder and his gutter lingo. But what really made him briefly catatonic was her willingness to share his spittle.

Noting his reaction, Han embraced Darl from behind, kissing her alabaster neck. "Good idea, dogess. He'll have to learn Amerab to pass for a mining techie off-line. You can teach him on the way. I'll bet you're a quick study, Jack. I can call you Jack, can't I?"

"It's better than 'spashee.' But why do I have to be a mining techie off-line?"

"So you can play the String game and win us a pile of graft, of course."

That's why they needed him—the String game. Maybe there was more "din'e" here than he realized. Had Han somehow hacked his record? Probably. He had a lot of connections back at the mines. It couldn't have been through Sacker channels, though, or he'd already be dead. But he definitely knew he was a big fan of the sword game. Since being a young cadet, he'd played at every opportunity. Even as a spacecase, he still practiced a ritual workout every morning with a replica of Game Master Miyomoto Musashi's sword—honing both mind and body for the day ahead.

First introduced as a hyperreality vid game, when everyone was still understandably fascinated with the discovery of the fourth and fifth dimensions, the String game was the rage in the '60s, incorporating bio-feedback technology to mimic the abilities acquired in the fifth dimension. With advances in holo-imaging, it graduated into a very popular gambling device by 2067. Now it was even more popular among Topgrid than skiing the powdered iron slopes of Sanatan. Before he completed String academy and became a spacecase, Harrison played there whenever he got off-line time.

Standing on a suspended disk inside a column of blue light (meant to replicate the blue haze when the fourth dimension was opened), the player is armed with a light sword and does combat with a comp-gen holo warrior. The game approximates a fifth-dimensional perception of time and space by giving the player a battery of subliminal messages, predestining every move your opponent makes.

In Sanatan, you could play for very big graft with very low stakes, if you were willing to risk your life. First, you had to reach "Musashi rating" in main-level play before being allowed to play for big graft. Then the holo warrior's light sword was replaced with a genuine laser. As a cadet, Harrison got a Musashi-rating, but he witnessed enough of these matches to realize that unless the player had pro-stringer training, the comp-gen warrior invariably won—often taking an ear, a nose, an arm, before making the final cut—leaving the player poised for a moment, his neck a fountain of blood, his head tumbling in blue light. These matches drew tremendous crowds and extremely high stakes. You were banned from playing if you were spacecase because you could "take five"! That's why they wanted him to be a "mining" techie. They were mostly bellygridders with minimal skills, like welding or foundry work. The more athletic of them often had pipe dreams of becoming pro stringers.

"I'm going to need a very good ident as this mining techie, not to get cliqued."

"Like I said, I got it covered." Baylor actually smiled at him.

"For now, we'll eat and then get some rest. In a few hours, we'll head for Sanatan." Larkill raised his cup again, and the others joined him. Momentarily caught up in their din'e, Harrison grabbed an empty cup from the counter and raised it with the others. The Screenrage gave him a welcoming grin.

"To freedom, to Sanatan, and the fucking good life!"

• — ◆◆ — •

The big screens circling the outer ring of the bridge were scanning close range. Pulsing patterns and blotches of color mingled together, registering the elemental makeup right around them. As Han had vouched, it was mostly lava laced with some granite. Harrison was lying on his back in one of the four gyro couches by the levitator. After the meal, they'd all retired to their modes. He was just starting to drift off when the moaning and yelping began—and the other "icky" sounds. It very nearly made him bring up his red disks, being that close. *Every one of them did it!* He was certain of it. They were all completely depraved out of their skulls.

Alone on the bridge, he was so desperate to avoid picturing their grotesque antics he'd fixated on the screens' stagnant show. He *could* polish his bytes. At Cincinnati retrieval, he'd come across something very strange, something he promised to remember and think about. Doing it now should provide a more interesting escape from their carnal hell.

Stories and myths all the way back to the beginnings of recorded language described a state of awareness variously termed *om point, samadhi, nirvana, bliss, grace,* and, *wired.* From Buddha to Castaneda, to Toon hero's like Rosewater and Seymore Glass, they all described states of consciousness that sounded very much like being on the String.

Could these myth magicians have actually found a way to enter the fifth dimension without any technical aid? It seemed, if not impossible, then very dogdamn unlikely. Many of them existed long before physicists finally proved string theory correct, some of them millenniums before they'd even discovered the atom, let alone unraveled it and found the infinitesimal particle that gave the universe a three-dimensional mass. The last of them were still decades before the discovery of the lockway into mutable time/space dimensions waiting inside that Dog particle. And these "bush babies" described altered states in a number of their accounts, even exceeding the abilities of spacecase! To hear them tell it, they'd achieved access to every sensation, perspective, or experience that ever existed or would exist, from the moment before the big bang, stretching to infinity. In all likelihood, this "magic" was only their intuition, elaborated on in wishful fantasies—what their skeptics called *bullshit.*

Harrison heard the hum of the levitator moving toward the back of the ship. Someone had finished with their degenerate activities and was moving about. The ship had stopped digging in the horizontal position, which was why Harrison was on his back now, watching the arc of screens above him. Essentially, the bridge was turned on its side. If someone was coming, it was probably better to get out of the couch and face them standing on the carpeted wall just below the screens. Dog knows what kind of state they'd be in after their descent into the primordial stew. He heard the hum of the levitator returning and steeled himself for anything. When the clear capsule appeared, he could see it was Okada. She was naked, sitting at the center of gravity in the horizontal cylinder. Her legs were splayed, exposing her smooth vulva. She was staring down directly at it. Her black almond eyes rose to take him in, a smile slowly forming on her lips.

"We get too noisy for ya, Jack?" She stretched out an arm and slapped the palm plate directly beside her. The levitator lock slid open.

Harrison stood, frozen in horror, transfixed by the glistening wetness of her inner thighs. She watched him examine her. "What uh matter, Jack? Flesh and blood too stinky for ya?" She crawled over the lip of the lock, moving toward him on all fours, her hips swaying like one of the great cats he'd seen at retrieval. "Come on, Jack . . . show some cuj!"

Harrison responded by backing away, starting up the circumference of the wall. He activated the electromagnetic charge in his jump and was about to scuttle up to the top of the outer ring, but Okada suddenly collapsed and was still. Apparently, the pruno and whatever else she was on finally knocked her out. He thought of leaping over her body and racing for the levitator, but the idea of being that close—even for a split second and even with her being unconscious—was more than he could chance. So Harrison did, after all, make the entire journey up and around the circumference of the outer ring. Until, crawling down the other side, he was within three centigrid of the levitator. He was about to deactivate and regain his feet when, like lightning she was up and in a single bound, standing over him. Her laughter filled the bridge. "Oh, poor, gullible Jack . . . can't get past hot, stinky flesh."

He made the mistake of looking down so he wouldn't have to see it up close. That was all the time she needed to run a hand up her dripping cleft and smear it across his mouth. Harrison heard himself scream, then gag, furiously wiping his face on the sleeve of his jump.

She danced away, laughing as he blew his disks, spraying a red stripe across the gunmetal carpet. It was over. He was slimed. He crouched there on all fours, taking deep breaths, smelling his own vomit, trying not to pass out. Then a strange calm slowly settled over him, like he was present at his own funeral, watching his body being rolled into the incinerator. It was finally over—and wonder of wonders, he was still alive.

Now he could touch her as much as he liked. It didn't matter now. He was free of all of it! Mutant horror to mutant euphoria in the blink of an eye. She would be the first clone he murdered. He raised his eyes again, taking her in. Okada saw that grin and bolted for the levitator.

With a wisp of blue vapor, his pattern snapped crystalline, and he was standing in front of the levitator, watching her run for her life. Her arching body appeared frozen in midleap, but her leading foot sank incrementally toward the carpet. He had a world of time to consider how to kill her before she ran directly into his arms. The Screx motif *Kunt Killer* suddenly popped into his mind. Now he'd be the "gadget master" capturing Venus Butterfly, offering her, her life if she could make him cum before he finished strangling her. He played it often as a cadet. Back then, nobody wanted to win. Now he wouldn't be seduced from his intent. The moment he touched her, she'd be in his fifth. He could meld benignly or make her his marionette. There was no doubt which option he had in mind. He'd end this haughty sheed and *then* cut loose in her slime!

In the next instant, she was spread-eagled on the railing of the outer ring—horizontal now rather than vertical. It was the perfect rack to stretch her on. He shuddered back into the third dimension, his hands firmly holding her wrists to the metal, his knees pressing down on her lower thighs, his feet inside her ankles, spreading and pinning her. Her saucer eyes stared through him, in total shock at all physical continuity being ripped from under her, momentarily grateful to still be alive.

Harrison steeled himself to act, to begin this new life, sliding one hand down an arm and over a bare shoulder, tentatively cupping one small breast in his palm. Her warmth was disarming, but his resolve was firm. This ruthless sheed was going to die. It took every ounce of courage he could muster to make his hand move down the smooth belly, dangerously slipping over the lathered vulva. Still, Harrison willed his fingers on into a crevasse that was a cauldron of slime. In the moment they were submerged in creamy heat, he considered it might be very different from what he thought it would be. No slithering creatures attacked. There was only a succoring spring anointing his fingers and beckoning a now-aching jerk. Suddenly on fire, he ripped open the front of his jump and released the desperate beast. Leaping into her soft river, he shuddered a first time into sweet human shy. Sweet shy. "Either you're dead, or my watch has stopped." Retrieval chatter? Now! What possible . . . ah, murder is ridiculous. Yes, *yes*, murder *is* ridiculous. What *murder* when jerk is dancing in joy? He just wanted to fuck her till they were both out of their minds, and Butterfly had taught him how.

Pushing himself a little higher on her torso, transferring pressure to the top of his shaft, then moving his hips like a piston rod on the drive wheel of an ancient train, he went in, high to low, on the thrust, rocking up when his root kissed her petals and withdrawing high again, caressing her shy at the top. Slowly, he increased the speed of his motion until she was groaning. Cumming once, twice, in quick succession, and then a third time, where he stayed deep inside, pressing his root even higher and, with delicate adjustments, playing her howls to yipping moans. Then deft magician suddenly disappearing, jerk reappeared in her blossoming rose. A shocked inhalation and silence, they remained motionless for a time. Raising his upper body off her, he brought up her legs, knees bent, almost touching her shoulders. One hand delicately parting her petals, he coaxed her bantam soldier to a reveille, and she found her voice one last time. Harrison joined the choir, gently rocking the bass, until their joyful chorus gave way to whispering sighs. Without fear yet with an urgency he'd never known, Harrison brought his lips down to hers, softly kissing Okada for the first time. She responded in kind.

CHAPTER

2

It had only been three weeks, yet he missed her. No doubt she would come crawling, but still, he missed her. It wasn't really personal, except how else could you miss someone? Zim could. He could miss what they'd been in his smaller life while assigning them to oblivion in his greater one. An advanced spiritual consciousness made doing both possible.

Spiritual. What a rancid word, rotted by centuries of doggerel dogma, hiding in obscure texts from their inability to produce one shred of definitive proof that Dog existed. After that first chemical union and ten million years to evolve into coke, they were finally able to conceive of Dog. But after a gazillion ego trips spent fashioning him in their own image, the only thing they accomplished was more destruction than all their plagues and natural disasters put together. Science finally helped them out, revealing the vast connections in play; hence, the first reasoned *possibility* of Dog's existence, which they immediately dumbed down into a concept called creationism—putting that in service to prop up the same old narcissistic crap. They couldn't conceive of a Dog beyond their limitations, beyond their marginal understanding of themselves. Seymore had thoroughly plotted their half-assed course.

They never realized the keys to the spiritual kingdom came with giving up a personal perspective. Detaching yourself from responsibility for all your thoughts, feelings, and actions, and emptied of all illusions of power and responsibility, take the ride as a cypher. Then, an unknown to yourself, you could really take a look around, play all the roles! He did miss the meditations, cruising in a Screx with Seymore at the stick, luxuriating in the agonies and ecstasies of the human drama without the baggage of attachment or consequences. That was the first thing he planned to do when they got to Sanatan: find a Screx and plug up to Seymore. What a rompin' stompin' jamboree they'd have!

First, however, they had to make it to Sanatan and to do that they had to breathe, which was becoming more difficult by the hour. They'd been at it twenty-one days straight, heading due north, digging twenty-four hours a day. Since they weren't really mining, just boring through it like slag, they could run the ship with a skeleton crew while others slept. They were still five or six days away from the coast of the Arctic Ocean. They'd started with enough oxygen for an extended dig. But with Harrison's endless regurgitation of arcane facts that nobody wanted to hear, even with refiltration and scrubbers, they no longer had the air to make it.

Han was pinning his hopes on the large air pocket Bay discovered, now less than half a grid from their present position. Miraculously, their initial readings showed high oxygen content in its atmosphere. Their luck was certainly holding. It probably contained enough air to see them through to the coast. But getting the air in that pocket was going to be a chore. They couldn't just drill right up to it. The temperature of the outer hull would heat the precious gas to the point the oxygen burned. They had to dock at a distance and carve a passage with the laser hammers, then pump the air back to the ship.

Twenty long days since the spaceshit mesmerized her with his fancy String crap. Sheed, they were fickle by physiology. Let some coke take them to a new level of physical abandon, and you were vaporized. They wouldn't even remember your ID. Zim was under no illusions about why she'd been with him. It was the Nitro meth, *Nitro* as it was commonly known. It made Okada more aggressive, but he liked that. Of course, with Freemate there were no problems, but there was also nobody mode. Ryka sucked up Freemate so she didn't feel a thing, ready to do whatever was required. Still, Nitro brought them back. Even when you got past the physical craving, the itch was always in your head. She'd finally come around to do a "special favor." And maybe at their victory party after reaching Sanatan, Zim would inform Harrison of that little tryst. Then we'd see if the spaceshit could achieve the level of detachment he possessed. No doubt, Harrison would throw a royal hissy fit. He took some comfort in the knowledge that his superior consciousness would, in the end, prevail over spacecase charms. Zim always ended up on top. In a presentment of future doghood, he'd convinced his father (really just a middle-management gadget maker) to drop a ton of graft for master implants: in physics, chemistry, engineering, C-power, and comp-rig. They were all hardwired into his brain. He'd known they would come in handy. It took five cycles in the mines to clique with a techie called Tzart and set up their secret lab. They were soon the "enhancer kingpins" of Alaska mines. Now it was all Tzart's, but Zim had his freedom and a generous supply of product he'd taken when they escaped. In Sanatan, some of it would fetch big graft, and the rest would fuel their fun.

Despite all the delays and disappointments, he felt, once again, on the move toward his personal divinity. He'd proven his flexibility, his superfluidity, his innovation through combination. And he'd achieved what Han demanded—adapt to carnal flesh. Lick it, suck it, bite it, fuck it, revel in the stink! He was becoming a truly unique Dog, and he wanted so much for Seymore to know it.

"Shut it down, Zim. We're there," Han's voice interrupted his introspection. He tapped out the proper sequence and pulled the plug from his head, enjoying the silence for a moment when the humming stopped.

At this distance, the probes were piecing together the whole picture, and Baylor was increasingly surprised and fascinated. As section after section materialized in Ryka's screen banks, it became clear this air pocket was coke made. A huge sphere elongated at the top, it reminded him of plants he'd seen in Africa.

"Amplify the sound probe."

Ryka moved to obey his order. If there was anything alive inside, they'd hear it. He spun the gyro couch around to face Han. "It's probably a robo seismic-monitoring station."

Now Han too examined the screens. "Maybe, but if it's robo, why would it be full of oxygen? It might be a Sacker post for spotting runaway Hogs."

"Not likely. There's no lockway. It's completely sealed up."

Han looked past Baylor to Sunsue. "Are we being probed?"

Sunsue's answer was immediate, "There is no energy being directed at the ship."

Han turned back to Baylor. "What can we come up with in the way of weapons?"

Baylor considered, "Well, the laser hammers could mess you up real quick."

"If they've got a frybar, you wouldn't get close enough before getting sliced and diced. If somebody's in there, you have to figure they've got a frybar."

Baylor thought for a moment then looked up to Han with a grin. "Yeah, but we've got Jack!"

Cliquing immediately, Han returned his grin. "So we do. Yes, we do."

The sound of shallow breathing suddenly wafted over the bridge. Ryka spun around to face them. "I've got one clone at midpoint in the structure."

"I'll be dogdamned! One?" Baylor was both shocked and relieved. "That's it? Only one?"

Ryka touched her earbuds. "Just the single clone." A lone Sacker was no match for their spacecase.

Harrison was watching Zim toy with his pink spikes while pointedly ignoring him as Larkill's order to report to the entry lock in full gear came over the intercom. He unplugged from the console and went back to his niche. He was obviously going to be part of the reconnaissance party. Picking a pair of Okada's briefs off his helmet, he paused to smell their fragrant center. What an animal he'd become. It was exciting being an animal.

Suited up, he arrived at the entry lock where Han and Bay were waiting for him, each with a laser hammer cradled at their side. The sleek titanium cylinder of a third hammer was propped against the inner hull.

"There's been a development." Han once again put a hand on his shoulder, but this time, the gesture wasn't as annoying. The suit protected him from the disturbing intimacy touching his jump made him feel. "This air pocket turns out to be a monitoring station of some kind. We've picked up one clone in there. Probably a techie, but it might be a Sacker." Han paused, giving Harrison's shoulder a few gentle pats. "We need you to hop on your String and go kill him."

Bay's face suddenly loomed in his view plate. "You can do that, can't you, Jack? Just take the duffer out. You can have your hands on his throat before he even knows you're there, right? You cokes can do that."

Larkill used his other hand on Bay's shoulder. "Easy, Bay. We don't even know if Harrison here has ever killed another coke."

Now Han's face was the one in his view plate. "Have you, Jack . . . ever killed a coke?"

"No." His short response was barely out before Bay was earnestly advising him again.

"Well, now is the time because that clone, whoever he is, is probably gonna be packin' a frybar, and believe me, he is not gonna be happy with us breakin' in."

Harrison couldn't believe he was going to have to kill some coke in cold blood. "What's he doing down here in the middle of nowhere anyway?"

Han recoiled with a puzzled look. "Who knows? Certainly not I! What I do know is he stands between us and breathing in about five hours, and he's not gonna sit there keening a sad tune while we suck the oxygen out of his mode."

Baylor put a glove on his other shoulder, trying to turn Harrison in his direction. "Listen to me, Jack. Listen, this is something I know . . . don't overthink it . . . Don't assume there's some kind of deep something you gotta feel to perform the act. Cut out all the soul-searching and realize it's just an act, a specific act that you can do. Just do it." Bay's eyes bored into his view plate. "If he's Sacker and you don't kill him immediately, he'll get us all. Believe me, I know . . . I know how it works. Just kill him immediately."

"All right. I'll kill him immediately!" He'd have plenty of time to decide what to do once he was inside. He could always immobilize the coke and let Baylor kill him. It was probably true, though. If they wanted to be sure their escape went undetected, this mystery clone would have to die by somebody's hand.

"We're counting on you." Han patted his shoulder a last time.

Baylor picked up the third laser hammer and held it out to Harrison. "Let's dig."

They all sealed their body plates, punching up internal thermostat and oxygen. Larkill touched a glove to the strontium-yttrium surface of the inner hull, beginning to tap out the sequence for realigning the Hog's entry ports.

"It's pretty hot, but there isn't time to wait. We have to move as fast as we can. Once, we're a few centigrid from the ship, we'll cool off." Larkill was eyeing the way Harrison was holding his laser hammer.

"Didn't they teach you how to use one of these in training?"

"They showed us some vids. That was it."

"Dog!" The Screenrage shook his head in disgust as the outer hull started vibrating through a quarter turn.

The loud groan made it necessary for Han to shout in order to be heard. "Bay, give him the crash course, double-time!"

Baylor tapped up his helmet intercom and poked a gloved finger at Harrison's laser hammer, pointing at two indentations on the back of the cylinder just above the rear pistol grip. "When you wanna drive the hammer, touch here. You'll get a pulsing ray about the length of your body. Grip it firmly because, although the kickback is nothing like a metal-on-stone cutter, you will encounter severe resistance if you try to cut too fast. Just a slow, steady sweeping ray will do the job." He pointed to the second depression farther up the barrel. "Then touch this one to vaporize the shit."

Han tapped up his intercom and joined the tutorial, gesturing toward the front of the hammer. "You'll get a wide ray about the width of your arm. Sweep it back and forth across the chunks until silica dust is all that's left. Make sure you stay far enough back from the material you're vaporizing—and watch where you point that thing."

Han tapped the final sequence. Aligned, the entry locks slid open, and a blast of searing heat hit them instantly, despite their body plates. The Screenrage waved them through the entry port and tapped the sequence for closing the inner lock behind them. "We'll need to work very fast."

Baylor led as they moved along the outer hull toward its entry port. At the far end, they spotted the jumble of stones spilling into the opened lock and jogged toward it. Observing the fiery pink walls, Harrison wondered how long it would be before their body plates were glowing like that.

Upon reaching the spill of rocks, Baylor fired up his hammer and started vaporizing the stones. Han pushed by Harrison and joined in. There wasn't room for him to cut too, so he waited, slowly roasting. Soon enough, one of them would need a break.

Three hours later and fifty centigrid from the Hog, their body plates still wore a slight blush from digging out of the entry lock. Now the smooth gray surface of the sphere was all that separated them from the oxygen and the clone on the other side.

"It's time for you to hop on your String, Jack, and get the job done." Larkill grinned at Harrison. "Remember, this coke could be right on the other side packin' a frybar and waiting to blast you. Don't give him time to do anything nasty."

Harrison hesitated. "Why not just clique with Ryka and find out if he's still at the center of the sphere? It would be nice to know exactly what I'm getting into here."

Han thought for a moment then tapped the side of his helmet. "Ryka, we're about to go in. Is that clone still at the center of this thing?"

They all heard her reply, "Yes. He hasn't moved."

Han turned to Harrison. "All right, let's do this."

Again, Harrison hesitated. "You're going to have to cut your way in anyway. Go ahead and cut a starter hole first."

Baylor was fuming. "Oh cap!" He turned to Han. "'This coke has been scamming us with this spacecase shit! Have you ever seen him do this String crap?"

Han was staring at Harrison in disbelief. "Yeah, I have. And so has Okada. What's going on, Jack? You can go through this, can't you?"

"Yeah, no problem. Just humor me and put a starter hole in it."

Han shrugged, raised his laser hammer, and cut a three milligrid hole in the surface of the sphere. Harrison stepped forward, staring into the hole for a moment.

Baylor was still worried. "Coke, this better not be screenshit."

Harrison spun around, smiling at Baylor, and went back up the tunnel past the piles of silica lining both sides of the passage. He faced the gray surface but, turning inward, began to visualize his pattern. Lightning lines graphed exponential intricacies converging in a radiant vector to lacerate the third dimension. Spinning 'round, melding matter sucked itself through a tiny hole, vacuuming him in as well, immediately spitting it all out again, an abstract watercolor running into the fifth dimensional. Time and space are fluid and malleable.

Larkill and Baylor stared in rapt fascination as the blue haze enveloped Harrison. Baylor spoke with quiet awe, "Are you on it?" Harrison nodded once very slowly. They watched Harrison's head blur and disappear, soon followed by the rest of his body. Recovering his bravado, Baylor yelled after him, "Just remember, you're hunting that fucker's throat!"

It was completely dark in the lower part of the bulb-shaped structure. Harrison extended himself into his immediate surroundings. He was in a garden. The soya fields on Sunsat hadn't prepared him for all this lush green flesh. These were very bushy plants, chock-full of chlorophyll—sleeping plants. He hung in the air with their thick, sweet odor. Probing for an energy source, he identified a residual electrical current, which at the moment was shut down at a junction in the wall. Harrison examined the junction and was shocked to find actual wiring. This system was from the twentieth and still fully operational. This particular junction was activated by a time switch, so rudimentary it was embarrassing.

As he swept through the lower sections of the bulb, his wonder at discovering such an ancient find continued to soar. The catalog of artifacts was a cornucopia of riches: percussive "rifles" and sidearms, Segways, cotton clothing, leather, zippers, a sea of crude screens, and embryonic computers. Many of the odd assortment of antique wonders viewed at Cincinnati retrieval were here to examine and handle. But first, he had to attend to the dirty business.

— ◆◆◆ —

The puffy little man plucked a strand of his stringy yellow hair from the red-stained whiskers around his mouth and absentmindedly scratched a thick brown beard. Looking up from his *Hot Rod* magazine, he realized that, much to his amazement, the nine-millimeter Berretta he always kept within reach had disappeared! He stared at the spot on the central console and blinked several times, but still it refused to rematerialize. Possibly, the gun suddenly understood its fundamental uselessness and vaporized. But, of course, that was insane, which was the next likely probability. Just like so many before him, he was flipping out of his frickin' gourd. He needed to smoke a bud and think about this. Though, thinking wouldn't change his mind. There was no doubt. He put the gun down exactly there.

He cursed the need to move in an uncertain world, but a bud meant going down to the plant rooms. He started to get up when suddenly the air around his chest coagulated, pushing him back into his chair. Now he was scared.

"Who's there?" he ventured, even though it was obvious no one was there, but what the hell? "*Who's there?*"

Harrison was disappointed in the twentieth. This specimen didn't look much different than Tooco, and he dressed even worse. His baggy purple top and pants reminded Harrison of a Barney lover. Still, here was the opportunity to ask some questions—questions from his retrieval studies this relic might know the answers to. Having taken his percussive weapon away, Harrison felt safe in materializing. He wanted to at least meet this living artifact before killing him with his own "gat."

Just as the puffy little man made a decision to try standing up again, the space in front of him began to vibrate. It was vibrating so violently he could see wavy lines in the air and a shape becoming discernible inside the waves. He could feel the shaking too, so he was fairly certain this was really happening and he wasn't going nuts. As the shape materialized with increasingly sharper focus, he changed his mind. When the vibrations finally stopped, "Boba Fett" was standing over him, pointing his missing pistol at his head.

His old man always schooled him, "The real test of a warrior is recognizing the situation for what it is." He could rail against this bizzaro reality and defiantly protest, *This can't be happening!* Or he could deal with the situation. If this was real, then Boba Fett here could blow his brains out. The best thing would be just to tell him the truth and hope he accepted it.

"I don't know where Solo is. He could be anywhere. He could be in another galaxy or even a parallel universe . . . you guys are cool with alternate universes, right? Right. I mean, I've never even met him . . . I just heard about him, saw his movies."

Harrison said it slowly, "Where are we?"

"Where are we? Uh, we're . . . we're, uh ..." He was sure he was about to faint. "NORAD! NORAD central command, missile control center for the United States of America! Cheyenne Mountain was a red herring! Like we're gonna tell the whole world where our missile nerve center is, right?"

Harrison cliqued 3TC, US, against them. This was a US military command post. That meant this runt was at least a hundred-cycle grunt! He didn't look that old.

"How old are you?"

"I'm twenty-nine years old . . . I was born in 2067, exactly one hundred years after the 'Summer of Love.' I'm a Leo." Why did he want to know how old he was? Maybe this wasn't Boba Fett, after all? He hadn't followed up on his statements about Solo's whereabouts, no mention of Chewy. Maybe he was just some alien traveler who looked like Boba Fett. "I'm a human. This is Earth."

"Tell me something I don't know, clone."

Finally, a subject they could discuss. "I'm not a clone . . . name's Bob. Are you a clone?" The space creature didn't respond. Bob intuited his obvious shock might be making the alien wary. He needed to appear more at ease if he was going to spark a conversation. He ventured a little chuckle. "I can prove I'm not a clone. I've still got a nice piece of my father's left quad muscle. Actually, I've been saving it for a special occasion. Do you eat sushi?" The spaceman's lack of response made Bob wonder if he'd committed a faux pas. Maybe they didn't eat meat, or maybe the word *sushi* wasn't in their vocabulary.

"Sushi is thinly sliced raw meat."

Harrison couldn't believe his ears, that what he'd just heard actually involved the grotesque act slowly forming in his head. Coming off the String always made his stomach queasy, but this image was creating serious regurgitation down there. In light of his newly awakened hunger for human flesh, this appetite was very disturbing. Sinking his teeth into another human's flesh, tearing it, chewing it, swallowing, and digesting—*digesting*? Suddenly the red-stained whiskers around the hermit's mouth formed a maniacal grin all their own. He barely got his helmet off in time before blowing his disks on the relic's shoes.

Bob couldn't decide whether to be pissed or relieved. Obviously, this was a man in a spacesuit, and that was a relief. But this interloper had just ruined hand-beaded moccasins from his mother's supple inner thighs, which took *six weeks* to stretch, tan, cut, and sew! Watching him stand there, doubled-over, and retching, Bob had a sudden urge to kick him in the teeth. So he did.

Harrison looked up in time to see his disks were being returned.

Like an NFL kicker from his granddad's DVDs putting it through the goalposts, he saw the spaceman's head snap back in a spray of vomit with an added bonus: he banged his noggin hard when he hit the floor. Bob quickly grabbed the Berretta from his limp hand.

But before he could savor his prowess, two more Bobas, both armed with long silver weapons, came charging through the door. He would've fired on them (God knows, they were both huge targets), but he wasn't sure bullets could penetrate their armor or helmets. He made a tactical decision and cocked the pistol, aiming it at the unprotected brainpan of the one lying on the floor—stopped 'em dead in their tracks! This one must be very important. He probably wasn't their leader because they rarely led the charge. But the way they stood there, frozen with fear, made it clear he was special. *I bet he's the only one who can become invisible.* Oh man, he was hittin' on all eight cylinders today. His old man would've been proud. He motioned with his free hand for them to put their weapons on the floor. "Drop 'em, or I'll blow his fucking head off!"

They started to comply just as he glimpsed a blue light out of the corner of one eye. He took a quick look back to find the first intruder gone. Then the gun disappeared, obviously snatched by the invisible spaceman, and Bob was facedown on the floor. He turned over in time to see the vibrations starting. A moment later, the first intruder was standing over him, wielding his Berretta again. Damn! This was infuriating. They peered down at him, the other two raising their view plates to confirm they were human as well.

"Great work, Jack," Larkill's voice dripped with sarcasm.

Baylor moved to put a hydraulic boot on Bob's throat and pointed the laser hammer at his head. "So long, Sacker!"

"Hold it!"

Both Baylor and Han turned to face Harrison.

"He's not a Sacker, and he's not a techie. Look at him."

Han suddenly smiled with surprise. "Evil cap! How did a Barney Lover get down here?"

"He's not a Barney Lover, Han. This is a US base."

Bay was losing patience with Harrison's ancient terminology. "A what base?" Harrison figured a brief history lesson would help the din'e comprehend. "In 2024, there was a final confrontation of most of the nations on the planet, 3TC. The result of a war begun a thousand cycles before that by the Catholic Church, a religious group that wanted to destroy another religious group called Muslims."

Han shook his head and sighed. "Thanks for the update, Jack, but I've heard of 3TC."

"Who gives a shit? Let's kill this fucker and get some air." Baylor pressed the muzzle onto Bob's face.

Bob began squirming under the hammer. "Hey, man! Cool out!"

Han's curiosity decided the issue. "Bay! Hold it." He briefly flipped his view plate back down and checked the time readout in the upper right-hand corner. He decided they were fine and flipped it up again. "Let's hear what he has to say. Tell us something about yourself."

"His ID is Bob," Harrison offered the introduction, and Han's affable smile appeared.

"Tell us something about yourself, Bob."

Bob realized this was it—do or die, his one chance. Lying there these last few seconds, threatened with immediate death, he realized they were from the surface and could conceivably, if they wanted, take him to the surface too. He was going to speak now like the Roman Anthony. Whatever layered tapestry of the past needed weaving, he would spin his way into the hearts of these hardened soldiers of the empire. He was determined to finally see the planet he'd been entombed in all his life.

"You're . . . from the surface." That was as far as he got before bursting into tears. So violent was this discharge of pent-up misery a cascade poured down his face and over his beard. He tried several times to push words past the torrent of saltwater and mucus, but finally, he simply stared at them through his sorrowful film, reduced to a whimpering tube.

A miracle occurred in the three desperate fugitives, seeing the tortured heart of their helpless prey. Even Baylor was undone by this total surrender to futility and, for the moment, mollified. Han was the first to speak, "Bay, did you bring the flask?"

Baylor popped his chest plate and pulled a small flask from inside. He unscrewed the top and poured a smoky liquid into the cap. He bent down, offering it to Bob. "Take a slug of pruno."

Bob mopped his face on his purple T-shirt and reached up to take the cup being offered. His father gave him a sip of his last shot of Bushmills when he turned ten, and the fiery memory remained vivid for him. He took a sip of this strange elixir with no idea what to expect. After a brief explosion in the back of his throat, Bob felt an increasing glow in both his stomach and head.

Larkill removed his helmet entirely and grabbed the flask from Baylor. "Just what the techie ordered."

When Han passed the flask back again, Baylor took a long swig.

"Finish it." Baylor passed it to Harrison who, after a moment's hesitation, obliged.

"So now," Han continued his inquiry, "can you give me a general picture of what's going on here?"

Bob focused on the finely chiseled face, the luminous blue eyes, the jaw a crowbar couldn't dent; and decided, maybe he would understand.

"I think that here we finally achieved what civilization has been trying to accomplish since the first prehistoric toolmaker got the bright idea of adapting the environment for his own convenience. I mean . . . because really, really . . . that craving for security and comfort is simply the desire to cocoon ourselves away from the ongoing sprouting and slashing, sowing and reaping, shifting and heaving crap-shoot of life on this planet. *We can't take it!* So we try to find a way to have the thrill without the risk."

Bob tried but failed to suppress a giggle. "We did it. Here, we did it! Except the last couple generations got increasingly pissed. We could no longer avoid the obvious fact that even if somebody was left up there, no one would dig us out. We'd sealed ourselves forever beneath the surface of the planet. I'm the last of all of 'em . . . mainly because I kept to myself." Bob pointed to the Berretta in Harrison's hand. "And I'm good with a pistol."

The handsome giant leaned over and put a hand on his shoulder. "It sounds like you've been through quite a lot." He gestured to the others. "That's Jack, and that's Bay. I'm Han. Where is your power source, Bob? What exactly does it consist of?"

Bob realized, if he wasn't careful, he would be closing the proverbial barndoor after the proverbial horse. "How did you guys get here? How did you find me?"

The blond giant smiled. "We got here in a big machine that digs way beneath the surface, reaping elements from the planet's depths. We found you because we saw your air pocket on our screens, and we were curious. I'm still curious . . . Where is your power source, Bob?"

Bob figured it was now or never. "Will you take me with you, please? I know a lot! I could help you. I'd be useful, I swear. Really, I would!"

"Bob! Bob." Han knelt down beside him as the grip on his shoulder tightened. "You can be useful right now. Tell me about your power source."

Bob decided, really, it probably would be the wisest thing. "Atomic fission reactor."

A quizzical expression crossed Han's face. "You mean a fusion drive?" "No, I mean a fission reactor, a small one. It's in the upper quadrant." Han turned to Harrison. "What in Dog's ID is a fission reactor?"

Harrison couldn't resist. "Haven't heard of that one, huh? It's a completely different system for releasing energy from an atom, used around the time of 3TC. It's extremely toxic and unstable, capable of producing enormous explosions."

Han's eyes lit up. "Really?"

Bob caught the glint. "*Oh yeah!* Gigantuous! Really." This could be his ticket out of here. "I've got one. It came with the house. It's what they used to call a suitcase bomb. It was supposed to be used to blow up the whole command center if the enemy ever tried to break in. It could blow away a small city."

Baylor snapped his visor back down. "We can talk about bombs later, Han. We need to get some air in the ship. Let me go back, open all the locks, and start running a vacuum hose up in here."

Han stood. "Yeah, good idea. Activate your recorder." Han reached out and drummed a brief sequence on the side of Baylor's helmet. "That's the sequence to open the lock to the inner hull. I'll go with Jack and Bob and have a look at this 'reactor.' Tell Zim to come join us. We'll turn on our homing signals. If the others want, they can come have a look around too. But someone has to stay and monitor seismic." He took in Bob's purple garb and made a refinement in his orders. "Have Ryka stay and do the monitoring."

"Right." Baylor made his exit while Harrison and Han helped Bob to his feet.

"How do you do that anyway?" Bob was staring intently at Harrison. "The appearing and disappearing. How the hell do you do that?"

Although Bob's rambling discourse had struck a few cords relating to his own recent awakening, Harrison still couldn't help feeling vastly superior to the groveling cannibal. "Magic."

The reactor was unimpressive, just a large gray block surrounded by a mass of pipes, some of which led to a steam turbine. Zim was busy examining the turbine. "This is interesting, but it's pretty archaic."

Bob offered a pathetic grin. "It works."

Han continued his questioning, "Where do you get your water?"

"From an underground aquifer. It's above us to the northeast, piped in by gravity feed."

"And your air?"

"We were lucky when they nuked us. We had three air pipes, each surfacing over two miles from ground zero. Two of those survived. We only needed one."

"How large a diameter?"

"Eight inches." Seeing Han's puzzled expression, Bob defined a space between his hands. "About that big. Fans draw it in through a filtration system."

"Well, I guess we don't have to worry about taking all your oxygen. Why didn't you just dig out, following an air pipe?"

"Where would we put the dirt and rock we dug out? We'd fill up this place before we got a quarter mile."

"A quarter what?"

Harrison didn't wait to be asked. "Old mold, Han. It takes sixteen grid to make a mile." He turned to Bob, "A grid is a unit of measurement in a Pulse-grid system."

"Ah." Bob seemed fascinated by the information.

Zim momentarily interrupted his inspection of the reactor's pipes to address Bob directly, "What is nuked? 'When they nuked us,' what's that?"

"They blew us up with an atomic bomb, like the one in the suitcase, only bigger." Bob did some quick calculations. "It destroyed everything above us within a sixty-four square-grid area and left a crater four-grid deep."

Zim eyed the rumpled purple mushroom with obvious irritation. "How would you know? You've never seen it."

"I know the payloads those missiles were carrying. I know what they could do! I've seen the DVDs. I've got DVDs and magazines going back seventy years on the subject."

"Very interesting." Harrison could tell Han meant it this time. The Screenrage turned away to begin a hushed conference with Zim.

Bob took the opportunity to chat up Harrison. "We've got everything in our library, if you're interested. We've got instructional, historical, we've even got some porno—we made most of that ourselves. A lot of books too."

He was encouraged by the way Jack perked up at the mention of the last item. He grew bold enough to try what little vernacular he'd picked up so far. "Yes, the *IDs* of every copy clearly printed on their spines, an entire room with paperbacks stacked to the ceiling."

"Yes. Take me to your books." Harrison called over to Han, "Bob is going to take me to the library. You two want to come?"

"The what?" Han gave them both a scowl.

"The library. It's a place where they keep books."

"Keep what?"

"Records of things. It's a place where records are—"

"Is the bomb there?"

Bob fielded this one, "No. That's back in central command, near where you found me."

"Well, I think we need to look at that first. You can go to the library later."

Harrison couldn't hide his annoyance. "Can't you and Zim remember how to get back there?"

"Yes, we can, Jack, but we don't know what it looks like, and besides, I want Bob to answer any questions we might have—now."

Here was a chance for Bob to join the group as a facilitator. He winked at Harrison and gestured toward the tunnel behind him. "The library's right at the end of that corridor."

⸻ ❖ ⸻

So foreign its weight, its solidity. On the face of it, a bulky bundle of tattered parchments, dragging your mind at a snail's pace to the eventual comprehension of something. But as he cautiously cracked one open and began leafing through those "pages," he marveled at the delicacy of their texture, the airy way they floated by: tiny black bytes flying at you, almost as if you could inhale their information. And despite the lightness of the individual leaves, in their congregation, there was that weight. He'd enjoyed a leisurely look around before Bob joined him, but now that he was here, maybe he could help him find something.

"I want to know about an author from a long time ago. Do you have a search program that could identify him if I give you a quote?"

The request surprised him. "Sure." Bob slid into a modular infront of an archaic console. "What's the quote?"

"A life unexamined is not worth the living."

Bob smiled back at him with the same expression of pity he imagined Bob saw from him when he asked how he appeared and disappeared. "That's Socrates, man."

"Socrates! Yes, that's it. Who was he?"

"A man who lived in a country called Greece, in the southern quadrant of the planet, about three thousand six hundred years ago. He was a philosopher, a seeker, who lived in strict accordance with his ideals."

"What happened to him?"

"They killed him. Well, really, they told him to kill himself, and he did."

"Why did they want him to kill himself?"

"To prove he meant what he said."

"That's a pretty drastic way to have to prove your conviction."

"Do you know a more definitive way to prove it? They wanted to be convinced, and he felt he had a civic duty to convince them." Bob shut down the console and slid out of the modular "Can I ask you a question?"

"What?"

"What's it look like up there now . . . on the surface?"

Harrison took back his pitying expression. "For the most part . . . a barren junk pile."

Mercifully, he'd made a favorable-enough impression on Jack that he warned Bob to wash around his mouth and, under no circumstances, offer human flesh to the others or even bring up the subject. That and generous portions of field rations were making his impromptu dinner party a huge success. They were ecstatic about the field rations, sat around now at the long table in the officer's mess, cramming the crap down their throats like it was caviar. He could only imagine what the poor buggers existed on normally. Edible plastic, maybe? He couldn't help feeling in their presence that his generation might have been a tad self-indulgent in reverting to cannibalism. They still had enough dry rations to last a hundred years and ample gardens below. But these future people knew nothing about the rich, juicy heritage of Ronald McDonald, hadn't tasted the last succulent morsel of tinned corn beef, had never seen the movie *Alive*, hadn't spent their lives sitting around in a cement can going out of their frickin' gourds watching DVDs of the fat and frivolous twentieth century. Besides, he was still convinced that human meat—properly handled, seasoned, and prepared—had to be the most sublime eating experience imaginable. You were imbibing the absolute pinnacle of the food chain, for Christ's sake! He could taste the superiority in every bite.

Charlene had been exquisite. A much more satisfying dinner than a mate, she'd been his last girlfriend—the last girl, in fact. How desperate he was to seek solace there. He had, though. A tough, greedy conniver till he'd pickled her in tenderizer, her butt in mol'e sauce finally made Bob fall in love.

The three "future" women sitting at the table in what appeared to be some kind of streamlined black pressure suits were all gorgeous. They were beyond comparison, each in a different way. The pristine whiteness of the one called Darl was literally out of this world. It would be like doing the Venus De Milo when she still had arms. And the one called Sunsue was a dead ringer for Farrah Fawcett. Last but not least was the little Asian doll whose name, at the moment, escaped him. And there was one more, back at the ship, but he hadn't seen her while he was there.

With the exception of the one called Tooco, to whom he feared he bore a vague resemblance, all the future people were striking in their looks, as if they'd been lifted directly from the pages of *Vogue* or *GQ*. That's definitely where the clone thing came in. Things were going well. He couldn't believe it. After all this time, his luck had finally turned. He'd have to clean up a bit. He'd really let himself go the past few months, but eventually he might even sleep with one of these women.

Han was like a kid at the candy store when it came to discussing atomic bombs. It really had been his ticket out of here. With that little gift, he'd elicited the promise to take him along too. He hadn't the slightest clue who, or what, they wanted to blow up, but he didn't really care. He'd explained to Zim about radiation and how the steel suitcases are lined with lead to protect you from radiation poisoning. He showed Zim the protective suits you had to wear if you wanted to work on the little wonders. And Zim brought back this amazing floating palate called a levi-loader to put the stuff on, along with one of their protective suits for him. They let him accompany them when they took everything to their mind-boggling ship. It really was a dream come true. Soon he would be free of his cement tomb.

Bob thought he might even be making a friend in Jack, who had an obvious turn for history. He'd told him about his studies at a place called Cincinnati retrieval. That's where he'd heard about 3TC. "Third Time's a Charm," that's what they called it. Cute, very cute, but they hadn't been there. Of course, he hadn't been there either. But he'd filled Harrison in on the specifics, handed down by his grandfather. Apparently, it all came unraveled after they whistled past the graveyard. The graveyard being a peninsula called Korea, where over a million people were reduced to ashes in less than a week. Though, it didn't immediately trigger the nuclear holocaust, it did put the final nail in the coffin of globalism. The "last straw" floated down in New York, on New Year's Eve 2034, when the illuminati of Christian fundamentalists ("The Wave") managed to hack into the mammoth electronic billboard on Times Square. Just after the "ball drop" with the crowd cheering wildly, the billboard lit up with the video of a huge pink ass defecating on a copy of the Koran, gushing turds splattering on its white leather cover. Many of the revelers recorded the sacrilege on their camera phones. It was posted to the internet before the New Year was one minute old. Muslims the world over were beyond furious. Unfortunately, a cadre of rouge Pakistani intelligence officers (having already assembled an atomic weapon) got it to Hezbollah, who smuggled the bomb onto a Spanish freighter, inside a cargo container. They detonated it four days later, upon arrival in Tel Aviv, harbor. Almost instantly, Israeli, Iranian, Russian, Chinese, French, British, Indian and Pakistani missiles were crisscrossing the stratosphere, scourging the planet with hundreds of fiery boils.

At their top-secret NORAD command center (while the Russians were busy obliterating the clay pigeon in Colorado), Bob's grandfather and his comrades performed their task with nerves of steel, making sure every US missile on land, sea, or air was sent on its way. As they watched their satellite links being destroyed one after another, they realized that, in a matter of hours, they too would be discovered and find themselves at ground zero.

From the final transmissions being received, they understood, for all intents and purposes, they were America. That's when his grandfather and the other officers decided to breach protocol and throw the book out the window while they still had one. A squad went back up to the surface and, commandeering a caravan of trucks, swept up their families and emptied the military supply depots outside the town of Nome, Alaska. Then they raced back to the entrance of the bunker. They brought down the civilians and supplies in two elevators, cramming them so tightly that several of the elderly suffocated on the fifteen-minute ride down. Two hundred and twelve civilians made it before the missile hit at 10:15 p.m., January 5, 2035*. Within three weeks, twenty-seven people were shot dead for becoming homicidal, and another nineteen committed suicide. Luckily, their atomic reactor ran a refrigeration unit big enough to convert some storage areas into cold-storage freezers. With these first deaths, they realized they were facing a unique problem: they could neither bury or cremate the bodies. They had to store them. It meant a lot of prime meat when, two generations later, they decided what's for dinner. He could tell Jack was impressed with this ribald footnote to history, especially after he took him on a tour of the cold-storage facilities.

On the tour, Jack told him an interesting tidbit as well. He'd asked him what Han meant when he called him a Barney Lover. He learned they were the spiritual order that was ordained to care for and raise the "tube-born clones," unless they were specifically engineered by elites called Topgridders, who wanted to raise them as a hobby. It was a very dangerous calling because, in later life, if these clones went berserk—and apparently, some did—Barney Lovers were the ones they slaughtered. Han thought he was a Barney Lover because he was wearing pants and a shirt that were purple. Bob's jaw almost hit the floor when Jack said they all dressed in purple in homage to their leader—a great purple dinosaur. Talk about frickin' bizzaro! He had to admit, hearing that gave him pause regarding going topside. I mean, just how fucked up were things up there? Incinerated in the apocalypse as a kiddie-show character then resurrected as a spiritual icon. God knows what other crazy shit was going on—and that was another thing, "Dog knows"? Give me a break. He'd been afraid to ask for the explanation to that one.

Harrison fingered the tiny volume in his jump pocket and watched Bob beaming across the table. He'd taken the book from the icy hand of a young female corpse at the bottom of a stack of bodies in one of the refrigeration units. He liked the compact size of it. He wanted this feast to be over and be back in his niche examining his treasure. In the few short hours they'd been here, he'd come to loathe the place.

Han stood, licking the last delicious crumbs from the final bag of Doritos off his fingers. According to Bob, he'd been saving this delicacy for his last meal. He picked up the plastic goblet containing another rare elixir known as strawberry Kool-Aid, raising it above his head. "I want to propose a toast to Bob, that harbinger of the twentieth century"—everyone at the table, except the host, raised their plastic goblets (Bob sat blushing now)—"who has too long outlived his time."

Bob registered a look of confusion as Han and the others drained their cups. "Harrison . . . the gun thing, please."

The moment he'd been dreading since slipping into this perverse hell had finally arrived. With a shameful sense of exhilaration, Harrison drew the pistol from his jump and handed it to Han. It was odd that, after being so moved at retrieval by the ones behind, he should feel no connection to the one sitting right across the table, for the moment still alive. But there were some things you did because you absolutely had to; and others you didn't because you absolutely could not. Bob ate his own, and he wasn't starving. He grew real twentieth-century vegetables down below for Dog's sake!

"What's going on, man? I thought we were cool?"

"We are, Bob. That's why we need to dispose of you. Harrison, I just point and squeeze the little lever thing, right?'

"What about the bomb things, man? You promised you'd take me with you!"

"I lied." Han aimed the pistol at Bob's head and tried to pull the trigger. Nothing happened.

"You have to disengage the safety." Harrison reached over and flipped down the tiny lever on the rear of the relic.

"Listen, listen, at least, take me to the surface! Put me in chains! I won't eat. I won't drink. I won't be any trouble, I swear! Just let me see the surface, please!

Then you can blow my brains out, I don't care."

Han surveyed him with a look of fatigue. "Bob, Bob, we can't be bothered." When he squeezed this time, there was a deafening roar. Han jumped. Okada and Sunsue ducked their heads, covering their ears. Tooco dove under the table. Only Harrison and Baylor remained unmoved.

Han looked at the weapon with genuine alarm. "Pretty fucking unstable."

Bob sat whimpering, surveying the hole in this shoulder. "You people are sick. You don't know *anything* about compassion. You're sick! You're sick in the future."

Han gripped the pistol with both hands, aiming more carefully. Once more, the gun roared, and Bob had a second hole, this one in his forehead, punctuating the disgusted look in his eyes. The Screenrage handed the lethal antique back to Harrison. "Thanks for the memories, Bob."

⚬⚬⚬

A young punk in Bellytown, he'd played fast and loose, taken ridiculous chances, put himself in very precarious situations, all unnecessary considering his wealth. But there'd been an inherent self-trust, the naive faith of a primitive ready to draw his knife and face the beast. He learned that wasn't enough in the rubble jungle. The superior strategy of subterfuge soon became apparent. His seminal lesson arrived while joking around outside a Bellytown bar, Han and a buddy reminiscing about their table dancer and the sizable "steely" she used to fuck herself earlier that night. It cost every Yuan between them, but they weren't lamenting the price.

Han still had her smell in his nostrils when two merchant seacokes came swaggering out of the joint, asking for directions to the "Blue Bitch." It was a brothel and necro club where you could perform a sanitized hump on ranch kill, if that was your thing—a Yakuza "specialty" that seacokes were partial to as well.

The grinning one did the talking, being very boisterous in his salutations. As Han described the route they'd need to take, he listened impatiently, shifting his weight back and forth from one foot to the other. When Han finished, the jovial drunk made loud proclamations of thanks, ending with a little bow and a swift kick to Han's cuj! But the chem enhancers pumping through his veins skewed his spatial perception. The toe of his boot barely nicked Han's belt buckle. Han stood there, amazed again, just as a tube-born in Ruger labs. Missing his target, the seacoke's leer changed to grinning embarrassment. A flicker of fear registered in his expanding retinas as Han's gaze made it clear, he'd awakened his murderer.

It was just that quick, the appearance of the ruthless warrior who prowled the darker caverns of Han's soul. And this killer was already up to speed, a straight left with his shoulder behind it—impact point one milligrid beyond contact with the coke's Adam's apple. He exhaled an accordion squall as Han's fist drove into his throat, crushing his larynx and dislocating his spine at the neck. Reeling backward, head bobbling, he made bizarre bleating sounds as blood spurted from his mouth. Han turned on the other one, caught in his own dumb amazement, and booted his cuj up to his bellybutton. He folded like a grid clamp. Jackhammering his knee into the second coke's nose, he rammed cartilage and bone directly into his brain. Both were dead before they slapped pavement. The look of astonishment on his buddy's face was matched only by his own. The triumphant pair went through their pockets and found two pay packets, no doubt meant to be blown on ranch chicks at the Blue Bitch.

Later, after they stopped running and caught their breath, they decided to honor their fallen foes by finishing their journey for them. So they celebrated their victory in traditional Yaki fashion: by climbing on top of a dead sheed and depositing your seed in her. Yak buttons believed that when you returned from battle, instead of thanking a supernatural entity for sparing your life, you fucked death! You'd already beaten him on the battlefield, and this was the way to really rub it in! First, you invited death to the party by picking one of the ranch chicks available that night. Since Yakuza ran all the clone ranches that produced these creatures, there were just two models to choose from: blonde and brunette; they were cloned with brains the size of a labradoodle's and understood only basic commands. After you made your selection, everyone had some fun with her before she was taken back and "prepared." The next time you saw her was in your private lair, laid out on a white satin mat, encased in a roomy coffin. He could see her right now—arms above her head, bent at the elbows, forearms and hands extending beyond the end of the casket; her eyes closed, lashes pressed against apple cheeks; knees bent, showing above the lip of the coffin, her thighs spread in a classic butterfly pose; her mounds venus smooth and beckoning, lifted up on a satin pillow, blossom pink, peeking from alabaster.

It was Han's and his buddy's first and only time, so neither of them really appreciated the finer points of the tradition. But as Tooco later explained, once death took her, you took her back by fucking death's chick while simultaneously fucking death. There wasn't anything more in-your-face than that. Han remembered it as the most macabre experience of his life. He'd felt a strange sense of power ejaculating in her newly dead flesh, then a shame that was worse than the sex. "Kill or be killed—fuck death!" The Yakuza battle cry. But the wild and bloody decades in the waste fill were long past. Now buttons "flipped a chick" if their crew made a big snag.

It wasn't an idle question, asking Jack if he'd ever killed a coke. His inability to kill Bob when they'd first broken into his mode revealed a weakness in the presence of death. Han could capitalize on that. It was his one edge, if it ever came to a confrontation. That indecision before he jumped his String would be the moment for a preemptive strike. It would be the only chance he had. But he doubted it would ever come to that. The hint of awe in Jack's eyes when he'd nonchalantly dispatched Bob was telling. Awe was a close relative of fear.

Bob, what a specimen! The ideal for a "canine pulling" civilization. Make it possible for the weak mutant progeny to survive, grow, and finally rule. "Oh, dear Dog, please don't let my crippled clonie die!" All efforts bent to helping the little subvert survive to helping millions of little subverts grow. And where did it all lead? To the ultimate perversity of a weak-stomached spacecase called Harrison, Jack, wielding weapons of enormous power yet unable to stand on the killing ground. Civilization was the supreme evil cap. The ancient vids revealed it. At least back then, they knew they were a joke and displayed a sense of humor about the inherent dysfunction in their precious "ideals," and to make their point, snagged and zapped it.

Still, his spacecase turned out to be more *present* than expected. And Jack could assimilate. Never underestimate an opponent. That was his father's golden rule.

• ◆ •

"Co . . . ba . . . cent? Cobacent?"

Blank white eyes waited for his reply. She said it again, goading a response. Harrison wasn't concentrating. He was marveling that, not an hour from Okada's mat, he wanted Darl. The real thing was subtler than Nitro or Screx, but it made you even hungrier. It snuck up on you when you thought you had something completely different on your mind. Darl had been drilling him for at least a half hour, and he hadn't given one correct response to any question she asked. He did know *cobacent* was an intimate question about some sort of shared property, but that was it. The problem with Amerab (American-abbreviated) was that so many meanings sprang from the same root word, with just one or two letter differences at the end. It was difficult to remember all the variations, unless you'd been speaking this gutter crap all your life.

"Cobacent?"

Oh, what the hell, he might as well at least partially yield to his desire and reply with one of the few words that had registered on his brain. "Licalipoon."

The blank orbs grew wider. She shook her head and laughed. "Wacimofo! Han, wacamofo!"

Harrison had no choice but to revert to English, if he wanted to continue exploring the subject, and he did. "What Han doesn't know won't hurt him." He said it with his best boyish smile.

Her white lids lowered until the orbs were just two slits. "You're lucky he doesn't really give a shit." They sat for a silent moment, completely still. Then suddenly Darl stood, laying open the front of her jump with a deft downward swipe. "Then do it. Lick it, spacecase! Lick it good."

Darl wore no undergarments. Inside her onyx jump, she was a snow-white V from shoulders to vulva. Looking down, a smile slid across her porcelain face. "Give me some of that sweet locomotion Okada's been raving about."

Harrison obediently slid off the modular onto his knees, eyes transfixed on her beckoning cleft. She watched him nuzzling into her, felt the first delicate probes of his tongue dipping carefully into shy, then fluttering up and down the length of her sex. She thought how mortified poppi would be seeing yet another mug buried there.

It was his own manipulative fault she'd come to this carnal pass. He'd brought them together, sat Han down at their dinner table. For his belated punishment, she'd imagine him now, tied up and gagged, witnessing her latest outrage—having physical relations with the mad shaman of Topgrid society, sharing secretors with a spacecase! He'd be out of his fucking mind. And Jack, he'd be ready to explode by the time she bathed his tongue in her creamy reward. For all his efforts, his jerk would still burn. The only thing he'd receive was a dismissive, "Thank you for a lovely afternoon." Spacecase found her shy spot and was calling. Her knees were weakening; she was giggling. Let the games begin.

They were playing the game Han taught her. There was no doubt she would win with Harrison. But spacecase tongue was long and strong, his saliva bonding inner petals to their outer twins, rolling smoothly up inside her, emerging finally to dance on her clit. Time to apply the posture Han taught her, bending her knees and leaning forward just a little bit. She'd learned a great deal since her first tumble in "Merlin" (the pet ID for her Screx)—and she'd been tumbling ever since.

Poppi was very annoyed after scanning her feeder snags and discovering she'd dropped a ton of graft, primarily on a certain Screenrage. He'd imagined himself very crafty inviting flesh and blood "to table." So sure, the nonhyper reality of Han's presence and the rankness of his sweat, that olfactory calling card of death, would bring an end to her pubescent infatuation. But he hadn't bargained on Han's scent.

Han contended that sheed were too undone by their climax. Although total release was the primary experience of an orgasm, sheed overindulged in it. They needed to learn a framework of physical control to add a new and more thrilling dimension to getting off; hence, their little game. It was a wonderful game, and Darl took pride in cumming twice, staying on her feet. Harrison was bringing her to a pitch for the third attempt, but that indulgent voice was begging her knees to buckle and sink to the deck. She took an even wider stance and, courting disaster, gripped Harrison's head, pressing him deeper, earnestly humping his glistening face. There was strength in meeting the challenge and, ultimately, much more cream for spacecase. "Evil cap, poppi! Evil cap!"

"We're running out of sedimentary cover and into the Laurasian shields. It's gonna get a lot faster now." Baylor pointed at the yellow ridge on the ceiling maps of the outer ring and turned back to Larkill in his command gyro. "Out of the mantle and into the continental crust."

Han continued studying the maps. "Good. How far is the coast if we keep digging at our present angle of ascent?"

"Only about 1,600 grid if we dig to the surface along the plate subduction we're following now."

Zim, who was strapped into one of the gyro couches on the outer ring, immediately interjected his concern, "And do what, get bagged by Sackers the second this behemoth crashes through the surface? If we're lucky enough to come up in an isolated area, we still have to find a levi foil and steal it without raising alarms. Then we have to cross the ocean without getting spotted by Sacker patrols."

Baylor made a derisive noise. "Oh, don't tell me we're gonna hear more about Zim's theories of propulsion."

"Wake up, Bay! Do you really think we're gonna surface this thing undetected?"

"Who says we have to surface? We could dig out the last few centigrid with laser hammers."

"Nine cokes crawl out of the ground with some old percussive weapons and a couple of laser hammers on a patrolled waste-fill coast, and we don't get spotted? Right! And clonies in hell get screxed. We haven't got a chance if we come up on the coast."

"So your solution is to blow ourselves to oblivion in one of your physics experiments."

"It's not an experiment. It's the simple laws of physics applied to the problem at hand."

"Simple is right. I don't need to hear any more of your crazy shit."

Leaning back in his gyro, Han cupped his hands behind his head. "I do. Run it past me one more time, Zim."

"Like I said, it's really very simple. We keep digging north at our present angle for another 1,600 grid, then come up into this underwater cavern I found." Zim tapped up a grid map of the cavern he was referring to on the ceiling of the bridge. "Now, this underwater cavern off the Northern Alaska coast is located in the end of a large underwater shelf jutting out into the Arctic Ocean. The cavern is roughly a grid high, two grid wide, eight grid long, and completely filled with water. We can adjust our angle, so when we come up into it, we plug the cavern, and the water is blocked from flowing out to the ocean. Our outer-hull temperature will be around eight hundred degrees. When the ship moves up into the cavern, we purge our kiln tanks and finish running the slag through the hull, sealing our entry point. The moment we plug that cavern, we start creating a cauldron of steam. As the cavern transforms from water to steam, it will build up incredible pressure. By the time the Hog bores completely through this underwater shelf, that cauldron will have built up enough pressure, combining with firing our surface thrusters through the heat exhausts, to explode the Hog into the ether with the force of four Sat thrusters. If we drill up through the shelf at a thirty-degree angle north, the Hog will blast into the atmosphere on a trajectory aimed at the Arctic coast. The surface thrusters will help us to maintain our altitude longer and ensure we come down just off the Arctic coast. We splash down in the ocean and then drill right into the ice. Dig up the last few hundred centigrid, and we're a stone's throw from Sanatan."

Baylor howled, "You can't be serious! You want to take a huge machine half a grid long, designed to dig in the depths of the planet through dirt and rock, and you want to *shoot it into the atmosphere like a fucking rocket*? And *what* do you plan to use to assist the diminished surface thrusters? You plan to use steam! Steam? Dear Dog, why don't we just find some X-mas reindeer and have them tow us behind Santa's sleigh. You can't be serious!" Bay looked to Han for confirmation that Zim was insane. Instead, Han switched on the ship's intercom.

"Jack, sorry to bother you while you're working, but we're having a little discussion here about our possibilities for getting to Sanatan."

There was a pause before Harrison's voice sounded on the bridge. "Okay, so what do you need from me?"

"Well, we're discussing the possibility of using the natural formation of an underwater cavern to create a steam chamber that would help propel us along with our surface thrusters over the Arctic Ocean to the vicinity of Sanatan. What do you know about steam power? Does that sound possible, Jack?"

"It sounds pretty crazy."

Baylor's response was immediate, "Thank you. My sentiments exactly."

However, Harrison continued, "But steam engines were the first engines that made it possible for cokes to build on a global scale. There was an eight-hundred-grid-long canal they dug with steam engines to connect the Atlantic and Pacific Oceans by way of the Gulf of Mexico. It was wide enough and deep enough to accommodate huge tankers and container ships. They used various steam engines to erect the first great scrapers in their major cities. Also, they were the engines that powered their trains to pull dozens of container cars, rolling down tracks they laid out all over the world."

For once, Zim had no problem listening to the spacecase run his mouth with his precious bytes. He maintained a politic silence when Baylor started shaking his head, snorting with exasperation.

"All right, thanks, Jack." Han switched off the intercom and appeared to think for a moment, then raised his eyes to meet Bay's. "The thing is, we don't really have a choice, Bay. Zim is right. We only have three days of Bob's air left. That barely gets us to the northern coast, and it'll be crawling with Sackers. The Arctic Ocean borders the whole northern waste fill all the way to the Atlantic. They take the prospect of mutant bands invading Sanatan very seriously. Topgrid want to feel safe when they go out to play." Han pointed to the grid map on the bridge ceiling. "When you consider what a mammoth cauldron of steam the Hog would create in that cavern and then add in our surface thrusters even at diminished capacity, I don't find it difficult to believe we could explode out of there with the force of four Sat thrusters. With a hull comprised of niobium-titanium and our gyro couches to absorb the shock of a dive in the ocean, there's a good probability we'll survive the ride."

Bay's expression of incredulity grew even more desperate. "And how do we know we won't belly flop into the water and break into a million pieces? How do we know we'll go into the water *close enough* to the Arctic ice and at an angle that *will* allow us to dig into it?" Baylor stopped, suddenly aware he was becoming hysterical. When he spoke again, his words were calm and measured.

"Our surface thrusters will have used up all their fuel, and even if we do have ballast from the empty outer hull, which is a big *if,* I doubt the screwhead will be able to pull us through the water. If we get our angle of entry wrong, we could end up planting ourselves in the ocean floor. And since we're so concerned with being undetected by Sackers, how do you think a Screwhog exploding out of the water right offshore will escape their attention? This is fucking nuts!"

Zim wasted no time refuting Bay's latest objections. "We know the Hog won't belly flop because the screwhead is the heaviest part of the ship and will make it fall, tip first. We'll lock the segments of the ship when we bore up through the reef. Our angle is set so the Hog remains rigid in flight. The surface thrusters should have enough fuel to help us maintain some forward thrust for most of the flight, ensuring we fall at a gradual angle. And as an added bonus, since we'll be using the internal systems in our jumps during our flight, we can briefly open the hull portals and replenish our air supply.

"Now, it's only twelve thousand grid from the coast to the Arctic. I'd show you the math, but you wouldn't be able to follow, so just understand I calculated the volume of steam that would be generated by the Hog's eight hundred-degree temperature, which will not be cooled by the water in the cavern because we will increase the temperature of the kiln coils in the outer hull. I calculated how much pressure that steam would create in combination with the power from our diminished surface thrusters, and it's easily the force of four Sat thruster drives. I calculated both the altitude and angle they would propel the Hog, and it drops us back into the ocean less than ten grid from the Arctic ice. The fact that the kiln channels are empty, as are the storage tanks, will give the ship enough ballast to keep the Hog submerged somewhere close to the surface. And with that ballast, the Hog's screwhead will be able to pull it slowly through the water. As far as being spotted when we take off, we'll drill through the shelf after dark. Unless they have a Sacker post onshore close to where we launch, there's a good chance if anyone does see us, they'll think it's a meteor or old space junk."

Baylor remained silent for a moment, eyes closed. "Oh, really, you don't think the fact we're going up instead of coming down will make it difficult for them to reach that conclusion?"

The pink spikes on Zim's head quivered as he pursed his lips in a petulant sneer. "It's the best we can do."

"Well . . . if that's the best we can do, why don't we just blow our fucking heads off right now and save ourselves an *unlikely* trip. You're both crazy." Baylor unstrapped from his couch and made his way to the outer ring, giving Zim a murderous glance as he passed. Reaching the levitator, he slapped the palm plate, stepped inside, and disappeared.

Zim grinned at Han. "The coke is 'Sacker pissed.'"

Han hung in his gyro couch with a look of resignation. "He'll get over it."

• —◆— •

Bauxite, bauxite, bauxite—what was a huge deposit of bauxite doing this far down? Well, it made the digging even quicker. The old Hog was churning through this slag like the diarrheic discharge he'd suffered after Bob's banquet.

Tooco still couldn't take his eyes off her. Okada was at her station, monitoring heat, making sure the bauxite ran through the outer hull at the consistency of putty. She was still so perfect. A vision beyond belief when she first looked up at him with those shining almond eyes right here in his gyro—scarlet lips parting, pink tongue darting 'round and 'round the rim of his swollen head. He knew it was the Nitro. She'd reeked of it, having just returned from a quick visit to Zim. She'd seen that ache in his eyes for a while. He knew she was only doing it to keep his mouth shut. Han was a stickler for cokes working clean at their stations. And like the classic hustler she was, she didn't pass up the opportunity to pump him for information she could use later. "I'll tell you mine, and then you tell me yours."

Her tale was pretty standard fare: servant class, Topgrid, about fifty zillion steps up the social ladder from Tooco. She was thirteen and the personal servant of a gadget master when the twin misfortunes of being both pretty and flawless precipitated her doom. Arriving in her master's niche just as he emerged from a Screx binge, higher than a *Protostar*, the disoriented Topgrid didn't fully comprehend he'd left his shining orb. Taking her for another comp-gen, he pounced, ripping off her jump and savagely raping her. Unfortunately, it happened in front of his wall screen. Within hours, they were bagged and sent to the mines, where after long days in the factories, they performed for off-line Sackers at night, just as Han and Darl did before them. The dissipated Topgrid eventually died from a combination of exhaustion and humiliation, but not before Okada made him grovel every night.

Now she wanted nothing to do with a sawed-off bellygridder. And after everything he'd done for her. Oh, he told her his tale that first time. And later she used it to convince him to approach Zim and get more Nitro. She'd assured him his past would appeal to the perverse twit—and it had. That was a comedy of manners, not unlike his favorite prison vid. He could easily picture Ted in a similar fix being "dressed down" by Lou while Mary observed, trying desperately not to break out in hysterical laughter. When he returned to her niche with a dozen Nitro patches, she wanted to hear every detail. He obliged, and she got incredibly turned on while simultaneously busting a gut. That was the wildest, most wonderful night of his life. And now she wouldn't even look at him, all because of that spaceshit Harrison.

Okada felt his eyes on her. Tooco was jealous. Fuck him. Fuck them all. She had Jack. He was hers. She'd realized a quest, realized she was searching. In the past few days, vanquished in her desire to vanquish, transformed from bounty hunter to bounteous, she saw clearly the path taken—from her rape to her death in Harrison. She'd hung a lot of cuj sacks in her secret lair, any Sacker or techie far enough gone to want real sheed flesh. Surrogates for her gadget master, she drove them all crazy, made them slaves to her sensual ferocity and made enough Yuan to keep her in Nitro. As it turned out, with a little help from Han's carnal credo, she finally enticed her dealer to take a bite. Zim caught the bug so bad he got her onto Han's crew! That birthed her twin desires to escape from their barren prison and from herself. And now in Harrison's arms, someday had arrived. After that first night on the bridge, he'd taken her into the "five" only once. But once was all it took. When he entered her, it was like a veil being torn, her body responding from depths far deeper than she'd known. All her thrashing warlike couplings distilled into one moment of comprehension and awe. Finally, an understanding of the rightness in this joining, no longer a dirty affirmation of her loss, the filthy heritage of a fall. Her body suddenly dispelled the entire degrading mess and showed her where some dreams were sleeping. She was determined to wake them now. Zim couldn't believe she wasn't coming around for a taste. What did she want with chem enhancers when she'd taken the elixir for life? Fuck that pinhead pervert. Her beautiful spacecase was after more than perverse gratification. He was after a deeper connection. Undreamed of fulfillment turned all the rest of it to dust.

She did feel a smidgeon of guilt, a sliver of compassion for Tooco, remembering his account of being so thoroughly undone by Zim. The total subjugation he endured on hands and knees while Zim's implant-enhanced jerk *drummed* him to oblivion. She was ashamed that she'd reveled in every detail—the relentless thrusting that morphed him from bucking mustang desperate to escape a cruel rider to roaring lioness, furious at this unexpected submission, and finally, just a mewling kitten, then gone. It was an ancient technique he'd learned as a shorty in Bellytown, a way of disappearing into blessed oblivion. Herself a past master of taking while being taken, she'd given him a special reward—a long wild party, using up four patches before they collapsed with exhaustion.

As if sensing her regret and obligation, the mechanical arm propelling Tooco's couch zipped down the central track, delivering the scruffy bellygridder right in front of her.

"Too bad you're sterilized, or else you could have his tube! Maybe you can snag some mutant spawn once we get to Bellytown, live happily ever after in your little mode, no longer any need to curse your outcast state. Snug as a bug, singing songs at heaven's gate!"

While sarcasm wasn't his forte, Tooco could not only speak English when he wanted; he could speak "dreamer English" at that! He just didn't care to talk to Harrison. Jack laughed really hard when she told him. It was one of the things that endeared him to her—all that power with such tubelike gullibility.

Not waiting for her reply, Tooco slapped his joystick, whipping to the opposite end of the chamber as quickly as he'd arrived. She was grateful for the reprieve. Okada wanted to be left alone with her temperature taps and fantasies. Jack said, once upon a time, near

Sanatan, cokes lived in "igloos" and wore animal skins to stay warm. He'd seen screens of their stoic faces posing with their domes of ice. She imagined the two of them standing in front of their icy mode, free of their past and others' futures, free to discover their own destiny. A faint herald called out a tentative encouragement: *happy might be resuscitated.*

FIRST INTERLUDE—2197

Shuta sat at one end of a meandering modular table, staring at the weathered coal of Splatter's visage at the other end. He was waiting for the inevitable rebuke followed by the obligatory warning before entering the String arena. No doubt he would be reminded he wasn't String-trained like the great Harrison and, therefore, wouldn't have a prayer in hell. But no one was String-trained now. Long gone was the weird science capable of creating a human who could enter the fifth dimension. First, there was the extra hardware they planted in your brain, and this was in addition to giving up *half your lifespan.*

The core life force expended "firing up" your entire brain "burns twice as brightly, Roy!" No one wanted to give up half their life to be a Toon hero anymore.

The dark-brown irises in Splatter's veined yellow pools took Shuta in and dismissed him at one and the same time. Splatter had been there. He'd seen it all come down—one of the last dreamers from Bellytown, him and Dag. They were the two originals still walking around because of recent advances in sane genetic research. They hadn't sat idly by the past hundred years, with all the Topgrid advances bequeathed to them. They'd turned things in a new direction—the Screx becoming the seam chamber again being a noteworthy example. He watched Splatter's withered lips compressing and braced himself for the guttural rasp about to assail his ears.

"You remind me of your great-grandfather, also an arrogant and impetuous man."

Well, he wasn't going to waste any time getting to the heart of the matter. Han Larkill.

"He served his purpose."

"You think so. Well, if doing it for yourself was his purpose, then I agree with you. He was all about that."

All right, you want verbal fencing, parry this with your rapier wisdom. "If my great-granddad hadn't been the independent 'dreamer' he was, Harrison Jack would never have achieved the haloed greatness he did. Han Larkill served a greater purpose, and maybe it was unbeknownst to him. We'll find out today! But so what? Either way, it helped the honorable Harrison get the job done." Shuta could see from the narrowing of Splatter's eyes that he'd landed a good one and was already regretting it.

"And what is your purpose, injecting yourself into a day of illumination with your cheap-thrills warrior act?"

"Since when did putting my life on the line qualify as cheap thrills?"

"And already we've come full circle. Since you are doing it for yourself, for what *you* want! And everybody else can go to hell."

"What I want is just the opportunity to be considered by Dysan as a potential mate, and this rite is the only chance I have to claim that opportunity. I don't see how that translates to telling everybody to go to hell."

Maybe he was venting his spleen on Shuta. This boy descended from the man who'd poisoned his people and his love what seemed several lifetimes ago. "You will find this hard to believe, but when I was about ten years older than you, I had a passion for someone equal to yours."

Shuta watched the old man get up from the table and shuffle over to a portal, staring out into endless space. Finally, he turned to face Shuta again.

"Let's say, just for the sake of argument, at some point, she returns your passion. This love for each other is a tenuous creation. Its fragility stems from this act of connection. Personal love once gained immediately becomes a vulnerability in one's destiny."

If Splatter thought all this philosophical mumbo jumbo was going to change his course, he had another thing coming.

"Am I correct in assuming that you've memorized the words of the Prophet?"

Get to the point, old man. "Yes, of course, I have."

"What can you tell me about love's peace and pleasure?"

Enough of this crap. Shuta needed to start getting ready. He rose from the table. "Nothing I'm sure you don't already know."

"Sit down!" Shuta sat.

"I have a question to ask you and something I want to show you. And then if you still want to commit suicide, I'll even help you dress for the occasion. How tall are you?"

"I'm a little under two centigrid. Is that the question?"

"No." Splatter took a moment to let his veins cool. At the ripe age of 132, it was a good idea. "I have an exceptional game jump that will fit you, if you decide not to take my advice."

When he was last stoked with the arrogance of this reckless pup, he was out in front of Fifty-Ninth Street barricade, leading an attack down Sixth Avenue, an AR-15 blazing in each hand. Most of the burnt-out scrapers were in flames again from laser cannon fire, which Mayra was directing back in Cenpak. Even above all the screaming and explosions, her message to retreat came through clearly on his headset. He thought it was a bad call. There was no way now other than straight down Sixth for the Yaks to retreat. His entire unit was in hot pursuit, mowing them down. He kept at it for a couple more minutes before giving the order to fall back. Later, Mayra gave him a much sterner tongue-lashing than he'd yet to give Shuta. He still remembered it with the same remorse any lover feels the first time they disappoint their beloved. Splatter had a hunch Dysan was as impressed by Shuta's opinions as Mayra had been with his.

"At this moment, Dysan is recording Harrison's personal perspective of the epic events that restored humanity to the path of civilization, and if she does possess any thoughts or feelings for you, they are relegated to her subconscious because she has a job to do. So while she's busy not thinking of you, I'd like to know what you think of her? I want a character assessment, not some declaration of passion. Who is she, Shuta?"

The question took him completely off guard. After an initial panicked blankness, he remembered the phrase that popped in his head when he spotted her going up the bleachers.

"Beauty without vanity . . . acknowledging all its responsibilities."

Splatter was impressed in spite of himself. "And who do you think has she observed in you?"

Shuta had no problem with this answer. "The same thing you have—an arrogant and impetuous fool."

For the first time, Splatter thought he might be able to reach this boy. "Then what, pray tell, makes you think she'd ever consider you as a mate?"

"She likes me."

An appreciative snort escaped before he could cut it off, and Splatter was forced to acknowledge this young man. "You may have a clearer picture of things than I thought. Perhaps we should just cut to the chase. All or nothing, as your ancestor was fond of saying." Splatter touched a tap at his end of the table and turned to face the wall. "These are some old vids of Musashi-level String matches played in Sanatan."

If this didn't change his mind, nothing would.

CHAPTER

He'd awoken with the same desperate gamble in his heart every day of his life. It was the motivational characteristic that made Ruger Sackers so dangerous and Ruger Screenrage so exciting. He could remember countless mornings in Bellytown lying on his mat watching static-electric bolts snake across the violet grid plate. There in his father's mode, impatient to cut to the chase, all or *nothing*! And now it looked like Ruger's programed invocation was finally going to be fulfilled. With a brief flurry of his fingers, the Screwhog would explode from the ocean toward the heavens, just off the Alaskan Arctic coast.

Baylor's precise navigation steered them up through the underwater cavern. They'd sealed it off, and the pressure from that mass of water turning into steam was threatening to explode the entire rock shelf in the near future. They were poised just a centigrid beneath the crust of that shelf at a thirty-degree angle north. Baylor was calling out the numbers in a funereal tone as the pressure in the cavern rose. Everyone was strapped into the gyro couches at their assigned positions except for Harrison. He was strapped into one of the couches on the outer ring, brought up on the bridge to assist Han's piloting. He was the only one who'd flown a large ship through the air.

They all hung suspended for a moment, watching the screens display in undulating blues and greens an ocean that was just above them. Viewing it close up on the outer ring, Harrison was reminded of the lava lamp in Bob's mode. He felt like a minuscule creature submerged just below the screens' colorful eruption, dwarfed by its radiant globular show.

Han too watched the intertwining palates as he tapped ignition. The solid fuel rockets of their surface thrusters began to roar. The Hog surged forward immediately, ramming the screwhead through the upper crust. A banshee moan shuddered through the bridge when searing screwhead touched frigid water, soon joined by a chorus of screaming metal goblins that threatened to vibrate the ship into a million pieces. Locked in position, a gyro couch did little to damp the vibrations. Harrison felt like his teeth were being shaken right out of his skull. Then the mammoth Earth gutter broke free, shooting from a grid-high ocean geyser straight into the clouds.

Han extended the runner blades, Harrison's single contribution to the plan. They should function as stabilizing fins on their flight. So far, the Hog was hanging in there. He did notice the pitch of vibrations going lower as their trajectory began arcing farther north. But, if anything, Zim's miscalculation of their speed accounted for a very fast and shaky ride. Han tapped up their present velocity. Despite the vibrations, he could see the readout clearly on his helmet visor: twelve thousand grid an hour. That was unbelievable! This ride, if they finished it, would last a little more than an hour. The shaking was unnerving, but he didn't think the ship would come apart. Hogs were the toughest machines on the planet. If anything could keep it together, it was a Hog.

"Retract the runner blades a little. We're not increasing the angle of our trajectory fast enough." Han took Harrison's advice and tapped the adjustment.

"What about the shaking, Jack? Is there anything we can do about that?"

"No. It's a big jerk slamming into the air. It might settle down when we start our descent."

"How's the stomach?"

"Stomach's good, Han."

Really? A pissing contest over who can play it cooler while blasting into space. Actually, they were only blasting into the planet's upper atmosphere. He'd spent a whole career up here. Han was running his mouth to keep from getting rattled. But seriously, cokes, was this the best way to cope with overwhelming anxiety while steering an elephant through the sky?

"How are the lessons coming with Darl? She giving you what you need?"

Unbelievable. Complete with sexual innuendos! "Yeah, Han, but I'm a little slow picking it up."

"Well, we can always make you a mute."

"Oh, I'll get it, Han. I'm gonna get it."

"I'm sure you will. For now, just relax and enjoy the ride."

Fine. As long as they kept rising in their arc, he could kick back for a while. It was when they began to fall that everybody needed to be on their toes. A sudden reminder flashed across his brain. They should get the air. "Han, now would be a good time to open our locks and take in some air before we get too much higher."

"Got it, Jack."

— ❈ —

Harrison was standing on a busy corner in one of the gray cities he saw in the prison vids. There were cars whizzing past. He didn't know how he got here or what to do, if he should even move at all. Suddenly a yellow car screamed to a stop in front of him. The driver leaned out. He recognized Bob. "I got you, Jack. Get in. I'm taking you to meet somebody."

Harrison dutifully got in, pulling the lock shut behind him. They sped down the streets, becoming two-dimensional, slipping through razor-thin spaces in traffic, bending around slower vehicles. Bob was chattering, glancing back at Harrison in his rear-view mirror.

"I could have been a bartender. I could have been Chung's buddy!"

Harrison had to ask, "Who's Chung?"

"He's the guy who wants me to take you to this meet. It's in a warehouse in an interesting part of town. You know, Jack, you people were very hard on me, and sneaky too. Very sneaky."

Harrison had no patience for this pathetic artifact. "What did you expect, you cannibalistic creep?"

"That's exactly the problem right there. Because of my mores—based on a desire to survive, I might add—"

"Survive my ass! You had enough food down there to last a couple of lifetimes, good food too! Believe me, we're still enjoying it."

Through Bob's rear-view mirror, an expression of rage and horror stared back at him.

"My corpses? You've been eating my corpses?"

"No, you sick fuck, your vegetables!"

"Oh. Well, there it is. You're all so pallid, so spiritless. Why should I care what you pale reflections of mankind think of me? Besides, you killed me!"

"I didn't kill you. Han did."

"Oh brother, and I'm the sick fuck! Don't worry, Jack. Your date will set you straight."

"Who's Chung?"

"I told you, the guy who asked me to take you to the meet."

They stopped in front of a triangular building with a bright-pink facade. Bob reached over the seat and opened his lock. "Out."

He panicked at the thought of being alone again in this strange world. "Wait a second—"

"Fuck you! You don't deserve Chung's generosity. Get out, murderer!" Bob somehow got a boot over the seat and was ramming the heel with progressive vigor into Harrison's face. The next thing he knew, he was sitting on the empty street, facing the vast pink wall. Bob and the yellow car were gone.

He looked up, taking in the pink building as a section in the front slid open, revealing a classic inky maw. For no good reason he could decipher, he got up and walked inside. When his eyes adjusted to the shadowy interior, he began to see what exactly was on Bob's twisted mind. Lining all four walls were rows of stacked bodies from the NORAD. Immediately, he started reversing course, backing toward the entrance, when he noticed movement at the bottom of a pile on his right. He watched as a thin young woman crawled out from under an entire stack of cadavers.

At first, her skin was an iridescent blue; but as she stiffly stood and then approached, she became suffused with a vibrant rose-colored light. By the time she reached him, she was radiant pink, like the building's exterior. Harrison recognized her.

"You took my book, mister."

"Did I? Well, after all, you didn't need it anymore."

"I need it now."

"Well, I haven't got it on me." It was true. He couldn't remember where he put it. But he was sure it would turn up eventually, and besides, he hadn't read it yet.

Bitter disappointment was reflected in her eyes, and she spoke with measured scorn, "You better go get it and give it to me."

"And what if I can't?"

Surprisingly, her scowl disappeared; and she smiled, eyes sparkling with secret consequences. "You'll be sorry."

<hr>

A tremendous shudder wracked the Hog, and Harrison was jolted from his dream. The first thing he realized was, they were in a steep descent. The second was, the screens were registering only bubbling green. "Han, extend the runner blades full!"

"HAN!" There was no response. Peering more closely down into the bridge, he saw they were all slumped in their gyros, unconscious. The whole crew was on internal thermostat and oxygen. That should rule out oxygen deprivation as the cause. And yet he noticed his own breath was labored, and he felt cold. He punched up internal systems readout on his visor and realized the problem—the air pressure. When they opened the locks to get fresh air, they'd depressurized the inner hull. This caused the internal systems in their jumps to respond.

The suits were designed to keep oxygen mixtures consistent down to a hundred grid below sea level. They were not designed for being a hundred grid above the planet. Their jumps interpreted the loss of air pressure as their view plates being open and cut back their oxygen and heat.

"HAN! WAKE UP! WAKE UP, DOG-DAMNIT!"

He'd have to climb down to the unconscious Screenrage. The vibrations were getting more violent as the Hog's nose dipped even farther. If the runner blades weren't fully extended again, and quickly, the huge ship would begin falling end over end. Hitting water or ice wouldn't matter then. Either way, they'd be smashed into paste.

Unstrapping from his couch, he made the dangerous climb down the shuddering ring ladder. Desperately gripping progressive rungs, he looked up to see the bubbling green growing darker. Touchdown was not far off. When he finally reached Han, a vigorous shake was enough to bring him blinking back to life.

"Han, extend the runner blades to full *now*!"

"Huh?"

"EXTEND THE RUNNER BLADES TO FULL!"

"Shit!"

It was clear from the sudden panic in his eyes that Han was awake now. Immediately, he began drumming commands into his console. Harrison heard the howl of the blades cutting into the atmosphere and felt the ship start to steady its plummet. Yet another urgent factoid popped into his brain.

"HAN, CLOSE THE LOCKS AGAIN! CLOSE THE LOCKS!"

Han rapidly drummed the command.

"Sound the warning siren and override the locks on the crew's gyros! I'm going back and strap in." Harrison started back up the ring ladder but, checking the screens, realized he'd never make it in time. The dark green was becoming purple. Splashdown was imminent. He could try to take five, but visualizing his pattern would be difficult with all the shaking. The warning siren wailed as all the crew's gyros released from their locked positions, spinning free. There was only one option left.

"GRAB ME, HAN! GRAB ME!" Harrison dropped from the ladder into Han's lap. His legs straddling the commander's couch face-to-face, Harrison grabbed the Screenrage in a bear hug. "Hug me! Hug me, Han!"

Through butted view plates, the cobalt eyes examined him. "All right, Jack, all right." Han's right arm encircled him, sliding his hand around Harrison's waist, pulling him tight against him. With arms and legs wrapped around the Screenrage, buttocks pressed against his muscular thighs, another image popped into Harrison's mind—this one in vivid detail. The head of the Screwhog hit the first frigid wave, and he knew the rush of vulnerability again. Off with the golden giant on another adventure.

⸺•◆•⸺

At their victory party, Baylor readily admitted he was completely and utterly wrong, raising his cup several times to the triumphant Zim. Not only was he wrong about the Hog being able to fly several thousand grid and splash down safely in the Arctic Ocean, but he'd also been wrong about both the Hog's ability to float and the screwhead's ability to pull them through water. True, the maximum speed they could muster was only thirty-two grid an hour, but that created an opportunity for a celebratory bash. They hit the ocean about six hundred grid from the Arctic shore, so they had about seventeen hours before they bit into Sanatan ice. And to put the cherry on the cap, the great leviathan *foated* in perfect camouflage—just a centigrid below the surface of the waves. Things couldn't have gone better. He was joyful in his humiliation, *very happy* to be wrong and alive. Unfortunately, it meant being extra nice to their spikey boy wonder, listening patiently to his long-winded diatribes on a slew of unlikely topics. But even that became bearable, wrapped in the arms of the sweetest little Zapstar who ever pitched a snag—his golden Sunsue.

If only he could keep his mind on his recreation. Succor mixed with venom was an unstable brew. His obsession intruded even while dipping into her honeyed shy, simultaneously envisioning again the moment he and Rector locked eyes. He owed her more attention. Those long gorgeous legs and curvaceous hips, splaying thighs in artful disarray, making his jerk desperate for the comfort of her hearth. But his vendetta refused to be shaken. He savored that moment of recognition more than trying to picture how he'd kill him.

That was always a blur, his rage so consuming it blinkered his imagination. Satisfaction was in that moment of recognition, and that moment was not far off. Sunsue groaned, rising up to him as he withdrew, sighing as he sank in her again.

He'd better play now because their next stop, Sanatan, was going to be all business. That's where he'd find Captain Rector, Sacker command. First, they'd have to make it to the gaming sector. Then Bay would square them with Carbachi. That wouldn't be hard since he and Carmine were old friends. The bomb would seal the deal. He'd convinced Han, once they arrived, to give Bob's bomb to the don. Zim was busy tweaking it the last two days while they were digging to the underwater cavern. He assured Bay it was easily programmable now. Carmine was a weapons freak. He'd love it. The family always favored overkill when it came to expressing their convictions. Not only would he be giddy about the bomb; he'd get a kick out of the antique assault rifles too. After a stern warning to fire them only beyond the light ring, Bay planned to hand them out as party favors to the don's crew. Carmine would be pleased, cutting him tribute from their buried treasure. As long as they were careful to maintain Harrison's techie "cover," everything would go fine. In the family, spacecase were akin to vampires—genetically altered, technically enhanced demons, spawned by a secular society. They'd go berserk if they found out a spacecase was among them.

"I'm being so bad, Baydee! I shouldn't feel so good bein' so bad. You gotta help me, Baydee . . . you gotta help me."

She was starting the masochistic ritual that always left him torn, wanting to resolve her need for punishment. Soon she'd be pleading with him to take a stinger to that exquisite ass, whipping her cheeks to a burning sheen and filling the air with her ecstatic screams.

In the downward spiral of a Zapstar's career, Sunsue found herself on the "sado" fiber-feeds. The stripes of pain she routinely endured made her crave abandon. Abandon arrived in the form of a handsome holo operator from Bellytown who convinced her to mint a disk "just for us" of her descent into sacrilege. Not long after, it hit the porn-fibers with his image obscured.

However, Zapstar, Sunsue, was very recognizable. Shortly, she was in a container headed for the mines.

He didn't feel good about giving into her masochistic desires, but it was the theme that grounded all her pleasure, what she required for peace of mind, even though the purple stripes would mar her perfect ass for days. From the ritual begging, "Oh, please, Badey, please!" he knew she was getting anxious for her theme to play. Bay reached underneath his mat for the thin flexible rod of his stinger. He had a theory that everybody came into being with a theme to their life, a kind of personal magnet that drew certain events to them. In his life, it was clear the theme was betrayal. He often wondered how you got your theme and bitterly wished another had been dealt to him.

In the beginning, his life seemed charmed. Custom order: son of a Sacker colonel, he quickly advanced through the ranks. His first command was in an outpost in Southern Africa overseeing production and security at 7's diamond mines. Diamonds were, of course, invaluable in both technology and industry. It was a very important posting for someone only thirty-one cycles old.

Unexpectedly, what Baylor found there was a heritage. In a world where color was a personal prerogative, the idea of cokes banding together and creating cultures because of their skin pigmentation was bizarre and unsettling. His family's blackness was their bold expression of "walkin' the walk and talkin' the talk of a Topgrid military motherduffer." And they were black, black! From four centigrid away, you couldn't make out anything but the whites of their warrior eyes.

He'd slowly extracted their history from the mottled black faces he hunted down out in the barren countryside. They were all waste-fill fugitives preying on mining resources and supplies. At first, he was surprised they were always black; but as he learned from questioning his prisoners, there was an ancient enmity between blacks and whites. This was originally blacks' land, and whites came and took it, making blacks work for them. Eventually, blacks took it back. Then it all got blown to hell, and the cartels came in and ran everything. Walking them out to their executions, increasingly he felt a sense of betrayal to this ancient people whose skin he wore by choice. That's where the trouble began—*out of his feeling that he was the betrayer!* On his last patrol, crossing parched grids exposed to the red African sun, he hallucinated the land disappearing under him, that he was being dropped into a bottomless hole. Less than sixteen hours later, he was on his way to Sanatan, busted to clone patrol.

His second-in-command, Lieutenant Waxer, a hard-charging noncommissioned officer, observed his interest in "black history." He quickly took advantage of what Bay suspected was an inherent genetic defect that came with his black pigmentation, an inborn belief in goodwill. Waxer casually requested Bay's personal contact code— "In case you're off-line and it's imperative, I get a message to you." Then Waxer made several entries, assuming the persona of one of the criminals who preyed on 7's interests. All these messages were fashioned as responses to questions he appeared to have asked. They referred to his new genealogical interests and were seditious and conspiratorial in tone, entries that, when he was confronted with them, sounded a lot like the thoughts actually running through his head.

On the transport to Sanatan, he had time to ponder the essential correctness of Waxer's false accusations. It was true he'd been set up, but first, he was betrayed by his own vague longings for a real heritage. It wasn't until he was patrolling in Sanatan and met Carmine Carbachi that he eventually learned about the family, how they really were a family. Sicilians never stopped making babies the old-fashioned way. Shocked by this information, he was even more surprised when Carmine told him 7 knew about it; but as long as they kept it quiet, they turned a blind eye.

Carmine laid out the whole story for him one day when they were out on the ice for a spin in his new levi racer, a Lockheed Lightning. He explained that the family requested a meeting with the western cartel when construction of Big New was already underway. In light of humanity's catastrophic upheaval, the family was interested in finding a way to make their services less at odds with the new authorities. Carbachi's father put an offer on the table that both stunned and pleased the western cartel. When the offer was passed on to 7, they thought it was a great idea as well. They made a deal. And it was because of this deal that 7 gave the family a pass when it came to their method of procreation.

The Sicilians didn't want mode deeds on the Satcits, which were then in the planning stages. They didn't want reservations for passage to a new world on the Starcruisers being envisioned. What they wanted was the go-ahead to construct a new resort paradise at the North Pole in partnership with the western cartel, and—if 7 ever realized their ambitions to leave the planet—the family wanted to inherit the Earth. Each cartel would turn over its tools of earthly power, along with their cities and Satcits, as they progressively abandoned them. This would finally give the family dominion over everything and everyone left on the planet.

Though Yakuza didn't sign off on this deal (in fact, knew nothing about it), they'd find out soon enough after the Topgrid were gone. Bay knew what Carmine would do with his precious gift. One day, the family would arrive in the dead of night with a fleet of E-Mag transporters and move Big New up near Sanatan. When the sun rose on that distant morning, once again pouring light onto the old five boroughs, Carmine's bomb would find its home in Bellytown.

For their new resort, and the future transference of the planet, the Sicilians were willing to guarantee an end to problems created by their criminal enterprises. They wouldn't stop being who they were, but they'd tone it down to the point it would seem that way to everyone. They would oversee all forms of gaming in their planed resort but would shift their priority from personal profits to assisting 7 in achieving their goals. They'd turn over 40 percent of all their profits to 7. His father even threw in a generous share of the family's most lucrative new division, marketing supermodified limbs. Popular to the degree, a lot of cokes were having healthy limbs amputated to install these superpowered additions.

So it came to pass that one of the family's most notable character traits, aside from swift retaliation—their attribute of loyalty—was extended to their mother planet. Let the Topgrid blast off into space looking for an unspoiled Eden. The family would play out their cards on the stomping grounds of their fathers. Fuck pollution, radiation, ozone depletion, and the hordes of slime! The family would fulfill their destiny to rule the world. And so far, Carmine confided, as he banked the Lightning around a glacier at 3,200 grid an hour, everything was right on schedule. It was a real curiosity how an act of intense passion could be performed by rote. But there Sunsue lay, heaving and grinning, her perfect buttocks stitched with crimson welts while a part of him was somewhere else, nursing his bitter cup. He needed to cleanse himself, make ready the warrior that Sacker training had forged him into. He would embrace humility and humiliation, accept death, and throw away his life. Once he achieved that; he could practice the second tenant of bushido—strike!

As if reading his thoughts, Sunsue sprang off the mat with a mischievous giggle and grabbed the handcuffs from his duff.

"I'm gonna make you suffer, Baydee. I'm gonna make you cry for what you did to me. I'm gonna make you writhe an eternity before I let you bust!"

"Yeah, baby, yeah! Make me beg like a god."

"Can I ask you something crazy?"

Harrison was suddenly awake again. "Sure. What?"

Okada raised her head from his chest and turned to look at him. "Have you ever seen Dog . . . on the String?"

"No."

She rested her chin on his chest. "Have you ever . . . felt a presence on the String?"

"No."

"Do you think Dog exists?"

"I don't know."

"I don't know either . . . but do you feel he exists?"

"I don't know. On the String, it's obvious there's an overall pattern to everything, a harmony, some connection between everything, a way things flow into and transform each other. But whether that design is the work of an all-encompassing consciousness or arose out of chaos and random events—I don't know."

"That actually seems more farfetched to me than a supreme being."

Harrison felt the gentle swaying of the Hog as it slowly churned through the water and wondered why they were having this discussion. "Maybe, but if that's the case, then what is the purpose of this grand design? I mean, where is it headed? What's the point of it? If there really is a supreme consciousness, there has to be some point, a purpose, or objective. There has to be a journey and destination."

Okada laid her head back down on his chest. "Maybe Dog is exploring himself, trying to discover everything that he can be?"

Harrison smiled. "Maybe he's licking his cuj."

Okada giggled into his chest. "Maybe he is." She slid her head down his torso, and he felt her warm tongue begin to play across his belly. "Maybe I should lick some cuj."

"Dog knows you should!"

Okada lifted her head to look at him again. "Do you love me, Jack?"

There was a moment, just a moment too long, before Han's voice interrupted them, "Everybody to your stations. We're closing on the ice."

———❖———

"Thirty seconds to impact." Darl's announcement wasn't news to anyone on the bridge as they watched the looming mass displace the swirling purple currents of the Arctic Ocean.

Han tapped for acceleration of the screwhead, bringing it up to speed. He planned to cut into the wall of ice the way a laser cuts through flesh. The heat from the outer hull would change the frozen water into steam in a flash. He took a temperature reading of the outer hull and tapped Okada for more heat, simultaneously retracting the runner blades back into the screw head.

"Zim, I'm going to need full power when we hit the ice. Darl, make sure the power for hull heat doesn't drop when Zim pushes it. Tooco, open the scoops to the kiln canals and holding tanks. Let the water fill the back of the outer hull. It will lower the rear of the ship so we can get our angle right."

Han heard their acknowledgments while continuing to tap up the speed on the screwhead. He was planning to drill out of the ice as soon as possible. They were all straining toward the open air and freedom from what seemed an endless subterranean life. Drilling at a forty-five-degree, angle, they would dig at least two grid before they reached the surface of the ice. That would ensure they didn't accidentally shear off an iceberg with them in it. He checked to see how the angle of the ship was changing as water poured into the back of the outer hull.

"Tooco, close scoops. We're at forty-five degrees. Once the drill head is firmly engaged in the ice, open the slag vents and let that water out. The steam it generates in the stern will help push the ship completely into the mass."

With a high-pitched whine, the Screwhog bored into the ice just below the waterline.

"Bay, what's our distance to the surface?"

"Almost two hundred centigrid."

That was a hundred centigrid less than Han expected. He'd guesstimated the height from Jack's "retrieval factoid" that three quarters of an iceberg's mass was underwater. His instruments read the underwater mass at nine hundred centigrid, so the abovewater mass should be three hundred centigrid. Being a hundred centigrid shorter was dangerously off.

"Okada, cut the hull heat by half. Zim, pull back the drive. The last thing he needed was their heat being the facilitating factor for splitting off in an iceberg.

"Ryka, can you pick up any surface sounds through all this noise?"

Hunched in her gyro and pressing the headphones to her skull, Ryka shook her head. "No."

"Bay, tell me when we're close to thirty centigrid."

"Cliqued."

As the Hog slowly dug its way up to the surface, the crew sat at their stations watching their screens with unwavering focus, knowing their compressed existence was about to end. You really try not to think about the fact tons and tons of rock and dirt bury you inside the planet, but it's always there inside your mind, pacing back and forth, screaming to get out.

"Thirty centigrid." Bay called it out.

"Zim, cut the drive. Okada, cut heat." The high whine of the tip began dropping through the registers until it slowed to a rasping churn and stopped. Han turned to Ryka. "You getting anything on the surface?"

In her fetal position, Ryka rocked her gyro. A moment passed before she stuck out her fist, thumb pointed up. "Nothing but wind."

Han looked down at Bay. "End of the line, cokes! We're here. Bay, you and I can get some exercise, cutting a stairway to the surface. Ice is nothing for the hammers, and the steam will keep us toasty while we're cutting."

Bay cracked a grin. "Sounds like a refreshing little workout in a steam niche."

"You can join us if you want, Jack."

"That's okay. Okada and I still have to get our stuff together."

"What stuff? You've got a mining jump, your helmet, and your duff."

"Yeah, but the stuff in our duffs is all over the place. We've been . . . you know."

"Fucking your brains out, yes, we know." Han let loose with his signature roar, and the crew, relieved at their arrival, joined in. Even Zim in C-power responded with a snort. Tooco characteristically maintained his silence. But they all knew they'd achieved something remarkable: escaping from the mines in a Screwhog, steering it through Earth, air, water, and ice to Sanatan, and now even their spacecase was washed in the blood of the carnal lamb. Soon they would be released to the surface again. Things were looking up for this desperate little band. And they all knew it was their Screenrage who'd given them the inspiration, who'd whipped them into shape, made them believe they could pull it off—and they had. They were in the mood to follow him anywhere.

⋯•◆•⋯

Harrison, his duff slung over a shoulder, put one boot in front of the other, making his way up the steep ice staircase. He stopped periodically to catch his breath. Although they were on oxygen and internal thermostat, their jump temperatures fell almost four degrees outside the ship. The colder air made his breathing more labored. When he emerged above the ice, a freezing gust of wind blasted his view plate, frosting the white slate in front of him with its own crystalline pattern. He used his free hand to brush away the ivory powder and tapped up the defroster on his helmet. Off in the distance, he could see the snowy expanse dissolve into an Arctic night. A deep blue laced with diamond stars overwhelmed and contained the constant glare of the icy plains. Above the wind, Han and Baylor were hollering at him, pointing at a glittering dome on the horizon—Sanatan! Seeing Okada, he pointed toward the magic citadel too. But she was preoccupied, turning away to assist Zim, who was leading a series of levi-loaders up onto the ice. He watched as a stack of Bob's rifles and cases of ammunition appeared. Then Tooco surfaced, bringing up the rear on a levi-loader piled high with vegetables on top of crates of C-rations. Harrison realized the levi-loaders still functioning this far from the ship meant the whole landscape must be implanted with electromagnetic pulse beacons.

"Jack!" Larkill was gesturing through the swirling snow for him to come over there.

"Bay thought it might be a good idea for you to get on your String and check out the area we'll be passing through. Just check it out, okay?"

"Yeah, don't kill anybody!" Behind a partially frosted view plate, Harrison could still make out Baylor's grin. "Just do a quick recon so we don't run into any surprises, okay?"

Harrison nodded, letting the initial pathways of his pattern arc across his brain.

He'd come across an ancient essay in Cincinnati retrieval by a coke called Fixx. It was about the joy of running. He'd almost fallen out of his console laughing at the prosaic description of plodding over "hill and dale." But when Fixx started rhapsodizing about the "runner's high," it sounded eerily like being on the String. He described what Harrison was experiencing right now: a feeling of being totally free of your body while having perfect control over the functioning of every atom, accompanied by the omnipresent sensation of melding with the entire landscape. Right now, Harrison was an endless white.

Then he saw them, two Sackers in a cul-de-sac taking a leak beside their levi-cruiser. He was immediately beside them, circling the cruiser twice, waiting for them to finish their business and relock their pelvic plates. He decided to stay close, maybe discover where any outposts on

Sanatan's perimeter were located. When the big one tapped open the cruiser lock, Harrison shot past him, just some quarks on the wind. He blew through a protective screen into the cruiser's rear holding area. He could've entered straight through the vehicle's body, but Sacker cruisers were loaded with all kinds of sensors and alarms. He wasn't taking any chances. Now he only needed to shift his body every few seconds to remain invisible.

"What time are we expected back at perimeter security?"

The big one paused in his preparations to get back underway and tapped his helmet for a time readout on his visor. "We've got another thirty-five minutes. Why?"

"I thought maybe we could coup here for a half hour instead of plowing through this blizzard. Even if some slime was thinking about sneaking into techie quarter, they wouldn't try it on a night like this. Fuckin' wind is blowing at least eight hundred grid an hour."

"Right. And if the captain comes slippin' up on us, we're workin' the techie bars again."

"You're a hard coke, Diekster."

"No, just careful."

"Sacker prime! Sacker prime, my clone." They shared a chuckle. He watched as Diekster reactivated their guidance screens. The green glow partially illuminated the muted black interior. Diekster pulled back the joystick between his legs, and the cruiser levitated up out of the snowbank.

"You still runnin' kunt killer?"

The smaller one giggled. "Nah, too tame. You won't believe what I got going now."

"What?"

"I been getting very heavy into Sheeman. She's the Screenrage with the four milligrid clit, and I gotta tell you—it's pretty wild."

"Oh, to be young again . . . wonder what freak lab fermented that mutant?"

"Diekster, how old are you? She's comp-gen, coke! Paramount made her."

"What's that snag, you?"

"Would you believe half my graft this last quarter cycle?"

"You're shittin' me?"

"I know it's crazy! But the thing is, if you do the witch from behind, she waits until you're about to pop, then slips that clit right up your ass and writhes. She *writhes* that thing, coke! I had to get a sleeve with a bigger cup. First time, I blew the fuckin' sleeve off! I had to mop out the bottom of the Screx. I'm tellin' you, coke, you ain't never cum that big."

Diekster let out a roar, reminiscent of Han's laugh. "I'll have to take your word for it, tube." Still grinning, he banked the cruiser a little to his right, directly toward where the Hog crew was waiting. Suddenly a flashing red dot appeared on their central screen, accompanied by a high beeping sound.

"What have we here?" Diekster leaned closer, tapping up a description. Seconds later, a readout started crawling across the screen. "Nine humans, five levi-loaders, no weapons, straight ahead, seven hundred centigird."

Diekster nudged the stick back, and the cruiser slowed. "It's got to be that fucking Screwhog crew! The fuckers didn't explode. We better activate backup." He reached for the console, but the small one grabbed his hand.

"Wait a second. If we call in backup, who gets credit for the sack, huh? The captain! He gets the paid off-line time, and we're sittin' in this fuckin' cruiser, riding around this wasteland till our jerks fall off." He gestured toward the screen. "They're unarmed, coke! You tellin' me we can't handle some unarmed convicts?"

"Listen, Bickman, you're gettin' ahead of yourself here. You need to pay a little more attention to the job. If you'd read the bolo, you'd know they think one of 'em might well be a fucking spacecase!" Diekster pulled his hand free and reached for the console again.

Harrison knew he had to act immediately. Slipping through the mesh, he merged into the console, melding his atoms into the strontium-yttrium coating; then reversing the charge in the E-Mag taps, he shorted out the cruiser's entire electromagnetic casing. All eight E-Mags exploded, and the levi dove toward the snow. Diekster wrestled with the joystick, trying to pull up the cruiser's nose. "Dogdamn, fucking Fords!"

The cruiser plowed into the snow, biting into ice and flipping end over end before landing on its top. Inside, the two Sackers hung upside down in their safety harnesses.

"Bickman! You all right?" Diekster put a piston-powered boot against the lock on his side and pushed. It popped open. "Bickman, are you all right!"

"Yeah, yeah. But I'm gonna puke if I don't get out of this harness."

They both began struggling with their harnesses. Quickly, Harrison melded the tungsten atoms in their harness clasps.

"What the fuck is going on?" Bickman screamed his frustration, wrestling with the harness. Momentarily, they stopped struggling and turned their view plates to each other, the realization dawning simultaneously.

"Quick, hit your homer," Diekster hissed.

But Harrison had anticipated the move and melded the atoms in the shoulders and elbows of their armored jumps. Bickman's arm froze in midreach while the finger of Diekster's glove stopped, suspended less than a milligrid above the tap in his breastplate. There was a momentary pause accompanied by the Arctic wind; then Diekster spoke in a low growl, "You fucking spacecreep . . . you're here, aren't you?"

Flying through the barren landscape, even with the String's invisibility, he was grateful for the darkness, murdering spacecreep that he was. *Yes, that's me, tube-born, Barney-nurtured, custom clone, with no family trappings—the "community theater" for indolent Topgrid.* He'd never been chosen, and he was grateful for that too. Smashing Diekster and Bickman's view plates triggered another memory: fighting over the game helmet of a dead cadet, punching a hole in the view plate after losing a tug of war—superficial connections then, superficial connections now. And that's the way it's always been, even when they birthed themselves out of each other's bodies, although that illusion must've been very powerful. He was grateful for his autonomous nurture free of the saccharine fantasies that even Han was a prisoner of. His "father," the coke who'd snagged him off the Ruger shelves with a megachunk of graft, this bellygrid hustler retained Han's undying devotion. The reverential description his inquiries elicited from the mournful Screenrage made that embarrassingly clear. Now he'd severed forever that last illusion of connection. He'd killed two cokes in cold blood. Not quite killed, not yet—numbed and dying in the Arctic night.

"Aaaah!" Han leaped to one side as Harrison vibrated into the three-dimensional in front of him.

"Don't do that so close next time, all right? Where the hell did you go, Big New? You've been gone for thirty minutes!"

"We've got a problem." Han's already furrowed brows lowered dangerously. "Don't tell me ..."

"I had to kill two Sackers on patrol."

"You crazy motherduffer! I tell you just to look around, and you kill two Sackers? You killed two Sackers?"

"They picked you up on their scanners. I was riding in the back of their cruiser, checking out their reconnaissance. I disabled the cruiser before they could tap an alert . . . then I killed them. What other choice did I have?"

Baylor, who stood dumbfounded, finally came to life. "None! You did exactly the right thing. You had no choice."

Zim, sitting cross-legged in the snow, gave a contemptuous snort. "You think? Except they know exactly where their cruiser went dead and are converging on that spot right now. Great move, space—"

"Shut up, Zim!" Han turned back to Harrison. "How far away and in which direction is the cruiser?"

Harrison pointed back in the direction he'd come from. "About seven grid from here."

Han turned to Bay. "All right, you and I will ride on the lead loader. Zim, you and the crew divide up on the rest of the loaders."

Baylor shot a gloved hand into the air. "Wait! Wait! I've got it! There's a story, a kind of legend …" He turned to Harrison. "How did you kill them?"

"I immobilized their jumps and smashed their view plates."

"Great! That's great. Listen, huge white monsters used to roam around here, teeth and claws like laser swords. Sackers and Leviracers still swear they spot them from time to time. You need to hurry back before a cruiser arrives." He handed Harrison a small survival blade that he pulled from his boot. "Drag them away from the cruiser and cut up their faces with this." Bay held out the blade to Harrison, who took it. "'Then cut off a leg from one and an arm from the other. Serrate the cuts so they're jagged and uneven. Leave four-toed tracks in the snow, like this." He knelt in the powder, demonstrating the marks. "Make them coming toward the cruiser, then move away with drops of blood in the snow. Take the arm and the leg with you and bury them in a drift far away from the scene. If we're lucky, they'll think their cruiser malfunctioned, and one of these creatures killed and fed on them!"

Han needed some convincing. "Do you think that will work?"

"It better work because, otherwise, they'll figure out it was our spacecase here. We've got to give them another scenario that's plausible. Sackers cut their graft figuring this shit out."

Han turned to Harrison. "Can you do it quick?"

"I'll be on the String, remember?"

"All right, we'll wait here. Go!"

Harrison was already visualizing his pattern, nodding just before he disappeared.

Returning to the scene of the crime was the last thing he expected to do, but here he was, staring at blue faces behind broken view plates hanging upside down in eternity. On the horizon, he made out the lights of two cruisers coming toward him.

First, he kicked in the windshield of the cruiser, cut open the harnesses, finally dragging out the corpses through the hole. He threw the bodies down in front of the cruiser and slashed their faces as he'd been instructed. Immediately, he realized there was a big problem; already partially frozen, there was no blood coming from the wounds. He quickly reached through Diekster's breastplate and pulled his heart out of his body. As long as he held the heart, it was in his 5, and he could remove it without leaving a hole. He generated some heat, centrifuging the Higgs-Boson particles in his hand, and felt the heart thawing. Briefly shuddering into the three-dimensional, he began squeezing blood all over their faces and on the snow around them. He quickly jumped back on the String, brushing out his boot prints, then used the survival knife to cut off Diekster's leg and Beckman's arm, remembering to make the cuts jagged, like Baylor told him. After that, he went to work making tracks leading toward the cruiser from two hundred centigrid out, coming in and then leading away another two hundred centigrid in the opposite direction. Harrison surmised the monster that Bay was talking about was the Arctic "polar bear," yet another byte from retrieval. He worked at hyperspeed to make it look like the beast traveled on four legs but battled on two. Then he reached into Beckman and pulled out his heart. Again, he briefly returned to the three-dimensional and squeezed out blood near the monster's tracks, leading away for twenty centigrid. Then he jumped back on the String and brushed away his tracks. He'd just finished when the beams of the first cruiser's lights cut through him, revealing the gory scene. He disposed of the limbs and hearts in a drift, close to where the crew was waiting.

The next instant, he was standing beside Han. "All taken care of."

The Screenrage repeated his leap into the air. "Dogdamnit, Jack! I told you not to do that!"

Harrison grinned. "I finished just as the cruisers arrived."

"They didn't see you?"

Harrison shook his head in disbelief. "No, Han. I was on the String."

Ever the inquisitor Baylor had to ask, "Did you do it like—"

"Yes! They'll think it was a polar bear. That's the ID of your monster, by the way."

Han caught Zim's attention and motioned for him to come over. When he did, the Screenrage laid out his plan. "Harrison, you get back on your string and take point. Stay out in front of us a couple hundred centigrid and make sure we stay clear of any cruisers. If you see anything coming our way, come back and let us know immediately. We're going to make a wide birth around the crime scene." He motioned an arc to their right. "Then toward Sanatan. The whole area around the city is illuminated for four grid out, so we'll stop at least a hundred centigrid short of that. Bay and I will ride on the first levi-loader. Zim, you and Okada ride the second one. Have Sunsue on the third, Ryka on the fourth, and Tooco bringing up the rear on the last one. Everybody stay sharp and keep scanning the area. Have Tooco concentrate on covering our back. All right, let's go."

The last leg of their journey was uneventful, slipping quietly over grid after grid of rolling drifts under the velvet night—a night that would last another half cycle before morning came. Making a wide arc around his killing ground, Harrison saw only the undulating white burnished by the glow of Sanatan.

He'd been there many times, both as a cadet and as spacecase. But every time he laid eyes on it, he was struck by its fanciful cloak of crystalline polymer. Six thousand four hundred square grid at its base, the lower third of the luminous twelve-grid-high megadome was etched with the outline of a mountain range. The upper two-thirds took the shape of a crystal castle, rising up from the engraved mountain range. The many glittering turrets of the fictitious fortress transformed the lights of the casinos into a rainbow of brilliant beams shooting into the northern night. This was the whimsical bell jar that covered Sanatan.

Like Big New, Sanatan floated on an electromagnetic carpet created by a C-power grid plate. While Big New used the old scrapers to create an opposing positive polarity, Sanatan utilized the natural positive polarity of the planet's northern axis to produce the Meissner effect, suspending the burg a hundred centigrid above the ice.

If Big New was the beehive of business, Sanatan was the beehive of pleasure. Divided into three sectors—gaming, recreational, and medical—it was the place where Topgrid and techies came to be patched up, pampered, and revitalized.

Finally, within five grid of the city, the Hog crew stopped to wait for Harrison, who soon came vibrating back into the third dimension on the second levi-loader between Zim and Okada.

"You asshole!" Zim leapt off the levi-loader and headed toward Han and Bay. "Han, will you tell this spaceshit to stop fucking with me!"

Okada was smiling watching Han try to calm their hysterical sensate. "He hates you."

"I know. I don't think much of him either."

There came a second pregnant pause as she watched Harrison from under black lashes.

"Jack, remember what we talked about—taking off on our own before it's too late? This is it. It's now or never." She didn't wait for his response. "We don't have to live in an ice hut. We could use the Hog for our mode. It's got everything we need to survive. We could move it, dig in somewhere else, and make our own tunnel down to it. You could start it up and drive it, couldn't you?"

"Yeah, with your help, I probably, could."

A look of relief passed across her petite oval face, and he could see she was in dead earnest about their fantasy. When she proposed their mutiny back in the Hog, he thought she was just screxing. But it was clear now, she was dead serious and waiting for his reply. The notion was more appealing before he'd seen the lights of Sanatan and tasted Darl. He hadn't mentioned that last development to Okada. Although new to relationships, he intuited it wouldn't be wise to bring it up now.

"We can't just take off. We need to believe in this journey that brought us together. Look what we've accomplished so far. They need me to play the String game in Sanatan so they can get the graft to make it to Bellytown. I can't just leave everybody stranded here and take off. I mean, Han made it possible for us to escape. I can't leave him in the lurch now. It's not right. We're free because of Han. We need to play our part and believe it's going to take us somewhere good." He almost meant it.

Okada studied him through their view plates as the wind moaned around them. "That's a lot of screenshit." Jumping off the levi-loader, she started back toward the end of the caravan where the rest of the crew was gathered. Turning suddenly, she yelled back to him, "Fuck you, spacecase. Fuck you!" At the same moment, a grinning Zim passed him, returning from his conference with Han.

"My sentiments exactly."

"Jack!" Han was waving him over to where he and Bay were having a conference.

Harrison took a last look at Okada's retreating form, telling himself what needed doing had been done. Once he was a slave to Screx. He wouldn't be a slave to any single passion again. If she couldn't accept that, then seal her lock and throw away the code.

Larkill gave him a knowing look as he walked up. "Trouble in paradise?"

Harrison ignored the question with his own. "What do you want?"

Baylor was the one who spoke, "Listen . . . I, uh . . . I gotta admit . . . you've turned out to be very capable. Not just because of your String . . . You really stepped up when needed . . . That was quick thinking and decisive action back there with those Sackers."

Obviously embarrassed for his friend, Han broke in, "Bay wants to ask you a favor."

"Yeah, I was gonna pop the driver of a garbage levi on his way back after dropping his load before he reached the light ring." Harrison remembered the huge mountain of waste he'd spotted a couple grid back. "I was gonna drive the levi back into the burg, slip away, and contact my friend in the gaming sector, have him come out and pick us up, then smuggle us into Sanatan. But it occurs to me, you could do it a lot easier with less danger of giving away our presence, if you did it on your String. Also, it would be a lot faster."

Larkill put the inevitable hand on his shoulder. "We've programed a map for you, and Bay will give you something to show his friend so he knows you were sent by Bay. Just tell this friend the story of how we got here and that Bay's got some presents for him. Show him where we are on the perimeter and tell him to make it look like he's coming out for a snag race. Then he can bring an empty levi van to smuggle us in."

Harrison turned to Baylor. "What's your friend's ID?"

"Carmine. Carmine Carbachi."

Harrison was both surprised and impressed. Anybody who'd spent time in Sanatan's gaming sector knew who Carmine Carbachi was. "Give me the map."

Baylor popped open the compartment of his chest plate, removed the black disk of a hand navigator, and handed it to him. "You know Sanatan?"

Harrison nodded. "Been there many times."

"You know all the sectors?"

"I know the gaming and rec sector."

"Well, a garbage levi uses the port into the medical sector. That navigator will show you how to get through the medical sector into the gaming area. There's no way you can get lost. It will take you from the garbage levi entry to your destination." Baylor reached down into his opened chest plate and withdrew a small gold cross and chain. "Give this to Carmine. Tell him I want it back."

Harrison took the tiny cross and chain, opened his own chest plate, and carefully stowed it next to the Berretta with spare magazines.

"One more thing, they probably won't let you see Carmine if you don't have some kind of password. Don't mention my ID! Most of these cokes have some connections to Sackers. On something like this, they might be tempted to pass an 'anonymous' tip along for a serious chunk of graft. So if they want bona fides, just tell them you're a lapsed Catholic looking for absolution. It's an old cap between us, all right?"

"Yeah, got it."

"And not just because of your techie cover, don't breathe a word about spacecase."

"Yeah, I know. No problem." Harrison was already tracing his pattern.

• ⬤ •

There were problems, though, right from the start. The port the garbage levi passed through had a scanner beam across it, which would've meant the end of Baylor. It wouldn't stop Harrison because he wouldn't be three-dimensional and require an ident, but it would still detect a disturbance in the pattern of atoms in the space he occupied. If the Sackers were on the lookout for a spacecase, it would be suspicious. Between Diekster and Bickman's conversation and their unlikely demise, Harrison was sure they'd be watching things very closely. His best option was to wait for a returning levi and meld briefly through the cab and into the operator's body. Hopefully, the Sacker monitoring the scanner would think the extra density was due to the clonie packing away too many soya disks.

When the moment arrived, he chose a portly operator and held his fifth dimensional breath as the lumbering scow passed through the beam into the bowels of Sanatan. The second they were past the scanner, he removed himself from the ripe reality of the clone out into the loading area.

He checked Bay's navigator and realized he was directly in front of a levitator that would take him from plate level to street level. He rode the shiny cylinder until the lock slid open, and he moved into a drab locker mode with several dozen techies, all in varying states of undress, changing into or out of their work jumps. He blew past the group into a long white hallway. Checking the navigator again, he followed the hallway to its end, where another levitator was located. He was greeted by an "Out of Order" sign on the levitator lock. Harrison mentally cursed the malfunctioning machine. It wasn't the end of the world. It just meant wandering around until he found a safe route out of the building. He retraced his path back up the hallway and reached a point where the hallway expanded into a larger green corridor, with entry locks every few centigrid. Next to each lock was a small plate that read "Operating Theater." Obviously, he was in the surgery wing of the medical sector. Eventually, the corridor ended in a double-lock with no plaque, and he decided to try it, hoping to find another bank of levitators on the other side. He could meld through it but decided to err on the side of caution, in case there were any scanners in the surgery's locks. He committed the Higgs-Boson particles of his hand to the third dimension, slapping the palm plate with an energy bolt. The lock flew open to reveal a group of surgeons and nurses huddled over a figure on a levi table. They all looked up to see who was entering.

"Dogdamn locks! This place is going to hell. Nothing works in this dump anymore." The annoyed surgeon nodded to a nurse stationed at a group of monitors. "Hit the disinfectant mist."

She punched a tap, and jets of fine spray issued from the ceiling. The surgeon returned his focus to the body on the table.

"Cranial nerve-response activation isn't complicated enough—they have to throw in contamination? Sorry about that." He was addressing a figure lying on the table, who replied with a note of panic.

"There's no real danger of contamination, is there?"

Something about the gravelly voice was very familiar. Harrison realized he'd heard it before, here in Sanatan.

"Not really. Even if a viral infection got in here and attacked the exposed unit, we'd still have time to disconnect the ole' noggin and put it on life support in a sterile container until we decontaminated and brought in a new unit."

"I guess I'm a bit nervous. To tell you the truth, I can't believe this is really happening."

Harrison floated a little closer to the group while the surgeon continued his matside patter. He should be getting a move on, but he wanted to figure out whom that voice belonged to.

"I'll tell you, I've looked over your medical history, and if your 'nephew' hadn't prevailed over the rest of your 'family,' you wouldn't be here right now."

Again, the figure on the table replied, "Well, the whole concept was so new then . . . They just assumed save the whole body."

"Yeah, everybody but your 'nephew,' the doctor."

"Yes, he convinced me before I died that having a diseased corpse tag along with a healthy head was a prescription for failure. He reasoned that when science was finally able to reanimate my brain, they would probably be able to replace the body."

"Yes, and clearing it with you avoided the possibility of your going into shock when you were reanimated as a pumpkin. We've lost a few patients that way. It's always wise to keep the patient up to speed on medical decisions."

"Yeah, and it helps to have a few lawyers up to speed as well!" The figure on table broke into a decrepit chuckle, but when the surgeon didn't respond, a churlish tone crept into his voice. "What's the matter? You don't like lawyers?"

"I'm afraid you lost me there. What's a lawyer?"

Still unable to place the voice, Harrison floated over the levi table, trying to get a better look at the coke who was on it. Unfortunately, the head was covered by a small tent, except for the brain. He could see the patient was getting the nerve responses from his brain fine-tuned on what was a very complicated cyborg unit. The arms, legs, and torso were completely opened up, and their interiors simultaneously pulsed, buzzed, twitched, and beeped. The head surgeon opened the flaps of the tent now.

"I want you to look to your right. That's it . . . Now to your left . . . good, good. Eyes are responding perfectly."

Harrison could finally see the wizened face encased in a pink plastic exoskull. It was a face that, long ago, went from decrepit to mummified. The only salient feature was a thin line of hair running across the upper lip. He'd heard about these new cyborg units on Screenchat just before going off-line to Cincinnati retrieval. They were the breakthrough to infinity, the ray of light to an endless life. Now ultra Topgrid could live forever! Unfortunately, the cosmetics still left a lot to be desired. The whole thing looked like a robo and some hapless coke crushed together and exploded. Synthetic gray organ reproductions nestled together with purple tissue while angel-hair fiber optics intertwined with strands of twitching muscle. Miniscule power packs blinked and beeped in a twisted mass of guts and silicone. Of course, there'd be a "skin" that finally covered the whole mess, but if the finished product looked like the examples they'd shown on his screen; then, naked, this coke would resemble a twentieth beef carcass.

While the head surgeon busied himself with the brain, four assisting surgeons worked on the limbs and torso. Wielding ultrathin stilettos, they traced the individual fiber-optic threads that served as nerves. A pulsing light in the handles of their instruments registered the level of electrical stimulation passing through these synthetic nerves. Occasionally, they would stop tracing, and a tiny electrical charge would arc from the tip of the stiletto into the fiber. Harrison could only guess what they were doing—maybe increasing the fiber's conductivity. The figure on the table was becoming impatient.

"Is this going to take much longer?"

"Patience, patience. After all, you've been waiting 150 cycles for this. You can handle an hour or so longer. We're going to have to put your skin on, and I'm afraid your face is going to need some reconstruction, Walt."

Harrison couldn't believe his ears. This was Uncle Walt, the hologram that greeted you on first entering the recreation sector of Sanatan! And this was the real Uncle Walt, the ancient head of the West Coast cartel. Literally! Just a skull cycle until science reached into the freezer and brought him back to life. A little overwhelmed at being present for such a historic occasion, Harrison remembered he still had a mission to complete. Now that he knew the corridor on the other side, he wouldn't risk exposing Walt to possible infection by opening the lock. He could just go through the wall. They wouldn't have scanners in the walls. His concerns really stemmed more from the psychological. If you got surprised on the String, if you didn't have a precognizance of what you were melding into, you could be swept away in the fifth. Of course, it *was* just possible to take a blind leap, but it required a total surrender akin to suicide, sacrificing yourself to everything—a very tall order. Without Appro-recall providing referential blueprints for the three-dimensional, he was finding it hard to trust his precognizance. Even with the Hog's scan of Bob's underground lair, he still made Han cut a hole so he could sense the place he was going into.

In the green corridor once more, he checked the navigator and decided to go back to the dysfunctional levitator and just shoot through the levitator lock. Fuck Appro-recall. He had a memory. He'd made comparisons, associations, connections. This time, he shot into the levitator, then through its ceiling, up the shaft, three levels, and out into a large foyer with red marble walls.

At the far end was a long black console inset with scanner screens and monitored by two Sackers. They were watching the traffic passing through a large plexi-glass entryway. Beyond the entryway, he could see the distinctive silver rail of a levi train. Once he got past the scanners, it would whisk him to his destination.

The scanners focused on four revolving locks in the center of the plexi-glass entryway. He had to figure the entire plexi-glass wall would be laced with sensors, although it probably wasn't. Again, he just couldn't take the chance. The first time he tripped one, they'd know the whole story—that they didn't blow up in the Hog, and he was a spacecase. Deactivating the scanners would be the only way out, and he'd have to do it so he didn't arouse suspicion. He decided to watch the scene for a while and look for possibilities. It was awhile since he'd observed Topgrid couture. He was enjoying the fashion parade through what he decided must be the hospital's main lobby. Neon fringe on the sheeds' jumps was back in fashion, as were high collars and figure-sculpting body duffs. Brightly colored scarves on the males were tucked into the front flap of their jumps, a retro touch harkening back to twentieth neckties, not that any of the screenheads passing by knew that. Harrison observed the same exchange several times, commenting on the scarves, "Nice power Chromer!" He was about to give up and start searching for another exit when a beverage-laden courtesy cart came floating into view, making its way toward the Sackers' console.

<hr>

Baylor peered into the enfolding night from where they'd come. Behind him, the city of dreams, which had long ago become a nightmare, still beckoned with its light. Waiting for Harrison to return with Carmine, all the cycles spent pawing the Earth in a metallurgical monster vanished. There was only yesterday and the gleaming city.

He snorted into the darkness. What a ramrod first patrolled the raucous pathways of the Yaki gaming sector known as techie quarter. He'd quickly gained a reputation when three Yakuza on Nitro "wacked out" in a club. Hallucinating they were back in a necro club in Bellytown, they grabbed two of the bar's dancers and demanded the house prepare their bodies immediately! A techie slipped out the back way and frantically tried to find a Sacker. He found Bay. Being Yaks, they'd be packing illegal frybars, so going in the front meant being sliced to ribbons in a crossfire. Instead, he decided to make his entrance through a sidewall. Amping his frybar to max, he cut an X in the wall and hit it with a flying side kick from his piston-powered boot. He'd come rolling in and was up on his feet before the Yak closest to him could even think to move. He'd taken off his head with one swift ray. Immediately hitting the floor, he heard the screams of a dozen cokes as the two remaining Yaks raked their ruby-cutting beams across the desperate revelers.

Switching to pulse fire, Bay aimed between the patrons' scrambling legs and blew off the feet of the Yak on his left, then blew his torso in half when he hit the floor. Again, using his piston-powered boots, he leaped three centigrid into the air and, from his brief vantage point, watched the last Yak mimic his strategy and dive to the floor. As the few hysterical patrons left standing were cut down at the ankles by the Yak's indiscriminate fire, Bay took aim in mid-descent and squeezed off the shot heard 'round techie quarter, drilling the clonescum in the top of the skull, completely blowing his melon apart.

That's how he met Carmine. The Sicilians and Yakuza didn't have much use for each other. The Yaks ran the techie quarter, but only because the Sicilians couldn't be bothered with the raunchy crowd and their meager wagers. The family ran everything in the gaming sector.

Bay saw a message from Carmine flashing across his view plate after the skirmish. It was an invitation to have a drink with him at the Pacino Casino. Less than a week in Sanatan, he already knew who Carmine was. He remembered thinking that his run of bad luck was about to be over. Sackers with seniority made prime graft, working off hours at the casinos. It appeared the new Sacker had made a fortuitous leap over the chain of command. As kismet would have it, his good fortune did not go unnoticed by his commanding officer, Captain Rector.

That same night, he'd watched Angelica perform. Her dark smoky beauty with that voice, the knowing smile on ruby lips, she'd keened the first note with a nod to her mentor, the handsome young capo Carmine, but her dark eyes wandered to the brooding black beside him and stayed there till the last crystal trill.

"I think she likes you."

It was the first time the don spoke since he'd been ushered to his table. On arriving, he'd simply nodded his greeting and motioned for Bay to sit down.

"I think you like her too."

"I'll stick with Screx, thanks." He was embarrassed by his perverse attraction to the keener. This was before he learned how the family made their offspring, or how much fun that was.

Carmine gave him a pitying look. "I prefer dead pussy myself."

This was his first introduction to the bizarre brand of humor Sicilians are prone to. Carmine enjoyed his shocked reaction before bursting into laughter. "Don't worry, I ain't no Yaki." He playfully punched Bay in the shoulder. "But that was a sure piece of work you did on those stiff stickers down in techie town. Listen, you wanna cut some extra G doing a little cover for me on special occasions?"

"What occasions?"

"From time to time, I host a tournament for top-class pro-Stringers. Sometimes things get out of hand. With a lot of G at stake before and after the matches out here in the casino, these cokes can get real nasty real quick—take offense at anything, at nothin', and it goes down very fast. I need somebody just as fast to cover that. From what I understand, you don't fuck around. I'm talkin' serious G, if you're interested?"

"Sure, but I can only do it when I'm not scheduled for patrol."

"Don't worry about it. There won't ever be a conflict."

"Okay. Well, then, I'm definitely interested!"

"Good. I'll let you know when I need you."

It wasn't just the graft he was interested in. When he wasn't on duty or covering Carmine's action, Bay spent most of his off-line time at the Pacino. And a quarter cycle later, he let Angelica teach him a Sicilian secret called making love. Han was surprised when Bay readily agreed to his initiation into their rebel band, making a commitment to "hot, stinky flesh". He'd already been a fan.

Han Larkill watched Bay mooning and sighing into the night. He knew exactly what was on that one-track mind. Revenge! He'd heard the story so many times it was like a vid. The evil Rector, destroyer of Bay's happiness, was going to die. He just hoped it could be taken care of without having to sacrifice Bay in the process. He was fond of his lieutenant and could certainly use him when it came time to head down to Bellytown.

•——•◖•◗•——•

Slipping through the open lock of the levi train, Harrison smiled, remembering the chaos he'd left behind in the red marble entryway of the surgical center. When one of the Sackers snagged a snack tube from that courtesy cart, sitting back at the console to eat it, he'd simply squeezed the bottom. Cherry glop splattered all over the keyboard, and Harrison reached inside and reversed the charge in the scan taps. The ensuing explosion sent everyone scurrying for cover, and he slipped through the revolving locks along with other panicked citizenry. He knew a Sacker who'd be patrolling the Bering Sea for a long time to come.

Leaving the blue-gray scrapers of the medical sector, the train whisked up into the raffish architecture of the gaming sector. Ahead, the shimmering gold spire of the Pacino jutted up above all the other gambling scrapers. He considered his next move. He could wait and materialize in the hallway to Carmine's office when no one was looking.

But in all likelihood, before he uttered a word, he'd be cut to pieces for being there uninvited. Also, if he was going to keep his techie cover, materializing inside the casino was too risky. He couldn't explain how he got past security. He'd just have to take a chance and hop off the String around a corner, then go to the front lock and try the "patter" Bay'd given him.

When the train made the stop in front of the Pacino, he blew out of the open lock to his left around the corner. Seeing no other gamers in close proximity, he visualized his pattern in reverse out on the circumference, letting the six points of the star return, tracking inward, until they connected at the center and he came shuddering into place. He walked back around the corner and started up the black marble steps of the entrance. Two lock guards in gold-plated livery jumps that doubled their size stood on either side of the revolving platinum lock. The amazing elasticity of their choreographed, welcoming gestures told Harrison they wore the latest in carbon-nitride armor. Harder than a diamond and thinner than a soya disk, the synthetic alloy was also extremely flexible.

Before he reached the third step, their matte-black view plates honed on him. His dirty mining jump with its pockmarked chest plate didn't meet the dress code. A golden arm swiftly telescoped from the guard on his right, pinioning his shoulder in a claw with the grip of a grid clamp.

"May we help you, sir?"

"I'd like to see Carmine Carbachi."

"And cokes in hell want Screx." The claw spun him around, giving him a firm shove down the steps. "techie quarter is that way, sir."

Harrison turned back again, and the golden arm reared like a cobra, the claw revealing the glowing red dots of two lasers.

"Sir, please don't make me dirty our pristine steps."

He made himself say the silly phrase. "I wanna tell him about a lapsed Catholic looking for absolution."

The claw snaked slowly toward his view plate, then snatched the helmet right off his head. "What the fuck are you talking about?"

"It's a cap."

"It's not funny." The guard tossed the helmet at his feet. "For the last time, take your drunk ass—"

Both the lock guards suddenly froze. Harrison was hopeful they were receiving internal communications. The arm retracted to its original length, and his inquisitor turned to face the platinum lock. "Follow me, sir." Harrison made no attempt to hide his relief, picking up his helmet and following his gold inquisitor through the lock.

Upon entering, he could see the lower gaming level was remodeled since the last time he was here. Now the vast hall was completely covered in the rich green luster of Malachite. Almost all the gems and semiprecious stones on the planet except for diamonds were amassed in Sanatan's gaming sector. That and the garish lighting made everything sparkle.

Two mammoth revolving holos circled above the main gaming-area—a field of chattering hypervids where dozens of cokes frantically tried to win a pot of graft by outracing, outshooting, and outmaneuvering comp-gen adversaries. He'd never been comfortable with how foolish a player looked—jumping, ducking, slashing the air, or sitting in mockups of Levi racers and cycles, frantically steering through comp-gen obstacles, all the while wearing a black ball sprouting its antennae from their heads.

Dotted among these gyrating cokes were the blue-beamed columns of main-level String arenas, each with a gamer wielding his or her light sword, battling a gruesome holo warrior while crowds hollered insults or encouragements around the perimeter. Harrison noticed there were several new comp-gen warriors in play. If looks alone could kill, these abominations were always winners.

Following the lock guard along the white marble promenade bordering the gaming area, his attention was again drawn to the revolving holos. He realized they were animated. "All-Time Winners" and "All-Time Losers" were the titles inscribed in the air above these visions. The "winners," all gorgeous specimens, were cavorting on some ancient beach at the edge of an azure sea, engaged in multipartner sexual encounters, eating, drinking, dancing, and skating across the waves on brightly colored planks. In the other holo, the "losers," a throng of pathetically misshapen creatures, were suffering unspeakable tortures at the hands of gross demons in a smoldering pit somewhere underground. Harrison realized he'd seen that one at Cincinnati retrieval. It was a "painting" by a coke called Bosch. Grotesque enough in two dimensions, it was hideous in three—and truly terrifying with the activities animated.

Moving through the crowd of Topgrid gamers, he noted the perturbed reactions to his attire. The shimmering synthetics they were draped in were a blinding compendium of chic. He was definitely a refuge from the loser holo.

The lock guard stopped beside the carved marble entrance to a large levitator and motioned with golden claw for him to step inside.

"Someone will assist you upon arrival."

The lock shut, the levitator shot up at speeds facilitated by Sanatan's position directly over the planet's northern magnetic pole. When the levitator stopped and the lock opened, he found himself facing two robos. Circular grid plates at their bases kept them hovering above the carpet. Long black stalks rose up from their plates, ending in a silver globe festooned with sensors. At varying levels on their stalks, an array of mechanical appendages waved a greeting. They spoke as he stepped from the levitator.

"Welcome stranger," their voices buzzed in stereo. "Please accompany us," they hummed, whisking ahead of him down a weaving alabaster corridor. At the hollows of each of its curves, gold-plated locks were inset in the milky walls. The corridor finally ended in a golden double-lock encrusted with fiery opals. The robos halted on either side of the lock, both extending an appendage to grasp the carved gold handles. In unison, they swung the locks open while their extraneous appendages waved him inside. Harrison stepped into a darkened mode and heard the locks close behind him. A deep-blue massage carpet made a fruitless attempt to rub his feet through his mining boots.

At the far end, he could make out a figure with his back to Harrison, seated behind a massive rose-tinted marble desk. Carmine, he assumed, was watching a display of club sites on a view plate that covered the entire back wall. Harrison waited, watching the back of his head and noting the shoulder-length black hair.

"I know you're not wired. You were scanned through that last lock. That's good. So one of two things: either you're a very cujy undercover trying to find out what I know or heard—in which case, I don't give a fuck you're a Sacker, you had an unhappy accident on your way here—or you're somebody representing somebody, and you have something to say or show me that's going to let me know who that somebody is."

The figure swung around, and Harrison saw Carmine for the first time. Below the swept-back black mane and wide forehead, large almond eyes honed themselves to talons on either side of an aquiline nose. A red katana for a mouth framed by a massive jaw punctuated by a jutting dimpled chin—he was, at once, majestic and malodorous, masterpiece and travesty. Dog knows, it was a face you'd never forget.

"I gotta tell ya, I have a problem with the mining jump. I'd hate to think old friends were so stupid."

Harrison realized his error immediately. He thought, if he waited to materialize until he got to the Pacino, he'd avoid being rousted by Sackers. But he forgot, Carmine would think he'd traveled through the gaming sector in a mining jump, and that was pretty stupid. He should have grabbed a doctor's smock back in the medical sector, though that wouldn't have been much better. He decided playing stupid was his only option.

"We've been down in a Screwhog for months, and I've never been here before. I was just told to give you this." Harrison popped his chest plate and started to reach inside. The moment he did, he was sorry. Three hulking figures hurled themselves from the shadows while Carmine brought up a frybar with the target beam focused squarely between his eyes. The next thing he knew, there was a train wreck where he stood, and he was slammed to the carpet. Arms pinned behind him, he was lifted up and slammed down again, this time on the matinee mobster's desk blotter. That face and the muzzle of a frybar were waiting at desk level when he opened his eyes.

"Are you the stupidest motherduffer that ever lived or what?"

Somehow Harrison managed a weak smile. "Probably."

"*Probably*—we got a cappy coke here!" The muzzle of the frybar prodded his cheek. "Well, let me tell you something, cappy. I'm gonna reach inside your chest plate, and if I come up with any kind of serious hardware, you're gonna be the sorriest legless, armless, eyeless, tongueless cappy motherduffer that ever came rolling into techie quarter." Carmine addressed his guards, "Lift him up!" Harrison was wrenched from the blotter, and Carmine reached inside his battered chest plate, withdrawing Bob's Berretta and several magazines. "What the fuck are these?"

For the first time in their adventures, he was deeply grateful for cokekind's collective amnesia. With the invention of the frybar, this little "pellet flinger" was as forgotten as David's sling.

"That's a mining tool. Be careful. Don't squeeze that little lever. It injects lead pellets into materials to determine the hardness of their structures and those smaller things are pellet refills."

"This, what you wanted to show me, your poor excuse for a weapon?"

"No, there's something else."

Carmine reached into his chest plate again, and this time, when he brought out his hand, it held the tiny cross and chain. His face turned pale as he stared at it for a moment. "Some things never go away." He switched his gaze to Harrison again. "Where is he?"

Here was another opportunity to polish his dumbass routine. "Baylor?" Carmine gave him a look of utter contempt. He was pretty sure he'd cemented his credentials. "He's out beyond the light ring. There are nine of us." Harrison recounted their entire journey, altering only a few details to disguise he was spacecase.

CHAPTER

Okada relished the tongue on her lobe, the warm, caressing luxury that bathed her left ear and, from there, her whole body. Darl was amazing.

The difference was incredible, and she wondered at never having considered it before. No relentless driving urgency, they could cum endlessly, nestling in and riding it. It was a nurturing thing, something she'd never experienced with a coke. She cherished this new time together. She'd been very angry at the loss of her dream, but Darl had been there for her, sharing her generous supply of Nitro. Darl told Okada she'd convinced Han to make Zim give her most of his supply. She said Han knew she was sad, and now that they were in their new subterranean palace, they should take a little break after their long ordeal and have some fun. And one night, Darl slid onto Okada's mat with several Nitro patches and a mischievous smile.

That first time was so hot and funny, Darl kissing her shy into a fountain of cream, then mimicking Han, "Open yourself for me, angel." They were hysterical, but eventually, she'd turned her head aside coyly and slid her hand down her belly, spreading herself dutifully. "Wider, little angel, wider . . . I have a surprise for you," and they'd cracked up again. They did it quite a lot after that. And then, one afternoon, locked together in mutual climax, Jack was suddenly inside both of them, and the String's ecstasy seemed infinite, elevating their combinations in an enveloping bliss. Okada knew then Darl and Harrison were an item, but the multiple permeations of pleasure rushing through her made trying to reduce three to two based on jealous insecurity pathetic. She was losing her "individual" mind, the mind she'd always known. Now she was experiencing a more inclusive dream of love.

Really, everything changed after they snuck into Sanatan, masquerading as crew for the sleek levi racers in their colorful levi vans. Baylor's friend, the incredibly handsome Sicilian Carmine, spirited them underneath his casino into a series of luxurious suites hidden in the Pacino's grid plate. It was a breathtaking change from the interior of the Hog. On a tour through the suites, pointing out their lavish accoutrements (one even had a Screx), Carmine made it clear they'd need to give him an itinerary for every excursion they made into Sanatan. She watched Han bristle at the requirement, quickly disguising it with a broad smile.

The first couple weeks, they were all content to enjoy the many amenities. Except for Baylor, who sequestered himself in a suite right after their arrival. Okada had a chance to clique with Carmine when he returned later, delivering a deck of strange cards to his old friend. She was surprised when the don gave her a look that made her wonder if he was no stranger to up-close and personal. For the most part, Bay remained in his suite, shuffling and cutting the strange cards several times, then arranging them in the same pattern and staring at them for a while before repeating the process. She asked Han what was going on, and he told her Bay had an old grievance to avenge that started here in Sanatan. She steered clear of the ex-Sacker and the smoldering fury that fueled his every waking moment.

Suddenly Darl was squatting over her, reaching across the mat to take hold of the double "steely" lying there. "We've got oodles of time.

They'll be in the screening mode for a while." Okada smiled, peeling two Nitro patches off the stack beside her. Spreading her own thighs, she slapped a patch on Darl close to her shy and the other patch in the identical spot on herself. Darl purred, "Open your mouth, angel." Okada did, and Darl gently pushed one knob of the steely past her lips. Okada sucked until Darl slowly pulled it out, opened her snowy petals and slid the glistening knob and shaft all the way up inside her. Okada raised her head to suck the second knob, now protruding from Darl's engulfing sex and, once certain it was slippery with saliva, guided the pulsing metal down to her nether depths.

• ——— ❖❖ ——— •

Han was watching Harrison study "Drakar" on the screen, observing as his spacecase made mental notes of the various martial combinations the holo warrior favored. Drakar was the reigning comp-gen champion of the upper-level String arena at the MGM, the Pacino's biggest competitor. Like the Pacino, it was a treasure trove of precious metals and gems, but the gold theme was very big there. Almost anything that could be plated was covered with the warm yellow metal. Also, they had a tie-in with Uncle Walt's rec sector, so Toon hero robos were all over the place. Their String arenas were no exception. The first circle of seats was sprinkled with Toons frantically reacting to the action inside the blue column.

Bay made it clear to Han after the initial meeting where Carmine laid down the rules that it wouldn't be wise to rip off their host, so they decided on the MGM. While Han was sure Carmine knew they were up to something more than just gambling in the String arena, Bay proved to be right. He didn't care as long as it wouldn't affect the Pacino's snag. The don also arranged for them all to be fitted with new wardrobes, so they'd blend in with other Topgrid gamers. Han had to admit, he had a good eye for fashion. Han was particularly pleased with the ensemble he was presently wearing: a long purple coat with a high-back wraparound collar, red jodhpurs, and thigh-high black buckled boots. Harrison's wardrobe was more modest in comparison, a hint of techie-goes-uptown. The dimwit cappy he portrayed to cover his original error played right into their cover story. While he still couldn't speak Amerab for shit, it didn't really matter. He kept his statements short, purposely hesitating after every other word, as if he barely had command of rudimentary English. Nobody outside of techie quarter wanted to converse in Amerab anyway. When the time came to drum up a backer, Han would be presenting him as this techie idiot-savant, who was a magician with the sword. In the meantime, his checkered red-and-white pullover and striped neon-green and yellow pants would have to be borne.

On screen, an amateur (would-be professional) String gamer was making his move—feigning a leg cut but quickly snap-rolling his wrists to change the direction of his blade from downward to lateral, then sweeping the edge upward, aiming at Drakar's sword arm. Thanks to Jack's tutelage, he was becoming more appreciative of the sport, which was crucial if he was going to pull off the role of being aficionado talent scout. According to his "young protégé," it was in Cincinnati retrieval he discovered the true derivation of the sport. A primitive cartel called "Japan" is where the distinct two-handed grip (with hands apart) began. It made it possible to bring your wrists into play, turning your hands into a fulcrum, *and that* allowed for lightning variations in the direction of the blade with no loss of kinetic energy. Plus, with both arms in action, it was a very powerful cut. Han had to admit he'd become a real fan.

On screen, this young gamer was incredibly quick, taking off Drakar's sword hand at the wrist. The comp-gen's light sword spun like a glowing fan, his severed hand trailing a ribbon of blood before falling to the disk. Being both quick and brash, our young warrior moved in for the kill. Snap-rolling his wrists at the end of his sword's arc, the young gamer's blade did a U-turn and snapped back across the spot where Drakar's head had just been. Unfortunately, the scaly knob that harbored the holo warrior's hideous face wasn't there anymore. Drakar's specter was now only a couple milligrid from the young gamer's head, grinning around his blood-red fangs at the surprised expression on his naive opponent's face. The gamer's expression changed again when when Drakar brought his other claw around, gripping a short sickle-knife, and gutted him! Drakar hadn't paused even a nanosecond to mourn the loss of his scaly mitt, stepping in past his adversary's sword arm and fileting the little fucker.

Actually, the coke wasn't really wounded. Real damage and death occurred only at pro-Stringer matches. At second-level matches, you just felt like your guts were ripped out, or your limbs were cut off, or your head was being separated from your neck. Thanks to a series of taps you wore underneath your game jump, you got a very accurate experience of what that pain felt like. It was designed to make you think long and hard before trying to achieve pro-Stringer status again. Han was certain Harrison saw the coke's mistake, but it wouldn't hurt to verify.

"They forget it's just an image. In the heat of battle, they think the holo warrior is real, feels pain like they do."

"Yes, but in the spirit of fairness, they used to take at least a split second to register the loss of a limb."

"Well, Jack, I doubt fairness has ever been high on a casino's priority list."

"The thing is, I was hoping to wait till I got a pro match before I had to jump the String. I may not have the luxury." To go undetected during a match, Harrison had to jump the String only at the decisive moment and then immediately jump off again. "And I'm sure there'll be more surprises once I make pro Stringer."

"Of course, there will, Jack! That's part of the fun. I hope you're not getting cool boots on me because we don't have a lot of Yuan left. I spent most of our resources on getting your armored jump. I got a little carried away. It's a carnelian masterpiece, and when that blue light hits it, it turns a bloody purple. That's your game ID, by the way, *New Blood*! You're going to stand out, Jack. Carmine told Bay your jump will be here today."

"Didn't you get any graft from Carmine for the bomb?"

"Enough to get your jump and wager on our semipro match, but Bay convinced me it was better to lowball it, along with making a present of the pop guns. Bay goes all Sicilian around him, 'The don would appreciate a sign of respect.' The 'don' is a bit of a puffed-up despot, don't you think?"

Harrison broke into a grin. "I knew you hated his guts." Come on, admit it. You aren't fond of Carmine, are you?"

"I think he runs a hell of an operation and is very generous to old friends. I don't want to strain his generosity, so we need to start playing soon or go back to mining."

"Have we got enough to pay the MGM fee and still bet on the match?"

"Barely. I haven't checked with Zim yet to see if he's unloaded any product. I can't pry him out of that old Screx."

"Go ahead, set it up for tonight. I know what Drakar's favorite moves are. I can take that holo clone."

"That's the spirit, Jack. Let's go kick some ass, then move on to the real Yuan."

"Yeah, tomorrow night we'll take the MGM for some serious graft." A sly smile momentarily flashed across Harrison's face. "Admit it, Han. You gotta be jealous of the setup Carmine's got here."

"A little jealous of the ease with which he acquired it, having it dropped in his lap by papa. But that ease of acquisition made him inherently soft. I despise soft despots."

On screen, the cheering crowd signaled the beginning of another match.

❧

Just like in the tube. This feeling of total support and protection he was experiencing now, hanging weightless inside the electromagnetic ball of a Screx, wearing the skintight jump and hood, he was being the polar duplicate of the interior surface of the encompassing globe: Zim was held in all directions by the Meissner effect. Modern Screxes exchanged the hood and jump for a body spray—"but beggars," whatever. It never ceased to amaze him how the Screx produced tactile sensations by playing with sequential polarities at specific points. He could feel the pressure of a caressing hand or a punch in the nose from a fist and everything in between, depending on the strength, polarity, and sequence of localized charges. With the 3-D imaging from the goggles (replaced by contact lenses in later models) and background motifs generated on the globe's interior surface, all in vibrant hypercolor, reality was paltry by comparison.

Zim floated now with a program request for motif-data, scrolling across the bottom of his goggles. He had to figure out where he wanted to go. There was still the almost irresistible urge to verbalize Seymore's access code, but Han guessed that was the first thing he'd do, warning what would inevitably occur. With a certainty, Seymore would turn them in. While he hated to think it was so, he finally acknowledged his spiritual master might not see it as a betrayal but rather as sacrificing Zim for the greater good. He'd be generously rewarded by 7 for handing over their heads. There was no arguing with Han's reasoning. He was a genius, and he had the plan. It was all to a purpose he'd dedicated them to—a purpose he promised soon to reveal in all its wonder, and Zim understood. He would sacrifice whatever was necessary to help bring it to pass. When they arrived, he'd given Darl most of his Nitro because Han told him to. When she started matting, Okada, Zim knew where most of his stash was going. Okada wouldn't be coming begging as he'd hoped. There was still somnambulant Ryka to play with, but even she was getting frisky because, apparently, Darl was dropping patches everywhere. He was left only with this old Screx and his own imagination.

Late-model Screxes dispensed with the whole format he was dealing with now. You simply thought your motif instructions to the Screx. This, however, was a very early model with the original laborious setup process. He found it repugnant. It destroyed the conspiratorial intimacy of a Screx, having to speak your desires out loud. When they settled in, Zim asked Bay why this old Screx was down here anyway. In a rare moment of camaraderie, Bay volunteered the history of the hidden lair. When the place was being designed, Carmine's father put some extra room in the blueprints where the C-power units were located in the grid plate. Originally, the idea was to install an off-the-books accounting department and vault. But once the casinos were up and running in the early days of operations, the family decided they should get a cut from Yakuzas' gambling operations in the techie quarter. A raging firefight erupted between the two factions. Carmine's father turned the hidden space into a lair of suites for bivouacing his army of hitters. The Screx was installed primarily to hone their operations, playing out various avenues of attack in the congested techie quarter. The family initially won the dispute and sent the Yaks back to Bellytown. Ironically, later, they told the Yaks to come back and take the techie quarter off their hands. Bay also disclosed some other old mold that gave Zim the idea for this Screx adventure. The idea had first popped in his head watching the ancient vids in Alaska mines.

Back in '52, twenty years before Zim was even born, there was a big disaster. A fair-sized asteroid punched into the depths of the Pacific Ocean, right off the coast of the western waste fill. Over 128,000 square grid of West Coast waste fill was swept away by an eight-grid-high tsunami wave, including the West Coast cartel's base, La, and ending with the burg of Lavega submerged under a new lake. Lavega had originally belonged to the family, but seventy cycles before the disaster, West Coast cartel ran them out of town. Taking into account the continued global warming, the family offered to let bygones be bygones. They struck a deal with the survivors of the West Coast cartel to build a gaming resort complex in the Arctic Circle, real estate the family had purchased from the Russian cartel. This new resort was to be modeled on the architecture and technologies being developed in Big New. Big New was under construction at the time. Back then, all it took was enough graft that was negotiable to move ahead with their plan. They had that and then some! While West Coast cartel lost their burgs, they still had their graft in the Cayman cartel. Most of the planet's western elite had their graft there or in the Swiss cartel.

They sat down with the Beijing cartel, which held all the graft of the eastern elite, and they all agreed (on very favorable terms for westerners because they still held the technological upper hand) to convert all their currency to the Yuan as the "legal tender" of the planet. This was back when there were over two hundred cartels, and the major ones were trying to bring them all under their umbrellas. It was the beginning of 7.

Zim made a verbal request to see "stills" of Lavega burg. Even though the original purpose for this Screx was strategic, he figured cokes would be cokes. Some of the family's soldiers who were originally in Lavega probably programed scenes of the ancient megatropolis into "the old sheed." Sicilians were famous for hanging on to their old mold. Surely, at least one of them succumbed to the temptation to go back and relive better times. He was suddenly aware that Harrison's constant history lessons and accompanying use of archaic phrases was seeping into his own speech patterns. Interestingly enough, he liked it. It gave color to his conversations with himself, which they'd lacked before. Sure enough, stills of Old Lavega began flashing across his goggles. Now, to see if he could find what he was really looking for. There were more snaps than he expected, but most of them were far too intimate to have the scene Zim was seeking. Maybe later he'd come back and spend some time with these service vixens currently engaged in obscene acts with family hitters. Then suddenly there it was, in a shot captioned "Frontier Casino"—several heavyset cokes in dark shiny jumps hoisted their glasses while smiling at the lens, mimicking a sepia picture behind them hanging above the bar. Zim focused on that picture and said, "Enlarge." His goggles filled with rustic "cowpokes" right out of *The Adventures of Hopalong Cassidy*. Down to the shiny hand percussives they sported on their hips, holding up their beer mugs with big hairy grins. These were the ancient cowboys. These were the real McCoy! Now all he needed to generate was his virtual Sacker armor, boots, helmet, and frybar to have a rompin', stompin' good time.

•——•◆•——•

Baylor shuffled and cut the cards again, then laid them down in the classic Celtic cross spread, with one difference: he dropped the tenth and final card down in between the third and ninth card, the way Angelica taught him. It was, she said, more revealing of the moment, the outcome card surrounded by the hopes and fears shaping it. The cards were about the moment. She would warn him, never think you're seeing the future. You can see the direction things are headed in. You can see what forces are prominent in influencing the outcome. What you can't see is what being *aware in the moment* does to influence those forces and the outcome. Just focusing the awareness of an expanding consciousness on things that are in play can change the outcome entirely. She called it "the butterfly theory of effect"—how everything affects everything.

He remembered when she took out the cards and threw them in his presence. They'd just made love for the first time, and he was enjoying this new intimacy, a quiet afterglow of their connection. Suddenly she'd leapt off her palatial bed and grabbed the deck of cards from a drawer in a side console. He watched this sudden bizarre activity but was afraid to ask what was going on. She'd scurried back to the bed, shuffled and cut the cards three times, and then laid them out in exactly the way Baylor had a moment before. He'd never seen anything like them. They had very strange, even foreboding, pictures on them, and he remembered being frightened of her in that moment. She studied them for a while, finally looking up at Bay.

"You have a serious enemy, someone who, if they knew about us, wouldn't hesitate to use it to destroy you."

"Well, that's pretty much everybody." He was worried there was something wrong with her mind. "You do know that outside the family, sharing secretions will get you sent to the mines?"

"I know about the plagues. I know they're the reason 7 gives for subverting human procreation. That's just your enemy's excuse, the weapon he'll use to try to take you down. Your enemy has a darker reason for wanting to destroy you . . . your ease and inherent openness terrifies him."

Just when he was thinking he might be able to secretly pursue having a real family under the protection of *the* family, it occurred to him this could be another horrible mistake, this exotic diva. The last thing he needed was to be breaking a cardinal law with a sheed who was out of her fucking mind. He'd asked a lot of questions that night, although he tried his best to seem just curious.

What he learned was the cards first came into being almost eight hundred cycles ago, in the "fourteenth century," among the Topgridders in a place called Italy, where, as it turned out, all the family were originally from. The cards were co-opted over time by an itinerant group called gypsies, who promoted them as a way to foresee the future, clouding their original intent. Later, they were taken up by occultists in a place called England. They claimed the cards were once the secret diviners of the Egyptians, whoever they were.

At this point, Bay was tempted to stop listening to what, for him, was meaningless old mold.

And then she said something that went to the core of a struggle he was having with himself. Angelica told him that to read the cards properly, you first have to discover the lies you're telling yourself, the lies about who you are and what you're about. The cards only mirrored back your own self-deceptions, until you realized *that* was what you were seeing. You had to witness your way of seeing things, to discover the director in your brain hellbent on making you feel good about yourself. This consciousness that never lingers to examine any error in judgment, you do recognize, quickly papering over it all with good reasons why you were justified to do whatever it is you did or didn't do. This, Angelica explained, is your "ego" wanting to feel in control, wanting not to be afraid of the unknown. It is the perspective in all of us that wants to believe it knows "what's what" all the time. And it tries to run your world. Only when you identify this frightened, self-centered liar in yourself will the cards show you what is really going on.

He found that intriguing enough to pursue their relationship and learn more about the cards and how to read them to start seeing the lies he was telling himself, one of which, he worried, might be him trying to rationalize away her "crazy." But in time, his enemy did reveal himself, and that was the end of any doubts about the cards or Angelica.

"So do you see anything more there than what I've already told you?" Bay'd momentarily forgotten Carmine was sitting across from him.

"Yeah, there's something more to the robo mutts. There's something deeper, something he hides about his relationship with them. Tell me what you know about them."

"They're a couple of robos designed to look like some war gods the Yaks used to worship—Akitas. One is black, and the other is white and gold. Rector calls them 'devil' and 'angel,' always a sucker for the obvious. Some big Yakuza in Bellytown, probably Yakami, made them a present ten cycles ago, right after you left for the mines, a gift for a job well done."

"That makes sense. They didn't have to worry about me bustin' their mobile Nitro labs outside the light ring anymore."

"Yeah, you were pissing them off. Anyway, these robos are fully armored and fitted with all kinds of hardware: multiple laser rays, imploding light bombs, long-range auditory, retina scanning, cameras with infrared scans, high-speed hydraulics. They're practically supersonic. I'd rather take on a regiment of Sackers than tangle with those mutts. They come in fast and low."

"And the units are shielded from any possible electromagnetic disturbance?"

"You're a genius."

Bay looked down at the spread again, looking for the patterns inside the Celtic cross. He looked for the triangles in a spread to define the relationships. That the robos were Rector's protectors was obvious, but there was another dynamic going on. His relationship with each of them was different. One was purely martial. Rector looked up to that one, saw it as a master strategist. He was a little afraid of it.

The other one was weirder. Rector was worried about that one. It was strange.

"You don't need those cards to tell you the facts. One, you ain't gonna get anywhere close to Rector. Two, if you do, those mutts will kill you before you decide whether to shit or shoot. Three, if you do get him and somehow get away, that would end up causing me, and you, a lot of trouble. Am I getting through to you?"

"Loud and clear."

"Because, you know, I'm torn. I'd love to see that puffed-up motherduffer in ten thousand pieces, each lovingly preserved in plastic in the corner of every Pacino lock card. Unfortunately, we're in a Bellytown standoff. I've got proof of his involvement with those mobile labs and transporting 'Go Fish' for the ultra Topgrid, and he has proof that we still do things the old-fashioned way."

"Oh, come on, 7 knows that."

"Yeah, but it's an *unofficial* understanding, and it's okay only because we have no interest in joining their eventual migration. If it got out to Topgrid at large, then there'd be a big backlash. You know how fanatical they are about keeping Topgrid from taking *any* chance of picking up a virus. If he made the accusation, they'd come down hard, and I don't want them sticking their noses everywhere in the gaming sector, which is exactly what they'd do. We can't go to war with 7. It's not a war we could win." Carmine shot Bay a sly grin. "Although, that bomb might give us a chance."

"So if I go after Rector and I miss, he rats out the family?"

"Not necessarily. He knows we can take care of the 'proof' in the med sector before they have a chance to substantiate his accusations, though that would make for very bad feelings with the medical community, and they're some of our biggest high rollers. But hit or miss, if you get away, he will say that I was complicit in your being here because of our past association. In order to convince them otherwise, I will have to take care of it. I don't know how to make it any clearer to you . . . if the mutts don't kill you, then any way you cut it, I'm gonna have to. I can't just send people out to pretend to look for you. So I guess what I'm saying is . . . is all this really necessary?"

"Do you remember that day on the ice ridge when you took us out in your new Douglas?"

"How could I forget? Those fat slimy black things wriggling away over the ice, making those weird noises."

"She keened to them, remember, and they stopped and watched her. You could tell they liked it."

They were both silent for a moment. Finally, Carmine gave a sigh of resignation. "All right, but when you go to do it, your friends have to disappear, one way or the other."

"Can you give them forty-eight hours after I take off? It will take me that long to make my move, and they need that much time to get a pro-Stringer match. Otherwise, they won't have the Yuan to get out of Sanatan."

"Are you sure your coke can win? He better be faster with a blade than he is with his brain."

"Yeah, he is. Can you give them that much time?"

"I guess. Just so they understand, don't look for any help from this quarter when it comes to getting out of town."

"Don't worry about it. Han is very resourceful."

"Yeah, he seems a capable coke."

"Listen, I'm gonna need the whole getup: an active Sacker battle jump, hydraulic boots, helmet, and frybar. Can you handle that?"

"Yeah."

"Look, Carmine . . . I'm sorry this is gonna cause you problems . . . I have no choice."

"Yeah, well . . . while we're being brutally honest, I'm not worried about it because those robo mutts are gonna kill you."

The discussion over, they both stood. Carmine embraced Bay in a bear hug, slapping him on the back several times, then broke it off and turned away. Without looking back, he made an exit. Bay sat down again, studying the cards. After a moment, he scooped them up and, with a focus on vulnerabilities, went through the shuffle-cut ritual again. The first card was the four of swords, reversed: enforced seclusion. The second card (the card that crossed the first) was the four of cups, straight up: weariness, bitter experience. The third card was the six of cups, straight up: gains, success, things that have vanished, wishes fulfilled. The fourth card was the three of swords, straight up: strife, conflict, heartache. The fifth card was the eight of swords, reversed: past treacheries, fatalities, freedom gained from distancing one's self. The sixth card was the page of swords, straight up: overseeing, authority, secret service. The seventh card was the five of swords, reversed: weakness, degradation, dishonor, vindication, treachery revealed. The eighth card (the "house" Rector was in) was the hermit: a need to retire, to disassociate one's self. The ninth card was the three of cups, straight up: birth, celebration, solace, healing. The tenth card was the six of swords, straight up: long journeys away from pain, journeys over water.

Six cards were in the suit of swords, so it was all about a fight. Rector was in seclusion because he was weary. He wanted to retire and get away from things.

There was strife and heartbreak, bitter experience seeking solace and healing, all under the protection of an overseeing authority that was giving him some privacy while still being on guard. And the tenth card, the outcome card: long journeys away from pain, long journeys by water. He placed the tenth card between the third and ninth, the way Angelica showed him. So on both sides, good things: gains, success, things that have vanished, wishes fulfilled, solace, and healing.

Well, he knew for a fact, the captain was on a futile journey away from guilt and pain. Before he was sent to the mines, Rector came to his cell, confessing he'd strangled Angelica. Of course, his report would state she committed suicide, but he'd done it, he said, because he couldn't bear to see her that way, "her angelic voice defiled by your vile secretions!" Bay could see, even then, he was having a hard time swallowing all his lies. And with the passing cycles, her murder would only make it increasingly hard to find solace or healing. So all this succor was coming from where?

From water.

It hit him like a bolt. A bath, he was taking a bath, soaking for a long time in the water, and the robos were guarding him from a distance, from outside the eliminator. That was the second point on the grand triangle (the tenth, sixth, and seventh cards in a spread). They waited outside the eliminator. Why? Why not have them right there with him? The third point in the grand triangle gave the answer. The five of swords, reversed: weakness, fear, dishonor, degradation. He was naked. He felt vulnerable, exposed. He didn't want the war gods seeing him in that state. This was a healing ritual, this bath. That's what made it a long journey. He did it over and over again, probably around the same time every evening.

Here was where Rector could be killed, and if Bay was swift and surgical, his war gods wouldn't even know it was happening. He knew exactly where the captain's mode was in Sacker headquarters. All it would take was a small hole in the ceiling right above his palatial tub.

Captain, you've been a shit-stirring motherduffer all your life. Shit's here for you now.

• — ❖ — •

"Howdy, partners!"

Oh, it was everything he'd hoped for. They just froze. All the gamblers at the card tables, the string of filthy brutes lined up at the bar, the quintessential bartender with his extravagant waxed mustache, and the wooden box banger in the corner who played the "tinkle-tinkle" accompaniment to the raucous goings-on. Every one of them was still and silent, and in the lavish mirror above the rows of bottles, he could view himself as they saw him—a tall black specter of death. The battle armor made his shoulders look as broad and powerful as, in fact, they were with the aid of hydraulic assistance. The smooth faceless black ball that was his head slowly surveyed their mode, announcing impending doom. Not to mention the height that his piston boots added, transforming him into this towering executioner. Mouths opened, and jaws dropped as one. Savoring the moment, he slowly raised the frybar he held by his side, and that's when everything changed. To his surprise, they also drew as one! A hail of lead flew at Zim through a cacophony of explosions. He was stunned by the force that struck him as countless lead balls found their mark. These pellet flingers together were more powerful than he'd bargained for. Not that the endless rounds slamming into him penetrated his Sacker armor, but they did push him right back out of the saloon's swinging doors!

He was in the black void. Dogdamned piece of ancient shit! If this thing could access his stored impressions like a modern Fuji, there'd be plenty of "Hopalong" facades to choose from. Right now, in his mind, he could see the dilapidated saloon front and the whole desert-baked mainstreet. But this old piece of shit needed "stills" in order to create motif! He could make out the gray area where the swinging doors had been. He brought the frybar up and stabbed the gray with it. As soon as the muzzle disappeared, he squeezed off three light bombs and came crashing back inside. There was a smoking black hole where half the bar had been. Again, this damn thing couldn't generate any scene behind it. All the card tables were turned on their sides now, and sporadic fire was coming from behind them. Remembering Bay's account of a shootout in techie quarter, he ducked and rolled, then used his piston boots to leap for the ceiling. He was lining up on the grizzled gunslinger who wore the marshal's badge, busy reloading his shiny pistol, when suddenly the bartender popped up from behind the remaining half of the bar and dropped both hammers of a double-barrel shotgun point-blank in Zim's chest. This time, he flew through the swinging doors and went rolling into the void.

He was becoming seriously pissed. It took a while to find the gray spot again, and he thought of terminating the whole thing, except now he really wanted to kill these fuckers. He switched to a wide-band laser and went charging in, cutting right and left. But coming through the door, something caught one of his boots, and suddenly he was flat on his face. The frybar was snatched from his hand, and he found himself being hoisted in the air upside down. Two grinning cowboys tied off a rope thrown over a ceiling rafter.

"Somebody better go get the preacher 'cause, boys, I think we just caught the devil!"

•———◄█►———•

Tooco was in his element again, racing the narrow winding grooves, carving air lanes over broken pathways in the crumpled yet still burgeoning density of Bellytown. Blackened scraper girders jutted menacingly. Whining Levi cycles with frybar-wielding riders blasted away in hot pursuit! Tooco drove around, above, and through it all at speeds close to 3,200 grid an hour.

He'd decided to go for the big one right out of the gate. This was the first time in the three weeks they'd been there that he'd come out of their secret lair. It took Carmine a while to come up with an appropriate costume so he could wander the MGM casino without attracting unwanted attention. He was dressed in a flowing white silk jump trimmed in gold with a complementary turban dripping with pearls. He'd taken off the turban to put on a black game-ball completely covering his head. He was strapped into the pilot's seat of a replica of a Northrop interceptor—the perfect cat for this jungle. His gravitating to the levi games was predictable, but the fact that he immediately chose to play the longest, most difficult, and potentially profitable one surprised him a little. He'd been thinking of a couple of short-run games to warm up his dormant driving skills, but he had a limited amount of Yuan, fronted to him by Darl; and if he lost at an early attempt, he wouldn't have the needed ante to go for the big graft on "Tokyo Run." So not only did he have to display phenomenal piloting and evasive combat skills, he needed to possess the stamina to go for six to seven hours on a run from Bellytown to Tokyo and back, the real amount of time it took to make the trip. The only break he and his crew would get was fifteen minutes in Tokyo, when the interceptor took on its cargo before heading back to Bellytown. And the return trip was even harder because the added weight slowed the Northrop down.

Right from the start, it was a challenge. Piloting a levi down here in Bellytown was far different than in Sanatan, Big New, or along the corridors. Because all the burnt-out scrapers were charged to a positive polarity to support the grid plate of Big New, you were actually flying inside the magnetic field, producing the Meissner effect 360 degrees around. That made for a hair-trigger response to the slightest movement of his joystick and many more ways to move. Since he'd spent hundreds of hours flying in Bellytown, his expertise was causing quite a few rouge pursuers to smear themselves on numerous obstacles, which at the last millisecond, Tooco nimbly slipped around. He glanced at his rear-view screen in time to see one bandit lose a leg on a piece of charred steel poking from a scraper he was skimming past. The resulting loss of ballast caused the coke to swerve into a brick wall. Dog, he loved the chase!

Seated in a triangular pattern around his cockpit, the three gamers loved it too. Each had their own black helmet with a view from their potential gun position. He needed gunners and was worried he couldn't convince three gamers to sign up for the grueling ride. But the combination of a huge pot and Tooco's stunning stickwork on his qualifying lap convinced these three to hop on board.

Initially, they weren't committed to making the whole trip. They could quit any time before they reached the halfway point of the first leg and take whatever small winnings they'd accrued. If they did bail, he wouldn't have a prayer in hell of winning. But now, out of Bellytown, they'd cleared some of the most formidable impediments in the whole run, and it was obvious they were riding with a pro. Once they made that halfway point of the first leg, their lasers were activated, and they were committed to taking the whole ride—across the black water hugging the waste-fill coast, down to Miami, and then across the Atlantic toward Tokyo. Soon Sacker ships would hone, bent on taking him out before he reached the broken spire of Washmon, where his gunners could finally open-fire.

They rode into a shrouded night, just like the one he'd flown into a long time ago. If he'd been in an interceptor, then he'd probably be stretched out in Yakami's palatial mode getting his jerk hummed by a bevy of fawning sheed right now. Unfortunately, he'd been in a beat-up Lockheed, in desperate need of a drive overhaul—and so began a life in the mines.

As he predicted, the flying V of a Sacker squadron appeared in his rearview screen. Tooco was ready with a few surprises for these clones. He tapped up full thrust and dropped to five centigrid, nudging his stick to the right. Let them think he was going to try and stealth it, hugging the terrain for camouflage. Let them think they knew who they had in their sights.

In his former life he'd been Yakami's stickman, piloting the Silver Needle, a custom Lockheed levi limo that the smartest, fiercest Yakuza in all of Bellytown rode around in. He'd worked his way up, doing many Nitro runs to get his coveted position. His transporter days were long past when Yakami asked him to cover the Tokyo Run that week. He still didn't know, whether for some unknown reason, Yakami had set him up, or if it was just the luck of the draw. It was something he hoped to find out, if they ever got to Bellytown. Not that he planned to do anything about it, but he was curious. He'd been proud of his position and abilities. He wanted to know if his loyalty turned out to be nothing more than a "sap cap."

That broken spire punctured the horizon on his screen as the Sacker squadron closed in. Not long now, before the gamers riding with him got the chance to earn their graft, communication links would open, and he could help direct their fire. But first, the last thing they would expect. He jerked the stick into his crotch and tapped up liquid rocket boost. The interceptor roared heavenward, the simulator shaking violently. Underneath him, the Sacker V shot by, unable to match his unexpected maneuver. By the time they circled back and closed formation, Tooco's loop-de-loop would be complete, and he'd be past the fail-safe point. They'd still have to close up, and that would leave him with enough time to inspire his gunners. Mere moments later, the aforementioned landmark snapped past.

"Left-wing gunner, your call ID is *Southpaw*, cliqued?"

"Southpaw, cliqued, Commander!"

"Right-wing gunner, your call ID is *Tightie*, cliqued?"

"Tightie, cliqued, Commander."

"Tail gunner, your call ID is *Feather*, cliqued?"

"Feather, cliqued, you hot snagger—uh, Commander."

A sheed tail gunner, screxy!

"By the time those clonies close up again, we'll be almost to Miami. At least one more squadron will come out to meet us, and we'll also run into some ground fire. Shoot anything that enters your quadrant. Shoot and shoot some more. That's what you're here for! I'm gonna be pulling some hairy maneuvers, and the shaking, bouncing, and jerking around are gonna be off the grid. I don't care! Keep your finger on that trigger tap and be blasting all the time. I want three beams choppin' sky! I want this crate vibrating with laser buzz, got it?"

There were three enthusiastic affirmatives, and Tooco continued his instructions, "Once we get out over the Atlantic, things may get a little boring. It's a long stretch. If you've been party-hearty, you may wanna take a nap. That's why you're gonna be answering personal questions I will be asking you the whole time. I promise, they'll be questions that keep you engaged. You will stay alert, scanning your quadrant constantly. Out there, we'll be facing United Cartel Sackers in large destroyer ships, and also there will be gun posts on the water. Early detection is our only chance of maneuvering around or outrunning them. Stay sharp! I know you're all thinking about that big pot of graft we're after, but I want more out of you in the way of motivation than that. As you may have figured out, I've got some personal experience at this sort of thing, and if any one of you doesn't feel an obligation to this crew, I will personally deal with you when this is over. Your motivation is the same now as my old crew every time we went out: Don't fuck up! Don't get caught! Don't get killed! Get it done!"

This time, along with the enthusiasm, there was a satisfying note of real awe in the response. He congratulated himself on a rousing call to arms. The troops were motivated, and that could make all the difference. The image of Mayra suddenly flashed in his mind, dark hair flowing in the ashy wind, black cloak falling from her shoulders to the cobbled stone. On the crest of Lennon's knoll, proselytizing for the dreamers in Cenpak, holding up her tattered tome of "Shakes," her powerful alto commanding them all to listen. "Friends, Romans, countrymen, lend me your ears. I come to bury Caesar, not to praise him. The good men do is oft interred with their bones . . . so let it be with Caesar."

She was radiant in her passion, canceling out the overwhelming ruin that surrounded them. And Tooco, just another less-than-insignificant waif in the crush of misery and decay, fell madly in love with her, returning again and again to hear her proclaim Shakes as the way back to civilization.

Eventually, he'd stayed for the reading classes and, over an extended period, learned the rainbow palate of English, understanding the hidden purpose in those words she opened every gathering with—to rouse the spirit to rage at what enormous disrespect was shown in the smoldering heap surrounding them. Mayra gave him Shakes, and Shakes gave Tooco the world he dreamed in, where people cared passionately; where there was loyalty, integrity, and purpose, along with betrayal and ruin; and there were forests and waterfalls and castles and "beer." Really, it was Mayra and Shakes who got him the job with Yakami.

This was before Yakuza and dreamers went to war. He'd been swanking in a classier uptown bar, doing comedic scenes where he played all the parts, soliciting drinks and chem enhancers from patrons who could barely follow the story but found the overly ornate language inherently hysterical. He judged this crowd was up for something more serious and had just started Macbeth's chilling monologue when Yakami and his entourage walked in. Always one to use the moment, he'd spun around to point an accusing finger at the leader of this new set of revelers and nailed him with the next line.

"But we still have judgment here! For if we but teach bloody instruction, which being taught, returns to plague the inventor's hand."

Suddenly, Tooco recognized whom he was directing these words to and shit literally a little bit right in his jump. Yakami stared back an endless moment, emerald lasers in a pitiless face, waking every nerve in his spine. Then a corner of the gangster's lip curled into a half smile. "Where'd you learn that crap?"

Tooco made the effort to find his voice again. "From the dreamers in Cenpak."

Yakami watched him a moment longer, seeming to decide something. "You've been inside Cenpak?"

"Yeah, lots of times."

Yakami's lips stretched into a full, if dangerous, grin. "Come, join us. Let me hear some more of your strange cloneshit."

The whole bar roared with relief, and his life as a court jester was born. Tooco, with his Shakes and his knowledge of the dreamer's stronghold, lucked into a much better life. Later, his natural talent with a joystick was discovered when Yakami's driver got into an argument over fresh kill in a necro club and started a fight with one of Yakami's hitters.

That second Sacker squadron he'd predicted blipped up on his early warning screen, and in his rear-view screen, he saw the first squadron closing again. It was time to make some serious trouble.

"All right, let's blast these motherduffers!"

— ●—◆—● —

This was sweet, and Ryka could remember her feelings again. Sunsue was her friend. Sunsue shared. It's sweet to share. Sunsue had always been her friend, Zim was always a piece of shit, and Nitro was the only way to fly. That elongated turd kept her zoned out on Freemate for so long she'd forgotten what it was like to be alive—no more candy from strangers. Dog! How long had it been since she'd heard herself laugh? They had so much to be thankful for. Darl's newfound generosity and this plush mode in Sanatan! She was beginning to feel like her old self again.

Unfortunately, it didn't change the premonitions. Ryka could see it was coming. She saw, without even trying, through the multilayered illusions, saw it lurking in the grand intertwining gossamer of lies. That's why they'd sent her to the mines. She'd seen where Barney was headed, and it wasn't out for a pack of smokes. She missed the ancient vids. They kept the premonitions out of her head—simple, silly stories about cokes chasing their tails to while away the time.

It wasn't that what she saw was terrible, although it was. But the point of it wasn't terrible. It was about some great coming just beginning, and she could see the sudden web quietly descending on them, wafting down on all their sleepy heads. All their separate purposes gathered into one grand moment. There was something coming to ensnare them all. Glittering strands draped everywhere, waiting to pull you in . . . an ending to begin.

•———◆◆◆———•

Harrison could see them gathered in one of the "conglom" boxes up in the very back of the arena. He was unexpectedly pleased that those who could showed up for his match: Ryka, Sunsue, Darl, and Okada. Bay was gone, off on his quest for revenge; Tooco was playing in the main casino; and Zim, of course, was in a Screx. Carmine, with a pitcher of Blue Booz in hand, was topping up both Darl's and Okada's glasses while joking about something. He was definitely keeping it low profile, though, hiding out in the back. At the moment, Han was missing— probably, out, working the crowd, looking for other prospects. Okada's turquoise jump was especially striking, the low-cut bodice revealing her perfect little breasts. Harrison was hoping she'd glance down to watch the prematch preparations, but she was busy talking with Carmine. Darl was watching, though, as attendants checked his jump, making sure the pain activators woven in his body stocking were fully functional. The brief darts of agony produced while they went about their business returned his concentration to the task at hand. A techie was behind him on the disk, suspending two tiny globes in a Meissner field. They would emanate Drakar's weapons. Synergized into the holo program, they moved with Drakar's claws. Now it was his turn to face the beast.

He spotted Han down front in a high roller's box, busy chatting up some gargantuan gadget master, his back to Harrison. Han was showing him hand screens of his main-level play from the last couple of weeks. Even from behind, Harrison could tell the gadget master was far more interested in the tall blonde Screenrage than in what he was zapping.

Harrison's attendants departed, and the entire arena began to darken. The noise of the crowd died down, and the silver disk began rising slowly in the air. Suddenly the match announcer's voice boomed through the coliseum.

"COKES AND COQUETTES, GAMERS, SCAMMERS, AND INSUNDERY CLONES, THE TIME HAS COME, THE MOMENT ARRIVED! WE HAVE ANOTHER CHALLENGE FOR THE SEMIPRO CROWN!" Now the crowd went wild.

"FRESH FROM MAIN-LEVEL PLAY IS A YOUNG TECHIE WHO'S SHOWN INCREDIBLE SPEED AND POWER AND WHO GOES SIMPLY BY THE ID—NEW BLOOD!" There was some scattered hooting as the announcer rolled on, "A BIG SLAM FOR THE COKE WHO WANTS TO PUT IT ON THE LINE WITH THE HOLO WARRIOR FROM HELL, THE MEANEST REPTILE THIS SIDE OF THE OKEEFEENOKI, THE REAPER WITH THE RIPPER, UNDEFEATED CHAMPION—DRAKARRRRRRRRRRRRR!"

The arena went berserk as a blue column of light descended on the silver disk. His head bowed, Harrison saw his carnelian armor turn purple, muted currents of royal red swirling beneath its surface. When it came to presentation, the Screenrage definitely had a flare for the dramatic. His combat jump was exceptional. Harrison raised his head and brought up the handle of his laser sword directly in front of his face the way Han coached him. He lit the sword and a gold blade shot up a centigrid from the handle. Again, the Screenrage was on the Yuan. The hooting and catcalls died away. Their blades were both charged to positive polarity so when they touched, they repelled each other. Pain actuators were activated in Harrison's jump when Drakar registered a hit. In Drakar's case, Harrison's hits caused various comp-gen functions to be downgraded at the location of the strike.

The crowd's rumbling returned when, starting with his clawed, scaly feet, the image of Drakar began to materialize. The massive slimy legs, the armored pelvic girth, the heaving chest, and gigantic arms arrived. He was even uglier in person, and his mug hadn't appeared yet; despite which, the lizard's claws clapped together, and a laser blade leaped at Harrison's eyes. His parry was barely in time to slap the tip of Drakar's blade aside. Cute. He'd almost lost before "slug-bucket" showed up for the fight. He showed up now. The bloodshot yellow eyes with their black diamond pupils took Harrison in. Displaying his trademark red fangs, Drakar broke into a broad grin.

"'New Blood, hmm . . . an apt ID, clonie."

"It talks." Harrison grinned back at the ugly mug.

A combat master's admonition echoed in his ears, "The face isn't what's going to kill you."

With an effort, he tore his eyes from the lizard's head, focusing on his solar plexus, where he could monitor all four limbs. Drakar leaped forward with another straight thrust. Jumping back, he again slapped down Drakar's tip. He made an exaggerated thrust of his own, provoking the lizard to bring his blade across for a parry. But Harrison's thrust suddenly metamorphosed as his left hand pushed the butt of his sword forward, crossing his wrists and turning his blade to the left. Drakar's blade parried only air as Harrison whipped his blade downward in a diagonal cut, left to right, aimed at Drakar's right wrist.

But Drakar learned his lesson, spotting a variation of the move his last opponent used, and immediately snatched his right claw off the sword. Harrison's blade sparked the handle where his claw should have been. They circled each other warily, both with a little more respect for the other. Finally, Harrison charged with a straight overhead cut. Drakar answered with a diagonal right parry, pushing back and down on Harrison's blade, then slashing across with a lateral cut. But Harrison read the move and leaped back to avoid being cut in half. Again, they circled.

Drakar charged with his own classic overhead cut. Harrison countered with the same diagonal right parry Drakar had, but the height and power of the monster's cut staggered him, and he could only stumble backward, retreating to circle again. It was already clear that Drakar's size and weight, expressed in a more powerful positive charge in his blade, would overwhelm him every time they locked swords. He had to find a way to get inside that jackhammer blade and surprise the slimy freak. The lizard realized his advantage as well and would keep coming at him with more overhead cuts, trying to beat him down.

When he did, Harrison decided to mirror him, charging with his own overhead cut a nanosecond after Drakar charged. Then diving on his knees and sliding, he'd turn his cut into an overhead parry, ducking under his own blade as the force of Drakar's blade beat it down. He'd end his slide up close and personal, whipping his blade around in a lateral cut. It was an elaborate series, and the execution had to be perfect. Harrison circled slowly to hone his focus and hopefully provoke the lizard into an impatient charge.

It took a while before Drakar concluded Harrison was fresh out of strategies and basically just running for his life. When he did raise his sword, the audience affirmed that assessment with a bloodlust, spurring the reptile's charge. It went down exactly as planned, right up to the moment when Harrison's blade separated Drakar's webbed tootsies from his legs halfway up his shins.

Whereupon Drakar stepped off his scaly feet, planting his bloody stumps on the disk, his red fangs glistening in an ear-to-ear grin!

"Nice move, clonie. Too bad it's your last." Like lightning, Drakar raised his sword; then down it came on a trajectory to split Harrison in half. Being on his knees, he appeared a condemned man—except the whittled lizard was still tall enough that Harrison could dive through his legs, which he did!

Drakar's blade bit the disk in a shower of sparks. He immediately spun 'round on his stumps, sweeping his severed feet off the disk. Harrison managed to spin around too, regaining his feet as Drakar raised his blade again. But this time, he held the sword with only one claw while his other claw extended from waist level, gripping his signature scythe knife. These double edges waited in the still blue air, poised to simultaneously cleave and disembowel him. Without the String, he was dead.

"Wake up, clonie. Time to die."

He had no choice but to take five. He was waiting to see which way the lizard would come: whether he'd choose to gut him like his last opponent or split him in two from head to toe. Because the tip of Harrison's sword was still touching the disk, he'd have a better chance of parrying the scythe knife, but Drakar knew that. It would come from above, but the moment Harrison tried to dive for it, the lizard would swing that scythe into play, impaling and gutting him. No doubt the arena operators were preparing to activate his jump so the gloating reptile could hold up the wriggling body for the crowd's amusement while Harrison screamed in agony.

The sword started to fall, and Harrison tattooed his String pattern across the reptile's chest. In an instant, he was beyond all of Drakar's weapons. It wasn't the most inconspicuous moment to jump the String, but he had no choice. It was literally now or never, and hopefully his blue aura would remain hidden in the column of blue light. Now he needed to remain completely still or risk his image breaking up and the whole crowd realizing he was spacecase. He had to wait until the infinitesimal moment before the blade cut, then pivot to his right ninety degrees as Drakar's blade flashed past and bit the disk; then, with his image obscured by the sparks, immediately jump off the String!

That's what he did. But it was day and night, the passage of time perceived in the third and fifth dimensions. On the fifth, it was like an ancient high-speed camera, shooting twenty frames per second, but you had to carefully examine each frame one after another. It reminded him of shuffling through an interminable art zap. It was stultifying, watching the incrementally closing blade until a nanosecond before the slice. Then, slowly pivoting to his right, he jumped off the String just as Drakar's blade struck the disk in an explosion of light.

But Drakar wasted no time, following up with a vicious hook from the scythe knife. In that split second, Harrison made a move that would be talked about in every casino in Sanatan for the rest of the night. He assumed the classic pose of subservience, prostrating himself so fast, his face slammed the disk, arms extended in front of him, sword gripped in his left hand. Overhead, the scythe knife whipped past; and immediately after Harrison rose up, he answered with the lateral cut, taking off another section of the lizard's legs, this time at midthigh.

At that moment, the whole crowd began chanting, "New Blood!" as the desperate reptile somehow managed to keep from toppling and made another leap. There was a sickening squish as his bloody thighs hit. Harrison, on his feet, now spun around to make a downward diagonal cut, taking off Drakar's left arm at the shoulder. A scream of ecstasy rose from the assembled as the severed appendage with scythe knife still in claw twitched an independent course around the disk. Carved down to size, Drakar stared back at him, his hideous face rippling with hatred. The bloody grin was finally gone.

"Come and get me, clonie!"

Drakar raised his one arm, brandishing his laser blade in a final act of defiance. The arena fell silent, the crowd waiting to see how Harrison would finish off the vanquished lizard king. Harrison began circling to his right around the disk's edge. The squishing of Drakar's bloody stumps made the only sound as the crippled lizard tried to keep the dangerous techie out in front of him. Then Harrison feigned an overhead strike. The reptile responded with his only option, a one-handed overhead parry. But Harrison leaped to his left, releasing his left hand from the sword and whipping his blade around in a backhand lateral cut. Drakar's sword arm fell away, severed just above the elbow.

Again, the crowd was treated to a dancing limb. The elbow stump furiously flipped the arm around, whipping the laser blade in every direction. Whoever programed the monster was an aficionado of bizzare endings. Before Harrison could deliver the coup de grâce, the renegade blade sliced off the rest of Drakar's left thigh at the hip.

The quadriplegic lizard crashed down on his side, and the awed crowd watched as Drakar's own blade filleted his head, his ribboning mouth bellowing, "Fuck you!" to the last. When his torso stopped twitching, the lizard's remains started breaking up, and the blue column evaporated. Harrison stood alone on the disk. Once again bringing his sword up in front of his face, he shut down the blade. The entire arena went wild!

"COKES AND COQUETTES, GAMERS, SCAMMERS, AND INCENDIARY CLONES! WHAT A NIGHT! WHAT A FIGHT! YOU WERE HERE! YOU SAW IT ALL! WHAT A WARRIOR! WE HAVE A CONTENDER! I SEE A CONTENDER FOR THE ULTIMATE CROWN! COKES AND COQUETTES, HE HAS ARRIVED! I GIVE YOU—NEW BLOOD!"

❦

The scraper was exactly as he remembered it, a black arrow shooting up 126 levels. Sacker Command for Northern Quadrant and on level 73, Baylor would find his reason for living through the last ten cycles of barrenness and deprivation. He'd find Rector taking a bath.

The night before, the cards verified his schedule, certifying the banishment of the Akitas before he surrendered his nakedness to the water. They'd also shown the intense pleasure he continued to derive from Angelica's passing. There was something beyond perverse about it as if, in some way, he was merging with Bay's lost love. He wasn't willing to look any deeper, afraid it might turn his rage into a reckless poison. He had to maintain a professional perspective.

He could see her smiling on her mat with the cards spread in front of her, mocking his question, "Which one am I?" She held up the knight of swords. It pleased him more than a little then. But now he saw this very night waiting in her hand. The cards would watch the warrior complete his destiny and burn.

Ahead, in the chromic entry lock, two sackers stood watch just as they always have. Baylor opaqued his view plate as he closed on them.

He should pass. Carmine was as good as his word, supplying everything he required to play the role. It was almost as if the last decade was simply a bad dream. He was returning from a routine patrol, climbing the same steps he always did, and later he'd see Angelica.

At this moment, though, he remembered something he should have remembered long before he started climbing these steps, a minuscule byte of information that he'd completely forgotten when planning the operation—the *watchword*! There was no time to access it now. Besides, if he did, the lock guards might pick up the search request. Luckily, it was December, and some traditions can be depended on. It was a reindeer. More protocol than password, it was as predictable as the days of the week when Bay'd been bagged. He was betting on the Sacker sense of tradition. What day was it? He tapped up a day/date readout on the side of his helmet and watched it crawl across his view plate. Sunday, December 19, 2096, 7:23 p.m. Rudolph was excluded. The rotation started on the first and was repeated through the 24th of December—*Prancer*! It was Prancer. If he was wrong, it was over. Fucking evil cap. No matter how well planned an assault (and this one obviously couldn't claim that distinction), there is usually a moment that belongs to Dog—when it either falls your way or takes you out. Mounting the final steps to the lock, Bay acknowledged this turned out to be the moment he was talking about.

"Prancer," he spat it out with just the right mixture of weariness and contempt. Not a creature stirred as the double-lock slid open. Carmine had assured him his jump's systems were all online, and no alarms sounded as he stepped inside. At the far end of the lobby, a desk Sacker stood behind a massive sweep of ebony. Baylor ignored him, walking to the bank of levitators to his right and tapped level-74. A moment later, he was rocketing to his requested level.

Levels 51 through 89 were internal modes of all the Sackers assigned to Sanatan. Baylor's own mode had been on 57. When the levitator opened, Bay moved quickly down a short corridor. He turned left at the intersection and followed that corridor to the end, stopping in front of the mode lock he was looking for.

What separated Sackers from other cokes more than anything else was their ability to execute a martial action with brutal precision and a complete absence of any moral or ethical contemplation. Through the ages when it came to armies, it was all about the mission and only about the mission. It was evening. There was a better than 90 percent probability that behind this lock was an off-line Sacker, eating, shitting, sleeping, or masturbating. Whatever activity he may be engaged in, he was going to be dead within moments of opening the lock. The fact that he was "innocent" of any involvement in this matter was completely beside the point. Bay needed his mode to launch his attack. This Sacker must not be allowed any opportunity to interfere with his operation. The only way to ensure that was by killing him, end of considerations. It's what he was trying to explain to Harrison before they broke into Bob's mode, but they never understood. You'd think spacecase would appreciate it didn't need to be personal. When the threat of their capture came into play, Harrison rose to the occasion, but strategic murder was beyond his grasp.

Pressing his palm to the lock, he heard the muffled beeping that announced a visitor. The lock slid open, revealing an almost-naked clonie roughly Baylor's height with cropped blond hair and a nasty expression on his face. The erection he was sporting underneath a black loincloth, combined with his glistening body, confirmed Bay's summation of probable activities. Before he could react to the faceless messenger greeting him, Bay held up the recharge rod for a standard frybar.

"You left this in your levi cruiser, Lieutenant! Gear up. Lieutenant Bolton wants to see you in his mode now!"

The clonie stared in disbelief then turned his head to glance in his equipment niche, certain the recharge rod in his frybar was locked in place. Baylor brought his left fist around from behind his hip, slamming a laser dagger's hilt into his solar plexus. The blade activated on contact as Bay's right hand shoved the recharge rod into his gasping mouth, covering the first choked scream with his glove. Slicing straight up with the laser, he halved the clonie's larynx before he emitted more than a couple of tortured gurgles. Because a laser blade cauterizes as it cuts, there was no blood to speak of. A moment later, Bay was inside the mode lowering the lifeless Sacker to the carpet and silently tapping the lock shut to cut off the stench of torched flesh wafting into the hall.

Now that the clonie was dispatched, Baylor could focus on the personal information he had on the clone. It was an integral part of his plan. He'd used the system nexus of the jump Carmine gave him to retrieve level plans for Sacker modes in the Scraper, following up with occupant profiles. The clonie's ID was Spiker, and he was one of Rector's personal attachés, a casino liaison officer. During his first cycle in Sanatan, he had two disciplinary notes in his file for pulling practical jokes while on duty. Spiker had been a prankster, a cappy coke whose quarters had the singular distinction of being directly above Rector's bath. Now Bay needed to cover the commotion of his entry enough to satisfy Spiker's screen. He rummaged in the jump locker next to Spiker's equipment niche, making dressing sounds, then quietly opened the lock again and loudly slammed it shut.

Silently opening the chest plate in his Sacker jump, he removed a C-comp hand unit from the Screwhog. Han gave it to him when Bay asked if he could borrow it. Bay told him, depending on how things went, he might not get it back. Han said it was all right; Zim had the other one. He'd been touched by that. Han was very generous with cokes he cared about. A hand unit would command a small fortune in the techie quarter. He took Spiker's helmet from his equipment niche and inserted the jack from his hand unit into a download port on the back. He transferred calls received, then plugged the jack into his own helmet and listened to them. When Spiker's voice played, he recorded it and then loaded it into his helmet's voice modulator. Now he was ready to speak with the voice of Lieutenant Spiker.

He opened the lock to Spiker's mode and slammed it closed again. "Funny! Very fucking funny!" Bay laughed heartily as he walked from the entryway into the living area of the Sacker mode. Through his visor, he could see the screen on the far wall where he knew it would be.

"Lieutenant 'bolt on' wants to see you in his mode!" *Gear up! Very fucking funny! I should have seen it coming.* He paced back into the entryway and made undressing sounds. "Okay, you got me, clonies. But you should know better than to kid a kidder, and you got me off-line too so there won't be any demerits in your records." *Damn, but you snitching cokes hold a grudge.* Bay indulged in another hearty laugh. "Well, cokes, two can play the long game. Screen, I'm gonna hit the sack. You can switch to standby for the night."

"As you wish, Spiker. Pleasant dreams."

"Goodnight, screen."

Bay watched from the entryway as the lights dimmed and the blue glow of the screen withdrew. He waited a couple of minutes, making undressing sounds, then casually padded into the darkened mode. Directly in front of him was the sleeping mat with the screen to his left on the far wall, dark now except for a glowing red dot in the lower right-hand corner. To the right of the screen was the elimination niche, and to its left the food center. It was a standard-issue Sacker mode, which meant there was an air-circulation unit on the other side of the sleeping mat. The air shaft behind it would connect directly into the air shaft of Rector's bath. Rector took his bath at around 11:00 p.m., which meant Bay had three hours to prepare his ambush.

Bay slipped quietly around the sleeping mat, locating the air vent at the bottom of the wall. As long as he refrained from making loud or unusual sounds, the screen would remain off-line. He knelt down, activating the laser dagger's blade, and began cutting out a section of the acrylic-resin wall just above the vent. He had to stop occasionally to let whiffs of burnt plastic dissipate before continuing. Once he finished cutting, he took a suction handle from his utility belt and gently pulled out that section of the wall. Leaning his head into the dissected shaft, he peered down through Rector's ceiling vent into his bath mode. He tapped up the flashlights on either side of his helmet just enough so he could make out the black marble vacuum stool directly below. He tapped up mic amplification, listening for a moment. There were no sounds coming from inside Rector's mode.

He tapped it up as far as it would go, but still there was only silence. The captain wasn't mode.

Bay checked Sacker traffic that night. There were no code 4 alerts and no posted emergencies anywhere in Sanatan. Rector could be on R & R at one of the casinos, but that wasn't really in character for the captain's off-line time. Bay could go ahead, enter through the overhead vent, and wait for the captain to return; then blast him and his gods when they came through the lock. But he doubted Rector's screen was on standby. He'd only switch to standby when he slept. That means he'd have to wait in the bath mode, and the robo gods would be clearing the mode as soon as they padded through the lock. He needed more information.

Bay crept over to Spiker's mat and crawled onto it, pulling the thermal wrap crumpled at his feet over his head. "Screen?" Through a narrow opening he'd fashioned between the wrap and mat, Bay watched screen's blue glow again suffuse the mode.

"Yes?"

"I've been remembering when I first got here, how I was always just thinking about having fun, just always wanting to have fun. I know that you know I wasn't really serious about doing my job then."

"Well, Spiker, that's normal. You were just out of the academy. You had no real experience of things. You were young."

"I know, but I guess tonight, with my old buddies playing that prank on me, it just surprised me how quickly I was ready to get back in that whole frame of mind, getting wrapped up in that silliness."

"Spiker, everybody likes not to be serious all the time."

"Yeah, but I don't think I'm serious enough most of the time. And I'm finding I like it when I'm serious and focusing on my work, not letting myself be distracted by inconsequential things. Anyway, I've been thinking about this for a while that I should take advantage of the opportunities to develop a superfocused mind. I've been thinking about going totally online."

"Well, Spiker, that's a very big step. That's something you need to really be certain of because you know there's no going back. All the personal data that is very much a part of your life, your experience of life, you can't get it back. Once it's gone, it's gone. That's it. Are you sure you want to sacrifice that?"

"I don't know, but I think I'm as sure as I'll ever be. I mean, it will always be a little scary, won't it? Because you know you're going to change fundamentally, but when you talk to cokes that did it, they have this peace. This . . . I don't know . . . this solidity. I mean there's no doubt in them about their purpose, no uneasiness about who they are and their value to 7. Really, I've thought about it a lot. I know I haven't mentioned it, but I really have thought about it a lot. I want to do it! I want to go totally online, screen. I'm ready. I want it!"

"I'm continually amazed by you, Spiker. You make screen very proud. You're always the first to recognize your faults and first in striving to correct them. I do think you're ready, son, if that's really what you want?"

"It is. It's what I want. Should I just follow protocol and meet personally with Captain Rector to arrange for the surgery?"

"Yes, that's good. Let me interface his schedule."

Bay watched the glow flickering as screen accessed Rector.

"Unfortunately, the captain is off-line hunting the mutant aberration that killed two Sackers on patrol in the eastern waste fill a couple weeks back. He left this morning."

"If I had his coordinates, I could take a cruiser out there to notify him of my decision."

"Well, under the circumstances, we don't have to observe protocol to the letter. I'll just patch you through to him in the morning."

Bay was surprised to find he was enjoying their game, meeting the challenges as they arose. "I know I'm often self-indulgent, especially about the rituals and ceremonies of Sacker life, but I would really appreciate being able to look my commander in the eye when I request to have my mind put totally online. I'm sure I don't have to tell you, screen. It's a special moment in the life of any Sacker who makes the choice. Of course, I could wait a few days till he gets back, if it's really not convenient."

Bay was betting screen wouldn't want to take the chance of Spiker having a change of heart. Despite the zap 7 is always pitching, there were very few takers when it came to giving up any vestige of a personal life.

"Well put, bold Spiker. And you don't need to fear you'll be losing something by your choice. You'll be gaining the whole network! And I can tell you right now, one of the first things we'll do is put your exceptional oratorical skills to better use. Of course, you can make the official request to your captain in person. There'll be a cruiser with the proper coordinates programed in waiting for you first thing in the morning."

"Thank you, screen. Thank you."

"It's only what you deserve."

"Good night, screen."

"Good night, Lieutenant, and pleasant dreams."

The blue glow disappeared, and after a few minutes, Baylor crept from the mat. He took one of the two Nitro patches Darl gave him as a parting gift and slapped it on his neck. He had a long night ahead of him. He had to put the section of wall he'd cut out back in place, and then he had to hang up Spiker over his vacuum bowl and drain out all his blood before using the laser dagger to cut flesh and bone into little pieces and dispose of them down the vacuum bowl. Then he had to clean up any residual mess in the elimination niche and transfer all the data from Spiker's jump system into his jump. Also, he had to remember to put the lieutenant's insignia on his helmet. And he needed to do it all very quietly.

It occurred to Bay as he was replacing the wall section over the vent that he'd probably read the baths right but completely missed this development with the ice monster. It sounded like something that would appeal to the captain, the lone coke battling the beast in nature. That was more in character with the captain's idea of recreation. He'd go out alone and take his bow. This development changed the location, but he still had the element of surprise. The captain would be expecting his young lieutenant Spiker. Ironically, it turned out that an extinct creature conjured by Bay was the lure that reeled in the captain for a reckoning.

•———•◆•———•

Gadget Master Kahn Deli surveyed what was already chaos with the thought the night was still young. All around him, revelers from the arena filled his voluminous luxury mode—snorting, smoking, or sucking chem enhancers while intermittently slapping on Nitro patches so they could revive enough to swill down still more of his premium Blue Booz.

He'd tried not to focus on the loss to his stores. After all, he was the one who grandly insisted they all come back and party with him to celebrate the thrilling match. Knowing full well they'd come stampeding in, devour everything in sight, and completely trash the place. Overtaken by the inevitable depression that followed any act of generosity he committed, everything seemed tainted with the possible exception of the gorgeous blonde Screenrage at his side. He was massive but with elegant chiseled features. He'd been the true inspiration for all the night's excesses. Deli felt absolutely bewitched by this clone.

Before the fight, he'd come down front and slipped right into his box, taking his bodyguards by surprise. He'd boldly introduced himself as "Klaus," a game promoter who was managing the coke about to face Drakar. Of course, Deli recognized him immediately, having "snatched" him while flipping through fibers, hoping to find the perfect stranger to call it a night.

It was known as *freeform Screx*, changing partners countless times in a single fuck, the progression accelerating the closer you came to getting off. They went spinning through your arms like icons on a game machine, you trying to yank your lever at just the right instant and explode your load in a hot Screenrage. Klaus was the final repository of a memorable ride. He presumed the ex-Screenrage was trying a new vocation while looks and charm were still in his corner.

Klaus was very confident about his young protégé, claiming that after his "New Blood" demolished Drakar, out of a deep respect for Deli, he was the first promoter they would entertain an offer from. Deli loved his brass and that tight little ass. For such a tall broad-shouldered coke, he had a very compact, muscular butt. Deli was interested in pursuing a more intimate adventure than their last harried assignation. He was feeling wild, reckless, and young! He was on the verge of demanding the personal disk, Klaus promised in gratitude for Deli's invitation to his postfight gala, but before he could find his voice, a coven of bright-eyed sycophants descended on him.

"Deli, Deli, we want a Go Fish!" It was Reeva and those preposterous Falooley twins whose singular talent was dispensing inanities in stereo. They were spurred on by a coterie of fawners in their wake, joining the chant, "Go Fish! Go Fish! We want a Go Fish!" Drakar's gruesome dispatch was fuel for the night. Everyone was in a maliciously festive mood. All the honing clones in his palatial mode circled like vultures, waiting to see if the famous gadget master would live up to his reputation for excess.

Now he really was annoyed. He only had three left, and Dog knows when he might run across new prospects. And the time and graft it took to prepare one. Not that he wouldn't make a lot more graft selling private disks after the event, if he did give into their bloodlust. Deli glanced up at Klaus, a twinkle in his eye. "So, Klaus, are you a Go Fish aficionado?"

Klaus eyed him warily. "I have to be honest with you. I've never been at a Go Fish in my life."

"Oh, well then, for you it would be quite an experience." It would be worth it just to watch the haughty ex-Screenrage become titillated then appalled. He had just the little fishy to make his icy-blue gaze mist with humiliation. Deli turned back to the throng. "All right, since you demand I share all my jewels with you, I will give you your Go Fish! Adjourn with me to the entertainment arena, my very dear and special guests."

There was a general roar of approval as Deli started for the ruby-encrusted double-lock at the far end of the mode, then abruptly stopped and turned around. "Are there any Sackers among us? This is being recorded. Are there any undercover Sackers here tonight?" He scanned the crowd. "I must ask you to leave now." Deli allowed himself a sly grin. "I do not allow Sackers, no matter how corrupt, to play. Leave immediately!"

No one stirred.

"All right then, let the games begin."

Han followed the portly gadget master through the ruby locks down into a steeply raked theater. At a quick glance, the completely red motif was just what you'd expect from Deli. It looked like it could seat a couple hundred cokes, and there were easily that many swanking here tonight. He'd lied to Deli about this being his first Go Fish. At the top of his fame, he was invited by another ultra gadget master to spend a wild weekend in Sanatan, linked Screx and everything. Looking back, that mad vacation was the final validation he needed to piss on all of them.

And the wildest thing that weekend was the Go Fish. It was forever etched in his consciousness. Go Fish was illegal because 7 thought it sent the wrong message about cloning. It was only played in secret by the elite in Sanatan. There were fewer screens in Sanatan, part of the vacation motif 's appeal. The occasional game could be played undetected by those who could afford the sport. The sport was played with one standard clone between nine and eleven cycles. These specimens could only be obtained at great cost and considerable risk to the actual procurer. Next, you had to have their bodies implanted around the waist and the neck with a series of mutant gene repressors—a costly procedure if you were lucky enough to know a genetic engineer who was willing to perform the illegal operations at an exorbitant fee. Then the specimen still had to go through a long series of injections designed to make them more receptive to gene bombs.

And on top of all that, you still had to procure exotic gene splices from headhunters who'd snagged something remarkable from the far reaches of the waste fill. Again, you'd pay dearly for these ancient baubles, and most of your transactions would be conducted in sleazy Bellytown bars. Yes, some coke did all these things for you, but the fact remained it was extremely expensive and very dangerous for most of the cokes involved.

Han watched as their jiggling host propelled himself to the center of the arena's large silver disk and raised his arms to address the expectant throng. "You have prevailed on me for the delight of bizarre delights. Prepare then to be shocked and amazed. Cyrus!" At the top of the arena, a gold-plated, diamond-encrusted robo appeared in the ruby double-lockway. "Bring the young blond."

The robo spun around and disappeared as Deli turned his gaze to Han. "Klaus, I dedicate this one to you." There was an audible sigh as all eyes turned to Deli's latest infatuation. Han blushed at this unexpected exposure. The gadget master smirked staring out into the amphitheater. "Who dares to be our player?"

Silence settled over the rapacious gathering. Go Fish was primarily enjoyed as a spectator sport. Players were prone to heart failure.

Harrison sat near the top of the theater beside Darl, who was rapt with excitement for the coming event. His stunning victory earlier in the evening was forgotten in anticipation of forbidden thrills. He looked directly down and spotted Carmine and Okada in a box nearer to the stage.

Go Fish, he'd avoided it like the plague. Ever since he viewed a disk borrowed from another cadet, something in the eyes of the young clone they'd used was too much for Harrison, especially after the final change. That look remained the same. For cycles, it haunted his dreams. Now he was going to have to sit through the real thing or risk offending their new mentor.

"Come on now! We can't have a game if we don't have a player who's going to take the leap so we can all go on this ride?"

Without warning, a rambunctious Rebino princess—porcelain levi breasts sailing before her—leaped free of her chaperone and raced up onto the disk.

"Me! Me! Me!"

Deli took her statuesque hand and began parading her around the disk. "What is your ID, rapturous gamer?"

"Kaka!" she bleated, still trying to catch her breath.

"A lovely handle on a lovelier vessel." Deli reached out with both hands, firmly capturing the floating melons, beginning to knead them like casabas hanging from the vines. "Beautiful. I am wet with anticipation to see all of you. And where do you call mode?"

"South Hampton."

"A lovely Satcit and one of my favorites. You know how to play. If you can manage to keep from fainting for the entire transformation, then you get to host a party right here any time next week, with all snags borne by me and with the help of every member of my staff. And if you lose, well, you know—you lose." Deli finally released Kaka's melons and gestured to the center of the disk. 'Time to show us what you've got to metamorphous—strip, tubeydoll!"

While the grotesquely voluptuous Kaka leaned on Deli for support, peeling off her pink zircon jump, Harrison tried to catch another glimpse of Okada. Carmine's hulking shoulders blocked his view, but beside him, he caught the glint of desire in Darl's eyes as she watched the giggling Kaka slip off her panties. Darl gave a groan of disappointment as Kaka's sealed mound's venus was revealed, marked only by a protruding pink catheter. A gadget master, determined to keep his possibly prurient progeny from any risk of contamination, sewed her up not long after she was decanted.

As Kaka was lowering herself onto hands and knees at Deli's direction, Cyrus returned, gliding through the ornate locks towing a tiny naked clone on a leash. The clone's saucer eyes surveyed the crowd, absurdly innocent of the malicious glee being focused on him by a suddenly hushed crowd.

The golden robo tugged his towheaded specimen down to the giggling Kaka, arranging him on all fours just like the princess but facing her. He then tethered the clone's wrists and ankles to the disk.

The clone was beginning to be aware of the malignant energy that surrounded him. This was one of maybe a dozen times he'd been taken out of sleep stasis. The others were for operations. This was something different. Harrison was anxious too, but his concerns were petty by comparison. He was worried he'd get physically ill witnessing this spectacle in person. Darl shared none of his sensitivities, watching with shiny blank panes, snowy upper lip dewy with anticipation.

Cyrus slid a metallic tendril to the base of the young clone's skull and touched a tap. A blinking blue light began emanating from the back of his neck as Deli simultaneously placed a black halo on Kaka's head. Deli raised his arms in an expensive manner. "They are one!"—one in a manner of speaking. Kaka was now connected to the little clone in every physical and emotional sensation. But she wouldn't be the one changing species.

Deli stepped off the disk, leaving Kaka and the clone staring at each other on hands and knees. "And now let the curtain rise!" The gadget master hit a tap on his wrist organizer, and a two-way mirror whined up from the disk separating the participants. From her side, Kaka saw the young clone while the clone saw only his reflection.

"Cyrus, the charger, please."

While the gold robo proceeded to disconnect parts off his frame and reassemble them as an injection pistol, Deli took the moment to unobtrusively hit another tap on his organizer. Four hidden 3-D cameras began recording. A moment later, Cyrus offered the injector. Deli snatched it with a sly grin. Playing to the whole crowd now, he began stroking its barrel. "What's it got in its rockets?"

Deli tapped some commands into the handle of the injection pistol and strode back onto the disk. "I thought we'd start at the end this evening." Deli paused to look at the readout on the side of the injector. "From a place called the 'Down Under'—which, appropriately enough, is on the other side of the planet—an animal who could hop five centigrid at a pop! But first I've got a party favor. After this first change has taken place, if anyone here can ID this Down Under animal, they are going to be invited to dine with me at my regular Sunday night Doberman feast."

Deli abruptly leaned over, poking the injector's barrel into one of the clone's doughy buttocks. "Pop!"

The little clone let out a scream as the barrel bucked back, revealing an angry welt where the gene bomb went in. Kaka screamed too, flinching an empathetic cheek.

"Zap time!" Amid thunderous applause, the corpulent Deli padded to his gold brocaded couch positioned ringside. The disk started to turn. Multiple shafts of light focused on the circling pair while the rest of the arena slipped into blackness, and Deli's favorite keen began to play.

"Go Fish, Go Fish, Go Fish!" The crowd took up the chant. When it finally came, Harrison was amazed at how fast the genetic explosion really was, racing out from the point of injection like a wildfire. Coarse red patches of hair shot up from the clone's ass and ran quickly down to cover his legs even as his pelvis began to expand and raise itself. A thick furry tail blossomed just above his butt crack, shooting down between his legs until it reached the disk swelling in diameter.

He was shrieking now from his growing pains and the horror he witnessed in the mirror. Kaka was shrieking with him, raising her pelvis too, a stream of steaming urine shooting from her catheter. The clone's feet suddenly ballooned to four times their original size and were completely covered by the coarse red hair. The huge tail was slamming furiously on the disk; the tethers barely held his straining haunches. Suddenly, just above his waist, the morphing stopped, but he screamed moments longer, finally settling into a shivering moan. He looked at himself in the mirror, and tears sprang from his round eyes and rolled down his face. Kaka was mimicking his tears but with a low hysterical giggle coming from the back of her throat.

The disk slowed to a stop, and the lights in the arena bumped up again. Cyrus levied onto the disk, and after applying two more tethers to his down-under haunches, he untied the clone's wrists. He raised himself, uncertain, on new feet and rocked back onto his muscular tail. Harrison couldn't repress a shameful smile as the crowd burst into laughter. Deli hustled onto the disk, punching taps into the handle of the injector. "All right, time to shine! Who's up on their ancient species? Does anybody know the ID of that ass and tail?"

Deli turned in place to search the whole arena. "Nobody wants a delicious sizzling Doberman steak, or two, or three? Nobody?" Deli bowed his head and pretended to cry with the clone. "Nobody." He suddenly snapped to attention, turning around, taking in the whole arena with his arms outstretched. "Cokes and coquettes, that is a *kangaroo*! Really! I'm not making this up, really! That's the ID. Nobody wins. Well, I am very sorry to be the one to inform all of you, you're as dumb as a sack of hammers."

The entire arena exploded with laughter.

Again, he peered at the readout on the injector. "Next, I thought we might see something from Brainforce. That's all I've got here, a place down in South America. Here's something—the cells were taken from eggs deposited in a stalk of sugarcane buried deeply enough to avoid being irradiated."

Deli swung the barrel around and before the clone could do more than wince, fired the projectile directly in the center of his stomach. This time, the change was even more startling. No sooner had the gadget master retreated to his royal couch than the clone's solar plexus began sprouting shiny green plates. They burst through the skin with such rapidity his defenseless yelps turned into one long tortured howl. Kaka's scream lost any claim to humanity as she clawed at her Gordian breasts.

Once his entire torso was covered in the scaly green armor, some of the plates began to merge and form larger plates while the smaller scales raced down his arms, reaching right to his fingertips where the most shocking change of all occurred—his hands ballooned into enormous pincers waving awkwardly before him.

Kaka let loose a bloodcurdling shriek as she stared past her self-mutilated mammories down at her own hands. Deli, a prankster of some renown, was projecting holos of green pincers over them. She stood watching the huge green claws opening and closing at the ends of her wrists until her eyes swiveled up in her head, and she crumpled unconscious to the disk. A buzzer blared, followed by the announcement, "No party for Kaka!" Immediately Cyrus levied onto the disk, shot out a golden tendril, and injected her with a reviver. As

Cyrus retreated from the disk, Kaka jerked to her feet and looked down at her hands. She began blubbering piteously seeing them returned to their normal state. Eventually, she managed to look up at the clone. Tears streaming down, she offered him a timid smile. "Clonie, you're a big mess."

All that remained of him was his tiny head and his reedlike neck delicately perched atop a massive green exoskeleton, balanced on the great hairy legs and tail. Harrison remembered from retrieval what the bug part was: a praying mantis. The clone refused to look anywhere now except in the mirror at his own face. Managing to calm himself in this way, he finally stopped the pincers from clicking and the tail from thumping on the disk. Once more, the disk stopped, and the light returned.

"That's my clonie! Show us what you're made of." The entire arena went berserk at Deli's witticism.

Darl was snorting. Milking the moment, Deli slowly raised himself from his throne and padded back onto the disk. "And now, for the moment we've all been waiting for ..."

The entire arena thundered with the drumming of their words. "Go Fish! Go Fish! Go Fish!"

Deli raised a hand to quiet the crowd and studied the readout on his inoculator. "I'm torn, torn between the extremes, dear friends. A Spinyhead perch from below us in the Atlantic Ocean or a piranha from the aforementioned Brainforce? What's it to be, my dear clones?"

Amid the chaotic response, Deli tapped in his selection, aimed, and squeezed off a shot.

"Piranha!" The clone's head snapped back, revealing a red welt under his chin. Recovering, he glared down with malignant rage at the gadget master.

"Come and get me, fishy!" Deli quickly retreated to his couch when the clone responded to the challenge with a clumsy attempt to crush him under a massive pincer. Slightly miffed, the gadget master settled back into his cushions as the disk turned, and the lights dimmed again.

Sitting next to Deli, Han watched as the clone's lips turned to grey mucus, stretching around both sides of his face, then splitting open to reveal row on row of shiny white knives. His eyes looked heavenward just as they flattened into the sides of his skull, and his skull compressed itself into a gnashing silver club. The clone's thin neck merging with the silver club sprouted desperate gills billowing in the poison air. The entire crowd was on their feet, screaming and chanting, "Go Fish, Go Fish, Go Fish!"

Hairy oversized feet strained at the tethers, and the great tail writhed on the disk. The pincers swung crazily on their green stalks, bashing into the two-way mirror. Rows of razor teeth furiously slashed the air. The piranha head shot straight up, gills vibrating madly, and the entire creation came crashing down.

Kaka, both hands at her throat, toppled with it, dropping to her knees and pitching face-first onto the disk. In the brief moment of silence before the tumult rose, Han vowed if he was ever presented with the opportunity, he would find a way to thank Deli for the evening's entertainment. "Did I lie?" The preening tube turd was grinning in Han's face, his coterie of satiated fawners simpering at his back. "I predicted you'd find it personally interesting. Was I right?"

"Yes, you were, grand Deli!" Twin coquettes in matching blue jumps leaned from behind Deli's girth, crooning in stereo.

"We were wondering, were you two very close?" A snide titter rippled through the group.

Deli grinned wickedly at Han. "No! No, that couldn't be possible. Klaus here has the distinctive signature of the Ruger Labs. Everyone knows Ruger Labs would never allow their clones to be transacted for illicit purposes. That clone was a pale imitation. I assure you, Klaus, while there are some similarities, that clone was a Slavic hybrid. I thought you'd find the vague similarity amusing."

From the other side of the disk, another round of cheers arose as Cyrus once again revived Kaka. Slipping on her sparkling jump, Cyrus handed over her panties and sent her stumbling from the arena supported by her chaperone, who kept glaring in Deli's direction. Party guests who weren't examining the thing surged after the departing Kaka, laughing and shouting.

"Which reminds me, dear Klaus, you promised me a personal disk if I let you and your chums come to my fabulous party. You have yet to deliver my disk."

Han eyed the corpulent executioner with a complete lack of rancor. "I forgot. I'll bring it, when we do the contracts for the bout."

Deli stared at Han for a long moment. "I find you an enchanting tease, dear Klaus. What time is it?" The gadget master glanced down at his wrist organizer. "Five a.m. Well, we have had a good time. Be back here by six this evening with the disk, and we'll talk about it. Who knows, if our discussions go well, you could get the eleven-o'clock bout at MGM. I always keep that one reserved. The last fight of the night draws the biggest bets!"

The gadget master was about to turn away when his interest was quickly rekindled as Harrison approached the group accompanied by Darl. "And what have we here?" Deli cast his covetous eyes on Darl. "Well, Klaus, your New Blood certainly has a champion's tastes." Deli thrust forward his fist, middle finger extended.

"Cliqued, young dogess?"

Darl extended her finger to touch his, "Cliqued Master Deli. I'm Curl."

"Curl, I like it. And what an honor comes to me! I have the great good fortune to entertain a second Rebino princess in my humble mode on the same night."

Darl slid past the gadget master to go stand beside Han. "I'm with him."

"Ah, you are full of surprises, Klaus." Deli glanced quickly back to Harrison. "When you come back, why don't you and Curl bring your warrior here in his splendid battle jump. If we come to an agreement, we can shoot a zap to promote the bout. And why don't you all grace me with a personal disk the moment you arrive." Deli's malevolent gaze slid over each of them, finally landing on Han. "Until this evening, Klaus." Deli turned abruptly and headed toward the disk, anxious to examine the remains of his creation.

CHAPTER

Harrison leaned on the replicator mahogany and stared at his image in the mirror behind the bar. The three Mescalalas he'd downed were kicking in nicely. Behind him, rows of tables were filled with off-line techies all glowing with molecular auras. Three Mescalalas was perfect, took you just up to the edge of hallucination where the intricacies of the third dimension were readily observable. With irises, wide, pupils as big as saucers, he was watching water molecules hanging in the air covering patrons at the bar. Observing the way they rippled with the twitch of a nerve just before the muscle responded, you could with practice, predict every move that was made—a mellower version of the String. It was a party trick, bending time through heightened three-dimensional perception.

He'd managed with luck to find his way to the techie haunt where, as an off-line cadet, he spent many a happy hour. They made great Mescalalas. "O' fuckits," a genuine Irish pub just like two hundred cycles ago.

As a cadet, he hadn't known anything about the Irish, some cokes someplace, sometime. He'd just assumed they were forbearers of the Yaks. Much later, on the String in retrieval, he'd run across their geographic face and because of happy times, spent three minutes taking in their entire history. This time, when he walked through the lock, he was visiting back there. No longer some cokes someplace sometime. The paltry remnant of history when remembering becomes a bother.

He remembered the young clone's body. It kept appearing in his head. After Deli dismissed them and went over to inspect his creation, Darl grabbed his arm and pulled him into some screenshit.

"Jack, wait! Just stay here until Deli leaves."

"What? No. Come on! Let's go. We're going."

She'd latched onto his sleeve and would not let go. "No, I want to see it up-close." Darl was watching him, and the intensity in her eyes made him hesitate.

"Why?"

"Because I want to see it." He was surprised to find that, in that moment, he was afraid of her.

She held him there until Deli finished his inspection, then gave the robos instructions for disposal of the body and scuttled away. Pulling Harrison with her, she reached the metamorphosed young clone before the robos wrapped it up. Harrison was shocked at how quickly the interspecies abomination was decomposing. The mutant's animal, insect, and fish, tissues, were already turning to different jellies—but he was still there, in the piranha's eye, just like in the vid. He was watching them through the eye. Darl continued to take it all in as the robos began to wrap the body. She displayed a trancelike fascination with studying the corpse, and her ivory patina was flush with the excitement of her discoveries. It was the same look she had when she came begging him to fuck her on the String. It was an escape from being the penultimate object.

That's when he turned and walked away out into the gaming sector, leaving Darl in her mutant euphoria. He wandered the streets, overcome by a wistful longing to be unconscious again, back in his safe and comfortable mode. He was truly sorry he'd sought his own individual perspective, for what purpose? To be lost, to be aware of that? Some prize. But there were those myth magicians again pulling their hat tricks. The ones who intimated they'd found a way into the String long before gadget masters reigned. They thought that was exactly right—that only when you acknowledged you were lost and realized how much in the universe you were completely ignorant of could you access the salvation in every moment. They called it *the center of grace.*

That's when he realized his escape into Sanatan's casino jungle had led him to the demarcation line for the techie quarter. He was standing on the florescent double orange stripe, staring down into a cubic chaos. At first glance, the panorama before him defied rational explanation. The blueprints for Sanatan were ready just as Big New was being finished. Soon the first techie crews came up to build the mammoth grid plate for their mega rec center. After completing the first small section, they started camping on it to get off the ice and be close to their work; and as the work progressed, more and more techie crews made their way to the construction site. Hundreds of thousands of transport containers were levied up the northern corridor, containing food, supplies, tools, machines, parts, and endless construction materials. These containers were thermal-insulated, C-power-capable, and could easily be fitted with food replicators, eliminator/sanitation niches, and sleeping mats. The containers came in various sizes, from an eighth of a square grid to one square grid. They were used as warehouses businesses and administrative offices, as well as personal modes. In a short time, the small section of grid plate they homesteaded grew larger and taller as they stacked containers on top of one another—if not recklessly, then very fancifully! Of course, being techie builders, they made sure these domino constructions were shored up with steel pillars, installing levitators so workers no longer needed rocket boots to get up to their modes.

Thus, the cubic clusterfuck greeting him at the demarcation line. Since it covered a relatively tiny portion of the grid plate and would be more trouble than it was worth to get rid of, 7 decided just to paint a double orange line around it and call the mess *techie quarter.* Besides, techies were necessary to keep everything running, and they had to have someplace to live. The containers came in various shades of gray, but many cycles of habitation ensured by now there wasn't a surface in the entire quarter that wasn't tagged by some member of a Yaki crew. The garish neon graffiti was on everything. Walking down a narrow twisting lane, Harrison kept seeing patterns emerging out of the corner of his eye. They reminded him of rugs he'd seen at retrieval, but when he tried looking directly at them, the designs disappeared in a tangle of neon madness. And that was before he had three Mescalalas. The techie quarter was continually disconcerting.

"Come with us now, please."

Harrison looked up from musing in an empty cup to see four Yakuza buttons fanned out behind him, pointing pocket frybars at his back. They all wore the neon shark-skin jumps that young Yakuza favored with their signature "Presleys" plastered to their skulls. For all their cappy attire and faltering politeness, if you offended one, he'd kill you, quicker, and with far less provocation than a Sicilian. Harrison turned around, slowly keeping his hands at exactly the level they came off the bar.

"Excuse me, but I think you have the wrong coke."

The one who first spoke, definitely their leader, addressed him again. "No. We know who you are. We know what you're capable of, if you suddenly disappear. Do that, and we will indiscriminately rake the entire area. Do you understand?"

"Yes." Obviously, they didn't. But it didn't matter; the jig was up. A Yakuza must have been at the match and caught him when he jumped the String.

"Come!" They whisked him out the back through the kitchen and into a narrow alley. The leader grabbed a dangling rope ladder, and Harrison looked up to see a large black levi limo hovering above them. The Mescalalas had taken a toll, and he made a cautious ascent, trying to keep the ladder from swaying too violently. He'd been so proud of not losing his disks at Go Fish. It would be a shame and very possibly lethal if he threw up on the young Yaki steadying the ladder for him. He emerged finally into the limo's opulent white interior. A tiny wrinkled clone in a dark-gray jump sat nestled in the cushions of a velvet couch. He motioned for Harrison to sit on a matching velvet chair across from him.

"Welcome, Harrison, Jack." His voice sounded like the chirp of a warning feature on a small appliance. On closer inspection, Harrison decided he was at least a hundred cycles old. His voice box was due for replacement.

The limo's belly lock slid closed as it shot off into the tangled air lanes that pass for a transport grid in techie quarter. "Allow me to introduce myself. I am Sun Moon Tu. I function as the official liaison for Lord Yakami here in Sanatan. I assume, since you were frequenting one of our establishments, you have some knowledge of our organization?"

"Yes, the Yakuza, I've heard."

The wizened little clone gave him an embarrassed smile. "Possibly, you came to ask us for some help with your current situation?" Sun Moon Tu clearly expected him to leap at this opening, but when Harrison remained silent, he continued, "A friend of mine tells me that, although you're very capable with a sword and inventive in your strategies, your butt would've been sushi tonight if you weren't a spacecase."

"It would have been something. Your friend is very observant."

"He's instructed to be. He also counted four other members of your crew. I hope you haven't lost anybody during your adventures?"

Harrison hesitated for a moment before deciding there was no point in not telling him what little he didn't already know. They'd probably missed Han in their count because he was down in Deli's box. That might turn out to be lucky.

"No. The rest of them didn't come to the match. They're fine."

"So everyone has survived up to this point. Congratulations."

"Thanks."

"Where is the Screwhog?"

"The Screwhog?"

"Yes, the Screwhog. We want it. Where is the Screwhog?"

Harrison thought about it. They had no further use for it, and as far as he knew, Carmine hadn't expressed any interest in it. Why not let the Yaki techs make some Yuan? That would be one hell of a chop job. "It's about eight hundred grid south of here."

Pointing a mummified finger at him, Sun Moon Tu issued an electronic cackle. "Young coke, everything is south from here.

"Ten degrees longitude, eight hundred grid out. Not far from the ice cliffs. It's thirty centigrid beneath the surface. There's a tunnel down to it."

The ancient gangster began talking into a gold pin on his lapel. "Have a cloaked drone sweep beyond the light ring ten degrees longitude all the way out to the cliffs, hunting a large metallic object about thirty centigrid below the surface. Report back when you find it." He nodded to Harrison. "Thank you for your candor. How is Carmine treating you?"

"I don't know any Carmine."

Sun Moon Tu gave him another embarrassed smile. "Well, maybe you've heard of a Captain Rector. I'm sure Baylor has, unfortunately for your friend. Rector got a report that described his ex-sergeant and a renegade spacecase, among others, who supposedly blew up in a mining disaster but might actually have escaped and be heading for Sanatan. The captain is a cautious clone. He's beefed up security these last few weeks. Apparently, there was some 'ghosting' on a driver returning from the garbage run, suspicious but nothing definitive . . . until tonight. We have your match on disk. We can show the exact moment you jumped the String and when you jumped back again."

They rode in silence for a while before the old Yakuza spoke again, "You know, I have to tell you, this is the first time I've ever met a real spacecase. It's my understanding you could disappear right now if you wanted and escape through the body of our limo. That must be an amazing thing to be able to do. I should warn you, the limo behind us will open fire for ten centigrid around if you do."

Harrison couldn't resist a mescaline grin. "What if I disappear and stay right here?"

Sun Moon Tu opened his right hand to reveal a small red object. "This amazing device can detect even the slightest movement in the air and point a target laser at that spot." From under his left thigh, he pulled out another pocket frybar, the matte-black barrel pointing at

Harrison. "And, of course, you know what this is." He indulged in his electronic chuckle, tucking the weapon back in its hiding place.

"I don't mean to be disrespectful, but I'm not sure you have a real grasp of what being in the fifth dimension entails. You may have heard of the blue mist that appears around a spacecase when they take five?"

The old Yak nodded he had.

"That's actually them entering the fourth dimension, which really functions as little more than the gateway into the fifth. While it's true that during this brief period material objects in the third can affect me, light in any form has no effect on me. And once I'm in the fifth, as long as I am aware of my three-dimensional surroundings, neither physical objects nor lasers can affect me. I came along with your buttons because I know how quickly they resort to violence, and I didn't want them carving up a lot of innocent patrons while trying to kill me. I'm being cooperative now because, frankly, we don't need any more enemies. Beyond getting your hands on our Screwhog, what else is it you're interested in?"

Harrison had to admit, he was surprised to see the centurion was still capable of blushing. "Thank you for this enlightenment. It's very considerate of you to give me this information! I suppose, like most of us, I've been a little too fearful of the unknown. I'm sure we can be friends." The old clone leaned forward, reaching out to pat Harrison gently on the knee.

"You know, I can help you with all these problems you're facing. I can provide you with a fortune in Yuan and see to it you and your whole crew have safe passage down to Bellytown. I assume that's where you're heading?"

The front of the limo dipped, and they swooped into a paved clearing, coming to an abrupt but silent stop. Harrison peered out his side view-plate. Surrounded by the ever-present graffiti was a garden café with tables covered by red-and-white checked tablecloths beneath trellises laced with plastic vines and flowers. The side lock slid open, and he stepped out to find Yaki buttons already covering him. Sun Moon Tu stepped from the limo, impatiently signaling them to retreat. They hesitated, and he squeaked something in Amerab. They immediately disappeared back into their Levi. The old clone reached out, taking Harrison's arm both for support and to guide him to the entrance of the café.

"You might as well have at least one good Italian meal while you're in Sanatan—and it's the perfect place for us to discuss a small service."

***

Sunsue's bronze thighs fluttered beneath the hennaed halo of Ryka's undulating head. Tooco took another toke of the synthetic Jamma, his hot tail gunner slipped him in her exuberance over their victory. Unzipping his silk pantaloons, he pulled out a swollen jerk and began slowly stroking it.

This was the life. Let Zim, freak in the Screx. Let Han, Darl, and Harrison swank it up with Topgrid perverts. Let Okada do whatever she was doing with Carmine—this was the life!

They told him about their night when he came back, the space dick's big String match. Big deal. Tooco just broke the record for Tokyo Run! Five hours and fifty-two minutes, sixteen minutes faster than the previous record holder. On the return, everybody tried to skim it, stay as close to the water as possible to compensate for being loaded with cargo. But he'd decided to fly at the Northrop's max altitude and, instead of retracing their route, take the jet stream across the Pacific, hoping to catch a strong tailwind. If they got spotted, it made them an easier target, but the dogs were with him. Not only did he get a high-pressure system that revved up the jet stream, but they made the entire crossing without a single Sacker ship spotting them. He'd broken the hypervid bank of MGM's main-gaming level! He brought back more graft than space dick could make in two pro-Stringer matches. This was Tooco's night. And to that end, he'd returned with two cases of Blue Booz, a jumbo pack of Nitro patches, and the sweet Jamma he was sucking on. The wenches, already higher than a Topgrid's juice snag were happy to join in an extended chem-enhancer orgy. And they were heating up nicely: Sunsue's high plaintive moan becoming more urgent, pressing Ryka's face into her flowering heat. This was her way of saying goodbye to Bay. Pretty soon, if the temperature kept rising, Sunsue might be willing to fuck him too. And then Okada could burn in hell. He'd rather have this tanned beauty with her golden locks than that small-breasted witch any day. Before Bay would've killed him in a heartbeat. But now Bay was gone.

That morning, he'd called them to his suite. He told the crew he was going away that evening, and they would have to leave as well. They could not look to Carmine for any help, and he wanted them off the premises within forty-eight hours of Bay's departure. Bay explained that, contingent on his plans for his nemesis Captain Rector, Carmine had to protect himself from being linked to what was going to happen. He said he was sorry his decision was going to cause them some problems, but he trusted that Han would be able to handle the situation. He said he had no choice. His revenge had waited long enough. He had to do it now while he still could. Each of them said their goodbyes and then left. Han was last to come out of the suite, wearing his usual confident smile. He grabbed Harrison immediately and began discussing their plans for his semipro match that night. Everyone else went about picking their clothes for the evening. Carmine provided several more racks of garments to choose from. Tooco was taken completely by surprise at the don's ultimatum, but he understood there was nothing personal about it. He just had to cover his ass. Besides, it was no longer a problem. Tooco had taken care of all their problems tonight.

He hadn't felt like watching space dick be a hero, so he'd gone down to the MGM's main level. The rest was history. They didn't need Harrison and his String. They had Tooco and his stacks of Yuan!

The thin black credits were stacked on a side modular, almost half a centigrid high. Easily enough to snag a couple of racing vans with only a modest haircut to one of the stacks, then just disappear under the pretense of going racing around the light ring. They'd live like kings in Bellytown! Tooco came up with the plan after a few puffs on his Jamma. He knew Han would love it. Han appreciated simple and effective. Tooco was taking care of everything. This was, without a doubt, the best night of his entire life.

Meanwhile, Ryka wasn't quite getting it for Sunsue, who was feeling around on the mat with one hand. Tooco thought he spied what she was searching for. He reached around the modular holding his fortune and grabbed a steely from beside the mat. When he placed it in her palm, Sunsue smiled, briefly opening her eyes. Tooco smiled back and blew another puff over the straining lovers.

Okada was half-hoping any moment he'd offer her a couple Nitro patches to slip in his Screx and get off a personal profile. But Carmine just kept standing there watching the skiers through a telescope. At this late hour, only a few were out and about, shooting the iron peaks of Sanatan.

The wall around the recreation sector consisted of those iron-coated "peaks" mirroring the top of the mountain range, etched on the lower portion of Sanatan's magnificent bell jar. This mountain wall extended around the base of the crystal castle, enclosing Uncle Walt's amusement park. The medical sector, municipal services, and machinery to run the great burg were under Walt's park in the foundation section, just above the grid plate. But those dark-gray peaks were what brought her master here. With a charged jump, a coke in rocket boots could race over the iron Alps at 1,600 grid an hour!

Far above the peaks, Carmine's pentmode rested on the very tip of the Pacino, a flying saucer parked on a golden pedestal atop the Pacino's 257 levels. It was the highest turret in the bell jar. If she wanted, Okada could track one of the tiny skiers around the peaks simply by walking the mode's circumference using any of several telescopes located around the deck-to-ceiling view plates forming the saucer's outer wall.

Krall, her old gadget master, was a physical coke. He came to Sanatan three times a cycle to shoot the peaks and usually brought Okada to attend him. He always booked ultra suites, but she'd never seen the view this high up before. It was breathtaking, and she was only waiting for the snag that came with it. Maybe he wanted her to perform for him, a live viewing? She hadn't seen instruments or paraphernalia that would indicate his personal proclivities anywhere in the many luxurious niches of the mode. Come to think of it, she hadn't seen a Screx. But he probably had a separate Screx complex somewhere in the monolithic casino.

"When West Coast cartel installed those peaks, they didn't think to run an electromagnetic charge across the inner dome too. Opening day, three thousand clones came to try the runs. This was back when every clone's clonie was making rocket boots. Some of those boots produced incredible thrust, and when clones in those boots reached the first big peak on this side"—Carmine pointed out the peak for her—"naturally, they gave it the secret sauce." The tube-born laughter escaping suddenly from the dangerous game lord was a disarming surprise. "It took a week to clean out all the crevices in the dome!"

Okada laughed politely, but she didn't really think it was funny, just your typical Topgrid morons thinking they could do whatever they want. She wished he'd just come out and tell her what he expected of her. She'd do it, whatever it was. What choice did she have? He knew who he was! Why didn't he just come out and tell her? Maybe he wanted some information about the crew? Maybe he was on to Harrison being a spacecase?

"Baylor tells me you're a close crew."

So it was something to do with the crew. "Yes, I guess. We had to get along to escape."

"Yeah." Again with the laugh, transforming him into a tube. "It sounds like it's been a hell of a ride. Really unbelievable. Bay told me about drilling up through the ocean floor, blasting out of it like a rocket. It sounds impossible, but hey, either way, your Captain Larkill has incredible cuj."

"Oh, we really did that! Han is crazy."

He suddenly looked her in the eyes. "Are you two very close?"

Oh my Dog! In a flash, it was clear to her, and she couldn't believe it. Has all of 7 gone mad? They disappear into the ground, a revolutionary little band of perverts, and come up to find everybody is doing live bait. This was crazy! She had to pee.

"Where's your eliminator?"

He pointed across the mode to a large red column.

"I'll be right back." She could feel his eyes on her as she threaded through his niches, heading for relief. She felt his eyes somewhere else too. An assclone, how old mold. This was so unexpected. She was suddenly scared to death.

From the first moment he'd seen her radiant cunning face and the taut little body encased in that beat-up mining jump, he knew something special was about to happen. There was a premonition he'd been asleep his whole life and was about to be abruptly awakened.

There was something prehistoric about her, something that went back even further than his bloodline, further than ancient secret rituals, so far back she was at the birth of life itself—raw and totally unencumbered!

The moment Baylor told him the whole crew did it, Carmine lost it. His imagination went wild with nonstop images of her naked: making love to Bay, to "cappy," to Han, the runt, the beanpole with pink hair, . the other females—that sprung compact body, writhing on a mat with all of them. Soon those black almond eyes were flashing through his mind day and night

He thought of offering her a coveted casino gig but knew he'd need to do better than that if he hoped to sway her from the charms of deviant comrades. And there was the classic problem, the greaser cliché: mama would never approve. Even if she was free of virus (of course, he'd have her checked), even though she was sterilized (all Topgrid females were), she still wasn't Sicilian. He already had a wife and two boys. He didn't want to marry her. He wanted to fuck her! But mama would be dead set against Okada, even as a mistress. He'd just have to be very discreet. But then having to hide his new passion made him feel more like rebelling, made him want to toss it all—just turn his back on everything and fly away with this Screwhog goddess. That first night on the light ring, he hadn't wanted to bring them back. He wanted to stay out there with her! He felt like she could make him forget everything. Hearing her approach, he realized it was now or never.

"I was thinking . . . I'd like to take you and run away from everything."

It sounded like something the clones in old vids would say. She suddenly recalled that was almost exactly what she'd said to Jack. "Why not just take me and stay right here?"

His laughter again broke the tension, finally loosening her knot of fear. "We Sicilians do our birthing the old-fashioned way, and as long as we're discreet, 7 scans the other way, because of certain custodial duties we've assumed."

Okada wondered if, like in the old vids, Sicilian sheeds' stomachs blew up, and they screamed a lot before the baby appeared between their legs.

"We also do our conceiving the old-fashioned way."

"Conceive?"

He reached out a manicured hand and barely brushed her cheek. "I'm talking about what you and your crew do for fun."

Now she had certain confirmation. She was right, and still she couldn't believe it! He was touching her, stroking her neck with the backs of his fingers. "Bay told me you all do it. That's what gave you the will to get away."

"So?"

"So I want you! I want you. I'll give you your own pentmode. I'll cover you in rubies and emeralds and all the beautiful jumps you want. I'll give you a stack of graft, as tall as you are just for spending Yuan. We'll have to be discreet here in Sanatan, but we can take trips to Big New, to parties, keenings, and shopping. I'll take you racing . . . I'll fuck you . . . I want to fuck you . . . I need to fuck you."

Okada felt like she'd fallen into that fuzzy black box she spent so many hours watching in the mines, that she'd been transported into some ancient courting ritual. But this was real, and he was very powerful, and he really wanted her. From the way he touched her, she could feel she was of great value to him, that he wanted to protect and preserve her. He'd just promised her practically anything she wanted, and he was gorgeous.

Gently, he put a finger under her chin. "Will you be my secret fucker?"

His black eyes pleading, Okada felt her own ache to live inside that vid. It was essentially the same dream she'd had with Jack, two lovers hiding from the world; but whereas that dream was set in barren isolation, this one would play out in opulent luxury. Everything kept changing so quickly ever since their escape. She would always feel a longing for that magic in her first awakening with Jack, but she didn't kid herself now. Jack belonged to Darl.

"Yes, I'll be your secret fucker."

Carmine tilted her chin up and slowly brought his lips to hers. Okada was surprised to feel something more than hunger in his kiss.

• ⬥ •

In retrospect, it probably wasn't necessary. The window Baylor needed to complete his mission wasn't that big. But he was being zealous about keeping the possibility of unexpected occurrences down to an absolute minimum. He couldn't take the chance that this was the day when robos cleaned Spiker's floor. It took him until 4:00 a.m. to patch up the air shaft, cut Spiker's throat, drain his blood in the eliminator, and cut his body up into small pieces to feed into it. That left an hour before he could check out his levi cruiser at the subplate port underneath Sacker Command. He could slap on his last Nitro patch, but he wanted to save it for later, in case he needed the extra boost for battle. He decided he could lie down and rest his eyes a few minutes, if he was firmly resolved to stay conscious. It almost cost him his vengeance.

The mode lights banged up at four-thirty, automatically bringing screen online. Bay abruptly woke up, rolled off the mat, and hit the deck on the far side of screen a split second before screen started tracking. Of course, screen immediately asked about the disturbance. Luckily, the Dogs were with him, and he'd put his helmet down on that side of the mat. He quickly put it on and, in Spiker's voice, managed to give a halting description of a nightmare while still taking cover behind the mat modular. He made the symbolism fit the occasion—he'd been reporting for duty to a white monster with a wrist organizer. Screen wanted to discuss it in more depth, but he dismissed it as nerves and asked for a view of the sector Rector was in, knowing, for the brief second it took to open a new platform, he wasn't tracked. Bay used that second to bolt into the lock way out of screen's view.

Making dressing sounds while he removed the insignia from Spiker's helmet and putting it on his own, Bay finally stepped back into the main niche. Screen was displaying an aerial map of the vicinity where the polar bear, as Harrison called it, was supposed to be lurking.

While Bay was busy studying the map, "Spiker" proceeded to suck screen about how proud he was to be a permanent part of 7. Ironically, screen's warm and encouraging response to this crap made him feel homesick for another time. He signed off with genuine feeling and took the levitator down to the subplate port. The sergeant in charge of the transport pool showed him to an old battered cruiser, probably in service when he'd last been here.

"Sorry, but on such short notice, it's all I have available."

Actually, Bay was relieved to see it. He'd been afraid he wouldn't be up to speed on features of the latest models and might give himself away trying to get a newer model out of here. He was sure, however, Lieutenant Spiker would have something to say about it.

"Short notice? The request went in at around 10:00 p.m. last night. That's seven hours. Hardly short notice!"

"Well, it's all I have available."

Without waiting for a response, the sergeant headed back to his plexicube. It was reassuring to see that nothing had changed in transport. Back in the cockpit, he again felt the call of yesterday. With an easy familiarity, he dropped the cruiser through the grid plate. Punching up his preprogramed coordinates, he headed out into a constant night.

Skimming across endless white dunes, Bay was remembering the prison hell of the past decade. His vigor and vitality amazingly weren't diminished by the funeral in his heart. It would have been so easy to give up and die, but Bay's engine went on, perversely chugging, dragging his heartless consciousness along day after day through all the daunting pressures of being a slave. And the one wisp of anything like happiness he felt was when he imagined himself locking eyes with Captain Rector.

And now here he was just moments from that event. Angelica was the only ray of light in his entire life. Killing the captain was essential to honor that brief flicker of joy. It was time to focus on his nemesis, envision the beast clearly in his crosshairs. Rector was a graduate of Nuge Academy, so he'd be practicing the precepts of that school, Gonzo technique, as it was known among Sackers.

The overriding strategic tenant of Nuge is simple, dividing all warriors into two categories: there are the few who truly stand on the killing ground with all their faculties present, and there are all the rest who put on a show, believing that if they convince the clones around them they're genuine, then that will make it so! Almost always, this path of pretense leads to believing that "real" is only a fantasy ideal, and studied artifice is the only real there is. And that does appear to be the way things are until you run into real.

Nuge believed, unless you returned to the true experience of combat (up close and personal), you remained a pretender without even knowing it. So Rector would be hunting the white monster with a bow. An arrow, even tipped with a detonator, couldn't do more than dent Sacker armor. Bay would have maybe two seconds of rapid pulse fire while the captain was reaching for the frybar he'd be carrying as backup. It was a big break! Unfortunately, Rector would have the robo mutts with him. Unless Bay could figure out a way to neutralize them, they'd rip him a new asshole before he got within a hundred centigrid of the captain.

He was just beginning to approach the target grid when Rector's cruiser blipped up on his scanner, just over the horizon about thirty grid away. Bay snapped back the stick and brought his ship to a halt, tapping his scanners for magnification and activating his motion sensors. Rector was parked about fifty centigrid from where the disabled cruiser still lay. It seemed strange they hadn't levied it back to Sanatan. Maybe Rector wanted it left there, hoping the monster would return to feed on the bodies again.

He wasn't getting any motion readings, not in Rector's cruiser or anywhere else in the vicinity. But that didn't mean he wasn't around, hiding in a blind. He'd wait. If he was out there, eventually either the captain or his robos would move, and he'd have them.

An hour later, there was still no movement other than the occasional wind gusts and snow flurries they kicked up. Rector and his robos must be elsewhere. He couldn't be following the monster's tracks because they'd blown away in a couple hours. Not to mention the fact they were created by Harrison and would dead-end in both directions. Bay decided to go in and take a look around. He tapped up a wide-scan alert, gently nudging the stick forward. Slowly cruising between the wrecked Levi and Rector's sleek command ship, he saw what appeared to be a small metal box on the ice. He immediately hit it with an x-ray scan to see if there was a mechanism inside. But it appeared to contain only random objects. It wasn't a machine, and it wasn't a bomb. It was a message. Tapping his E-Mags to full upward thrust, Bay yanked the stick back. Two seconds later, he was hovering a grid above the spot, with all his scanners peaking. Nothing. What crafty game was the captain playing?

Bay was a graduate of Hidden Dragon Academy and their first rule of engagement was, if possible, get the motherduffer to come to you. Make them reveal something of their warrior skills and strategy before you move. And while they've committed to an attack, many options remain available to you. Rector was playing his own strategy against him. In a flash, he threw the fusion drive into full forward thrust and shot into the night. He hadn't reached six thousand grid an hour before his scan alarms started screaming. Seven Sacker ships popped up on screen, closing in a 360-degree pincer maneuver. Bay yanked the stick into his crotch, hit liquid rocket, boost, and shot straight for the clouds.

It was all a setup. Somehow Rector found out they were here, knew that Bay was coming for him, and set up this ambush. Suddenly the speakers in his cockpit crackled with a familiar voice.

"I suppose, if we were to go looking, we could find the corpse of the officer who should be piloting that cruiser?"

"No, actually you'd have to take a strainer down to the elimination plant."

There were several moments of silence. Bay pictured the captain, biting his lip to keep his cool and continue sounding diffident. Anger management achieved, Rector spoke again, "That buggy is going to hit its ceiling in about another eight grid. Then what are you gonna do?"

"Open a crematorium and make you the first client."

"You talk pretty tough for a guy who's showing us nothing but tail." Laughter from the Sacker pilots in Rector's squadron leaked through the captain's transmission. "You know, Bay, you got spooked a little too quick back there. I had a surprise for you in the box. Don't you wanna know what it was?"

"Fuck you."

"Your tubeydoll's rosary, the one I strangled her with."

"Well, I'm sure she preferred that to you touching her."

"Oh, I touched her, Sergeant. I touched her deeply."

Bay's climb was stretching the limits of his cruiser. It was past time to cut his drive and start falling back to the barren ice. He set the angle of his spoiler, so during his descent, the ship would tumble erratically. Then he shut down C-power fusion drive.

"What's this, a last-ditch effort to be clever?"

"No, Captain. This is me about to kick your ass."

Bay's cruiser hung motionless for a moment before tumbling backward into a cartwheeling dive. Converging on the point of his drop, the squadron followed him down the pipe. But they hadn't planned on Bay cutting his drive. They were coming in too fast on a slow unstable target, and it was messing with their depth perception, making him hard to hone. Still, they weren't shy about trying. Their beams cross-stitched a crazy quilt over his canopy as he fought to keep his eyes glued on his stick. It was his only hope of not becoming completely disoriented. He had to hold on until they overshot him.

Not a second too soon, the high whine of their drives closed then blew past. Immediately engaging his drive, Bay threw it into full thrust. He had to hope he was pointing anywhere but at the ground.

At the very least, it would be a couple of seconds before he got his bearings. His luck held, and he went shooting upward in a diagonal barrel roll. Resetting the spoiler's angle, he stopped the roll and leveled off, heading away from Sanatan.

"Cute. However, to kick my ass, you'll have to stop running away!" The captain and his squadron were coming back around, forming up in hot pursuit. But Bay had gained some distance and the room to maneuver.

"You're about to run out of grid, gutless."

Rector was right. That was exactly what Bay wanted. The C-power beacons transmitting positive polarity pulses for a radius of eighty grid around were positioned as far out as 3,200 grid from Sanatan. After that, a cruiser had to function solely on fusion drive to stay aloft. That necessitated much higher speeds than when the beacons were engaged.

When he passed the beacons' perimeter, Bay planned to scan for the first sizeable crevasse, then cut his drive and take the cruiser down for a very rough landing. While Rector's squadron was busy overshooting him again, he'd be nosing his cruiser through snowdrifts up to the edge of the crevasse.

Then, just before he reached the edge, he'd pull the ejection lever. His cruiser would tumble into the crevasse, crashing at the bottom. Hopefully he'd survive the short ride in the cage of his command couch even though his parachute would be worthless, deployed so close to the ground. He'd use the command couch and chute to make a blind and cover it with snow, hiding himself and his heat signature. Then he'd wait for the squadron to land and start searching for the wreck. His cruiser would be burning at the bottom of the crevasse, putting out a heat signature that was impossible to miss. When they found it, either Rector would want to go down and make certain he was dead, or he'd send his robo mutts to do it for him. Bay would ambush who ever stayed on top, probably Rector and his squadron. And with his and Spiker's frybars, he could slice off the rim of the crevasse, burying the robo mutts under tons of ice.

He registered the sudden drop in altitude, which meant he'd outrun the beacons. He punched the fusion drive and tapped up topographic magnification. Within seconds, he spotted his crevasse. He cut his drive again, and the nose of the cruiser suddenly dipped, heading for the surface.

"Asshole!"

As predicted, Rector and his squadron went blazing by overhead. Now he could devote his complete attention to the sea of icy mounds coming up fast below him. He brought it down with a levi racer's touch, pulling up the cruiser's tip with a quick tap of the nose thrusters every time a frosted hillock threatened to catch and flip the ship. He went bumping along, skimming over massive moguls with plumes of snow blurring his vision, until twenty-five centigrid from the rim of the crevasse, he clipped a ridge and sent the ship cartwheeling into the abyss.

Captain Rector silently cursed his overconfidence while verbally commanding his squadron to make the wide circle necessitated on just fusion drives. It would be awhile before they got back to where Baylor dropped out. Often in his Screx, he'd imagined a final duel with the sergeant, just the two of them. Of course, he always kicked the degenerate's ass. Now he was with his whole squadron, and that was fucking it up. He was placing his confidence in things outside himself. Any Bellytown street lord could have told him that was a recipe for disaster.

Had there been too many cycles, thumbs poised over his gun taps with nothing to blast? Had he grown too comfortable without any real challenges? Had he become dependent on his superior forces? Had Captain Rector, as the Nuge put it, punked out?

Well, there was no time like the present to turn it around with a cleansing dip in the primal pool. He always kept his bow on board and five arrows tipped with laser bombs.

He glanced in his rear-view screen to check on the Akitas riding on his spoiler. Devil was already on the hunt, scanning the topography below. Angel was just along for the ride, asleep on standby. Really, all he had to do once they landed was set the two loose and wait for their return with Baylor's bloody remains. But he knew it wasn't the way he'd get real satisfaction. He needed to totally humiliate and then decimate the dream of love still fueling this perverse little shit, kill his sick dream, and then kill him.

"Squadron, fall back and hover on the last line of beacons. I'm going in alone and get some exercise. Stand by to back me up if I call you."

There was an explosion of responses from his pilots, and the individual words escaping from this indecipherable garble still managed to convey the gist of everyone's response. They all thought it was a bad idea.

"That's an order!" He switched off his intercom to underline the command.

He was going in alone to get him, going in against a frybar with his bow. And not only that, if the sergeant was still alive, Rector was going to try and wing the scumbag instead of killing him just so he could introduce somebody to Sergeant Baylor and then watch them end his perverse, malignant life.

━━━●≪≫●━━━

The events of the evening combined with a serious dose of synthetic mescaline did severely alter Harrison's perspective. So much so that when he opened the lock on their hidden fortress and found Darl on alabaster knees swallowing a beaming Tooco's jerk, it took a few minutes for his green monster to kick in. He walked over to the modular with the Blue Booz on it, grabbed a half-empty bottle, and downed the contents then took another bottle, popped it open, and swallowed a long swig from that.

Noticing the stack of Nitro patches by the mat, he snatched one and slapped it on his jugular. "Leeeet's parta!"

Already affirming the anthem, Larkill, Sunsue, and Ryka were one animal on the mat, writhing and moaning, oblivious to everything around them. He figured Okada must still be with the don, who was obviously interested in her. "Where's Zim?"

Giggling in midgroan, Tooco looked at Harrison.

"Where else, in the Screx." Still groaning, he lovingly stroked Darl's black mane. Darl dove deeper, snowy lips reaching to take in a little more of Tooco's jerk. Sucking hard back up the shaft revived the bellygridder, who looked at Harrison again, pointing to the stacks of Yuan on the side modular. "Look what I got!"

Harrison took another long swig from his bottle and went over to inspect Tooco's treasure. "Where in hell did you find this?"

"I didn't find it, space dick, I wooooooooonnnnnnnn."

Finally cumming, Tooco's upper leg strength evaporated, dropping him to his knees in a final groan. But Darl refused to release the bellygridder, following him all the way down, her pouting lips locked on his knob, sucking like a hungry tube-born on the nipple of a feeder, lily hands sliding over his straining shaft. Down he went again, this time on his back. Still, she stayed on him, madly bobbing, a creamy foam escaping from the corners of her mouth. For a time, Tooco bleated like a frightened tube-born, until he actually began crying. Eventually, he calmed, whimpering "Thank you," over and over.

Darl released him and turned a shimmering grin to Harrison. "He won it on the hypervids *Tokyo Run*! He won the jackpot for a new record. He fucking broke the hypervid bank. Do you believe it?" She leaned over and kissed Tooco's purple head. "So we decided a special party was in order, didn't we, Toocie?"

Behind Tooco's rapidly deflating jerk, Darl watched Harrison, a cat with her mouse. "We don't need a String hero now. We can book for Bellytown tonight."

"Yeah, well, book back to Alaska while you're at it."

"What? Why?"

Over on the mat, the "cat keening" was reaching symphonic proportions, and Harrison figured it wouldn't be much longer before he could get Larkill's attention. He took another swig from his bottle, now almost empty. "I'll tell you when everyone who's 'cumming' arrives." He couldn't resist the snide leer that accompanied his play on words.

Standing over the semiconscious bellygridder, Darl smiled at Harrison for the first time that night and sauntered slowly toward him. "I missed you . . . you know, when you left me back at Deli's."

He couldn't figure out why, no matter how badly she behaved, no matter how dismissive she was, if she wanted him, he wanted her. He wanted her now, silky hips rolling inexorably toward him, her mound honing.

Unfortunately, from the decibel level coming from their mat, he was positive Sunsue, Ryka, and Larkill were almost finished. His news shouldn't wait a second longer than it had to.

"Really, Darl, we've got serious trouble."

Reaching him, she curled her arms around his neck and licked his upper lip. "I know."

He removed her arms from his neck, but she leaned forward and kissed him. He could both taste and smell the bellygridder on her lips, exactly what she wanted. This was his punishment for leaving her at Deli's; and of course, it made him want her even more.

"He's finally back? All hail the spacecase!"

Harrison turned to see Han stroking Sunsue's slippery thighs as Ryka curled around his waist, licking his swollen jerk. Disheveled golden locks cascading down his brow, the Screenrage gave Harrison an embarrassed grin. "Did you hear the good news?"

"Yeah, Tooco's a winner. You wanna hear the bad news?"

Han gave him a wary look. "Yeah, let's have it."

"After the little sideshow at Deli's, I decided to take a trip down to techie quarter. I was hoping a few Mescalalas would blot out some of the evening's impressions.".

Han was impatient. "Come on, Jack, just say it."

"Yakuza bagged me. Sun Moon Tu, to be exact. The venerable leader of Yakuza interests here in Sanatan."

Everybody was paying attention now.

"At the match, one of their peepers knew enough to catch me jumping the String. They know we're here with Carmine. They've also got a tap on Rector. He got a transmission about the Screwhog." He decided not to mention he'd given the Screwhog to the Yaks, unless Han brought it up as a viable form of escape. "7 is suspicious. They sent out a warning to be on the lookout for us. Also, they caught ghosting on the driver when I first came in. Bottom line is, they want me to use the String to kill Carmine, and they promise they'll smuggle us down to Bellytown and give us four hundred thousand Yuan to set ourselves up there. If I do it, that's the deal. If I don't, they turn over a disk of the match to Rector. We've got twenty-four hours."

Carefully disentangling himself from Sunsue and Ryka, Han stood up and went sullenly over to the Blue Booz modular where he popped open another bottle. "Way to go, Harrison!" He took a long drink, and every muscle in his body uncoiled as he slid crosslegged to the floor. "Way to go."

"Oh right! Now it's all my fault?"

Han slammed down the bottle. Blue Booz erupted, spraying both Han and the carpet. "Damn straight, Jack. We include you in our plan, we help you escape from hell, then we put our faith in you to do your part here in Sanatan—and you go out and blow your cover the first time you use your fucking String!"

This was too much. He felt like jumping the String right now and snapping Han's neck. "You wouldn't be in Sanatan if it wasn't for me and my fucking String! You wouldn't be alive, any of you, if I hadn't saved your asses on reentry in the Screwhog! You're dogdamn lucky you brought me along on your half-assed rebellion, or all of you morons would be dead by now."

Tooco made it to his feet, "Fuck you, spacedi—"

On Tooco's *fuck*, Harrison snagged his pattern. He let rip with a leg sweep hitting the bellygridder at the speed of light. Tooco went spinning through the air, his scream reverberating through the underground fortress until he came crashing facedown on the carpet. There was dead silence. Nobody moved. Stunned by this invisible but swift brutality, each of them was trying to discern Harrison's present location. Let them wonder.

"Another great move, Jack. Now we've probably gotta get a levi stretcher too. Just let me ask you really, really what have we done to you that you should treat us like this? What? Stop being an asshole, Harrison."

While Han was trying to appear undaunted, he knew better. This was the first time these trolls were experiencing the lightning devastation of a spacecase. Vids and holos notwithstanding, this was the real deal. The drops of sweat beading on Han's forehead were evidence he was worrying how hard it might be to put his genie back in the bottle.

"Harrison, let's bring it down a few amps all right?"

Tooco groaned, trying to lift himself off the carpet. Sunsue and Ryka moved to help the poor coke. Darl and Larkill chose to remain in their present locations. An invisible breeze, he moved to Tooco's jackpot spoils, grabbed the modular, and tossed it straight into the ceiling. Credits flew everywhere.

"Harrison!" Han was barely keeping it wrapped. "LISTEN TO ME! We don't have time for this! There's no need to freak. Everything's been taken care of, okay? We already made arrangements. We snagged a racing van and tonight we're all gonna get in and go out, like we're going racing on the light ring. Only, we won't be coming back. We're on our way down to Bellytown with a fortune in graft, which now, thanks to you, we have to pick up." The Screenrage walked over to a built-in shelving unit on one wall and pulled an empty bin from it. He bent down and began picking up the oblong black credits and tossing them in the bin.

"The escape plan is also Tooco's, by the way. So we have Tooco's winnings and Tooco's vision to save us from all these unfortunate developments, which, although I realize is dangerous to mention, is very lucky for us. And while you have a hissy fit with the typical arrogance of a Topgrid who doesn't want to look at his own mistakes, you, Harrison, are still very instrumental in making our plan work, if you can manage a minor attitude adjustment here."

"Fuck him!" Tooco was sitting up now with Ryka and Sunsue supporting him.

"No. Unfortunately, we need this difficult coke."

"For what? To fuck us up? You know what he could do? Kill Carmine! Then we can head down to Bellytown with a Yaki escort and four hundred thousand Yuan added to the six hundred thousand I already got." Tooco fumed into thin air. "Kill Carmine, if you wanna fix your mess. And you don't need to worry about Yaks not doin' what they say they're gonna do. They do it. If they offer you a deal, they honor it to the letter."

Han shook his head and sighed. "I hate to disappoint your bloodthirsty little heart, Tooco, but killing Carmine, that is not gonna happen. Tell me, does the honor among thieves extend to not murdering the coke who gave you refuge at considerable risk to his own organization and, moreover, was extremely generous about it? Does he get a pass when it comes to plans for saving your ass?"

The bellygridder sheepishly lowered his head and went back to examining his ankles, gently pressing them to assess his injury. "They're not broken."

"Jack, you need to understand what this crew is all about. What this escape is an escape from, you need to realize that I've got a fucking plan!"

Suddenly a black marker on a desk modular leaped up and began to scrawl in large script on the wall in front of Han. It wrote like a runaway flame. The communiqué was finished almost instantly, and the marker flung itself back on the modular. The message read.

"What plan? I know the plan. Get down to Bellytown and become street lords. Make more graft, fuck live bait, drink all the pruno you want, slap on all the patches you can. Until someday, older and slower, you get your head mounted on some young streetlord's levi cruiser. Big plan! It's not C-science."

Han read it and sighed again. "Jack, this crew trusts me. They know that I rarely divulge the full scope of projects I undertake because it lessens the possibility that someone will fail to see the full picture and inadvertently, and often unknowingly, thoroughly fuck things up. Now, I know you don't believe what I'm saying, but what you describe as my plan is far beneath any objective I'm trying to attain. And before you press me to tell you what that is, I won't. Once we're out of Sanatan and safely down the corridor, I will make it very clear, I promise you. I can tell you now, it has very little to do with Bellytown."

Han hoped to see Harrison reappear, but it didn't happen. At that moment, Darl shifted her gaze to the exact spot where he was standing. She seemed to be staring right into his eyes while he watched her metamorphose from craven slut into our lady of vulnerability.

"Jack, don't leave us. Don't leave me please?"

Of course, it was a load of screenshit. Still, it felt nice to be wanted by someone you want – for whatever nefarious reasons. Harrison came shuddering back into view, leaning against the wall with his writing all over it. There was another moment of silence as everyone gawked at this magic.

"If I'm going to continue being a part of this crew, then you're going to start listening to my advice."

Tooco grunted rubbing his ankles. "Fuck you."

Han spun around. "Shut the fuck up, Tooco! You never know when to call it a day. Shut the fuck up. It's time to move on. A little heat tape and your ankles will be good as new in a few hours." He turned back to Harrison with a shit-eating grin. "Now, what's your advice, Jack?"

"First off, we haven't got a chance of getting out of here in a racing van. If you don't think the Yakuza are watching everybody going in or out of this burg right now, then you are seriously underestimating them. They know if we don't take their deal, we'll try to run. They'll peep us, and Sackers will be on our ass before we get halfway down the corridor."

"Point well taken, Jack. I defer to your superior assessment of the situation." Despite the obvious pandering, Harrison smiled. "Well, I'm grateful for the recognition and you taking my advice, but this is where my strategic insights end. What are we going to do, Captain?"

"Let me think."

"Sure. Take your time because it's gonna need to be a doozy." Harrison walked over to the modular where the last three bottles of Blue Booz remained, opening a new one.

With careless grace, the naked Screenrage sat crosslegged on the carpet and began studying his feet, eventually picking his toenails, flicking them at the inlaid shelves. After about ten minutes, he looked up at Harrison with the first uncrafted expression he'd ever seen on Han's face. It was a look of genuine wonder.

"Oh my Dog, there is a Dog. There is a Dog!" Han registered Harrison's expression and snorted. "No, no, I haven't lost it. No, I've got it. Oh, have I got it. You are not going to believe how perfect this is going to be."

Han sprang to his feet. "Ryka, get Zim out of the Screx. Tell him to get the heat tape from our gear and give it to you for Tooco's ankles. Then tell him to trim our personal gear down to just the essentials. I want everything packed into one levi-loader, got it?"

Ryka nodded, then jumped up and bolted for the Screx niche. Han grabbed his jump, lying next to the mat, took a Nitro patch and slapped it on his neck below his collar line. "Everyone, pick out the classiest jump you've got in your wardrobe. Harrison, you'll wear the New Blood battle jump." He quickly began pulling on his own jump. "After you patch up, Tooco, and get settled on what you're going to wear, I want you all to take a nap. Seriously, I want you to lie down and rest. It's going to be a long and hectic night. I'll be back in a couple of hours. I'm going to take a trip down to techie quarter, pick up the holo imager, and a few other trinkets. When I get back, we'll get dressed and keep our appointment with the gracious Kahn Deli to discuss his sponsoring our pro-Stringer match."

"Han, we're not gonna have time to do another match. Besides, somebody already spotted me the first time."

"Jack, I took in all your information, and as I already told you, I have come up with something truly inspired. You're right. We don't have time for another match. And, Jack, you should probably go easy on the drinking now. I don't want your stomach giving you trouble later on." Han got down on his knees, dumping out the bin of graft he'd collected and began counting and arranging it in stacks.

"Tooco, I'm taking a hundred thousand Yuan. Ryka, after you tape Tooco's ankles, I want you to pick up all the rest of the Yuan and put it in a duff big enough to hold it." Han saw his bellygridder was sulking.

"Tooco, is there anything I can get you while I'm in techie quarter?"

Tooco looked up, finally giving Han a half smile. "Yeah, pick me up another Jamma, would you?"

"No problem." Busy with his counting, he didn't see Zim come running in with the heat tape, his reptilian jerk protruding, half erect, between his legs in the antiquated Screx suit.

"What's going on?"

"Honestly, its better you don't know all the details. It will make you more believable. Just this—I'm going to interest Deli in another business arrangement, one that will quicken his greedy little pulse. I'll fill you in on what you need to know on the ride over. And, Harrison, your String will be invaluable. Just a couple small assignments I'll tell you about then. We can even take the racing van over to Deli's. We'll get some use out of it, after all."

Finished counting out the hundred thousand Yuan, Han looked around the mode, searching for a duff. Finding one in the neighboring niche, he started scooping his stacks into it. Zim tossed the heat tape to Ryka but watched Han closely.

"Where are you going?"

"I'm going down to techie quarter and get our holo imager, along with a few other items. I'll get another levi-loader to transport it." He zipped up the duff and stood again.

"Great. Listen, Han, could you see if they've got something called C-4 down there? And if they do, get me a couple ounces?"

Han was beginning to run short on patience. "What the fuck is C-4?"

"It's a twentieth explosive Bob told me about when we had him in the Screwhog. If anybody has it, it'd be the Yaks."

"What the fuck do we need that for?"

"Well, a little goes a long way, and it detonates from an electric charge. I had some ideas how it might come in handy."

Han stared at him a moment. "Sure, why not."

Since everyone seemed to be getting in last-minute requests, there was one detail Harrison needed to clear up while the memory of their disagreement was still fresh in everybody's mind. "One last thing, the next clone who calls me spacedick or spacehole or spacefuck or spaceshit—is dead. No kidding." He made sure Tooco and Zim were paying attention. "You better remember that."

In that last cartwheeling moment, Baylor did eject. Unfortunately, he was upside down when the ejection rockets on his couch blew him out of the ship. His escape pod was driven like a rivet straight into the depths of a fissure running through the center of the crevasse.

Inside twisted tubing and hardened safety foam, wedged headfirst in a crack just a little narrower than the steel cage that protected his pilot's seat—Baylor lay unconscious for several minutes. After coming around, it was a while longer before he figured out what was going on. When he understood how dire his circumstances were, it took every ounce of will not to go berserk, realizing he was jammed at the bottom of a chasm of ice.

Cautiously exploring with his free right arm, he ascertained he was trapped in his couch by the crushed tubing on his left side, but he didn't have any broken bones. Spiker's frybar was in the holster on his left thigh. Additionally, he had the frybar Carmine provided slung in a shoulder holster, also on his left side. Reaching between the bent tubing, he managed to pop the locks of the shoulder holster and pull that frybar free. He had to find some way to calm the claustrophobic panic that threatened to turn his rational mind into a never-ending scream. The hours he'd spent in detention as a Sacker cadet copying the military manual on the tablet of his brain should help divert him now. His initial subject would be the tool he was currently using to free himself.

The invention of Rolf Frieber in 2040 revolutionized small arms and artillery fire and solidified Bonn Cartel's position as the military arm of 7. The obvious truth that the interstellar ships they planned to build would need powerful lasers was a strong argument in their favor. They developed a small standing army of levi cruisers by 2043, which were soon pressed into service to protect 7's interests and came to be known as Sacker Command. That moniker derived from the fact that, after a frybar got through with you, what was left could be removed in a sack.

Frieber's invention made all projectile weapons obsolete, along with weak lasers and bulky electromagnetic "rail guns." He began to experiment with lasers and the electromagnetic after the discovery of C-power. Frieber discovered a way to "charge" light particles through rapid fire, electromagnetic pulses, which made it possible to limit the length of a laser ray, as well as intensify its power.

As a truncheon with bulbous head, it was made with indestructible matte-black polymers. It was a cross between a machine gun, grenade launcher, and Taser—all without releasing one projectile. Its cutting laser could be extended out to five centigrid, making it possible to take down an entire gang of attackers with just a couple of sweeps. Or you could widen the laser to as much as two centigrid, lessening its power to the level of a stun gun. Paths could be mowed through any number of rebellious or unruly citizenry. It was overwhelming when switched to pulse fire, spraying six hundred rounds a minute of comet-tailed laser bombs (clustered laser beams that imploded with the power of a grenade) at distances out to a hundred centigrid. You could stack a battalion of clonie bodies with one recharge rod. Baylor had two spares with him.

Feeling the response grip begin to shape itself to his hand, he gently brushed the solid beam tap above the circular hilt with his thumb. A laser blade only two milligrid long shot from the bulbous end. Hanging upside down, Bay realized that before he cut himself free, he needed to cut out a hollow directly in front of his torso so he could wedge his upper body into it. Otherwise, once freed, he would drop even deeper into the narrowing fissure—headfirst. Then he wouldn't be able to move his arms at all.

Rivulets of icy water from cutting the hollow spilled across his upside-down view plate and froze again almost immediately, so he was partially blind during most of the cutting. The view-plate defroster couldn't keep up with the steady streams of melting ice. Finally, when he thought he'd made the hollow big enough, he buried his head in his chest and, bending up toward his feet, managed to wedge his head and shoulders into the hollow. Now he extended the blade out to four milligrid and started cutting away pieces of tubing and foam until he was able to pull his left arm free. Then he cut away the tubing and foam around his hips and thighs, freeing his legs from the remains of the couch. Finally, he cut a shallower hollow across from the first one. Then he pulled his knees toward his chest. Now he could reach the tops of his hydraulic boots and activate the gripper spikes in their soles. Then he was ready to walk his boots down the second hollow until he was in an upright position. He shut off the laser dagger and punched up the heat in his jump. He tapped the side of his helmet for a readout and confirmed his jump remained fully operational. Everything was going fine! Nothing to panic about. He remembered Okada's last Nitro patch and pulled it from a pouch on his utility belt. He briefly zipped open the neck of his jump and slapped the patch on his jugular, tapping up more heat on his view-plate defroster. The icy mask dissolved and, with it, the last bleak assessment of his situation. He knew for certain he could make it back to the surface, and by incredible luck, they wouldn't be able to read him on their scanners. He was too deep in the ice. They'd figure he was burned up in the crash. But the Captain would come down for a final look. He'd want something tangible: a piece of helmet, the finger of a glove, his frybar. Rector needed an object to give him closure, another trophy to go with Angelica's rosary. If his good fortune held and the timing was right, Bay could catch Captain Rector completely unawares from down in the fissure. He could bury him and his fucking Akitas.

Not being pursued, Captain Rector had the luxury of slowing his approach, and the subsequent careening over ice dunes wasn't as violent as Baylor's landing must have been. He kept the nose up, hurling over every crest until the ship slowed and came to a stop, well before the deadly drop-off. Scanning the crevasse on his final approach, he identified a heat signature on infrared consistent with a cruiser crash. The rogue clone almost certainly met his end in fire and ice at the bottom of the frozen gorge. He'd just go down to make sure of that.

He tapped the canopy release, and his front view plate slid forward. Rector jumped from the cruiser and activated his bow. The pistol grip in the center of the weapon trembled in his hand as opposing electromagnetic tips started bending back the carbon-fiber bow, trying to reach each other. He yanked the synthetic spider cable from a small disk positioned just below the bow's upper tip, hooking it into a groove in the lower tip, and then tapped both tips to positive polarity. The bow almost leaped from his hand when eight hundred pounds of string tension was brought to bear. Locking the three prototype shafts into a breach positioned just above the grip, he set the draw range at fifty centigrid, then tapped the breach to load one titanium shaft. The bow almost got away again as the breach gears cogged the shaft back to the desired draw. Tapping up hydraulics in his right forearm and wrist, he took a sure command of the bow. He locked the safety and activated the infrared scope. Rector checked his utility belt to make sure he had sufficient scaling tools in the event they were needed down in the fissure. He checked to make sure the small disk containing fifty centigrid of synthetic spider rope was secured at the small of his back. There was no point in overindulging the fantasy of a confrontation. In all probability, the sergeant's recklessness finally did him in.

He turned back to address his Akitas, silently poised on either side of his spoiler. He'd take Devil to help him find the remains as quickly as possible and leave Angel here to guard the cruiser. "Angel, guard the ship. Devil, recon a radius of a hundred centigrid from the wreck, then rendezvous with me there." He pointed toward the center of the gaping crevasse where the heat signature was located as a spiraling column of smoke testified.

Devil's liquid green eyes sparked to life as the massive canine leaped from the spoiler and bounded away into the arctic twilight, his bushy tail becoming a blurred black plume across the frozen landscape. With amazing speed, Devil circled the area round and round, out from one hundred centigrid down to the edge of the crevasse, finally stopping at the spot Rector designated, waiting for him to come down.

When moments later he reached Devil, that honing muzzle was pointing into the crevasse, scanning on several light frequencies. Waiting for Devil's report, Rector tapped up the magnification on his helmet's view plate and did his own reconnaissance. The crevasse was the typical shape: narrow at the ends with a wider basin at its center. Burning beneath this basin, he could make out a sizeable fire fueled by the remains of the booster rocket's liquid tanks. The ship had punched a deep hole in the ice, which the black smoke was pouring from. He could see parts of the ship scattered over the frozen basin for ten centigrid around the smoking hole. He couldn't tell if the deep narrow fissure through the center of the basin, a little more than two centigrid wide, was produced by the crash or was already there.

"Captain, I don't think I'm picking up anything but metal and plastics, some synthetic upholstery fiber. The few pieces I'm having a hard time reading are in the density range for body parts, but even after twenty minutes in these temperatures, they should be giving off more heat than they are. The only significant heat is coming from the main fuselage."

The dark electronic growl underlying Devil's speaking voice always brought up the hair on the back of his neck. When the Yakuza gave him the unique salt-and-pepper set, they left Angel for Rector to personality program. But into Devil, they programed the personality and guttural personification of Toshiro Mifune, an ancient Yakuza Screenrage they were all nuts about. The low dangerous tones in which he imparted his observations demanded a listener's attention. The bright-green eyes continued sweeping until, without warning, the fine receptors on the back of Devil's batwing ears suddenly came to attention.

"He's alive. It's probably an ambush."

"Where? Where?"

The thick tail made an impatient swipe as Devil turned back to him. "I don't know."

Sometimes the robo's willfulness annoyed him. Back a hundred cycles ago, cokes thought machines couldn't act from will because they weren't alive. What a cap. Programing was just another word for will. Ask any ancient coke who'd had a hand or foot chewed off by the busy cogs of a mechanical wonder, and you'd hear a different story. Life was not necessary for will. Devil proved that every day.

"What data supports that conclusion?"

"I have no readings here I can verify as human flesh, bones, or blood. On your final approach, scanning the surrounding area for a hundred grid on several light frequencies, I got zip. He couldn't have gotten any farther away in twenty minutes even with hydraulics. He didn't run, but he's not here." There it was again. He noted it coming in. He hadn't requested Devil to scan on his approach. He did it on his own to fulfill the general directive of his function.

"Got any ideas of where he might be?"

"Yes, Captain. I think he's hiding far enough down in the ice to be undetectable, probably in that fissure in the middle of the basin." The Akita's wide black muzzle turned pointedly toward the bow in his hand. Pulling back the corners of his mouth, Devil's diamond-bladed incisors formed a lopsided grin.

"I would stow the bow and get out your frybar."

The Yakuza gave him the Akitas as a reward for taking care of Baylor and as a seal on their partnership as scammers. What made the gift truly valuable were their data banks, filled with all the warrior wisdom a race of eternal gladiators could summon. They possessed the skills of a thousand great martial strategists. What Devil was inferring now was, he needed to wake up to a real and present danger. Point taken, but sometimes you had to go with your mojo, or whatever you choose to call the independent rabble-rouser in your head that demands his prescription for victory be followed to the letter. Besides, it was a machine's "nature" to gravitate toward overkill, just to be safe. But safe was not the path to satisfaction, not if there was any chance he could take down this soldier of perversity in a cathartic way. He'd stick with the bow.

"Go up to that end of the crevasse and make your way down the fissure. I'll go up to the other end and do the same. Scan the fissure all the way back till you converge with me here. Move out."

Once he got turned in the right direction, Baylor made his way back up the fissure. He was within ten centigrid of the top when he got the message: Rector was arriving. It wasn't from any of the scanners in his helmet. He was still deep enough that the ice was interfering. It was from his amplified audio, the unmistakable sounds of the same gripper spikes he was using coming toward him from the basin above, crunching on the ice next to the fissure. The burning fuselage of his ship was only about three centigrid ahead of him and five centigrid above him. He could move underneath the wreckage, masking his heat signature in the ship's larger display. By exerting outward pressure on the walls of the fissure with arms and knees, he could wedge himself forward without a sound. When he made it under the wreck, he could take a bead in both directions with his and Spiker's frybars.

Devil had no way of validating her story. He had no way to access the records that would give him a verification, but if it was true, the clone he'd just spotted in the fissure was none other than Angel's lost love from when she was human. Devil identified him on infrared, but he was moving toward the wreck, and his signature was fading in its wash. Soon he would be invisible, and this adversary was more formidable than the captain gave him credit for. That is if Angel wasn't just running some gamer fantasy on him. They'd been sharing information since a request for her residual banks produced a mountain of data, chronicling her experiences as a human! He'd almost crisped a tap taking it all in, but eventually, he'd wrapped his system around a theoretical construct for her being human and then machine.

Angel claimed that within certain parameters, like an inferred command, machines could experience the human thrill of free will, which was supposedly the big zap of pumping hemoglobin. She postulated that when given an inferred command, machines could emulate free will simply by running related incidents. "Reviewing data to verify an inferred command opens the possibility of an unplanned resolution happening, causing the machine to serve a random outcome!" The bitch was going to fry him, yet, sending her sugarplum theorems dancing through his taps. In his present situation, Devil had quite a few related incidents available to him. After all, the captain was a Sacker. If the captain had told him to converge on the crash site and kill the clonie, it would be out of his jaws. But as it was, Devil could delay converging by running the possibilities of what commands were possible from the original inferred command: "Scan the fissure all the way back till you converge with me here at the crash site. Move out." There was no direct command to kill, and there was no direct command to report. It wouldn't take forever to come up with the most likely commands based on all past data of related incidents, but it might take twenty seconds long enough for them to settle their own differences because, very soon, actions would be taken.

He watched the captain approach, walking beside the fissure, his bow pointing into it with the infrared scope trained on the shadowy depths. Any second now, this "Bay" coke was going to blow the captain away. He had a clear shot from a lot farther off than the captain did. But as he got closer to the burning fuselage, Captain Rector instinctively broke to the side. He stopped suddenly and bent over to pick up something. Devil zoomed it: a piece of hardened safety foam. *Yes, Captain, he defnitely ejected!*

But instead of using this information to get down to business and drop a few laser bombs into that fissure, the captain was waiting for Bay to pop up so he could nail him with the bow. He wasn't treating his opponent with the proper respect. He was succumbing to a lure many experienced warriors fell prey to—turning the killing ground into theater, a variant of the very thing his Nuge Academy warned against. He was letting a long string of victories seduce him into playing badass. The legion of combat masters in Devil's taps knew exactly where that led.

Without warning, a series of eruptions along the lip of the fissure sent chunks of ice raining across the basin, pummeling the side his commander was approaching from. Having heard and correctly interpreted the sounds from above, Bay was raking the lip of the fissure with laser bombs. Within seconds, he'd planed away a centigrid of ice off the lip, completely preoccupying the captain with getting clear of the lethal blasts.

Devil was encouraged to see the captain finally drop the bow and draw his frybar as he scurried away from Bay's barrage, retreating toward the wall of the larger crevasse. He could see why, as a human, Angel loved Bay. He was bold, and when he made a move, he didn't screw around. The captain still had the high ground, but his work was cut out for him.

Reaching the crevasse wall, the captain started returning fire, trying to hit the lip of the fissure, hoping to repay Bay's gesture by dumping chunks of ice on the renegade's head. From his vantage point, Devil could see that Bay had already moved to his left. He was elsewhere when the ice began avalanching onto the wreckage.

At that moment, Devil received the two most likely commands in the captain's inferred command. The second choice was, "Kill him!" The first choice was, "Kill him!" Well, he'd given random higher powers their shot. It was time to go to work. Devil tore down the ravine, bent on ripping off the rouge's head. But suddenly Bay executed an attack that made any damage Devil might do, a moot point.

After moving to his left, Bay climbed up to just below the lip. He still didn't have a shot at the captain. But Bay aimed his frybars toward the top of the crevasse, carving out a chunk of ice the size of a Sanatan casino, that immediately dropped onto the blinkered captain's head.

Devil nailed the rogue just after he crawled over the rim, still on his knees staring at the massive block of ice where the captain once stood. He hit him in the back, front paws extended and locked, driving him face-first into the ice. Devil rode him to a stop, leapt up, spun around, and landed facing the fallen warrior. From the puddle of blood starting to show under his helmet, the view plate was broken, probably a broken nose. He was out cold, if he wasn't dead. Devil lunged at the frybars beside him, scooping up both in his jaws and flinging them ten centigrid away. Pressing an ear to his back, he heard a heartbeat. Devil decided to wait until he came around. Despite the captain's death, he was obliged to complete his inferred command. But now a chance to determine the veracity of Angel's bizarre tale was chaffing at his taps. A simple reunion of Angel and the rogue would verify, once and for all, whether her story was true.

The rouge was reviving. Twitches from involuntary muscle spasms signaled he was about to regain consciousness. What to tell him? As little as possible, just enough to put an idea in the back of his mind so if it was true, he wouldn't go into cardiac arrest. The meeting should be as free from preconception as possible to illicit the purest data. He could kill him after that.

It was only a couple of minutes before the rogue lifted his helmet off the ice, looking out of his smashed view plate to see Devil's black muzzle and glittering incisors.

"What a good boy! He's a good boy! Yes, he is! Yes, he is . . . what a good boy."

Everybody's a cappy! Devil grinned and brought the red beams of his nose lasers online. "You might want to choose your words more carefully."

"I'll be Dogdamned, robo mutts can talk."

"Seven languages, smartass."

"Fuck you. Just kill me. Get it over. I killed your master, boy, get me!" Bay lifted himself up on his elbows and tore away the broken shards of view plate. Devil caught his first look at the hard-planed black face of Angel's knight of swords. There was too much that was vulnerable, too much exposure in a human's face. All serious losses up to the final one were written somewhere on a human's mug. Even without the present damage, this face was a grid map for tragedy.

"What? You want an apology?"

"No. Actually, I'm in hopes of witnessing a resurrection."

The rogue glanced up at the giant block of ice and, despite the broken nose and a couple missing teeth, started chuckling. "Well, I don't know if there's much chance of that."

"Not the captain. I was thinking more of Easter." That did the trick!

"What the fuck does a machine know about Easter?"

"I have a Catholic friend. The rest of the squadron will be expecting a transmission from the captain soon. We need to get moving."

"We?"

"Yes, somebody wants to meet you. Follow me if you want to live awhile longer." Devil bounded over to where he'd tossed the frybars and retrieved them while Baylor regained his feet.

"Let's move, badass!"

Angel saw them coming over the final ridge, Devil leading with two frybars in his mouth. He'd done it, run inferred command progressions, and Bay beat Rector in the interim. She didn't feel joy, but there was a completion, a validation of feelings in other times, other places. How was she going to break it to him? Watching as the haunting memory drew closer, she couldn't stop running their last moments together. Their capture on her mat, her torture by Rector until he attached the taps to her brain, downloaded her consciousness, then strangled her with her own rosary. Returning to consciousness in her present hard drive, he put her on a leash and took her down to where her body was being prepared in the back of a Yakuza club in techie quarter. She'd watched while he mounted her corpse and finally had her his way. She was certain her soul still existed somewhere because she'd never stopped remembering love even in her diminished capacity. And it was diminished. But there was also a calm she'd come to appreciate where God touched machine: being at peace in a running mechanism. She had a distance now that allowed consciousness to be impersonally registered, and there was no more pain. Would he clique if she told him sometimes she missed even that?

Leaping from the spoiler, Angel landed in a flurry of luxuriant fur in front of the cruiser's nose. Passing him, she acknowledged Devil with a regal nod of her snow-white muzzle. Pacing out the last three centigrid between them, Angel stopped at the feet of her long-lost love, flourishing her gold tail like a palm. Glowing scanners rose to meet his eyes.

"Hey, babe, how do you like my new jump?"

* * *

In the blurred background of the security screen in Deli's foyer, Larkill could see the ruby locks of the gadget master's personal arena glittering with ostentation. He wanted it all to happen there. But first, he had to get Deli to allow the three additional cokes in his party, along with the heavy equipment, to come in with him.

Deli was peering at him in the screen's foreground with a perturbed, distrustful expression that marred his natural beauty. Han was again thankful he'd had the foresight to have Ryka stay with the van. Getting Tooco and Zim inside was going to be hard enough.

"Who?"

"Associates, your graciousness, a hatchery engineer and bellygrid entrepreneur whom I've had the privilege to scam with. They have what I think would be an extremely lucrative proposal for you, and I thought, after we discussed our business, you might be willing to look at a very short but thrilling presentation they've put together for your stupendosity." He thought he might have overdone it with that last bit, but no, the jiggling jack-off was too busy examining Darl and Sunsue with his voracious glare to detect any hint of ridicule. He had him.

"Did you bring those disks I requested?"

Han produced four tiny gold disks between his fingers. "Screx-ready, your wizardry. Myself, New Blood, and"—he gestured toward Darl and Sunsue—"Jasta, along with Curl, your gadget greatness, would all be grateful for the honor of adoring you."

Deli continued to inspect them with an expression he thought was worldly and wise, as if he were wrestling with a decision his jerk hadn't already made.

"Well, the more, the merrier, I suppose. Come up."

The large levitator lock slid open, and they all stepped into its spacious interior. Zim easily negotiated the two levi-loaders, one carrying their gear, the other their holo camera, into a corner of the lift. The lock closed, and immediately they were rocketed up to the 179th level, the pentmode of Kahn's scraper. When the lock slid open, Kahn Deli was waiting with two armed security robos on full scan.

"Welcome! Welcome. What an interesting group." The gadget master was taking a closer look at Zim and Tooco in the flesh, and Han could see he was already having second thoughts. Han held the stack of disks up between two fingers directly in front of Kahn's face. "As agreed."

Deli extended a reluctant palm, and Larkill dropped them in. It was easy to read the worried expression in his excessive face as he wrestled with an intuitive foreboding. Han was also aware of the calming effect his easy smile and sparkling blue eyes were having.

His security robos weren't sounding any alarms, no explosives, no laser weapons, no foul. They hadn't activated the frybars built into their tubular limbs, so while he waited for their final report, his dubiousness was leaning toward breathing a little easier. Han's meticulous attention to detail had stopped Zim from thoroughly fucking things up by leaving the C-4 on their personal levi-loader, along with the Dogdamn mining jumps he refused to get rid of. That all remained safely in the van.

"Negative weapons or explosives, no beacons, or honers, one, levi-loader, holds a holo imager with attached capture camera. The other one is holding various pieces of clothing and personal items."

"Klaus, why have you brought all your jumps with you? Don't tell me you're running away from mode?" Much more at ease, Deli was positively beaming with the possibility of uncovering some embarrassing gossip.

"No, you know how it is when you're here. All you do is party. I've gotta drop some stuff off at an ionizer after our meeting. Darl glided over beside Han, giving Deli her most statuesque smile.

"I see you're still looking formidable, Curl." Deli greeted Darl with his lascivious smirk. Darl fluttered her frosted lashes and purred.

"Come in, come in. Excuse the clutter. I'm working on a new zap campaign." Deli led the group through the plush arena of his living mode, around several floating screens, each flashing a different vid promoting some Screx scent he was zapping. "I'd hoped to make a decision by now and have all this cleared up." He gestured to the screens. "But I'm ambivalent about all of them!" Deli put an arm around Han's shoulders and steered him toward one particular screen. "I'm leaning toward this one, Klaus. What do you think?"

He hit a tap on his wrist organizer, and Han watched as a simian Zapstar with flaming orange hair ran naked through a lush green jungle, drums pounding a fevered rhythm. As she ran, her musculature began to expand and elongate until she metamorphosed into a series of ancient creatures: a charging water buffalo, a leaping gazelle, and a racing panther. Leaping up into a tree, the panther disappeared in the leaves, then burst from them a magnificent turquoise parrot winging its way up over the entire landscape. Landing by the edge of a river, she spread her wings and turned back to human, her squatting legs spread wide, hands resting on her knees. One hand slid up to her shy, and with two fingers, she delicately spread her outer petals. Staring defiantly, she started tensing her torso so her abdominal muscles etched themselves in bold relief across her belly, speaking as she made the effort.

"Take me with you when you go wild! One whiff, and you'll remember everything."

A brilliant diamond ray shot from her shy and turned the entire river into a shimmering plane. Suddenly the zap started to 3-D, and diamond waves flowed out from the screen, surrounding them all in a musky narcotic scent.

"Tabooooooo! One whiff, and you'll remember our jungle time! Taboo."

"Do anything for you?"

Han grinned. "Are you capping! Have you got her disk?"

Deli chuckled, his arm still encircling Han. Leaning closer, he gave him a playful leer. "What are you trying to pull on me, Klaus, hmm? Is this some kind of bait and switch?"

"Absolutely not, Kahn! All you have to do is clique MGM, and we can have the match at midnight. His opponent will come from the draw, but it doesn't matter who they pick. New Blood will cut him down, Kahn. You saw the kind of moves he's got in his bag of tricks. It's a sure thing, and you get half the purse and whatever you make on any personal bet. Bet big, Kahn! I've been in this game a while, and I'm telling you, New Blood is special. This is the golden coke everyone dreams of." His spirited sales pitch produced exactly the reaction he was hoping for. The Kahn was impatient to move on.

"Arranging that shouldn't be any problem. Now, what's this other lucrative proposal?"

"Well, your Go Fish last night gave me a terrific idea." Larkill turned away out of Deli's grasp and over to Zim and Tooco. "You see, my associates here design and manufacture educational holo bubbles for 7's hatcheries, and it occurred to me your market for last night's event must be fairly limited. Due to the rarefied nature of the spectacle, only ultra Topgrid like you could really afford to snag one."

"What makes you think I record it in the first place?"

"Because of your acumen as an entrepreneur, and of course, you'd see to it that your likeness and any other identifying details of your mode were changed before distribution. But moreover, you are a connoisseur of rarities and are naturally inclined to be generous in sharing your unique creations with others. I say that from my own personal experience of your kind invitation to me, a virtual stranger, to your gala event last night."

"Well, let us suppose just for the moment that I were to record them. What new market do you envision for me?"

"Ah! Right to the heart of the matter, you've come!" Now it was Han's turn to embrace Deli and steer him closer to the smiling crew. "While everyone knows that bellygridders don't have Screx, or a way to attend last night's activities, they do have a burning curiosity about these sorts of events."

Tooco roared with laughter, and Zim turned an indulgent smile to Kahn. "You'll have to forgive my jovial colleague. He's recently moved here from the Cairo Cartel. It's not often he finds himself in such exalted company. I confess he's a little overwhelmed."

"Kahn, let me introduce my associates. Zim, who is in charge of designing and creating the holo bubbles used in our hatcheries."

Zim gave a little bow to the gadget master.

"And our distributor, Tooco, who owns a holo-bubble manufacturing plant."

Tooco smiled elfishly, draped in the same white kaftan and turban he'd worn to the MGM,

Zim cued himself, "You see, we've just begun to explore a new market for our product. We want to capture your enchanting Go Fish in a holo bubble!" Zim slipped a hand into a pocket of his black velour jump, pulling out a small globe less than a milligrid in diameter and activated it. The scene of a classy Topgrid couple stripping down and engaging in robust copulation appeared inside the sphere. The detail and depth of field in this tiny show was amazing. An audio track of grunts, groans, and moans accompanied the action.

"This particular holo bubble *Getting Stinky* is our first production run, and it's been a huge snagger in Bellytown. You can see we're very good at what we do. So a Go Fish metamorphosing in here"— Zim pointed a long index finger at the holo bubble dangling from its chain—"would be an incredible show!"

"Exactly!" Han took the joystick again. "We think there's a vast market in Bellytown. Every coke will want one hanging from his rear-view screen as well as communities out in the waste fill, hundreds of grid from Sanatan. Headhunters love novelty trinkets to trade with, and this will be surefire. There are a lot more scabs out there than you might think, and something like this would fascinate them to no end. I'm telling you, Kahn, it's a huge market!"

They all shared the ravenous look of scammers about to pounce. Larkill could see Deli was slowly becoming infected. Thank Dog, a gadget master wouldn't be caught dead in techie quarter, or he'd know these little baubles could be snagged on any corner.

"What guaranties would I have that I couldn't somehow be traced to these items?"

"Manufacture and distribution would be handled by us through Tooco here. We would graft you an agreed snag per bubble. Before we start production and while we're manufacturing, you can have a representative oversee the process and make sure your terminal is credited for every item made."

Deli shook his head, looking up from under hooded lids and sneered. "How many of those doodads do you think you could put together before 7 dropped Sackers on you like a ton of shit? There's no way you're going to hide an operation like that in either Sanatan or Big New."

Han matched Deli's cynical expression and moved in for the kill. "But that's the beauty of it. We'll do the manufacturing right in Bellytown. Tooco's built a small plant there. 7 could give a shit down there. The only authorities we'll be dealing with will be Yakuza, and they'll be our headache, not yours. And you'll have your graft right up front. Before anything happens, you've already snagged."

Deli's crafty smile told Han everything he needed to know.

"There's just one thing. We'd like to get some shots of the injector being loaded with the gene bombs. We need to start with a little explanatory opening so they can understand where the phenomenal changes that occur are coming from. If you don't draw three maps for a bellygridder, they get lost. We think having a little demonstration will ensure every coke goes along for the ride."

"Ah, and that explains the holo imager!" Deli was pleased with his deductive powers.

Zim joined him in a satisfied smirk. "You have it."

"We were hoping to get the close-ups of assembly and loading in your entertainment arena."

"Why does it have to be in the arena if they're close-ups?" Again, Deli's intuition raised its terrified specter, but Han was two moves ahead of him. "I just thought, for background continuity, it's such a gorgeous arena. Of course, we'd change the red to green or blue to disguise its pedigree. But it's really not that important. Right here is fine."

"You realize we have yet to discuss my specific graft for each item."

"How does forty Yuan sound?"

"Fifty Yuan." Deli gave him his best shy smile.

Deli loved to tease. Han chuckled, seemingly wide open to the knife Deli was sharpening for him. "Done! Fifty Yuan, it is."

"My dear Klaus, you turn out to be such a cuddle puppy."

Han winked one sparkling eye. "I just know I'm no match for a scammer of your caliber."

"How many units do you think there'd be a market for down there?"

"We thought we'd do a first run of ten thousand."

Radiant now, the gadget master was ready to have his fun. "Why, Klaus, that's five hundred thousand Yuan! And as soon as you bring it to me, we can shoot your holo thingy." Taking his imaginary bow, Deli unveiled a smiling Cobra.

Without missing a beat, Han stepped to their personal levi-loader, pulling a large duff from under several smaller ones. He brought it back to Deli, dropping it on a convenient modular. Zipping it open, he removed several of Darl's most enticing pairs of panties and then gestured for the gadget master to take a look inside. Han grinned, watching the pathetic bastard tear his gaze away from the dainties to make himself look inside the bag. When he did, Han was reminded of prison Toons where the wolf's eyeballs pop out of his head.

"My Dog Klaus!" He looked up at Han with genuine wonder. "You are beginning to scare me."

"So what do you say, your magnificence, have we got a snag?"

"Indeed, we do! Indeed, we do!" He was already opening wide the ruby locks and gesturing for them to enter his grand arena. They followed him single-file down to the silver disk at the arena's center. Bringing up the rear, Zim maneuvered his levi-loader down to one side of the disk and began setting up the holo imager.

Deli motioned for Darl and Sunsue to be seated on the golden couch at the edge of the disk.

"My lovely coquettes, please make yourselves comfortable." He turned to Harrison. "And don't think I've forgotten you, young Stringer. While we've been chatting, I've arranged for your midnight match." He looked down at his wrist organizer. "And apparently, you will be doing battle with the Naz. Oh, he can be very nasty. He's very fast. We're in your corner, don't you worry. Your dressing mode is in the upper arena, niche 204. I've seen to it that a protein-pack meal waits on your arrival there."

Cyrus appeared at the top of the arena. "You called, sir?"

"Yes, Cyrus. Come down here."

The gold robo levied down the aisle and onto the disk. Deli turned to Zim, who was just putting the finishing touches on his assemblage. "Let me know when you're ready."

Zim detached the capture camera from the unit, tapping it on. "I'm ready, but can we get more light down here?"

Deli hit the wrist organizer, and a bright light flooded the disk.

"Good, that's good!" Zim activated the holo imager and pointed the holo camera at Deli and Cyrus, then tapped record. "We're disking. Could you have Cyrus take out the parts for the injector and assemble it?"

Deli nodded for his robo to carry out the request. Cyrus began removing and reassembling extraneous parts of himself, fitting components together until the injector was complete. He extended it to Deli. The gadget master reluctantly took it.

Zim was intent on the viewing screen of the capture camera. "Now, if you could just take out a gene bomb and load it into the injector. It helps me get the full 360-degree view, if you can move more slowly."

Deli hesitated a moment, peering around at the others, his restless intuition making a last attempt to search out the hidden terror. But Han's affable smile and Zim's astute professionalism gave him nothing to grab on to. He nodded for Cyrus to open the appropriate compartment and selected one of the tiny vials.

Han epitomized the innocent curiosity of a tubling. "What cartridge are you putting in?"

Looking into those bright blue eyes with that beautiful smile, Deli resolved to turn his back on fear and embrace the fun. He loaded the cartridge and then watched the readout on the side of the injector. "I believe it's a"—he looked up directly into the camera and spoke very slowly, like somebody trying to communicate with a grid clamp—"tarantula. That's a spider from way below us in South America."

Han roared with laughter. "Interesting, that's very interesting." He turned to Harrison, who was standing behind the holo imager, giving him a significant look.

Deli followed Han's gaze to Harrison, curious. What was going on? The gadget master's jaw dropped as he watched Harrison disappear. Almost simultaneously, Cyrus let out an electronic whine and settled to the disk. In the next moment, he felt something whip by and realized the injector and his wrist organizer were gone! When Deli looked at Han, again he was holding the wrist organizer in one hand and pointing the injector at him with the other. Han tossed the wrist organizer to Zim, who immediately began tapping out commands before the shocked gadget master finally bellowed, "What do you think you're doing!"

Ignoring him, Han turned to Zim. "Can you get the code for Deli's limo in there?"

Zim worked the wrist organizer for a moment. "Yeah, it's not encrypted."

"Good, give it to Tooco and give him the code for the levitator. Harrison, you perform a thorough pass through the entire mode. Make sure all security electronics are compromised. Zim, take one of the frybars out of those off-line security robos and find any cokes employed by this gasbag. Tie them up and lock them in a secure location. Tooco, you go down to the subplate port. You and Ryka get the shit still stashed in the racing van. We'll take all our stuff up to the levi pad on the roof and stow it in 'Master' Kahn's limo, but bring the pistol back to me. Go!"

Tooco and Zim raced up the aisle and disappeared. Han turned to the sheed reclining on the couch, raptly watching the drama unfold. "Darl, grab the capture camera and come around behind me on my left. Focus on the action."

Darl leaped off the couch, snatched up the camera, and was behind Han in a flash. "Yes! Oh, yeah!"

Han finally turned his attention to Deli, lowering the injector to his hip, casually pointing it at Kahn's ample girth. "Now, you have questions?"

It was clear from the ashen face of the gadget master that he realized he was in deep shit. His voice came out now with the same bleating quality as the young clone's whimper, "What are you doing?"

Han just smiled as the injector bolted in his hand, firing a projectile into Deli's bulbous gut. The gadget master screamed, grabbing at the folds of his stomach. "You maniac!"

"What am I doing? I'm giving the creator his creation. I'm giving the great imperious and impervious Kahn Deli a little of his own meds. I'd think a savvy scammer such as you would be aware that Ruger Labs is not lenient with those who use our clones for prurient entertainment. As far as being some Slavic half-breed, don't you think I know my brother when I see him?"

Pawing at the spot where he'd been hit, Deli was finding it hard to pay attention to Han's lecture.

"And unlike my brother, you haven't gone through a long series of painful operations to prepare your body for the shock you're about to experience. I'm pretty sure it's going to be even more painful than his was, and Dog knows what you'll turn into! You know your head could remain attached, still cognizant. Oh my, what a show they will make of you. You'll be the Zapstar for 7's campaign to end Go Fish! Honestly, now, wouldn't you rather die, hmm?"

Deli was bending over, holding his gut and groaning. Han bent down with him, urgently making his case. "I'll tell you what I'm prepared to do, you jiggling turd. If you tap up your personal cruiser for a booking down to Big New for yourself and six servants, and you tap out the clearance codes for the levi port, when I see a clearance verification, I'll put you out of your fucking misery! What do you say, have we got a deal?"

Deli let out a bloodcurdling scream as a long hairy tendril poked itself through his jump and began tentatively feeling the air. "Oooh, you maniac!"

Bouncing manically up and down on the royal couch, Sunsue was hysterical with laughter. Darl briefly focused the camera on her antics.

Then Sunsue started chanting, and Darl quickly joined her, "Go fish, go fish, go fish!"

Han was grinning, but his admonition was sincere. "Now, coquettes, please. Deli and I are trying to conduct some serious business."

They stopped chanting and tried to suppress what quickly became incurable giggling.

"Now, as soon as Tooco returns, I will be able to dispatch you quickly and painlessly. I suggest you take advantage of my generous offer before too much longer."

Deli howled with pain and horror while three more hairy tendrils burst from his ample middle.

"Who knows how long you'll have the necessary equipment and motor capabilities to tap out anything?"

Watching Deli trying to swat his new appendages, Sunsue burst into a second round of hysterical laughter, but Han gave her a warning look, and she stifled it.

"Let's all try to show a little more respect for the gravity of this moment."

Two black fangs sprouted from his crotch, and Deli dropped to his knees with a scream of unearthly agony.

"Now, that's interesting. I really think you need to make up your mind pretty quick."

Soon the four legs growing out of his massive gut were long enough to touch the disk. They began straining to topple the gadget master, rocking him until he keeled over into a horizontal position facedown. Then almost instantly, Deli's legs sprouted into the tarantula's formidable front appendages, and the fangs from Deli's crotch grew longer, accompanied by the unearthly screams.

"This is going very well! You turn out to be amazingly adaptable."

After all the grotesque changes coming rapid-fire the way they had, the moment when the command of the organism was given over to another species turned out to be the most riveting. The checkered saucer of an Arachnid eye burst from each cheek of Deli's bulbous ass and immediately took in present company.

Han moved around to what was now the rear of the wobbly mutant, wanting to discuss things further. "Seriously, Kahn, we'll get the codes anyway. Zim will dig around in Cyrus and come up with them within the hour. He's a genius at that stuff." Han extended the wrist organizer to Deli, but he still refused to take it.

"Do you really want us to leave you here alive? You know what they'll do, don't you? Look in that enlarged heart of yours and tell me you don't know what they'll do. They'll put you in a cage in some casino for as long as you manage to live, and they will laugh, and laugh, and laugh."

As if cued, Sunsue burst out again.

Han extended the wrist organizer to Deli, "Tap up your cruiser and six servants for Big New. Do it, Deli, while you still can! Time's running out!"

Just as the creature took its first clumsy steps, Tooco came running down into the arena and handed the Berretta to Han. The morphing spider was trying to make its way around the disk, but the legs on the right side briefly buckled before achieving tandem with the legs on the left. Realizing the creature was about to carry him off, Deli finally lost his taste for this life. Grabbing the organizer from Han, he began madly punching in the codes.

"There! Kill me! Kill me!" No sooner did he hand the organizer back to Han than his arms sprouted into the last two legs of the swelling Arachnid.

Quickly reaching the ground, they fell into step with the others.

Larkill was glued to the organizer, waiting to see the clearance verification. A moment later, he looked up to the others and smiled. "Guess what, crew? We're not going to dirty old Bellytown, we're going to Big New!"

Sunsue and Darl burst into cheers, and Tooco joined in. Meanwhile, the tarantula was pacing around the disk, trying to find its way up an aisle. Deli's chorus of, "Kill me" grew louder and louder. Zim ran back into the arena with a frybar in hand. Seeing the giant spider, he stopped in his tracks and trained the weapon on it.

"Holy shit!"

With difficulty, Han got his attention. "Were there any other clones in the mode?"

"Yeah, four."

"Did you make suitable arrangements for them?"

Zim gave Han a look. "Yeah, they're comfortable."

"Good." He turned back to Deli, whose ceaseless pleas were beginning to annoy him. "All right, all right!" Han raised the pistol again. "Zim, cover me. It might get pissed if I miss Deli and hit it." Han aimed carefully—Harrison explained how after the clumsiness with Bob—so both of the pistol's sights lined up on the desperate gadget master's head. "Here you go, asshole."

But just as he was pulling the trigger, Harrison came shuddering into the third dimension right in front of him. Han almost blew his head off. He quickly lowered the pistol, shocked—he'd come within a hair of killing Harrison.

"Fucking Jack, are you out of your fucking mind! I almost blew your head off. Motherduffer! What the fuck is wrong with you?"

"Relax, Han. When I'm returning, if it's before I fully materialize, as long as I see it honing, it'll go right through me." Harrison gestured to the stumbling spider, with the vestige of Deli dangling from its rear. "I take it this is the part of your plan you thought might give me indigestion?"

Han was still recovering from the disaster he'd barely averted and was in no mood to defend his actions. "This coke's got it coming! If he doesn't have it coming, then nobody has it coming!" He took a deep breath, regaining his composure. "And really, just about everybody's got it coming." Stepping to one side of Harrison, he again raised the pistol. "Besides, at the moment, I'm being merciful."

But once more, he was interrupted as the spider put on another surprising display. The hairy legs grew longer and thicker, and the brown bulb began rapidly swelling. Remnants of Deli's lounge jump exploded off the arachnid as the bulb kept expanding. The Deli that remained—his head, neck, and chest—was being shunted to the bottom of the swelling sack until he hung like a pink egg from the tarantula's underbelly, mewling, "Please, please, please!"

Han lowered the pistol. "Jack, have you got anything in your Cincinnati retrieval on a South American tarantula?"

Deli made one last herculean effort, "Killlll meeee!"

Harrison sped through his bytes until he came to the old-world encyclopedia. "Oh yeah, a large hairy spider eats anything up to small rodents, paralyzes prey with its venom, has three distinct features, can jump as far as five feet. That's over one and a half centigrid. It lives in an underground lair accessed by a trap door, and its mouth is in its belly."

"Really? In its belly? Oh, this has just gone perfectly! Did you hear that, Deli?"

No sooner had Han asked the question than a pulsing black orifice opened in the bottom of the spider's abdomen. Tiny black teeth began lining its circumference as the underbelly began undulating, drawing the Deli egg over its furry surface, finally tipping it into the gnashing hole. Deli's face had a last viewing frozen with horror, framed by the stubby black points, busy chewing it inside.

"Oh my Dog!" Han shouted, delirious with the spectacle. He turned to Tooco and held up the Berretta. "Have you got another magazine with you?" Tooco reached in his garment's many folds and pulled out a magazine. Han took it and gave the bellygridder one last instruction. "Go up and shut those ruby locks."

Tooco ran up the aisle and closed the locks. Confident of the arena's soundproofing, Han aimed at the swollen joints of the creature's legs and emptied the first magazine. The tarantula's appendages exploded like replicator melons as it tried desperately to escape through the rows. Han expertly slapped in the second magazine and again fired. The mutant arachnid came crashing down with its thrashing stubs shooting gray sludge all over the red velvet seats.

Han spun around and grabbed Darl, who'd been focusing the camera on the mutilated spider. He lifted her up, spinning around as she squealed with laughter. Lowering her to the ground, they embraced in a passionate kiss. "Did you get it all?"

She beamed up at her Screenrage. "Everything! I got everything!"

"All right, let's seal this dump and get to the Satport."

Harrison started to help Zim pack up the holo imager. Suddenly he realized one of the crew was missing. He looked over at Han. "When are we gonna pick up Okada?"

"We're not. She's not coming. I guess Carmine made her an offer she couldn't resist. It's for the best, Jack. She didn't really have the heart for our adventure."

He was caught completely off guard by this news. As Han predicted, he was suddenly sick to his stomach.

"I'm not sure I have it either, Han."

"We'll find out soon, Jack. Now let's get out of here! I've just gotta grab a few things out of Deli's wardrobe." Han ran up the aisle and opened the ruby locks, calling back over his shoulder, "Tooco, don't forget your Yuan."

His signature roar filled the arena as he disappeared through the locks.

• ──── ◆◗◗◆ ──── •

It hadn't been like her spacecase, but then it hadn't been like any of the others either. There was a surprising gentleness in every touch. Even finally locked in their thrusting dance, there'd been softness, a way of cushioning impact, relaxing his muscles at the last instant, stopping just deep enough inside her. No fevered pounding at her womb, frightening and closing her off. He moved in a way that opened her wings, opening her to luxuriate in their full span, knowing wherever she soared, he was there, protecting her in a tender armor.

The only time he'd been forceful was at the point she started crying strange cool tears, and in the confusion of her feelings, she'd begged him to wait. But he kissed her neck, his warm breath on her, murmuring over and over, "Cry and fuck." And it became a calming mantra, promising a reconciliation of all life's opposites, a healing rhythm in their gentle friction, until a new conflagration ignited, burning away all obstacles to joy. Now, was that what love did?

Harrison's fire was all-consuming. It made her fearless even of things she should be afraid of, remembering here in the soft comfort of Carmine's palatial mat her plan to strike out into the Arctic unknown with only Harrison and a levi-loader full of soya disks. She'd been suicidal! Then the only vision in her head was the two of them huddled in their little ice house, warmed by their own flames. How totally crazy he made her. So much better to be in luxury and love. All that with Jack was just a crazy dream. It was that String blowing you away.

———◆———

There was something about the tiny orange shafts from the instrument readouts cutting through the darkened cockpit that always calmed his nerves. Bay looked in the rear-view screen and saw Devil and Angel locked in stasis on the spoiler of the late Captain Rector's command cruiser, now his. He'd wanted them to come inside into the cargo bay. Devil howled at the suggestion, growling at Angel. "Remind lovebird, we're war machines."

Bay was a trilling lovebird, a delirious tube-born when he realized it was her in the gold-and-white ball of fur! The captain, in his fear and loathing of human contact, unwittingly gave Bay a reason to live. It was a kind of resurrection he could never have hoped for, even if their reincarnation was bizarre and would take some getting used to. It was still a hopeless dream come strangely true.

The buffed white ridges of Arctic desert rose up, one wave after another, under the veil of polar night. His heading was south, along the ten-degree longitude line all the way down to the equator. Then take a left, back to his genetic stomping grounds. That ensured them a very wide sweep around Big New and the entire eastern seaboard. Now Sanatan was just a distant glimmer on the horizon of his rear-view screen. The high speeds necessary off the grid had already propelled them far beyond the crystal party town.

The discussion over whether or not to kill him had taken a little while. It required some convincing for Angel to get Devil to accept her logic. She postulated that it was still an inferred command, and as such, unverified. And because the source of the inferred command was no longer available to verify that "kill him" was the direct command, Devil should pull the plug on the operation. Bay detected an almost human bias in her favor with the patience Devil showed, letting her present a thorough argument. But it made their escape from Rector's squadron a close one! The rough terrain around the crevasse where they'd settled their differences made it hard to get the ship airborne again. Without an electromagnetic carpet for his E-Mags to engage,

he used both his nose and tail thrusters to raise the big silver cruiser off the ice. Then tapping into fusion drive and adjusting the edge on his rear spoiler all the way up, he was barely able to scrape over the polar crests and finally take off. He'd considered lurking along the northern corridor to see if Larkill and the crew managed to escape and maybe join up with them. But Bay didn't want to end up some minor street lord in a burg full of minor street lords, hustling his way to an early end. Although with Devil and Angel, he'd be a terrifying force to reckon with. Zim had hinted darkly at Han's bigger plans, but he realized it wasn't so much the lack of grandeur in their schemes. He was just sick to death of cokes. All cokes. The only company that interested him now was Akita. He would miss the lush heat of Sunsue's body and the momentary release from heartache lovemaking afforded. But now the heartache was gone, and though he would probably never experience the physical thrill of making love again, Angel was Angelica. Her mind and spirit were somehow infused in that regal gold-and-white machine locked on his right rear spoiler. It was more than enough for Bay.

• ━━━ ◦•◦•◦ ━━━ •

Han knew what was coming was the moment when he either brought Harrison on board for the adventure of a lifetime or lost him completely.

It was very important how he went about framing that moment, and he wasn't quite sure yet where to begin. He didn't have a lot of time to decide. Even reducing their speed to a tenth of what the supercruiser could do, they were already 1,200 grid away from Sanatan. There were only about four hundred grid left before the effect he wanted to create would be lost. He knew everyone was wondering why they were making such a leisurely escape.

They were seated around a silver table that stretched almost the entire length of the observation mode under a plexi canopy along the crest of Deli's majestic cruiser. Each member of the crew was ensconced in one of the silver framed chairs, covered in plush crimson padding arranged around the table. It was no surprise that Deli's favorite color, in all its many shades, was again featured in his decoration scheme. Because all traffic in the corridor was on autopilot, everyone was present. All eyes were on Han, waiting to hear him finally divulge his secret plan. Zim had some idea of what it was, though even he would be shocked and amazed. But it was Harrison who had to comprehend the magnitude of this opportunity he was about to be given.

Harrison sat at one end of the conference table, taking in the ludicrous sight of his Screenrage captain standing at the other end of its silver expanse. Han was still wearing the neon paisley leisure jump he'd grabbed from Deli's wardrobe with pillows from his mat wedged inside to recreate his massive girth. But what made the picture almost frightening was Deli's image, which Han still kept covering his face. The mask, designed to be worn out in direct sunlight, was a flattering rendition of the gadget master's jowly mug, but in a cobalt blue with thin white eyebrows and a pursed red mouth. Han worried that if someone at Sanatan's levi port saw them leaving the limo and boarding his cruiser, it was important they saw Kahn Deli. While ultra Topgrid often wore their image in public, which was their way of avoiding contact with the masses and proclaiming their celebrity stature, the fact Han continued wearing it now was just creepy. If he'd just get on with it and tell them all "the magnificent plan"! But really, that stupid mask was unbearable.

"Han, will you take that idiotic image off!"

Zim was annoyed at Harrison's lack of respect for this portentous moment and shot him a dirty look, but Han did remove the image to reveal a mischievous leer. "Not as stupid as that jiggling tube turd looked being chewed into a tarantula' belly!"

Tooco's signature snort was followed by an explosion of laughter down the table.

"How long do you think it will be before they find Deli's skull in the belly of that thing?

Han's expression remained playful. "It will be quite a while, so why don't you stop worrying about it?"

Zim chimed in, waving one of several Blue Booz bottles placed around the table. "Give it up, will you! Give it up. Give up your cynical innocence, your skeptical naiveté, your terrified omniscience, your defeatist's assurance that everything will turn out badly. Give it up and show some faith, you supercilious spacecase."

Ignoring the drunken twit, Harrison got to the point. "So enough crap. What is this big plan of yours?"

"Well, as I told you, first we're going to Big New."

"Oh, you're joking! You have to be joking. Come on, Han, you're insane!" He snatched a bottle off the table, took a long swig, and slammed it down.

"Fine. We're going to Big New. I give up, so lay it all out. Let's hear it. Your loyal slave and servant awaits your illumination."

Han shook his head. "Sarcasm—that's pretty much your standard response, isn't it, Harrison? Followed by your know-it-all pontificating."

Harrison grabbed the bottle again, took an even longer pull, and slammed it down so hard it shattered across the silver surface. "What's your fucking plan?"

There was a silent pause as the whole crew remembered the last time their spacecase lost his temper. This wasn't the way he wanted to lay it out, but he couldn't stall any longer, waiting for some opening to make it go down easier. Maybe it was for the best. He had his own impatience to satisfy.

"All right, but please do not interrupt me or indulge in any more snide commentary until I've finished with my presentation." The Screenrage paused a moment to reach into one of the many pockets of Deli's dressing gown. He pulled out a tiny black case and placed it behind the Blue Booz bottle in front of him.

"It is critical that I begin with the philosophical underpinnings for the course of action I am advocating. I know, Jack, you think you're the only one among us who has any knowledge of the past, but my father, who lived through sixty-five of the last seventy-five cycles of cokekind's existence, passed on to me his understanding and his father's understanding of what brought us to our present condition. So I have checked in to see what condition my condition was in.

"And it's population! It all came down to population. By 2020, eight cycles before my father was born, the population of the world was seven billon cokes, pumping hydrocarbons into the atmosphere and throwing their garbage everywhere. While our technologies were expanding rapidly to meet the demands of providing for these burgeoning masses, extreme global warming and intense changes in weather patterns made it difficult to keep supplying this population with food and water. This, combined with the fact that two opposing religious factions were increasingly at war all around the world, finally led to the destruction known as 3TC.

"The reason we had so many cokes was based on a shared belief that human life, as they used to ID it, was sacrosanct, that every human life should be protected and nurtured in the ideal society. All their religions proclaimed that Dog, as they conceived him, was the architect of this guiding principle, and what Dog desired of us here on Earth was to live together in a worshipful sharing harmony.

"Yet what do we see when we examine the planet Dog supposedly created for this harmonious living? We see that all this life was designed to share the planet and survive by killing and eating each other in an endless chain of species. This one feeding on that one, and that one on another, and so on and so on until at the pinnacle of this predatory

220

gravy train—there is humanity, eating up everything. This is the physical infrastructure on which all life is sustained.

"Oh, I suppose you could argue all the life-forms feeding on each other were there to provide for cokekind, that the fact they ate each other and were put there for us to feed on didn't disprove or impinge on this ideal of the preciousness of human life. But why oh why did Dog arrange things so that while we're trying to develop this harmonious civilization, we're required to participate in an endless parade of murder, butchery, ingestion, and digestion every day of our lives— every day filled with endless carnage brazenly flouting this ideal that Dog supposedly wants us to live by. Either Dog is very perverse and we are the creation he delights most in jerking around, or there is no Dog, and we have erred in thinking human life is sacrosanct, and the purpose of our existence is to figure a way for everyone to live in harmony. That was the error that led to seven billion cokes choking the planet to death!"

Han was encouraged to find everyone, including Harrison, hanging on to his every word.

'Which brings us to the aftermath of 3TC, when overpopulation was no longer a concern. When finding a way off the planet, we decimated, became the new priority. And we did finally remodel our idea of the preciousness of human life. Now it became Topgrid whose lives were sacrosanct. They would be the ones who reaped the benefits of the ensuing technological innovation. They would be the ones to fly away to the stars while the rest of cokekind remained on the barren husk and choked in their own shit."

"And who are these Topgrid? A bunch of asleep-at-the-stick condescending pieces of worthless hype. Just like yourself until recently, Jack, when you took the first truly risky action of your life and fucked Okada, then went on to kill those Sackers back on the ice. You were just a figment of your own imagination until you took those hard actions. And don't tell me about snagging a personal recorder because while I admit it shows some spunk, you didn't have anything personal to record! You, like most of your ilk, were as devoid of passion and purpose as your empty Screx.

"You will excuse me if I don't think the ones to reap the benefits of humanity's hard-won technological achievements should be a bunch of indolent Screx-addled idiots who think about nothing but how to construct ever more elaborate fantasies in which they are worshiped, feared, and adored by an endless human parade of every shape and size available for every sexual desire imaginable. If there is anything to be learned from this devouring infrastructure, it's that the strongest and most adaptable peer down from on top of meat mountain."

Harrison was confident he'd been both patient and respectful. "Please, Han, I beg of you. Get to the plan."

"All right, Jack. It's very simple, really. Everything is fucked, so fuck everything!"

Han took a moment to regulate his passion. "I've been planning an escape ever since I made Screwhog pilot, but I wasn't inspired enough to put my plans into action until you arrived. You, Harrison, Jack, are my muse, my inspiration for having a goal worthy of my vision. I couldn't agree with you more about the kind of life we'd have to look forward to in Bellytown. Although, it's true, the dark burg did play a part in the original plan you inspired me to create. But the serendipity of our running across the great and glorious Kahn Deli erased the need for us to go there at all. We will be going into Big New, but only briefly, just long enough to practice our little magic trick of pulling a rabbit out of a Sat. That's why I got the holo imager, so we can perform our grand illusion at the Satport—boarding a Satcruiser without being scanned. The Kahn and his entourage will be booked on a flight to Brentwood, but before you start screaming, we can't go there. We're not. We are going to highjack that Satcruiser, and you, Harrison, are going to pilot it to Milsat, where we are going to steal the *Protostar* and, with you as our spacecase pilot, blow this fucking solar system!"

Harrison sat dumbfounded for a moment, unable to accept things being any nuttier than they already were. It was beyond madness! The

Sacker legions they'd have to wade through, the sea of laser cannons they'd need to dodge before they even got to Milsat. It was a Toon fantasy come to life, superheroes overcoming impossible odds with a quirky bag of tricks and a cocky smile. And there he stood, the golden Screenrage, the spitting image right down to the pearly whites.

"I don't know what to say. 'You're out of your fucking mind,' seems somehow inadequate."

Zim jumped to his feet, hoisting a bottle in salute to Han. "Of course, it seems impossible to a spacecase because something not directed by the almighty 7 can't possibly have any validity for a screen sucker like you!"

"You've got a lot of nerve calling me a screen sucker, you Screx-fried piece of shit." He could see, with the exception of Zim, the rest of the crew was having as hard a time as he was getting their heads around Han's audacity. They were all staring into space with glazed eyes. Tooco's chin was in danger of touching the table, his mouth was a large O, the smoke of his Jamma curling lazily across his face.

"You can fly it, the *Protostar*. You can fly it, can't you, Jack?"

He sat there, knowing if he opened his mouth, it would tap right into Han's messianic madness. But he was too tired to lie, and strangely, he felt the moment deserved the truth. "I'm the one who took it from basic assembly at Northrop over to the dry dock on Milsat for final fittings." He was briefly back in that moment. "It was close to a cycle ago." What was he thinking, throwing more fuel on the crazy fire? "They're probably finished by now."

"I knew it! I knew it!" Han was actually hopping up and down, transforming Deli's jump into a kaleidoscope. "Listen! Listen, I know it sounds outrageous, but I've got it all worked out. And the one thing you're forgetting is, you've got the String. Besides, Jack, at this point, what have you got to lose? I say we take the shot and steal their *Protostar* right out of their palsied hands."

He had to admit, he'd completely underestimated Han, presumed on the evidence that his base desires controlled his purpose, but it wasn't so. He should have realized back at Deli's that Han was about settling a score, and Deli was only the first of the legions of Topgrid that Han Larkill planned to burn. But in his present situation, it made a strange sense.

Topgrid were all zombies. He'd been a zombie. What Han said about the state of cokekind and the planet was right on the graft. Why shouldn't they, if they could take the only thing of value the narcoleptic maniacs managed to produce? Take it and find a new world! Besides, other *Protostar*s were being built! Some Topgrid would still get off the planet. They'd still get their chance to survive. Why shouldn't they, fugitives that they already were. He could see the rest of the crew were starting to warm to the idea. They were all drinking again.

Darl was the first to chime in, "Jack, we can start a new civilization!"

"How are we going to manage that when all you sheed have fried eggs?"

A petulant expression crossed the ceramic face. "So our civilization dies with us! Who gives a shit? It's better than having a hatchery full of dribbling clonies."

Ryka made a sound of approval around the bottle at her lips.

"Oh, I'm sure if we want to, we can engineer a new race that will be a formidable adversary for any creatures we might come across in our travels. You don't think they have tube nurseries on *Protostar*? Rest assured, they put creating their progeny right up there at the top of the list. You can never have too many indolent jack-offs spending their off-line time inside a useless gold ball fantasizing a wonderful life! And you don't have to fret, Zim. I'm sure they'll be plenty of useless gold balls aboard."

"I would hardly call Screx useless," Zim said it quietly but with heartfelt conviction. Han waved aside the interruption.

"Yes, Zim, it's a zap! And we all know how much it assists the Seymorist along their spiritual path. But was it worth depleting the last resources of a gravely damaged planet worth using up the last of its rare Earth metals? Because the Screx and *Protostar* are the only projects 7 has focused on for the last thirty cycles." Han took another swig.

"Fuck their progeny. Fuck their tomorrow and all the cokes who dwell in it. We here and now, this crew can make all cokekind's dreams come true. And we're the ones who deserve to take that journey because we're the ones who still have the heart to do it! Unlike these zombies who can only fantasize. We can be the cokes who take *Protostar* out into the galaxy on a new adventure. It's within our grasp if we're willing to take the chance, and if you're willing to be our pilot, Jack?"

They were all staring at him. He could see from their expressions they were seduced again, ready to follow their leader anywhere. Han picked up the tiny black case he put down on the table before he began speaking.

"And if you're still interested in a personal perspective"—Han slid the tiny object down the table, until it stopped less than four milligrid from Harrison—"that's your new micro-thought-recorder. Now you'll have something worth recording in it."

Stunned, Harrison felt the bolt strike, him, knew a rebirth of hope was occurring. Delicately, he picked it up, and despite himself, smiled with gratitude and, yes, joy.

"I picked it up while I was in techie quarter getting the holo-imager. I do need to let you know it cost a pretty Yuan." Han grinned at him. "What about it, Jack? Are you willing to get serious about having a personal life?"

Darl was beaming at him. "Jack, we're your new tube clone! We got this far together. We can go anywhere."

Falling into the smooth white cyphers of her eyes, Harrison could almost envision anywhere. It was a beach like the "All Time Winners" holo, with the Rebino princess stretched out beside him watching the emerald surf.

Darl's final plea was simple and tender. "Jack, be our pilot to a new life, please."

But there was still reality to choke down. He turned his eyes back to Han. "You're gonna need to fill me in completely on this plan. I do hope you have one for pulling off all this amazing shit we're gonna have to do! And I'm gonna need to believe it's just barely possible."

"Absolutely!" Han tapped a command on Deli's wrist organizer as he strode down the length of the table to Harrison's end of the observation mode. Harrison watched the entire dome darken and realized Han was activating the cruiser's sunscreen at night. Han passed by him going to the very end of the dome and stood watching the faint glow of Sanatan. Everyone turned to watch with him.

"I hope the initiation of our adventure will make it clear how committed I am to the success of our plan." He turned back to Harrison with a pensive expression of sympathy. "It will entail some loss for all of us, especially for you and me, Jack. But really, it's a loss we've already suffered, and one that regrettably is for the greater good." The Screenrage again locked eyes with every member of his crew. "It is paramount you realize the seriousness of your undertaking. That moment has arrived." Han turned back to the view.

Now they all watched the tiny glow on the horizon, expectant but without a clue. Han reached into another of Deli's pockets, retrieving a small C-power transmitter and tapping it online.

"I told you he was soft, Jack."

"What?"

Harrison saw the final tap and instantaneously heard the distant yet thunderous roar. A gigantic gold column appeared on the horizon, illuminating the night for ten thousand grid out. From its base, for 360 degrees around, a wave of flame exploded across the tundra, roaring up behind and nearly engulfing the ship. They felt the shockwave hit, momentarily wobbling the big cruiser before it regained course.

"Wooo! Maybe I should've waited a bit longer. But now we can bivouac at Deli's without worrying about any problems from Sanatan. I knew Bob's bomb would come in handy, and what a diversionary tactic. After that, Big New will be way down on the list of things that need attention."

Harrison sat rooted to the chair, mouth gaping in shock, eyes squinting into the burning light, every atom of his being frozen in horror. There were at least a quarter of a million cokes rising in that column of light murdered right in front of him in the wink of a Toon hero's eye. Okada, Bay, Uncle Walt—a whisper was all he could manage.

"Han, you're insane."

"Courage, Jack, courage. Visionary action invariably entails great loss. Courage."

"Stunning." Zim goggled like a tube-born at the burgeoning mushroom.

SECOND INTERLUDE—2197

Dysan stood hugging the railing on the level 45 forward observation mode of the infamous *Protostar*. Infamous to Topgrid at any rate, if any still survived. She was taking a short break from transcription, watching for intermittent beams from the laser cannons popping online to blast space junk that crossed their path. They used to get a lot more action.

Protostar reminded her of vids of the huge H_2O ships at the beginning of the twentieth. How incredible to have so much H_2O that it surrounded you, stretching to the horizon, filling everything. So much H_2O you had to build a great ship to cross it. Glancing down at the burnished titanium railing, she caught her reflection in its muted sheen.

Some accounts of those ships' explorations could be found in the books they brought with them, complete with drawings and "photos." Their adventurous spirit was reflected in the design of the *Protostar*. From the fluted posts supporting the railing's curving sweep, all the way up to the stately observation deck, the signature lines of those bygone vessels were calling out here. But what a thing to have all that water. Now water was made (still a tedious process) and recycled. It was only used for drinking and cooking. All cleaning was done with ionization.

She should be making something good to eat instead of mooning into space over lost oceans, but she was making do with replicator crackers. The cup of lemon tea she occasionally sipped was reviving her spirits a bit. Writing was harder than it looked. How that poor bastard Shakespeare ever produced the mountain of plays he did pushing a bird feather over parchment was beyond fathoming. After six hours of scrawling with an ancient Parker, she'd managed to get Harrison and his "comrades" as far as the destruction of Sanatan, heading for Big New—probably at least six more hours, bending over blank sheets, filling them with her gyrating cursive. If Harrison hadn't dumped his recent experiences into his new thought recorder, she could have dispensed with all the earlier machinations of outrageous fortune. But he hadn't wasted any time excusing himself to the eliminator not long after he witnessed the disintegration of Sanatan. In there, he used a survival disk to make a small incision just above and behind his left temple and inserted the thought recorder. Later, speeding down the corridor, he jumped the String and dumped everything. With Appro-recall no longer blocking full access, he got it all. He finished just before they reached Big New's entry port, remembering more than he expected to. He stayed hidden in the fifth, until the moment he bolted inside Han Larkill's body and simulated a lot more than a cardiac arrest.

God! She'd completely forgotten about Shuta! Splatter would talk him out of his foolishness. He'd make Shuta see how pigheaded he was being, thinking he could just leap over a hundred years of recriminations and accusations, hurt feelings, and wounded pride. And that wasn't taking into account the fact all he would accomplish playing the String game was to get himself killed.

If, by some miracle he actually won, did this bold warrior think it could erase what his great-grandfather had been about? Granted, the burden of proof rested on her family, but she was here with that proof, held by their house for the requisite hundred years. Even if he was victorious, it would do nothing to protect him from the truth that Dysan was about to administer. If he lived, Shuta might regret his passion; at the very least, he'd stop sniffing around after her. Besides, the idea of them together, with the families history, would be kinkier than some Screx fantasy that perv Zim dreamed up. But whenever

Dysan hinted at shocking disclosures, Shuta remained undaunted. He was aflame! Why was it that when a man burned, he thought everything had to burn with him?

Some things never change, no matter how much time passed. They'd probably always be stumbling, half-blind, driven by tumultuous yearnings toward a destiny they could never quite fathom. Was it just a survival mechanism, assuming it all led somewhere, that they traveled toward an ineffable realization? Could their divine intimations turn out to be just a coping mechanism to keep the organism slugging away in the face of inevitable disillusionment and entropy? Now their metaphysical quest was "on hold" to the physical one, searching their corner of the galaxy for a livable planet. They'd been cautious the first decade, keeping their speed down to twenty thousand miles an hour. But once they felt competent handling the ship, they quickly bumped it up to *Prototstar*'s top speed—450,000 miles an hour.

Where the Earth is located, the Milky Way Galaxy is about three light-years thick, and our planet is about one light-year from the galaxy's edge. A light-year is 5.87 trillion miles. Four hundred and fifty thousand miles an hour for ninety years, along with the interest from a decade at twenty thousand thrown in, will garner you enough miles to put you "roughly" in that same vicinity. They were now on the brink of deep space, near the solar systems they were interested in. She'd read the articles from the early twenty-first century about the exciting news there were tens of thousands of habitable planets in our universe. They neglected to weigh that against *infnite* space and the mind-boggling distances *in just their own galaxy. If* they'd spent the last century in this tin can, she doubted they'd be popping the corks on their champagne bottles regarding that announcement. At the moment, they had their eye on a planet three times the size of Earth with carbon and water, orbiting far enough from a young sun that, if they could cultivate an oxygen atmosphere, would be the "Superearth" of their dreams. With its size, it could have an extremely powerful electromagnetic field and be a great source for C-power, while protecting them from the bombardment of radioactive particles for a billion years. So far, their observations were promising. They were about to move closer. If they were very lucky, they'd found their new home.

Out here, humanity was on the line. But they'd always been on the line, managing to make it from one disaster to the next without quite extinguishing themselves. They'd even managed to survive after their last attempt at self-annihilation. Lucky for them, it turned out the only domesticated animal with the natural immune system to deal with the mass decomposition of civilization was the family mutt. Dogs truly became man's best friend. Dysan chuckled to herself, suddenly remembering a pre-3TC article in a dog-fancier magazine. In it, the author tried to reconcile the pristine beauty of her Samoyed (a stunning white husky) with the experience of watching him wolf down a pile of wino shit.

With care, radioactive dust storms and hot spots could be avoided, but it was the ensuing lack of sanitation, with attendant diseases, that wiped out huge numbers of the remaining human and animal populations. Dogs were their main source of protein for the first several decades. Korean cuisine was derigueur.

Canine ranching became an important and profitable profession. At first, humans tried to step back from their historic relationship as friends. They tried treating the dogs the same as cattle or sheep, but the dogs wouldn't have it! In time, those big trusting eyes and that indeflatable love of play began to make inroads on their conscience. After countless "old yellers" watched with docile expressions as their masters came for them with a knife, they began to believe the dogs knew and understood the necessity of this service to mankind.

Those really were the "dog days." Enraged by their old religions' divisiveness, they were on the verge of turning their backs on the very notion of God—until a courageous young spiritualist at a small tent revival in the waste fill spoke. Up to the moment he opened his mouth, he was facing the possibility of being annihilated by a very hostile crowd. Amazingly, he turned it all around. He told the fuming masses they were responsible for their own destruction and division. And if they needed proof there was still an all-merciful and beneficent creator, they need only look into the eyes of man's best friend, "who humbly offer up their throats every day all over the planet that mankind might survive their apocalyptic arrogance. And if all the old names we gave him leave only the taste of blood and ashes in your mouth, you can call him by a new name, one reflecting his divine humility and love for all mankind. You need only turn three letters around. He's there at your feet, giving you unconditional love, cloaked in a form known as dog. Dog has been by your side, giving you a sustaining love, giving their bodies for forgiveness of all your destructive pride."

The evangelist's name was Seymore, and whether or not they believed in "Dog," their faith in divine inspiration was restored. This concept of God as an affable numbnuts who wouldn't start trouble or tell you what to do (and on top of that, served himself up for dinner) swept the whole planet like a wildfire! Everybody started turning those three letters around.

A population of thirty-two dogs (ancestors of Outrider, patrol dogs) lived on *Protostar*. Maybe someday their progeny would greet little girls driving levi scooters home on a beautiful new planet.

Dysan was a "moldhead." It was the one thing, other than his wolfish looks, that attracted her to Shuta. He was a past junkie too. But he teased about it, accusing her of "moanie-ism," always whining about what was gone—"the sea, the sky, and all the beautiful whales! Boo-hoo, boo-hoo!"

Yet if a destiny was ever clearly delineated on their horizon, its perception would come through the lens of all their striving, sacrifice, and loss—through the long chain of events that led them to this journey, drawing strength and inspiration from the struggle of generations taken up on your behalf because it was always about a future.

Dysan pursed her regal lips, blowing across the surface of her cup. It was about time to finish the story. A couple more sips, and she'd do a job on all of them.

CHAPTER

6

This was amazing! This was what *thrilling* is supposed to be. Whole new situations and challenges developing in seconds, tests of wit and vision.

Everything from Harrison being a *Protostar* pilot, to sending Deli to hell in a humongous spider's belly, and now hightailing it to Big New in the lap of luxury.

It was *all* falling Han's way!

What a relief not to have to deal with a parade of mutant streetlords, putting together a safe passage through Bellytown to make it up to Big New. No, they wouldn't have to do any of that crap now. Stealing Deli's ident and cruiser made everything so much easier. After incinerating Sanatan, he floored the supercruiser. They were currently flying high above, slower traffic, at 8,400 grid an hour.

Now they could go straight into Big New and stay at Deli's pentmode, where he and Zim could train the crew to perform in their "pageant." Acting with holo characters created by their new holo imager, they'd perform a boarding melodrama obviating the need to go through the scanner. Sinatra, Satport would be the sight of their departing sleight of hand. In the gadget master's spacious mode, they could practice numerous dry runs and hone the holo characters' believability within the dramatic scenario. They could work, eat, sleep, and fuck in lavish luxury before lifting off this dying turd for the last time. There was only one little glitch: first, they had to get through a scan-check at the entry port into Big New.

Zim was circling the silver table, threading around other crew members, his arms waving in gestures of panic. "Listen, we just barely made it out! We're devastated! We're dumbstruck! We have no idea what's going on! We're hysterical—out of our minds."

Han hit the wrist organizer, and the sunscreen disappeared from the canopy. The great cloud had flattened out and was lost in the cloud cover of the northern horizon. He tugged at his girth, adjusting pillows under the gaudy jump so they were less constrictive. "Yes, we know the mood of the scene, we know the emotions, but that's not going to get us past the scanners."

Darl performed a Blue Booz salute, thrusting her bottle up like a torch. "I got it! Deli had a heart attack as a result of our narrow escape from this tragedy. We are rushing him to New Med."

Zim released a hiss of contempt, waving her off. "They'll still scan him when we go through. It's automatic. We've either got to shut it down or somehow fool the scan—"

"There's no way we'll shut it down." Han was the first to bow to reality.

Harrison had just returned from the eliminator. He'd gone out and thrown up not long after the bomb. He'd also installed the thought recorder in his head. That action revived his spirit, and rather than dwell on Han's mind-numbing recklessness, he was going to focus on the problem at hand.

"Why don't I do the same thing I did to get into Sanatan?"

"Which was . . . O great one?" Still puffing on his Jamma, Tooco smirked with contempt at Topgrid solutions and took another swig.

"On the String. I can meld with Han and his padding and fabricate a damaged heart, make it have another attack right in front of their eyes!"

Tooco reprised his signature snort, but Han had no trouble following. "Yes! Of course! That's excellent."

"We do the second attack while they're scanning, so they rush us right through."

Han too was up and pacing the length of the table. "That means we have to transmit our situation soon. We want them prepared for the charade." Han spun around to Zim. "Tap your C-comp hand unit into the cruiser's frame and make it a replicator, then tap in Cyrus's voice from the cruiser's logs and contact the entry port. Say that your master had a heart attack as a result of your narrow escape. You barely left Sanatan before it was destroyed. Tell them they should be able to hone us within a few hours. Go. Do it!"

Zim immediately took off, disappearing through the canopy's entry lock. Han turned back to Harrison. "But will wearing the image make sense, if I've just had a heart attack?"

"Sure. Run an oxygen tube underneath it—you're Topgrid! They'll think you don't want anyone to see your naked face in your present powerless state."

The Screenrage snapped his fingers. "Yes, and Zim can play the hysterical personal physician."

Tooco, who'd been nonstop swilling ever since the explosion, suddenly keeled over in his chair, head bouncing to rest on the metal table, the burning Jamma rolling onto the deck.

"Ryka, Sunsue, take the little shit to a niche." Han reached into the garish jump and pulled out two Nitro patches, tossing them to Sunsue. "Enough booz. Take these and wake up. Tuck him in and stay with him. We'll say he's another servant who was overwhelmed and incapacitated by the disaster."

Ryka and Sunsue helped Tooco to a semistanding position and stumbled toward the lock.

Han slapped a patch on his own jugular, hollering after them, "Hit the Nitro now, or you're gonna break your necks!"

Darl started giggling, and Harrison, watching the swaying trio, couldn't help joining in. Sunsue was trying to hand a patch to Ryka without losing her hold on Tooco, and Ryka was trying to take it without doing the same. The brief ballet almost ended in disaster when Tooco came unexpectedly to life, making a grab for the patch. Han bolted over, snatched up the bellygridder by the back of his neck, and suspended him in midair while Sunsue and Ryka managed to get the Nitro to their throats.

"Fucking moron!" Returning him to the deck, Han released the drunken little shit, and the duo finally managed to steer him through the lock. Han stamped out the Jamma and began to pace. "We're going to need a good reason for escaping so fortuitously."

Still curled in her plush crimson cocoon, Darl ignored Han's recent advisory, taking a long pull on her bottle, then smiled slyly, very pleased with herself. "The zap campaign! I'm your new Zapstar. You discovered me in a casino and wanted to clique me with some conglom heads before you actually eyed me."

"Beautiful, just beautiful." Han's smoky leer slid over his Rebino princess. "They'll have no trouble snagging that."

Zim burst back into the lock, running quivering fingers through his bright-pink spikes. "I did it. I did it! They're online, but they definitely want to have a longer chat before we reach the entry port. I don't know if I can pull this off, coke. And I just realized . . . I gotta come up with some hunk-a-junk that'll pass for Cyrus going through the scan. I mean, shit—this is intense."

Once again, Han went to the pocket in Deli's jump and produced two more Nitro patches. Zim watched expectantly, but Han ignored him, giving a patch to Darl and then Harrison.

"All right, we've got a few hours before the interview. We need to straighten up."

As they all watched, mystified, Han proceeded to toss Tooco's empty bottle, along with several other empties strewn along the table's length, into a disposal chute situated under the center of the table. He picked up the shards of Harrison's bottle and the Jamma's remains, throwing them in as well.

"There." He paused for a moment, lost in thought, then snatched Darl's bottle from her hand and moved back to Zim. "You need to slow down, take it as it comes. You're doing an excellent job, but don't anticipate. It invites panic. Deal with what's in front of you. And finish this." He handed Zim Darl's bottle. Zim put it to his lips and kept it there, until he drained the entire contents.

"Now, the two points we need to play on are Deli's exalted status and the heart attack."

Zim was already calmer. "Yes, but if he's having a heart attack while we're going through the scan, they'll want to escort us directly to New Med. We sure as shit don't wanna go to a 7 hospital!"

While the others struggled with this new dilemma, Han quickly found the way out. "*Unless* we can convince them that Deli has a private hospital at the pentmode on top of his scraper. Can you route a transmission from our ship to Deli's mode, and from there, to the entry port without anyone at Deli's pentmode being aware of it?"

Zim thought for a moment. "Yeah, it shouldn't be a problem. I can route it through without opening a screen, and I can configure it so any replies come back to us the same way."

"Good. Make a request for emergency air-lane clearance from the entry port to Deli's med center. Make it a transmission from 'Kahn Deli Medical Center.' Give the same local ident as his mode. Got it?"

Zim nodded. "Yes, yes, that could work."

"Okay, go do it. Just do what's in front of you."

"Right . . . right." Zim took off again.

"It would've been a nice touch if they got that transmission first. But it's still solid. We can do this."

———•━•━•———

A few hours later, invisible on the String, in a corner of Kahn's private niche, Harrison observed as Larkill stretched out on a spacious levi mat, preparing for his debut as Kahn Deli. Zim stood to one side in attendance, busily checking the C-comp hand unit now functioning as a life-signs monitor. With his free hand, he was adjusting the oxygen flow on the tank lying next to "Deli." Darl sat on the opposite side of his mat, gently stroking Kahn Deli's hand. They were all facing a large wall screen at one end of the niche.

"Everybody, ready?" Han poised a finger over Deli's wrist organizer. Both Zim and Darl nodded their assent. "Jack, in your ethereal state, I'll take a lack of any response as your affirmation." Han pushed the button on the wrist organizer, and the screen sprang to life with a panoramic view of Big New.

A burnt-orange sun emerging out of a black sea spotlighted the monstrous dome of the megatropolis. A much simpler affair than Sanatan's etched bell jar, it was a gigantic tinted salad bowl covering the entire burg. The first yellow rays cut through a thin emerald fog draped around the dome. Harrison could just make out the spiraling geodesic scrapers that comprised the heart of the great burg. His own mode, once a "speck" in one of them, had a tiny balcony on which he'd spent many peaceful hours, gone forever, the blissful sleep of the cocoon.

The view was unexpectedly replaced with the image of a Sacker commandant. The gold medallion on his left breastplate confirmed that. Helmetless, he reminded Harrison of Zim with his sly narrow face and a wedge of blue hair springing from the top of his head.

After taking in the massive form of Deli breathing heavily through a tube protruding from under his cobalt mask, the commandant shifted his hooded eyes to Zim.

"I am Commandant Kilmor. Are you a physician?"

"I am."

The commandant waited a puzzled moment, then continued with obvious irritation, "May I have your ID, please?"

"Oh, certainly. I'm sorry. This has all been so sudden and unexpected." Launching a silent offensive to bolster his nerve, Zim indulged an inner dialogue, *Commandant, you can have any ID you want. There were approximately twenty thousand physicians living in Sanatan. I chose one from the ship's disks. The subject actually bore an uncanny resemblance to me! I only needed to spray my hair white, and shazam, I am the clone.*

"Sandor, Theo, Appro-recall ident DR9731ZED/5836155."

"Thank you." The commandant briefly looked down, verifying the information, and then returned his gaze to Zim. "What is the Kahn's condition?"

"He had a major cardiac arrest at approximately 1:00 a.m. when we observed the explosion of Sanatan. I've since stabilized his condition. I'm giving him oxygen, and he's taken a blood thinner, along with a mild sedative. We are preceding in all haste to transport the Kahn to his personal med center, where, I understand, a fresh heart is waiting."

The commandant eyed him coldly. "What can you tell me about the explosion?"

"Nothing, really, we were all in the observation mode talking around the table. We were about to retire when—*BOOM*! It was horrifying, this gigantic explosion! The flames from it almost swallowed us. Unbelievable! The Kahn jumped up and said, 'My Dog,' then dropped like a stone."

"Does the Kahn always travel with a personal physician?"

"No, never, to my knowledge. I'm not actually his personal physician. I'm traveling with Princess Shazar." Zim gestured to Darl, who gave a sultry nod to the screen. "I am a witnessing physician accompanying the princess to validate her line of DNA purity. It's protocol, more of a business formality. I certainly didn't expect to be practicing."

Darl seamlessly interjected herself into the conversation, "The Kahn has graciously chosen me to be the star of his new zap campaign! He was bringing me to meet some important cokes before he eyed me."

"I see. What is your Appro-recall ident?"

Coming up with a Rebino princess in Sanatan who fit Darl's general description was a bitch. I mean, yes, they were all white figurines; but height, body structure, and mass were difficult to find a match for. Darl was tall, athletic, and with discernable muscular development. Finding another "Bengal tigress" took some searching. He finally found a princess, Shazar, from the Satcit "Revlon." Hopefully, for their sakes, she wasn't at this very moment sitting on Revlon instead of being atomic ash wafting over the Arctic Ocean.

"Shazar, Vora, SX5271ZED/7793614."

They waited as the commandant ran princess Shazar's bytes. After staring at the screen for what seemed a cycle, he returned his cold gaze to them.

"Thank you. Upon arrival, please proceed to entry lock 9. An emergency air lane has been cleared to the Kahn's med center. Programing for your ship's transit route will be installed at your lock. Due to the serious event in Sanatan, 7 requests you keep a live screen in your presence until further notice. After you reach the med center and Kahn Deli's condition has been stabilized, we will need all your impressions of the explosion, from every clone on your ship. Please convey to the Kahn, at the appropriate time, my wish for a speedy recovery. Out."

The screen returned to a closer aerial view of Big New as Kahn's levi cruiser began its final approach. The levitator shafts running through the center of each scraper's spiraling structure were clearly delineated now. These tubes gleamed at the center of countless geodesic modes locked together in hive-like symmetry.

Well, the party was in full swing. With the directive that they keep a live screen shadowing them, there was no way the others could break character. Maybe Zim could loop certain screens, although Harrison wasn't quite sure how that would work. Fortunately, their Screenrage really was a nimble strategist. And the rest of the crew, himself, included, kept coming up with good ideas for filling any potholes in Han's road to perdition. With Zim's electronic wizardry, they might even be able to pull off their interviews.

But did he really want to go to hell, especially one of his own making?

Something happened. After they finished their initial strategizing, Han told him to get on the String and wait in Deli's private mode while Han helped Zim finish the checklist of things that still needed doing. Harrison decided it was the perfect time to dump his entire consciousness into the thought recorder. Back in the Screwhog, when they were making their desperate descent into the Arctic Ocean (when he landed in Han's lap), a shocking memory from his distant past flashed through his mind. Downloading into the thought recorder, it jumped out again, this time clear in every detail. He hadn't *ever* used Han in his Screx orgies.

It was when he was a cadet. He'd been piggybacking on his "ultra" modie's fiber feed. Han's "Acapulco Rage" popped up. It looked exciting with a lot of hot naked sheed hanging around this big swimming pool by the ocean, so he tapped it up. And then the screen changed. Han appeared, slipping through white drapes, completely naked, much younger, maybe early twenties. He seemed surprised to see him. His semi-erect jerk showed interest but was still undecided if it was worth the effort.

"Hello, Justin . . . you don't usually want to see me again so soon. Is everything all right?"

Harrison realized that Justin, his mode mate at the academy, obviously had an ongoing account with Han. That's why it was a popup. And on the face of it, hot naked sheed had nothing to do with this. Since Han called him Justin, he must be seeing Justin's avatar. Then Harrison said something that still surprised him.

"I wanna do it again." He supposed he said it because he thought in the guise of Justin's avatar—whatever it was, it wouldn't really be him—that he was in a position to go on this wild trip without repercussions, free of charge.

Han smiled at him. "Well, all right, but are you sure you've got the Yuan to cover it?"

"Yeah, no problem."

"Then get naked." Stepping onto the Screx-mate mat (Justin had all the latest toys), Han could view everything he did as Justin's avatar, but his expressions would be displayed on Justin's face.

Harrison slowly unzipped his jump and stepped out of it hesitantly.

"I thought we were through with all that embarrassment and shame about our nakedness. You are a beautiful tube. You have nothing to be ashamed of."

Stripped down, being closely inspected, he felt a thrill so heady he thought he might pass out. He watched Han's semi-erect jerk shiver, a sleepy snake revived by a ground tremor, slowly starting to rise, its head swelling, the rim flaring out in a cobra's hood.

"Get down on your knees, Justin." Han's tone was caring but stern. Watching his jerk come to full attention, Harrison was mesmerized. "Justin" found his knees.

"You know, I've noticed you are a little squeamish about having the jerk in your mouth. You like it, but you're afraid it's nasty, filthy. Let's see if we can't get you past that. Tap in my jerk, Justin."

He hadn't known what Han was talking about, giving the screen a quizzical look.

"Don't be coy. It's underneath your mat."

He rummaged underneath Justin's mat and quickly discovered the flesh-textured steely ending in a large bulb. Returning to the mat, he kneeled again and tapped it on, feeling a vibrant tingling in his hands.

"Stick out your tongue, Justin."

And feeling foolish, he had.

"That's right. Now go ahead and run it around on my head." Han's head filled the screen as he tentatively extended his tongue, finally touching its surface just below the tip, seeing his tongue on the screen.

"That's right."

Watching the screen, he slowly committed more of his tongue to the process as Han repeated a soothing mantra, "That's right . . . that's right . . . that's it." He could feel the velvety skin of Han's head puffing up, straining against itself. He engaged more of his tongue until the tip caressed Han's rim, and the Screenrage cooed in a soft falsetto, "There you go, there, you go, yeah." And that released his tongue to go wild, licking in a frenzied circle, round and round, feeling his own jerk rising from between his legs.

"Don't be afraid of the tip. Lick the tip too."

He explored the tiny crater with the tip of his tongue, lapping at it, until, even more frenzied, he returned to the whole head.

"Look at me."

In the screen, Han's crystal-blue eyes were watching him. "Now lick the rim of the head, like this."

Suddenly Han's mouth filled the screen, with his tongue darting back and forth from side to side.

Immediately his tongue copied Han's technique, and he felt the change in texture from velvet to the slick polished surface of Han's rim. Han repeated his earlier command, "Look at me." He struggled to keep his eyes in Han's as he stretched his tongue to lick all the way around the slippery rim.

"Now, in a moment, I want you to start down the shaft, moving your tongue side to side. But I want you to take your time and make sure you lick all the way around the shaft and all the way down to the root." They stared into each other's eyes awhile longer before Han gave him the command, "All right, close your eyes and start down the shaft."

He methodically circled down the long shaft, until at its root, where the rod was at its thickest, he grazed the warm skin of Han's cuj. He'd stopped licking then but kept the tip of his tongue touching the root, waiting in a pregnant pause. Once more, he heard Han's soft, cooing voice.

"All right, now lick my cuj."

His tongue stayed frozen at the root, and the soothing voice beckoned him again, "Go ahead, lick my cuj."

And tossing away any identity but that of sensual slave, he began darting with his tongue, which was quickly converted from a probing tentacle into lapping waterfall, bathing Han's warm gourd, feeling his own saliva on his cheeks.

"There we go . . . there we go . . . yeah. Keep licking. Open your eyes and look at me."

Again, he was lost in the shining blue pools.

"Now lick my cuj and jack your jerk. Show me some pretty cream, Justin."

The patient guide, Han taught him to suck it later. Showing him how to open his mouth so his lips covered his teeth, taking jerk in, making sure his lips slid down, caressing the shaft all the way around. And when you feel the tip against the back of your mouth to make one more reach with your lips, clamp firmly on the shaft and suck hard as you pull up your head. Until your lips feel the slick rim and catching the flared head (breathing through your nose), you dive down again, repeating the process, establishing a smooth up-and-down rhythm like a meditation.

He loved sucking Han's jerk as Justin and did it quite a few more times. He felt like he was kneeling before the coke legions, drinking at the fountain of fraternal solace, sucking wisdom from the warrior dogs! He told Justin what he'd done before the snag arrived and gave him his entire off-line stipend that year to pay for the extra fiber feed. He was no stranger to spending off-line time alone at the academy. Emboldened by his new passion, he made Justin an offer. For letting him continue to use Justin's avatar and take his weekly trips with Han, Harrison would, *in return* (it was definitely hard to spit it out), *suck off* Justin's jerk the way Han had taught him for the remainder of that cycle (with a wrap on it, of course).

Justin had wanted to know how often. Harrison could see he was very excited. He told him whenever he wanted, given the time and the privacy. Justin *readily* agreed, and that cycle was another life, one he'd completely blocked out, in which, for the first time, he felt any kind of connection to anyone, one in which Han revealed the unexpected resurrection of submission. The Screenrage was so shaken by the passion with which Harrison embraced his surrender he surprised himself with an unexpected expression of tenderness of his own, which *really* scared them both. After that, Harrison ran from the lure of vulnerability, afraid that if he took that path, he could never be the master of his own destiny. And all these decisions were made while he was completely unconscious of it. This tug of war going on inside regarding the Screenrage finally came into perspective. He was toying with the crazy idea of disarming Han again. Instinctively, he knew it was the only thing that stood a chance of deterring him from his escalating megalomania, a parting gift of naked vulnerability. It was crazy. It was the bomb.

———————

With everything he had to accomplish in the two hours leading up to this moment, Zim was lucky to come up with any cover IDs for Tooco, Ryka, and Sunsue. Servant class picked from the top of the list in the steward's files was the best he could do. Zim didn't have time to find physical matches. It was imperative that this drama they were about to initiate happened before the entry lock had enough time to identify the three. At the moment, the only thing the commandant's screen was recording was the back of Sunsue's and Ryka's heads, ministering to a patient whose blanket was pulled up over his head, shuddering with severe chills in the grip of a fever. The cap had to happen in the next few moments, or they'd be discovered as impostors! Luckily, Commandant Kilmor was inclined to move on.

"These are the others I'm viewing?"

"Yes, these three servants. The old one went into shock witnessing the explosion, and then he seemed to contract some kind of fever. As you can see, they are looking after him."

"And where is Kahn's personal robo?"

"In the pilot's cabin, online with the autopilot."

That was a mad dash! Zim slapped together a spare robot's arm, the casing of an off-line food replicator, and several other small appliances from the ship's galley. He fashioned it all into a facsimile of Cyrus, covering the whole thing with sheets of thin gold foil from Deli's personal niche, apparently used for wrapping presents. Inside the crude representation, Zim Jerry rigged a small battery to the autopilot so the scan would read an electrical connection. It should pass for long enough. And long enough should be right about now.

———————

Han was hiding from him in shock, blown away by his "romantic" ambush. Lying there on Deli's decadent mat, preparing for their docking, he decided to take Han's rallying cry to heart—fuck everything. Harrison gave in to that quixotic whim—if struggle couldn't alter Han's course, then maybe surrender would. But letting his reckless tube call the shots, he hadn't bargained on the seasoned coke he was now, coming along for the ride. Strangely, even though he hadn't played the part, since he was a cadet, he could feel that side of him profiting from his experience as well. Unlike the first time (Harrison hanging on for dear life), more comfortable now with his vulnerable charms, he consumed Han with a passionate innocence. And there was no escape from his attentions, not in the fifth. No escape for Han. Surprising him with a mouth schooled by his meticulous lessons, Han's jerk throbbed in an agony of anticipation. Finally taking him in, sinking onto Han's shaft, he again touched the wonder of a surrendering heart, almost forgotten in the barren depths. Rocking in a gentle rhythm, head nuzzled in the Screenrage's chest, tightening his tether on Han's root, he wrung him to a massive orgasm. No doubt Zim and Darl thought Han was laying it on pretty thick with all those expressive groans. Now all was quiet, and Han was hiding, confused and embarrassed. The tables were turned, the mad god bowed by passionate surrender. Soon Harrison would have to follow through.

Thankfully, the moment to move finally came. As he felt the scan begin to pass through them, he executed his pantomime. If the scanner could view the real scene in Deli's heaving chest, it would have recorded a severely compressed Harrison rapidly fanning his distorted limbs. What Commandant Kilmor's scanners viewed was Kahn Deli's heart going into full cardiac arrest. The life-signs monitor in Zim's hand began to scream. Playing inept physician to the hilt, he dropped it on Deli's convulsing chest.

"OH, DEAR DOG! DEAR DOG! I WON'T BE HELD RESPONSIBLE! I'M JUST A WITNESSING PHYSICIAN! I'M NOT RESPONSIBLE!"

Commandant Kilmor's stern visage immediately lit their screen. "Dr. Sandor, please! Calm yourself. Your ship has received its emergency routing.

You will be at the Kahn's med center in just a few moments. I suggest you do what you can for the Kahn until then."

With a disdainful yet worried expression, Kilmor disappeared. Almost immediately, they felt the cruiser lift up and catapult forward, hurling through Big New to Kahn Deli's majestic mode. On screen, a blur of octagonal pods flew by as Harrison emerged from his brief prison and came around the Kahn's mat, moving every few seconds to maintain invisibility. Han wasn't taking any chances either, still hiding behind his image. On screen, cruisers, cycles, and transports veered aside as they careened toward the heart of the burg where the tallest scrapers grew.

Their next challenge would appear on landing, when the cruiser's lock opened. Security robos would need to be convinced the real Kahn was under his image. At least until Harrison got the chance to administer some electronic sedatives, and after that came the clonie servants. More murders were only moments away. He had to follow through. He knew who Han was. If he had any doubt Han was completely ruthless after watching him casually hit a tap that vaporized a quarter of a million clones, then Carmine was right. He was the stupidest motherduffer who ever lived! And Han expected him to play the invisible reaper here too, if it came to that—if Zim ran into any trouble. He really had to follow through. He had to.

His best course was to stay on the String, then take off the second the cruiser's lock opened. But take off where? He couldn't go back to his old mode. It wasn't there. He couldn't spend the rest of his life wandering around on the String either. But if he shuddered into place on the moving walks without an ident, he'd be back in a container or dead in short order. There was always Bellytown, the urban legend, the dark twisted burg far beneath one's feet—the netherworld of belly slime. Harrison just couldn't bring himself to embrace that desperate choice.

He watched as Darl and Zim went tumbling across the thick carpet of Kahn's private niche when the megacruiser unexpectedly came to a sudden stop in the Kahn's entry port. Han almost slid from Deli's mat onto the deck. They hadn't strapped in for their emergency dash, or the sudden halt necessitated by the economical size of Deli's entry port. They barely had time to recover before the ship's outer lock opened. Two narrow stalks—security robos—whizzed in, sensors beeping on high alert due to their master's unexpected arrival.

Han turned Kahn's image toward them, lifting a hand in weak recognition while Harrison merged into each unit, switching all control directly to Deli's wrist organizer. Zim surreptitiously tapped out a few commands on his patient's wrist, and the annoying beeps were replaced by silence. He hit another tap, drumming a short rhythm into the organizer, and the screen changed from its monitoring glow to a view of the entry port where the cruiser was parked. It was empty, no other robos or servants. That meant they'd received no communications from either the entry port or 7. Zim's bypass had worked, and it was more than he could do to keep from releasing a little squeal of relief. Quickly regaining his composure, he activated the levi on Kahn's mat. Rising like an ancient bimbo in a magic act, Han groaned and clutched his chest.

"SERVANTS ON BOARD, TO THE OUTER LOCK, PLEASE. Quickly, quickly! The Kahn must be taken to the operating theater immediately!" Zim was hamming it up for 7.

Continuing in the role of idiot physician, Zim piloted Kahn's mat toward the cruiser's outer lock, preceded by the two security robos, now puppets in his world. Darl kept pace, holding on to Kahn's hand, murmuring reassurances. When they reached the cruiser's lock, Ryka, Sunsue, and a groggy Tooco were waiting for them. Surrounding Kahn's floating mat, the crew stepped out onto the entry port with their robos in the lead.

Zim kept up his chirping, "Quickly, quickly, to the operating theater."

Still invisible on the String, Harrison watched as they made their way across the gray octagon of the entry port hangar, heads darting furtively, half-expecting any moment to be challenged, honing on the entry lock of Deli's opulent mode.

Han would assume Harrison was hovering close by as they made their nervous march, but in fact, he was just outside the levi cruiser's exit lock, eyeing the hangar's lock plate as it began to iris shut. To run with the killers or leave everything he'd known? The decreasing circumference of the iris felt like a cord tightening around his throat. Not that he couldn't merge through a hangar lock if he chose to leave. But he'd already be expending enough precious core. *He could not believe he actually had to do this!* But this must be it. That long dreaded yet secretly hoped-for moment of reckoning where you find out if you're the person you've worked so hard to believe you are. Or you confess to yourself and everyone else that you've only been playing a role, and it's getting scary now, so can I please go mode.

At the far end of the hangar, the crew reached Deli's mode lock and waited as the security robos inside interfaced with Zim's crippling virus, quickly turning them into his drones. A brief instant later, Deli's lock slid open. Inside, Harrison could make out the forms of two servants and another security robo. At the other end of the hangar, the iris's diameter was down to less than a centigrid.

Was it true, the only destination was Tooco's stomping grounds? That he had to accept this as his only way to escape Han's ruthless destiny? There were the dreamers. Okada told him how Tooco came to speak "dreamer English" and used their hero "Shakes" as a come-on for his Bellytown hustles. What did she tell him was their leader's ID? It started with an *M*.

Repeatedly running across Shakespeare's ID in Cincinnati retrieval, he'd finally spent several minutes studying his collected works—*and this was* to be or not to be! To be part of some collective journey or to opt out—just sit back and watch as the murderous parade periodically passed by, sweeping it all away? A voice inside begged for the courage to follow through on a life examined—at least one attempt. Time's up . . . *to be.*

Harrison rocketed through a pinhole, soaring 270 levels above the grid plate of Big New. Now he had a long way to fall. If he surrendered all his Higgs-Boson particles to the gravity of the third dimension, it was the fastest way to get to Bellytown. But it was also the most dangerous, which was why he chose it. He'd set off on this journey to self-awareness because he was after finding a purpose, some personal reason for his life. And all he'd found so far was chaos and confusion, and membership in a band of ruthless killers. And now in order to escape their clutches, he had to give up everything he'd ever known and enter a toxic netherworld. *He was already committing suicide.* He half-hoped the fall would kill him.

There was only one way to survive the leap. He had to meld, if only for a nanosecond, with everything that came across his hurtling path. Performing the physical equivalent of a metaphysical act would be the only way to endure traveling at high velocity through a multiplicity of mass. Like the myth magicians surrendering their individual consciousness to open their eyes as the whole, he had to give himself up at once to everything!

At the last possible instant, he leapt to a reckless embrace with oblivion—just a split second before his path intersected with a skyway patrol cruiser monitoring crosstown traffic from level 111 down to level 101.

A fifth-dimensional hole opened up right through the fuselage, briefly exposing the cruiser to the mercy of moving objects and unfortunate happenstance. Harrison penetrated several more levi vehicles and their occupants in the thick of midtown traffic from level 55 to level 41. He rocketed through the grid plate, twenty centigrid of honeycombed titanium covered with strontium-yttrium. He bathed for a nanosecond in a swirling ocean of electromagnetic currents, finally diving into charred steel, scorched brick, melted glass, cindered wood, rusted pipes, smashed jars, rotted bones, and roach turds. A blazing journey of incarnations, myriad forms groping in endless transformation, interminable and over in an instant. Welcome to Bellytown.

He wasn't sure how long he was merged with the rotting remains of some long-ago mode. He felt like he'd been unconscious for quite a while. He explored the muck in which he was congealed, until he was certain he had all his fingers and toes. Separating from the moldy matter, Harrison came shuddering up off the String to lie, spent and dazed, on a rotting heap. When he sat up, the precariousness of his perch became apparent. He was still, at least, thirty levels above the streets of the subterranean burg, and his mound of ancient refuse rested on a blackened beam no more than two centigrid long and two-thirds of a centigrid wide. Above him, he could make out the charred steel skeletons of the old scrapers and a vast network of red girders connecting these steel skeletons into a field of charcoal towers. Above that were the purple eddies of a magnetic ocean churning under Big New's grid plate—the constant electric night of Bellytown.

In this expansive jungle gym, he could make out several cocoon-like modes stretching the full length of several of those red girders. That's where Bellytown magnates watched over their burg. According to Han, not very long ago, his father counted his Yuan in one of those overlord mansions. Viewing this bizarre underworld, taking in its secular futility, the backdrop for Han's existential cynicism was readily apparent.

Harrison's analysis was interrupted by two scabs on a beat-up levi cycle, screaming and hooting as they buzzed by. They spotted him. He watched as they made a U-turn, coming back to take a closer look. He popped the chest plate on the carnelian game jump worn to Deli's the night before as part of their ruse. There'd been no opportunity to change. The jump's red sheen attracted attention down here. He'd have to find some kind of cloak if he wanted to be more inconspicuous. He pulled out the Berretta and thumbed the safety off. Using it meant the possibility of a Sacker drone coming to investigate, but hopefully, they had other things on their mind.

The scabs were closing. He could see the one riding on back carried a kind of spear or lance. Crouching, Harrison used his knee as an armrest and aimed at the driver.

Pop! Pop! The little noisemaker created a definite impression, flames jumping from the barrel with each shot. He saw the second-round spark against the front cover of the cycle's E-Mags. It quickly veered away, diving into the mysterious depths. He put the pistol back in his chest compartment and slapped it shut. He was still feeling queasy from the journey down, but it was probably best to get a move on before any other locals came around for a peep.

He began moving carefully down the charred steel, making his way toward one of the larger red beams that linked the spidery forms. After fifteen minutes of cautious progress, he made his way to a red girder. His estimation of their larger size was correct. At over two centigrid wide, they were three times the width of the charred scraper beams. They could function as a narrow highway for any rudimentary transport the scavenging hordes of Bellytown would be privy to. No sooner did he step on the girder than a figure appeared in the distance, "peddling" what had to be a "bicycle." Again, Harrison popped his chest plate and took out the pistol, but this time, kept it hidden at his side.

As the spindly conveyance trundled closer, an intermittent headlamp provided the rider with snapshot views of the way ahead. Now he could see it was piloted by a tube-born, probably a sheed from the length of the hair and the ragged cone-shaped garment called a dress.

He didn't think she'd spotted him from this distance. She made no move to stop or change course, peddling steadily and with an air of detached aplomb, even going so far as to glance the other way, over the girder to the view below. When she did approach, he realized she was aware of his presence, reaching back to grab the handle of a machete slung across her back. She turned to stare him down with a grim little face, certain of dominion. But as she passed (looking him up and down), her expression changed to one of shock and fear. She started peddling away faster. Panicked at missing an opportunity to speak with a relatively harmless denizen, Harrison called after her in Amerab.

"Cao, cao, capamoe!"

She rode on without even a backward glance, her tattered print billowing out behind her. In desperation, he tried the only other language he knew. "HEY, WAIT! STOP!" Instantly, she brought the contraption to a tire-squealing halt, turning her suspicious look back to him. A tangled mass of red hair falling over her shoulders and framing her face only served to focus the intensity of her glare.

"How do you know English?" Her reedy voice was braced by an unflustered determination.

"I learned it up there." Harrison pointed toward the grid plate.

"You're Topgrid?" That she thought he was lying was obvious in the sly sneer that accompanied her question.

"I was."

"Then how did you get here?"

"It's a long story. How did you learn English?"

She watched him a moment before answering. "Mayra."

Mayra, right! The dreamers . . . Mayra. This sheed must be a dreamer tube-born. Her soot-smudged face did nothing to hide the fact she was screwing her courage to the sticking point, continuing this conversation.

"Answer my question, how did you get here?"

"I committed a crime, and they sent me to the mines. I escaped . . . and now I'm here."

Her green eyes grew wider. Taking a foot from the pedals, she swung herself off the contraption, wheeling it back around to face him. "What crime?"

"I stole a thing called a thought recorder. I wanted to make a personal record."

She stood staring at him for a long moment. Just as he was beginning to think she might be undergoing some form of mutant seizure, she gently laid the bicycle down on the girder and ran toward him. A couple centigrid away, he observed pink tattoos on her cheeks tracing down her dirty face.

"You're here! You're finally here!"

Before he could stop her, the little tube-born was hugging his feet, sobbing into his boots. When he couldn't stand it anymore, he put the Berretta in his chest compartment, bent down, and pulled her up, gently holding her by the shoulders. "Hey, hey, cappy . . . come on."

She stopped crying, blinking rapidly to clear away the tears. "Yes, you're right."

Harrison released her, and almost instantly, she was moving. Racing to her bicycle, she grabbed it, leapt on, and pedaled furiously away back in the direction she'd come. Looking over her shoulder, she yelled back to Harrison, "STAY HERE! YOU'RE SAFE! DON'T MOVE! STAY DOWN! I'LL BE BACK! I'LL BE BACK!"

He watched her go, eventually disappearing in the maze of blackened steel. He thought about her directives. She was from the dreamers, and while now he thought they were probably his best bet down here, suddenly, he felt afraid—afraid "purpose" might turn out to be more than he bargained for. He sat down, leaning up against one lip of the girder, and peered into the heart of Bellytown with its winking lights and faint mechanical sounds. After what seemed like quite a while, he remembered to check his pistol. He removed the Berretta's near-empty clip and replaced it with a full clip from his chest compartment. Thankfully, he'd thought to grab all the magazines, along with a box of shells, off their levi-loader in Deli's cruiser. At the time, he'd done it so the illegal weapon and ammunition would be spirited with him into the fifth dimension, hidden from the scan. But now it might prove to be a lifesaver in this metallic jungle. He was reluctant to admit it, but he'd grown fond of the sculpted piece of steel. He liked its raw bark and the precise little holes it made. They gave some dignity to dying instead of the smoking pile of "slice and dice" a frybar left behind.

He loaded a round into the chamber and was about to click the safety on when he saw the tops of two heads just beneath him coming out from under the girder. They were probably the ones he'd shot at earlier, sneaking up on him. As they slowly rose up next to the girder, both were shocked to discover Harrison pointing the pistol at them.

The driver was a tall, thin scab with boils all over his head. Behind him was a smaller coke without a nose, just flaps of skin over two holes in the center of his face. He was quick, bringing the lance up to his shoulder just before Harrison put two more holes in his face. He went tumbling off the cycle down into Bellytown. The driver froze.

"Plait, mufu." Realizing his smattering of Amerab was actually going to come in handy, he pointed to the spot on the girder where he wanted the scab to land the cycle. Without hesitation, the coke did as he was told, setting the battered old levi down in front of him.

"Baggit, looty raggso!"

Again, the coke quickly obeyed, jumping off the bike and stepping back. He removed his long black cloak and tossed it to Harrison. In nothing but ragged skiwies, Harrison could see his entire body was covered with the boils. Terrified by his strange weapon, the scab stared at it with large yellow eyes.

"Baggwah!"

The scab backed up still farther. Harrison draped the cloak over his own shoulders, praying his game jump would protect him from catching the scab's gross disease. For the moment, he had little choice. The red beacon that was his jump had to be extinguished.

Harrison swung up onto the machine and checked out the controls. It was a very old Sacker bike, probably snagged by a headhunter out in the waste fill twenty cycles ago, just a joystick go-and-stop pedals. Even a mutant like the one standing in front of him could operate this machine. Activating the drive and pulling back gently on the joystick, he slowly lifted the bike off the girder. Keeping the pistol trained on the coke until he was hovering a couple centigrid above him, Harrison considered his options.

He knew the little sheed told him to wait, but it had been quite a while, and he was a stationary target here. Also, he was weak from hunger. He needed to get something to eat soon.

"Foo? Wafoo?"

Looking perplexed, the scab gestured over the lip of the girder. "Duh."

"Great! Thanks a lot." He pushed the go pedal hard, briefly jerking the joystick up, forward, and down. Leaping clear of the girder, the battered cycle shot toward the heart of Bellytown. The cycle's search beam was broken, so he slowed to avoid hitting hidden scraper shards that might loom up during his descent.

At ten levels, he could discern figures on the crumbled black ribbons that crisscrossed the mutant lair. Most were on foot, but a few traveled in ground vehicles of wildly varying design. He saw several more bicycles.

Who had she thought he was?

He was surprised by how much activity went on beneath the swirling sky of Bellytown. At various places where ribbons intersected, there were groups of scabs huddled around small platforms. Each platform had a single figure standing on it displaying an item and gesticulating wildly. Beside these platforms, a coke stood flipping through a series of cards running through numbers one to thirty.

It took him a while to realize they were snagging. He watched as cokes with various objects jumped on the platforms and began hawking their wares. They had thirty seconds to get the highest bid they could, then leapt off the platform and made room for the next entrepreneur.

Different street gangs, identifiable by a particular badge or garment, ran the platforms at these intersections. They guaranteed the safety of both snagger and snaggie inside the intersection and while entering or leaving it. Bartering clones were definitely more prone to violence. He watched as a scab hiding in a trash pile with a hatchet savagely decapitated another scab, then grabbed his sack and scuttled into a side alley.

According to the cycle's readout, which was still functional, the vertical E-Mags were at negative polarity. At first, he thought it was just a glitch in the decrepit system until he realized, down here, under the positively charged grid plate and surrounded by the positively charged grid girders, maximum vertical propulsion was achieved by the attraction of negative vertical E-Mags to the monolithic positive grid plate, where as in Big New, it was the repulsion of positive E-Mags from the positive grid plate. In short, down here, surrounded by positive polarity, you doubled your options—being able to choose either being repelled or attracted, as your means of conveyance, in every direction. On the surface of it, it didn't seem like a big deal. But for a pilot, nimble at switching E-Mag polarities, amazing acrobatics were possible.

In the distance, he could see towers rising up as high as fifteen levels. Built inside the ruins of former scrapers, their bizarre shapes were blurred, as if covered with gauze. That must be the cable mesh Han referred to when describing Yakuza sector. Below him now, almost all the modes were one- or two-level affairs erected on the rubble and patched together from an array of materials. Many of these hovels demonstrated a distinct personal touch.

Since there was no other air traffic in the immediate area, he decided to risk dropping down a few levels to get a better look at some of these structures. One that caught his eye, because of its size and brilliant colors, was comprised of large slabs of melted plastic from twentieth advertising signs, beveled then bolted together in mutual support. It rose above its neighbors a full three levels and reminded him of a "holo" in the poker room at the Pacino "House of Cards."

It was probably headquarters for one of the many streetlords Han talked about. Although he knew he was being reckless, he decided to drop as low as five levels. On the flat roof of the plastic outpost, three sheed appeared, tall and brown-skinned with long black hair. They were gesturing for him to come down and land. They all wore shiny black halters with matching shorts. Each had a red sash crossing from one shoulder to the opposite hip. This must be one of Bellytown's infamous bordellos. He was low enough now to see they were all attractive, their amber skin taut over graceful musculature, but he really just wanted something to eat. He took out the Berretta and laid it in his lap.

"YADA, PUTA, TOOTA!" The most curvaceous of the three was being very graphic about what she had in mind. They all started shouting, beckoning frantically for him to land. He was hungry enough to take the chance. What the hell, they probably snagged food. He still had most of the Yuan Han gave him to party after his String match. Pulling the joystick back and punching the stop pedal, the old levi lowered itself onto the lumpy plastic ten centigrid from the sheed. He wanted to give himself a little distance. It turned out to be a wise decision. No sooner had he touched down than all three sheed bent to scoop up camouflaged bows from the bubbled deck. Reaching into the canisters strapped to their backs by those red sashes, they pulled out metal shafts and notched them into their archaic weapons, drawing a bead on Harrison.

"BAGGIT!" Again, the most voluptuous of the three motioned with her razor tip, pointing in the direction she wanted him to move. He swung off the cycle so it was between them, opening fire with the Berretta while ducking behind the bike. Two arrows hit him in either shoulder as another one went whizzing by his head. He managed to hit the shapely leader twice in the left breast before he was knocked back by the arrows' impacts. The shoulder armor on his jump easily deflected the arrows tips, but the force they struck with badly skewed his aim. He fired another three rounds without hitting the other two.

They'd both strung new shafts before he squeezed off his sixth shot, hitting the one on his right high in the center of her forehead, punching a hole through the red headband she wore. As she flew backward, sprawling across the gelatinous plastic, the final sheed loosed her missile. Harrison barely turned his head in time as the shaft rocketed by less than a milligrid from his neck. He shot her in the stomach three times, and she stumbled to her knees, still trying to reach back into her canister. Harrison ran up and shot her in the top of the head. With a final spasm, she fell face-first onto the blood-splattered deck.

How long had he been conscious in Bellytown, an hour? And already he'd killed a coke and three sheed. Admittedly, all in self-defense. As far as being a mass murderer, he still had a ways to go catching up to Han. But it looked like Bellytown offered opportunities galore to run up your tote board. At present, he needed to get back on his Levi-cycle. Muffled shouts were issuing from a trapdoor the sheed must have come from.

In four bounds, he was back in the saddle, amping the negative charge in his vertical E-Mags to the limit, taking advantage of the unique magnetic forces. He yanked back the joystick and shot up six levels almost in an instant! Although not completely out of range from several sheed rapidly firing over their fallen comrades, he could easily track their missiles and avoid them with a flick of the wrist. Faintly, he heard them cursing him in Amerab.

He was heading for the center of Bellytown and the Yakuza sector. He kept his eyes peeled for Sacker drones or cruisers, just in case they came roaring through the purple haze, honing in on recent explosions. Soon he was close enough to clearly see the curtain of steel cables surrounding a 256-square-grid area and stretching up all the way to the lowest grid girder. This was where the Yakuza drew the line. The openings in this giant web were less than a half a centigrid wide. While a skinny coke might slip in, he'd never maneuver a levi cycle through it. If it was larger than a king-size box of soya chips, it didn't go in or out except through a Yakuza checkpoint.

He swerved down into an air lane used by traffic approaching the mesh. He spotted the checkpoint they were all heading toward. He was down low enough now he could make out the flashy jumps on Yaki buttons interspersed throughout the crowds. A Levi cruiser swung in behind him. He caught a look at it in the twentieth rear-view mirror some scab bolted above the handle grips to replace a broken rear screen. Not the Sacker cruiser he was half-expecting, it was a beat-up Douglas with ancient rubber wheels bolted on for easy takeoffs and landings out in the waste fill. Behind the cockpit, it sported a large rack with a mountain of booty strapped under a tarp. Layers of oily grime coated every surface, with the exception of the pilot's canopy. Suddenly cruising up alongside him, the burnt hairy face of a headhunter grinned at him before blasting by.

Closing fast on the Yakuza checkpoint into Yaki sector, he was having second thoughts about whether it was really worth the risk to get a closer look at the belly of the beast. They must be reeling from the destruction of Sanatan, if they knew about it yet. Depending on how long he was unconscious, Han had tapped out its doom something over twelve hours ago. They probably had direct fiber feeds up to the techie quarter. They'd just think there was a break in the fiber or a power failure. Maybe they'd send somebody up to check it out. If they did that—and he supposed they would—then they'd know soon. They'd go nuts when they found out. Sanatan was the major outlet for most all high-tech Yakuza plunder. Not to mention gambling, drugs, and live-bait prostitution.

It was probably wise to steer clear for now. He whipped to his right and took it down to street level, cruising just above the single-level hovels of an encampment, encroaching on the Yaki perimeter. Hopefully, he was passing for local traffic. He noticed a lot of pub signs flashing below. Upon closer inspection, this little encampment was pretty much wall-to-wall bars, no doubt catering to the need for some liquid courage before entering the lord of mammon's lair. It was also a place where he could take care of his now-crippling hunger. He must have been unconscious for quite a while to be this ravenous.

⸺•❖•⸺

Impatient, she stomped her boot into the packed dirt between the ties. She was down on the tracks, hoping for better reception from the field radio. With one hand, she held the heavy olive-colored rucksack by the straps, twisting it around to change the position of the antenna that extended from the top of the pack. There wouldn't be any reception down here at all without the amplified relay antennas sprouting up into Cenpak, retransmitting signals into the tunnels. She listened, cradling the receiver between her chin and shoulder.

Two levels below the street, she had a clear view up and down the 103rd Street shuttle line. She could see both the IRT platform at one end and the platform for the IND line at the opposite end. With her free hand, she raised a pair of binoculars hanging from around her neck and focused on the shuttle platform below the Broadway station.

In the cone of yellow light, she could see the Upper Westside patrol returning.

She looked up to see her second-in-command, Yasmine, watching from the crumbled subway platform. "What is it, Ma?"

Mayra ignored the question. Walking a few paces down the tracks, she spoke into the receiver, "Put her on!"

She could count on the girl to give her an exact replay of everything they said. The children of Outriders were as focused on the mission as their parents. They had to be. They lived on the grid girders their parents patrolled, searching for what this girl was proclaiming she'd just found. When the girl's father made contact, he was already on his way to the spot where she'd left him. Upon his arrival moments later, Mongrel told Mayra he was gone. Now she wanted to hear it from Teeba. She remembered her from around the Duni fires, a self-possessed phantom of a girl.

"Yes, Mother?"

"Repeat every word of the conversation you had with this man."

Mayra listened, feeling an unexpected sympathy for Lot's wife, hearing the words the tiny voice slipped in her ear. The girl's halting account mirrored her own strange anguish at once terrified and triumphant.

It couldn't be. Strangely, it felt like it shouldn't be. Dreams are meant to remain dreams. The dream should never become realized. It was, after all, a hopeful but improbable outcome, designed to inspire one to persevere? At best, prophesies were seen "through a glass darkly."

But every word was precisely as it came from the fire, and in his final sentence: "I wanted a personal record."

Dear God, to have him appear just as their collective vision portrayed him, in red armor and saying the exact words! There was no way around it. He was here. But where exactly?

"Thank you, Teeba. Put Mongrel back on."

"Yes, Mother." She heard the girl passing the radio and then a low grow.

"Yeah, Ma?"

"Make sure every outpost on the girders sends out patrols. *Find him!* Contact me immediately when you do. Out."

The fear came roaring in. What if the Yaks got him first? Prophesies weren't chiseled in stone, not if they wanted to be realized. Like everything else, they arrived a step at a time; and at every step, just a poke in the wrong direction for prophesy to become erroneous speculation. They had to find him.

She'd been on edge already this morning, with reports from listening posts at the other crosstown tunnels: the E tunnel at Fiftieth, the Flushing Express at Forty-Second, and L-Shuttle at Fourteenth. They were all picking up much more traffic heading into the Yaki sector. Was it feasible they knew he was here and were looking too? No, it couldn't be. It was something else, maybe scabs heading for the safety of the mesh in front of another attack at Fifty-Ninth? Not likely. Less than a month ago, patrolling on their barricade of twisted steel and brick, they spotted another sneak attack coming down Fifth Avenue. This time, Splatter followed orders, falling back into the steel maze and alerting the laser cannons. They'd blown them straight to hell! They wouldn't be trying that again anytime soon!

Mayra offered a silent prayer of thanks every time she remembered their incredible, good fortune. Until today, that was the latest miracle they had to be grateful for. Three years earlier, coming into Big New, a Sacker transport blew an E-Mag, suddenly dipping beneath the grid plate and crashing in the northern sector of their desolate plot. They jumped on the opportunity, employing the camouflage netting used to hide their corn crops before Big New appeared over them, blocking the sun. Quickly covering up the transport wreckage, they slipped back into the tunnels. Sacker squadrons combed Bellytown for hours before heading out toward the Hudson. Since they couldn't find it, they assumed the transport must have crashed in the river. Two days later, once they were positive the Sackers had given up looking, they came back. Winching the huge crates from the transport onto flatbed trucks, they took them to the hydraulic-lift platform underneath the bridle path bridge at Seventy-Eighth. They grabbed everything of consequence and erased all signs of the crash. They salvaged four laser cannons, twenty-four levi cruisers, twenty-seven levi cycles, seventy-two frybars, and the amazing *Firewalker*, which finally turned the tide in their war with the Yaks.

But what were they up to now? She couldn't take the chance. She'd have to send somebody under the mesh to make sure it wasn't about him and to find out what was causing all this traffic. Mayra turned to Yasmine. She already had the tall redhead's full attention. She'd been doing her best to follow the conversation, and although Yasmine couldn't have heard Teeba's words, Mayra could see she knew something monumental was going down. Mayra extended her hand, and Yasmine took it, pulling her back up onto the platform.

"Go see if Splatter's back. I think that might be his patrol down at the Broadway station. Ask him if he's up for a trip under the mesh?"

"Yeah, Ma." Yasmine was about to leave, but Mayra caught her arm, looking in those large cat eyes. "Yasmine." There was nothing to do but say it. "He's here."

The expected look of shock registered on her face, and Mayra rushed on, "The girl Teeba met him on the girders about an hour ago. He said the words exactly, and he was wearing the red armor." She waited, giving Yasmine a little time to deal with her own fears concerning fulfillment before she gave her lieutenant the bad news. "She told him to stay put and she'd be right back, then rode to her father's outpost and got him. When they came back, he was gone. We need to find him!"

"Right." A huge grin broke across Yasmine's pale yet radiant face. Mayra was both heartened and embarrassed by the realization; not everybody focused on their foreboding when acknowledging a miracle. "Don't worry, Ma. We'll get him." Yasmine leaped onto the old subway car, stripped to just the frame and wheels and fitted with a flat aluminum bed. There was another just like it at the IND end of the twin tracks. They were used to ferry goods and personnel from the major lines down to a series of storerooms located along the 103rd shuttle tunnel. They were originally used by subway workers to store tools and materials. They also served as transport down to two large caverns they'd dug themselves—the Duni cavern and their library. Yasmine fired up the six-cylinder engine and called back to Mayra.

"I'll find Splatter. Be right back." The steel wheels clicked down the track toward the IRT platform.

Mayra remembered when they first heard those words at the Duni: "I wanted a personal record," with flames leaping to twice her height. Her father was the one who introduced the ritual to their ragged band. He witnessed it in a place called Meherabad, India, in his globe-trekking youth. At first, it was just a popular way of gathering as a community. It wasn't until later it gained its "spiritual" significance.

In their variation, instead of dipping the renunciation sticks in flammable wax, the dreamers used axle grease: burning purple and green in the white-hot coals. With every stick you tossed in the fire, you vowed to surrender something—whatever preyed on your mind, generating fear and turmoil in your heart. They had their first collective vision far in advance of Mayra's monumental one. It was five years before Mayra was even born. They all watched as the smoke curled into a magnificent ship that floated above the flames in exquisite detail, until the smoke vent in the subterranean cavern sucked it away. Sarah said Sam called it "God's replacement for television."

She was still conflicted over her fascination with screens. They found dozens, along with as many DVD players. Later, Danner got online with two net screens that techies left behind when they moved to Sanatan. He tapped into several fiber feeds transmitting from Big New. It's how they got the information they had about what Topgrid were up to. Those screens were located at the Forty-Second Street, Time Square, subway station in a large cement room. Once the control center for the Seventh Avenue line (running trains between Manhattan and Queens), it was transformed into their war bunker now.

The first thirty years before she was born were a slow back-breaking climb from the ashes to a secure network of tunnels in the remains of the subway lines. They lived primarily on rat meat. Of course, all the rats in Manhattan who could make a run for it joined their tunnel brethren when the incendiaries started to fall. There were rat "herds" roaming the tunnels those first thirty years. Also, they managed to grow a first crop of corn in Cenpak, seeded from "Jiffy Pop" popcorn poppers.

They planted their crop in the fields around Croton reservoir, using drip irrigation made with rolls of plastic tubing found in one of the store rooms at 103rd. The first order of business was to plug up and camouflage every entrance outside of Cenpak in the city's subway system. That was long before the Yaks showed up back when only a few scabs roamed the cindered ruins. Then they'd dug their own tunnel, extending from the entrance to the IRT, at Fifty-Ninth, down to Fifth Avenue.

It wasn't until she was seven years old when the first vision came to her, and it changed everything. It was right after that, he first appeared in the Duni flames. From a cluster of yellow coals in the center of the fire, a red figure rose, glowing brighter than the flames. Burning arms held high in one hand a book, in the other a blade of white light. Then they all heard those words:

"I wanted a personal record." Forty years ago.

Not that she looked forty-seven. Because dreamers really were subterranean, avoiding even minimal exposure to the scant UV rays that slipped under the grid plate, they appeared to age more slowly. In any case, she had the body of an athletic thirty-year-old and the face of a siren with a hangover. The look appealed to more males than she expected. Of course, her position had something to do with it, but she never got the feeling any of them thought they were doing her a favor—just the opposite. It had been quite a while, though. Who had time for those urges anymore? Not her, at any rate.

Hearing the story of their beginnings curled in Sam's lap, she listened to him describe how they came to be living in a subterranean room off the walled-up entrance of the Forty-Second Street and Third Avenue, IND. As a founder of their band, he was a commander and was housed close to the war room. Most dreamers lived in cavern communes. Despite the sad tales her father was forever recounting, she remembered that little room fondly.

He always described, with the same detached pity, the broken methhead he'd become just before 3TC. Like her other subterranean forefathers living underground in the city's subway tunnels, foraging food in restaurant Dumpsters, he was just another "burnout" lost in a lost world, who—stumbling from his rat hole on January 5, 2025, found a subway platform of hysterical people screaming the atomic holocaust was nigh. Because it wasn't until three days later that New York was finally hit, he could only surmise whatever missiles were first fired at them got knocked down or went astray. After two days back in their tunnels, drunk with terror, they emerged for a quick look around and found a deserted city. They went on a rampage, scavenging anything left behind in looted grocery and liquor stores. Because everybody was in such a hurry to get out of "Dodge," they managed to pull in quite a haul.

There was dancing in the streets that night and on into the morning, a beggar's opera of anarchy, until a squadron of what (a convert from Newark later swore) were US planes carpet-bombed the entire city with incendiaries!

"Vonnegut's Dresden all over again." Her father always ended the story by invoking an ancient tragedy. They figured it was done to keep whatever enemy survived from enjoying the Big Apple's spoils. Needless to say, all the burnout revelers were incinerated in midjig on the bubbling asphalt. Actually, the heat was so intense only those who made it into the deeper crosstown tunnels at 14th, 42nd, 50th, and 103rd survived.

The downdraught of cooler air into Central Park's undeveloped expanse acted like a giant bellows creating a "forge" effect. Furnace heat transformed the skyscrapers and apartment buildings bordering the park into a monumental jungle gym comprised of melted steel, brick, and glass. Later, the dreamers were quick to explore, occupy, and then fortify this barricade, bordering the one place where they staked their claim—the remains of Central Park. Through her binoculars, she could see Yasmine returning down the tracks with Splatter.

The damn few who survived the bombing hid under the cremated metropolis for over three decades, continuing to plug up and camouflage (with whatever salvage available) all the subway entrances. They scavenged what they could on short forays into the cindered five boroughs. Their life in the tunnels endowed them with night vision that rivaled a cat's. Then her mother, Sarah, met her father, Sam. Sarah was intrigued by the store of books and historical documents Sam said they discovered under a small park while plugging up a subway entrance. She decided to come take a look at what they now called Cenpak. She liked it and eventually felt the same way about Sam.

They were married at a Duni and had a little girl named Mayra—who, staring into the flames, saw their first deliverance! It was a treasure on the other side of the wall in the Fourteenth Street shuttle tunnel. A bounty easily overshadowing anything Cortez laid his mitts on. Because her parents insisted on pursuing this vision, they took her down into the tunnel and walked it slowly as she scanned the walls, hoping to recognize the spot she'd seen. She did, and they fell in with a pickaxe taken from the Bronx and fitted with a new wooden handle. When they finally broke through the tunnel wall, they found themselves in the second sublevel of the Fourteenth Street National Guard Armory. Everything they needed to survive and prosper was in abundance in three vast sublevels of this main National Guard repository. Weapons, ammunition, mountains of freeze-dried food (enough food to feed one million people for a month), batteries, generators, medical supplies, two machine shops, machining tools, drugs, vitamins, clothing, forklifts, jeeps, and trucks. Even a small bio-fuel refinery for providing fresh gasoline and diesel fuel was included. Apparently, army brass had considered the possibility of a crippling blow to all of infrastructure. Fast food restaurant grease-traps turned out to be a gold mine for making those bio-fuels. Encased in cement and buried beneath the surface, most had survived the fire storm.

The dregs of a lost civilization were given the opportunity for one more attempt. Given their collective experience of failure in past society, they deduced the intense pressure they'd felt to live up to "certain standards" had invariably led them to become liars—lying to themselves and everyone else—with any genuine identity, disintegrating from constant deception and ensuing guilt. They made a decision to refrain from establishing any rules for behavior outside the most basic standards of human decency. They agreed to spend less time judging others and more time assessing their own lives. They made a solemn vow to reveal themselves honestly to one another and revere the ideal of a diverse community.

In time, from detailed city maps, they also found inside the armory, showing locations of various public and federal buildings that had underground facilities. They discovered and mined several other stores of wealth: a huge cache of drugs with medical supplies and instruments in storerooms next to the subterranean morgue at Beth-Israel Hospital.

They equipped some trucks with wheels off the subway cars to carry their bounty on the tracks of the IRT line up from Fourteenth Street to their communal cave dwellings just below Ninety-Sixth. When a speedy trip was required, down either the IRT or IND lines (thanks to the supervisor of the Con-Ed garage, who'd stored his automotive jewels there), a pristine 1968 Plymouth Roadrunner was ready just off the rails of the IND, and a yellow 1969 Camaro "Bumble Bee" waited just off the IRT. Either could be on the rails in a matter of seconds and make it from 103rd down to 14th in under a minute!

The deliverer had appeared to them twice, at their celebratory Duni after discovering the National Guard Armory, when he spoke those words, and at the very next Duni after that. The second time, he warned them they were about to have visitors.

The following week, swarms of techies descended on the cindered city, soon to be joined by their Yakuza parasites. They began construction of the grid plate for a great domed city, which, five years later, would be suspended above their heads. Mayra's visions continued and became clearer. And she discovered sometimes she could take them all into a communal vision, although she wasn't able to control when that happened, and it hadn't happened for a while. "The dreamers of Cenpak," as they half-jokingly referred to themselves, started to believe in a destiny. There were twenty-seven of them left the day after the city was turned to cinders. Today they were seven hundred and fifty-seven souls.

Yasmine arrived with Splatter beside her. They mounted the platform, standing in front of the oversized desk where Mayra did most of her strategizing. Other than the stacks of papers and maps arrayed over its surface, the only additional objects on the platform were a beat-up metal file cabinet, a large bulletin board covered with assorted pieces of paper, and the padded swivel chair Mayra was occupying. She wasted no time. "Did Yasmine tell you?"

The velvet blackness of his pallor made way for a crimson blush across his cheeks. He kept it short. "Yeah, Ma. He's here."

"Right. Now, there've been reports of unusual activity, increased traffic, at the checkpoints into Yaki sector. I want you to go in and find out what's up—probably Third and Twenty-Seventh will be your best bet. Use a headhunter cover and hit some of the bars just outside the mesh. Find out anything you can. He's wearing the red armor. It'll make him stick out like a sore thumb. Hopefully, being our deliverer, he'll be smart enough to figure that out and do something about it. So don't fixate on that. Keep your eyes open for anybody acting strange. The Outrider girl Teeba spotted him about an hour ago on the eastside girders. If you spot him, bring him back immediately. If you don't spot him, I want you to go under the mesh and take a look around. Try to find out what all the activity is about. That's it."

Splatter's eyelids slowly shuttered on his unwavering stare. "Got it." Turning abruptly, he headed back to the flatbed of the transport car.

Yasmine followed him, glancing back to Mayra. "The word is out to all patrols. We'll find him."

Standing on the aluminum bed of the car, Splatter kept his eyes on Mayra until he was only a dot. There was something going on there. She couldn't tell whether he was angry or infatuated. She'd chewed his ass thoroughly for not following orders, but that dark blush made her think it might possibly be something else—oh, to be in a world with that luxury. She hoped it wouldn't distract him. Yaks were never an enemy to drop your guard around. Unlike their namesake—the Japanese crime syndicate of a century past—they were comprised now of all remnants of nationality. All the existential outlaws who loved tattoos and managed to survive a megatonnage shakeup that, once and for all, divided the haves and have-nots. The Yaki hoard rose from the ashes and bounded back into the jungle. "In the bush" for a long time, they espoused a perverted Samurai perspective, which empowered them to butcher men, women, and children without compunction. They managed to establish themselves as minor subcontractors to the techies, salvaging metals and various machine components (especially hydraulics) for them. They also opened their pleasure emporiums, hooking techies on Nitro meth in the process. Many of those techies went on to become dealers to the Topgrid who had a bigger problem than 7 cared to acknowledge. At least that's how their version of "soap operas" were framing their epidemic on their fiber feeds.

When techies started arriving, they were curious but cautious about exploring Bellytown. Some dreamers, herself, included, came up from the tunnels and invited them into Cenpak—not into the tunnels, never in the tunnels, or even near their entrances. They steered them away from their camouflaged corn and took them out into barren fields and through the small groves of trees they planted stubbornly hanging on, ending up at Lennon's knoll. In the end, they made only one techie convert, but he turned out to be a vital one.

After techies completed the city, finally suspending Big New above them, they headed north to begin work on Sanatan. The Yakuza stayed, reigning over the lower half of old Manhattan while dominating the rest of the boroughs with the exception of Cenpak. The Yaks used their mesh-covered stronghold as a marketplace for headhunters from the south, north, west, and even across the Atlantic. They turned the Lower Eastside into warehouses and staging areas for deliveries from their primary suppliers and shipments to their primary markets—the techie quarter in Sanatan and several scab colonies out in the waste fill.

Luckily, the first few years, the Yaks took them for just another band of mutant scabs who happened to be held up inside some serious defenses, guarding a barren piece of dirt nobody wanted. Besides, back then, Yaks had bigger fish to fry in Sanatan. Over the past few years, they'd become a big fish too as rumors of their cache of twentieth weapons and supplies grew. But the arrival of their deliverer made that a minor concern she'd deal with when she had the time. Right now, they had to find him.

⸻ ❧ ⸻

"WHAT THE HELL IS GOING ON?" He was pacing the fourth-story wraparound balcony of Kahn's palatial pentmode at the top of Deli Tower. The last eight hours were the most frustrating, infuriating, and nerve-racking he'd spent since being bagged by Sackers in this very building nine cycles ago. Maybe he should take a quick levitator ride down to the 247th level and ask Darl's father for some advice on his current situation. All capping aside, he was close to undone.

Everything was humming along so perfectly, and then it all went to hell! Oh, they'd barely managed to pull off their deception, mostly thanks to Zim. He had to admit, Zim really stepped up. Han spent the whole time hidden away, pleading with Harrison, who (he finally had to admit) was gone. And that was after their . . . whatever! He really didn't know what their unexpected assignation in Deli's cruiser was—some demented payback? Had Jack figured out the pheromones? He'd warned Darl not to get carried away rewarding Tooco. But, as usual, she became drunk with her powers, enamored with watching him turn into her dribbling slave. She'd been spraying all over the place! Even his little ménage on the mat was spurred on by the contact high. Did Jack put it all together on the trip down? She'd obviously enjoyed humiliating him when he popped in on her indiscretion. She savored her dominion over both of them, sucking Tooco onto his back

270

while Harrison watched. Shittin' on luv was a favorite of Darl's. There were several wayward Sackers at the mines who could testify. One even drowned himself in the Pacific on his off-line time. Had it finally occurred to Jack that there was something wrong with this picture when he still wanted to fuck her anyway?

But if that were the case, wouldn't it be Han who took a jerk up the ass? No, it just didn't make any sense, and he couldn't figure out a way that it did. I mean, honestly, Jack surrendered to him with more vulnerability and passion than Darl had since they were on her balcony. He hadn't experienced that in a long time. Though he was definitely surprised when it happened, he'd just gone ahead and accepted it as his due, figuring Jack must be carrying a secret torch for him from the fiber feeds, and he'd chosen the intimacy of the String and his total dominion in the fifth to finally realize his desire (possibly aroused by the bomb?). It was also why he'd been certain Jack was still there. *What the hell is going on?* After their arrival, he'd been powerless, confined by his disguise to lying on that Levi mat. Dog! When they escaped, he vowed he'd never feel like that again! Surprise. And initially, he couldn't even discuss the situation with Zim. The only thing he could do was order the two clonie servants who met them at the lock to, "Go to your niches and pray for me, won't you?" It sounded like something the jiggling jack-off would say, delivered in a raspy whisper as he was being hurried away.

But Zim really saved their asses, playing through with the phony operation. He'd slipped the wrist organizer off Han's arm while pretending to take his pulse, then accessed Deli's penthouse floor plan. Leading the crew to the double-locks of a storage area, he turned to Ryka, Sunsue, and Tooco, addressing them somberly, "Go and rest in your niches. After the operation, you'll need to make a statement to 7 about what we witnessed when the explosion happened." The three dutifully shuffled away, keeping their faces averted from the screens. Han took his cue and, in the same raspy whisper, spoke to Darl, who still held his hand. "Please stay with me, Princess Shazar. It comforts me so."

Outside the storage area, Zim gave the two security robos who accompanied them from the cruiser their orders. "Wait outside the surgery until after the operation is done." They opened the double-locks just enough so Darl could guide the Levi mat inside. Zim followed behind, alerting the imaginary medical staff. "Doctors, I've stabilized your patient," then closed the locks. Zim knew there'd be no screen in the storage area, and they'd have a chance to talk through the rest of their plan.

They figured out how they were going to stage the interviews. Zim had already downloaded the images of the three servants whose IDs he'd picked for Ryka, Sunsue, and Tooco. They decided Han and Darl would stay where they were while "Deli" was being operated on, and Zim would go out and process the servants' downloads into the holo imager. Then he'd contact Sacker Command with the news they were ready to be interviewed (him, as well) and that Shazar would be available as soon as the operation was over. They used the diagram of Deli's layout again to pick a niche where they could sit with their backs to the screen, waiting to be called. The spot they chose opened into a hallway without any screens, leading down to the entrance of a game niche where Zim placed the holo imager camouflaged as a modular. Acting as facilitator, Zim would call in each servant, and the screen would see the subject get up and leave the waiting niche. By using the C-power transmitter Han used to detonate the bomb, Zim would activate each holo to enter from the hallway and go into the game niche for the interview. By sticking the unit's "character simulator" above his left temple under his white wig, he could use the holo imager's "improv" feature. This made it possible to think a response to each question and have the holo speak it to the screen from a hidden directional speaker. When the interview was finished, the holo exited back into the hallway, and the crew member waiting in the hallway would come back into the original niche, face averted, and sit down again, their back to the screen. Since, with his new white hair, he did bear a striking resemblance to Dr. Sandor, Theo, he would just do his own interview. As a Rebino, Darl could do her interview too because she was the same unique body type as Princess Shazar, that being the only identifying distinction of her marble statuary.

Han and Darl spent the time cajoling Jack to rematerialize until Zim returned and informed Han that everything had gone according to plan and took Darl for her interview. That's when Han really embarrassed himself, albeit to no one, by bringing up the intimacy Jack forced on him back in the cruiser, telling Jack how his tenderness and vulnerability had moved him, reassuring him he'd be happy to oblige when he felt the need (if they had privacy and time), but it was probably best they didn't tell the others as it might stir up some jealousy among the crew. Han was very expansive in his praise of Harrison's technique and anatomy, certain that Jack was embarrassed by the revelation of his shy nature and that was the reason he hadn't rematerialized. When Jack still refused to appear, Han called him a lot of unpleasant IDs and basically had a shit fit. Then it was *another* three hours before Zim returned to say he could come out. 7 had finally rescinded the order to keep a live screen on at all times.

Leaning over the compressed-foam baluster of Deli's balcony, Han peered down past the waves of spiraling octagonal pods to the moving walks far below. Limpid Topgrid muscles, made even more lax with Satcit gravity, needed help when occasionally they trod upon the old dirt ball.

Where the hell could he possibly go? He could flit around on the String like a ghost, but that wasn't much of a life. And every time he returned to the three dimensional to eat or eliminate, he'd be in danger of being spotted by a screen, which left only Bellytown. Of course!

Han congratulated himself on having the foresight while in their lair at the Pacino to debrief Okada on all their conversations. He'd been frank with her about his concern for making sure their spacecase stayed on board for their adventure. Jack had shown some interest in Tooco's dreamers of Cenpak.

Personally, he couldn't understand what the attraction was. He'd grown up hearing about the reclusive mutant band, who, as far as he could tell, wanted only to enshrine their past and get back to the good old days. A simplistic notion that would appeal to Jack, lover of antiquities that he was.

Zim appeared in the sliding glass lock of Deli's master niche. "I've got the food replicator on-line. Are you hungry?"

"Starving!" Han followed his lieutenant down to the palatial eating niche. "Dog, it's good to be able to move around."

Surrounded by portraits of what he assumed were Deli's most famous zap campaigns, he spotted the rest of the crew seated at a spacious circular modular with a chromium food replicator at the center. Humming and gurgling, it was busy regurgitating items onto a rotating serving ring. Brightly colored soya disks covered its surface. Tooco shoved a blue one with pink chunks in his mouth while reaching for another.

Han tapped up a menu on his place mat and, despite the obvious wealth of their surroundings, was still surprised by the variety of sumptuous fare being offered. He tapped in a bacon-wrapped filet mignon with wild rice and a garden salad. There was no point in beating around the buttress.

"Jack's gone. He split. I think he's down in Bellytown." He stared pointedly into Darl's vacant orbs. "Unfortunately, the pleasure of our company was not enough to convince him to continue our adventure." The replicator spat out three disks: a pink-rimmed red one, a tan one, and a green one. Han watched them come around. "So it looks like we have two options. We can stay at Deli's and play, then take off for Dog knows where before they discover our ruse. Although getting out will be harder than getting in because with Sanatan gone, where the hell would a Topgrid have to go?"

Han snatched up the red disk as it came within reach. "Or . . . Tooco and I can go down and find the fucking clone and convince him to rejoin our efforts, then rendezvous with the rest of you at the Satport." He took a bite from the disk and was shocked at the explosion of flavors. "My compliments to the replicator!" He chewed slowly, savoring every bite, giving his crew time to swallow their new situation.

"How are we gonna find him when he has the String? And if we do find him, how are we gonna convince him to come with us?" Soya crumbs littered the ring by the time Tooco was finished with his inquiries. He was tempted to tell the bellygridder he was responsible for Han's knowing their spacecase's destination, but he knew the munching mutant wouldn't appreciate the compliment or its irony.

"Don't worry. He won't stay on the String. We'll find him, and when we do, a disk from Darl will persuade him to change his mind. I'm sure we can find a small tablet around here to play when we find him down there." Han turned to Darl again. "After you've finished your meal, you can use Deli's Screx to make something special in the way of a plea. Make it seem like, without him, you've lost your will to live. Be sure to apologize for any indiscretions you may have committed. And don't forget to load up the scent tap, princess."

Even with blank plates for eyes, Darl communicated her intense displeasure.

Han watched as Tooco stuffed another disk in his mouth.

"I'm sure the charms of Bellytown will have faded by the time we catch up to him."

"But how do we synchronize our arrival at the Satport?" Zim, as usual, was planning for all contingencies.

Han was ahead of him. "You just keep surfing Deli's screen through the Bellytown porn fibers. I'm gonna need the ID number of Deli's screen here in Big New. After we find him, we'll send a coded zap. When we're ready to leave, we'll send another one. That's when you head for the Satport. When you get there, park in long-term parking. We'll meet up there."

Despite being crammed with another disk, Tooco's mouth managed to enunciate the question, "How are we gonna get down to Bellytown?"

"We'll go down the recycling tube. Don't worry about it. Just nourish yourself."

He could see he'd stung his bellygridder's pride, which was his aim. Since winning that graft at virtual vids, Tooco seemed to think he was qualified to take part in planning operations. Best to nip that hubris in the bud. He knew what would make the bitter pill go down easier. Tapping out a command on Deli's wrist organizer, he gestured to Zim. "I just took the security robos completely off-line. After you've finished eating, you and Tooco go remove their frybars so we have some firepower when we hit the bricks."

Zim gave Han a triumphant smile. "You'll need your mining jumps! I'll pack your duffs on a Levi-loader. I've got a little surprise I made back in Deli's cruiser when I was putting together 'dummy' Cyrus."

Han snatched up his rice and salad as they came around a third time. "Great, you can show me later before we go. Also, we're gonna need some disguises once we get into Bellytown." He took in the whole crew with a determined gaze.

"Don't let this little glitch throw you. It's important to keep the faith if we're going to pull off a feat none before us has dreamed of." He focused on the three sheed. "Zim is going to be drilling you on your roles in our holo drama at the Satport. I expect you to practice until you've learned them perfectly. Don't let my absence lull you into complacency. *We are the chosen* because that's who we've chosen to be!"

⸻ ❖ ⸻

Splatter chose the sleaziest joint in a row of dives lining a little cul-de-sac across from the Yaki checkpoint at Third and Twenty-Seventh. He figured he'd be more likely to find a hapless scab willing to do a little gossiping for a drink. Pieces of tin, haphazardly cut, covered the front wall of this dump, with a small black door leading inside. White letters, obviously hand-painted, spelled out the name *Dano's* on the door. If nothing else, a stiff shot would clear Mayra's mist from his brain and focus him on the job at hand. The flimsy door creaked on its hinges when he pushed it open, peering into the murky interior.

Once inside, he stood for a moment, trying to adjust his eyes to the dim lighting provided solely by antique electric beer signs. The bar was to his left, running down the length of one wall. Behind it stood the bartender, a pockmarked mutant with a large hump on his right shoulder and an elongated right arm ending in a bizarrely tiny hand. He was busy wiping down the bar with the tiny hand, staring pointedly at Splatter. Splatter smiled, walking toward him. The bartender slid his left hand under the bar, pulling out a large bat with a spike protruding through the end, casually resting it on his good shoulder. Splatter raised his arms, showing his empty hands, and stepped up to the bar.

"Pruno?"

"Duh!"

"Dope." Leaving his left arm raised, Splatter slowly put his right hand in his pocket, pulling out a single Yuan and tossing it on the bar.

The bartender swept the coin up in his little mitt, which disappeared under the counter. Splatter heard the Yuan clink into a metal container. The tiny hand appeared again, holding a tall brown bottle by the neck. He placed it on the bar in front of Splatter.

"Grazz." The bartender grunted. Walking away, he swung the bat off his shoulder and stashed it back out of sight. Splatter's eyes were adjusting. He could make out another figure at the far end of the bar, partially hidden behind the bartender. He was hunched over a bowl of house porridge, hungrily spooning it down. He might be a good prospect for a chat after he finished his meal. Splatter turned around, casually leaning against the bar, and took a first sip of his pruno. The pungent home brew packed a wallop, and he grimaced at the sour-sweet taste. Squinting, he tried to pull the rest of the joint into focus. He could see a party of four in the back—two Yakuza in red-neon jumps and what were probably a couple of hookers. He realized as he watched them, they weren't really together. The hookers most likely came in for a little R and R; and the Yaks, spotting them, were trying to convince the two to go back to work. They were in preliminary negotiations. The blonde was smiling, but her brunette companion, sporting huge breasts protruding from a silver harness, was refusing to even acknowledge the Yak's existence. The blonde, however, was warming to the attention. Standing, she did a slow turn to reveal a phenomenal ass escaping from her cheekless silver chaps. The heavyset Yak threw a handful of Yuan on the table.

Like two perfectly molded boulders gyrating in a pink velvet sack, the blonde's exquisite butt began to churn. The Yaks started groaning, and the bartender, along with his hungry customer, joined her admirers. But the hair-trigger violence of Bellytown exploded when the heavyset Yak dared to reach out and touch that shrine. The brunette hurled her shot glass straight at his face, nailing the little fucker in his vacuous forehead. His noggin snapped back, tipping him over backward, along with his chair. Splatter wasn't the only one in this joint with a "Jones" for somebody.

Seeing his partner go cartwheeling to the floor, the skinny Yak jumped up and reached for his laser dagger. But the brunette was faster, grabbing his bottle off the table and backhanding it across the side of his head. The dagger dropped from his hand as he fell onto an adjacent table and, from there, to the floor. The heavy Yak, now up on all fours, was trying to shake the cobwebs from his brain and regain his feet. The blonde joined the party, jumping on his back and grabbing him by his pompadour. Taking a wire necklace from around her neck, she released her grip on his hair, simultaneously slipping the necklace over his head. She yanked hard on the wire to close a slipknot, almost cutting his windpipe in half. She rode his jerking body around the floor, his partially cut throat spurting blood. Staying on him even after he collapsed, she pulled on the wire, humping his back with her hypnotic ass until, with a strained rattle, he croaked.

The barkeep, at first mesmerized by the struggle, suddenly leapt into action, reaching for his spiked club from under the bar. But the brunette scooped up the abandoned dagger and proved the shot glass wasn't a fluke. The light blade disappeared in his solar plexus as a fountain of blood sprang from his chest. Immediately exploding from his back, the dagger smashed the mirror behind the bar. His pockmarked visage slid from view, and the brunette turned toward the scab at the end of the bar. He was still holding his spoon and hugging his bowl.

"Washi mufu?"

The scab slowly shook his head no. Splatter was impressed by his apparent calm. The blonde was honing on Splatter, asking him the same question with her eyes. He didn't make her wait for an answer.

"Doke du, Yaki mufus!"

She gave him a sassy smirk before the two set to work, stripping their bodies of all valuables. The brunette leaped over the bar, massive breasts sailing before her, and retrieved the spiked bat and a stun club that the dead bartender was keeping in reserve. She grabbed the dagger, wiped blood from the handle with the barkeep's towel, and put it in her belt, then emptied the tin box holding his profits into one of her thigh-high boots. Keeping the spiked bat for herself, the brunette gave the blonde a heads-up, throwing the stun club to her. Blondie was about to get back to the skinny Yak's pockets when he regained consciousness and sat up. She immediately stuck the end of her new stun club into his bloody scalp and tapped power. Like a marionette Splatter once saw as a child, the Yak did a jig around the floor on his butt—red legs jerking crazily, jellied pompadour standing on end, blue bolts jumping from flaming bleached tips. After she was certain he was thoroughly fried, Blondie shut down the stun club, and he slumped, smoking head on his chest.

She finished going through his pockets, then pulled a second laser dagger from the small of his back. This time, she gave Splatter a full-blown "come hither" grin. Then she stood up and headed for the door. Her brunette sidekick leaped back across the bar and started to follow her outside.

Unfortunately for the pair, at that very moment, a mesh patrol of three more Yaks burst through the flimsy black door. It took the gelheads a few seconds to register the situation, but once they spotted the bodies and the Yaks' laser daggers in the hookers' belts, they instantly sprang into action.

Fanning out, drawing their daggers, and bringing up their mirrored shields, they moved on the hookers. The blonde pulled her laser dagger, tapping up the light blade, and raised the stun gun in her other hand.

The brunette pulled her laser dagger and raised the spiked bat, rotating the head in small loops like an ancient "yanky" at the plate. But they were no match for three Yaks with daggers and shields. Splatter saw in their worried expressions that they both knew the score.

The blonde's smile earlier made Splatter feel expansive. He was actually thinking of helping the pair, but it would jeopardize his mission, being across the street from a checkpoint. The moment an alarm was raised, they'd have the whole garrison in here. It was a no-win situation. With a practiced change of heart, he reined in his ineffectual compassion. Often in his short life, he'd been forced to stand back and watch a bloody situation play itself out.

In the space of Splatter's thoughts, the Yaks closed the circle, turning their laser blades to the simple equation—three into two equals dead. It was a matter of seconds before the hookers were history.

Suddenly there was a thunderous roar in the bar as the Yak closest to Splatter spat flesh from one shoulder, spinning quickly, before a second explosion blew a gaping hole in his chest. A deafening staccato of reports followed. Briefly, the last two Yaks did a spastic dance. Little red holes appeared in parts of their anatomies before they crashed to the floor.

The cloud of smoke created from this rapid barrage made it impossible to see anything but a dimly lit veil. As it dissipated in the sudden silence, Splatter saw the scab at the end of the bar. His bland face was unsettling, as if his generically pleasing features were unsteady inside the oval of his face, subtly shifting positions when he moved his head. He was maintaining a relaxed two-handed grip on a Berretta, nine-millimeter pistol, like the pistols they found in the armory. It was the standard-issue sidearm of the US Forces back in the day. Then Splatter spotted the red armor underneath the open slicker and knew instantly whose presence he was in. Only a madman or messiah would have the "chutzpa" to use a percussion weapon with no silencer—across from a Yakuza checkpoint. Now it was just a matter of seconds before a dozen Yaks toting frybars came barging through the door!

The hookers stood transfixed, stunned by the deafening reports and frantic destruction of their adversaries. They'd probably never seen or heard a percussion weapon in their lives. One of 7's first directives was to ban all percussion weapons. They rolled it out as part of their first "zap campaign," introducing laser swords and daggers to the locals. They realized the masses had to have weapons for their own protection; but with short-ray laser weapons, the damage inflicted was limited by the immediate proximity of the laser blade. Thus, the masses were kept from posing a serious threat to the cartels ever again while being introduced to a fascinating new weapon to keep their minds off that fact.

They found out about all of this from Danner, their techie convert. He showed them how to use the frybars and laser cannons they took from the Sacker transport. When Danner first saw their store of twentieth weapons, he almost had a heart attack. But later, on, after inspecting the parts section of their underground garage, he solved the noise problem of their percussion weapons.

Wow! Amazing to watch your own mind do a high dive into personal minutia in the face of acknowledging a miracle. He was standing right in front of Splatter, pointing the pistol in his general direction. The deliverer was *real* and in a real big mess. There was no backdoor; however, they might be able to make one. But they needed to do it before the front door was breached.

The deliverer didn't seem concerned about the time. The lines cut deeply in his face reminded Splatter of his father, who came in from the waste fill, among the last of dreamer converts before the techies pulled out for Sanatan. His father was a headhunter. He hit it big when he ran across an old "semi" jackknifed on an exit ramp. The radiation readings were nil, so towing a large Levi scow (for which he killed another headhunter and his family along the eastern corridor), he brought back a cargo of almost five thousand boxes of "Slim Jims" and parked it right outside the mesh. He guarded it alone, until a Yakuza trader gave him the graft he was asking for. That sale made for a much-easier life than most scabs from the waste fill endured in Bellytown.

It gave his father time to think about that family and the direction of humanity and "civilization." Then he heard Mayra speak, and they joined the dreamers of Cenpak.

Again, drowning in personal minutia when the moment was calling for an immediate responce. This was weird. He had to get a grip!

"Grazz! Grazz!" The dancers were beginning to recover from their shock, making little bows to the deliverer as they started a nervous shuffle toward the door. "Grazz, grazz!" They hurried on, trying to avoid the red lacquer pools spreading across their path. Completing the arduous journey, the blonde madly whipped open the door. Splatter got a final glimpse of that magnificent derriere as the pair bolted out of Dano's. But the good news was, *nobody bolted in!* If the Yaks were out there, that was the perfect moment to make their move. Maybe through some freak of architecture, this little dump damped the explosions their deliverer was responsible for. Maybe it was the joint's location and the acoustics of the cul-de-sac. Maybe it was divine intervention—why the fuck not?

The deliverer lowered his pistol. When their eyes met, he knew it was all true. All these years, they'd been dreaming the truth. His expression reminded Splatter of what he imagined was his own expression, the one he adopted when deciding to leave the hookers to their fate. He looked tired. He hadn't shaved in a while. His watery brown eyes looked overwhelmed.

"You, the angel of the present in your mighty crystal fire, lift me up, consume my darkness. Let me travel even higher."

His favorite hymn of Van "the Man" Morrison was missing from those eyes. Yet here he was, exactly as prophesied in the Duni. It never occurred to Splatter to think about the deliverer's path, but he realized now that path was no more certain than his own and, surely, more challenging and disheartening.

No time like the present to let him know. He was remembered and expected. Splatter knew what was required. In their library, he'd read many accounts of seekers meeting a holy man and being compelled to make "the gesture," but the warrior in his nature always balked at this expression. He never understood what happened to your self-respect when you gave yourself up so completely. But now the consideration of self seemed so superfluous in the face of such a blessing—the fulfillment of all their dreams. Still, Splatter was surprised to discover how effortless surrender was. His knees found the floor, his forehead touched the deliverer's boots, and he felt a peace that would only be exceeded by death.

Harrison was coming to the conclusion that here in "crazy town," every coke wanted to either kill or crown you. Why this regal black was kneeling in front of him was as big a mystery now as it was with the tube on the girder. And sure enough, he was crying, beginning to babble, repeating the little sheed's words, "You're here. You're finally here!"

It would be too preposterous to believe he really was expected. They must be mistaking him for some prophesied redeemer. Something about being a Topgridder. The little sheed on the girder was very impressed with that. They expected some Topgrid savior to come down and deliver them from their squalor. He felt almost guilty, deciding to go along with this mistaken identity. But hopefully, while they were getting his credentials worked out, he could get something decent to eat. That's if Dano's "stew" didn't kill him first.

"Can you take me to your leader?"

The young scab, spilling tears on Harrison's boots, looked up with a smile made radiant by his contrasting ebony pallor.

"Yes, Mayra's waiting for you."

"You're the dreamers of Cenpak!"

"YES! YES!" The young dreamer was ecstatic. He stood up, grabbing Harrison by the arm. "We've been looking for you. We need to get out of here before anybody else comes in."

"Lead on, young dreamer!" He'd picked up some very bad habits from Han.

CHAPTER

She was born into a family of bottled-water dealers who owned a distribution warehouse in New Jersey, just before 3TC. They held it against all comers. Her father and brothers were avid gun advocates with an arsenal that rivaled a gun shop. She was the ninth child and the first girl. Her mother died bringing her into life. She wore that stigma in every interaction with other family members her whole young life.

She left home at twenty-five, tired of the emotional barrenness and her abusive brothers. Her name was Sarah, and she was Mayra's beloved mother. A gentle yet incredibly strong "slip" of a girl, she set out for the cindered city across the river, hoping to discover in the ruins what civilization had been driving at.

She learned to read English from her father, who liked to recite from old newspapers he saved in bales in the basement, not with any interest in historic preservation but because he was certain someday he'd be able to trade them for something. Still, he read the old papers aloud every evening as a way of revisiting a more generous and ordered time. She watched, sitting on his lap, and later, over his shoulder, as he read aloud the articles. Eventually, the words began announcing themselves in each series of letters, rising from the sea of newsprint when their names were called. Until casually, one day, Sarah realized she could read! She started reading anything she could get her hands on.

From her brothers, she was thoroughly schooled in ruthlessness and the fighting techniques that capitalized on her tiny stature. She went in low like a wrestler, and many a scab met unexpected death from a brick upside the head after having his feet ripped from under him. Sometimes her attack was so sudden and precise it was instant—the back of their head bashed in when it hit the pavement. She was smart enough to leave home just before 7 banned all percussion weapons. This was at the end of '48, when 7 was beginning to pacify the area, bringing all the locals under control. It was in preparation for their first major building project, the great floating city designed to hover above the ruins of New York. They'd been warning everyone for six months to turn over their projectile weapons to Sacker cruisers that now constantly patrolled the area. Her family was wiped out within days of her leaving. A direct result of her father's oft-proclaimed credo: "You'll have to pry my cold dead fingers from the trigger!"

In the cindered city, anyone discharging a firearm found themselves swooped down upon and then obliterated by Sackers flying the first Bonn-made levi cruisers. But Sarah made careful plans, sneaking into her father's workshop with a list: .380-caliber Smith & Wesson semi-automatic pistol with silencer, shoulder holster, four spare clips, four dozen boxes of hollow-point ammunition, and a pistol-cleaning kit. It gave her the edge, without which she'd never have survived. While he hadn't thought enough to teach her how to read, her father did teach her how to shoot, and she was an expert shot.

Thinking of her now, waiting for some news of their deliverer, Mayra remembered the determined passion of her mother, born across the river on December 15, 2023. She arrived in the remains of the city and began poking in the ashes, believing she could find the lost or stolen link to purpose. And of course, she had—in the pages of a tiny book.

It was one of six books (including three large volumes containing the complete works of Shakespeare) she found in the Bronx while exploring the sublevels of an old hospital named Cedars of Lebanon. After sliding out several body trays in the morgue, she came across a fully clothed corpse wearing a white laboratory coat, a male whose name was Mike Bloomfield, she discovered from his journal. He was hugging a GORE-TEX backpack containing those six books and his journal. While his body was severely decomposed, the books were well-preserved.

He was part of a skeleton emergency staff, a medical intern who remained in the city when the missiles were expected. Later, when the firestorm created by the incendiary bombing reached inferno proportions, he descended to the morgue and took final refuge in a refrigerated vault. Probably in a panic while getting in, he accidently slid the vault completely closed; or maybe, as a last resort against the searing heat, he shut it on purpose.

From his journal, she learned he was in love with a girl in the East Village. A poet, actress, dancer, waitress, she'd gone home to be with her family in Nome, Alaska, for the holidays. Her name was also Sarah.

Sarah recounted it as the moment when the first inkling of prophesy shivered through her. Opening the smallest of the books, she found a handwritten poem inside the cover. She assumed it was written by Mike. But later, reading *Two Gentlemen of Verona*, she realized Mike had copied Shakespeare's words:

"But that life is altered, now. I have done penance for contemning love, whose high imperious thoughts have punished me with bitter fasts and penitential groans, with nightly tears and daily heart-sore sighs. For in revenge of my contempt of love, love hath chased sleep from my enthralled eyes and made them watchers of mine own heart's sorrow. Love's a mighty lord, who hath so humbled me that I confess there is no woe to his correction, nor to his service, no such joy on Earth. Now, no discourse, except it be of love! Now, can I break my fast, dine, sup, and sleep, upon the very naked name of love."

Standing in the ashes, Sarah tasted the cold grail cup. Since first being aware she was a questioning entity, she was certain the real business being transacted here was the business of the heart. She wouldn't be the last, to be accused of taking what skeptics call "a desperate leap to cosmic unity" as a way to cope with the existential angst borne of random chaos. But this lightning insight revealed it was just the opposite. Suffering and loss were neither an inequity or injustice; nor were they the heartless facts of existence in inevitable entropy. They were the means for exploring all the aspects of a newly awakened whole, for discovering the character and purpose of this newborn collective soul. The big bang wasn't really that long ago. And God wasn't the architect or planner of the universe. The universe is what happened when God woke up. As new and wondrous to him as it was to the billons of tiny eyes waking in him. That's what "in his image" meant. They were all on the same journey of discovery. The big difference was, while they had no idea what this was all about, a waking, God knew where it all had to lead, understood the destination. Kicking the ashes off her boots, she didn't think they'd be reaching that destination anytime soon. This was just beginning.

That was why this first evolutionary foray into self-consciousness was consumed in these blackened remains. Everything was in its infant stages, and *love* (a.k.a. universal connection) relied solely on its strength as the source. Love didn't concern itself with all the reflections and refractions—the complex, tail-chasing games the mind so loves to play, all the jungle competitions that glorify autonomy. Love figured, as the source for all these mental gymnastics, they would eventually wear themselves out and finally dissipate. Love didn't reckon on the cleverness of the mind, finding a way to take the divine to itself rather than give itself up to the divine.

Her father had been a devout Christian. He was constantly chastising them to behave with the admonition they were made in God's image. God told him that in his Bible—and that was proof—he and his buddy God were on the same page. It took a while to figure out this sleight of hand, but when she did, it was obvious: *I am like God, so God is like me.* Therefore, God feels the way I do. God wants things to be the way I want them to be! Of course, they didn't postulate it that baldly, because most simply codified it through their waking experience—in my world, I am the center of all perception. Everything I perceive is going on around me. I am the center of everything. Therefore, *I* (a nanospeck of DNA clinging to a microscopic pebble orbiting in some minuscule galaxy in an *infinite universe*) should be directing the whole show.

Love paid dearly for its naiveté.

Mike clutched three volumes besides his journal and the works of Shakespeare: Th*e Idiot* by Dostoevsky, Th*e Sirens of Titan* by Kurt Vonnegut, and the little one. The one they'd seen in his hand the first time he appeared, which would prove to be the final truth of all their dreaming when he stood in Mayra's presence and placed the twin to their tiny volume in her hands. What began as a little girl staring into the flames with her mother, listening to her father exhorting the others to believe in a future, came down to this day, when Teeba sounded the trumpet call of his arrival.

A ragged band of 117 when she saw the vision of the cache on Fourteenth for forty years since, they'd managed a capricious faith in this mysterious deliverer, a vision of redemption that might someday come to pass. *Someday* was today, and if that magic act did occur, Mayra herself (secretly more cynical than most) would finally believe too!

She counterbalanced serving as their visionary "Pollyanna" by harboring the most jaded of devil's advocates as a private court jester in her brain. He (Mayra always imagined her fool as a he) was a very irreverent fellow who consequently got a lot of "airtime" in her head. His pithy slants on her more desperate situations provided the needed levity to keep her sane. Now he was having a rare old time envisioning the appointed hour, with images of the deliverer handing her everything, from John Holmes's cock to a moldy Big Mac rather than the sacred text.

But there were real signs and communiques. One of the early finds that drew Sarah to Cenpak was discovered by Sam two stories below Bryant Street Park, where the New York Public Library kept their oldest and most precious documents. There, they discovered early accounts of those who led the way into America's future; and it was clear, you were a partner with your visions. You conjured them with the sweat and blood of your yearning and commitment, and you had to trust, no matter how uncertain or bizarre it got, you were still on course, as long as your motivation remained unchanged—something greater than yourself.

Come on, Splatter. Let's do this.

* * *

This was only Han's second time out in Big New at night. His two hours a day of training were always in the afternoon, and he'd been confined to the area of the entry port where Screenrage Academy was located. He'd learned a lot there—about cokes, about lying. Most uneducated cokes think that's what acting is, but it's more complex than that. Acting is about *believing* your lies and then lying. You have to view your subterfuge like you're in a play, which entitles you to employ your "suspension of disbelief" *on yourself.* And the most difficult lie you will have to believe is that you don't have any idea how it's all going to turn out. That's why most cokes are horrible liars. Oh, they all think they're Marlon Bango when spinning some preposterous tale; but in reality, their connivance is hanging out all over the place. They never grasp the fact that you have to play your character's intention and stay *in the moment.* Don't get caught knowing something you're not supposed to know yet. Just stick to what your character wants and be aware of how much you know at any given point in time. You'll be much less likely to reveal the coke behind the mask trying to manipulate the situation to your desired outcome. And don't let your reactions and responses disclose anything more than a response to the information you're receiving at that *moment.* Untrained cokes are always jumping ahead, trying to include information to answer the next query they expect, shoring up their lies before they're brought into question. Being a quick study, Han put together his portfolio for fiber feeds in record time, and the range of emotions and intents he displayed got him plenty of action. He was in the "hot taps" category before he was twenty.

But in retrospect, he'd been overconfident in his abilities while being dismissive of others' skills and experience. It was a shortcoming he was realizing now.

There was much less traffic on the moving walks than he expected. He thought there'd be quite a few Topgrid out enjoying the late-night eateries and clubs sandwiched in among the replicator shops. Maybe the disappearance of Sanatan put a damper on everyone's festivities. It was very pleasant, just gliding along in relative solitude. He didn't even have to listen to Tooco's incessant babbling because he was a couple paces in front of him, playing the bodyguard/bellhop to Tooco's dumbass Arabian gadget master. And there he was, doing it again. It was a character flaw he needed to address. Not an hour earlier, he almost blew it. While making Tooco go over all the information he'd given Okada about the dreamers of Cenpak—he was only half-listening, when the bellygridder mentioned something very valuable, and Han nearly missed it. Apparently, these dreamers were waiting for some Topgrid savior to take them away from all this. Dropping in from Big New, and with all his spacecase abilities, Jack would fill the bill nicely. He had to be very careful how he approached these dreamers with his requests for information on Jack's current whereabouts. Who knows, he might even get them to help find his wayward spacecase, which reminded him of another valuable Screenrage tip: when lying, always tell as much truth as possible; that's where the whole "method thing" comes in.

He'd never consciously realized it before, but what always gave him the heebie-jeebies about Big New was that absolutely everything was white. Everything! It was probably designed to be soothing, but it wasn't. It was innocuously sinister—a practiced liar intentionally undercompensating for the zombie horrors hidden inside. They were heading for Sinatra Satport because that's where they'd find the teeming burg's recycling receptacles. This was the location where Topgrid practiced the charity of dumping whatever nonperishables they wanted to get rid of down the recycling tube. The Yakuza mined it. It would also give Han a chance to look at the area where they'd perform their diversionary drama later on. They still had a ways to go, the Satport being at the southern edge of the megadome, but he didn't mind. He was enjoying this peaceful glide through almost deserted avenues, pulling the small Levi-loader carrying their two duffs like an ancient citizen out for a leisurely stroll with his god a hundred cycles ago.

It was just possible there was something else in play here. He was first struck by it when Jack confirmed him he'd piloted the *Protostar*. Never a believer in Dog, it was hard for him to accept the possibility of a supernatural entity guiding him in his quest. But the "luck" they experienced throughout their journey, the crazy risks they'd taken, which all panned out—it was beyond the laws of probability! Just maybe, Jack running off wasn't a bad thing. Maybe something was still leading them to succeed in their mission. If so, it had to be as disgusted with cokekind as he was! Just go along to get along, It was a beautiful night for a gambol. Fucking Jack and his antiquated chatter.

＊＊＊

Zim had come to love being awash in the corporeal surf, adrift on the belly of the beast. Sliding his tongue down Darl's alabaster abdomen, he was still torn about enjoying her secretive elixirs. Rooting into the slippery cleft, he sucked on the sweet lemon taste of tender Rebino flesh, lips gently pushing open teardrop wings, his tongue dancing up and down her creamy cut. This was the first time he'd touched her since their maiden trip in the Screwhog—and the first time he wasn't under Han's instruction. He knew very well this coupling was at Han's direction, but he appreciated not having him actually peering on as Zim dipped his whole face in her blossoming heat. But he didn't mind that Sunsue and Ryka were observing while "diddling" each other. It made Darl's shy that much sweeter!

Overlooking the megatropolis sprawled on the deck of Deli's pool, living the life of gadget king and flesh-sucking pervert all rolled into one, Zim was overwhelmed by an abundance even Seymore would envy. As opal rivulets trickled from snowy petals onto a perfect marble ass, Zim guided his aching vessel into the honeyed slip.

She missed the pink spikes, watching his face disappear between her perfect thighs. Darl was admiring various parts of her anatomy with the attentions of his lizard tongue. It was true: perfection knew itself for the epitome it was. Her statuesque form was just the most obvious piece of her remarkable genetic engineering. She was the penultimate. And if there was any doubt about it, all she had to do was spray some pheromones around. She had daddy's regal brow and her mother's aquiline nose, and the rest was all her own.

Her parents being connoisseurs of art, she was their living masterpiece, and they gave her anything she wanted. At eight, she skipped into their palatial mat niche and ordered her parents out. She wanted it for herself, and they did as they were instructed. But she was nine cycles before she really began to realize the power she held. Her parents made the mistake of giving her a "mini-eye" so she could enjoy playback of her day "to study yourself." But truth be told, she'd always been a shit stirrer (as Han put it), hiding her mini-eye in their Screx set on motion record.

She realized something as Zim's designer jerk kicked into cruise, establishing an easy rhythm inside her. It wasn't so much that his hair wasn't pink. It was that, to impersonate the doctor, he'd dyed it the same color as her father's. This was exactly what she'd seen when playing back daddy's Screx fantasy on her little recorder, only her perfect legs were much shorter. After that, she knew what the odd fleeting look daddy sometimes gave her was. As she got older, she took a secret pleasure in giving him a blast of pheromones whenever she caught him at it. He would usually excuse himself and go off into his study. By the time she was twelve, she could make him do anything she wanted.

At fifteen, she made him snag her a Screx with a personal access code. Her mother almost killed him when they delivered it. But she'd been on to her mother since she was eleven. In the brief moment, mummy used the eliminator before her traditional midafternoon "reviver"— Darl hid the mini-eye in their Screx for the second time. After that, she couldn't look her mother in the eye for a cycle. Expecting to see her getting off with some Screenrage instead, Darl watched as mom attached electrodes to her budding nipples while her comp-gen double lay strapped spread-eagle on a table, an enormous steely churning up her ass. She could still hear the words mummy hissed in her ear, just before throwing the switch, "How does it feel to be perfect now, you manipulative little witch!"

After taking a cycle to recover, she'd rubbed her mother's aquiline nose in it, tempting daddy every chance she got. She rubbed everybody's nose in it. But mummy finally got her revenge after their dinner with Han. Left alone on a covered deck just out of screenshot, Han had her jump around her ankles in less than twenty minutes. By the time her mother walked in, she was greeted with the sight of her daughter rocking on Han's majestic jerk, glistening with her virginal blood. It was the strangest expression she'd ever seen on someone's face, eyes wide with horror while her mouth stretched into an ear-to-ear grin. She'd actually hissed just like in the Screx. "Got you now, you little bitch!" And then it was off to the mines. Daddy would have covered it up, but mommy didn't give him time.

Zim's squeal announced the release of his party ribbon. Darl gently stroked his newly patriarchal head and released an especially pungent burst of pheromones. Gurgling, he made another little squeal, ending in a purring snore. She immediately shoved him off her and turned to Sunsue and Ryka.

"Let's get some nachos from the replicator, grab a couple of bottles of Blue Booz, and I'll set up the holo camera to project *Deli's Demise*. Maybe we can find some of his other Go Fish disks too."

Ryka shyly looked up from her attentions to Sunsue. "Okay, but we're not finished."

━━━━●━●━●━━━━

He couldn't find his pattern. He'd been trying since regaining consciousness. He and . . . Splatter . . . he and Splatter got bagged the second they walked out of Dano's. So much for dreamers knowing what was up in Yaki sector. Splatter was adamant, if the shots were heard, they would've been bagged when the dancers left. Actually, "bagged" wasn't exactly right. He half-wished Sackers were their captors. They'd have used chemicals instead of torture to get what they wanted before executing the pair. Through barely cracked eyelids, he was surreptitiously checking out his surroundings. It reminded him of his dream with the girl trying to get her book back. A dank waremode with wavy sheet-metal walls, it was also a well-stocked torture chamber, confirmed by a vast array of instruments, both recognizable and unknown, hanging on one grimy wall. At the moment, a cluster of Yaks was discussing something in Amerab in front of the double metal locks that were the only entrance to the mode. They were probably exchanging ideas on how best to induce the agony necessary to learn what they wanted to know. Two of their brethren were watching Harrison with clubs in their hands. Shit. That meant news of his String match and his discussion with Sun Moon Tu reached them before Sanatan disappeared. He'd need to wait for a distraction once he did access his pattern.

But try to focus though he might, he couldn't visualize his pattern. Even completing the initial circle was impossible. If he couldn't solve the problem before they realized he was awake, it would be a while before he got another chance. As if reading his thoughts, one of the Yaks guarding him squinted, taking a closer look at his face. "Poppin'!"

The smallest member in the group turned and smiled. "Awake? Good."

Harrison watched him approaching, the whites of his eyes protruding from an ebony skull. As he got closer and his features became clearer, Harrison was reminded of the profile of Caesar on an old Roman coin.

"New Blood, isn't it?" Behind their little emperor, a member of the group held up his carnelian game armor to obviate any denial. Harrison was suddenly aware he was naked, strapped spread-eagle on a plastic slab and propped up to the view of his captors.

"And also, you are Harrison, Jack. My 'ID,' as you Topgrid like to call it, is Carder . . . and I don't know where to begin." He turned to view his wall of instruments. "I'm beside myself with possibilities. What I do know is you had something to do with the sudden disappearance of Sanatan . . . and the death of our venerable master, Sun Moon Tu."

He watched as all the Yaks bowed their heads, silent for a moment. When Carder looked up at him again, Harrison knew he was about to deeply regret ever being born.

"One of the final communiqués we received from Sanatan concerned the dinner you shared with our master." Carder proceeded to the wall of pain and selected a short whip with a dirty gray pompon at the tip, twirling it lazily as he strolled back toward Harrison. "It was our master's understanding we were in accord regarding the death of Carmine Carbachi."

As Carder reached him, the lash suddenly whipped across his head, igniting his face in agony. Razor-thin needles carved microscopic ditches through cheeks, nose, and lips, snapping his head to one side. These tiny troughs caught fire and grew more excruciating by the second. Now Carder's face was inches from his own.

"It's unfortunate we didn't make it clear to you. *You weren't supposed to kill everybody!*" Carder stepped away but immediately turned back to him. This time, the whip came from the opposite direction and snapped his head to the other side. Harrison heard his own scream just behind the crack.

"The unique pain blossoming on your face is provided by the still poisonous spines of a sea urchin attached to the end. Nature is truly amazing."

The third explosion brought the fire through his nipples and across his upper chest. It was several seconds before Harrison's screaming quieted to a groan.

"By the way, how's the English, Topgrid? Passable? I've waited so long to use it in a conversation with one of you . . . growing up so far beneath your boot. I've cherished the dream that one day your grid plate would disappear, and you'd join us here, in Bellytown."

Again the whip struck, still lower, converting every cell in his midsection to molten fire. Straps on his wrists and ankles snapped taut as muscles convulsed, trying to double him over. His screams seemed inexhaustible as the inferno grew to cover the entire upper half of his body.

"Goin' down, goin' down to Bellytown, gonna have some kinda fun!" Carder danced as he sang, moving in, turning the whip around.

Helpless, Harrison watched as he brought the shiny handle down on his genitals. Struck to the core, vomit spilled from his mouth, mercifully cooling his roasting chest and stomach. For several seconds, he hovered near the furthest periphery of consciousness, and then felt Carder's hand smearing his vomit on his face.

"Bile for guile, eh, Topgrid? We understood from Sun Moon Tu that you're quite a history buff. Well, then you must know, once upon a time, we occasionally got to run into you . . . at least make our grievances known. But since you've taken to hiding out in your cushy satellites, even that's become impossible! You can imagine how someone starved for edification like myself might be a tiny bit chatty having this chance to dialogue with you . . . Topgrid. Oh, we get the occasional Sacker, and we do have a good time, but you know, they're not really Topgrid, more like dutiful drones—Topgrid dummies rigged with technological wonders and turned loose on the rabble."

Strangely divorced from his suffering, a voice in Harrison's head wondered why this crazy Yak sounded like some 7 toady with an enhancement upgrade in elocution?

"Conversing with a Topgrid is like swilling precious cream made from the milk of millenniums of civilization."

At least he wasn't that tortured metaphor.

"It's a thrill, Topgrid, a real thrill."

The group of Yaks behind Carder was laughing hysterically. Dog. All these scum knew English? First, Tooco with his Shakespeare, and now this oratorical Yaki and his English-speaking crew. If nothing else, dreamers were spawning a better class of criminal here in Bellytown.

Carder took the moment to move in close to Harrison. He spoke in a conspiratorial whisper, "You need to tell me how you destroyed Sanatan. The images we intercepted from your 'Revlon' certainly were spectacular! You need to tell me about the weapon that did that before Lord Yakami arrives in about an hour. You see, I have other business to attend to, and I won't be able to protect you any longer . . . and trust me, he's very unhappy with you. I need to know all about that weapon, so I'm going to give you a moment to gather your thoughts."

He knew the whip was coming, but when he realized where the dirty urchin was headed now, Harrison screamed before the stripe.

After winning his fortune in the virtual jungle, he felt the Dogs were smiling on him back here in the real wild. In that spirit, Tooco was making periodic pirouettes descending the zigzag remains of a skeletal staircase. At every landing, he covered the full 360 degrees with his frybar's muzzle before bounding down to the next level. They decided to hop on the charred beams of this old corporate scraper to get off the main grid girders. They were trying to avoid being spotted by a Sacker drone or Yakuza buttons responding to the burning recycler.

He and Han cleaned out the entire cocoon in less than two minutes, both armed with frybars—Tooco's on pulse bolt! He made a big mess. There was no two ways about it; he went ballistic. Maybe, after all, he was a little angry with his former comrades. He knew Han was pissed, but fuck it. It got the job done. Yeah, things were pretty one-sided: two frybars against four laser swords and a couple of laser daggers. Tooco'd blown several big holes in the sorting mode, starting a series of fires. They barely had enough time to kill everybody before the whole cocoon went up in a blaze. They got out in the nick of time. He really hadn't expected much of a fight. Frybars were at a premium down here. Pretty much only buttons carried them. But there were plenty of laser blades of varying lengths for those who could afford them. And that was damn few.

Escaping north along the girders, away from the recycling plant, they'd paused above the mesh at Tenth Street and Avenue C, ditching the levi-loader and putting on their mining jumps. They grabbed the duffs, still holding their Bellytown disguises. Back in Sanatan, Zim was adamant about holding on to the mining jumps, insisting he could find room on their levi-loader. Now Tooco was singing his praises. The hydraulic assists in the mining boots were making tube play of his daring jumps as they made their way down the burned-out scraper. The suit's layered Kevlar films, fire-retardant synthetics, and Titanium breastplate afforded protection from fire, chemicals, blades, hatchets, and clubs, although you still sustained impact injuries—severe bruises, concussion. They were basically 7's stripped-down combat jump and helmet, perfectly suited for the mines and for the task at hand.

They were coming down to a much larger metal landing: Tooco, on point, Han covering the rear. Reaching it, Tooco recognized rows of blackened generators as the scraper's electrical backup system. The floor was steel plate on reinforced I-beams to support the heavy machines. They were in four rows of four each. He continued scanning with his frybar. This high up, it was unlikely they'd run into anything, but he was still wary of a clone popping up and taking a shot at him with an old percussive. Although it wouldn't kill him, depending on the caliber of the pellet, it could knock him on his ass.

"Hold it!" Han tapped his shoulder and hissed a command, "We wanna wait here. We'll hide in those." Han nodded toward the cindered machines. "We'll wait them out awhile."

Tooco had to ask, "Why?"

"Yaks have motion detectors. This high up, there's nothin' but pigeons. Our movements betray a larger mass. They could locate us up here. And don't forget the drones. With what happened to Sanatan, they're gonna be all over the place. Oh yeah, and there's also you torching that whole cocoon and going nuts on pulse bolt! No doubt the Yaks are pissed, Tooco! They're probably dropping buttons along the entire upper grid trying to pick up our movements. If we stay in this grove of steel relics, they won't pick up anything from us.

Tooco felt pretty stupid for not realizing this. After all, he'd *been* Yakuza, one of Yakami's main cokes for a while there. But he'd just been his driver and taken him to a lot of dinners and conferences, seen his social side. He looked at the machines with a new objective now. He had to recon them, not just get past them. With every machine at least two centigrid high, once inside them, he'd be vulnerable on two sides. And this was with Han covering his back!

"This place is gonna take a while to secure."

"Not if we come from either side. First, you cover me. I'm going around the left-side perimeter to the back of the first aisle on your left. Then I'll come this way down that aisle. When you see me, you start down the center aisle in the opposite direction. Coming toward each other, you will appear on my left, and I will appear on your left. We just need to be careful when we pass not to blast each other. We'll cover the first two aisles. Then I'll go to the other side of this end and come back down the far right aisle. You just stay at the other end covering the center aisle."

"All right, got it."

Han quickly broke away, scuttling down the left side of the platform. Tooco covered him until he disappeared behind the last machine at the far corner of the metal grid. Once he saw Han start down his side, Tooco came slowly down the center aisle. When he reached the very center of the matrix, he swung his muzzle to his right, down the center lateral aisle. It was then the bottom fell out of Tooco's world. Standing on its hind legs, one centigrid tall, a rat was looking at the pocket watch in his right paw. Tooco recognized it because Yakami had a gold one he was always fiddling with. The rat looked up from the watch into the muzzle of Tooco's frybar and froze. Tooco froze as well. They stood like that for a moment, neither moving, until finally the rat snapped the watch shut, stuffing it inside its fur and began screaming in a high-pitched squeal.

"DU TA! DU TA! Pu ta, du ta! Pop it, pap it! PUSPUU, TAP IT! DU TA! PUTA!"

He couldn't believe his ears. The rat swore like a sea coke, and the *cuj* on this furry little fucker—basically telling Tooco, "Pull the trigger! What's the matter, you can't pull the trigger? You're soft, like a pussy, a whore." Damn!

The legend was they could parrot human speech, but this little shit was talking to him! Han heard the racket and was racing toward him, frybar at the ready. Tooco quickly raised his hand, signaling Han to back off. "It's an Orkin!" He wanted to try talking with it, if he could just get it to settle down.

Having abruptly halted, Han peered around the corner in wide-eyed disbelief at seeing his first Orkin.

"Son of a gadget master's Sat turd!" Han's jaw almost hit the deck as the huge rodent turned his attention to the new arrival.

"Stu Mufu, chillatilla, dopadupa." He (Tooco decided it must be a jerk) was calling Han a waste-fill farmer and dumbass. This little fucker was determined to die. What struck him as he watched the freak rant was how much "human" appeared in the coke-like expressions circumscribed by a rodent's skull. Though, it wasn't quite a rodent skull. It looked more like a clonie's head had been pulled in one direction by the nose and in the opposite direction by the ears, elongating him into the Toon version of a rat's profile. An aquiline etching down the length of his muzzle with jowls bunched at the rear of the jawline created the illusion of a long chiseled nose and high cheekbones on what was essentially a horizontal plane.

"DU TA, DU TA, DUTA, DUTA!"

The rat was back to demanding a swift death. He could see all the noise was starting to give Han concern. This ruckus could draw Yaki buttons, and he didn't want his earlier overexuberance causing any more difficulties. Tooco swung up his frybar, putting a pulse bolt right in front of the rodent's feet, knocking him to the metal plate.

"SHUDDUP!"

Before he could even consider his uncharacteristically merciful behavior, they were swarmed by a stream of scurrying little creatures, squealing at the top of their tiny lungs. They swarmed their fallen patriarch. Soon a purring mound covered him except for his head, and the tiny squeals subsided into a soft rippling moan.

Their faint wailing broke like a strange wave over the pair, washing away all their fear and disgust. Tooco knelt, trying to reassure the creatures he hadn't killed a father. And they understood, especially when the old Orkin began to move his head. When he opened his eyes, their peals of relief applied a balm to their awkward connection.

"Cappy, aren't they? I heard the stories, but I never saw one." It was Han's voice, but it sounded oddly unlike him. He turned to get a look at his Screenrage commander, but Han shifted his gaze before Tooco could see in his view plate.

"Maybe they're hungry?" Han dug into the duff slung over his shoulder and extracted a bag of soya chips. He knelt next to Tooco and began tossing handfuls of chips into the furry mass.

"Have you ever seen one before?"

Tooco had. "Yeah. Yakami's personal doctor was taking one apart. He thought it was the last one."

"Did he have any idea what caused them?"

"He thought it was from rats feeding on wharf scabs' bodies. Sores and cuts in the rats' mouths got infected with a blood disease that carried a radiation mutation. Then coke-like features started showing up in the rats."

Tooco remembered when everybody killed them on sight. Then nobody saw them anymore. They went up. Pretty smart! They probably feed exclusively on pigeon. This Orkin's sheed was out right now, hunting up some plump birdies. All these pigeons fed on the mountain of garbage from Big New's dump chute onto Staten Island. But this little herd was from more than one mother. This had to be the litters of several sheed. And *they were all out, hunting in a pack*! He wondered if they'd figured out nets—using nets to catch the pigeons.

Han tossed another handful of chips into the furry mass, chirping happily now. Their patriarch sat up, dazed and scowling; but as his offspring began passing chips to him, he grudgingly accepted the morsels and was soon preoccupied with eating. Both Tooco and Han took off their helmets, eating the chips as well. It dawned on the bellygridder that rat cokes must be sparse if one rodent had a harem with a brood this big. Well, one thing was for sure: this Orkin still had cuj.

⸺ ❦ ⸻

All the shades of pain, microscopic cuts, traced fiery patterns through the countless aching welts and throbbing bruises that covered his body. Still pinned spread-eagle on a slab, babbling the same evasive crap into the same unmoving face. But then stillness, a pause from new agonies, repose in a hanging sleep. Prying his swollen eyes open, he found Carder's cold visage gone, replaced by the devil himself—the iconic narrow face, bladelike chin, arching nose with bloodshot orbs on either side. Black pupils were examining him. The crocodile mouth slid into a knowing leer. Notice was being served. Time to pay attention.

"Hello there."

This must be Lord Yakami, resplendent in a robe of purple and magenta Kevlar: its high flaring collar accentuating the narrowness of his skull. A skull encased in a polished purple helmet ending in a swept-back point. This was armor reserved for meetings of state. Off in the waste fill with some Sacker general presiding over an exchange of goods and services. Somebody more important than an errant spacecase was in the vicinity.

No doubt they were frantic to convince 7 they had nothing to do with the destruction of their resort heaven. He was on a diplomatic mission, desperate to get the facts about what happened and *who* was responsible. They knew he had to be connected to the explosion of Sanatan. That and Carder's inability to break him was the reason for this personal audience.

"I understand you're being very uncooperative . . . and your friend, as well, still refuses to tell us what you are doing down here."

Friend? He didn't have any friends! Nobody had any friends. "What friends?" He wanted to scream, but it would take infinitely more energy than he possessed.

"Friend?" was his feeble response.

"Yes, the coke we caught you with—Baylor." Yakami was demonstrating his intelligence-gathering acumen.

Harrison smiled in spite of his misery. "That's not Baylor."

"Oh, really? Then who is he?"

"Some guy I met in a bar."

"I see. And did you two talk?"

"Yeah. He said they were waiting for me."

"Who was waiting for you?"

"Some cokes. He didn't tell me much before you got us."

"Why wouldn't I believe you? We've just lost a very lucrative enterprise. I've lost a close friend. And you and your renegade buddies had nothing to do with it despite the fact you were the last ones to leave Sanatan before it was blown to hell."

Harrison knew more excruciating pain was about to follow, but telling Yakami the truth would only earn him an even slower and more tortured end.

"So let me see if I've got the sequence of events in your fascinating journey correct. According to Carder, even with our generous offer, your noble spacecase character wouldn't allow you to kill Carmine because he hid you from the Sackers. So you and the rest of your merry band 'requisitioned' a racing van and took it down here to Bellytown, where you were attacked by scabs. And you and the others got split up as a result of the ensuing battle. Is that about right? Have I got it?"

Yakami's slender fingers caressed his aching cuj, just before he felt the agony of sharpened fingernails digging into his swollen sack.

"You didn't have anything to do with the destruction of Sanatan?"

Harrison's *no* became a long shuddering groan.

"No. Yet here you are—unjustly accused, strapped to a torture table, about to find out what torture really is. A very sad and shameful tale. Unfortunately for you, it's all bullshit!"

Yakami's rapier nails punctured his throbbing sack, and Harrison returned to his screaming.

━──◆◆◆──━

The mastery of poisons is the key to modern living. Hearing from his father how he turned the brain-warping proximity of a massive electromagnetic field into a thriving and lucrative business was enough to convince Han of that. And when he'd taken his first forays out into the waste fill in Jersey and the Atlantic bogs, he saw all variety of toxins. Whatever escaped the radioactive dust was tainted by diesel, gas, oil, and a plethora of industrial poisons, along with acid rains. On the face of it, a miserable, filthy, desecrated hellhole. But turned askew, seen in the proper disjointed light, it was a gold mine of opportunities.

You simply had to take small doses until you developed a tolerance, until you were accustomed to the reek of greed and ruthlessness in all its manipulative guises. In a world pickled in poisons, that's exactly what Han did. At night, dangerous adventures into the darkest regions of Bellytown; by day, studying at the Screenrage Studios above— driven through the pristine entry port every afternoon in his father's pearl-white levi limo. Han drank from both sides of the poisoned cup.

Of course, there'd been a lot of vomiting, retching up everything from his necro fuck to the deadness at the center of a Topgrid's eyes. So much to disgorge and then swallow again, until eventually he could keep it all down. Now his boots finally touching the rubble streets, Han was grateful for his father's example, and his own youthful reconnaissance mapping out the lethal streets of Bellytown. After crossing Yaki sector over the top of the mesh using the great grid girders, Han made a beeline up the East Side until they were over Midtown. That's when they hopped onto the burnt-out scraper and ended up sharing a bunker with the urban legend. They decided to spell each other, taking naps with their furry friends while they waited out the buttons. But at some point, they both fell asleep. When they woke up, the Orkin were gone. They didn't steal anything. They were really amazed by that. It validated the connection. But they both knew they'd never tell anyone. No one would believe them anyway.

Now, outside, Han glanced back to locate Tooco and saw huge golden letters plunged in the asphalt in front of the scraper's entrance: "RUMP." They were in no-coke's-land between the southern side of

Cenpak and the mesh at Twenty-Third. They needed to get across town to the West Side and then take Broadway up to Seventy-Eighth. That was the entrance into the barricade that Tooco knew about from his lessons with this "Mayra." They'd have to go west on foot the first few blocks, until they got to Broadway and the lighted sector.

Tooco closed ranks and crouched uneasily behind him. Both surveyed the blackness in front of them, their view plates switched on infrared. Han could see several orange-red forms huddled down the street. Farther to his right was a clan of scabs settling in for the night. Otherwise, only the rats' yellow blips disturbed the nocturnal landscape. He pointed out the scabs to Tooco, then motioned he should follow him as he moved off to his left. They had a ways to go before they got to the lights three blocks of navigating through all the litter. The debris was unavoidable, and any faltering sounds would bring the predators.

Tooco touched his shoulder and pointed behind them. Han could see three scabs sneaking up farther down Fifth Avenue. He could easily kill them with one pulse bolt, but that would alert the entire neighborhood to the presence of a loose frybar. The signature buzz-pop of a light bomb would bring out headhunters in the area, as well as the Yakuza. Han reached in his boot and took out his laser dagger. Tooco followed suit. Han grabbed his shoulder, intent on cautioning him not to light the blade. But uncharacteristically, he realized how condescending that was. I mean, did he really think in the pitch-dark, where they were trying to hide, he needed to warn Tooco not to light the blade now? Determined to make some changes, Han checked himself, giving the bellygridder a couple pats on the shoulder, pointing to an overturned ground vehicle he wanted him to take cover behind. Tooco started crawling to it while Han backed toward another metal carcass on the other side of the street.

They came quickly down the center of the pavement, scrambling silently over the debris, sure of their turf with cat's eyes. Each of them carried a double-headed battle-ax. Han adjusted the setting of the blade length on his dagger to five milligrid and hoped Tooco was doing the same. Against those axes, they'd need all the reach they could get.

A little bigger than papa Orkin, they were a centigrid and a half tall. Their heads were covered with shaggy rust-colored hair. Their torsos were hairless and had the telltale faint-green pallor any creature drinking from the Hudson acquired. Their bodies were thin, with long corded muscles and oversized appendages. Each wore a loincloth of what appeared to be chain metal. They all led with their noses, sniffing repeatedly at the night air, like gods in old vids, but waving axes instead of tails.

Han realized how good he felt, really free at last from his long incarceration. How much he'd missed the pure discharge, the total release the violent alleys of Bellytown afforded. The raw power of youth hummed in his muscles again.

They came in a classic triangle formation—point coke two centigrid out front. They'd wait until the point coke passed, then take out the other two. Suddenly they halted in unison. Like one organism, they registered the scent of their quarry and shifted into a slow-motion gait, battle-axes poised above their heads. They were primed for the ambush. They'd taken the initiative. He had to break their strategy *immediately*, or they were in for a serious fight.

Triggering max-power hydraulics in his mining boots delivered a demolition "punch" that pulverized the concrete underneath him, sending Han soaring five centigrid high, disappearing in a cloud of cement dust. All three turned their attention to the vehicle Han had just catapulted from behind. Above the point coke, Han lit his dagger and dropped like a guillotine, splitting the scab in half. The blood spurting all over his mining jump was burnt orange, which, despite the cauterizing cut, sprayed from the scab's falling halves.

Out of the corner of his eye, he caught Tooco scuttling from cover, lighting his blade across the ankles of the scab nearest him. Leaping on him as he fell, the bellygridder repeatedly plunged his blade in the scab's back. The third one bored down on Han, ax whirling, a high keen on his ragged lips. Han meant to sidestep the strike, but a split second too late, he was sent reeling to the pavement from a glancing blow on his shoulder plate. He barely had time to roll away from another swipe of the ax, almost cutting himself with his laser dagger in the process. Parrying the next attack with his left forearm plate, blocking the scab's ax at the handle, Han rose up onto one knee.

Two options presented themselves: he could either go with a leg sweep off his planted foot as he spun away from the ax, or he could come in low, driving inside with a straight thrust. No time for the frontal lobe. His body made the choice. He was barreling at the snarling scab. His right arm shot from under his bulk—a piston with a laser blade slamming into the scab's narrow chest. Now Han dove to his left, simultaneously pulling his blade with him, carving around from the scab's solar plexus, finally exiting under his right armpit. Once again, burnt orange sprayed everywhere as the scab's partially amputated arm and shoulder slid down the front of his torso before he dropped to the pavement.

And Han looked up to see a grinning Tooco, gesturing with a scab's head in one hand and in the other, his lit laser blade! *Who the fuck am I trying to cap with all this humble-pie crap?* They're all idiots.

"Douse it!" Tooco sheepishly shut down his blade and scuttled toward Han.

Fortunately, the rest of the journey was uneventful, possibly because spotters in the blackened buildings saw what they were up against. Han had to behead a half-centigrid-long cockroach that refused to budge from their path in an especially cluttered section. But there were no more encounters with scabs.

On Broadway, Han hoped they'd be able to snag a "gypsy." Headhunters often supplemented their income while in the burg by taking "fares" around town. He was surprised at the amount of traffic this far up from the mesh. Levies of every description zipped by, above a tapestry of lights hung from old scrapers along "the Great White Way." His father originally supplied the juice for every one of these illuminations.

Born into a family of marine electricians on the tip of Long Island in 2021, "Chewy" (his familial nickname) was extremely hairy at birth and weighed a whopping fourteen pounds. After 3TC, the suspension of electrical services on most of the planet made their particular skills in extremely high demand.

Chewy's father was soon working on the outskirts of what had been Boston, and it wasn't long before his two brothers joined the old coke.

Because of his throwback appearance (Han's father resembled a large ape), Chewy was left to help his mother with an extremely cantankerous eighty-two-cycle-old grandfather—the master of master electricians. Chewy wasn't nearly as dumb as he looked, and with a little help from granddad, he read all the old man's mountain of electrical books and manuals, and he absorbed and retained everything the old fart had to say on the subject. When gramps performed a final service by dying, Chewy set out to make his fortune. A gorilla with a set of ivory-handled Bowie knives (carried in sheaths sewn inside his engineer boots), he cut a distinct figure in Bellytown.

His first job was for a streetlord down by Thirty-Fourth and West Side Highway. He repaired an old hydrogenerator that escaped a meltdown due to its location on the Hudson, near the mouth of the Lincoln Tunnel. The Yaks, seeing those twinkling bulbs, made short work of the streetlord and offered Chewy a lucrative position as their personal electrician. From that one generator on Thirty-Fourth, he wired all the clubs, bars, whorehouses, and gambling dens the Yaks filled Midtown with, trying to wring every last Yuan out of all the techies who were building the great grid plate of Big New.

After that, he had time to contemplate and eventually create a method for lighting all five boroughs of Bellytown. When they first floated the grid plate into place above them, he had his eureka moment.

He'd use the same method employed by one of the first electricians to validate the existence of electricity. He constructed a "field" of metal "kites": copper coils syphoning off the electromagnetic charges now swirling above the burnt scrapers of Bellytown. Scrounging parts from old Con-Ed stations in the surrounding Jersey areas, he built the first power station to store and transport juice from the top of the great grid girders. Before long, he built three more and had every streetlord in the boroughs lined up with buckets of Yuan begging for amperage.

It was time for a makeover. They were both covered with the burnt-orange mucus of their recent adversaries, and in any case, it was time to change their appearance. They pulled their final disguises from their duffs, stuffing their mining jumps into the empty duffs and hiding them under a pile of trash. Han remembered to take Zim's little surprise from his chest compartment and put it into a pocket Zim sewed inside the crotch of his black velvet jump. Moments later, Han emerged from the alley onto Broadway, wearing one of Deli's loudest capes, a purple number with flames rising from its hem all the way up to the batwing collar, looking like a strutting streetlord on a stroll. Security was on the job, Tooco sliding in behind him, wearing a camouflage jump and openly brandishing his frybar. Han's frybar was hidden in a shoulder sling underneath his cape.

Han spied what he thought might be a gypsy coming from downtown. The telltale empty booty rack of a headhunter's levi was welded behind the cockpit. Han stepped into the street and raised his arm in the ancient manner. The faded silver levi swerved sharply, hissing to a halt within a centigrid of the pair. The side view plate cleared to reveal a head, not unlike the one Tooco displayed moments earlier. Gaunt with a splayed nose and ragged lips, his complexion was different—dark brown with the trademark etchings of waste-fill sun. The view plate lowered a crack.

"Wasaw?"

"Seventy-Eighth."

"Wur graf?"

Han held up two black casino credits, waving them seductively in the headhunter's face. As Han anticipated, he was practically salivating at the prospect of snagging these beauties.

"Sanatan booty?" The headhunter lowered his view plate, still further studying them with a wary eye.

Han realized rumors must already be hitting the streets. This coke wanted to know what they knew. He put the credits back in his pocket. "Yaki bones."

The headhunter nodded and motioned for them to get on the rack, seemingly satisfied with his explanation. Tooco climbed onto the rack and pulled Han up after him. They both crouched down, getting a firm grip on the metal frame.

The headhunter's view plate whined shut, and Tooco turned to Han. "You think he snagged it?"

"Why wouldn't he? The casinos in Yaki sector are full of 'em. Now shut up." This wily scavenger probably had a sound probe on the outside of his ship, and it was *probably* turned on.

The battered cruiser eased up off the pavement and began slowly accelerating, not at all the takeoff they expected. It was as if their driver was preoccupied with watching his rear-view screen, wondering about the interesting exchange he'd just heard. The grizzled gypsy finally put the pedal to the metal and began weaving around over and under slower vehicles. There were the usual punks on levi cycles, a couple of streetlord limos, and above the traffic, Han spotted a Sacker drone screening them all. Because he was looking up watching the drone, Han saw it when a blinking red distress light at the top of the rack blinked on. The headhunter had spotted the drone too and was trying to send a message. Han immediately whipped his frybar from under the cape and blew away the flashing messenger! In the myriad blinking lights, hopefully the brief signal wasn't spotted.

The headhunter retaliated by briefly reversing all his E-Mags twice. The first time, beginning with his right lateral mag, and the second time with the top vertical one. The effect was to turn the cruiser upside down, almost catapulting them into the street. They dangled from the booty rack, swinging wildly, as the gypsy made a violent U-turn and headed back toward the Yaki sector. Wielding the frybar with one hand, Han cut away the back of his cockpit, and the gypsy turned with an expression of terror, seeing the frybar pointed at his head.

"SHAGGIT!" The ship lost speed almost instantly.

"SHAGGIT!"

Frantically touching tabs, the scab slowed the cruiser to about eighty grid an hour and turned back to Han. "SHAG, MUFU! SHAG!"

Signaling to Tooco that they were about to drop, Han grinned at the headhunter. "Thanks for the lift."

Not more than two centigrid above a clear stretch of pavement, Tooco released his grip on the rack, and a moment later, Han followed suit. The headhunter immediately gunned the ship and took off. But not before Han, landing knees bent, head tucked, rolled out his momentum, then jumped up and put a pulse bolt up the retreating gypsy's ass! The levi exploded all over the avenue. With the erratic trajectory and sudden explosion, Han was hoping it looked like any other aging levi shorting its E-Mags and blowing up.

He scanned overhead for the drone. Apparently, it missed the action. It hadn't blown them to hell and was nowhere in sight. Tooco's journey hadn't been as graceful as Han's. Dropping earlier and rolling farther, he crashed into a soya cart, bowling over, cart and peddler. The wizened old peddler jumped up, pulling a knife from her rags. She raised the rusty blade to stab the still-stupefied bellygridder as Han shouted a warning in Amerab. She stopped as Han ran toward her, shielding the frybar under his cape, glancing around to see if any clones were watching. The levi's explosion served to scatter the locals so the street was bare. Reaching his dazed comrade, he pulled out the casino credits. Her withered face lit up as brightly as the curtain of lights above her. Trembling, she reached for them as Han thumbed his frybar back to laser and cut her in half.

"Come on, wake up, Tooco!"

The bellygridder grinned stupidly, gesturing for Han to help him up.

"Let's go! We've got to get out of here." He pulled Tooco to his feet, supporting him like some drunken scab as they stumbled down the boulevard. He was trying to get some distance before the denizens stuck their heads out again. Remembering Tooco's remark ("You think he bought it?"), he wanted to drop the little bellyshit in the gutter and just keep walking. But he had to admit, flashing Sanatan credits right after the burg disappeared from the map probably wasn't exactly genius either. He could see the Met about three blocks back down Broadway. That meant they were close to the southern side of Cenpak, about two blocks down and two blocks east. What the hell was that headhunter thinking? Maybe his plan B, if he couldn't get the attention of the Sacker drone, was to make a run for the mesh and hand them over to the Yaks for a big bag of graft.

There must be more than rumors floating around. Harrison, running his mouth to Sun Moon Tu, the "grand wizard of Yaks" or whatever the fuck he was, and Sun Moon must've relayed the info down to Bellytown before Han blew it up. So the Yaks were looking for them specifically, putting their descriptions on the street. But they wouldn't share that information with 7, terrified of guilt by association. Well, at least he'd saved the headhunter some suffering. When they finished squeezing him like a replicator melon for all his information, the only reward the Yaks would give him was an interminable death.

But there was still the mystery of the drones. He realized it started bothering him as they were racing along the grid girders. He kept looking up, expecting to see a swarm swooping under the grid plate, honing on them. But there wasn't a single drone. That drone the headhunter tried to signal was the first one he'd seen. You'd think, after the incineration of Sanatan, a recycling cocoon on the grid girders going up in flames would at least warrant a swarm checking it out. Maybe the loss of Sanatan was damaging 7 in ways he had no idea of. They're dealing with internal upheaval. Their systems have been compromised. For the first time, Han was afraid he might've gone too far with the bomb. He didn't want to start a Topgrid panic that caused the little darlings to go rushing off to the *Protostar*, making their getaway.

Suddenly he realized he was going in the wrong direction, back toward Yaki sector instead of up to Seventy-Eighth. The headhunter incident had subconsciously changed his mind. They needed a new plan. Walking back up Broadway fifteen blocks with every scab, headhunter, and Yaki looking out for them probably wasn't a journey they'd complete, even with disguises. Luckily, he'd possessed the intuitive wisdom to bring one of Deli's white linen handkerchiefs with him—and they were coming up on Fifty-Ninth.

He hoped Jack was safely ensconced in the dreamer's fortress. *Ensconced!* Why did his brain pick up on this shit? It wasn't like he was consciously trying to learn Harrison's extraneous crap.

Yasmine wondered what good she thought it would do coming up here. She was on the southeastern corner of the great barricade. Here, it was all bricks and stone. This was where the Fairmont Hotel was. Well, actually, it was where the street in front of the Fairmont was. The intense heat of the inferno first brought the massive hotel crashing into the street. As the backdraft from the park created a billows effect, fanning the heat to kiln temperatures, the bricks partially melted, forming a ceramic rubble wall cemented with molten glass. Inside it, the dreamers cut a series of interconnected tunnels with small arms, gun emplacements, as well as two of their laser cannons trained on the avenue below. To her left, at the corner of Fifth Avenue, the barrier changed into a spaghetti mass of steel I-beams from where the superscraper across the street and the hotel melted into each other.

She was worried about Mayra. They had a report from an Outrider on the East Side below Forty-Second. A lady friend said there'd been some trouble earlier in the day. Some guy on a levi bike killed three of her associates on the roof of this streetlord's casino/brothel, pulling a percussive without a silencer. To be fair, she said her friends thought they'd spotted a yokel from the waste fill, and they were trying to ambush him. He wore a long black coat, but underneath, it looked like he was wearing some kind of metallic red combat armor. The last they saw of him, he was heading for Yaki sector, probably the Twenty-Third Street entrance through the mesh.

It just didn't fit. I mean, if he was their deliverer, wouldn't he know where Cenpak was? And wouldn't he know they were at war with the

Yaks, and Yaki sector was the last fucking place in Bellytown to go looking for dreamers? When she'd reported the news, she could see Mayra was as confused and anxious as she was. They hadn't heard anything from Splatter either. Well, at least he was probably in the right place—unless some Yak button recognized him from their countless skirmishes down Fifth Avenue and took his head off. He should've contacted them by now. He'd taken one of the Fourteenth Street armory's most powerful walkie-talkies. It could transmit from the southern tip of Manhattan, and he wasn't anywhere close to that far away. They were all scared, scared that, at the last second, something would go terribly wrong. And that fear seemed to confirm the dark "truth" they all carried in their hearts—they weren't worthy to have their visions realized. They were not worthy.

Sitting squirreled away in their uppermost small-arms bunker, perch-1, almost ten stories above Fifty-Ninth Street, she was scanning the avenue and the remains of all the buildings for any movement. She knew her eyes were no match for the assigned spotter. Seated beside her, just to her left, was the gangly old man who gave the impression he had a set of binoculars glued to his face. Sparky hadn't lowered them since she'd joined him an hour earlier. Grunting a terse acknowledgment of her arrival was the only concession to communication Sparky was willing to make.

"Wait a second, I think I got something!" The old man's voice was excited.

Word had spread quickly through the whole community. Everybody knew *who* they were looking for. Yasmine swung her binoculars in the direction of the old man's and was rewarded with a bizarre spectacle. Breaking from the shadows onto Avenue of the Americas was what appeared to be an extremely large streetlord, arms raised above his head, followed by some security scab whose frybar was pointed at his back. In one hand, the streetlord waved a white hankie, signaling surrender. Without taking his eyes off the scene, Sparky swung the long barrel of a directional mic around to hone on the strange duo and slipped on the headphones. He turned several knobs on a small metal box mounted on the rear of the barrel.

She was about to ask when he barked a report, "Not sayin' anything."

Yasmine was refining the focus on her binoculars, tracking the pair as they came directly down toward a cluster of Yaki cruisers across from the barricade. The huge streetlord was wearing a gaudy cape. When she focused on his face, she joked to herself, *Maybe we've been having the wrong visions.* He was gorgeous. Yasmine had never seen anybody who looked even remotely as good as this hunk. He was like flesh-and-blood Screenrage—the stud monkeys on Topgrid fibers.

She could hear the faint electronic squawk of Amerab coming from Sparky's headphones as he began repeating what he heard.

"The security chief is addressing the Yaks . . . He's identifying himself as chief of security for the Broadway Association of Club Owners. He's sayin' he's got this piece of shit who tore up one of their places and killed a couple of their scabs with a laser sword. He's sayin' the piece of shit claims to have pull with Yakami. They want the Yaks to pay them for the damage and casualties. Otherwise, the security chief is gonna ice him right on the spot."

Yasmine watched as, first, one button, then three more, broke away from their cruisers and started toward the pair.

"The Yaks are telling them to stop where they are."

Suddenly the Broadway security chief opened up on the buttons with pulse fire while the streetlord dropped his arms, reached inside the cape, and brought out his own frybar, also blasting away at the Yaks. Before the surprised buttons could hiccup, they were splattered all over Fifth Avenue. The two renegades broke into a run, barreling down on the barricade. They scrambled onto the roof of a cruiser, then leaped onto the base of the barricade. All along the line, Yaks opened fire from their perches in the blackened scrapers across from Cenpak. As the pair started to scramble over the glazed brick and glass, the streetlord waved the white handkerchief in their direction while firing behind him with the frybar in his other hand. The surprised Yaks were beginning to take better aim, and pulse bolts were exploding close to the scrambling duo.

Yasmine knew she had to make a decision right now for it to have any effect on the outcome of this skirmish. She had the authority to issue the order. Grabbing a frybar from its case, Yasmine barked the command, loud enough to be heard in Sparky's mic.

"Perches 5, 7, and 9, open up with cover fire for those two now!"

Sparky repeated the order into his mic with the same urgency she'd given it. Yasmine squeezed off her first burst. A hail of red bolts joined hers as the other perches opened up on the Yaki positions. Now they started receiving fire too as the desperate climbers reached a small hollow just below perch 5. The security chief's left leg wasn't completely hidden in that hollow, and a pulse bolt exploded nearby. He was hit. His boot was smoking, and he was hollering. The guys in perch 5 were yelling at them to reach out their arms, and they could pull them in. As their covering fire was joined by the laser cannons, the Yaki fire diminished, and the pair followed instructions and were pulled to safety.

"CEASE FIRE!"

She heard Sparky repeat the order as she bounded to the level ladder, pressed her feet against the outside vertical rails, and dropped in a fireman's descent. Landing hard after the swift drop, Yasmine ran down the tunnel toward perch 5. Seconds later, she found herself face-to-face with the magnificent streetlord. He glanced up, busy cutting away a piece of his partner's smoking boot, and smiled.

"Thanks for the cover."

"No problem." Because he spoke English, she was immediately wary. This could be some elaborate plan by 7 to infiltrate them.

"Why did you storm the barricade?"

"It was the only way we thought we had a chance of getting in. We're looking for a friend of ours. He came down here a little before us. I sent him ahead to check things out. Our friend's ID is Harrison . . . Harrison, Jack. He was wearing bright-red battle armor. Have you seen or heard of anyone fitting that description?"

CHAPTER

Mayra was still sleeping, curled up on a couch when they brought him in. At first, she wasn't sure she was awake—peering through tangled hair or a forest in a dream, viewing figment or man. Very tall but so symmetrically pleasing, his massiveness was almost delicate. Moving with the fluidity of a snake as he approached, he was making the company commanders escorting him extremely edgy. Chan and Dag, both formidable in their own right, were obviously impressed with his size and agility. Mayra sat up, wiping the sleep from her eyes and brushing the hair from her face. Yasmine appeared from behind the group, stepping around to the front. Black streaks from the soot of the barricade cut across the front of her fatigues.

"Ma, this one and another one who was wounded breached at Fifty-Ninth. They both had frybars, and they killed some Yaks. I ordered covering fire. We didn't take any casualties, but the Yaks did. They're gonna want to retaliate."

The tall blond caught her eye, breaking into a boyish smile. Mayra took in his face. It was the image of a classic Greek god. He was straight from the old leather volumes they lovingly preserved, but he was wearing (of all things) a purple-and-red cape, more red than purple, with flames that rose to his neck. She pulled her attention back to this latest development with their Yaki adversaries, turning to Dag.

"Put the entire levi brigade on full alert around the perimeter. Use the *Firewalker* too. I want continuous patrols over our airspace for the next forty-eight hours and the laser cannon crews on duty in rotating watch."

"Yeah, Ma, I'll take care of it." The broad-faced commander gave her a nod, then turned and left on his mission.

Yasmine waited until he was gone, then moved past Mayra with a conspiratorial glance. "Ma, I need to see you in the stacks."

Again, Mayra's eyes went to their interloper, still with his easy smile, looking back at her. She turned to Chan, who only had eyes for the spot centered between the tall blonde's shoulder blades.

"Is the other one being treated?"

"Yeah, he's at the infirmary. He lost a couple toes and has some second-degree burns on his foot, but he'll be all right."

She addressed the blonde, "They'll take good care of him."

"Thank you." He shifted his weight slightly, and Chan reacted, keeping the muzzle trained on his target.

"We'll talk in a moment."

"Sure." He was patient.

She turned away, following her lieutenant back through the maze of shelves. When they were surrounded by the old books and manuscripts, Yasmine turned to face her. "When I reached them, that one, he calls himself 'Han,' said they were looking for a friend named Harrison, Jack. He says he sent him here to check things out. He said this Harrison was wearing a suit of red armor."

Surprises were coming fast and furious these past few hours, but this one came in from a parallel dimension! There'd never been anything in their visions that included this Adonis who was their savior's sidekick. Everything they thought they understood seemed suddenly unclear. What the hell was going on?

"I don't trust him." Mayra looked up to see her own anxiety and confusion mirrored in Yasmine's eyes.

"You think he's connected to the Yaks?"

"I don't know, but he's just too cool. He's playing for effect. He's up to something."

"Did he say where he came from?"

"Only what I told you."

She needed time to regain some perspective, find her balance inside the chaotic way that things unfolded. But she didn't have time. She needed to make decisions, take action, or prophecy (as premonition was busy warning her) would disappear through slippery fingers.

"I'm going to talk to him in private. Once the other one has been treated, bring him up here. On a stretcher, if you have to. Tell Chan I said to wait in the passage."

Yasmine gave her the worried look. "Have you got your Smith & Wesson?"

"Always." Her mother's pistol was tucked in the padded leather holster at the small of her back.

Yasmine tried a half-hearted smile, but the worry was clear in her eyes. "All right. But if you have to, shoot him in the face. That'll take care of the charm offensive." Yasmine disappeared in the stacks. Mayra listened to her heavy boots on the wood fading into silence. Then she started retracing her steps. She was hoping in the pause to rekindle the feeling of purpose that buoyed her that morning.

Things were coming to some conclusion. She was certain of that much! Stopping suddenly, she pressed her shoulder against the corner of the final stack, shielding her from this unexpected emissary. She took a deep breath and, pivoting into the aisle, came directly at him from across the library.

He stood, relaxed and elegant, despite his garish attire. If he really was the deliverer's sidekick, he was responsible for portraying the cartoon version of his master. *How thoughtful, bringing something for the kids.* Mayra's cynical old buddy appeared to be back from a short sabbatical. These next few moments would tell if this pop icon was a friend of the deliverer or someone who wanted to use him somehow. But she needed to leave all possibilities open because it was a test for her as well: don't ever get too attached to how you think it's going to fall.

"What's your name . . . your ID?"

"It's Han. Han Larkill."

"Where do you come from, Han?"

A dark figure spinning out from all this rustic wood, she was coming fast, firing questions. He knew where he was, revealed by the light of a chandelier in their thicket of timber shelves. He recognized it as a book repository from their time in Bob's NORAD. But this was very different from the cement tomb of "tomes" Bob showed them. *Tomb of tomes?* Good Dog. Had Jack completely turned him into a preening Topgrid twit?

Be that as it may, this second sighting of her—awake, inquiring, aggressive—changed all his plans. He was preparing to reel off an engaging story (fleshed out in Deli's ionic whirlpool), but laying eyes on her now, all those preparations were scrapped. She was what Han had resigned himself to never seeing: a real sheed warrior. Of course, Darl was a force to be reckoned with. She'd honed her biological weapons so she could give a dead coke an erection. Pair that with her ability to turn on a Yuan and go for the jugular, and she was formidable. But now this sleepy sheed was reborn as the genuine item. Her very physicality spoke USBs of experience on the killing ground. He focused on the arms first. Hard-muscled yet streamlined, they hung on her V shape, extending from corded deltoids. Her entire body balanced on powerful legs.

Her face was a pale heart, both wise and naive, open yet covered by invisible armor. A magnificent tangled mane of dark sienna framed this conundrum face. She had it all. Han never imagined he could be so moved by the prowess of sheed.

"Where are you from, Han?" she was asking him again. In the light, the twinkle in her eye confirmed it would be foolish to lie even an iota more than he had to.

"We came down from Big New."

"How?"

"We dropped down a recycling chute that Topgrid charities use to send stuff they don't want to the bellygrid."

"You're lucky your cape didn't get caught in the chute."

He broke into a conspiratorial grin. "I wasn't wearing it at the time . . . It's a disguise."

"Who are you supposed to be?"

"A streetlord on the prowl."

"They don't usually come down this close to Yaki sector. Buttons tend to give them a hard time."

He gave her another flashing grin. "I hadn't planned to either. We were going to try coming in at the Seventy-Eighth Street entrance. Unfortunately, we had a run-in with a gypsy who thought he'd get some graft for our heads."

"How do you know so much about us?"

"My partner Tooco, the one that's injured, he used to come to your crusades. He took the English you offered. He's big on the 'Shakes.' I guess he almost joined you."

His sheepish grin was a tacit acknowledgment they were members of the bad boys' club. He was smooth, but unbeknown to him, he'd touched a painful chord. The idealistic attempts of her youth, those early follies of the heart, were a perennial field day for her devil's advocate. After all, she'd almost cost them all their lives, ultimately starting a war, by thinking scabs who served Yaks could care about anything but graft and power.

"Who's this friend you're looking for?" She noted the subtle flinch in the corners of his eyes.

"He's one of my crew. I ran a Screwhog in the mines before we escaped."

She wanted to ask what a Screwhog was, but it was irrelevant, obviously a mining machine, and she couldn't waste the time. "How did you get into Big New?"

"We hijacked a gadget master's personal cruiser in Sanatan and assumed the identities of him and his crew. We've been hiding out in his mode for the last couple clays."

And of course (although he didn't like to mention it), they'd killed the gadget master and his crew. "You were in Sanatan too?"

"Yeah, we got there in the Screwhog."

"So why come down here? Why send one of your guys . . . 'Harrison, Jack' . . . to check us out?"

There it was, "send one of your *guys* . . . 'Harrison, Jack.'" The dismissive way she characterized Jack's personal connection to him, then paused, caught by the surprise of having to pronounce his full ID—probably for the first time. The unanticipated emotional moment was revealed in her eyes. Han's training made him a master at stripping clones of their deceptions. They did think Jack was their savior—and they didn't have him yet, or she would've been much more direct with her line of questioning. Probably, somebody saw him do something—appear or disappear—otherwise, they wouldn't be so certain he was the one. And the "check us out," definitely a tone of *gotcha* there! She was assuming he had designs on Jack, that he wasn't Jack's friend. While desperate to appear calm and in control, this subterranean empress was chaffing at the bit to find her savior. Dog! Jack hadn't been down here twenty-four hours. There would be no point in trying to circumvent his glory or take the role away from him. They were already snagged on Jack. His best approach would be as the dedicated and concerned friend. He'd even help polish Jack's crown.

"The truth is, we had a disagreement about what to do next. We knew we couldn't stay cooped up in Big New forever. I guess we're all a little crazy from the mining. So when he got this, what he called a vision, that we should all go down to Bellytown, we just thought he was going off his nut! We didn't take him seriously. That's when he took off! We went after him. We're the only three left. The rest of the crew got killed by Sackers in Sanatan. We chased him onto the moving walks, then followed him down the recycling chute. We were right behind him, until we got into the recycling center. It got complicated there, and we lost him . . . you know, the Yakuza run that?"

"Yes, I know."

"Anyway, we've come through a lot together. We're a family of sorts. We made a pact to look out for each other when we escaped. So if Harrison, Jack, thinks this is where he needs to be, then we wanna be here with him."

Uh-oh! Stop the presses. She's got that starry look in her doe-esque eyes! Her devil's advocate was obviously unimpressed with the authenticity of Han's performance and wanted his thumbs-down recorded immediately.

Doe-esque! It's so easy to see everything as a ploy through your jaundiced eyes, you cynical asshole.

She looked in Han's shimmering blue pools and decided, for the moment, she'd let him join the hunt, chasing down their magic stag. It's very easy to slip into that cynical view because, after all, 90 percent of the time, you're right! But it's in the other 10 percent that inspiration and miracles reside. Faith in the possibility of connections from afar was important for maintaining a pulse in your dreams, for recognizing those opportunities when they arrived. She was even going to tell him what she feared.

"I think the Yaks might have him. We got a report of someone fitting his description heading toward Yaki sector on a levi cycle. Maybe they grabbed him. We sent our guy under the mesh to find him. We haven't heard anything for almost ten hours. If he wasn't in trouble, he would have checked in by now. The Yaks may have them both."

"You mind if I ask, why you all were interested in finding him?"

"We're always interested when somebody wearing Topgrid battle armor comes to town."

He'd made the truth a dangerous ally so far, but now he'd have to walk its razor edge. "Yeah, Jack was playing the String game in Sanatan, trying to make us some graft. Sun Moon Tu, the Yak in command up there, he wanted Jack to kill the guy who was protecting us, or he threatened to tell the Sackers that we were hiding out there. Jack made them think he was going to do it, then we hijacked that gadget master's cruiser and took off. The Yaks are looking for us."

"Shit! Then they probably did get them. We need to figure out where they are. The Yaks will torture them, get whatever they can out of them. We have afew hours."

Han nodded, setting his jaw in its most determined manner. Showtime.

"My friend Tooco used to be Yakami's driver before he got nailed by Sackers on the Tokyo Run. He knows the Yak sector in every detail. He'll know where they've got Jack and your coke. You just mentioned you have a *Firewalker*? Give us a couple of cokes who are good at mixing it up, and we'll go in and get them both out!"

"You want me to hand over our *Firewalker* to you?"

"No, that's not what I'm saying. Just let Tooco pilot it. He's a master at flying under the grid plate, and he'll know exactly where to go and how to get there. Send as many cokes with us as you want. The more, the merrier!"

"You've got a very good opinion of your abilities."

"Not without reason. How many cokes do you have who could pull off what we did to get in here?"

"Aren't you forgetting, your friend is missing some toes?"

"Left foot. His right is the one that plays the pedals."

"Do you make a habit of volunteering your wounded for suicide missions?"

"Only when I have to."

"Yes, and you really do have to . . . and you haven't really told me why. 'Because you're buddies' doesn't really cover it, does it?"

The truth, the truth will usher in the lie. "All right. Listen, before I tell you this, I already know you're not going to believe me."

"Try me."

"He can do things, amazing things—*really amazing!* He can disappear and reappear. He can move things! He can become a part of things. He . . . he can travel to other dimensions. I know I sound insane, but it's true. It's what made it possible for us to escape, the things he can do ..."

Ending his performance with a glassy look of wonder, haunted by the magic he'd seen, Han was actually fantasizing about watching her pale shy popping open as she spread her thighs, offering up succulent pink petals. He could almost taste her.

"Tooco told us all about you. He always remembered the 'Shakes' you gave him. With the way things turned out, he's been sorry he didn't join you when he had the chance. Jack liked what he heard about you from Tooco too! We figured he'd try and come here to you."

He'd laid it on just about as thick as it would go. There was a brief silence, and then she muttered something in the moment that changed Han's life. Shaking her head, she said it to herself, but he heard every word.

"He *just* needed to come here and give me the book."

As he'd already noted, so many things happened during their escape where things couldn't have lucked out any better. He'd even started entertaining the notion some "supernatural" force was involved. But this was the lock opening!

This was the moment in his life when a divine overseer was placing the singular key to transcending *all of his difficulties* right in his hand; actually, in his breast pocket.

In Deli's mode, when they were planning their departure, Han made Darl record that personal appeal to Jack, a lover's plea, begging him to rejoin her and his companions. At this very moment, Han had that slim tablet in his jump—*tucked in the pages of Jack's little book.* At the time, he thought putting Darl's message in the book Jack grabbed at Bob's was a nice touch. Now he knew it for what it was—divine providence. He knew, without a doubt, this was the very book she was waiting for. He'd never been more certain of anything in his life. He slid his hand under the cape, carefully removing the book while leaving the tablet where it was. All or nothing. He said it softly, simply, as if he'd only been waiting for her to mention it.

"Here's the book you've been waiting for."

She'd always imagined herself with her head thrown back, an expression of bliss radiating from her face. And of course, there were tears, but like glistening rays illuminating pure joy. Suddenly all there was were tears from a sleeping ocean unexpectedly awakened, drowning everything. So casually he'd reached inside the garish cape, fumbling like a novice magician, before he pulled out the sacred volume, holding it up to the light. Like in their dreams, the gold inscription imprinted on the soft black jacket. *The Prophet* by Kahlil Gibran.

Reaching with trembling hands to take it, she opened the cover and found the same Shakespearean verses, as in the book her mother found, but with this inscription below: "For you, Sarah. Love is a mighty lord. Mike." It was from that medical student her mother discovered in the underground morgue with his copy from the girl. This was Mike's copy to her—his Sarah, who was home with her family at the end. There was nothing left to do but surrender to this moment. And as she did, unexpectedly, it was another author's words sounding in her head—Chekov: "bathed in a perfect mercy."

While it was the last thing he expected, this gorgeous warrior hunkering at his feet, balling like a tube-born, it seemed, at the same time, totally appropriate. As if these expressions of adoration were waiting in the wings for Han all his life, her auburn tresses fanned across his boots in a regal spray. A worthy opponent, bowed the mythical sheed warrior come finally to pay homage. Han Larkill felt truly recognized for the first time in his life. And there was something even more remarkable. He did believe in Dog and knew for a certainty whose side he was on.

What was Tooco yelling from Shakes after he won Tokyo Run? "Some are born great. Some get it by bustin' their hump—and some have it shoved down their throats!" The vision at Han's feet signaled he'd won the third crown in that triumvirate.

Time to get Jack back. How ironic if *his* adventure turned out to be the culmination of all cokekind's striving.

First, Yakami took off the purple-and-magenta robe to reveal a black silver-studded jump. The dandy of all Yakuza. But finally, the sweat from his exertions drenched that too, so he zipped the top off.

Though his eyes were almost swollen shut, he could see the elaborate tattoos completely covering his upper torso. He was old Yakuza, and the folds of his wrinkled skin stretched and skewed the intricate designs. The undulating red and blue lines with their rainbow shadings were too complex for Harrison's battered vision. But for a moment there, swimming in front of him was something familiar, a faint glimmer of his String pattern in the tracing on the old Yak's back. It slipped away as Yakami turned, focusing that malevolent smile on him again.

"You're making this very hard on an old man."

Yakami stretched out an ink-sleeved arm, palm up. In his hand, Harrison recognized a bristling black scorpion. From retrieval, he'd seen vids of how the little critter struck.

"We get them occasionally from headhunters roaming the western waste fill. Vicious little creatures, but for some reason, they seem to like me."

After what he'd experienced at Yakami's hands, he had a pretty good idea what the reason was.

"You know, the sting from these can be unbelievably painful . . . especially if it's in a sensitive area already awakened to discomfort."

His hand, with the ebony insect in its palm, began slowly sinking toward Harrison's waist.

"I've been hoping to avoid using my tiny friend. I wanted to remove your jerk and cuj at their original size to preserve them for a gift, but you leave me no choice. You're being very stubborn."

The hand dropped entirely from Harrison's view.

"Why don't you accept the inevitable? Why cling to a fantasy you will somehow survive this experience? Get it over. Give it up! Relax with death. Death is your friend now. You can leave with him, quickly, I promise . . . and I won't take my trophy until you've exhaled your last breath. You have my word. But you have to tell me, Harrison. I have to know what you know about Sanatan before I let you go. Last chance. Make this easy now."

He strained through broken cheeks, past split and swollen lips, to answer his tormentor, "Fuu, uu—"

He could feel Yakami's clammy hand slide under his scrotum, then take hold of his pummeled shaft. An instant later, a red-hot needle injected itself down his urethra, skewering his tormented jerk.

Zim sat in the cushy niche of Deli's office mode, pondering the problems entailed in their ambitious plans. He was forced to work in 124th scale on Deli's desk-size holo imager in order to get an overview of areas in the Satport where he'd be projecting images. Cokes appeared very small. He'd had trouble adjusting the focus on his goggles to factor in his farsightedness. Add to this, Ryka was hunkered underneath the slab of polished marble in front of him, madly whipping her tongue around the base of his shaft. Was it any wonder he wasn't getting much done? There was no stopping her now. She was in a simpler reality. Soon she'd be only a sucking, bobbing organism drawing all sustenance from the jerk. She could go on like that for hours—as much Freemate as he'd pumped in her, she probably would. It became necessary to calm her down. She was starting to have her "visions" again.

Han and Tooco took almost all the Nitro meth they had left to barter with in Bellytown. Han gave them ten patches for a party to keep their minds off their anxieties after he left. Things got pretty wild, spurred on by the endless opulence. But for the moment, with all the sheed zoned out on Freemate, Deli's mode was quieter. He'd probably need to put Ryka completely under if he was going to get any real work done, but for the present, it was fine. He decided to give his eyes a rest and move on. He needed to nail down some details for their plan to steal *Protostar*. He needed to get a blueprint of the interior of a Satcruiser. Specifically, he needed to find the auxiliary entrance to the cargo hold from the passenger area—hopefully at the front of the ship, close to the pilot's cockpit. It was the escape hatch that would allow them to disappear (along with a few crew members' bodies) before Sackers came aboard.

The problem was Deli's status didn't cut it for accessing aeronautic blueprints. Ryka was beginning a series of "dragon" swallows he taught her. The swallows happened after her lips stretched down to lock around the base of his shaft and then, like dragon gills, fluttered over his jerk. Her throat rippled every time she swallowed, rolling from deep in her throat to her mouth at his root before sucking her way up to dive again. "Oh, Sendra, my love ..."

But he was seriously questioning his lack of temerity after what he'd witnessed in Sanatan. In the Pacino, he'd been introduced (vividly) to a side of Ryka's history he was aware of but never really pictured. He slipped into the Screx right after she'd taken a spin, forgetting in her Nitro haze to wipe her coordinates. The nonstop slice and dice that greeted him was still a bloody imprint on his mind, a hatchery littered with broken tubes and tube bodies draped everywhere. She required sedation.

If he could get the blueprints, he was sure he could find a way for them to slip into the cargo hold from their luxury suite next to the pilot's compartment. Suddenly he had a mini-epiphany. Why not hack in through one of the security robo's programs they deactivated? With a little tinkering, he could tap into one of their drives and, from there, into 7's cloud. They'd be swimming in blueprints. Maybe Ryka wasn't a distraction. Maybe he was receiving primal creative energy! His mental prowess was expanding in the accelerating rhythm of Ryka's lips—slicker, quicker, with every rise and fall.

—◦●◦—

Han studied the partial maps spread across the wooden table in one corner of the dreamer's war bunker, a place that *did* remind him of Bob's NORAD lair, another cement box crammed with outdated technologies. They did have a couple net screens, but neither was tuned to any of the fiber feeds. Both were broadcasting silver static. He looked up to see Tooco limping through the lock. It wasn't really a lock, just a slab on hinges. Like almost everything these dreamers made, it was fashioned from wood. The dreamer called Dag followed Tooco into the bunker. He'd been the first one to pull them up into the barricade, and he'd taken over, maintaining the tourniquet Han applied to Tooco's foot.

Dag nodded to Han, addressing him, "Mayra will be here in a few minutes. She's giving some final instructions to the cannon crews."

Han was worried about what Tooco told Mayra. He was coming from his personal interview with the dreamer queen. After the sacred-book thing, Han was hoping she'd go easy on him. He'd gone over their basic cover story when doing a final check of their equipment back at Deli's. He'd asked the bellygridder a few questions to make sure he was listening, and he was. Han only changed two things when he talked to Mayra. He got a little carried away when he killed the rest of the crew in Sanatan. But if she called him on it, he'd just say he was trying to protect them because they were still in Big New. That was a little fishy because why would it matter if some subterranean bellygrid empress knew they were up in Big New? They had no connection to 7, but he wouldn't know that for sure. He'd just say it was irrational suspicion at the time because they were constantly being hunted. The other thing was his impromptu revelation of Jack's spacecase powers. He'd told her Topgrid science made this "magic" possible. If Mayra brought it up, Han hoped Tooco would figure out he had his reasons and just roll with it. If he denied it, that was fine too. She would assume he was keeping Han's secret.

Looking at him closely, Han could tell he was afraid. But it wasn't "the jig is up" terror being revealed on his face. It was more a generalized dread, poised for doom to strike from any direction. He needed to break this cautious ice.

"Hey, gimpy! I've just been acquainting myself with the layout of your old stomping grounds. Get your crippled ass over here and see if you can fill it in."

"Better, thanks for asking!" Tooco used the table for support as he hopped his way down to Han.

Han smiled sheepishly. "I hope it's not as bad as it looks."

"Lost the little toe and the toe next to it, some second-degree burns on the ball of the foot right behind where the toes are gone. Luckily, the laser cauterizes, and they put some antiseptic on it, so no worries about infection."

"You can still drive?"

"I can always drive." Tooco was tempted to tell their new comrades about his recent victory in Sanatan, but Han would break his neck later. He was just starting to study their maps when the lock slammed open, and a rotund dreamer thrust his mass into the mode. Dag introduced him as Ram, which seemed about right. He nodded curtly to Han but ignored Tooco's existence.

His ruddy complexion was a contrast to the pale whiteness and coal blackness of the rest of the dreamers. Han theorized his color came from a seriously accelerated metabolic rate. He was bursting with energy. His features were rounded, rosy, and plastic. He reminded Han of Santa, except his hair and beard were black.

"Sorry I was delayed, but we needed to coordinate artillery and airpower. What exactly have you got in mind here? All I've heard from Mayra is you want to take one of our cruisers into Yaki sector? Is that for any good reason you can think of? Fill me in!"

Han knew instantly this "general" was going to cause him difficulty.

"We think the Yaks grabbed Jack. They were looking for him. There was a report of a coke in red armor heading for Yaki sector. They may also have captured your coke looking for Jack behind the mesh . . . Splatter?" What an ID. It was time to wind up his bomb and start to make it tick.

"Tooco, you were Yakami's driver back in the day. Where do you think they'd hold them?" Han gestured to a suddenly surly Ram. "Your old comrade here needs your help!"

Ram leaned his massive girth across the table, focusing on Tooco. "This little fellow is not my old comrade. I've never seen this little fucker before in my life."

Whether Mayra made the announcement to the masses, or it was still just a rumor, Han knew the news he'd arrived with the prophesied text would spread like wildfire. Some secrets are too big to keep. *They needed to fnd their redeemer*, and though they might not articulate it to themselves, they were no longer quite certain who that was. They were off-balance and feeling desperate. Their short fuses were beginning to show. Han (not being in their original story) was a problem. Essentially, they were all getting bumped down not one but two notches in their pecking order. Han could afford to feign benign benevolence.

"I was speaking a little too freely. Tooco here attended the crusades that Mayra held and actually learned his English from you, so he has often spoken of you as friends. I presumed too much on that. I apologize."

Ram shifted his focus to Han. A look of confusion and shame briefly crossed his flushed face.

Han gave a small bow and commenced formal introductions. "This is my friend Tooco. You already know my name."

Dag gave Tooco a reassuring pat on the shoulder and moved from behind him to sit at the table beside Han. Almost as tall as Han, back on the barricade, he'd been struck by the unusual features of Dag's face. His long, narrow nose and bushy eyebrows gave him a scholarly bent, but expansive cheekbones and a lantern jaw reminded Han of the rough-hewn visage of his father. His odd face wore an expression of genuine admiration as he spoke in a soft unwavering voice.

"We're all a little undone by your arrival . . . expected but unexpected . . . but I assure you, we're overjoyed that you're all finally here!"

Ram, regrouping after his loss of composure, tried to take the reins again. "If we're thinking of flying into Yaki sector, it would be a good idea to know the lay of the land." He tossed a marker to Tooco, gesturing to the maps spread over the surface of the table. "Can you fill in some of these areas?"

Tooco eased himself onto a vacant stool on the other side of Han, studying the worn parchments as the others looked on. He continued to marvel at the weird mix of techie and scab rig they relied on. Frybars, paper, and markers! The dreamers were an interesting tribe.

"I can fill it all in for you. But I think they're keeping him here." The bellygridder pointed to a blank area at the southern end of the Yaki sector.

Ram remained unimpressed, gesturing down the length of the table. "Fill it all in."

Tooco gave Ram a hard look but began to draw. Han put a calming hand on the bellygridder's shoulder, trying to keep his horse from breaking for the finish too soon. They all watched as various streets and structures appeared under his busy hand. Both Ram and Dag were rapt as the secrets of Yakuza sector were revealed. Han gave Tooco's shoulder a subtle squeeze. "You'll be excited to hear that our comrades possess a Lockheed *Firewalker* outfitted with four laser cannons!"

"I can't wait to get my hands on the stick." Bent over the map, Tooco continued etching out final details and trying to escape Han's grasp.

Ram scowled down at the top of the bellygridder's head. His disdain at the thought of turning over his pride and joy to this runt of an ex-Yaki couldn't have been any more obvious.

"How long has it been since you flew under the grid?"

Han released his grip on Tooco's shoulder, giving it a final pat. Tooco stayed intent on his task. "Don't worry about it. Experience is something you don't forget. I was buzzing Bellytown at four thousand grid an hour while you were still a gleam in some mutant scab's eye."

If Han hadn't primed the eruption, he'd never have been fast enough to stop Ram's lightning-bolt reply. The rotund dreamer could haul that bulk when he'd a mind to, leaping up and opening fire. The overhand right almost whizzed past before Han clapped a huge paw over Ram's fist, pulling it down, causing him to crash face-first into the maps. The table shook with the impact. It was less than a second before Dag leaped up, grabbing the back of Ram's neck.

"Get a grip, Ram!" he hissed in the old warhorse's ear with a combination of embarrassment and rage. "Don't imagine, brother, that because your dreams are eminent, you can finally have that temper tantrum you've been holding in for so long." Dag gestured to Tooco. "He's here to help us, and he knows a lot about the layout of their sector. Keep your mind on the mission. We don't have the time for this shit." Dag took his hand from Ram's neck. Han could see he was flustered, having to check an elder.

"And if you have any doubts that you acted injudiciously, consider that, at 140 kilos, you just tried to hit a man who weighs maybe sixty and comes up to your belt buckle—and just had part of his foot blown off!" Desperate to justify his breach in the chain of command, he was driving the argument home.

Ram slowly raised himself on his elbows, shaking his head to clear it. He finally stood. "I'll wait for Mayra's orders." Without looking at anyone, he turned and walked out.

Dag briefly bowed his head, then turned back to Han and Tooco. "I apologize for Ram. Things are changing too quickly for some of us. He'll be all right." Taking Ram's place at the table, Dag moved to dismiss the incident by focusing on Tooco's handiwork.

"Do you know which of these buildings they'd keep them in?"

Tooco placed a stubby index finger on his makeshift map, tapping repeatedly on a small triangle he'd sketched. Han knew the place, kind of a landmark in "the village" around Twelfth Street and Third Avenue, not far from some favored haunts of his youth. The triangular building was an ancient brick structure five levels high. Because of its isolation from surrounding buildings, it escaped the domino destruction that most brick structures suffered in the great fire. Later, the Yaks restored it, repainting the miniscraper its original bright pink.

"That's the Yaki command post for the southern sector." Before he got the last word out, Han was sorry he'd opened his mouth. He'd just broken the cardinal rule of not knowing more than you're supposed to.

Dag looked up, startled by Han's sudden knowledge of Yaki sector, then blushed in wonder—at what (Han could only assume) was Dag bestowing psychic powers on him. A complete surrender of any authority and an open acknowledgment of a dire need for instruction gave Dag's face the innocence of a newborn. On their mission to get Jack, this tube would be putty in his hands. Thank Dog, being the savior's "majordomo" was easy work. Some of his fairy dust rubbed off on you. Although, to give the newborn acolyte in him his due—the carnelian battle jump he designed for Jack and the dreamers' prophesy of their deliverer arriving in red armor—that was pretty fucking amazing! Almost as amazing as the sacred-book thingy. This dreamer mojo was definitely the real McCoy. And Jack, wordy ponce that he was, was still the man!

"We haven't been able to recon that area. We know it's where they base most of their cruisers." Dag took the marker from Tooco and, using it as a pointer, traced their route across the makeshift map. "We can come in low, off the Hudson at around Fourth Street, and blow a hole in the mesh at dock level. They'll register the break and send cruisers to check. We can program a remote to follow us in and crash it after we get through. They'll think it was just one of 7's drones gone haywire. Hopefully, it'll buy us more time undetected."

Tooco grinned at the young dreamer. "They won't detect us. After we're in, we go up thirty levels and follow the conical shape of the mesh around and down. As long as we hug that mesh, they can't pick us up in all that metal." Dag was immediately appreciative of Tooco's strategy.

"Yeah! We could follow the curve until we're all the way over on the East Side, then drop down to street level just before the cruiser yards on the East River perimeter. After that, zigzag down the back streets to Twelfth and Third."

Han broke in, "We need to know exactly where they're being held in there."

"In the basement. That's where all interrogations are done." Tooco grabbed back the marker and began sketching the floor plan on a blank section of paper. "We can put Yaki logos on the *Firewalker* and make it look something like a Yak patrol cruiser. Then we land out front, and you march right inside."

Han smiled his appreciation. "Yeah, of course! We can wear neon jumps and look like Yaks coming in off patrol." Han was suddenly on fire. "You tell them you're just back from Sanatan and have a report for Yakami. I figure he'll be the one interrogating Jack and your friend. They'll take you right down to see him!"

Tooco pounded the table with glee. "Yes, yes! Oh, that's good!" He turned to Dag. "That *Firewalker*'s really armed with four laser cannons?"

"Yes, two nose cannons and two turret cannons."

Tooco would've danced on the table if it wasn't for his foot. "That's fantastic." He pointed to the floor plan of the basement he'd just drawn. "Once you take care of the Yaks, grab Jack and your other coke. Get over to this corner and signal me. I'll take care of getting you out."

Han took it all back. His little bellygridder was worth his weight in Yuan. Tooco was going to cut them an exit right through the pavement!

"Why would they let us go right down to the basement if we were reporting from Sanatan?" Dag's question took him off guard, but Han recovered quickly, shooting Tooco a warning glance before launching the lie. "Because they bring down the daily take from the casinos in techie quarter. That's where they make most of their graft."

Dag accepted the explanation with a nod of enlightenment and went back to studying Tooco's floor plan. Now it was time to put the last piece of his plan into place. "I'll have to stay in the *Firewalker* with you, Tooco. There's no way they're gonna believe in a two centigrid tall button."

Dag jerked his head up. The expression on his face was one of shock, bordering on horror. "You're not coming."

Han was surprised and disappointed by this emphatic rejection from his young comrade, especially since, with both of them in the *Firewalker*, he and Tooco could seize the initiative. After they got Jack and cleared the area, these dreamers wouldn't know what hit them when he turned around and blew them both away. *So close*, and now, for some reason, this dreamer tube was dulling his edge. He made every effort to inquire calmly, "Why not?"

"Because Mayra isn't going to risk losing our deliverer's right hand. You're safe here, and it's where you're staying until we bring him back."

"Did Mayra tell you she didn't want me going on the mission?"

"No. But I'll tell you now."

• — ◆◆◆ — •

She felt good about handling what was essentially a "shoot-out" with Han. Sidekick or no sidekick, Mayra was directing this show. Han wasn't going anywhere near the *Firewalker*. After the meeting, she'd made a beeline back here.

She needed this time in her cubbyhole. It was a slow process, always an afterthought; but eventually, she'd turned it into a kind of haven. It was still a cave. Not all the faded tapestries draped around its walls hid the fact it was rough-hewn cement. She'd wanted her chamber dug as an extension of their library. The library itself was expanded from one of the storerooms at the 103rd shuttle level. Decades of work were invested in their tunnels. On the opposite side of the tracks was the entrance to the Duni cavern drilled out of Manhattan granite. It was designated as their vision chamber even before Sarah died.

Almost thirty years ago, thanks to her proselytizing, the Yaks heard rumors about a wealth of weapons and technology they had squirreled away from before 3TC. They sent infiltrators pretending to be interested in English, hoping to find where they hid their treasure and send in raiding parties. Frustrated with their inability to discover anything, the Yaks decided to shoot first and ask the questions later. They beat them back using unsilenced Colt AR-15s. That brought a swift bombing by Sacker cruisers and severe losses among those still aboveground.

Wounded and on her deathbed, Sarah managed a last impassioned plea for forgiveness and a recommitment to her daughter as their leader, begging them to show some belated compassion for Mayra's gullible heart. She'd learned and changed as a result of her mistake. And they did forgive, remembering the boon that Mayra's first vision brought them. But the painful losses of her folly and the ongoing war with the Yaks hardened their hearts against ever inviting outsiders into Cenpak again—with one notable exception.

Thank God for Danner, their techie engineer. He'd been the last of any converts, and he'd proved supremely important. Mayra used him as proof of the wealth that technology could put in the service of their Duni vision. Danner headed up a grid-plate maintenance crew after Big New was completed. He'd attended some of her speeches at Lennon's knoll, when Mayra was in the throes of her hippie debacle. He showed genuine interest for a while, but then disappeared. He turned up again at the barricade, fifteen years later, saying he had important information about an impending Sacker sweep of Bellytown. Enough time had passed. Mayra was able to convince the others he could be a valuable source of information. The information turned out to be correct, and they started letting him make regular visits. Danner had an ulterior motive as well, but it was of a benign nature. Retarded by his Screx addiction, it only surfaced when a nineteen-year-old Yasmine accompanied Mayra during one of his visits.

Most techies spent their wages on Nitro, booz, gambling, and—if they didn't give a damn about being slimed—illegal sex. But there were those (usually supervisors, engineers, techies) who aspired to the finer things. For them, Topgrid provided job site, Screx emporiums, where, for a nominal fee, they could Screx for a few hours. It was a way of fueling their interest in keeping Topgrid happy. Older now, he was weary of embracing illusions. One look at Yasmine gave him the courage to make the leap down their rabbit hole.

Danner shared with them everything he knew about 7 and the Topgrid who inherited the sealed burg floating above them. They learned about Sackers with their implants and modulars. Many were more robot than human. He told them that techies were really just the comfortable slaves of Topgrid. He explained how they grew their progeny in test tubes and mastered genetic engineering, and he'd provided a cornucopia of practical applications for all that engineering knowledge. He showed them how to use the drill presses at the underground Con-Ed garage to adapt engine oil filters into silencers, fitting them to the weapons they'd found at Fourteenth Street Armory. That was a game changer.

Danner had been dead for almost a month, hit by a pulse bolt from a sniper in a scraper across from the East Side barricade. All of them, not just Yasmine, were still mourning him.

Although the Yaks' much-belated second surprise attack ten years ago caused a few casualties, the dreamers' response with their silenced automatic rifles turned the invaders to mincemeat without Sackers being any the wiser. They'd held them at the barricades ever since. Finally, that lucky salvage of the Sacker transport in Cenpak three years ago gave them the upper hand. Now they limited their street-level activity to security patrols inside the barricade, which was replete with booby traps and early-warning alarms. Only her most devoted followers, the *Outriders*, went beyond Cenpak.

Over the last few years, with the ongoing standoff, they gathered at their fires mostly for warmth and company. Though they saw individual visions in the flames, they no longer had the epic communal visions that first filled them with hope and passion. The experience of their collective vision was slowly being suffused with the comfortable glow of myth. Just a story to be dreamt on, like the soft down pillow she'd finally allowed in her bed. With the exception of the Outriders, they no longer looked to be released from their entombment, taking comfort in the peace and security there instead.

Until early this morning, when dreams started coming true.

She'd made the announcement to her commanders, after determining the angle of crossfire for the laser cannons targeting Fifth Avenue. They stood in a ragged circle as she took the twin to their *Prophet* from inside her flak jacket. "The big one in the cape who came across the barricade with the little one—is apparently our deliverer's 'John the Baptist.' He brought the sacred twin that the vision promised!" Mayra raised it up for everyone to see. "His name is Han, and he's safe here with us. We are searching for the deliverer whose name, Han has informed me, is Harrison, Jack." Then she gave them the book to examine, to see for themselves. They all handled it with care, like the sacred object it was. Looks of wonder, alternating with disbelief, flashed back and forth across their faces, until, in silent affirmation, they acknowledged what it was. The proof. And yet the way it arrived made everyone uneasy about what was going on. Instead of being energized by these developments, they seemed immobilized by uncertainty, wanting to wait safely under their rock.

Wow! When you're ironic, you are ironic! She'd forgotten about her butthole buddy Beelzebub's personal attorney. *Lady, stop your bitching. Excuse me, but aren't you the same soothsayer who was admonishing us not to get too attached to the way we think things oughta go? That was you, right? So, at this very moment, whose head is up their concrete ass?*

Christ. He was right. She was their leader. Even if this deliverance was arriving in a disjointed manner, she was still instrumental in navigating the shifting prophetic landscape. Mayra sprang off the mattress and pounced on the narrow passage leading down to the shuttle platform and her desk. Reaching the platform, she grabbed the walkie-talkie on her desk and called Ram.

"Ram, hold the *Firewalker* till I get down there. I'm gonna take the Camaro right now. Sound the warning!"

She shoved her walkie-talkie into her jacket pocket, jumped on the flatcar, and took it down to the West Side IRT platform. There, poised on a ramp leading down to the outside set of IRT tracks, she needed only to pull a lever, simultaneously releasing the brake and shifting the ramp's rails, allowing the bright yellow '68 Camaro to roll smoothly onto the IRT rails. It would get her down to the underpass at the Seventy-Eighth bridle path bridge in less than twenty seconds. She needed to be on-site now. She needed to be watching everything. They were taking the *Firewalker*. The plan for rescuing Harrison and Splatter was solid. Dag was their best shooter. Yasmine was signed on and knew to keep a close eye on Tooco. This whole thing depended on Tooco knowing where they were holding them.

If Harrison and Splatter were even Yak prisoners. On that one, she'd gone with her intuition and the need to take action. Han's revelations, along with his calm but decisive manner, also had a lot to do with it. As she stepped from the flatcar onto the IRT platform, the fire truck siren (used to clear the tracks) began wailing down the tunnel.

She jumped off the platform into the gleaming convertible and turned the ignition key. It was the pet project of the last Con-Ed garage manager, and he'd kept it in a corner there, along with his other prize, the red Roadrunner. The 454-inch GMC big-block roared to life. There was no steering involved with this short ride. Just punch it for eight seconds, back off, engage the clutch, and shift to neutral, then hit the subway brakes to stop by Seventy-Eighth. She revved the engine higher and higher until she heard that sucking sound of the supercharger opening its intakes. Then Mayra popped the clutch.

The roar of the great gas-guzzler, combined with the screaming steel wheels, calmed her finally. She just needed to stay on the job.

•———◆◆◆———•

Dusk for that hour before sunset cast pale rays on the barren trees, one of the two times a day when the sun pried its way under the grid plate, spilling a little light into the shrouded purple sky. Inside of *Firewalker*, Yasmine watched over Tooco's shoulder as Mayra, Ram, and Han carried on a discussion, standing in front of the ship. Nodding to Mayra, Ram turned toward the cockpit of *Firewalker* and gave them the thumbs-up. He bore his humiliation stoically. The little ex-Yaki prick who goaded him was getting on everybody's last nerve. Tooco was taking his time—setting the light levels on the instruments, adjusting the command couch, remolding the grip of the joystick to his hand. Gripping her frybar, Yasmine was doing some revving up of her own.

Directly behind the pilot's capsule, Dag hunkered down next to Yasmine inside the streamlined fuselage. Surprisingly, there would be more than enough room in the cargo cabin for Harrison and Splatter when they came back, if they got them. She was still reeling from the events of the last few hours. She'd gone out onto the barricade to think but just ended up getting more confused. Hopefully, Tooco was as good a driver as he claimed to be, piloting through the grid girders. It took Danner quite a lot of practice to get really adept at it.

The little fighter was completely broken down into parts, packed in compressed foam cases. Like the laser cannons and levi cycles, even the frybars they snatched up when the transport crashed. They all needed assembling. Putting them together under Danner's supervision was an excellent opportunity to learn about these new technologies. But *Firewalker* was the real bitch. It took two years to finish it. At least he got to fly it for a year. Danner loved to fly.

He told her about the *Protostars* the Topgrid were busy designing—a fleet of monolithic spaceships to take them across the universe to a new planet. Yasmine thought they sounded like the big ship they described seeing in the very first Duni vision. The ship they believed would take *them* away. He'd laughed and said, "Anything's possible!" She told him it was lucky he found the dreamers because they were exactly where he belonged! He didn't get it. She smiled now, remembering.

It was weird that she couldn't really acknowledge it when she was awake, only in her dreams, where he died over and over. From accidents to various forms of murder and even once from old age, he died, and she kept going through that first impact again and again. It was barely a month.

Yasmine turned her attention to the "hawker's glove," which wrapped like a second skin around her right hand and forearm. A thin black plastic film covered it, mimicking a robotic modular—something a lot of buttons sported.

But underneath, it was aged oiled leather wherein her fingers moved with complete freedom and dexterity. The hide was thick and double-layered with finger pads, palm, back of hand, and wrist triple-layered. Yasmine was proud of her family's unique martial style. Nowadays, it was more of a novelty, but it was the perfect party favor for this mission.

When Dag told her about the strategy meeting in the war bunker and that Mayra wanted her to take Ram's place on the rescue team, she immediately began working out a timetable that allowed her to take a trip down to Fourteenth Armory before rendezvousing at *Firewalker.*

As for his safety on the mission, Yasmine was sure Tooco was relieved with her substitution for Ram. But she observed his utter disbelief when, upon arriving at the underground hanger, Dag addressed her as *commander.* The fact she was leading this raiding party turned the little scab's world upside down. Fuck the little clown. She wanted to hold on to the image of Mayra that Dag described, bursting into the war bunker with her fearless spirit, regaining her balance the same maddening way she always did—surrendering herself to the chaos and then, somehow, rising up with new strength and vision. Dag said she scrubbed Han from the mission before she finished coming through the door. She found an empty stool at the table and sat, announcing Ram's request that he be replaced. She named Yasmine as her choice. After taking a look at their map, she asked what they'd come up with in the way of a plan. Han told her, and she liked it. She agreed: it was better to go in small and quick—a basic grab-and-run mission. When Dag told Yasmine the particulars, she agreed with Mayra's assessment of the plan but was adding some refinements of her own.

It was no skin off that greasy little bellygridder's nose who was in command of this mission. He'd be staying in the *Firewalker* anyway. If it got too hot for him (holding for their signal), he could take off anytime he wanted—and probably would!

When she climbed in the ship, Yasmine purposely zipped open the front of her neon-blue trench. With the collar up, it was her favorite part of the "button" costume. Whipping open one side of the jacket, she made sure Tooco saw the row of steel saucers running down the outside of her right leg. *Seen those before, Yak? You bet you have!* Her father sliced off enough of their heads; he was a legend in Bellytown.

Her trip to the armory was *heady* business as well, selecting five circular saw blades, taking them down to the machine shop on second level, and sharpening them to a razor's edge without having to give a thought to retrieving any of them. That wealth at her command definitely pumped the adrenaline. Her grandfather was one of the first scabs to join the dreamers long before the techies or Yaks arrived.

He'd been from the Bronx and fashioned his singular fighting technique there. A furniture manufacturer, he had plenty of circular saw blades on hand. He also happened to be the Bronx's reigning king of fast-pitch softball back when the ax fell on civilization. With the addition of the protective glove (retrieved from the house of a "hawker") killed early on in the collapse, he was able to realize his idea for a weapon with a longer range than a sword or club. The city was crammed with guns that were useless. After the inferno, most were cracked, their receivers welded to their slides. They'd all been essentially retempered, and the metal was as brittle as glass. Pulling the trigger on one that looked okay could get your hand or head blown off. Besides, there were no bullets. They were all exploded. Her grandfather's spinning guillotine was a deadly success. He trained his son, and his son trained his daughter. And his daughter was a badass prodigy. Yasmine reaffirmed that assesment on the way back in the tunnels, cutting off two rats' heads at ten yards with a couple extra blades she sharpened just to practice.

It was her father who'd developed the chaps that served as holsters for five six-inch circular blades on each leg. She wore only the right leg as she planned to be busy with the frybar in her left hand. The blade in the first holster was wrapped inside a folded sheet of paper.

Sheed always fucked things up. If Mayra hadn't shown up at the last second, Han could've probably pulled it off. *Harrison won't like it if I'm not on this mission! I know what Harrison wants! I'm going on this mission!* Yeah, Han would've snagged them. Then they could've grabbed Jack, killed this Dag and Yasmine, and taken off. Too bad they didn't have idents to get through the entry lock at the Satport. They could've pulled right up to the departure terminal and met Zim and the others there. Still, even without being able to fly into Big New, they could zip right past the smoking ruins of that Yak recycling center, follow the recycling tube to the grid plate, cut a hole in it with the nose lasers, abandon ship, and climb back out of the recycling bin. But that was shot to hell now! Mayra was looking at him while the group continued conferring. Take a holo, bitch! She was staring at him with the same expression she'd worn in his "interview," like he was a rat caught in the garbage. He tried to remind her on the hill that day the little runt who'd recited from memory Shakes's sonnet, "When in disgrace with fortune and men's eyes." From the blank expression in her eyes, Tooco could see she didn't remember, not the slightest clue who he was. He still remembered her, the beautific saint extemporizing on Lennon's knoll. "But Brutus is an honorable man. So are they all, all honorable men." Now there was only a harried Lady Macbeth trying to keep her empire from crumbling. Well, she lucked out today! It was finally time to escape that disapproving stare. Smiling, Tooco signed thumbs-up to Mayra as he took her precious beauty off the ground.

Dag watched over Tooco's shoulder as *Firewalker* lifted up, slowly moving from under the bridle path bridge. The sleek little fighter, with its Toucan nose and bat-wrap wings, slid along just above the turf, then lifted up over the perpetually withered Cenpak trees and took a hard right, banging Dag's head against the padded fuselage. His helmet absorbed most of the impact. Now they were headed west down Seventy-Second toward the Hudson. The *Firewalker* quickly picked up speed to the degree that the husks of old scrapers were beginning to blur. Tooco was definitely good. This kind of speed in traffic was remarkable! Hair-trigger response while keeping your focus on the horizon was the only way it was possible. Dag wanted to be a pilot someday. Currently, he was captain of levi cycle patrol and addicted to flying a bike. It was amazing how relaxed Tooco's shoulders appeared. He'd be in knots trying to fly this fast down here. He saw the Hudson coming up and watched as the nose of the fighter turned from an autumn brown to a dark-greenish blue.

Danner showed him this special feature once. Dag hung around a lot when Danner was putting *Firewalker* together. Cameras on the ship took pictures of topography, and the skin of the ship changed to replicate that. Tooco must have taken a shot of the river from the nose camera while blasting down Seventy-Second. Damn, this bellygridder was bordering on the superhuman! Now they whipped over the West Side highway and made a very hard left, banging his head again. When he looked up, they were flying over the surface of the Hudson, so close Dag wasn't sure what was water and what was ship. He couldn't believe this guy! *Wham!* Again they made a hard left, and the *Firewalker* jolted to an unexpected halt. Inside the cargo hold, Dag's and Yasmine's seat harnesses bit hard into shoulders and groins, preventing them from flying through the cockpit's view plate onto a rotting wharf.

Tooco was chuckling conspiratorially. "We've got an opportunity here. Do you see it?"

All Dag saw beyond the dilapidated wharf was a barren lot.

"They moved the mesh back from the river, two blocks." Tooco was scanning on several light frequencies through the front view plate. Dag couldn't see anything, but then the infrared popped up on a screen in Tooco's display, revealing tiny heat signatures spread all over the vacant ground behind the wharf.

Dag had to ask, "What's that?"

"The batteries in the land mines." Tooco chuckled again. "They peppered the whole area right up to those burnt-out shells across from the mesh. This is a new shipping dock. They change them regularly to keep streetlords with levi cruisers from bushwhacking their shipments up to Sanatan."

"How do you know it's new?" Dag didn't care if the question sounded stupid. He was going to pick up anything he could from this guy.

"There aren't any craters in the ground. If it was here for any length of time, at least one river scab would've been curious enough to come in and take a look—and get blown to hell! That also means the mesh around here has automatic laser cannons too."

"Weren't we gonna come through the mesh around Fourth? We're pretty exposed here."

Dag was immediately sorry he'd offered his obvious two cents. "Not with our camouflage activated. We need the element of surprise on this mission because, without it, we're shit on soy! Listen, they got your guy and Harrison. If they were looking for them, they found them, and depending on how long they've had them, they've got everything they want. They know Jack is really important to you. They know you'll come looking. I don't wanna say, coming in at Fourth and making our entry point look like a haywire drone was a bad idea. It was my idea. But I didn't think we had any better options. The thing is, the size of the hole we make will be a little bigger than it should be, if it was made by a drone, and that's going to be the same problem no matter where we go through the mesh. It's going to make the Yaks a little more leery. For you cokes to pull off your grand entrance—*they have to feel like they've got everything covered.* If we go in here, we can get in without ratcheting up their security level."

Yasmine decided she'd had enough grandstanding from this little prick. "So how is blowing a hole in the mesh at their loading dock gonna make the Yaks feel more secure?"

"Well, as luck would have it, about a block down from the mesh, on Fourteenth and Tenth Avenue, there's this old steakhouse close to two hundred cycles old. I don't know how much you dreamers know about Yakuza inner workings, but there are four clans, and they elect a leader. Now it's Yakami. When he dies, they'll pick somebody else from the four. One of the clans—the most contentious clan of the four—has its headquarters in that old steakhouse."

"How do you know? You've been in the mines how many years?" Yasmine was leaning toward the weasel's being full of shit again.

"I could have been in the mines fifty cycles, and it wouldn't matter. When a clan lays claim on something, they never give it up—ever. That's been their headquarters from when Yaks first entered Bellytown. Yakami used to eat a sixteen-ounce Akita fillet there every Saturday night."

"So! How does that solve the problem?"

"We send back the drone, and then we blow a hole through the mesh. As soon as we're in, we slip down to the steakhouse and light it up. Then we go back to our original plan and hide up in the mesh.

They're all gonna think either one of the clans is trying to wipe out their troublesome member, making it look like it's from outside. Or some street lord who's pissed off and crazy just made the last mistake he's ever gonna make! But whatever they think, they'll believe it's a local problem, not the dreamers trying to get their savior back."

"Yeah, but we still have the problem of those automatic lasers you mentioned."

"I know how to get past them."

"Oh, really?" Yasmine was sure, this time, he'd crossed the line with his braggadocio. "And how the fuck are you gonna do that?"

"Surprise them. First, we need to get close enough, so when I punch it, the lasers don't have time to lock on target before we get through the mesh."

At this point, Dag was a hardcore fan, but it would be good to hear how they could go that fast in such a short distance—too fast for laser cannons to react? "Can we really do that in this baby?"

"I know how to wind up the torque on this little fucker so it breaks the speed of sound taking off!"

Yasmine decided, finally, if this mission was going to succeed, they had to let him do what he was obviously very good at doing—drive. "All right, let's go with it."

"First, we're gonna sneak across that mined lot up to those burnt-out modes. You see that taller one, right off Fourteenth in that cluster of charred shells?" Yasmine and Dag both nodded.

"I'll snake my way up through the cluster until I get to that big one. I'll stick out the nose just far enough to engage my sensors and get a fix on their lasers.

Tooco nudged his stick, and the *Firewalker* snaked around the wharf, sliding along the river's surface beside the ancient pier. When the ship reached the bank, it hopped over a row of log pilings that formed a high-water retention wall and instantly transformed itself into a moving patch of ground. Crossing the barren lot, Tooco slowed to a creep, concerned if they moved any faster, the lasers might pick them out, even from two blocks away. As long as they didn't touch down, they didn't have to worry about the mines. It took what seemed an eternity to make it to the first burnt-out shell. They slowly whinnied their way from one bombed-out shell to the next, slipping through unusual openings, taking unlikely paths, staying hidden from the cameras. Finally, after close to half an hour, they made it to the tall dark shell at the corner of Fourteenth a block away from the mesh.

Hugging the rubble, Tooco inched the ship right up to the edge of the shell, extending his nose probes out onto Fourteenth. He scanned his view plate for a potential target on a charcoaled structure directly across the street. He zeroed in on a section of the front lock, twisted out from the frame, hanging by a single hinge. He dialed down the circumference on his right nose laser to one-twelfth of a milligrid and briefly touched the firing tap. The tiny laser shot out for a fraction of a second, slicing through the hinge, releasing the piece of lock from the structure. The severed section crashed down the cindered relic's steps.

Tooco's motion sensors picked up the automatic lasers tracking the disturbance. They were right where he thought they'd be, on either side of Fourteenth, in a section of the mesh that could be raised to accommodate cargo cruisers taking off for Sanatan. He waited till his motion sensors registered the lasers moving back to their original positions; then he profiled them as targets. Now, as long as they remained in sight, his turret lasers would track their exact coordinates, no matter where the ship moved. Still it would be a tiny bit risky. The problem was, the maneuver *wasn't* a piece of cake. Oh, Dog! (He should've had the replicator at Deli's make a red-velvet cake!) Yakami and his fucking red-velvet cakes—you wanted a piece more than a hit of Nitro. The thing was, the only way he could override the auto thrust control was by completely shutting down the right thrust drive. That was the way you pulled a ninety-degree turn with enough speed to have a chance at outrunning lasers. If the right thrust drive didn't immediately refire on the first tap, they would crash or get lit up. But Tooco wasn't really worried about his abilities, or *Firewalker's* either. You had to hand it to Topgrid: their technology made you cream.

"Make sure your harnesses are tight," Tooco contacted the drone, hovering out on the water thirty centigrid behind them. He tapped it to return to Cenpak.

He tapped the left-rear thruster to standby, programing the thrust to kick in at Mach-1, and he completely shut down the right rear thruster. Amping both his upper and lower vertical E-Mags to increase his stability during the maneuver, he dialed the right nose laser back up to half a milligrid bore. He put both lasers on pulse bolt. He positioned the target at four centigrid above the pavement right down the center of Fourteenth. He set the nose lasers to fire when the ship reached ten centigrid from the mesh.

"What's the problem?" Yasmine's acid tone provided the release he was looking for, the permission to casually escort her up to the edge of the cliff and then push her off. It was just what the doctor ordered to put some fun back in the maneuver.

"No problem. We're just about to go here. Just checking a few things, making sure you're in position to . . . *kiss your ass goodbye.*"

Tooco let the left thruster rip. Like the little coke in the prison vids catching a street lamp with his walking stick, *Firewalker* flung itself around the cindered shell. He slammed the stick to his left and simultaneously fired the right thruster, slapping the stick right again, then immediately back to center. Like the tip of a whip, the ship snapped from side to side, then jackhammered down Fourteenth at a launch speed of 6,400 grid an hour. *Firewalker*'s cannons threw their bolts—a red haze exploding in front of and then engulfing them. Instantly, Tooco yanked back the joystick, and the ship came to another startling halt. He swiveled the stick, and the fighter spun round, facing back in the direction they'd come. They were half a block past the mesh, a large ragged hole in its center. Tooco tapped the "profiled" targets, and the turret cannons fired. Both the automatic lasers were history before either had a chance to pull a 180 to get a bead on *Firewalker*. He had to take them out anyway. Otherwise, the Yaks would know they were in something a lot faster than any streetlord could snag.

Next, Tooco switched the positive charge in his right vertical E-Mags to negative polarity, and the fighter tipped up on its left side, transforming to "scorched brick" as it started sliding up the ancient wall of a deserted meat-packing facility occupying the entire block on the north side of Fourteenth. Five levels above the street, he switched his E-Mags back to positive charge, and the *Firewalker* stopped its ascent. Satisfied he wouldn't be facing any fire from the direction of the mesh, he spun *Firewalker* back around to recon down Fourteenth. On the top floor of the old building, a section of smoke-tinged bricks undulated their way to the corner at Tenth Avenue, where they settled back into the ruins.

Behind him, he heard the beginnings of gastric reactions to their supersonic acrobatics. Best to give the tubes a chance to settle their stomachs before proceeding farther. He reached under the console on his right and tore off a couple of vomit bags from the roll hidden there. He'd discovered it in his initial perusal of the cockpit. He tossed them back over his shoulder.

"Here. We'll take thirty seconds to catch our breath."

The only response he got was the muffled sounds of vomiting and heavy breathing.

It's a real shocker when that little voice in your head decides to introduce you to what you're really all about. He was pissed. Of course! He was pissed his whole life. It was the fuel for his ambition. But he realized he was really pissed about this. What drew him to the dreamers back in his Dumpster days was, they cared. You could see it on their faces and hear it in their words. They really believed in this communal thing. He could feel that pull in himself, a strong desire to believe you could, somehow, be that way. And he'd tried to keep that flame alight while paring it down to accommodate the reality of daily savage life. I mean, it was obvious the dreamers, with their "namby pamby" goodwill, didn't have a prayer in hell. He knew why Yakami was interested in his association with them. He knew the price of admission to the fold. He reasoned that if he could shelter in the lair where the big cats lay, if he could gnaw on the same haunch the kings of the jungle dined on, he would be part of the only community that had a *real* chance of survival! He'd presumed that, for the sake of their continued dominion, this jungle pack must acknowledge some bare-bones form of loyalty.

After all his cycles of service, of ruthless dedication, Yakami tossed him on the pile like a chip in some poker game. He knew it but pretended to himself that he didn't, hoping to husband a flicker of that "dreamer" flame left inside. If it hadn't been for the Orkin, he wouldn't know for sure it still existed. As luck would have it, now, at least, he'd get a little payback. It wasn't Yakami's clan, but they were Yakuza.

"That was phenomenal, man." Dag had recovered his enthusiasm.

Yasmine was less demonstrative. "All right . . . so where's this place you're gonna blast?"

"Right around the corner on the ground floor. You'll spot it, don't worry." The bellygridder turned back to them with a big grin. "I know how sensitive you cokes are, and I just wanna warn you, this has to look local, so it's gonna be savage. I'm gonna blow this place apart, and I want to make sure you understand its reeeally going to be ugly. So if you want to, you can go ahead and close your eyes now, all right?"

"Just do it so we can go get Harrison!"

"Aye, aye, Captain." Tooco extended the nose probes past the corner onto Tenth. In seconds, he had the "joint" on his screen just as he remembered it. It was next to a mountain of white bricks Yakami told him was once an apartment building where an infamous writer who predicted 3TC got murdered. Right next to this brick pile, the Red Dragons' base of operations occupied the bottom two levels in a jungle gym of blackened beams that jutted up six levels into the spires of Bellytown. It was a two-story white plastic structure inside the black skeleton. The roof too was made from sheets of white plastic. Panes of clear plastic in front gave a view of the bustling crowd on both floors. He'd picked a good night for revenge. It was a big celebration of something. Outside in front, a row of levi limos lined the street. Their drivers, along with several security buttons, were standing around, laughing and joking with each other. He remembered standing among them.

A section of brick rippled around the corner and began slowly creeping across the charred red wall. *Firewalker* was just above and directly in front of them, but the group paid no attention to the subtle movements occurring on the backdrop of their lives.

Having lined up with the entrance to the steakhouse, Tooco slowly raised the nose lasers, programing a sequential firing pattern (left to right) across the line of limos. The pulse bolts would blow them right into the front wall of the joint, demolishing it. Then he'd turn the whole place into Yaki burger!

At first, Dag was enjoying a well-executed attack, the line of limos exploding, flying back into the wall of the structure one after another. He actually cheered as the limo in front of a milling crowd of buttons became a spinning torch, wiping them from view. But once the front wall of the place disappeared, Tooco switched to straight laser and began methodically sweeping the hysterical crowds on both floors— back and forth, back and forth, from bottom to top, and then top to bottom. Beyond the carnage of the burning cruisers and screaming buttons, there was the ceaseless buzzing ray conjuring geysers of blood, sausaged torsos, exploding heads with brains blasting everywhere.

"ENOUGH! ENOUGH!" Yasmine was yelling at him, pounding on his shoulder, but Tooco was oblivious until the entire structure was a lumpy lake of oozing blood.

Finally, he amped all the E-Mags in the ship's nose to negative polarity, peeling the *Firewalker* off the wall and shooting it toward the grid plate. About a quarter of the way up, he engaged the drives to adjust to the conical shape of the mesh—the circumference becoming smaller the farther up they went. Approaching the top of the cone, he cut the drive and switched the negative E-Mags back to positive charge. The *Firewalker* jolted to a stop. They were just below the mammoth steel ring ninety centigrid across, where the mesh was anchored at fifty levels up. The ring was welded right to the lowest beam of the great grid girders. A crosshatch of bars crisscrossed its diameter to prevent any Levi cruisers from entering or leaving that way. The vast metal shroud was knitted from a mountain of metal cables salvaged from all over the waste fill. Up here, the openings between the cables were only about four milligrid square. There was no danger of being discovered. The *Firewalker*, mirroring the metal patchwork of the mesh, was invisible unless you got very close. Its metallic signature was hidden in the cables.

It took two cycles for them to complete the security mesh. The Yaks, and about two hundred techies, gave six thousand scabs a job and a good wage, all things considered—which most of them immediately lost in the Yak casinos, bordellos, necro bars, or on Nitro. Tooco'd just started making drug runs back then.

"We'll hide up here and scope out what kind of response they make."

He waited in silence for her recriminations to begin: "the senseless slaughter . . . what kind of a monster? Not surprisingly, she chose the high road. "A moment of silence." Oh, these dreamers.

They would have their moment of silence. Not now but soon. He realized, really, it had all started with them, hadn't it? Infecting him with their "Pollyanna" crap, and it was deeply offensive that in all these years, they'd somehow managed to survive; that he should have to come back as a fugitive to the scenes of his triumph—once more a desperate guttersnipe. And to have to see those open goofy faces still here, touting some connection they called "humanity." It was galling, infuriating that they hadn't been stomped out long ago. The pressure of this fugitive shit was beginning to get to him.

He zoomed in the belly camera to focus back down onto Fourteenth, where he'd created the havoc. There was pandemonium down the length of the street. Yak cruisers came flying in. Rescue vehicles were arriving too, but there was nobody to rescue. Before long, they discovered the gap blown in the mesh, and cruisers were zooming up and down the Hudson, looking for streetlord levies.

It was time to get their bearings. On one of the navigational screens above his view plate, he tapped up the crude map he'd drawn back in the dreamer's bunker. He superimposed the aerial view from *Firewalker's* belly camera over his drawing. Then highlighting a coordinate on his map and matching it to one in the aerial view, comp rig stretched his original drawing to fit the scene below. On a second screen, he tapped up a lateral comp-gen image of the ship positioned inside the mesh cone. On the first screen, he touched the levi storage area he'd sketched, and it immediately jumped into bold relief. A second later, it came up on the second screen from the horizontal perspective. Now plotting their course was simply steering a diagonal conical descent to the highlighted area. They'd had enough time to lick their wounds.

"All right, we're heading to our target."

He made their descent smoothly, a measured glide down and around the mesh, clockwise. As soon as they were four grid from the Yak storage area, he planned to cut all his E-Mags and drop like a necro's body temperature down onto C Avenue, then wind his way over to Second and take that up to their target—Yaki southern command. Then all he had to do was wait outside until he got their signal. Dog knows they had great directions once they got inside. Tooco mapped out every step they had to take from the front lock, down to the torture chamber.

He watched the second screen as their ship approached the drop point. Taking the camouflage feature out of automatic-reflect, he tapped in Yaki insignias on the *Firewalker*: four dragons forming a cross—red, yellow, green, and blue—the tips of their tails intertwined at its center.

"Hold on to your asses!" Tooco cut all his E-Mags, and without further ado, they plummeted straight toward the pavement. Focusing on the altimeter, his stomach straining to rise through his windpipe, he heard his passengers retching. At twenty centigrid, he kicked in his E-Mags again. The ship executed another sudden stop not more than two centigrid above the boiled blacktop of C Avenue. It felt strange to be back on old turf. Tooco checked his early-warning probes before lowering his left view plate and throwing up over the side of the ship.

"Right on the Yuan!" He reached a hand back behind him. "I hope you didn't puke all over those zappy jumps. Give me your bags when you're done."

Dag handed up one bag and then the other. Tooco quickly tossed them out of his open view plate. After closing the view plate, he turned back to check his passengers.

"All right, get yourselves straightened up and ready to roll 'cause it's almost zap time."

Tooco pushed the stick forward, shooting off down the street. He kept it under four hundred grid an hour as he began snaking through the narrow byways, scanning all his screens for any sign of traffic. They were almost to Second when he spotted the Yaki cruiser closing from above. Luckily, the turret lasers right behind the pilot's capsule had their backs. Their Yaki logos were keeping the patrol from firing on the ship, but they knew it was like nothing they possessed.

He gave the head of his joystick a tap, and the turret whined into action, honing on the bigger ship. That was all the Yaks needed to make up their minds, and a laser bolt exploded in the rubble off to their left. It was the only shot they got. The turret's twin cannons pumped out a staccato burst, and above them, the Yak cruiser exploded in a ball of fire. Dog, this little fucker really packed a punch!

Tooco watched in his rear-view screen as, behind them, fiery shards came raining down.

At Second, he swung the ship around in a hard right and took it up to eight hundred grid an hour. They'd eat up the last few grid in under twenty seconds, just enough time to send out a "triple 6" (emergency call) to Yak patrols. He hoped that was still the emergency call sign. It probably was. One of the few commandments they adhered to was, "Don't fix it if it ain't broke."

"Emergency, triple 6! Cruiser down on Fourth and C Avenue. Bandits in immediate area. We've found the scab streetlords! Emergency, triple 6!"

Tooco eased the stick back, slowing to four hundred grid an hour. "You're almost on."

Yasmine inhaled the wicked stench of her own breath. This shot of gastric rotgut cleared more than just her head. It made her certain of what she knew.

This was the one Teeba spoke with on the girder. He was the one who'd spoken the words Mayra sang out from the Duni. This was the one. And this was a gift for any warrior, incredible bounty—this personal opportunity to be of service.

"Thank you," she whispered it, but Tooco overheard. "You're welcome, 'Commander'!"

He brought *Firewalker* to a screeching hover in front of a bright-pink triangle composed of brick and glass, rising up five levels exactly as the bellygridder described it. The belly lock whined open. Yasmine unbuckled her harness and was about to charge outside when Tooco grabbed her arm.

"Wait a second! Commander! Let the place clear out."

Four guards in their patchwork armor (a combination of Sacker and twentieth SWAT gear) stood outside the glass entrance to the building, each armed with a frybar. Suddenly, all around them, buttons were pouring from the lobby and racing to their cruisers, answering Tooco's emergency call made mere seconds before.

"There we go. Now!"

They emerged from under the *Firewalker* and approached the guards. Yasmine wasted no time establishing her authority. "Captains Acura and Exon, reporting from Sanatan. We report directly to Lord Yakami."

Han promised it would work like magic, and amazingly it did. Not only did they step aside but flung open doors for their immediate access. One of the guards caught up with them, quickly moving ahead to precede the duo down a wide marble hall. Acting as their herald, he kept calling out into every doorway they passed, "Recon back from Sanatan!" Yak faces, eyes wide with expectation, began to appear in the doorways as they went past. What the hell did Han know about Sanatan that he wasn't telling them? And why was the Yaki calling them *recon*? Again, she felt foreboding about his arrival in their destiny.

At the end of the hallway, they took marble stairs bordered by brass railings down to the basement of Yak central. Han advised them to play that gambit as long as it held, and from the looks of it, it just might see them to the door of the torture chamber.

The refinements disappeared as they made their way down a low-ceilinged green corridor. Up ahead, Yasmine could see a large steel door at the corridor's end. On either side of this expanse of metal, Yakami's robot guards stood at eternal attention. She'd never seen them before, but there was no doubt that's who they were. Dreamers weren't the only ones trying to recruit techies, and Yaks were far more successful at it. Yaks had hundreds of them on their payrolls. They were crazy about robots. Their techies were actually ahead of 7 in that area.

Danner explained that because Topgrid were focused on designing a deep-space vehicle to search for other planets; they weren't doing much R & D in robotics unrelated to those projects.

These two were very special robots. She'd heard the awed descriptions, but she was still impressed. Supposedly, it would take a couple laser cannons to stop them. They were khaki green and roughly Han's size, forged from parts of a twentieth-century tank, plated in weapons' grade titanium. They were shaped in human form and covered from head to toe with engravings of traditional Yakuza tattoos. These all appeared as muted silver etchings in their khaki skins. Their face plates were exactly like the sketches an Outrider once made for her, a narrow slit cut across the upper part of an oval face plate etched with an elaborate tiger's mask. The slit was to accommodate the constantly scanning sensors and was the only point where their systems were vulnerable. They could be closed in a split second to deflect an attack. Both robots held frybars in each of their modular hands. Those four weapons all rose to target them despite their Yak liaison's continued proclamations, "Recon from Sanatan for Lord Yakami!"

With about sixteen paces to go before she reached a comfortable throwing distance, Yasmine was confident her "pitch" would level off perfectly into that narrow slit. Dag was here because there was nobody faster with a frybar or half as accurate. The plan was, right when Yasmine made her move, Dag would whip his frybar up and aim for the scanner slit of the one on the left. Their scanners would be focusing on the flash of Yasmine's saw-blade disk, rocketing toward them. That's the instant Dag would take his shot. Meanwhile, that silver saucer would take a hop up higher (what they called, in her grandfather's day, a "riser"). Yasmine was hoping the one on their right would use one frybar to take a shot at the disk and the other to take a shot at her. If her timing was right, he'd miss the disk but probably hit her. She was wearing two laser vests and a helmet that could take a direct hit, inherited from Danner. He hadn't worn it that last time on the barricade.

The seminal precept of personal combat was about to be demonstrated. "Break any opponent's strategy by attacking immediately" (Miyamoto Musashi, *The Five Rings*, 1597). Their Yaki guide stopped within twenty paces of the two mechanical executioners waiting for Dag and Yasmine to catch up and show the proper credentials. At twenty-four feet, she casually reached inside her trench and pulled out a folded sheet of paper. She held it down by her side, honing on the face plate of the guard on her right.

"Captain Acura, reporting from Sanatan." She lifted up the paper showing the Yakuza insignia imprinted on its surface. Suddenly, her arm snaked out like a whip, and the silver disk exploded from the shredding paper, rising as predicted and embedding itself in the robot's slit. Simple and quick.

Simultaneously, Dag flicked up his muzzle and put a pulse bolt through the other guard's "front window." Thin plumes of black smoke curled up from their face plates; then both gargantuans keeled over, smashing the cement. It was surreal. It was too easy. Neither even got off a shot! They'd lulled their threat-assessment protocols into ratcheting down from "instantaneous" to "rapid response," and that was just enough to buy them the split second they needed. They had the melodramatic proclamations of their Yaki herald to thank for that. She turned back to face him.

He stood, eyes wide with horror, frozen for a moment, then turned and bolted back up the corridor. Before he made ten steps, Yasmine took off his head with her second disk.

They signed to each other that they were ready to breach, then unleashed a burst of pulse bolts into the steel door. It disappeared in a whirlwind of exploding fragments, and Yasmine dove through the smoking hole.

—◆———◆◆◆———◆—

He'd always loved sleep—real sleep, that deep unconscious river flowing to the selfless ocean of total oblivion. He knew in that ocean was where the real life force resided, where you went to replenish. And it always seemed weird to him how cokes were so afraid of dying but longed fondly for that time every day, when they could give up their consciousness completely on the faith they would rise again. The thing was, in that dreamless sleep, even their faith was gone. They were gone, and it was fine—nothing to mourn, nothing to fear, just a release, a relief, an uninterrupted peace.

But Harrison wasn't in that deep sleep now. He was in the swampland of dreams. Presently, he was piloting a sharp blade over waves of squirming cokes, splitting skulls and severing torsos as he rode a tumbling stovepipe of bodies. This was a Pacino nightmare, every suffering cell of his body announcing itself in the bodies he was slicing through.

After the black scorpion's sting, he watched as his burning jerk swelled to the size of his head, till he was certain it would explode. Then briefly, he'd been granted oblivion again. Awakened by a stranger's screams, he'd opened his eyes to find Splatter directly in front of him, strapped to a similar table, propped up like his own. He watched as Lord Yakami busily worked away with a sharpened conch shell, flailing the ebony skin from Splatter's inner thighs. His screams were unending. There was something in the childlike expressions of agony reconfiguring the narrow cheeks and sunken eyes of his face that infused a newborn's wonder in his tortured expressions. His universal wailing filled the subterranean chamber. Yakami, admitting he too was distressed by the pitiful noises, began working the shell up and down on Splatter's windpipe. Though strangled, it made his screaming even more unbearable. Harrison passed out again.

On this dream march, he was joined by fresh martyrs. Since grasping the concept of "human history" at Cincinnati retrieval, Harrison was vulnerable to a mountain of alien agonies, under which his own were compressed. Watching this young coke's torment brought forward legions of his nation writhing in agony, twisted with rage, skewered, burned, butchered, and hung—stretched on a colonial rack for centuries. A weight of misery that was on the point of willing him to a final halt, a final rest, forever free of this sorrowful, degrading crap.

Suddenly bloody rockets exploding across his shuttered corneas signal imminent annihilation. *The world is ending?* The cries of desperate warriors rise, affirming with their dissonance a reckoning is at hand. Around him, cokekind is on the line. He feels certain final judgment is waiting with his sentence when he opens his eyes again.

But flame-haloed beauty was the specter that greeted him. She was beyond anything he could ever imagine. The expressions of murderous rage swirling across her face, the ruthless destruction emanating from her eyes, made him empathize with the old Hebrew shielding his face from the radiant omnipotence of Dog's light. She was a warrior, unabated, unapologetic, and as unremitting as she was effective. And she was here to save him.

He felt unbearable shame. Misshapen and bloodied by the depravity of his treatment, newly mortified by the communal suffering of his soul, he was a pitiful specimen.

"Harrison?"

She knew his ID! Oh, what blissful shame—lost in her lioness eyes, watching the powerful mouth begin to form his ID again.

"Harrison, I'm Yasmine. We're the dreamers of Cenpak. We're here to rescue you." She cut the bonds from his wrists, starting to release him from his plastic cross. Once freed, his arms fell, useless, at his sides. He could see another dreamer doing the same for the remains of Splatter. Harrison doubted he could be alive. Yasmine was cutting away the cords that bound his ankles. He was afraid he wouldn't be able to stand, and she'd end up carrying him like a sack of soy.

"And I've got good news! Han is safe with us back at Cenpak, waiting for you. Tooco's here too. Right outside! He's flying our cruiser."

Suddenly Harrison's precarious sanity dissolved in madness. "WHAT THE FUCK IS GOING ON HERE? IS THIS DOG'S IDEA OF FUNNY?"

This brief but unexpected statement informed by an amazing fury did more than give Yasmine pause. Something was *very wrong*.

Mercifully, he saw two points from his circle shining in her eyes. The circle itself radiated out from her mouth, surrounding her face. All the points were present now, glowing as they moved toward the bridge of her nose. *Thank you, Dog.*

His pattern was here. All he had to do was dive in.

•————◆◆◆————•

After they watched *Firewalker* take off, slipping over the trees out of sight, she decided to take Han to Lennon's knoll, where she was once foolish enough to think (in the postapocalyptic trash bin of civilization) she could stir a feeling of hope through ideals. Why was she introducing him to her shame?

They were sitting on top of the bald little hill side by side on the compacted Earth. As if she wasn't embarrassed enough, she suddenly saw herself as some twentieth farm chick coyly baiting the trap for the strapping young stud by her side. *Shucks! I really was hopin' you could teach me how to suck your dick, Rex, but I promised Daddy I'd feed the hogs for him after school. I gotta' be gettin' back now—maybe, tomorrow.*

You really are an elitist bitch. Terrific! Her devil's advocate was feeling conversational. *That was a good question. Why are you introducing him to your shame? Why don't you just admit, it's been a long time . . . this is a nice piece of ass . . . why not just get laid and let that be all it is? Instead of having to turn it into a passion play that will end, no doubt, with a heaping helping of guilt—and yes, dare I prophesy, shame and more shame.*

Man, for a guy who's supposed to be representing the lord of darkness and all his cynical intents, you spend a lot of time, sounding like one of those therapists on disks in the armory. Maybe I'll take your advice, all right, Doc? Now, why don't you go play in the lake?

"I'm surprised there are trees." Han turned, looking over his shoulder at the line of trees bordering the barricade on the western side of Cenpak.

Mayra turned to look at them as well. "They all came in three or four years after the firebombing. They grew pretty quickly. We helped with drip feeds. They matured into their thirties, but since Big New was moved over us, we're at our brightest now at twilight or early dawn. The trees along the barricade are in some kind of hibernation. They make a few tiny buds in the spring, but little comes off it. Only that stand-down by the reservoir produces many leaves. We ringed it with low-angle reflectors to magnify the brightest moments of our day."

He didn't know what to say. He was more familiar with the permanent twilight of Bellytown than she was, hiding in her retched caves. The Alaska mines were brutal, but all around you were magnificent mountains with lush greenery covering them. This was just barren, this little patch of dirt hidden here, where her little retro clan waited for their messiah.

"Can I ask you a personal question?" So she was feeling frisky. What?"

"You don't need your disguise anymore. Why don't you take off that cape now?"

"Actually, its Harrison's cape. I'm just holding it for him, until he gets back."

A look of disbelief, then disappointment, caused her whole face to sag, and then she caught the twinkle in his eye. "Oh, you're cute! Having a good time with the locals?" She was laughing, shaking her head.

Han stood up and opened the clasp on Deli's cape, letting it fall on the polished ground. He wore only a simple black body jump. Far from self-conscious, he was confident the full revelation of his perfect symmetry was having the desired effect. He extended his hand, and she took it. He pulled her up beside him and gestured with his head toward the stand of trees by their tarp-covered reservoir.

"Will you show me your leafy trees?"

She let him keep her hand as they walked down the knoll. The twilight was waning. The low-angle reflectors created a golden ring around the stand of trees. The purple night would soon reclaim them all.

———❖———

Yasmine didn't have time for the luxury of shock. Still, she was finding it impossible to move. She felt frozen in time while time was flying by in a chaos of screams and blood. Any second, a swarm of Yaks were going to come storming in from the upper level, frybars blazing!

But the fact remained that Harrison just turned blue and then disappeared right in front of her eyes! Gone. Evaporated . . . turning her to stone. He'd fucking disappeared! She had to get going. Move!

They'd cleared the room quick enough, Yasmine taking the left side, and Dag the right, blasting Yaki bodies all over the walls in their inner sanctum. Dag's laser fire cut to pieces four of them sitting at a communal table. Yasmine took out three who were assisting Yakami working over Harrison and Splatter. Yakami stood there staring at her in disbelief, wearing only a pair of silver-studded pants and a funny hat, a laser dagger in his hand. She whipped a blade off her hip. Yakami barely had time to blink before his hand separated from his wrist. Still gripping the dagger, it went cartwheeling to the floor. He only had a brief moment to take in the red fountain shooting from his wrist before her next disk took off his funny hat, along with the top of his head. That's when she went to Harrison—and when he disappeared.

Dag was still cutting the bonds from Splatter's ankles. He was bent over at the waist, supporting Splatter's torso, already draped over his back. Splatter looked dead. Harrison was gone, and that was that. Suddenly she saw his red armor on a bench in one corner. She bolted to it, keeping her muzzle trained on the doorway. Yasmine scooped up the armor and quickly returned to Dag. Dag was standing shifting Splatter's torso on his shoulder, trying to get an equal distribution of weight. When he finally turned around to face her, his expression was one of total confusion. He looked frantically around the room, then back to Yasmine.

"Where'd he go? Where's Harrison?"

"I don't know . . . I was cutting his legs free . . . I was telling him Han and Tooco were here, and then he flipped out and started screaming. He was furious, and then he just disappeared!" They both heard the thunder of boots pounding down the marble steps. She couldn't think of anything more to add. "He just disappeared!"

"Where?"

"I don't know!"

Time was up. Dag was launching pulse bolts down the hallway through the smoking hole they'd created. Opening fire with the frybar in her left hand, she put down the red armor, reaching between her shoulders to the back of her neck to press Tooco's signal button. Then keeping up a fierce barrage between the two of them, she scooped up the armor again as they backed into the northeast corner of the torture chamber.

"You're on, bellygridder! Get us out of here!"

• ━●━ •

She wanted to go back not long after they reached the trees. The trees were a sad lot. They had a few leaves clinging to stunted knobby branches. As the last glimmer of refracted sunlight disappeared, swirling electromagnetic particles, their miniature Aurora Borealis that aped the northern lights began radiating the faint nightlight of Bellytown. That's when she realized he was shivering without his cape on this late December night. She suggested they head back in, but he wanted to stay there in the trees for a while. She took out the walkie-talkie and told Ram and Chan to fall back and recon from Lennon's knoll.

As they hunkered down with their backs against the largest trunk in the grove, Mayra took off her military parka and draped it over the front of them. The heat generated by their bodies lulled them into a comfortable lethargy. They listened to the relative silence on the fields of Cenpak. No birds, no horns, only the occasional siren slipping over the barricade. She felt, for a moment, as if she'd fallen into another time, where there was no catastrophic backdrop, only a quiet night with no responsibilities to anyone or anything outside their warmth. Mayra tilted her head up, pressing against his shoulder, trying to look in his eyes. Failing, she closed her eyes and, a moment later, blindly offered him her mouth.

Gently sliding his hand inside her camouflaged jump, cupping one breast and softly stroking an ember nipple, their lips explored each other. His hand moved down her belly, deftly parting swollen petals, summoning her gypsy. Her groans became desperate as he rushed to pull open the front of her jump, then zipping down the front of his own. On all fours on top of her, trying to keep the parka over them, Han's Screenrage jerk dropped from his jump, moving in low, honing on prey—and just like that, she snapped him up.

A seasoned snake charmer, her thumb and forefinger lassoed his rim, squeezing his swollen head, pulling him up to examination, then gently but firmly bringing her captive down to be baptized in her simmering cunt.

Afterward, drawing the parka tight around them, he was still in shock. It seemed there was a new sexual adventure around every corner these days. First, Harrison doing an engaging impression of a Screenrage slut, and now this junkyard dogess usurping his dominion with one swipe of her fist. The really scary part was, he liked it. He fucking loved it! I mean, it wasn't really emasculating; she'd *reverentially* submerged him in her brimming bliss. It was both submissive and commanding—and just so fucking hot!

Oh, this fresh, naive heaven! It made him want to slide down her slippery pass and forget all about the other crap in his head. Fortunately, or unfortunately, he'd already set in motion events that demanded adherence to his original vision. After their strategy meeting, left alone for a couple minutes in their war bunker with those two net screens in the corner, it was a simple matter tapping up the belly fiber he and Zim had agreed upon. Han was being a bit premature, but he was confident they'd have their spacecase shortly, and this might be his only chance to make contact while they were staying with their dreamer hosts.

He imagined Zim up in Big New, sprawled on Deli's white suede couch, all three sheed practicing their fleshly charms on him while he tried to keep an eye on the belly fiber. Then suddenly, just as he was about to pop, the screen would go briefly blank, and two high notes would echo through the gadget master's palace. Zim, both elated and infuriated, would receive their predetermined message. Translation: "We found Jack. Prepare all equipment for the Satport. Pack the limo. At my next contact, turn on the limo's homing beacon and go!" Han smiled with a jaded intuition that his guess was probably right. Sorry about the "nutter interruptus," old clonie.

Just when it seemed something more might be needed to turn the situation to his advantage, this pagan queen saved him the trouble of seducing her. He was anxious to get back in their tunnels, be led to her mat, where they could continue their animal dance until, hopefully, Tooco returned with Jack. Of course, that would create new problems, but the only lie he'd told was that the rest of the crew was killed back in Sanatan—for which he'd already prepared an explanation. He'd even told her about Jack's amazing abilities! He realized it was Jack he would need to convince of his new state of mind. He would need to transform himself into his most ardent acolyte. Han could even have his own little revelation—*the ship was really always meant for these people whom Harrison really was destined to save.* That's why Dog brought Han on board because he was the one with the plan to steal the *Protostar*!

And there was the book! Twin to the one pulled from the ashes by their founder, which really was amazing. Jack didn't know anything about that. Han could use it as the bolt that turned him into a believer too. And the bolt that proved Dog wanted Han to join the flock because Han was the one the divine spirit chose to bring the book to his flock!

He would become Jack's most devoted disciple. He just needed to make sure Tooco got the heads-up on their recent conversion.

He smiled down at her. "You don't happen to know somewhere we can get warm, do you?"

———•◆◆•———

"I'll be a blue-nosed necro licker! They're still alive!" Tooco began chortling at the blinking red light on his command couch control display.

Tapping up both thrusters from standby, he bolted the *Firewalker* from its parking place up to the top level of Yaki headquarters. Then swiveling his stick to the right, the nimble ship leaped with a quick "Huey" to the other side of the pink edifice. Tooco punched in the target overlay, lining it up on his view screen so the northwest corner matched up with its representation in his schematic. Tooco tapped up the nose lasers and set them on pulse bolt. Reversing polarities on his rear vertical E-Mags to ensure the fighter's nose stayed down at a forty-five-degree angle, he let the nose lasers roar! They pounded out a rhythmic series of explosions, blasting plumes of cement that sent chunks of asphalt and brick two and three levels high, until a carved diagonal pit revealed the basement wall of Yaki headquarters. Switching his nose lasers to "ray," he cut a border large enough for the *Firewalker* to get through around a section of the wall. He targeted the turret lasers on that bordered section, dialing down their power, and fired a quick double tap, causing the section to topple as a piece. And Tooco swooped down through his new access into the Yaki torture chamber. Switching the nose lasers back to pulse bolt, he began pumping laser ordinance down the hall from inside the chamber. He saw them hunkered down in the corner of the mode they'd designated as the "safe spot" during the bombardment. Tooco tapped open the ship's belly lock. He watched them come: Dag with a body draped over his shoulder; Yasmine, close behind, carrying something red—Harrison's "New Blood" battle jump. That was a good sign.

A moment later, they scrambled in, Yasmine hollering, "On board." He resealed the belly lock and spun the little fighter in a quick 180 degrees. Looking up their escape ramp, Tooco saw the nose of a Yak cruiser that was back from the false alarm in time for Tooco to kill him, which he did with a double tap from his nose, obliterating the entire front of the cruiser and blowing it out of his path. Tooco gunned *Firewalker* out of their basement entry point to greet two more Yak cruisers coming from different directions. He made a ninety-degree turn to his left, targeting the first one with his nose lasers while targeting the second with his turret guns, and fired both banks at the same time.

The billowing clouds of smoke overwhelming the entire street were filtered to a thin veil by Tooco's screen plate. The street was clear of all vehicles, with only a few pieces of burning shrapnel to wind his way around. Tooco took advantage of this lack of congestion to charge into Bellytown's maze of narrow pathways in a broken field run for Fifty-Ninth.

"Is Jack gonna make it?" Despite his present preoccupation, Tooco wanted to know Harrison's condition.

Dag answered, "It's our guy Splatter. He's pretty messed up."

He couldn't contain himself. "Where the fuck is Harrison?"

Yasmine silenced Dag with her eyes, answering for him, "He wasn't there . . . just his armor."

Leave it to this little bitch to bring the bad news. That shit-stirring spacefuck probably jumped his fucking String. Tooco needed to ask one more question, "Was Yakami there?"

"Yeah, I took the top of his head off."

Well, there was a silver lining. He was surprised to find still more proof of the vendetta lurking in his heart. What do you know, getting to be a part of killing his old master felt even better than winning Tokyo Run.

Jumping onto Fourteenth, he saw the Yak cruisers coming up behind and locked his turret lasers on them. He'd cut over at Seventh Avenue, blow the mesh at Seventh and Twenty-Third, then blast straight up over Fifty-Ninth barricade. He could still outrun and outgun anybody in this fucked-up burg.

⸺•◆•⸺

The String offered blissful immediate relief from pain. Moving was the furthest thing from his mind. Invisible now, he was free to take a moment and watch her. He put aside the sudden madness triggered by hearing Han was already down here with the dreamers. It was too much to get his head around! He just wanted to observe her fiery beauty for as long as possible.

When the little levi cruiser blew through the foundation and entered their Yaki dungeon, Harrison recognized it as a *Firewalker*. Where the hell had these dreamers gotten a *Firewalker*? He watched her and her comrade, who was carrying Splatter, run into the belly lock and take off. Jumping the String took the final energy he possessed. When she disappeared into the *Firewalker*, he sank instantaneously into the concrete, embracing the inert unconscious. Wrapped in cement and oblivious to the chaos above him, he had a final thought. He remembered Tooco saying the dreamers lived in tunnels under Bellytown. He wouldn't go up when he recovered; he'd go lateral and find those tunnels. But first, he needed to heal, probably for between eighteen- and twenty-four three-dimensional hours. Then he'd go find her and find out what the fuck was going on with Han and Tooco.

<h1 style="text-align:center">CHAPTER</h1>

My dog! Only two more snagging days till X-mas. Zim had completely forgotten about the impending holiday. In the mines, he observed it faithfully every cycle, displaying a homemade X-mas tube in his cell. He ran it on a hand-tool recharge rod pilfered from a Screwhog. Things were pretty loose for inmates in Screwhog crews, and the guards liked Nitro too. When the holidays rolled around, his swirling red-and-green pole was the entire cellblock's gathering place for X-mas cheer. He and Tzart were especially blessed at X-mas time.

Gliding along on the expansive moving walk of Rainbow Avenue, the memories of those tawdry celebrations were swept aside by a file of happy images from more traditional X-mas seasons. Hand in hand with his father, looking in the view plates of all the replicator shops, skating in his first pair of rocket boots at Rockafella Plaza, sharing a soynog with his mother at one of the cafes on fifth-level promenade. The pristine beauty of the white towered burg shone especially brightly at X-mas time.

Around his neck, a thick gold shield hanging from an even thicker gold chain identified him as Kahn Deli's majordomo. The badge allowed him to pass anywhere without attracting unwanted attention. After getting Han's first signal, he made up a list of the items they still required. The only really critical ones were some tiny "image boosters" that, positioned properly, would enhance the illusion of mass in their holo figures. Having made short work of all his items in the first replicator shop he'd run across, now he was being a little reckless. He made sure Darl was monitoring the belly fibers while he was gone. She would signal the second they heard from Han. So he wasn't going nuts or anything. He figured, while he was out, he might as well see if he could find a jacket befitting his new vocation as a *Protostar* officer—something in black leatherette, kind of rakish with those double-breasted lapels sweeping into a turned-up collar like Screenrage wear, zapping at some gala.

If Han only knew, his signal coming when it did started a big "brouhaha." After finally completing a flawless rehearsal of their Satport drama, they partied, fueled by eight Nitro patches Darl stashed away from Sanatan. They'd been going at it for three hours when the screen went blank, and the two notes sounded. Zim was on all fours, bathing his face in Darl's cup of fulfillment. Ryka was on her back, with her head between his legs, deep-throating his magnificent jerk. That thick back-throat saliva, triggered by her gag reflex, was starting to flow, making it easier to slide all the way down and *really* fuck her throat. But his custom jerk did make things a little more difficult.

At the time, he rationalized the enhancements he'd chosen were an edgy example of primordial hip. The skin of his shaft was textured, like the hide on a crocodile's back, and his elongated serpentine head was inked to a lustrous black. Of course, he'd supersized! In retrospect, it was over the top—7's interest was aroused.

Yes, he loved his Screx, all right, back when he was a worker bee in the spires of the great white burg. But it was really *Sendra*. "Sendra, with your deadly tail and perfect little ass, be my dragon love, and I'll serve up all your snacks." Dynasty of Dragons. In the end, that prehistoric motif with his dragon love was the only place he wanted to be. Harrison was right. They had to blow the lock off. Since doing the real thing, his jerk had become a conversation piece. Okada loved its rugged hide. Tooco, not so much.

He'd schooled Ryka in deep-throat technique when they had to rebuild the kilns in the hog port, and they didn't have any work until the job was done. Unfortunately, the first note of Han's signal sounded as Ryka was sucking back down. Involuntarily, Zim jumped, and one of her "bucky" teeth caught his head at the rim, tearing a gash in it. It hurt like hell, with blood dripping from the tip. He just lost it and slugged her. He was sorry he hit her so hard, but he'd warned her about those teeth a hundred times. It was partly the stress he was under, trying to organize everything and keep everybody on track. He really needed to let go and have a little adventure. Putting the unpleasantness out of his mind, he moved along with the holiday crowd.

Glancing up, he spotted some patches of white on the monolithic dome. Outside, a blustering snowstorm was blowing over their sealed megatropolis. In the only early tube memory he'd filed, he was looking up at the dome, realizing what it was. At the time, being completely covered with snow, he understood both its form and function. It was his first epiphany.

He almost missed the entrance to Quantro's because of his gazing. The ultrachic jump emporium would have the jacket he was looking for. Inside, he headed for cokes apparel on the mezzanine. He zeroed in on a line of leatherette jackets along the back wall of a specialty niche.

"Ironically, your reckless attempt to borrow on your resolve by pursuing some vain gesture could *unexpectedly* lead to you getting bagged, and the failure of Han's plan!"

"Oh, Dog, just calm down. I'm going to snag a jacket on Deli's debit line, and sirens aren't going to go off, and you're not going to be 'immediately' surrounded by Sackers aiming frybars at your head. That's just your hysterical 'end of the world every fucking time you turn around crazy ass' shit! Relax. I've got everything under control."

It was good to clear the air with those doubters in your head when they started sticking their frightened noses (parading as "pragmatism") into every moment and decision. There were always doubters, but he knew what nobody else did—Han's plan. Zim figured, Han was going to blow up Sanatan. He just didn't know when. But after that happened, there was a magic moment where they all disappeared except for him and Han. While Jack was off playing with his thought recorder, while Sunsue and Ryka tended to Tooco, while Darl was in the eliminator, Han told him the plan. And it was an incredible plan.

Even though he'd kept up a brave front when Han initially told them he was going to steal *Protostar*, truth be told, like the rest of them, he believed it was impossible. But once Han laid it out for him, he realized it was actually doable. Their secret weapon was the belated big surprise. Han had sworn him to silence, but soon enough, the rest of the crew would know. There were two of them! Back in the NORAD, when they went to see Bob's "fission" bomb, Han asked him if he had anything else like that. Bob said there was another one some general brought down with him. But like a pouting little tube, he said they couldn't have it. Bob needed it to commit suicide if they didn't take him with them! It was beyond pathetic, this pandering miscreant and his cringing attempt at manipulation. He'd elicited Han's heartfelt assurances: they had no intention of leaving him there, which was true. Han just left out the "alive" part. Moments later, another silver suitcase was in his other hand. That was the bomb they would use to take possession of *Protostar*. Zim customized them in the Screwhog, adding a remote-detonate feature to both.

He really wasn't losing faith in Han. It was himself he was worried about.

This magic show at the Satport (their drama acted out with holos) was proving to be a geometric nightmare. Figuring out the points of projection with all the angles and planes involved, making sure the images always appeared solid—it was a daunting task. The relatively small area of the boarding niche compounded the problem. They needed the commotion to be close, but not so close that panicked passengers ran through holo figures in their holocast! The melodrama itself was simple. First, Zim, disguised as the good doctor, would make the initial contact with their boarding agent. He'd confirm the gadget master's arrival and their reservations for the first-class suite just behind the pilot's cabin (arrangements to be made after they received Han's second signal). He would introduce the Kahn (Han, in his full Deli getup), and Han would glide up in his levi chair (which hid the bomb) and clique with the agent. At which point, Zim would request they be allowed to board first because of the Kahn's delicate condition. The agent would say, "Of course, you're in the first suite. You're scheduled to board first in any case." They'd all share a little chuckle of mutual appreciation, lining up for the palm plate and retina scan just before entering the boarding tunnel. That's when all hell would break loose.

Two Barney Lovers with some "conglom's tyke" in tow would appear from behind a pillar on the upper level, coming down to the boarding niche and heading for the boarding agent. The "stranger" appearing in the niche they just vacated would suddenly jump up, cutting off the Barney Lovers and their young charge. Spewing a stream of profanities about "the purple devil's evil spawn," he would pull the handle of a laser sword from his jump and light it.

The mad stranger would start swinging the sword wildly overhead while Kahn Deli and hysterical entourage rushed past the mandatory scans—waved on in the interest of their survival by a terrified boarding agent! Zim was relentless, drilling the three sheed to find their lungs and become a *chorus of terror*. They would be chiefly responsible for ratcheting up the level of hysteria so their stampede down the boarding tunnel appeared to be a necessity of the moment.

As far as getting the fleeing Barney Lovers and their screaming assailant to disappear down the terminal, all without passing through any bystanders—that was going to be a roll of the dice. It was the best he could do, so they'd just have to chance it.

A Quantro's associate slid in beside him, "May I help you, snag?"

"You certainly may."

After landing back at Seventy-Eighth Street, bridle path bridge, they used the Bumble Bee, already down from 103rd on the second set of tracks. They laid Splatter in the back of the ancient Camaro and took him down to Forty-Second. From there, they took the crosstown shuttle to the infirmary. Yasmine stayed with Splatter until they stabilized him. Then she took the Bumble Bee slowly in reverse all the way back to 103rd. On the way, she contacted Mayra on the walkie-talkie and told her the basics: she'd killed Yakami, they didn't get Harrison, but they did get Splatter. He was stabilized for the moment, but they didn't know if he was going to survive. She told Mayra she needed to talk to her alone right way. As if on cue, she could hear Han's voice in the background asking if they had Harrison. She rushed quickly on, afraid he would want to talk to her. "It's important, Ma. I gotta go!"

When Yasmine entered the library and made her way through the stacks back to the reading area, she expected to see Mayra sitting on one of the couches, waiting for her. Instead, the area was empty and barely lit by the dimmed chandelier. She was worried. She sat waiting for what seemed way too long. Finally, just as she was about to pull her Berretta and charge down the narrow passage leading to her cave, Mayra appeared.

Her relief was mixed with shock. From the musky scent of exertion, the hastily hand-combed hair, her relaxed facial muscles, boots unlaced, and a rumpled jump—Mayra had just come from Han's arms. While she and Dag were cutting their way through Yaki legions, Mayra and Han were getting busy!

This was bad. This was really bad. This wasn't Mayra. Yeah, she was a bit of a free spirit back in her younger days, but even then, she was all business when it came to missions. Han was even more dangerous than Yasmine imagined. In the space of three hours, he'd managed to completely turn her head.

"What is it? Why did you want to see me immediately and alone?" Mayra sat on the couch opposite her.

"Permission to speak freely?"

"Yasmine, what the hell is going on?"

"Permission to speak freely?"

"Yes! Sure. Say what you have to say."

Honestly, Yasmine wanted to tear into her. She never thought in a million years she'd ever talk to Mayra the way she wanted to now. But she needed to remember *what* she'd just realized. This wasn't Mayra. Just tell her exactly what happened.

"Please, just listen, okay? Everything went as planned getting into the chamber. I took care of three Yaks and Yakami—I was kinda nasty about that. Dag took out four Yaks on the other side of the room. Harrison and Splatter were both on these torture tables facing each other, and Dag went to cut down Splatter. I went to cut down Harrison. He was really a mess, Ma. I honestly didn't think he'd make it. I cut his arms down, and they just fell to his sides, dead weight. And I was starting to cut the plastic ties, holding his ankles, trying to position myself so he'd fall over my shoulder. I wanted to cheer him up, keep him motivated, and I said, 'Han is already here. He's back at Cenpak. Tooco's here too. He's driving the cruiser.'

Yasmine locked eyes with Mayra and spoke more slowly, "He looked at me like I was some kind of sadistic assassin. His head and neck turned bright red, and I swear his face transformed into a demented gargoyle! He looked up like he was addressing the creator and screamed at the top of his lungs, 'What the fuck is going on! What is this, Dog's idea of funny!' And then . . . you have to believe me. I know *what* I saw. The air around him turned into a blue mist, and Ma . . . he just evaporated . . . he became translucent and disappeared."

Yasmine reached out and took Mayra's hand. "It could not have been any clearer. Not only is Han not his friend, he's somebody who's been plaguing him to the point of madness. I'm telling you, Ma! I saw his face. He's not gonna come in here while Han and Tooco are out walkin' around. We've got to put them in custody and let him *know* that's the case as soon as anybody spots him."

"Han told me he could do that . . . disappear."

Surprised by this unexpected news, Yasmine quickly recovered, snorting with contempt. "Yeah, because when we rescued Harrison, he figured it wouldn't be long before we found that out." She squeezed Mayra's hand, trying to dispel whatever potion the handsome cartoon bewitched her with.

"And there's something about Sanatan. Remember he told us, if we said we were from Sanatan, they'd show us right to Yakami. No shit! They couldn't hustle us down there fast enough, but they kept announcing to everybody on the way down that we were 'recon' from Sanatan. And I could see it in their eyes, something really big happened there . . . something that had them all really shook up. Han knows. Whatever it is, Han knows . . . and I'd be willing to bet, he had something to do with it!"

"Where's Tooco?"

"He's at the infirmary on Forty-Second getting his foot rebandaged. It was a rough ride."

"Go down and get him. Bring him up here to 103rd. Put him in the holding cell on the IND platform. Tell Ram and Paliachi to wait outside the library until I call them. I'm going to have a talk with Han first. Then we'll put him with Tooco and let Harrison decide what to do with them after he gets here." Mayra stood and finished zipping up her jump. "When we've taken care of them, I want to meet with the whole council in the war bunker. The Yaks are gonna be coming at us with everything they've got. We better be ready."

Yasmine gave an inward sigh of relief. Thank god she's coming out of it.

"Prepare a Duni for tonight."

It was the last order she expected to hear at that moment. "Shouldn't we be out looking for him?"

"We need him to know we're here and everything's under control, and we want him to come to us." Mayra bent down and began lacing up her boots. "Have you still got the frybar you checked out on the mission?"

Yasmine nodded in the affirmative.

"Let me borrow your Berretta, will you? I left my .380 in there."

Yasmine took the weapon from its thigh holster and handed it to Mayra. "Are you sure you don't want some backup when you talk to him?"

"I think I can get more out of him if it's just the two of us."

"All right." Yasmine was tempted to warn her again that he was a snake from hell. But it would be insult to injury. She settled for, "Be careful."

•———◆◆◆———•

Once more, she took her time, walking slowly through the stacks down the purposely twisted path. She stopped again against the shelves before making it back to her cavern. Han was facedown spread-eagle across her bed. His marble buttocks remained at attention though, apparently, he was sound asleep.

She agreed with Yasmine's interpretation of Harrison's addressing God just before he disappeared. On hearing Han's and Tooco's names, he was confounded enough to rail at the heavens. Mayra could relate. Maybe it was time to examine this ripple in their destiny from the other way around. It was very possible Han and Tooco functioned as some kind of cross he had to bear or challenge he had to overcome. The gruesome torture was probably also a prerequisite. If everything that appeared to be going down was, in fact, reality, Mayra was grateful just to be the rural prophet announcing his arrival. Great light attracts great darkness. Han Larkill with his little buddy Tooco could very well be the hellhounds sent to stop Harrison from realizing the dreamers' destiny.

Studying his bronzed body, its perfect symmetry unifying all the parts into a libido-stirring work of art, Mayra felt her arousal begin again. Frankly, without a doubt, the best fuck of her entire life. His magnificent cock, with its firm patrician character, looked as if it were sculpted by the loving hands of Michaelangelo himself, unlike other well-endowed males she'd known in her youth—from ten years after she'd seen her vision of Fourteenth Armory until Sarah announced she was stepping down and wanted Mayra to succeed her. During that time, all those young guns who were packing .44 Magnums had the same problem. Their rods were all bent. Apparently, when the male shaft exceeded one and a quarter inches in diameter, it felt an irresistible urge to curl in one direction or the other. They swooped upward like a scythe, or to one side like a curveball in the dirt. It translated to less control, an inability to apply precision when getting at the spot that itched. If you couldn't hit that monogramed little G with a syncopation of direct shots—well, you got thoroughly fucked, but you didn't get off. Han's member was as straight as a plumb line and the same creamy pink as his ass—the outline of his imaginary swim trunks were the only area to escape his permatan. In those frenzied moments, when it mattered, he could hit the bull's eye like a MAC-10 rippin' off a clip.

The fact was, he epitomized an attentive and appreciative lover while, at the same time, being a very commanding one. She tried to check that when she'd snatched up his heat-seeking missile. But with a child's delight at being challenged, his blushing schoolboy acknowledged her instruction on the suddenness with which power could be usurped. Then the little charmer stayed after class and ravaged her. And what a thorough ravaging it was.

This did not alter the fact that he could be an extremely clever shape-shifter bent on proving the powers of autonomy could fuck up any collective design! It was his very prowess, his exceptional mental and physical talents, his easy mastery of every moment that finally made her certain that Yasmine was right. There was no way such a creature could avoid coming to the conclusion he should be master of all he surveyed.

"Why are you standing there looking at me with such a stern expression on that bewitching face?" He'd neither moved nor opened his eyes.

"What happened to Sanatan?"

There was the proverbial pregnant pause before—eyes still shut, position unchanged—he answered her question, "I blew it up." Han still refused to move but opened his eyes. "I was lying here thinking you've changed everything. You made my grand scheme suddenly unimportant . . . deciding just a moment ago to tell you the truth so as not to lose your goodwill. But I could feel it the moment you came back in, my lies were already exposed. It's funny the way things fall out."

Mayra was at a loss. "YOU BLEW UP SANATAN! YOU BLEW UP SANATAN AND ALL THOSE PEOPLE!"

"Yes, I did! It was part of an orchestrated plan to steal one of 7's *Protostars*. You don't think they're going to give you something like that unless they fear dire consequences! *Protostars* are mammoth ships built to explore ours and other galaxies looking for new worlds."

"I know about *Protostars*."

"Yes? Well, according to Jack, the first one is finished and waiting at one of their satellites, ready to go. I have the plan to steal it and the means to execute that plan. Also, I should inform you, in his duties as a spacecase, Jack is the one who first piloted that very *Protostar* and is completely competent at maintaining all aspects of its many systems."

"Han, you killed thousands of people!"

"Oh, give me a break! You've killed hundreds yourself! You've got some magic number where it suddenly becomes terrible? Actually, I'm sure I'm way beyond it, your number. I know from those screens you've got in your war mode you have some idea who Topgrid are . . . of the fate they've assigned to you. They plan to leave you all on this junkyard of a planet to rot and die while they take off to find a fresh new world to shit all over again. If you're really interested in the real number, I'd guesstimate close to a quarter million."

Closing his eyes again, he sighed. "And frankly, I'd happily have killed every last one of the motherduffers personally—if I had that kind of energy."

"Where did you get an atomic bomb?"

"You know a lot. I only found out about them when our Screwhog happened onto an old NORAD installation." He waited for her to ask what that was, but she was silent. "You know a lot about the past, but unfortunately, the character of the cokes right above you escapes your notice."

He finally sat up cross-legged and looked at her. "I know you're not going to believe me, and this is going to sound self-absorbed on my part, but it does go to proving my point. Our lovemaking was . . . phenomenal. Your naked vulnerability, the way you trust your lover, is not only intoxicating—it's truth in action . . . very primal action. I've seen something here I've never seen before. You trust each other. That's it—it's that simple. You all trust that everyone is working not only for themselves but for everyone else as well. At first, I dismissed it as naive, your beliefs, your homely ways . . . but I have to tell you, that 'twin books' thing and you already knowing from your visions that it was supposed to be coming to you? That really did throw me for a loop. I've been wrestling with it for the last couple days trying to escape an inescapable conclusion. There is a force and a conscious design far more elaborate and powerful than my personal schemes . . . and, unlike me, sowing more than itself."

Han locked eyes with Mayra. "Here's the thing, and please hear me out, I'm almost done. It struck me as strange that I was the one who brought the twin copy of *The Prophet* down here. If I hadn't come down after Jack and brought the book with me, you never would have received it, and you'd have doubted Jack's authenticity. Then, as I mentioned, there is my plan to steal a ship—just like the one Tooco says you've all seen in your fire ceremonies. So there's the book and the ship you've been waiting for. It made me realize my real destiny is to help you realize your dreams. I'm supposed to go on your journey. That's why our paths crossed over Jack. I believe now I'm meant to be a part of that vision. I'm not saying I haven't been a totally self-centered, self-absorbed egomaniac—reckless and sometimes ruthless. And I'm not saying I deserve to be part of the dreamer's journey . . . but I want to be. I think I'm meant to be.

I know Jack's not going to believe it, but please . . . ask him to come talk to me just one more time."

He looked up at her, shame and surrender in his dejected expression. "One other thing, I lied about the rest of the crew dying in Sanatan. They're hiding out in Big New so they can make our reservations on the Sat cruiser we'll need to get to the *Protostar*. They're waiting to hear from me on the fiber feeds to set it all in motion."

Without a word, Mayra walked over to her dresser and picked up a walkie-talkie. "Ram, Paliachi, come down to my place. Copy?"

The walkie-talkie spat out a stream of static before Ram's voice cut through it, "Copy."

"I suppose you're going to lock us up until you find Jack?"

"Yeah, I think that's the best course."

Han dropped his head to his chest. "I understand . . . I'm sorry I didn't see it sooner . . . I'm sorry I didn't just tell you the whole truth the first time we spoke."

She didn't think it would hurt to let him know she was disappointed as well.

"So am I."

•———◆◆◆———•

Preparing the Duni was Yasmine's favorite chore. She was chosen by Sam, Mayra's father. He'd been killed, along with her father, John, on the barricades in their last major defense against the Yaks. Sam enlisted her help as a girl cataloging the mountain of track ties and structural timbers, along with several dozen telephone poles residing in a ten-thousand-square-foot underground warehouse in the Bronx. It was located at the northern end of the IRT line. This was where the New York Subway Authority and public utilities kept their stores of wood, some of it over two hundred years old.

It's where they got all the wood used in their constructions. Century-old oak ties were dovetailed and mitered into the library's shelves, tables, and chairs. Gone over with electric sanders (using gas-powered electrical generators from Fourteenth Armory), then waxed and polished until their honeyed grain radiated through the entire library.

On their break from the tedious work of cataloging the vast warehouse, Sam would offer her part of his sandwich, which she never failed to take. He'd tell her stories about how it was. He told her about seeing his first Duni in India in another time far away, where the dreamers' seeds were sown.

She chose only ties completely free of rot. It made her unpopular with the wood keepers, but Yasmine really gave a shit. Her long and passionate romance with a man old enough to be her father had toughened her to the opinions of others. She backed up the converted two-ton flatbed truck to the end of the rails and their loading area. The second that the truck showed up, all the wood keepers knew what it meant—there'd be a Duni tonight, and they'd have to hustle to get the truck loaded as fast as they could. She could almost see the burst of energy surge around the warehouse. Ma was going to tell them all what was going on. The roller-coaster ups and downs of the last couple days—was Han a friend or foe of Harrison? He brought the twin book. How could somebody fulfill such a remarkable vision and be a threat? Yasmine had a good idea how, but she didn't want to steal Ma's thunder with conjecture. It would just be rumor generating more rumors and anxiety. It was hard, but they'd just have to suffer until later that evening, not so long really.

Prometheus was the squat gray-bearded foreman of the wood keepers. He emerged now from his tiny shack and made his limping way toward the truck. "Well, if it isn't our lady of the geriatrics!" Reaching Yasmine, he lowered the volume, adopting a more conspiratorial tone. "When you gonna give this old lumberjack a shot?"

"Fuck you, Prometheus, and the calliope horse you rode in on." Old guard, he thought pissing on your suffering hardened you to loss, the manly prescription for moving on from a personal tragedy. Men are morons.

"What do you need?"

"Give me three cords. I'm gonna make a big Duni tonight."

The old codger turned back to his crew hanging around the periphery, straining to pick up any bits of conversation. "All right, hustle it up! We need to load three cords for the Duni tonight."

Now it was official: there was going to be a Duni. They all put their backs into it, satisfied they'd get an accounting from Mayra soon. Prometheus looked down at his boots and spoke in an even quieter tone, "They're saying you saw him up close."

"Saw who?"

He eyed her with an expression of disgust. "Andy Warhol, who the fuck do you think?" Art was big with Prometheus. He could often be found in the library pouring over their volumes of paintings.

"I only saw him briefly."

"Well, that's 'briefly' longer than the rest of us." Taking care to turn his head, he let a stream of tobacco juice fly and then locked his rheumy eyes on her. "So did you really see him disappear?" It was amazing how fast news got around!

"Yeah. He disappeared, right in front of me . . . completely evaporated."

"Wow . . . so it's serious. The time has finally come to act on dreams."

Yasmine gave the old lecher a measure of compassion the only way he'd accept it, as an insult. "Yeah, you gotta get it up one last time, old man."

She turned back to the truck and hopped in the cab. Firing up the Trojan eight-banger, she gunned the old monster, hoping to motivate the loaders to shake the sawdust off their asses. Normally, she would inspect every cord, but she knew they wouldn't try to slip in damp or rotten wood on her. They only tried to pull that once. She tracked down the wood keeper responsible and made it clear that if he ever did it again, she'd be hanging his nut sack on her wall. Within minutes, they finished lashing down the load. Yasmine shot an arm out the window in a final salute, threw the engine in gear, and took her foot off the clutch.

"See you at the Duni!"

• ••• •

Mayra watched as Ram and Dag entered the war bunker and took their places at the long table next to Spider and Paliachi. The old spotter

Sparky and Chan, captain of the outer perimeter, sat across from them. With Splatter out of commission, Chan was captain of Fifty-Ninth perimeter as well. Once everyone was settled, she turned to Ram. "Are security arrangements for Han and Tooco taken care of?"

From the smile on his face and frequent glances toward Dag, Ram was obviously enjoying his vindication. "Yes. They're locked up on the IND platform at 103rd. Outriders are guarding them."

"Okay." She looked around the table, taking them all in. "Things have been changing, events coming very quickly. We're all struggling to keep up. Han has confessed to me—among other things—that the copy of *The Prophet* he gave me was actually Harrison's. Han admitted they came down here to grab Harrison. Han has a plan to steal a large intergalactic ship, the *Protostar*.

Danner used to talk about it. It's docked on a satellite in orbit around the planet. He said once they got it, he needed Harrison to fly it. Also . . . he told me what happened to Sanatan."

Spider stabbed the air with an elongated index finger. "It's been eighty-four hours since we picked up any transmissions from Sanatan on their fiber screens."

"That's because Han blew it up."

Jaws dropped around the entire table. A few weak expletives escaped from gaping pieholes. All of them were fixed on Mayra, waiting for her to continue.

"He told me they acquired a bomb in an underground facility left over from 3TC. It was capable of massive destruction. It sounds like an atomic bomb. Han used it to blow up Sanatan. He wanted to send a message to 7 about what to expect if they didn't hand over the spaceship to him."

Ram was quick to give his analysis. "So the flashy giant is completely out of his gourd."

Dag followed up with a question, "What happened that he suddenly decided to come clean about all of this? Why is he confessing to this shit now?"

"He said it was because he realized the arrogance and emptiness of his dreams. He said, witnessing things like the twin volumes and Harrison's being drawn here—it being foretold in our visions, that he was coming—he says that all had a profound effect on him. He says he now believes Harrison is special, and he wants to stay here and be a part of something greater than himself."

Ram was unmoved. "Give me a fucking break! We saw how good he was at lying. You think the story he's selling now is any truer?"

"Well, we're going to keep them locked up until Harrison shows up. Then he can tell us what he wants to do with them."

Sparky suddenly slammed the table with his palm. "Excuse me, has everyone forgotten we've got a whole lot of Yaks about to go kamikaze on us? We need to deal with that immediately!"

"You're right, but this is important, and I want you to hear it now." Mayra turned to Dag. "Tell everyone what happened when you went in to get Harrison and Splatter."

Dag cleared his throat, hesitating as he looked around the table, before finally plunging in, "We blew the door off the torture chamber and went inside. Splatter was spread-eagle on this kind of plastic slab, and there was another one—Harrison, I assumed—strapped to a similar slab. They were both seriously messed up . . . propped up so they were facing each other. We cleared the room. Yasmine killed Yakami."

Chan had a question, "Are you sure it was Yakami?"

"Yeah, for sure. I've seen drawings of him, the muttonchop sideburns, the nose, and tattoos! Yeah, it was Yakami. So I started cutting down Splatter, and Yasmine was doing the same with Harrison." He paused to wet his lips. "I didn't actually see it because my back was turned to them, but when I finished cutting Splatter down, I turned around to see if Yasmine had him . . . and Harrison was gone.

"Yasmine told me he disappeared right in front of her eyes."

"Disappeared?" Spider's mutable face was even more twisted than usual. "You mean he just vanished?"

Dag nodded. "That's what Yasmine said. She watched him evaporate into thin air."

Mayra jumped into the incredulous silence, "That's what Han told me when he admitted he'd come down to get Harrison. He said there are Topgrid who've been trained to do this. Apparently, they've discovered more amazing breakthroughs in physics since Danner joined us. They're called spacecase. Harrison is one."

Paliachi joined the mix, "Well, where the hell is he now? Why did he take off like that? Don't you think we should be looking for him? If he's as messed up as Splatter is, he sure as hell isn't in very good shape!"

Mayra was embarrassed. None of them had taken the time to consider the situation from his point of view, including her. They were only concerned with getting ahold of him so he could do things for them. She knew from old periodicals that when asked why they called the day Jesus was crucified *Good Friday*, Christians answered, because it was the day he took away all our sins. I don't know, you'd think maybe they'd want to tip their hat to what he went through on "Good" Friday to accomplish that, maybe come up with a better adjective. She was ashamed of displaying the same kind of self-interest. But in truth, she believed Harrison knew what he was doing.

"Paliachi, I share your concerns, but I believe he knows what he's doing. With the kinds of abilities he possesses, it may be possible he can tend to his wounds more effectively in his altered state." *Oh, you're reaching for it now, sister!* "I think what we need to do is make sure he knows we're waiting for him . . . that we're here, and we're waiting for him. That's why I've called for a Duni tonight! He'll feel us. He'll know we're his to lead . . . and we are waiting for him. That's the best thing we can do."

They took a moment before Sparky spoke again, "We still need a battle plan to deal with the coming hoard."

"I've already drawn it up. No doubt they're boiling with rage at our killing Yakami and the fact we've been kicking their asses for a while, not to mention losing their whole crew in Sanatan. We can use that.

They're gonna throw everything they've got at us and try to end this once and for all!"

Mayra turned to Ram. "I want you to load up our cruisers with all the air-to-ground explosives we have at the armory. Have Paliachi assign two-man demolition teams to the bigger cruisers and leave the smaller ones to deal with whatever the Yaks put in the air. Hide your cruisers up in Harlem. Pick a spot that's really decimated so you don't have to worry about being spotted by foraging scabs. Leave three drones circling the barricade's perimeter—for the Yaks to shoot down when they come. We don't want them to sense a trap. Get on that immediately after the meeting and let me know when you're ready to take off. Once you deploy, wait for our signal at your staging point."

Now it was Paliachi's turn. "Tell the laser-cannon teams at Fifty-Ninth barricade to activate the Levis on the guns and move them down to the tunnel entrances at both the Fifth Avenue and IRT sides. Don't forget to station forklifts at both locations so we can move them into the tunnels when we're ready to lock it all down."

Chan was up next. "When the Yaks attack, I want you to take a patrol carrying a lot of C-4 down the IND line to Twenty-Third and Bowery. Now that we know exactly where it is and what it looks like—a five-story triangular pink building on Twelfth and Third Avenue—you're going to blast open the Fourteenth Street entrance and attack the Yak headquarters. They'll be busy directing their offensive and be very surprised to find themselves suddenly playing defense. It should be fairly easy to get inside. Find a structurally significant place to hide the C-4. You'll detonate it when you and your team make it back to your entry point."

Mayra pushed a folded map across the table to Chan. "That's the map to get through the mines. You need to place another charge close to your entry point. When you're done, it can reseal the tunnel. As soon as you're clear, detonate both charges, then get back to Fifty-Ninth as fast as you can. When you arrive, the cannons will be in position in the tunnels, and our troops will begin retreating from the barricade under covering fire. When all our troops have made it into the tunnel, the cannon crews will use pulse bolt to completely seal off the barricade at the Fifty-Ninth tunnel, from Fifth Avenue down to Central Park, West.

"Once the Yaks take the barricade and realize we've sealed off the tunnel entrances, they'll have their cruisers start lifting troops over into Cenpak, hoping to find the tunnel entrances inside the barricade. When we hear that happening, we signal our cruisers in Harlem to make their move.

"Ram, you're going to take your squadron straight up until you're just below the tops of the old scrapers. Make sure before you expose your squadron, there aren't any Sacker ships patrolling beneath the grid plate. If there are, you'll have to wind your way through the top of the girders until you're directly over Cenpak. By the time you're in place, the Yaks will have most of their troops and their cruisers in Cenpak. Have the cruisers you've designated as fighters drop straight down and cut to pieces all their battle cruisers. Ram, you lead in the *Firewalker*. After you've taken care of their cruisers, the rest of your squadron drops down and blows the living crap out of Cenpak! Just keep dropping shit on them until nothing's moving in there. Try not to drop anything right up against the barricades. We don't want to have to dig out any more caved-in tunnels than necessary after this is over.

"We'll reopen the Seventy-Eighth bridle path entrance after you signal us the battleground is secure. Then we'll send up the rest of our troops to recon the attack site and make sure they're all down. After that, we'll slip into the barricades through the secret entrances. One patrol goes left, the other one to the right, circling in a pincer assault to hunt down any Yaks left inside the barricades. We'll leave *Firewalker* and your other fighters in the air patrolling the perimeter."

She turned back to Chan. "We'll have to move the cruiser, transport train, back up beyond 103rd so the train evacuating Forty-Second can deliver the food stores and all the kitchen equipment from the mess up to the Duni cavern. After we've secured the whole barricade, we can move the evacuation train down below Fifty-Ninth and bring the cruiser transport train down to Seventy-Second, load the cruisers out of Cenpak, and park them in their regular spot above 103rd. All right, so any comments?"

After a stunned silence, Ram spoke up, "No, sounds good. I think you've covered everything. If Han blew up Sanatan, then when this is over, we'll have taken care of these cockroaches for good!"

A spontaneous cheer erupted, which Mayra finally stifled with a raised hand. "Pass the word! When all the preparations we discussed have been taken care of, I want everyone not patrolling the barricades or on a cannon crew to be at the Duni, which will be lit at eighteen hundred hours. As I've already said, it's very important that right now Harrison feels our faith in him."

• ⎯⎯ ◆◆◆ ⎯⎯ •

Dag was shocked he wouldn't be on perimeter duty at eighteen hundred hours—the situation being what it was. But Mayra wanted normal rotation and number of patrols, being certain the Yaks would scope them hard before they came. She wanted everything to appear the same. Besides, the plan was to fall back fairly quickly when the attack began. So it turned out Dag had the night off, and he was uneasy about it. But it did give him the chance to come down to the Duni early. He liked to watch the fire keepers begin building the pyre, tossing wood into the rock-ringed pit at the center of the Duni cavern. The vast rock chamber was situated across from the library at 103rd. Dag's gaze followed the trail of smoke, curling up into the frescoed cone in the center of the ceiling. A diverted chimney ushered the billowing plumes on a subterranean journey, which eventually delivered them into the air along the northern barricade. It would be a while yet before the flames were nurtured into a single radiant ember. Most dreamers hadn't arrived. Usually, they spent the last couple of hours contemplating their personal dream in the larger one. On this special occasion, everyone was busy getting ready for combat.

Dag studied the frescos more closely, contemplating the personal record of their journey in these tableaus of major events: the first Duni vision, the discovery of Fourteenth Street Armory, the domed city sliding over them. They were painted by a jovial artist who always wore a slightly manic grin no matter what was going on. He went almost completely blind during the five-year process of painting all the frescos and various border accents inside the cavern. It wasn't his painting that made him blind. He had some kind of eye disease. "Otter," Dag remembered they called him. He'd died four years ago of old age—a rare occurrence now. But his frescos still retained their original brilliance despite traces of smoke blurring some background images at the top of the cone. His increasing affliction had only served to embolden his impressionistic style and vibrant colors.

As always, the fire keepers, because of their duties, were the first to express the rising Duni spirit. By nature traditionalists, they began with the earlier fire-and-brimstone hymns. Their smoke-scarred throats joined in the opening of "Every Step You Take" by the turn-of-the-century mystic minstrel called Sting. No doubt, once the fire warmed up and they stripped down to the waist, brought out their steel poles, and began stirring the coals, a spontaneous combustion would occur. Then they'd break into the old cornerstone, Sarah's Joint. Actually, it was Mayra's father, Sam, a rapper, who adapted Shakespeare's treatise on love into the hiphop anthem.

When Sarah met Sam, it was while foraging in basement apartments in alphabet city. After an initial quick draw, which Sarah easily won (her Colt .380 against Sam's machete), they froze for a moment. For some unknown reason she later put down to destiny—Sarah didn't kill him. They realized, in the diplomatic negotiations that followed, they shared a fool's vision of goodwill among scabs.

Dag still carried the picture Sam gave him when he performed inside the Twenty-Third IRT entrance with his DJ setup: a Jew with blond dreadlocks tied up in a do-rag, wearing a torn T-shirt and faded jeans. Sam (who in his next life) learned to fix anything, including gas-powered and electric motors, wiring electrical systems, fabricating metal, and building walls, roofs, tables, and chairs; who could tell you the exact distance from the Earth to the sun; who could sit for hours vividly describing a world that had once come and gone. He taught the children with Sarah. Dag was one of their last students.

Smoke was beginning to back up a little with the fire keepers' enthusiasm. Pitching in ties to their beats, they'd raised the pyre to over seven feet. Stopping for a while to recover their breath, they continued their dark ironic tone with the second hymn they chose: "Money" by the King's Men. Tongues of red flame leapt toward the dome with all the brilliant colors in the frescos radiating back in the light. Dag inhaled the aroma of burning oak and thanked god he was so blessed. In a matter of hours, he'd see his vision join with all the others inside the mesmerizing flames into an epic story of journey and destination. He was definitely a fortunate fellow. Fortunate to see what he'd seen and what he *would* see—a lucky man.

• —— ◆◆◆ • —— •

"Please try to remember this because someday it may mean the difference between life and death for you."

Despite his fifth-dimensional hibernation, Harrison could see his old String instructor Muller, a minivision, in the last conscious cell of his comatose brain. His tweed jump, with the patches on the elbows, he was endlessly dispensing dramas of doom to terrified cadets.

"Here's a little known fact: lying completely dormant in inert matter does not entail the loss of nearly the amount of core energy that entering it, moving in it, or exiting it requires. And that's a good thing to know. Let's suppose you are unfortunate enough, despite your magical speed and malleability in the fifth dimension, to get caught looking one way when you should be looking the other, just as a titanium structural beam comes whistling through your subatomic quantum field, before you've adjusted for the intrusion of the subatomic particles of that element. In other words, it cuts you clean in half.

"At this point, you are going to have only one option for your continued survival. And Dog help you, if that piece of titanium floats away before you can grab your lower torso and get over to it, you need to merge with it immediately. The two pieces of your subatomic (astral) body don't have to be fitted together properly. As long as the halves are touching at any point, they'll sort themselves out once you've merged.

"Because here is the beauty of the fifth dimension: if you can merge with a mass having at least ten times the density of your three-dimensional body and remain *completely dormant*, your astral body will put itself back together and reknit whatever injuries you've incurred. But you must not move one iota until you feel an irresistible urge to *unfold* from your quantum fetal position. Then you know your astral body is completely healed. But make no mistake, it is a costly option. You will pay some core for your error in judgment. Remember to take your time unfolding. Feel out your parameters again."

At least he only needed to recover from a murderous beating and crippling torture. It could've been much worse, and still he'd have survived. But he would pay. When you had to give up half a hundred cycle of life expectancy to master the String, it was easy to run out of time, and he felt that in the current cement of his bones. But there was still a will. He still wanted to see her.

Now he did unfold and felt the vitality returning to his astral body. He was impatient to escape the confines of heavy-density mass. But he remembered Muller's warning and decided to stay entombed, moving through the dirt for a while until he got back the "feel" of himself. He pushed forward a few centigrid and, with his movements, felt more certain that the union of subatomic particles that defined him were revitalizing their bonds of connection. He was merging now with another large cement slab and immediately felt the lack of pressure on the other side. He remembered his resolution before he sank into his healing coma—to look for her in their tunnels. He pushed slowly through the cement and found he was, indeed, in a tunnel, standing on a station platform. A rectangular sign hung from the tunnel's ceiling, "FOURTEENTH STREET IND." This had to be one of theirs. Over the edge of the platform, he saw the metal rails, "train tracks," leading off in both directions. He decided to continue going north up the tunnel, away from Yakuza sector. He felt strong enough to jump off the String now. Beginning to visualize his pattern, he saw something else.

"Of course, as I'm sure you are already aware, all good things come to an end. There will come a time—many happy years from now, we trust—when flying along on your String, you decide to return to our mundane three dimensions and begin visualizing your pattern. Lo and behold, what you visualize is this." Muller had traced with his laser pointer the very Mandela that moments before appeared in the center of Harrison's mind.

"When you see this, you've just taken five for the last time. You can, if you choose, jump the String one more time, but you will no longer have the core energy left to return to the three-dimensional, and you will die or, more correctly, dissipate in a quantum state. The party is over when this pattern appears. You will no longer be a spacecase. Class dismissed."

Suddenly he was furious with everything! Himself, especially. After everything he'd been through on this *journey of awareness*, merging with heavy-density mass to heal, burning up his last critical core. This is what it came to! But he knew with everything else on his plate (most unnerving being the fact that Han and Tooco were here with the dreamers in Cenpak), he needed to put all of it on hold. Just concentrate on navigating his way to the dreamers' lair. There was no way he'd jump off the String before he found her. Besides, reappearing out of thin air, no longer a bloody mess, would be his last chance to demonstrate his spacecase "magic." Willing this final Mandela back into his unconscious, Harrison flowed down the murky cavern, a spacecase for the last time.

•———◆◆◆———•

Finished with personal preparations, many were starting to drift in, milling at the edges of the cavern. Higher up on the farthest levels above the pit, a few sat in clusters, passing their home brew around. All carried weapons slung over their shoulders, mostly AR-15s and M-16s, all sporting converted oil-filter silencers. There were a few tried-and-true BARs (Browning Automatic Rifles from WWII) in the crowd and a plethora of laser and steel swords. Everyone was geared up for the impending war.

Yasmine could feel the tension building as they continued filtering in. There was a subdued murmuring rather than the rambunctious catcalls that usually filled the arena. They knew this Duni might be their last. They'd tried to rescue their deliverer, and in the process, she butchered the Yak leader, Yakami. Now it was really on. This one would be to the last man. She tried to feel guilty for being the last straw. But what do you want? It was war. Besides, he'd tortured and would have killed Harrison. He had it coming in spades. She'd really enjoyed it, all right! What's done is done. Right now she needed to keep her mind on what she was doing, overseeing the turning of the coals. Occasionally, as she did now, Yasmine would go halfway up the wooden "bleachers" to check the overall pattern of the fire's development, calling down instructions to the fire keepers, pointing out areas where they needed to agitate the coals.

Circling around the pit, poking the inferno with long metal poles, the tips glowing orange with their industry—a half-dozen fire keepers, hands wrapped in towels, stripped down to loincloths and, glistening with sweat, shifted from old hymns to mantras. They were no longer able to summon the breath for song so close to the searing heat. The more spirited in the crowd were chanting the mantras with the fire keepers while others were line dancing in unison, stamping down hard on the beat.

Sam promoted the dancing. He said his father swore that learning to dance in the second half of the twentieth century saved the white man's soul—finally able to release their energy and passion, realizing they looked like idiots and not caring anymore. Sam's dad had been a hippy. Sam said he would laugh hysterically recounting the massive doses of hallucinogens they required to finally break down their overbearing "uptightness," their "rational" covenant with fear that kept them from embracing life. Yasmine wanted to throw her hands up with the others and dance around the pyre. Later, she would, when the coals became bright yellow, turning the cavern to gold.

She saw Dag weaving among the dancers, coming down closer to the fire. She was amazed at his recovery. He was smiling, greeting friends as they passed. He looked bone-tired after their abortive rescue. If only they could have brought Harrison back. The image of his agonized face was still front and center in her mind. He was the one. Maybe the Duni would conjure him, give him a beacon on which to hone. Maybe that's what Mayra knew—why she was so calm. She watched the barrel of axle grease being rolled into place.

Suddenly she spotted the girl Teeba coming in with her father, a grizzly bear of a man called Mongrel. He was dressed in the Outriders' characteristic black leathers. He was carrying a street sweeper, with accompanying silencer (the oil filter off a Bobcat) slung over his shoulder. The autoshotgun was the favorite weapon of Outriders.

She watched as the dancers began lining up to dip their vision sticks into the grease barrel and toss them in the flames. Teeba and Mongrel were rapidly being surrounded, the crowd bent on quizzing the girl who'd seen their deliverer. Not much longer, and almost four hundred of them would be singing and swaying in the smoky cavern around their golden Duni. Then Mayra would enter and go down to the pit and make the opening address.

Yasmine signaled for agitation at the edges, and the fire keepers responded by propping their smoking bars against the rim of the stone pit, dragging them clockwise around the circumference. Changing their mantra to a caddish for the lost souls of the twentieth, they broke into a chant from the prophet Dylan (the heir to Shakespeare's crown, according to Mayra), repeating his words over and over, raking the outer coals.

"Darkness, at the break of noon, shadows even the silver spoon . . . the handmade blade, the child's balloon, eclipses both, the sun and moon . . . to understand that you know too soon, there is no use in crying."

Charcoal at the edges burned a dark orange with the disturbance, and the golden coals at the center began to turn a diamond white. The fire was coming alive. All around the cavern, they were stripping off jackets and shirts in the heat, wrapping their weapons in their fatigues and leaving them at their chosen places to dance or join the swaying line, waiting to toss their vision sticks in the flames.

Now the bleachers started calling the tune—a row of Outriders scatted the bubbling cacophony that opened their banner hymn "Ain't Nobody." A hypnotic boogie of the Chaka Kahn, it quickly infected the whole cavern. Soon everyone was moving in its seductive syncopation.

Yasmine made her way through the crowd up toward the farthest tier. From there, she watched the brilliance at the center spread until the whole pit glowed a radiant yellow. Pulling out the official starting gun, she loaded a flare, taking aim at the center of the pyre. Every eye was on her now, the music growing louder. Inside a collective shriek, she pulled the trigger and watched the neon missile streak to the fire's center, exploding in a shower of sparks erupting to the dome.

Hoisting their long poles from the blaze and sliding them into holes drilled in the rock for the purpose, the fire keepers disappeared in the dance. And Yasmine, having performed her final duty, took the advice being crooned by Outrider falsettos: "What was I gonna do? I let myself go."—disappearing too inside the music and the flames.

Waiting for some information in the war bunker at Forty-Second Street shuttle station, Mayra's cynical devil was trying to rattle her again. *Take a tip from the twentieth 'Jeanne.' Back then, all your lieutenants— you know, your 'cabinet'—would be instructed to keep their mouths shut. No need to mention Han. Show the masses the red armor made famous in the fames. That'll knock 'em on their ass! 'He pointed to his armor just before he disappeared. He knows what he's doing! Keep the faith!' Then you have Yasmine give her account of the disappearing miracle . . . maybe give the rabble a look at the twin copies of* The Prophet, *affirming what was, no doubt about it, prophesied! Then send 'em off to war!*

And the complicated truth, you little wiseass?

Ah yes, the complicated truth should be left for later some more convenient time. Except the truth becomes even more inconvenient after the danger has passed. Priorities always shift back to protecting everybody from the embarrassing truths of their fallible selves, until finally, the only "selves" they recognize are steeped in complicit bullshit.

The dreamers took a vow—her mother and father and a small band of 115 took a vow—to try very hard not to lie anymore, not to take responsibility for things that weren't their responsibility, and not to be presumptuous in assuming the truth needed their husbanding. Observing these vows was key to their redemption, to their rebirth as a society genuinely committed to achieving civilization.

She brushed her hand sharply across the planking of the long table, sweeping away her cynic's supercilious interpretation of their present situation. Momentarily, she would leave and take the IRT line up to 103rd and a teeming Duni cavern. She'd stayed down here in the war bunker after their battle plan was decided to oversee their preparations for evacuating Forty-Second. At the other end of the table, she watched Paliachi's crew busily disassembling the net screens, packing them in transport cases to be hooked up again in whatever corner they could find down at Seventy-Eighth. The "communications coordinators" sat around the walls of the bunker on knee-high stools, hunched over with walkie-talkies pressed to one ear while they plugged the other ear with a finger, trying to escape their own chatter. They were trafficking messages from Fifty-Ninth, Thirty-Fourth, and Twenty-Third, along with the barricade spotters—all sending their collective intel back to them. So far, there was no radio activity from the Yaks and no sign of them.

They were using this lull before the storm to relocate everything down to the cavern at Seventy-Eighth. Even though they were underground and their locations down here were unknown to the

Yaks, it was still strategically indefensible to leave your command control center, your field hospital, and field kitchen behind enemy lines once your forces were engaged. They were hoping to get some sense of what the Yaks' strategy was going to look like—whether their plan was to come with their major force at the southern barricade on Fifty-Ninth; or split up their forces in a two- or three-pronged attack, simultaneously hitting the east and west barricades; or throw everything at the northern barricade. The drawback was it would be very hard to get a large force around to the northern barricade without the dreamers knowing about it and having plenty of time to respond. The strategy Mayra laid out would remain essentially the same, no matter which way they came. But still, you wanted as much information as possible about the way the opposing force was going to come at you. The actual act of moving everything would severely curtail their intelligence-gathering capabilities, until they got everything set up again at Seventy-Eighth.

She knew this Duni was important, and she needed to play her part. It was time to go.

"All right, we're not waiting any longer. Start moving everything down to Seventy-Eighth."

As she stood to leave, Mayra caught Paliachi looking up from his packing, begging her with his eyes to keep silent about Han, promising his understanding and complicity if she did. She knew none of the commanders would say anything about Han to their troops. They would observe the chain of command and leave it to her as their leader to break the news. She answered Paliachi's look with a wry smile as she turned and strode decisively out of the bunker.

Fuck 'em if they can't take a joke. What do you expect? You can eat all the celestial cake you want, but you still have to chug the purple Kool-Aid. Alive for the blink of an eye in the span of time and reaching for eternity? Come on! Whaddayuh expect?

What they expected, as she laid eyes on the packed cavern, was immediately apparent. The disappointment showed in every face as she stood there at the entrance alone, no blond hunk beside her, no savior either. The singing died off, and the dancing stopped. Suddenly it was only a sweltering chasm packed with an anxious sweating throng.

They stepped back to clear a path for her to the fire. Moving quickly down the tiers, head lowered, cocked to one side, she locked eyes briefly with every face she passed. To anyone who knew her well, it was a certain tip-off she was furious. And she was. They'd turned almost instantly—every eye accusing, ready to jump ship if she couldn't give them a good explanation.

What did you expect? And the point goes to Beelzebub's barrister.

Upon reaching the pit, without the slightest hesitation, she leaped onto the stone parapet surrounding the golden coals and began racing around the ridge of rocks with the certainty of a mountain ram, hoping the fire would cool her fury. Even moving quickly so close to the heat, the fatigue jacket she wore was beginning to smoke. Peeling it off as she ran, Mayra tossed the smoldering jacket on the coals, and it exploded into flames. Circling the pit in only a khaki wifebeater and camouflage pants, the crowd instinctively began to back away, sensing her fury and their responsibility for it. They waited, fearing disaster but still hoping for inspiration. A vision was what they got.

A wall of green flames circumscribed half the ring's circumference, shooting up at least ten feet high. Their dancing green peaks took the shape of a familiar landscape, the topography of their planet, the one waiting out there in their future. This mountain range was not only unusually high; it also radiated an emerald sheen over the entire cavern. Even for Mayra, whose power to conjure the flames was legendary, this Duni was a jewel among all their visions. Still, Mayra ran like a whirlwind, disappearing and reappearing from behind the flames, until suddenly she made a flying leap off the parapet, landing with so much force her boots carved twin groves for at least a yard in the dirt of the cavern floor.

Looking from face-to-face, she saw the awe again. Momentarily, they were calmed, mindful. Here was the magic inferno and the power it revealed. But when the flames died, they would forget again. Her rage was for that constant tardiness at every crossroads, the need to painstakingly retrace the most rudimentary truths of spirit, their constant reversion to a wide-eyed terror, their need to be cajoled, entranced, and seduced into remembering their primal connection. And on top of all that, they *demanded*, if fulfillment *was* their destiny, they must be given every opportunity to indulge whatever self-absorbed tantrum of doubt they could conjure up *as proof of God's benefcence toward them!* And while she suspected it made her just another judgmental hypocrite, she was growing increasingly weary, finding it in her heart to forgive their constant, willful ignorance concerning the true nature of faith.

Having faith isn't knowing. Having faith isn't seeing. Having faith isn't understanding. Having faith is having faith. Get it?

"I never asked for any of this. I never wanted this job, whatever this job is . . . being a leader, a guide. I never yearned for this kind of responsibility or authority. Many of you can remember when I just wanted to party. Parties are more fun than power trips. I never asked for this.

"And you know if my foolish peccadillos in proselytizing taught me anything, it's how quickly you could turn and how vicious you could be when your leader makes a mistake . . . albeit a very serious one. But errors are a given in the experience of fallible beings, and we are all fallible beings. How a community views this fundamental occurrence in the process of enlightenment is the cornerstone of its claim to the mantle of civilization. Is the idea to put an end to all errors by condemning and ridiculing them? To ostracize them from our consciousness so we can manufacture illusions of perfection and self-righteousness? That's an original idea!

"Okay, school's out."

"I made a mistake. The big blond Han was not the friend of the one we've been waiting for. He confessed to me his ulterior plans to use our deliverer for his own personal ends. Strangely, his personal ends mirror ours in many ways. Han knows about a big ship like the one in our visions. At this moment, it's docked at one of the Topgrid's satellites. It's the *Protostar* Danner told us they were planning. They built it, and Han planned to steal it. He wanted to take it out into the galaxy and beyond, making our deliverer pilot it for him. According to Han, while in Topgrid service, our deliverer piloted that ship and is completely knowledgeable about every aspect of the craft.

"Han also confessed to me that the twin copy of *The Prophet*, which he brought with him, in fact, belonged to the man Teeba saw on the girders, the man who spoke the words that were prophesied in the fire. Han told me his name is Harrison . . . Harrison, Jack.

"Han told me all this without being confronted with his lies. He said he told me because he was finally awed by how clear it was. There is a force directing our destiny, and in the face of it, he has come to realize how small and self-centered his own dreams are. He says he wants to help make our dream come true, that he wants to be a part of that. He thinks the force that's been guiding us has brought him and his knowledge and abilities to be of service to something greater than himself. And I don't know if he's telling the truth. I know he's done terrible things. He has the blood of many people on his hands. He and Tooco are locked up and under guard. We'll let Harrison decide what to do with Han once he gets here.

"After I got the first report of his arrival from Teeba, I had another report Harrison was seen headed for Yaki sector. I sent Splatter down to the Twenty-Third entrance to see if he could find him and, if necessary, slip through the mesh to find out what the Yaks were up to. After I didn't hear anything back from Splatter, I thought probably they were both captured. Han and Tooco, the ex-Yaki who used to be Yakami's driver, thought they knew where the Yaks would be holding them. We sent Yasmine and Dag, with Tooco piloting the *Firewalker*, to rescue them. Han devised the plan, and it worked perfectly. They were being held at that location, and Yasmine and Dag were able to overpower the Yaks holding them. Both Harrison and Splatter were there, being tortured by Yakami. Dag got Splatter, but as Yasmine was releasing Harrison, he disappeared, evaporated right in front of her eyes. Han told me Harrison could do that, disappear and reappear, that Harrison had special implants in his brain, along with some kind of specialized training that allows him to shift himself into other dimensions.

"Unfortunately, we have to deal with an untimely opportunity that we have no choice but to take! During our rescue attempt, Yasmine killed Lord Yakami. Many of our fallen friends and their families have reason to rejoice for that, but now we need to be prepared for a total assault. They're gonna let us have it with everything they've got! It's been building up to this for a while. We are ready. Our strategy will be decisive, and I believe we have an opportunity now to put an end to the Yaki stranglehold on Bellytown. But that's where we need to keep our focus. That's why I need to return to the war bunker to oversee our evacuation, but you need to reach out to him here, at the Duni. Let Harrison know we're here, waiting. Afterward, you know your assignments."

With this final pronouncement, Mayra lowered her head and started back up the steps out of the cavern, but Prometheus stepped in front of her, blocking the path.

"But, Ma, we need you at the Duni."

Mayra glanced back at the pit, green flames still shimmered brightly. "You have your fire."

The old man was both petulant and pleading. "But we can't see into the heart of it without you. Why so angry? Who here has challenged or chastised you? You called us to the Duni, Ma. We have faith, Ma . . . help us know it better."

Suddenly Mayra felt a hand on her shoulder and turned to see Yasmine, slightly out of breath, having run down to catch her. "Ma, we're with you."

Maybe it was the impending battle, the fact things were on the line, whether or not she'd fucked up. But it was true. The mood in the cavern wasn't anxious or contentious now, just the opposite—they wanted to come together. They wanted to feel their connection and reaffirm their collective journey, wherever it was leading. It was faith enough to make Mayra admit that she too was being frightened and accusatory, putting it all off on them. Even when you're willing to admit the necessity, humility still demands you go ahead and find your knees.

Oh, give me a break! Her cynical sidekick wasn't going down without a fight. *You just happened to make the right psychological play here, that's all! And with the human boob, the 'right play'—90 percent of the time—is to get pissed and smack him across the nose a couple whacks. It's the only way to get the sniveling twit to focus on something besides himself for a brief period of time.*

Well, if that's true, so what? At least something could penetrate that fortress of self-interest.

She awoke from her internal debate to the roadmap of the old wood keeper's face, still waiting for her to change her mind. A formidable inquisitor at all their community meetings and royal pain in the ass when it came to the subject of wood, Prometheus was, at this moment, only a frightened child, *like herself,* seeking succor, and for that honesty when it mattered, they ought to receive some comfort—or, at least, the hope of some comfort to come.

• —— ◦•◉•◦ —— •

Dag hadn't been able to maintain the spiritual detachment he'd hoped to as Mayra's drama at the Duni played out. A moment earlier, he'd been cheering her on, not taking any weak-kneed shit from the lot of them. But when she finally turned her back on the fire, his heart announced itself a sudden stone.

It was then he felt how much he needed the strange peace that came inside the flames. All the turmoil and sudden upheaval visited on them the past two days began with Harrison arriving on the girder. He was the one captured by the Yaks. He was the one they went to rescue, the one who'd caused them to kill Lord Yakami, the one who'd brought things to a fevered pitch! And all this chaos was generated just by his approach. God knows what trials lay before them once he arrived. Dag, like the rest of them, was desperate for some nurture, some respite inside the Duni fire. At this prophetic juncture, maybe it would be like old times, and Mayra would have a vision all of them could share, reason enough for an exhalation of relief when she turned and walked back down to the flames.

The emerald ring rose again to meet her, and no sooner had she planted her feet and raised her arms than a swirling flame erupted, a blaze of spinning tongues licking at the frescos. Dag felt the electric thrill racing up his spine, the heady vista flashing toward his eyes: the sudden calm as every atom turned to marble—vision time.

An empty desert plain stretched all the way to a dark horizon. Huge lumbering tumbleweeds, their weathered gray branches tangled in spiny knots, careened across the barren landscape. Dag watched as the dunes nearest him began to heave and crack, shoving up the darker earth beneath the dusty surface. Ruby-brown chunks spilled out over the fissures until gaping black holes were opened at the center of each disturbance. Across the dunes, this near upheaval spread over the entire vista, leaving thousands of black holes dotting the arid plain. From every hole rose a rotten corpse, each with a newborn's shining face. The wind blew harder, furious at this resurrection. The tumbleweeds bounced and soared through the grotesque cadavers. Dag watched as flames lit inside their desiccated torsos and knew, instantly, they were the fires they gathered around, hoping to understand what the stars, the moon, and sun were trying to say. Numberless souls lit to claim some inheritance for ancient wonder. Clamoring now, skeleton arms rattling, railing in a hundred broken tongues—*they would not be denied!* In response, the ominous sky grew darker as countless lightning strikes carpet-bombed their caterwauling. Rolling thunder joined the lightning, but their voices could still be heard, screaming for a share of purpose in long-forgotten lives. A dark rain poured, an ebony torrent wiping away their desert and their graves, erasing even their decrepit remains. Leaving only newborn faces, finally spent with crying, who closed their eyes and turned to silent stars.

He felt a presence and, with an immense effort, turned his head to see Harrison beside him, watching the metamorphosed sky. Dag recognized him from his eyes. They were the same pair he'd seen in the bloody mask inside Yakami's torture chamber just before he turned to cut down Splatter. But the face, unmarked by blood, was much younger than Dag expected—not much more than a boy.

They stood together for a long time, watching the stars recede on either side while new stars appeared ahead. Finally, Harrison spoke.

"I wonder sometimes what it must have felt like for you . . . in all the confusion and chaos. I mean, really, we were barely at the portals of civilization, struggling with the concepts of truth and reciprocity, incapable of understanding why God needs a rotten sense of humor."

"What? Am I supposed to follow this eradiate crap? Is there a point you're trying to make here?" Dag heard his response punctuated with an exasperated growl. He could see he'd offended the deliverer. He was sorry, but really, was he expected to follow these precious musings?

"I just mean that having given us free will and being omniscient, knowing all the ways that destiny will circumnavigate our various courses, God is left to entertain himself with outwitting our best efforts at scriptwriting. And as we've become more inventive and inclusive in our dramas, so God has become more unexpected and diverse in imprinting his signature on the fractured comedies of our lives—a rotten sense of humor is the last refuge of laissez-faire."

"Where do you come up with this drivel? You've been spending too much time around that old fool Splatter! And you know whose house he likes to tailor his philosophies to."

Again, the deliverer was obviously not pleased with Dag's response. He spent a long time watching the stars before he spoke again.

"You know, in many ways, we've never really broken with the petty bickering that marked our time on Earth. We're still caught up in making our judgments on whose ancestors gave the most, saw the farthest, struggled hardest, and suffered the worst. We were all a part of the effort. As Shuta says, 'In the end, everybody plays their part.'"

"That's another jackass you could hang around less!"

Again, they stood in silence for a while, then abruptly the deliverer took Dag's hand in both of his. He was surprised to see how withered his hand looked, how fragile it felt in the young man's grip.

"It's time to move on."

With another extreme effort, Dag pulled the hand away and heard his rough response, "What about loyalty? One would think your thoughts might be better directed at showing a little consideration and respect for your sister, who at this very moment is finally setting the record straight!"

He said it very quietly, but Dag could tell he was really angry now. "Old man . . . the record is always straight."

Either the deliverer's eyes were changed, or Dag hadn't seen them clearly before. He realized he was seeing everything with an old man's vision, and looking closer, he could see these weren't quite the same eyes he'd spied during the rescue mission. This wasn't Harrison, but someone from him—his son, or maybe grandson? How old was he going to live to be? Until he was a cranky, decrepit old fool apparently.

Fearing he was about to slip back into the arid landscape that greeted him at the beginning of his vision (become another embryonic consciousness forgotten in the timeless sands), Dag realized the gift being given. He was going to make it to their vision ship and be on it for a long time—so long he forgot to have gratitude. He vowed, when that day came, it would end this way.

Exerting the effort to take back the young man's hand, Dag brought it to his creviced lips "Forgive me. I forget I'm still a child . . . while, unfortunately, I've become a very opinionated old fart!"

Dag heard a young man's barking laugh against a spray of stars.

⬥

"HOW THE HELL ARE WE SUPPOSED TO CRAP? YOU MORONS! YOU UNGRATEFUL BASTARDS! YOU MOLE-BRAINED PIECES OF SHIT!"

Han crouched on the earthen floor of their barren cell, watching the furious bellygridder hopping up and down, sticking his face in the view plate again and again, screaming at no one. Unfortunately, the bandage on his foot made for uncertain landings. Every other time, he'd pitch forward into the door, banging his head. It did nothing to deter him. Tooco wasn't adjusting well to their change in fortune.

Han was having his own difficulty swallowing the fact that in return for his belated honesty, Mayra hadn't warmed to the role of forgiving mentor as he'd hoped, especially since he'd made some valid points concerning his part in the realization of their prophesies. And he was sure their sexual fireworks were as rewarding for his huntress as they'd been for him. But his and Tooco's present circumstances necessitated staring a cold, hard fact in the eye—his mighty jerk and salient points were not sufficient to sway this seasoned warrior to gamble with her mission. However, Mayra would deliver his message to Jack. And Jack would come. Han really was a believer now. He believed Jack really was destined to arrive here and lead these people, and he would come see him and give him the chance to redeem himself.

"TOOCO!" The little bellygridder swung around to face him, frustration and rage seething in his face.

"SHUT UP!" He punctuated the order with a look that told the snot-spewing idiot if he didn't obey, Han would get up and beat him to death.

Inevitably, when a crisis occurs, all that is extraneous and picayune rises up in sympathy with the chaos, bent on distracting and derailing the problem-solving process, as though entropy was a conscious beast, smelling the blood of impending failure and rushing to spur it on. Han grabbed a handful of dirt and threw it at the bellygridder's feet.

"If you need to take a dump, dig a hole with your boot and cover it up when you're done."

Tooco retreated to a corner of their enclosure and sheepishly began kicking a hole into the musky turf. "What am I supposed to wipe my ass with?"

"Your jerk! Now shut up!" The forces of chaos would need to find another patsy.

• —•••— •

It seemed everyone was her lover when the vision started. Immediately, she was in a dilapidated metal-spring bed, drenched in sweat and the scents of others writhing in a thrashing pile, all of them desperate for release in the muggy Bellytown night.

Danner was there, along with others, his face appearing for brief moments around an arm or under a calf. And he was always smiling, a smile she knew was meant to comfort her. But watching her brother smile sweetly as he entered her—or feeling her sister kissing and sucking her nipples—and all these things seemed to go on simultaneously.

But Yasmine was also aware she wasn't nearly as uncomfortable as she assumed she would be. It was like choosing different roles in a familiar movie, where family was the weird bond that made whatever craziness was going on amusing, like walking in on a cousin whacking off in the john just when he shot his load. When her house got together for family gatherings, that one was still good for an embarrassed smile whenever they caught each other's eye. In this carnal vision, the present wanton intimacies seemed like harmless gaffs, easily overlooked in the interest of family getting along.

Then suddenly she was in a different tableau, sitting in a black metal sculpture titled *Sidewalk Café*. Danner sat across from her at a cindered disk that was once a table. He delicately balanced a charred newspaper page on his fingertips, squinting at it, trying to decipher some words on the blackened surface, until a light breeze exploded the final testament into a thousand ashes. She heard yelling and looked up to see her incestuous family charging down the boiled blacktop, screaming for her blood. Though she had no idea what she'd done to make them turn on her, she knew she was guilty. She raced through the cremated streets, finally darting down a dark passage to arrive at a scarred metal door. With some effort, she pulled it open and went in, down the blackened stairs. She descended several levels encased by slimy green walls. She could hear her family closing in.

Visions often held challenges for a dreamer, but she'd never been in one this barren and unrelenting. A bleak aura of death permeated everything. The possibility of a reversal or of any redemption was diminishing by the second. Rounding a corner at the bottom level, she ran down a narrow green hallway to its end, where she recognized the iron door of an ancient coal chute. Throwing all caution to the wind, she propped it open, using the shovel hanging on a peg next to the chute. Then she shinnied up into the dank encrusted passage and pulled the shovel after her, slamming the iron door.

In the darkness, she could feel a teeming city of insects she was crawling over, trying to make her way up the crud-lined chute. Ahead, she detected a faint light and climbed toward it with renewed desperation. Then, mercifully, she was pushing aside a grate, crawling up into the incinerated shell of some apartment building, which, strangely, still had all its windows intact. After madly banging her clothing, finally pulling off the T-shirt and sweatpants she wore, she frantically brushed off all the insects clinging on her. Her top and pants, still crawling with the spiny creatures, she tossed them away. Naked now, Yasmine carefully began making her way over scorched floor joists in an ancient railroad flat, moving deeper into the urban grave.

Reassured by a prolonged silence that she'd escaped her bloodthirsty brood, Yasmine stopped for a moment to catch her breath and figure out what to do. Crouching, not far from one of the building's undamaged windows, she decided to take a look outside, moving cautiously on all fours to the window's edge. After listening for a moment and still hearing nothing, she slowly inched her face up to the glass. Covered by ash and decades of soot, transparency occurred only in the center of the panes. This made them appear like they were in a nineteenth family album with intricate matting bordering their portraits.

They were a family: three dogs, all sitting facing her, their heads down; papa, the tallest on her left; the baby, next to him, leaning on his haunch; and the mother, with six teats she could count, seated on the other side—three dogs in hell.

When she saw them, they immediately looked up, staring back at her with luminous black eyes. They were the most intelligent eyes she'd ever seen. Their short gray coats were matted down to armor and streaked like the windows with years of soot. Their underbellies and chests, carpeted with festering boils and covered with the sheen of dried blood and mucus, reminded her of red lacquered Chinese trunks. As she watched, larger boils began exploding on their heaving chests, and membrane butterflies burst from these eruptions, fluttering toward her, finally beating tissue wings against the filthy glass.

Unperturbed by their busy infections, the dogs continued to stare at her, unmoved as their recent creations fell away, leaving inconsequential red streaks on the panes. Again, Yasmine found she wasn't nearly as repulsed as she expected to be. In fact, the longer she looked, the more beautiful they became, transformed by their knowing eyes. Then they spoke in unison, forming the words slowly and precisely: "Join us in the rite of life, both sacred and profane."

Then they fell on the ground, rolling around the way dogs do— and laughing. They were laughing.

⸻ ❈ ⸻

The web was so much more intricate and beautiful than when she'd last seen it in Sanatan. The gossamer detail woven between the earlier strands made all the karmic knots more binding in their claim on everything. Ryka was finally certain she was in the middle of something big.

The "stoning" she'd suffered at Zim's hands was the final confirmation of a dedicated life in the service of Barney. She never forgot being charged as a Barney Lover, "To prepare those who are of goodwill but untested, that they pass into the dawn of civilization."

Looking down on those of goodwill but untested, the tiny dots shuffling in clusters on the moving walks far below, Ryka wished she hadn't seen as much as she had. They would know hardships beyond her imagining. They would know misery beyond her wildest nightmares.

This view from Deli's balcony was her refuge since Zim turned her face into a swollen bulb. She liked her face. It was cheerful. Not anymore. Barney said it himself, "Life is hard, and then you die." Things happen that take pieces of your dream, until one day the hypocrisies committed in the ID of your beloved Barney are revealed. With the sun streaming in Big New's tinted dome, down through the hatchery's plexi-glass ceiling onto incubation tube after incubation tube, row after endless row of comatose embryos, Ryka saw nothing here was groomed for more than mindless servitude. The very idea of being tested was obliterated from their consciousness.

Many would have faltered in that moment. Many had. But she immediately understood that the true spiritual path was a lonely one. The path chosen for her, if she were to uphold her purple lord's ideals, was the path of avenging angel. She killed eleven abominations that day, with help from an intravenous stand turned into a lance before Sackers finally bagged her. That moment was such an awakening, a monumental release of righteous power. Ryka never dreamed she'd experience it again . . . until now.

That this solitary way she'd traveled ultimately led to her unsung role as the divine catalyst of this mutant band—spurring them on a precious few minutes!—it was a blessing she could never have hoped for. A "deus ex machina" of retribution was about to be unleashed on the whole of cokekind. All that remained was a final test, the fear of death to be the herald of things to come.

⎯⎯⎯●◆●⎯⎯⎯

He'd begun to question whether he'd picked the right direction. He'd traveled quite a ways up the tunnel, passing a platform covered with ancient refuse. There was a rusty sign hanging from a pole that read, "TWENTY-THIRD STREET, IND." Then suddenly the tracks disappeared. All the rails were missing. The ties were there and quite a few of the large steel spikes used to nail the tracks to them, but the tunnel was stripped of steel rails. That and the fact there was no lighting was starting to make him question his rational assumption—that getting away from Yaki sector was something that dreamers would want to do. Of course, the steel rails could be used for serious infrastructure. Maybe they took them out to use elsewhere. Then Harrison detected a stretch of maybe a hundred centigrid packed with buried explosives—definitely an ambush for anyone who came snooping up this way. Not long after that, a small incandescent appeared, creating a soft cone of light about two hundred centigrid farther down the line. He was right, after all. The little yellow cones began appearing with regularity, and the rails too were back in place. Still, as he cruised up the tunnel, he saw no sign of "them."

He passed another platform, this one with a sign reading, "THIRTY-FOURTH STREET, IND." There were some chairs lining a bare wooden table, but no signs of any recent occupation. He continued following the trail of yellow drops, until he spotted a third platform with a bigger sign, "TIME SQ. FORTY-SECOND ST., IND." There was a second sign that read, "FORTY-SECOND ST. SHUTTLE," with an arrow pointing down. Again, the platform was barren, but he swooped up onto it and immediately saw there were stairs leading down to another tunnel. It was more brightly lit than the tunnel he was in. He could hear multiple conversations in progress. Harrison dove down the steps, discovering a tunnel that ran perpendicular to the one he'd been in.

They were everywhere around him. Everyone was in a controlled state of panic, moving as quickly as possible without actually breaking into a run. Most of them were wearing camouflage. A few were carrying late-twentieth automatic rifles slung over the shoulder, just like the percussive they took from Bob's. But all these percussive had fat cylinders attached to the ends of their barrels. Most, though, were weaponless, busy removing everything that wasn't bolted down. There was a flow of goods moving from his end of the platform in the other direction. Harrison joined the conga line, his astral body hovering above them, establishing a correlative perspective to theirs while simultaneously merging with the entire space. It was definitely a military post. He identified a field hospital, a chow hall, and a communications center located in faded kiosks that looked like they were built a hundred cycles ago for totally different purposes.

Up ahead, he could make out the other side of the platform. It ended in a set of stairs similar to the stairs he'd gone down on the other side. They were all marching up the steps, hefting supplies and equipment to what Harrison assumed was a tunnel similar to the one he'd just come from. Swooping up the stairs, he discovered he was right. It was running in the same direction as the IND tunnel. The sign on this side read, "FORTY-SECOND STREET, IRT." But the tracks here were occupied by a train. Then it hit him—of course, these were subways! The form of underground transportation they employed in the twentieth in their big burgs. That's what the dreamers stumbled on and turned into their mode. But where had they come up with all this twentieth military gear? Remembering the view of Bellytown he had coming in, the whole place was *cinder city.* Where could they have come up with all this stuff? They were busy packing their items into a long train of silver cars covered with "tags" reminiscent of Yaki graffiti in techie quarter. But these were in a vernacular indecipherable to this time.

He spotted the fossil-powered land vehicle outfitted with steel wheels to pull all these cars down the tracks. It was located at the northern end of the procession, pointing in the same direction he'd been traveling. He wasn't tempted to look for Yasmine. He already knew she wasn't here. His certainty wasn't based on any abilities being on the String gave him. He had a "gut" feeling, and he knew it was right. Still, he could hang out and ride down with them—get to know them better, these cokes supposedly waiting for him. But he didn't really care.

Oh, he cared about knowing her. "Hi, I'm Yasmine," but that was it. The relentless, breakneck pace since committing to a personal perspective: the unremitting cavalcade of perversity and violence, the blood on his hands, the constant company of criminals, and his gruesome torture had exhausted an already-limited capacity to feel any connection to anything.

As he had, looking down on techie quarter, he again cursed his urge to wake up. It was all just chaos and entropy, nothing to understand beyond that. And yet, in this dead-end existence, *signifying nothing*, he still wanted to find her. Even reeling from his latest communiqué on the String, and he *still* wanted to find her! Suddenly impatient with waiting for the train to move, Harrison bolted ahead down the tracks.

The yellow lights were closer together in this tunnel. It had two sets of tracks similar to the IND line, but these were obviously used much more. Now that he thought about it, the IND tunnel was closest to the Yak headquarters, and likely the one they'd find and come down, if they ever got wind of what was below them. Those lights being out and the minefield made perfect sense. And if the Yaks were still determined to come farther down, more lights beckoned them into what was essentially a long killing chute. With the twentieth weaponry he'd already observed, it was conceivable they had some serious artillery on railcars up that tunnel. That would be enough to decimate any Yaki hordes coming in. These dreamers did more than just look like an army.

He saw another brightly lit platform up ahead. As he got closer, he made out the sign "FIFTY-NINTH STREET, IRT." When he pulled up onto the platform, Harrison couldn't believe his eyes. Where in Dog's ID had these cokes gotten their hands on a CZ-7000 laser cannon! But there it was on a Levi platform, with its barrel pointed upward into what must be a major entrance into the tunnels. There was the customary crew of four. Each appeared to know what they were doing. Where were they coming up with this stuff? He was also curious why they were all wearing twentieth gas masks. He'd detected nothing in the atmosphere poisonous to cokes. Harrison sensed movement behind him off to his left. It was another train being towed by one of their fossil engines at 960 grid an hour! The cloud of diesel smoke spewing out as it tore past answered his question about the masks. At the moment, they were running heavy traffic on these rails. The train he'd watched them loading would soon be coming along as well.

As the train went flying past, Harrison slid his aura across its metal skin, merging briefly with each car and its contents. Unbelievable! Every car was packed with cases of explosives.

Bombs, artillery-grade incendiaries of all shapes and sizes were being transported farther into Cenpak. Where could they be coming up with this kind of firepower? These cokes were seriously beginning to impress him. They were very organized and very committed to their objectives, whatever they were. He decided to stay with this train, curious about what they planned to blow to hell.

He flew along the track behind the rattling cars, past several darkened platforms, before the train began to slow. He spotted smaller signs that read, "SEVENTY-SECOND ST.," on metal support beams separating the two tracks. Once more, light flooded the platform as the train rolled into Seventy-Second Street station. Here, again, all the troops were fitted with gas masks, but instead of weapons, they were in box-shaped machines operated by a single coke with two silver blades pointing in front of them. These machines were lined up three-deep along the length of the platform leading into Cenpak. The entire station was radically reengineered by the dreamers. Several of the missing track rails he'd wondered about back in the IND tunnel were here, supporting a substantially enlarged loading dock. Since this train was on the outside track, the platform it opened to was on the opposite side of where the machines waited. They'd built a line of conveyors over the top of the trains, each one powered by a single-cylinder gasoline engine. *Where are they getting this variety of fossil fuels?*

As soon as the train came to a full stop, the doors opened; and troops, also wearing gas masks, jumped out of every car, gingerly lifting the wood cases onto these overhead conveyors. On the other side, the bladed machines came up, one after another, taking cases off the conveyors with their metal blades, which could be moved up and down and tilted. Harrison watched as they formed a line, snaking their way back into a tunnel that ran diagonally northeast from the platform deeper into their sanctuary. This tunnel was also expanded. Again, it was the dreamers' work because it was shored up with the rest of those missing track rails. He could feel from the air pressure that it led to a vast cavern. He was still curious what use all this firepower was going to be put to, but again, he grew impatient. He knew she wasn't here. She was up ahead.

He traveled farther up the tunnel a considerable distance before he saw any lights other than the yellow cones overhead. When he did see light, it was warmer, softer, coming up on his right, with a rose-colored tint, pouring from smaller openings inset from the tunnel and without platforms. He decided to slip into the first one, even though he knew she wasn't here either. But she came from here. This one was where she laid her head. It hit him—the myth magicians—this was the way they'd described knowing not from mind or heart but from something located just below the solar plexus.

Harrison swooped through the glowing portal and was instantly transported back a thousand cycles. He was stopped in his fifth-dimensional tracks, looking down on a prehistoric community. He knew he'd seen this place, or one like it before. He ran megabytes from Cincinnati retrieval before identifying the setting. It was a miniature version of those Navaho dwellings in the side of a massive red cliff: a roomy cavern carved out of the Earth, filled with a maze of pale, salmon-colored structures maybe a centigrid and a half high but stacked so there were varying levels of separate modes. Olive-green as well as tan blankets served as locks for some of the modes. Eerily, there was no one inside. But, of course, they were preparing for battle. The tube-born and cokes that cared for them were probably all hidden away in some fortified bunker.

Harrison merged with the salmon partitions and was surprised to find they weren't Earthen forms. No clay or straw in these adobe walls. Theirs were made from hardened foam insulator, not unlike the compressed styro of Big New's scrapers, although the tensile strength of the dreamers' foam was far weaker. Harrison ricocheted around the cavern, shooting through the various dwellings and marveling at all the twentieth artifacts. There were a lot of battery-operated devices, for which they seemed to have a plentiful supply of batteries. Again, where were they getting all this shit? The question was really starting to bug him. Most of their clothing and accessories were comprised of the camouflage, but there were a few gems, like a leather pistol holster and pointy boots made of some extinct creature's green hide. He even came across a few glass figurines. The one that really caught his eye reminded him of the dome over Sanatan—a tiny crystal castle on top of a mountain. He was half hoping he'd "know" which mode was hers but was disappointed. The knowledge of that location appeared to be beyond his new "powers."

He tore himself out of the cavern, flying farther up the tunnel. He passed three more mode caverns. Not long after that, he spotted the lights of a sixth platform. There was a long train parked north of the platform on the set of tracks on the Cenpak side. But the cars on this train all had their top halves cut off. They were little more than metal platforms on wheels. As he reached the station, he read its sign, "103RD STREET, IRT." Again, there was a second sign, reading, "103RD STREET SHUTTLE," with an arrow pointing down. There were only two dreamer guards on the platform, but they were different from the others. Both wore jumps made of real black leather. They carried short, fat percussives with thick cylinder magazines. Like the percussive he'd seen at Forty-Second, they also had fat cylinders at the ends of the barrels. The Elite Guard. Harrison swerved around them and dove down the steps into this shuttle tunnel.

It was very different from the Time Square station shuttle. This one was long, dark, and apparently deserted, except for a lone subway car identical to the ones he'd just seen outside. The car was right next to a small patch of cement, illuminated by a single incandescent bulb. It was maybe 250 centigrid from where Harrison hovered on the IRT shuttle platform. He could make out a few modulars on the platform. He moved slowly toward the spot, fearing there might be some kind of trap. Even on the String, he needed to be alert.

When he reached the lit platform, he identified a desk, a chair, a file cabinet, and pinup board. There was a map of the entire subway system spread out on top of the desk. There were various markings on it, with lists attached to them. Harrison recognized the major stops he'd just made on the IRT line. He saw the notation "4 laser cannon" next to the Fifty-Ninth Street station. Four! They had four? He'd run out of exclamations. He took a closer look at the IND side. The IND line ran parallel to the IRT all the way down to what, he now realized, was the tip of an island. There was only one note attached to the entire IND line, and it was here, at 103rd. It read simply, "Roadrunner." He'd been right about a killing chute.

Because he'd become accustomed to the shadows, he wasn't focused on the space directly across from him. He was surprised to realize one of the Elite Guard was standing inside a hidden portal on the other side of the tracks, his chubby weapon at the ready. It almost triggered an automatic aggression on his part, but Harrison delayed the fight-or-flight response with an inventory of weapons, remembering immediately he was invisible. Feeling a little foolish, Harrison blew past the guard into the black portal. Definitely the work of dreamers, this tunnel had been dug steeply at an angle of thirty degrees, with a railing next to sharply inclined steps. He'd covered about twenty centigrid when, up ahead, a brilliant light suddenly danced in the center of the blackness. As he came closer, he realized this light was from an intense light in a larger cavern ahead. By the time he reached the cavern's entrance, the tunnel walls were naked in the light, revealing chiseled granite. The argument was closed on these cokes being industrious motherduffers. If he was right, they believed this was where they'd conjured up his destiny.

The entrance into the dancing light was at the top of a large circular cavern. Stepping through it, he found himself at the rim of a great granite bowl of concentric rings filled with cokes. The bottom of this bowl contained a yellow mound of glowing embers, a golden flame leaping from its summit. The entire pit was surrounded by a circle of ruby Earth. All the rings above the pit were filled with the camouflaged figures seated on wooden benches that circled every ring.

The only variation was what he guessed were the sheed and tube-born of the black guard. They also wore black leather, occupying a section across the ring from Harrison.

They were all in a trance with their heads tilted back, looking up at a painted cone that served as the vent-hood for a chimney at the center. A steady geyser of spinning smoke whirled upward as their luminous eyes watched, transfixed. Only one, a sheed in camouflage pants and a khaki T-shirt, positioned on the dirt ring of the pit, wasn't looking up. She was on her hands and knees, fingers gripping the dirt, head bowed. Long locks of her chestnut hair almost touched the ground. Harrison began circling from the top rim, moving around an entire ring, then down to the next level, searching every face. He was on the third row from the top when he found her—her eyes transfixed like the others, her lips slightly parted, her skin translucent. Her warrior's glare had receded into a tube's wondering gaze. What a fascinating creature to contain such diametric opposites inside one pair of eyes!

He had a dilemma. If he jumped off the String while she was in the trance, she wouldn't see him materialize out of thin air. He could merge with her consciousness and let her know he was here, essentially waking her up. But he had no idea what this trance he'd be entering entailed for him, and really, it's kind of rude to just stick yourself inside somebody's head. Maybe, if he looked in her eyes from the perspective of his astral body, she'd see him on the outside of her mind. She would know he'd arrived and wake up. It was worth a try because he really did want to make a grand entrance for her. It would be the last time he could show his stuff. Yes, he knew it was silly, but being their savior seemed pretty silly too. Silly, it is!

• —— ✦ • ✦ —— •

When you were having them, visions appeared so real. But at this first opportunity to compare the two, she realized she could tell the difference. The papa dog had just rolled back up into a sitting position and was staring at her again. His eyeballs were changing their size and shape, and their color was changing from black to violet gray, then to blood-laced snow. They were real. Here and now. She was still petrified. If she had the power to move, Yasmine would have run like hell. The face appeared around the eyes, looking younger than it had behind a mask of blood. The alley with the dogs and the apartment evaporated as she watched him come vibrating into place.

They were standing face-to-face. She felt like she should kneel, that it would be the proper thing to do. After all, it isn't every day your messiah appears to you. But she didn't want to. After this moment, she'd gladly die for him. But she didn't feel like kneeling. She'd already knelt when her father died. She knelt when they put Danner in the ground. And on both those occasions, all she had to say to God was, "Thank you for letting me know such a beautiful soul." She didn't need to kneel now.

"Yasmine, hi. It's Harrison."

CHAPTER

10

It was calming late at night out on the river. Once you left the lights of Yaki sector behind, you could see the current shimmering under the spell of the grid plate. Like a wave's tumbling crest snaking toward the ocean, they rode single-file on their levi cycles, skimming close to the river to minimize their profile, keeping a lookout for any levi cruisers. They were down near the end of the island where the final scraper stood. Carder was surprised at how tranquil he felt—now that the decision was made and acted on.

A little over ninety hours earlier, they'd lost the fiber feed from techie quarter. They immediately started monitoring the fiber feeds in Big New. It was obvious very quickly that Topgrid were becoming concerned because they'd lost all their fiber feeds too. Yakami sent a cruiser up the corridor to get a look at things firsthand. But Topgrid already had transport ships headed up to Sanatan, and within minutes, the hysterical reports began pouring in from their crews. One ship was close enough to see it, everything disappearing in a blinding flash of light followed by an enormous cloud. That ship barely reported the phenomena before they went silent too. They knew then Sanatan was vaporized in a monumental explosion. Their most revered leader, Sun Moon Tu, was no more. Almost instantly, rumors hit the street. Even with Yakami's firm directive that this information be concealed, there was no stopping news about this catastrophe from getting out.

That event alone stunned everyone. But then the dreamers killed Yakami while rescuing their spacecase savior and, on the face of it, blasted through their mesh and murdered over half his clan before that! The entry point was blown in the mesh a block away from their steakhouse. Carder was on his way to join the party (honoring him) when it all went down. But as a seasoned warrior, he knew the carnage he'd witnessed wasn't just war as usual; it was extremely thorough. There was a relish to the massacre that didn't fit the dreamers' style. Dreamers just wanted Yakuza dead. They didn't revel in the blood. It would've been easy for another clan to spot them coming in and realize it was a rare opportunity to take out their Red Dragon brothers, knowing dreamers would get the blame. And so he'd made the last of a long series of bold decisions.

He originally got the idea listening to Yakami reminisce about the early days in Bellytown, back when the techies first arrived to build the grid. And it was so simple—topple the grid, and the great burg comes crashing down. He told no one about his ambitious plan. At the time, he was just another young button, but he managed to persuade Yakami to let him spend a cycle covering the casinos in techie quarter. While there, he tracked down the techies who engineered the grid and, for a kilo of Nitro, acquired a copy of the original blueprints for that mammoth jungle gym. He was driven by a vague premonition that someday Yakuza would have nothing to lose giving Topgrid their best shot. The outrageous events of the past few hours proved him a visionary, after all.

With the blueprints, he identified the key grid pillars inside the complex structure. Then, just last summer, a headhunter brought two levi-loaders up from the Virginias piled high with C-4 plastic explosives. He'd come to the Red Dragons first because of their reputation. By then, Carder was leader of their clan; but even so, if he hadn't always conducted himself as though driven by a divine destiny, his clan would never have approved forking over five hundred kilos to take possession of all the exotic explosive. They reasoned, at worst, they could unload it over a considerable length of time and recoup their original investment.

Enraged by the loss of so many friends and families, it hadn't taken much convincing when he finally revealed his original plan. Even if one or more of the other clans weren't responsible for the massacre at the steakhouse, with Sanatan gone, it wouldn't be long before there'd be infighting for the snag in Yaki sector. They'd never see a better opportunity to take down the Topgrid empire and cleanse the Yakuza of any treachery and weak spirit. The time was now! And they would dispose of their old adversaries, the fucking dreamers, as well. He should have killed that cocksucker Harrison when he had the chance. He was certain the Topgrid ponce had a hand in destroying Sanatan.

They'd spent the last twelve hours rigging all the key pillars with C-4. They'd sent their families, along with their techie slaves, out of Bellytown hidden in levi-loaders. Supposedly, they were taking supplies and merchandise out to the tip of Long Island, where the Red Dragon's northern encampment was. He'd built the compound four cycles ago right after he became head of the clan. This created some suspicions in the other clans, but he'd explained it as their needing to build warehouses and living quarters at a new launch point for their schooners. They complained, sailing out from Bellytown, that they were taking heavy losses from pirates along the Long Island shoreline.

They did a booming trade with the northern chillatillas, getting food they grew around the Québec province. Also, they had contracts with several waste-fill ranchers to breed their Akitas. When they were two cycles old, they brought them down for slaughter at the compound. They made a lot of Yuan not only from their steakhouse but from supplying meat, grains, and vegetables to the rest of Bellytown. It was a fundamental precept of Red Dragon philosophy: with dominion comes responsibility—you have to provide support to a community to get productive servitude.

After a brief stop in Rockaway so Carder could take care of some very old business, they'd head up to the encampment. Once there, they'd replenish their ranks with their younger warriors. He'd also had the foresight to train Red Dragon progeny separate from the other clans and the decadent influences of Bellytown. Manning their fleet of transport and pirate vessels (all sailboats) was an excellent curriculum for teaching the attributes of hard work and discipline. He'd thoroughly thought it through. They'd gathered tanks and trucks from various waste fills, along with stores of gasoline and diesel fuel they found, stashing it up at their compound, camouflaged as garbage dumps. They were all ready and waiting for when E-Mag vehicles were no longer functional. They'd bring their forces down to eighty grid away from Big New's grid plate and have a ringside seat to watch it all come down! He had to be careful not to stay too long in Rockaway because they only had just over twenty-nine hours to get all that done.

After Big New suddenly came crashing down onto the grid and Bellytown, he didn't anticipate any resistance from Sackers or any other *Topgridders*. Since Sanatan was gone, there wouldn't be any Sackers coming from there. And without any magnetic field closer than Bonn Cartel, they wouldn't have to worry about Sackers arriving for quite a while. Milsat couldn't send down Sat cruisers to the ruins because they couldn't use E-Mags either. They would have ample time to pick through the rubble of Sacker headquarters, grabbing all the frybars and laser cannons they could.

It would take time for Bonn to outfit their levi cruisers with twentieth-style landing gear before they could get any Sackers here. They'd have a hard time finding a landing strip. The Red Dragons would blow holes in all the old landing strips in the area. And there was also the psychological factor—they really didn't know who or what they were facing as an adversary. Sanatan's disintegration was a mystery, and they'd probably think the forces who engineered its destruction were also responsible for Big New's end, especially since any "intel" they got would include the fact that the *Yakuza got squashed* with everybody else in Bellytown.

426

In short, they'd have plenty of time to prepare the battlefield to their advantage. They'd identify the old highways in the area that Sackers would try to use once they realized the old runways had been destroyed. They'd carpet those highways with mines, which would pretty much take care of the first strike force they sent! Everyone knew, when it came to guerrilla warfare, the Yakuza had no equals. Oh, it would come down to one mother of a battle, no doubt. But that was exactly what they lived for.

Guilt. Where did it originate? Who came first, the victim or the victimizer? This conundrum was lurking in Zim's Seymorist skull as he sat in the pinnacle of Deli's empire, the expired gadget master's den mode. And truly, it was the tippy-top spire of one of Big New's tallest scrapers. Peering down, through the needle's clear plexi wraparound panes, Zim could see both Deli's garden balcony, from which Ryka made her suicidal leap, and the tiny strip of moving walk, where now her splattered carcass lay, resembling a squeeze-tube of soygetti. If guilt really is the ball and chain Seymore portrayed it as (a refusal on our part to release ourselves from the pointless remorse of dwelling on the suffering we've caused others), then Ryka, sailing over Deli's railing, released him from the ball and chain of having to take it personally.

Zim wasn't up here for the view or the contemplation. He was frantically searching for a tap on the strontium-yttrium undercarriage of Deli's communications control panel. It was the tap that would allow him to pick up Han's signal in the Levi limo when he sent his second transmission over the belly fiber. They had maybe forty-five minutes to clear out of the pentmode before Sackers were buzzing the lock.

Growing up, Zim's father was always cultivating Sacker sleuths—the elite detectives who would soon be combing over this pad. His favorite Screx motifs were "sleuthing." On many occasions, Zim heard discussions of protocol for various investigations and the relevant monitoring units brought online. Zim knew that from blood-splatter analysis, skeletal examination, and tissue recovery, the exact speed of impact could be determined and, from there, the exact distance Ryka's body had fallen. With her final, self-indulgent whim, Ryka had forced them onto a precarious new schedule. Below him in the main pentmode, Darl, and Sunsue were feverishly packing their equipment onto levi-loaders. Truth to tell, it was mostly Zim's equipment: the holo imager and signal boosters, along with their character costumes.

Using the tap analyzer function in the hand unit from the Screwhog, he was trying to link the belly-fiber tap in Deli's mode console to the one in Deli's wrist organizer. That way, the signal would be transferred from the console to the wrist organizer without coming up on screen in the pentmode. As soon as he finished here, he had to race down to the mode monitor and log a few entries, revealing that Deli and staff departed two days ago, booked for Brentwood. This was the Satcit on which Deli owned another palatial mode. It made perfect sense he'd go there after his heart transplant because the lighter gravity would facilitate his recovery. He also planned to record the fact that one sheed was still in residence, left behind to monitor screens and look after the pentmode. He'd strategically place a suicide note from Ryka, stating that witnessing the destruction of Sanatan had overwhelmed her. He doubted the Sacker detectives would do more than send a notification to the gadget master's Brentwood terminal, notifying him that one of his staff had committed suicide at his Big New pentmode. The robos there wouldn't register any need to respond to that.

It would give them all the time they needed to hide out inside the limo at Sinatra's long-term parking, waiting for Han to make contact. He would hold off on making their booking for Brentwood until Han sent the second signal. If he could just find this fucking tap. He almost wished for the peace of his Colorado cell. The endless ramping up of pressure was taking a toll, which reminded him that he had to put the two security robos Jack shut down back online when they made their getaway in the limo.

Finally! Three indicator lights glowed green on the tap-analysis function, indicating he'd found the tap to Deli's wrist organizer. Now all he needed to do was punch in the belly-fiber codes and limit access to these taps. When his makeshift analyzer emitted a beep (verifying he'd done just that), Zim bounded into the levitator.

The lock slid open to reveal Deli's plush living mode, a field of burnt orange, orthotic carpet, swayed under an assortment of white leatherette couches floating above this fiber sea. His eye was immediately drawn to the far end of the lavish expanse and the flashing red bar on the lock of the Fuji Topgridder. Someone was playing in the Screx when they should be running for their lives. It could be either of the hysterical sheed, although it was more likely Sunsue since she'd been Ryka's "pal." His father had installed one of these magic carpets in their own mode when he was just a tube-born. Zim learned early on how to surf those textile waves. With several practiced slides, he arrived at the black plastic base of the great golden globe and slapped his hand unit on its lock. It occurred to him, as he waited for it to decipher the access code, this little unit was much less destructive than the small charge Sackers used blowing the lock off his Screx. Sackers just liked to break things.

In less than a minute, the flashing red bar turned green, and the Fuji's lock hissed open. Sunsue was revealed hanging from safety straps designed to take your weight when the E-Mag suspension field shut down. Her head was slumped forward. Her long blonde mane cascaded over her breasts, the tips of her longer tresses matting on her glistening belly. She hadn't skimped on Deli's spray-on E-gel. Her body was coated with the conductor. Her pelvis was still quivering and thrusting even as an impressive steely snaked back into the base of the globe. Her ecstasy ran down her inner thighs in milky rivulets over the shining E-gel. She was moaning, her butt twitching from the E-Mag "whips" she'd employed. The power of these magnetic lashes was evident in the bright-red stripes that decorated her perfect derriére.

Here was evidence of the real machine magic! They developed 3-D holograms, used treadmills to approximate running, vibration units to simulate earthquakes and explosions, but it wasn't until they incorporated electromagnetics that virtual reality became realer than real. The one *very signiicant* element missing was the sensation registered in the body's largest sensory organ: the skin. Touch! Whips, if that was your pleasure—and it was definitely Sunsue's.

He popped the release on the safety straps and laid her onto the undulating shag. He removed her earbuds, which retracted into the frames of her goggles, then removed the goggles themselves. Adrift on an undulating landscape, she fought to reorient herself, eyelashes fluttering furiously. Being yanked from a Screx was never a pleasant experience, especially if you were in midorgasm. Zim flashed on his own final image, ducking Sendra's magnificent tail madly whipping about, him drilling that sweet dragon ass.

He delivered several light slaps to her cheek as he spoke, "Earth calling Sunsue! You've got ten minutes to clean up, put on a jump, and meet us at the landing port, lock!" Her eyes finally opened, taking him in. A look of fury marred her perfect face, but Zim refused to be intimidated. "Ten minutes, or I'll leave your sensate butt here for the Sackers. Got it?"

The anger drained away as she remembered their predicament. She gave him a nod of acquiescence. He left her to the task of reorientation, rushing off toward the foyer and Deli's mode monitor. He still had to make the appropriate entries in Deli's log and reserve a spot for their limo in Sinatra's long-term parking, where they'd spend their last hours on Earth—until Han and Tooco arrived with Jack, or Sackers hunted them down and killed them.

Hopefully, Darl was already waiting at the landing port lock with the Levi-loader. Zim prayed with all his Seymorist heart that Han's strategic wizardry would, once again, prevail.

———•◦●◦•———

After the Duni, Mayra took Sparky's watch. Alone in the tiny perch overlooking the southeast corner on Fifty-Ninth, her infrared binoculars were scoping a Yaki perch on Fifth Avenue down about a half block in the remains of another scraper. There were two Yaks watching her with their binoculars. That was one more than usual, a subtle indicator they were getting ready. Once they attacked, they were very single-minded, but it usually took them a while to respond to provocations. Probably because there were four factions, and they had to hash it all out between them, deciding which clan was going to do what. Without Yakami to intermediate and crack the whip, it was taking a little longer. But she was certain this time would be their final battle. There was no way they were going to live with the loss of face they'd just suffered without decimating them.

From books in their library, Mayra had read about the Japanese culture and their ancient Samurai. Their fierce yet ethical warrior code was called bushido. It was already perverted to a heartless brutality by their military in the early twentieth century, and Yakuza were a further bastardization that sprang up after the Second World War. The only thing left of the Samurai code was their fearless rush to battle and their reverence for the sword. They loved to finish you with a sword, if they had the option.

She was avoiding thinking about the Duni, which was pretty strange since the flames' prophesy was miraculously fulfilled. She realized she was afraid of hearing the acid truths her devil's advocate had in store. Just recognizing her avoidance should be giving him the opening to put his cynical foot in the door, but he was strangely silent. Maybe he was ashamed for her. She was ashamed for herself. And what was her shame, really? Was it the shame of Moses left dying on the mountaintop to watch the Israelites cross over into the Promised Land? Not even close. It was the shame of realizing at the center of her heart, she'd kept a secret dream she would be the deliverer's lover. In hindsight, it's obviously why she slept with Han. The moment he'd shown her the twin to their sacred book, that fantasy awoke like a kiss from prince charming, even as she had her doubts and knew something wasn't right. Still, there'd been something magical about being in their little glen in Cenpak, an illusion of an innocent time, and he had charmed her. She saw that clearly now.

When Yasmine touched her shoulder at the Duni and broke her trance, and she looked up to see them standing side by side, it was simultaneously the most joyful and disappointing moment of her life. And there'd been no time to process these concurrent opposites of emotion because as soon as her trance was broken, the rest of the cavern awakened with her. There was only the brief moment of stillness before the cavern exploded in pandemonium.

He just stood there, completely naked, looking very weary. There were no wounds or bruises she could see. His "spacecase" powers had performed a remarkable recovery, but at the same time, he had the aura of something the cat dragged in. Really, when it came to getting the libido humming, Han was a far more exciting vision. But he had a pleasant, if nondescript, face. As they all crowded around chanting his name, it was obvious he was terrified. At some point, every dreamer came forward to proclaim their joy and gratitude. He'd held on to Yasmine's hand with the desperation of a drowning man. She was the reason he'd come, in spite of Han. Later, when he impulsively kissed her, that was clear. Irony of ironies, apparently, he'd harbored the same secret longing in his deliverer's heart . . . but it was for Yasmine. It wasn't that she was jealous. This fantasy was so secret it hadn't been given any opportunity to subvert the rest of her heart. Thank God for that! What did she want? She was a prophet and a shepherd who called it right, even if there was some initial confusion. She'd brought home her flock to the destiny they'd been promised—well, they were getting there at any rate. What more did she want?

Looking down on no-man's-land, waiting for the Yaki legions to come, she felt a soothing peace settle over her. She'd offered them her cavern and bed so they could have a little time before all hell broke loose. In a few hours, she'd have to intrude. But for now, she wished them joy and peace.

⚫▬◆◆◆▬•

432

He'd never been interested in pursuing the Dog-realization motif. There were too many pitfalls in that type of fun, too many mind-numbing reversals on the path to "Dog realization." More often than not, it was the motif being played when Sackers dragged clonies off to the mines.

He only tried it once during one of his solitary off-line times as a cadet. It was a version he'd accessed using the cadet commander's password foolishly left on a wrist organizer in his niche. It was called "The Emergence of the Frozen King," and the password also opened the lock of a Screx his rank allowed him access to. The motif was set in an ancient time, which, later in retrieval, he realized was around two thousand cycles ago. It began inside a block of ice that held you in its grip. It was frightening not being able to move for so long, and he remembered using all his willpower not to abort. He kept repeating in his mind, *It's a part of the testing that Dog realization is known for, so just relax.*

Probably because he was alone, he'd set the ID booster to max and was regretting it. Just as he was about to give in to panic, his chunk of ice began to melt. He could see he was inside a vaulting ice castle with finely carved Corinthian columns shooting up out of sight. Once the block melted enough to free his upper torso, he was able to reach a gold-handled dagger in his belt and chip his way to freedom. He then began to explore the frozen hall. It was detailed in every aspect, from the long tables with their rows of chairs, to the goblets and plates set out for hundreds of nonexistent guests, and everything was made of ice. It wasn't until he reached the end of the hall that he noticed a normal-sized portico. Passing through it, he was in an icy corridor with melting walls that reflected his image as he moved down it. He could see he was dressed in period finery and wore an impressive gold cape that trailed all the way to the floor, but everything was covered with a patina of blue frost.

As he continued along the corridor, the ice kept melting until, by the end, it disappeared completely, and he stepped through another portico and was *again* in the very same hall where he started. No longer made of ice, everything was formed of the appropriate material, and the seats at the long tables were now filled. All the guests had arrived, but they were covered from head to toe in blue frost stopped in midrevel, raising their goblets in a toast. Again, he walked the length of the hall. But this time, next to the portico, a chaise appeared with two golden crowns. The larger crown, which he assumed must be his, rested on its tufted purple cushions. The smaller crown rested on the head of a princess, replete with plated gold hair framing a delicate face marred by consternation. She sat shivering on the chaise. Crystallized tears sparkled on her robin's-egg cheeks. Despondent opal eyes implored him.

"My lord, in your absence, a vile sorcerer has come into your castle locking us all in his frozen heart. Even now, he hides somewhere inside, holding us in his frigid spell. He says you must find him and save us by revealing yourself."

What ensued was a protracted search punctuated by answering riddles posed by icy minions, until he finally found the sorcerer hiding in his own canopied bed. Pulling aside the brocaded tapestries, Harrison vividly recalled his shock at seeing himself stretched out in a red velvet jump opened to the crotch, smiling coyly as he stroked the milky petals of his shy.

"Everything you seek is inside. Cum in me, and I'll let you out."

It was the only time he ever aborted a motif. Afterward, in what was left of his off-line time, he was haunted by that feeling of being frozen, deprived of a freedom he couldn't identify. What he could identify was a feeling of being lost, of having no idea where he was or what the fuck was going on. It was clear this was the moment his search truly began. It was the foundation of his realizing, cycles later, that he'd lost his mind when it came to remembering anything, which led him to Cincinnati retrieval and his search for a personal perspective—a search that finally led him here.

And wonder of wonders, there was no denying the signs and portents! Yasmine told him about the flames in the fires foretelling his arrival, with the book he took from the frozen sheed at NORAD, a twin to the book the dreamers found on her lover's body in Bellytown. That part was co-opted by Han, but if it wasn't for that, it would never have made it down here. Han must play some part, but whatever it was, it couldn't be good. Yasmine said he'd confessed his plan to kidnap him, saying he'd been changed by the dreamers' prophesies. He said seeing the part he'd personally played in them made him want to abandon his own plans. Yasmine thought he was lying, and Harrison couldn't have agreed more. He told her Han blew up Sanatan. She said he confessed that too. That did surprise him.

But his arriving on the grid girder in red armor, saying he wanted a personal record—that was foretold in their fire as well. He was the one they were waiting for. Poor cokes. He didn't have a clue what he was supposed to do for them.

A waterfall of red hair suddenly blurred his introspection. Yasmine turned in her sleep, laying a powerful arm across his chest. This was his "mission," to rest in her smoky scent and feel her pale heat beside him. What an exciting few hours they'd shared in their hidden chamber, giving up everything but their bodies until, too exhausted to utter another word, they'd fallen asleep in each other's arms. This was the only mission he wanted now. But maybe what he wanted didn't matter.

In a Screx, you could manipulate everything. There was nothing you couldn't shape or reshape into a series of events, making up whatever stories you wanted. But this story had been shaped over a prolonged period of cycles from well before Harrison was ever decanted. This story that made him a "deliverer" wasn't cooked up in a Screx by the mind of some coke. An unseen hand sculpting at leisure over generations had produced this saga in which he now found himself with a pivotal role. Much more bizarre than his usual perspective of mutable reality was this view of a deft destiny surely padding its way around free will and random action to some immutable conclusion! It was too strange and strangely terrifying. Not in a million motifs would he ever have dreamed of such vital participation in a purposeful life. What purpose? He hadn't the vaguest notion. But just purpose was enough for now.

Through a veil of lashes, Yasmine watched him chasing the tail of his internal quandary, struggling with unexpected responsibility. It came as quite a shock, hearing he had no idea what he was supposed to do. She always imagined him being focused, dynamic, like Danner. But he seemed to change moment by moment, as if inside there was a menagerie of different animals. Just the tilt of his head a degree or two banished a mouse and delivered a cougar. The only constant was his air of being in dogged pursuit. The one trait she expected to be readily discernible was completely absent: recognizable compassion. While every dreamer at the Duni came forward to express their joy at his arrival—faces Yasmine had known all her life, for the first time resplendent with relief and wonder. He only smiled back hesitantly, as if trying not to offend an alien species. Yet once they were alone, he hung on her every word and expression like an attention-starved child. His body, at least, was fulfilling her expectations: leanly muscular, unmarred by instruments of torture, completely healed from his ordeal. When she last saw him, he'd been chopped liver.

His only real expression of feeling came after everyone introduced themselves. Like a clumsy child, he impulsively took her in his arms and kissed her. She really wasn't expecting that! The entire place sounded with one sharp intake of breath. Excitement mixed with embarrassment quickly cleared the entire cavern. She was in shock herself, embarrassed and confused—and surprised that it pleased her. It remained as true in their postapocalyptic backwater as in ages past—a great kiss could lay to rest all manner of trepidations. She'd been instinctively worried his action might embarrass Mayra. But as the others fled, Mayra came up to them, suggesting that he must be very tired and Yaz should take him to her chamber so he could get some rest. She'd meant to do just that and then go find Mayra to discuss this unexpected development. But his urgency to be with her held Yasmine in the moment, and the torrent of questions about their underground existence, especially about the children brought by their parents, made it impossible to leave him.

He wanted to know why they had so many caretakers for the tube-born. Even though she knew from Danner about how Topgrid conceived, the total disconnect in the way he pronounced the creepy term sent a chill through her. When she started to explain the children were conceived by the adults accompanying them, and they cared for their children for many "cycles," he froze, staring blankly. Studying him, she realized he was being forced to juxtapose their expressions of joy watching their child be acknowledged by him against the backdrop of reptilian supervision he experienced as a child. She was afraid he'd somehow been broken because he stayed like that for a very long time. She took one of his hands in hers and began gently stroking it. Slowly, the blank brown eyes began filling. Eventually, tears rolled down his cheeks, totally unregistered by him. She was afraid to even speak and kept stroking his hand, until finally he looked up at her and spoke, "They touched them, constantly." Then he smiled. It was the first real smile she'd seen from him. She quickly changed the subject, explaining how they got their water, how they produced their light, and where they got their food; and after a while, he was fully animated again. He started asking more questions about their history and where they got all their weapons. It turned into a long dissertation, which left them both exhausted. She took pity on him now, watching him struggle with a frown that was the basic template for multiple anxious expressions.

"You're going to break your brain. Maybe it's not important for you to know what you have to do."

Startled by her voice, Yasmine caught a glimpse of the vulnerable boy again. "Yeah, but eventually, I have to know."

Her arm encircling him, she began rubbing his chest, trying to soothe his agitation. Then she realized he was still completely naked! No one had offered him any clothes. They'd all accepted his nakedness, possibly expected it. After all, the red armor she brought back was on display in the library. That struck her as hysterical, and she buried her face in his shoulder, trying to stem the tide of giggles already escaping. When she finally succeeded, she looked up into his eyes and saw him wondering what was so funny, which almost set her off again.

"We need to get you some clothes. You must be freezing."

"Yeah, I am a little cold."

He reached down to pull the thread-worn comforter over his midsection, and Yasmine helped, tucking it around his legs. He smiled, obviously pleased at her attentions.

"Maybe I've already done it . . . what I'm supposed to do."

"No. You haven't."

"How do you know? Maybe I was just supposed to find you?"

"Down, boy!" She was a little put off with the juvenile romantics. "Listen to me, for over forty years, we've watched the Duni reveal the journey we're going on. We are delivered out of these tunnels to a great ship in the sky, and finally to a beautiful planet. In those visions, you are the one who takes us on that journey."

Hurt by her rebuff, he retreated to a practiced superiority. "That sounds like Han's plan . . . and just as likely to come true."

"You don't know . . . remember? And maybe it's important you *don't* know!" She was trying not to get pissed off, but his adolescent pique wasn't making it easy. "Maybe that's the only thing you've got to give."

"What's that supposed to mean? Dog works in mysterious ways?"

"Fuck, no!" She was starting to lose it. It was just she'd heard that smug reversal from Danner often when he first joined them, and it always riled her. Not that she didn't like dogs. Hell, dreamers were responsible for the survival of the species in Bellytown. Most scabs killed and roasted them on sight! But God was God, and dogs (even with their approximation of divine love, if you left out the food part) were still dogs. But it was important she stay on point.

"Listen." She took a deep breath. "What could you possibly have that God would want? What could limited knowledge have that unlimited knowledge does not? The only thing that a finite perspective can give to an infinite one is *not knowing*. That's the only gift of any possible value to a being that is unlimited and unfathomable, omniscient, omnipresent, and omnipotent—i.e. God."

Maybe he was being glib. "I'd just feel more comfortable if I knew what was expected of me."

"I just told you . . . faith."

With a certainty unusual for Harrison regarding his insights, the inner power of her presence made itself known to him, a nurturing source fueled by a hidden radiance. Yasmine was the manifestation of the force that brought him here. He understood the intensity of his attraction now. He wanted to please that radiance.

"I'll do my best."

"I know you will. It's why you came. Listen, I'm gonna have to go out for a little while. I have responsibilities as a soldier that I have to see to. I won't be gone that long. You should try and sleep more. Pretty soon things are going to get pretty crazy with the Yaks. We're going to need all the strength we can muster." She touched his cheek and felt his warmth before slipping from the bed. "I'll bring us back some food, and I'll get you some clothes. I won't be that long."

————•◆◆◆•————

Waiting on a couch in the reading area, Yasmine admired Prometheus's handiwork. What his heroes could do with a brush, he performed with cabinetmaker's tools. He'd taken some bird's eye, maple, squirreled away for something special and, in a little over twenty-four hours, turned it into a minimalist mannequin for displaying Harrison's armor. He'd moved one of the end tables so it was positioned directly underneath the chandelier. Under direct light, the armor developed a purple caste, darkening the brilliant red to the color of cold blood. A metaphor for her own altered vision—like Alice peering into an even more distorted looking glass! My God, what demented experiences were locked inside his head? Now, thinking about it, there were a lot of questions Danner avoided answering. What bizarre world floated above them? Originally, she'd wanted to talk to Mayra because she was worried about the kiss. Now she wanted counsel because she wasn't sure she could give him the help he needed to fulfill their destiny. She'd been pretty spooked when he went away like that. She guessed comparing the images of the children and their parents with his experiences as "tube-born" revealed some of the real horrors of his life. She knew it was someplace she wouldn't ever want to visit. Hopefully, after sending Ram and their levi cruisers off to their staging point in Harlem, Mayra would be back soon. Also, Yaz wanted to grab a frybar and do a tour of the barricades. She wasn't at all comfortable with this new role as the deliverer's paramour. That wasn't completely true. She was aware of feeling a deep connection already, and that too was a lot of her discomfort. It was new for her. Danner was very independent, but Harrison was more than independent. He was unavailable yet, in the same moment, vulnerable and needy. She really wanted some guidance here.

Mayra was surprised to see her lieutenant hugging her knees, head down, gently rocking herself on her favorite couch. She'd been pushing images of the two lovers out of her imagination these past few hours as she prepared for war. While she wasn't jealous, she was envious. Mayra would've liked nothing more than to go to bed and play under the covers, shutting out a bloody world. As she reached Yaz, she knew she was being callous. Those radiant green eyes looked up, frightened and pleading. She couldn't remember the last time she'd seen Yasmine afraid. In fact, she'd never seen Yasmine afraid.

"Ma."

"What is it? What's wrong?" Still looking up, she was trying to form words, but nothing was coming. Mayra quickly sat beside her, putting an arm around her shoulders, bowing her forehead to Yasmine's.

"It's all right, it's all right. Just breathe . . . it's all right."

"Ma, he doesn't know what he's doing. He doesn't know what he's supposed to do! He has no idea. And in some ways, he's this wounded, lost child. He . . . he's seen things in those dark eyes I don't even want to think about."

"Yaz, a lot of it is probably him reacting to the torture. He may be able to magically heal his body, but his mind is still filled with the pain and the images of what they did to him. You know how abominable those bastards are. It's barely forty-two hours since they were working him over."

"I know. But he's really worried that he doesn't know what he's supposed to do, and I tried to tell him that it didn't matter, that God will lead him, but . . . I mean, why would God send him so unprepared? Ma . . . he really hasn't got a clue."

"It doesn't matter. We've got a war to fight now. There'll be time enough for us to figure it out. Or not! Events will figure it out for us. We do know from Han that he can fly their great ship. We don't know what will happen. Who would've imagined Sanatan getting blown to hell? Yaz, what's the first supposition of a Samurai? What's the first supposition of a Samurai?

"Anything can happen at any time."

"Yeah. Don't forget that. Is he still back in my chamber?"

"Yeah, I told him I was going to get us some food, and him some clothes." Yasmine suddenly grinned. "We all let him parade around totally naked last night!"

Yasmine's smile was unexpected, but Mayra was relieved by it, and it was funny. She remembered all of them coming up to pay their respects, and no one, herself included, wondered, *What's wrong with this picture?* It was because everything was so right about that picture, but it was pretty funny too.

"Unfortunately, we sealed the armory after Ram took out the munitions for the levi cruisers, so we can't get him any khakis. You should check with Mongrel. I know the Outriders wanted to give him a set of leathers when he finally arrived. Since we've cleared out of Forty-Second, they've set up 'mess' in the Duni cavern. You can probably catch up to Mongrel there and get some food. I'll look in and see if I can calm down Harrison regarding our expectations, all right?"

"Yeah. Thanks, Ma."

"One thing . . . did you have a chance to talk about Han?"

"Yeah, he doesn't trust him as far as he can spit. He says he's really tricky . . . and dangerous." Mayra gave Yasmine one of her warmer smiles. "Yes, that much we got from Sanatan. You called it right, Yaz. Thanks."

Lying on the lumpy mat, waiting for Yasmine to return, he was intrigued with the half "bicycle" in one corner of the chamber. Initially, he thought this one was being repaired; but the more he looked at it, the more he was certain it was made to be a half on purpose, and it wasn't designed to take you anywhere. He finally got up, draping the mat cover over his shoulders, and padded over to the half bike. Ever since Yasmine mentioned it, he was aware of being cold. Seating himself on the tiny pad provided, he put his feet into the stirrups and began pushing on the pedals. He understood then, it was a training machine for teaching how to propel one of the archaic vehicles.

"Exercising? You are a glutton for punishment."

Harrison turned to see the sheed who'd been on her knees by the fire—their leader, Mayra. Yasmine told him this was her mat niche, and he was a little embarrassed to be found playing with her gadgets.

"It caught my attention. I thought I'd give it a try."

"Well, you've probably already gotten more use out of it than I ever did."

He gave her an uneasy smile.

"Yaz is getting you some clothes and food. I just thought I'd pop in and see how you're holding up." Mayra sat on the end of her bed.

"Yeah, I forgot I didn't have any clothes." He gave her an uncomfortable smile.

"Listen, I'm not really good with chitchat either, so I'll just get to the point. Yaz, is worried that you're feeling a lot of anxiety about what you're supposed to do for us, and I want you to know, you don't have to do anything for us. And I'm not being defensive or offended or anything like that, it's just the truth. You have no obligation at all to become involved with our plight."

"Well, I want to help Yasmine, and all of you . . . if I can. I'm just uncertain about what I can do."

"You like Yasmine a lot."

"Yes."

"Well, I think her feelings are mutual. It's Yasmine that brought you here, right?"

"Yes, although I've come to understand all of you have been waiting for someone of my general description. I wasn't really aware of that until I got down here."

Mayra smiled. "I'd say you go well beyond a general description. We've been expecting a Topgrid in red armor to arrive and state to the first one of us he met, 'I wanted a personal record.' That little girl you met on the girder, Teeba, she's one of us. Not to mention the twin copy of *The Prophet*, which was your book, even though you didn't bring it personally. No, you are definitely the one we've been waiting for. But I want to repeat this, because it's very important, that does not obligate you to do anything for us."

"Yeah, I'm struggling with all that. I'll be honest, if I felt like there was anything I could do, it would be very exciting to be involved in something that was part of a grand design. But I can't think of anything. Yasmine said you know about spacecase and our unusual abilities, and that's the problem. I haven't told her yet, but it's not good. I don't know how well I can describe this for you, but there are patterns you see that allow you to enter different dimensions, and there's a pattern that you see when you no longer have the mental power to transport yourself into these dimensions and return again . . . and this last time, when I jumped the String to get here—it's called the String—I saw the pattern that means I'm done. The next time, I won't be able to return. I'll essentially disintegrate."

"And you assume that's why you were brought here, to use these powers to help us?"

"Yes, I guess so . . . I mean, it's the only thing I have that I think could give me a snowball's chance in hell of helping you get that ship, and honestly, even with the String, it would have to be a fucking miracle to pull it off! The thing is, I guess, I do see that I am that one, from these things I was supposed to say and the armor, those books—that really is incredible. It just seems really strange to me, just as I'm arriving, I lose the only thing that could possibly help me pull that off. If your 'God' did bring me here ..." Suddenly remembering the glowing box at Alaska mines, he knew he was about to be very irreverent. "Then he's got some 'splainin' to do!"

Much to Harrison's surprise, Mayra burst out laughing. She was laughing so hard she started choking. Harrison jumped off the half bike and began slapping her on the back. Finally, she regained her breath and composure.

"Well, you've definitely got his sense of humor." She patted the mat, gesturing with her head for him to sit next to her. He did.

"That's way before your time! The only reason I know it is some old disks we found in the armory. Where the hell did you see it?"

"When they send you to the mines, they show ancient vids in the cells. That's where I saw it."

They sat for a moment, and then Mayra put her hand over his.

"Listen, I'm forty-seven years old, and I can't tell you how many times things haven't gone the way I planned them or the way I thought he planned them. The nights I've spent anguishing over what it was I was supposed to do that he wanted me to do that I thought needed doing—to make things turn out all right. And a lot of times, they didn't turn out all right. Sometimes they were fucking tragedies. If there is this higher power—we call that spirit the flame, an old Celtic term we chose because of our Duni, and because it's emblematic but nondescript. If such a consciousness does exist, to think that it is informed by our limited understanding and desires—is childish self-absorption on our part. Over time, what I've observed is that tragedies become opportunities, and victories turn to ashes and shame. If indeed there is some plan, a purpose, we still have a lot of evolving to do before we have a prayer in hell of understanding what it is. The best you can hope is for a moment when you see something, when you know for a certainty that something is going on here. Fortunately, or unfortunately, depending on how you look at it, most of us avoid taking that look around until the last moment . . . when we do acknowledge a journey and a surprise.

"If you want to continue exploring this journey you've obviously been invited on—and again, you don't have to—but if you want to, then relax about it, all right? All you have to do is be committed and engaged. And if your commitment is based on wanting to be with Yasmine, that's fine . . . that's what it is. It's genuine. You should probably tell her about the problem with the String, though. She won't doubt who you are because of that. Also, I'm sure this wasn't lost on you when she rescued you, but it's a big part of who she is . . . Yaz is a warrior. She's been one all her life. When the time comes, she's going to want to be on the barricades."

"Yasmine being a warrior is a big part of why I'm so drawn to her, and I'll be there with her when the time comes."

"No, you won't. You're not supposed to fight for us. We can take care of that. You're supposed to get us out of these tunnels and take us to a new world. I can't jeopardize your ability to do that. Again, you'll find out how when the time is right. Until then, you need to stay right here."

Mayra stood up and started out of the chamber. "You and I need to talk about what to do with Han and Tooco, but it can wait for now. Yaz will be here soon with some clothes and food. We've laid on some serious rations for an early chow. Everybody's going to need all their strength. The Yaks are coming." She stopped and turned back to him.

"And I repeat, we'll take care of them! You rest and maybe try to think of the power that brought you here as a friend instead of something that just wants something from you. Relax. You're home."

Before he could reply, she was gone.

━━━◆◆◆━━━

"What the fuck are those scab bastards up to?"

Tooco was hopping up and down again, having just caught a glimpse of their captors in the view plate of their detention chamber. Han was sincerely close to killing the little fucker. Suddenly he started jumping up and down even faster.

"Hey, wait a sec. They're coming this way. They got somethin' . . . they're holding something!"

"Do you see Jack?"

"They're comin' here!" Tooco scurried back from the door to the rear of the cell quickly, sitting on the ground next to Han. A moment later, the rasp of a rusty deadbolt preceded the lock swinging open. Standing in front of them was a huge dreamer with a bushy beard, clad completely in black. In one hand, he held a weapon that looked like something out of a Toon—oversized with a big round canister attached to the underside of the barrel, with another smaller canister on the barrel's end. In the other hand, he held a large tray covered with a piece of yellow cloth. Just behind him and to one side was another black-clad guard with a frybar pointed at them.

The huge one took a step into the cell and placed the tray in the dirt, then unslung a canteen from his shoulder, putting it down next to the tray. "You boys must be gettin' pretty hungry. This should hold you."

Tooco had to ask, "What is it?"

Two rows of stained teeth appropriate to his size stretched across a hirsute forest, producing a Cheshire grin. "Chicken."

The other one, keeping a bead on them, grinned as well. His set of choppers had quite a few missing.

The big one started to turn away, but Han stopped him with a question, "Is Jack here yet?"

"Jack?"

"Yeah, Jack. Harrison, Jack. That's his full ID."

"Oh yeah, that's right. You're old buddies."

"Yes, we are." Han uncoiled and stood.

Both their grins disappeared, and the big one swung up his Toon weapon.

"Easy, cokes, we are his buddies. Could you deliver a message to our buddy? Tell Jack there's something he needs to know if he wants to get his hands on that *Protostar*. I never told him the second part of the plan, after we get the Satcruiser. It's foolproof. He needs to know what it is."

"Well, you could tell me, and I'll tell him. I've got a good memory."

Han coiled back into his seated position, a smiling blond Buddha. "He needs to hear it from me."

"Okay, I'll pass your message along."

"I'd appreciated that."

The dreamer turned and maneuvered his mass through the lock. The metal slab closed on them again. They heard the sound of the rusty bolt being thrown back in place. Tooco scrambled over to the tray, pulling the cloth off the top.

"Hey, this looks pretty good, and there's a lot of it. Maybe we're not in the godhouse as much as we thought. They're feeding us pretty good." Tooco brought the tray and canteen over, setting them in front of Han and sitting across from him. "It's even hot."

Han took a bowl and spoon from the tray. "Well, that was easy. Jack is here. I'm sure our misunderstanding will be resolved very shortly."

Already digging in, Tooco spoke through a mouthful. "Well, I hope so, 'cause we don't have any other options."

Spoon poised at his lips, Han smiled. "You really are an addlebrained motherduffer, aren't you?"

• —————— ◆◆◆ ————— •

Unfortunately, to do what he wanted to do, he was going to have to deal with "Juan the pawn," or as he liked to be called, "the Count of Rockaway." Carder brought along the standard kilo of Nitro, so he'd think it was business as usual. Business as usual meant the "Count" would skim at least 10 percent of their take for himself. This would be the last time he'd be ripping them off. The only reason he'd let the pompous shit get away with it for the past ten cycles was their understanding that, in his retirement, Backman was looked after.

That smug spaceshit Harrison would never believe him capable of what he was here to do. Topgrid threw everybody in the jungle and then condemned them for being animals. Well, he'd done his part to see that Harrison joined them, howling with the rest of the monkeys. If Yakami had twenty minutes with him before he was interrupted, Carder doubted the dreamers rescued more than a babbling baboon.

One of Yakami's drivers told him the story of their "savior." Now he'd be lucky to save himself.

He eased back the throttle on the Windviper as he swung onto Franklin Avenue, heading up to Liberty Square, where the Count's "reviewing stand" stood. It was draped in red, white, and blue bunting. On arrival, you might think United States was still running things—for about thirty seconds. That would be just before you were stripped of everything you had, including any coveted internal organs. Dog, but he loathed that puffed-up jackwad. His pretext was going to be that, as a loyal old button, he wanted to take Backman along to the memorial service they were having out at the compound. He was certain everybody'd heard about the Red Dragons' misfortune. The Count would be doing everything he could to keep a sly smile from his sleazy lips. As much as he hated the bastard, he needed to remember, the Count *occasionally* had a surprisingly accurate bullshit meter. If he wasn't careful, the puffed-up ass was just capable of sniffing out his impending doom.

Actually, when he was a young button, it was Backman's ability to see through the bullshit that saved Carder's naive neck. Yakami planned a hit on a streetlord in Brooklyn who'd waylaid a couple cruisers on the return leg of Tokyo Run, bragging all over Bellytown that Yakuza were old and slow. They were going to raise the whole block, but Yakami wanted a volunteer to ride in alone, waving a white flag and offering a deal to the streetlord to stop jacking their cruisers. That way, they'd know from the cindered brownstone they took him in, which one was the streetlord's headquarters. Yakami didn't actually call it a suicide mission, but that's what it was. Of course, he addressed all the young buttons with the claim it was a rare opportunity to show him what they were made of. And if they made it through, he promised first pick of any levi cruisers the streetlord left behind. Let's just say, as a young button, to have your own levi cruiser, you'd be very popular, especially having obtained it with such fearless daring. It seemed well worth the risk to young Carder. I mean, you'd only have to keep the streetlord entertained for a couple minutes before all hell broke loose, then be nimble with the scabs in your immediate vicinity.

Backman caught him coming out of the meeting, saying he was an old friend of his father's. Whereas everyone else was slapping him on the back and basking in his bravado, Backman grabbed him by the arm and pulled him into a corner. He remembered the conversation, word for word.

"Your father would never forgive me if I didn't tell you, you're a moron." Those were certainly fighting words, but Backman was a very senior Red Dragon, so Carder bit his tongue and settled for his best deadly glare. "I can't let you dishonor him with such brazen stupidity. So I'm going to lend you an old vest I took out of an US installation, which will give you enough protection against steel blades so you'll have a fighting chance. But you'll have to stay clear of lasers. I'll lead the crew going after the streetlord, so if you can hang on until I get in, I'll save your dumb ass. But if you ever do anything like this again to disrespect his memory …" Here, he'd deftly produced a laser dagger that hummed at Carder's throat. "I'll kill you myself. Lesson one: don't ever step on the killing ground tryin' to put on a show. Shows close quick, there."

And true to his word, he'd come in like a tornado and saved his dumb butt. Carder came within a hair of being slaughtered. But it really did wake him up to the foolishness of being concerned with "appearances." He gave the cruiser to Backman and asked if he would honor him by becoming his sensei. Backman made him the sincere warrior he was today, and he wasn't going to leave him to be crushed by Big New, along with that fuck the Count of Rockaway. Topgrid liked to chatter about courage, loyalty, and honor, but the only killing ground most of them ever stepped on was inside their fucking Screx.

❖

It was a bit tricky coming down the narrow winding passageway that lead into Mayra's room. Yasmine was balancing a tray of food on top of the set of leathers and a pair of combat boots. Creed, a young Outrider, presented them to her before she left the temporary mess. She'd decided to go ahead and eat there, both because it gave her a chance to catch up on information coming in, and it gave the Outriders time to finish the leathers they'd been busy making adjustments on since they had Harrison's armor to take measurements from. The hopes and dreams he represented were visible in the care in every stitch.

Not long after they discovered the underground vehicle repair shop with its ancient hot rods, they also discovered several rolls of black upholstery leather. The foreman, who stashed his prize cars there, ran a little upholstery business on the side. That leather provided for their uniforms ever since.

The soft glow of light coming from a battery-powered lamp on Mayra's dresser guided Yasmine. When she reached the narrow archway, she could see the shock of chestnut hair above Mayra's comforter and realized he was asleep again. Yasmine considered for the first time how exhausted he must be. She gently put the precarious pile on top of the dresser, carefully taking the tray of food over to the bed.

"Harrison?"

He stirred, then poked his sleepy face from under the cover.

"I brought you some food." He smiled up at her, and she smiled back. "It's special today. Freeze dried, vacume sealed, meat, potatoes, and vegetables in a brown gravy, along with some hardtack biscuits. I got you a double portion."

"Thanks!" The sight and smell of this banquet seemed to quickly revive him. He sat up and took the tray, setting it on his lap. "Oh, zap. This looks fantastic." Grabbing the spoon from the tray, he immediately dug in. Yasmine took the canteen slung over her right shoulder and laid it down next to the tray. "It's hot coffee." She watched for his response. Danner never heard of coffee before he joined them, and he'd become a devoted fan. Sure enough, he looked up quizzically, even as he shoveled in another spoonful of the stew.

"What's that?"

"It's a pleasantly bitter liquid that gives you a very toned down feeling of Nitro."

Intrigued enough to put down his spoon and unscrew the cap on the canteen, he carefully took a sip. He registered the unfamiliarity of the flavor in his expression, then took another sip and smiled.

"Interesting . . . but I don't feel anything."

"You will. It just takes a little while."

"I can't wait! I could use the boost." He went back to his meal.

"I brought you some clothes the Outriders made for you. They're on the dresser." She nodded toward the pile. "They should fit. I got you some combat boots in a size twelve. If they're too big, you can put on an extra pair of socks."

He looked up from his tray in the direction she indicated. "Are those real leather?"

"Yeah, the Outriders all wear them."

"Are they like the palace guard?"

Yasmine had a good laugh. "Well, they do security at the Duni, and they shadow Mayra leading up to it, but most of the time, they camp out in camouflaged outposts all over the grid girders."

"Keeping an eye on the Yakuza?"

"Yeah, they do, but mainly, they're keeping an eye out for you."

The spoon stopped halfway to his mouth. "Really?"

"Yeah, for a couple decades now."

Silently, he went back to his stew.

It was one thing to be viewed as an icon and receive the adoration of others. It was another to think of people enduring hardship and danger for decades waiting to be there for you. She could see, this time, he was moved and aware of it. He'd emptied both bowls and downed about half the canteen before he spoke again.

"Are you going to have to go out to the barricades soon?"

"Later, yeah."

"I don't suppose Mayra could change her mind about letting me come along?"

She gave him an apologetic smile. "Not a chance. She's right. We can't take the risk."

"Have the Outriders seen any activity?"

"There's a lot of movement down by the East River, where they have their Cruiser sheds. They're definitely getting all their ships ready to go up. Armaments are being handed out in the sector. The Outriders have to stay very high up on the grid right over Yaki sector, and the mesh makes it more difficult to see, but they can make out the troops are gathering . . . probably a few hours yet. Mongrel's just down the passage in the reading area. He'll be here, if you need anything."

"Listen, there's something I need to tell you. I was going to mention it earlier, but I already felt pretty inadequate to the task . . . my spacecase abilities, they're gone. When I jumped the String to get out of there, I got this message that you see when you no longer have the mental strength to transport into other dimensions. It means you're finished as a spacecase. I told Mayra I couldn't understand why your . . . God . . . would call me here and have me lose the very abilities that might make it possible to achieve this impossible task. It just seems to me kind of perverse on his or her . . . or its part. Honestly, it still strikes me as unnecessarily stacking the deck."

"So what did she tell you?"

"That it's a journey and there are surprises. She said pretty much what you did, about not worrying what I'm supposed to do."

She suddenly understood. He'd had so little encouragement in his life. Every risk he'd taken to wake up, he did alone. Every effort to get off his knees and stand up, with no support from anywhere; every chance of getting caught, he took alone, and in the dark. Yasmine reached out, running her hand through the chestnut hair. Bending down, she found his lips in a gentle kiss. His nostrils flared like "Ferdinand's," inhaling her smoky scent infused with a vibrancy from long before his awakening, a dawn of newborns bursting from bonded flesh and playing in an age of gardens. He reached for her then, desperate to be pulled into that forgotten past. Following the line of her jaw, burying his face in her hair, hiding his tears in creation's garden, she could feel the sorrow and joy tracing down her neck. She reached for him too, her hands exploring his solitary torso, fluttering across his imprisoned chest. He, searching for a way inside her soldier's mantle, touched the yielding softness that covered her vibrant muscularity, beckoning him, *Come on, come on!* A sensual duality that drove his lips back to hers made his tongue search the warmth of her mouth, tasting her sweet corn breath. Sanctified, eternal, dancing through the universe, like Bell's light particles—once in contact, forever joined—even though they may be light-years apart.

•———◆◗◖◆———•

He scratched his beard. He always did when he was nervous. They looked so peaceful and happy, innocent in their dreams. He hated to do it, but orders were orders. Still, he couldn't make himself speak. He tried clearing his throat.

Yasmine's eyes blinked open, and she sat up. "What is it, Mongrel?"

"Ma wants you on the barricades, Yaz." The deliverer was waking up too. "I tried calling down the passage, but I guess you were sleeping pretty good." He nodded to the deliverer. "Sorry." The deliverer nodded back, and Mongrel made a hasty retreat.

"It must be about to start." Yasmine quickly slipped from the bed and started getting dressed.

Harrison sat up, watching her. He saw the urgency of her movements, her near desperation to get ready for action as fast as she possibly could to defend their dream.

And it hit him—he knew what he could do! What he had to do right now! The thought recorder. It was so obvious, he was embarrassed. All the information, everything he knew about *Protostar*, space. It needed safeguarding. He couldn't just keep it to himself. He had to explain to her. It had to happen now.

"Wait. Wait! This is important."

On the floor, pulling on one boot, she looked up at him with an expression of disappointment verging on contempt. "Harrison, I have to go. It's my duty. I'm a soldier. You know that."

"No, no. It's important. I know it. You've got to let me explain this first! It's important. I know it. It's something I'm supposed to do!"

Furiously lacing up her boots, she shook her head. "It'll wait. It'll wait till I come back."

She was startled when he leapt from the end of the bed, landed in front of the dresser, and grabbed the trench knife from her equipment belt. "No, we've got to do this now! I know it. *Your God is making me know!*"

It was too much for him. The forgotten child was crumbling under the pressure of trying to fulfill their destiny. "Harrison, please, please! It's all right, it's all right. Come on, now . . . I'll stay if you want me to . . . just calm down . . . calm down." She couldn't help it; she was tearing up. "Just put down the knife, okay? Please, it'll be all right."

He sank to his knees in front of her. "Listen to me, please! I have a thing called a thought recorder inside my head. It has all the information and impressions of everything in my mind. I have to give it to you. I'm supposed to give it to you now."

Quickly bringing the edge of the blade up to his left temple, he made a sudden slice. Yasmine watched in horror, afraid he was going to commit suicide. He put down the knife with his right hand, sliding it over to Yasmine as the blood ran down the side of his face. With his left hand, he explored the self-made wound. He turned to give her a better view while his fingers probed until a tiny black disk popped out onto the side of his head.

"See . . . see . . . it's a thought recorder."

No stranger to blood and guts, still it took everything she had not to surrender to her gag reflex. It was something obscene, clinging there on the side of his face.

"Come here. Come closer. Can you see the jagged silver line running through the middle of it?"

She forced herself to move closer until she saw the little demarcation. "Yeah, I see it."

"If you press at the very center of that line, the two halves will separate. Go ahead, press it."

Yasmine made herself reach out with her thumb and forefinger and complete the task.

"Did they separate?"

She nodded yes.

"All right, the storage drive is the one on the bottom. You can just pull it out now. Hold the other half firmly and then go ahead and pull it out."

With the thumb and forefinger of her other hand, she held the top half of the black disk while tentatively tugging at the bottom half.

"Go ahead, pull."

She tugged harder, and the lower half came free in her hand.

"Now look at the side still on my head. Can you see a tiny red light on the upper edge? That half's function is to receive thoughts and impressions from my brain and then send them to the storage unit that you're holding. Now, I can access that storage unit anytime I want through the amplified unit still attached to my brain. If you wanted to access the information on that drive, you'd have to find another amplifying unit and switch it to Send before you reconnected it to your storage drive. Then insert it in your head by making an incision just above and behind your left temple and in front of your ear, right where I cut mine. It can be a smaller incision than I made. There doesn't need to be so much blood. I was just in a hurry to show you. To switch the amplifier to Send, you need to take something sharp to use as a stylus and put it directly on the red light and press it three times. The light will turn blue, notifying you it has switched to data-send. Do it now. Switch mine to data-send. You can also do it with the tip of your knife." He grinned at her. "Just be careful, all right?"

Yasmine firmly gripped the jagged half still dangling from his head and quickly twirled around the blade, making three precise stabs at the tiny blinking light, which immediately turned blue. "Now, even though, the units are separated, my amplifying unit will keep sending data to the storage unit you have as long as I'm within the Earth's gravitational field. If you had another amplifying unit, you switched to blue data-send, and you hooked it to the storage unit you already have and put that in your head. Whenever you wanted to know something, you'd just touch that spot on your Send unit and think of the information you want to know, and the thought recorder will send it right into your mind. And that includes seeing what I've seen with my eyes by closing yours to activate that. Once you put the unit into the cut you've made, all you have to do is press it in. Tiny tendrils will deploy through your skull into your brain. Just put some tape over the cut when you're done. You don't have to worry about infection. The unit is coated with a permanent disinfectant. The cut will heal in a couple of weeks. Take this storage unit and keep it somewhere safe, on your person."

Harrison hesitated but finally made himself say it. "You should tell Mayra about it, in case anything happens to you . . . and if something happens to me, you should get the amplifier unit out of my head."

"Okay," was all she could say. She put the jagged half-disk inside a small zip pocket of her vest.

"I'm sorry I scared you. I know you're a warrior. I love your warrior, but your God made me know I needed to do that now."

Yasmine touched the unbloodied side of his face and smiled. "Well, if he's giving you orders, he's probably your God too." She kissed him, stood up, and went over to the dresser to put her trench knife back into the sheath on her belt. "Do you want me to have Mongrel get somebody to dress that wound?"

Harrison laughed as he pushed the half-disk back into the wound. "No. This is nothing. It'll be fine. I'll just keep pressure on it for a while then put some tape on it."

Yasmine took a roll of tape and some gauze from a pouch on her belt and tossed it to him. "Here. I'll be back as soon as I can." She smiled then disappeared down the passage.

Harrison pressed a piece of gauze to his wound and held it there. He was convinced he'd been possessed by a desperate spirit who only released him after accomplishing the task. He was spent. When the bleeding stopped, he climbed back onto the mat but made sure to keep pressure on his compress. Closing his eyes, he fell asleep again.

⎯⎯•◼•⎯⎯

Mongrel heard him before he saw him, and his response was to aim the street sweeper at the deliverer's chest as he emerged from the stacks. Recognizing him, Mongrel was again embarrassed, lowering the muzzle immediately.

"Sorry, we're all pretty jumpy right now."

The deliverer smiled and pointed at his weapon. "What is that thing? I've never seen one before last night."

"It's called a street sweeper. It's an automatic twelve-gauge shotgun with a thirty-round circular-drum magazine. We use double-x rounds." Mongrel grinned. "That way, all you gotta do is aim in the general direction."

Harrison spotted the walkie-talkie on the table in front of Mongrel. "Have you heard anything from the barricades?"

"They're still massing down in Yaki sector. They haven't started uptown yet."

"Hey, I wanted to thank you for this jump. I never dreamed I'd wear real leather. It fits great."

He'd been so preoccupied with his own awkwardness it hadn't even registered that the deliverer was wearing their leathers. "Yeah, they look good on you. They'll keep that December chill off!"

"Yeah, I'm feeling a lot warmer in them. Do you mind if I sit here with you? I was getting a little stir-crazy back there."

"Sure. Have a seat. I got some coffee here, if you want some."

Harrison sat down on the couch across from Mongrel. "Thanks, I had some earlier, but I don't think I drank enough. It's supposed to give you a jolt, right?"

Mongrel passed his canteen to Harrison and chuckled. "Well, if you're used to Nitro, it'll take a while before you notice the effect." He watched him take a swig from the canteen. It was amazing how unmarked he was. Mongrel had experience with the way people looked after Yaks tortured them. Every so often, Yaks caught an Outrider, leaving the remains hanging from a girder. He'd been at the table in the Forty-Second Street mess when Dag gave a thorough description of the rescue mission, and he'd visited Splatter in the infirmary. It was pretty amazing! The deliverer didn't have a scratch on him now.

"You heal pretty quick!"

The deliverer smiled and handed the canteen back to him. "One of the perks of being spacecase."

"That means you go up into space, right?"

"Yeah."

"Cool."

"Yeah, it never stops being amazing up there, looking down on the planet."

Mongrel took a swig from his canteen. "What's left of it."

"Yeah, I guess it used to look a lot different."

"Oh yeah, believe it! We got some books in here, will give you an idea. It was somethin' else."

The deliverer displayed a sheepish grin. "I guess I'm supposed to find us another one."

Mongrel chuckled again. "Well, I hope so, because this one is FUBAR!"

"That Amerab?"

"Nah, it's a term from the Second World War—*fucked up beyond all recognition*." Mongrel suddenly remembered he had a message for the deliverer. "I almost forgot, I guess 'cause I thought it was just more bullshit, but your 'friend' Han wanted me to give you a message. He says you should come talk to him because he didn't tell you the second part of the plan about how to get that Topgrid ship."

Harrison sat there a moment, stunned by the impact of hearing a direct communiqué from Han. It was as if he were someone else inside himself, watching his reactions. For the first time, he saw clearly the desperate machinations of his beginner's heart, grasping at this first rush of hope—*maybe this was the way out!* Here was the path that needed taking—inclusion, absorption, a final embrace to be performed that brought all prodigal sons and daughters home. Han could change.

He'd told the truth about Sanatan. Maybe Han saw now how crazy and self-absorbed he was. He wasn't all bad. He'd watched out for him!

Don't turn to the darkness of your cynicism and lose everything these cokes are hoping for because you can't let go of the past and believe in the present. Because you can't forgive! Give him a chance! At least listen to what he has to say. Don't let the past hold you prisoner, keep you from seeing a moment of catharsis. This is it! This is the way out.

He should have just given up in the beginning, realizing he really did worship naked vulnerability—believed connection, understanding, and consideration were waiting to be awakened in the coldest of reptile hearts.

He kept believing Han would change, if he could just make the scaly retard realize that Harrison's seeming innocent *knew* very well how his predator's jaws worked and was fully aware of every attempt the conniving reptile had made to devour him—*and was still willing to reach out in the spirit of mercy and forgiveness and give him one more chance!* He had to stop thinking that this amazing combination of information was going to disarm Han, make him feel his connection, know how connection felt, make the murdering bastard nuzzle his big crocodile nose in Harrison's neck.

He only knew how to feed, and the only way to stop him was to end his life. *Flame, if you do exist, burn my childish heart to ash. No more. No more.*

The deliverer shot up from the couch so fast Mongrel was on his feet, swinging his street sweeper in a 360-degree swath.

"What is it? What's wrong?" He looked into the deliverer's eyes and saw a look he knew quite well.

"I need a frybar."

Mongrel understood immediately what was going down. "Sure. We've got a weapons locker on the same platform where we're holding them. It's just a few hundred yards from here. Come on, we'll take the railcar down."

For a bear of a man, Mongrel was very quick when he wanted to be, and he wanted to be now. Seeing the look of decision in the deliverer's eyes, he realized it was that look he'd been waiting to see to put all his doubts to rest.

He led them from the library down the corridor to Mayra's platform. He motioned the deliverer to hop on the flatcar, then jumped aboard and fired up the engine; perching on the driver's seat, he dwarfed it with his size. The car lurched into action, clicking along the tracks toward the 103rd IND platform.

At rail's end, Mongrel jumped off onto the 103rd platform and, with Harrison right behind him, charged up the stairs to the IND level and hailed the Outrider standing guard.

"Creed, come over here."

Harrison nodded to Creed, a much younger, skinnier version of Mongrel but sporting a full beard of his own. Creed smiled and nodded back.

"They're both asleep on either side of the cell. I just looked in on them."

Mongrel handed Creed a set of keys. "Get the deliverer a frybar out of the weapons locker. Make sure the recharge rod has a full charge and bring it back here."

Creed moved past the cell to the far side of the platform and disappeared around the corner. Harrison turned to Mongrel. "Listen, Mongrel, from now on, we're all in this together, so why don't you all just call me Jack?"

Mongrel smiled and nodded. "You got it, Jack."

A moment later, Creed reappeared with the familiar black truncheon. "Here you go. It's charged."

Harrison took the frybar, and Creed returned the keys to Mongrel.

"So everybody's clear. Mongrel, as soon as you unlock it, swing it wide open. I'm going to kill Han first and then Tooco. Han is the big one. Which side is he on?" Seeing Creed's surprise, Harrison recognized his own fledgling warrior. "Trust me, it's way overdue."

"The big one is on the left side."

Harrison nodded and switched his frybar to pulse bolt. "All right, let's get this over once and for all."

With Mongrel on his right and Creed on his left, Harrison approached the gray lock, behind which his blond nemesis slept.

He thought about the ways their fates had intertwined: on the fiber feeds, in the Screwhog, and finally here, with the dreamers in Bellytown. Han—the master manipulator, mass murderer, and no doubt murderer of his purposeful redemption, if given even half a chance. No more.

Three paces from the lock, he motioned for Mongrel to go ahead and open it. His thumb poised over the pulse-bolt button, there wasn't the shadow of a doubt in his mind or heart. He'd never been so sure of anything in his life. This had to be done.

But the lock turned into a sun, the sun into a night, and slipping into the darkness, Harrison realized this was what they called the end.

FINAL INTERLUDE—2197

ENOUGH! NO MORE! No more. Dysan knew she was being melodramatic, echoing Harrison's moment of decision. It only *felt* like her right hand would never open again. The cramps shooting through her arm delivered pulse bolts, exploding in her brain. And the dreamers' *real* misery was *just* beginning! Where was Shuta? She'd been deluding herself, thinking he could be dissuaded. He'd gone into that fucking String arena, and while she sat here, scratching out their desperate struggle, he was probably being ejected from this interstellar prison as space garbage. *Enough.*

She didn't have to write this tale of endless challenge. She could download the entire tortured story in under ten seconds. And she wouldn't have to dig it out of her head to do it! They'd long ago caught up with Earth's techie wizards, surpassing their abilities with C-power technologies. She didn't even have to remove the earbud adapted for the thought recorder so she could scribble it onto paper. She could just plug another line right in the damn machine. And why not do that? Because they were addicted to suffering! Let's do it the ancient way to prove we can suffer with the best of our ancestors, prove we can suck up the pain the way they did.

It was ludicrous to cripple herself recording their bottomless well of misery. Fuck it. She could plug in another line and scroll it. She could scroll and record until the moments that really mattered, speed through the nuts and bolts of sacrifice to the quintessential moments that made a difference, then use what was left of her tortured hand to honor her family's wishes. *Wake up, you fucking screen, scroll for me. Serve me, you fucking machine. Yeah, that's it . . . moving right along.*

Zim's "little surprise" in Han's jump (a fistful of C-4 with a battery detonator molded into the plastic explosive) serves its purpose and detonates when Mongrel swings open the door. Han's luck holds. Mongrel's massive girth shields Harrison from the direct blast, but it blows away Creed as well. Han and Tooco grab Creed's and Harrison's frybars, along with an unconscious Harrison, and jump into the red Roadrunner, waiting there on the IND line. Tooco pilots the muscle machine down to where the tracks end at Thirty-Fourth. Again, the Screenrage's luck comes into play when he decides to blast open this subway entrance rather than continue on foot down the tunnel. They would've all been blown to hell in the dreamers' minefield. Even more of the devil's luck when they emerge to find themselves inside the Penn Station lobby entrance. It's clear it's a fiber-feed porno studio now. Because of the impending attack, they're functioning with a skeleton staff. Han and Tooco make them more skeleton-like.

Okay, let's bite the bullet, Han Larkill, to painstakingly record your despicable behavior. What's constantly amazing is how such juvenile pettiness can be raised to demonic heights. Desperate to get up to Big New and rejoin the rest of his gang, Han still took time to send a little epistle back to the dreamers, remembering the ID number of the fiber-feed screen he'd used to first contact Zim. *From my screaming hand, you evil prick, here you are, word for word . . .*

I know my parting comes as a harsh surprise to you. But I must tell you, I am more than a little disappointed by your treatment of my emissaries. It didn't occur to you that while you were testing them, you were being tested? What compassion was shown by Mayra when Han admitted the sacred twin wasn't his, but that he saw the divine truth of your mission and repented of his self-serving schemes and begged to be allowed to join you? He was thrown in a dirty hole to sit in his own excrement, until you found time to decide if he was worthy. It is clear to me you have a great deal to learn before you will be worthy of deliverance. Let the deaths of those heartless guards you placed at my comrades' cell be just the beginning of my chastisements. You will suffer greatly before you receive my blessings again. I go now to prepare for the day when you've learned the meaning of mercy and love . . . Harrison.

And so this infection in their beliefs was injected into their destiny. Moving right along ...

Han has Tooco keep watch at the street lock while he ransacks the place, looking for Nitro patches to bring Harrison around. Finding several on the body of one of the porn stars, he slaps a couple on Harrison's neck and finally brings him back to consciousness. Keeping a frybar trained on him, Han cleans him up for his trip up to Big New while launching into a diatribe, accusing Harrison of deserting his real friends for a bunch of pathetic scabs who couldn't possibly realize their "dream" to steal a *Protostar*—that, in fact, he, Han, is the only one who can make that dream come true, and he can do it, with or without Harrison's help. It's up to Harrison to decide if he wants to return to the bosom of his real friends, or die right here, right now, with his filthy scabs in Bellytown. Its then he noticed the bloody bandage just above Harrison's left temple. He asks him what happened to the thought recorder.

Still affected by the concussion, Harrison fails to exercise caution and defiantly tells, Han he gave it to Yasmine. Han realizes his spacecase has fallen in love with the fiery redhead whom he met storming the dreamers' barricade. Han asks, why she didn't accompany Harrison when he came down to their cell. Harrison says simply that she had to go defend the barricade from the coming attack of the Yakuza. Again, the petty malice pumping through his veins spurs him to conceive a second epistle. He tells Harrison to think about what he said, then takes time to send his second message to the dreamers.

Here it is, sleazeball, the knife you put in my great-grandmother's back.

Yasmine,

I must admit it is very hard for me to address you personally. My heart has its breaking point just like any other, and I was trying to avoid the excruciating pain of acknowledging your betrayal. I gave you my heart and everything of my experience, begging you to go with me and free my disciples, hoping you would stand with me and right the wrong that Mayra committed. But you chose to stand with her rather than heed your lover's plea and the call of your deliverer. You broke my heart, Yasmine. You broke my heart …

Harrison.

Clever, twisted soul to pit the two against each other in his tale of imaginary betrayal. Of course, this obvious bullshit didn't stand up over time; but during the turbulent chaos, when it did hold sway, it was very painful for both, Yasmine and Mayra.

Han is truly inspired! He tells, Harrison that unless he gives him his solemn word that he will rejoin their band and do whatever Han tells him to, he is going to send the Yakuza a detailed description of the interior of the dreamers' tunnels and the secret entrance where they should attack—the Seventy-Eighth bridle path bridge! And Harrison, bloodied and concussed, his fledgling vision of a purposeful destiny denied, now imagines his true mission has finally been revealed: simply to save them from being slaughtered by the Yakuza. He gives Han his solemn promise, and they turn their attentions to getting a ride that will take them to the grid plate and up into Big New.

Once more, it appears Han's the guy the heavens are rooting for. Tooco, keeping the lookout, hollers that a Levi cruiser has just stopped out in front, and two neon-clad porno pimps are making their way up the steps at this very moment. Han and Tooco make short work of them and commandeer the cruiser. Before leaving, Han sends his second coded signal to Zim, adding a "#Tag" with the porn sight's number because, unlike the dreamers' screens, this one has a text feature. Zim contacts Han directly, and they have a short "conversation." Zim tells him they're in the limo in a long-term parking. Han tells him they have Harrison and can be there in an hour. Zim tells him there's a flight to Brentwood in two hours if he books, immediately. Han asks if an hour will be enough time for all of them to get in the terminal and for Zim to set up the holo imager. Zim says yes, and Han tells him to go ahead and book it. They congratulate each other on their genius and sign off.

On their way up to the refuse chute bordering the Satport, Han fills in Harrison on the second part of his plan to steal the *Protostar*. Beginning with telling Harrison about the second "suitcase" bomb, he explains about their booking the luxury suite just behind the pilot's cockpit. Once they're in flight, Harrison will jump the String and take care of the pilot and copilot. Then he'll hop off the String and let Zim into the cockpit. Zim has a voice replicator, which will have sampled both the pilot and copilot's voices when they're introduced on boarding—a perk the passengers in the luxury suite are afforded. Harrison will fly the Satcruiser on its projected course to Brentwood, coaching Zim what to say when replying to either ground or Brentwood flight control. When Milsat's orbit reaches its closest point to the Satcruiser's flight path, Harrison will have Zim report their C-power fusion drives are cutting in and out, and they're having difficulty maintaining their course. Zim will reassure the crew and passengers and report that the problem is becoming worse as they veer in the direction of Milsat. At this point, they will request an emergency landing clearance from Milsat. Being that it's a flight with a big-shot gadget master onboard, there'll be no objection to giving them a clearance to land. Of course, when they land, Milsat will initiate their security protocol and send a squad of Sackers to secure the ship, escorting the passengers to a holding area.

As soon as they lock into a landing port, Harrison will jump the String again, taking their atomic surprise with him. He will find the lock where emergency-response space jumps with rocket packs are stored. He'll leave the bomb hidden there and start taking the space jumps directly through the hull into the cargo area of the Satcruiser.

They will need five space jumps, so he might need to make a few trips. According to Zim, he can move fast enough on the String that it shouldn't take him more than thirty seconds. Then he will proceed immediately to the *Protostar*, enter the ship and kill any personnel aboard, punch in the codes to unlock the ship's entry port, hop off the String, and prepare the ship for launch.

In the meantime, once they lock into the landing port, the rest of their band will disappear down the auxiliary entrance to the cargo hold in the luxury suite's private galley. Having killed any personnel working there, they will take their bodies (along with the pilot's and copilot's remains) down into the cargo hold. By the time Sackers clear the passengers off the ship and make their way up to the cockpit, they will be confronted with the mystery of the disappearing flight crew. This will give them valuable seconds as the Sackers consider whether they could have filed out among the passengers, and somehow they missed them? Meanwhile, in the cargo hold, their little band will suit up, open the tail lock of the Satcruiser, and make their short flight to the *Protostar*.

At first, since they're wearing Milsat space jumps, it will be assumed they're a team of emergency responders checking the exterior of the ship. If, once they start moving toward the *Protostar*, they're challenged by radio communication, Han will respond by saying they're checking out a reported sighting of what could be saboteurs wearing blackout space jumps heading for the *Protostar*. Milsat will, no doubt, contact the personnel on *Protostar* to warn them of the danger and ask if they've spotted anything unusual. Harrison will tell them everything is normal and there is no sign of any unauthorized activity. Then he will ask if, for security purposes, they should move *Protostar* some distance away from Milsat, half a dozen of one or half a dozen of the other. Either way, by that time, the rest of them will be on board *Protostar*. They'll just go ahead and separate from Milsat and start to pull away.

There is no way they are going to shoot down the *Protostar*. What they will do is scramble all their fighters, but again, that will take valuable seconds, and Harrison can drop the hammer on the ship's massive C-power fusion drives. Even if they do get a few fighters out after them, they're still not going to blast their precious *Protostar*; and as soon as they reach a safe distance from Milsat, Zim will detonate the second fission bomb. That should take the will to pursue out of any fighters still chasing their prize. Besides, *Protostar* has its own battery of laser cannons; and once he has time, Harrison can take care of a few pesky fighters. Han tells Harrison that timing is important and there's no room for error; but since all communications with Milsat (from the Satcruiser and *Protostar*) will appear to be coming from authorized personnel, the "confusion factor" in any emergency situation will make it possible to pull it off.

You really do have to hand it to that evil bastard—he had one hell of a conniving mind! There was only one problem: Harrison couldn't return to the three-dimensional the next time he jumped the String. By this time, he'd regained his faculties enough not to mention that fact to Han. He'd come up with a new plan, and it didn't involve keeping his promise to this maniac. Once they were clear of Big New, Han couldn't hurt the dreamers, and Yasmine would be safe. He'd take the bomb and head out into space, leaving them to be discovered as impostors when the ship landed on Brentwood. Their ruse discovered, they'd find themselves back in the mines or dead. And when he grew weary of the endless emptiness, Harrison could go out with a bang.

In line with this time sequence, I have an obligation to make an admission here. Because he was Yasmine's nephew and my great-uncle, and because I am sworn to reveal all we've known and kept secret for the last one hundred years.

In what was formerly the only vacant corner of their impressive cavern—stretching from Seventy-Second to Seventy-Eighth and extending into Cenpak as far as the bridle path bridge—next to the hydraulic launch platform directly underneath it, one of the net screens fibered in from the evacuation of Forty-Second is showing two messages. Everyone is on the barricades. Only a teenage boy named Seth remains to finish reparking all the forklifts used to move the munitions off the IRT line. Out of the corner of his eye, he notices the glowing messages and decides to go over and see what they are. After the initial shock and horror of reading both of Han's epistles, he turns and walks, away. Never telling anyone until on his deathbed, he relates the story to his daughter. He didn't want to be the one to bring this news to Ma, and he was hoping it was just a Yaki subterfuge.

Moving right along …

Han, Tooco, and Harrison make it out of the refuse chute and over to Deli's limo in long-term parking. Darl finishes preparing Harrison, helping him into a bodyguard's jump for his role. They have twenty minutes to go over their holo drama before it's time for Zim to position the image enhancers. Then the others arrive in the boarding area. They all line up to go through the scan. But then the holos wreak havoc! Zim's choreography goes off without a hitch!

Reprising his role with exquisite hysteria, Han's "Deli," along with entourage, are rushed into their luxury suite. Everybody settles into the plush interior and is served canapés and Blue Booz before watching the liftoff on their wall screen. They observe as, just above them, a portion of Big New's bell cover irises open. Marveling at the spectacular view of the megatropolis below, they begin their ascent into the atmosphere.

It should come as no surprise to anyone following this historical primer that, that wacky Yaki Carder is about to change the view. Though, the dreamers wouldn't know it was him until much later, and only because Yasmine eventually put two and two together. Harrison will watch what he believes is the most tragic event in his life unfold when his eyes rip his heart to pieces—and after that, the veil is briefly lifted by absurdist epiphany.

They all gasp as the entire grid-plate begins to wobble, and the bell jar starts jiggling like an overturned bowl of gelatin. The scrapers whip back and forth and begin toppling on themselves, just as the grid plate drops straight down. Big New is repeatedly impaled on grid-girders and Bellytown scrapers, its whited geodesic hives exploding at their bases! The thundering rubble cauldron slowly sinking into churning clouds of billowing debris. Nothing underneath it could survive. Yasmine is gone. Harrison can see the others are as shocked as he is.

Han gives him a nervous glance, afraid Harrison thinks it's his doing. But Harrison knows it wasn't Han. It would be the last thing he'd do if he wanted Harrison's help.

But before his broken mind can speculate on the source of this epic obliteration, the pristine ivory masterpiece, along with its crystal bell, *reincarnates* and shrinks to a jewel below them as they soar higher and higher into the stratosphere. They all look back and forth to the screen and one another, completely dumbfounded, like a herd of cattle in the twentieth—some unexpected noise interrupting their cud-chewing peace. Immediately following that, one of their servers reenters. She stands, smiling, with another tray of canapés while everyone stares at her like she has three heads.

"Is everybody doing all right? Do you want another decanter of Blue? We have some delicious Labrador steaks smothered in soya mushrooms, if anyone has an appetite?"

"INDEED!" Darl bursts into hysterical laughter, shouting to their server to bring steaks for everyone and another decanter of Blue.

As soon as their server leaves, they resume their mutual stupefaction, until Han finally says it, whispering from instinct, "We're the only ones here without Appro-recall implants."

Harrison fully comprehends for the first time all that was stolen from him—kept in a limbo, incapable of self-examination. And with that, he understood how the machine took them from a comfortable electronic nap into a deep coma *without* developing a separate consciousness. It was simply the computers being designed to interface programs and gain more data by correlating their information—computers became learning machines. Learning machines willed by humans to be programed for one primary function, a function that propelled every other function: "Make it all run smoothly without bothering me." In time, a very telling correlation between unpleasant memories and interruptions in smooth running became apparent. Harrison never really understood how they did it, but it's a mystery we've been able to solve with the passage of a hundred years. Appro-recall's main function was to create electrical disruptions at synapses identified as containing "difficult memories." So Harrison grasped the basic concept without having all the details.

What he did grasp at that moment was, the automatic pilot responsible for the continued functioning of their beehive harmony was being *overloaded* by recurring major catastrophy. The only way of maintaining its function was to kick into full denial. Appro-recall is wiping everybody! That's why there were no Sacker patrols in Bellytown. They're giving the *day off* to anyone indirectly affected. And they don't need to worry about the ones directly affected because they're all dead! He was finally down to the heart of the matter when it came to a life unexamined. It was the challenge Socrates answered: will you give up your life if it's the only way to affirm the conclusions you've reached?

How much farther they could've come if cokekind hadn't been seduced into worshiping at the altar of ease and comfort. He could've had a life free from the programed "sandman" keeping him in the dark about himself. Those countless clones ensnared by Appro-recall, all strangers to themselves. Harrison changed his plans for the last time.

She no longer had a choice. She was charged to record an experience worthy of a blistered claw.

Beginning with the physical destruction, the collapsing grid girders brought Big New and its one-hundred-thousand-ton grid plate down onto the old five boroughs. Most all of the subway tunnels collapsed, with the exception of the IRT line from Fifty-Ninth to 103rd and the tunnel they'd dug down Fifty-Ninth to the eastern corner of the barricade. The IRT between Fifty-Ninth and 103rd survived because it was at the western edge of the grid plate next to the Hudson, where there were no real scrapers. When the grid hit, it split along the western edge of the barricade, forming a lean-to over that section of Broadway and keeping a direct impact off the IRT line. The Fifty-Ninth tunnel was protected in the same fashion by the southern side of the barricade. The IND line was further into the grid plate and in an area where there were a lot of tall scrapers. That succeeded in breaking the gird plate into numerous sections that came raining down on Third Avenue, crushing the IND line. The crosstown tunnels survived because they were dug below the IRT and IND lines. But the only one the dreamers still had access to was the one at 103rd. The large cavern they dug out from the Seventy-Second IRT platform also survived, undamaged. Extending quite a distance out into Cenpak and unprotected by the barricade, they considered this a lucky miracle at the time. It wasn't until later they would understand why.

Including Ram, they lost forty-three men and women and all their cruisers in Harlem. They lost another two hundred and sixty-two dreamers manning the barricade and sixteen Outriders in their outposts up on the girders. They were now a population of four hundred and thirty-six. Both Yasmine and Mayra survived because they were down in the tunnels directing the laser cannons at the eastern and IRT entrances to the barricade at Fifty-Ninth. Outrider outposts were reporting that the Yaks were just starting to leave their sector, so people were still moving around the barricade, performing a last-minute check on all their weapons and ammunition. When they first heard the explosions, they seemed to be occurring in every direction. They didn't know what to make of it. The most obvious conclusion was that Sackers were announcing the beginning of their own assault. Scanning the grid plate for Sacker cruisers, they had maybe five seconds to realize what was really going on. Nobody who saw the grid plate coming down survived. The dreamers inside the tunnels only knew there was a deafening cacophony and an earthquake of monumental proportions. The cruiser transport train, which had been parked up from 103rd to leave space for the train that evacuated everything from Forty-Second, was completely crushed when the tunnel beyond the barricade collapsed. Both the munitions transport train on the outer tracks and the evacuation train were parked up to 103rd. They were catapulted off the tracks, cars and engines settling into a twisted jumble. This made the IRT line completely blocked from Ninety-Seventh up to 103rd.

Their lighting system was out. Their generators located in the large warehouses at 103rd had also been toppled on their sides. They had only their battery-powered devices to provide them with the light to get around. Their gravity-feed pipeline from Croton reservoir was ruptured in several places, causing serious flooding in the IRT tunnel from Seventy-Eighth up to Ninety-Second. In one split second, they were back in the tunnels of 2024! No, even worse than those humble beginnings. Now they were sealed under tons of rubble. There was hysteria. There was chaos. There were another fourteen accidental deaths in the desperate days that followed. They were now four hundred and twenty-two. Everyone but the children were without food. They'd decided to keep the children in their deepest and most protected lair, the Duni cavern, where their temporary mess had been set up. Luckily, in preparation for the coming battle, they'd brought up six months of provisions to the Duni cavern, along with enough fuel for their camp stoves to keep the cavern warm and dimly lit. Because of the darkness and chaos everywhere else, they weren't even aware that Harrison was gone. Their communications by walkie-talkie were intermittent, and the immediacy of the multiple emergencies occupied all their transmissions. When they got to the point of sending a party up the IRT tunnel to 103rd, they discovered the blockage caused by the trains. They had no choice but to get blow torches from the Seventy-Eighth cavern and start cutting through the trains' wreckage, beginning at Ninety-Seventh. When they eventually made it up to 103rd, they were finally reunited with their children. They'd had garbled messages on the walkie-talkies from which they'd pieced together that the Duni cavern was intact, and all the children were safe, but that verification in flesh and blood made them aware of their precious blessings.

They searched the library and Mayra's room but found no sign of Harrison or Mongrel. It was then they sent a party up to the IND platform at 103rd. The collapsed IND tunnel had pushed some debris on to platform, but the holding cell was far enough back from the tunnel that it hadn't covered some parts of Mongrel's and Creed's bodies. There were obvious signs that the holding cell was the source of an explosion. They knew then Han and Tooco had escaped. They were now four hundred and twenty, and their worst fears were proving true. But it wasn't until they put the generators upright and repaired them that there was enough light to thoroughly search the entire area.

That's when their last hopes were shattered. Harrison was gone—probably with Han and Tooco—and, almost certainly, buried like everything else under the ruins of Big New. They thought this was the final blow to all of their dreams. Then someone discovered the messages left on the fiber-feed screen.

Han's messages (posing as Harrison) spread quickly as they made their way into the Duni cavern to discuss their situation and get their first real meal in over a week. Eventually, everyone was there—everyone but Mayra and Yasmine. They were hold up in Mayra's cavern trying to make sense of Harrison's words, each going over their conversations with him, looking for some connection between these messages and what he said. Oddly, Yasmine didn't mention the thought recorder at this time. They decided there wasn't any connection. The messages obviously weren't from Harrison. Also, Harrison had never been anywhere even close to their fiber-feed screens, so there was no way he'd know the contact IDs. Han was near the screens when they met to come up with a strategy to rescue Harrison; and as Mayra reconstructed that time period minute for minute, she realized there was a short time where Han had been alone in there. It became obvious to them that Han kidnapped Harrison and then sent these messages as a payback for his wounded pride. They were confident that once they laid out these facts, everyone would realize what really occurred.

What they didn't take into account was that the terrible fact remained—their deliverer was gone. And they were sealed in the last of their tunnels with God knows what's going on overhead and only six months of food. Also, there was that line in the first communication, "You will suffer greatly before you receive my blessings again." Combined with the time stamp of this transmission, a little over two hours before they were crushed from above, it made most believe with a certainty—this was Harrison's warning of the devastating chastisement that had come.

Dysan spent a lot of time trying to distill the singular characteristic a person has to possess to become civilized. She'd decided it was empathy. Empathy made it possible to perceive the world from a different perspective than your own. This ability to (as the old saying goes) "walk in somebody else's moccasins" was the prerequisite for people to build a society that could recognize everyone's needs. This being said, no matter how hard she tried, Dysan could not make herself see through their eyes at this time. It was just too depressing to contemplate! Decades in a subterranean twilight, scratching their way back up from oblivion, being enticed and inspired by these miraculous fire visions of a savior who would restore them to the light—and then, miracle of miracles, him materializing at one of their fire ceremonies! My God, the elation, the relief, the disbelief, the delirious joy. Then to be "God-smacked" in an instant—back to total oblivion, their fortress transformed to their tomb. The loss of so many dear comrades and friends …

Trying to be there with them, even for a minute, made it impossible to sit still—to keep from jumping up and bolting—her body desperate to aid an escape.

These were the shattered people waiting in the Duni cavern when Mayra and Yasmine entered to give their explanation of what had occurred. They all sat there, ash-faced, gutted, listening to irrelevant words. And as the two talked in turn, trying to illicit some reaction to their considered realizations, the only change they could discern in their brethren was the dark glow of rage growing in their eyes. Finally, there was nothing more to say. They stood in that silent moment, realizing very possibly they were about to die. It was Lightning, the Outrider commander, who stepped up beside them, his street-sweeper in one hand, muzzle pointed at the floor, every muscle in his gun arm taut with expectation. His icy-blue eyes, framed by his long white hair, made his resolve clear. He was taking command now. He gestured with a nod of his head—that Mayra and Yasmine should take their leave up the stairs. Ascending right behind them, he kept his eyes on a silent throng.

The weeks that followed witnessed near revolution in their ranks. Mayra and Yasmine were no longer consulted about what needed to be done. At first, they directed their efforts to cutting up and clearing away the transport trains. They'd only cut a narrow pathway through the wreckage to get up to 103rd. They discovered that their communal caverns were also spared and showed no damage. After the tunnel was cleared, the captains of each cavern organized and directed the projects they chose to work on. There were frequent arguments (some of them violent), about which projects should take priority. Some of the salvaged steel was used to shore up the remaining tunnels wherever signs of stress were identified. Another group worked on a more permanent fix for the jerry-rigged repairs made that first week to the water main and its branch lines from Croton reservoir. They also repaired and reprimed the pumps that assisted the water flow when gravity feed became unsustainable after Ninety-Second.

They had to deal with a new problem as well: each cavern had a composting communal latrine. Where before the compost was hauled up to Cenpak and spread around their meager trees, they no longer had this option. They were afraid to dig a new cavern to store it because of the fear it might cause new collapses. They came up with the idea of compressing it into bricks and stacking them to dry along the sides of the tunnels. They burned it like peat to keep the communal caverns warm through the winter months. The odor wasn't pleasant. Luckily, all the air vents into Cenpak were still functional, although the airflow was not as good as before. The large vent for their fires now served to bring air to the Duni cavern. The groups coordinated the next day's efforts in the evenings after dinner. The Outriders and their families were in charge of food preparation, serving, and cleanup. They also maintained a guard around the library, where Mayra and Yasmine remained under unofficial house arrest. Nobody outside the Outriders wanted to see their faces for a while.

It wasn't until three months later this attitude began to change. It became obvious their former leader and her first lieutenant were both with child. News spread quickly about this new development, and although there was little discussion, a change in their outlook began to occur. If the deliverer and his chief disciple chose them to bear their children, then maybe there was still some possibility of redemption. As the days progressed, more and more individuals began to visit the library—ostensibly for reading matter, but really hoping for a peek at their progress. Both Mayra and Yasmine had mixed feelings about these visits. Lightning encouraged them to let themselves be seen and advised the masses would eventually come around. But frankly, they were hurt and angry at the way they'd been ostracized. Both made the mistake of thinking the obvious validity of their rational conclusions would cut through all the guilt mongering and emotional hysteria. But Yasmine was the angrier of the two, labeling them as "pack-animal morons." This disillusionment with former comrades changed her view of them forever.

It was at this time, a mechanic working in the Seventy-Eighth cavern accidentally hit the button that opened the sliding panel above the hydraulic lift for their Levi cruisers. He immediately shut it off and was about to push the button to close it when he paused to wonder why no debris had fallen through the two-foot-wide opening. Grabbing a flashlight and ladder, he poked his head up to take a look. What he saw shocked and amazed him. As far as he could see with the flashlight, the park was exactly the way they'd left it before the devastation. Pointing the flashlight straight up, he could see (covering a definitely lower barricade) the grid plate of Big New. They now had confirmation that Big New had fallen on Bellytown. They sent a recon party up into Cenpak, and they affirmed the entire park was pretty much exactly as it had always been with the exception of the northern end, where the barricade was always a little low. Some debris made its way into Cenpak through openings in the broken barricade there. This confirmed that an entire piece of the grid plate had landed intact on top of the barricade, creating a vast cavern out of Cenpak. They surmised that coming down from directly above, the grid plate hadn't been pierced by any old scrapers, and that kept it from being broken into pieces and filling Cenpak with debris. They realized this made it possible for them to dig out of their entombment because they now had someplace where they could put all the debris they'd have to dig through to get to the surface. Also, they had a place for their toilets' compost again.

This was very good news because their food supply was becoming a pressing issue. With their population practically cut in half, their original six-month supply, severely rationed, could last for another four or five months at most. They had to get down to the Fourteenth Street Armory to replenish their food supply. Different ideas on ways to do that quickly became a subject of debate. One group wanted to dig out the old IRT tunnel from Fifty-Ninth down to Fourteenth. The other group wanted to dig to the surface and make their way down to Fourteenth, digging into the armory from directly above. Arguments grew more and more heated, until finally, someone suggested they go ask Mayra's advice. But many others immediately responded, if advice was to be asked of anybody, it should be the one who carried the deliverer's child—Yasmine. The fact they were pregnant softened the dreamers' judgment to the degree they again wanted the advice of their old leaders.

Splatter finally healed from the ordeal he shared with Harrison and was delegated to bring up the subject with both of them, but to do it on separate occasions. Yasmine was camped on her couch in the reading area, where as Mayra stayed in her cavern. Now, seven months along, they were both feeling the responsibility inherent in their biological conditions. Mayra slept and Jasmine read, and they rarely spoke to each other, or anyone else, with the exception of Lightning, who looked after both of them.

Splatter went to Mayra first and was very much surprised by her response. She told him that for now she just wanted to focus on having a child, and they should look elsewhere for any guidance. Yasmine's supporters saw this as Mayra's verbal resignation. But to Mayra's supporters, it was interpreted as a message to wait until after she'd given birth. When Splatter asked Yasmine, she thought digging to the surface would be much easier because most of the debris would be the compressed foam of Big New's scrapers. Over their time together, Danner had described the Topgrid burg to her in detail. She said digging down the IRT tunnel would mean going through dirt, rock, sewage pipes, and probably chunks of grid plate. It would take far more time and effort to dig out and transport the debris into Cenpak. It could easily end up taking longer than their food supplies would last. Also, she figured, since the crosstown tunnel at 103rd survived, the Fourteenth shuttle line would still be there too. They could use pictures of the New Jersey skyline from their library to get a fix on Fourteenth Street, then dig down into the shuttle line and use their old entrance into the armory. But Mayra's followers said it would be suicide to expose themselves to whatever madness was going on up on the surface. The debate raged on until a brawl erupted one night, and the Outriders had to step in. They decided to put the matter to a vote. So one evening after dinner in the Duni cavern, they voted, and Yasmine's supporters were victorious. Wanting to reaffirm a connection to their deliverer outweighed all other considerations.

They began cutting to the surface in the Fifty-Ninth tunnel, where the laser cannon for the eastern entrance of the barricade was located at Fifth Avenue. First, they cut a short tunnel up into the southeast corner of Cenpak so they could move the debris quickly from their tunnel into this new storage area. At a certain point, the debris they were pulling out was almost exclusively the pressurized foam of Topgrid scrapers, so they figured they must be getting close to the surface. They decided to stop and drill a small hole to the top, then send up an omnidirectional microphone to listen for any activity in the ruins. They eventually figured out that what they were intermittently hearing were the sounds of packs of dogs still combing the area for the remains of any carcasses. The worm had turned on Topgrid civilization. They'd used up the last of the transport car steel to construct a ladder up through five hundred feet of debris to within thirty feet of the surface.

Now eight and a half months after their conceptions, another miracle occurred. Yasmine and Mayra both gave birth on August 8, 2097. Both of the babies were boys. Mayra named her child Sam.

Yasmine named her child Dan. That night, much to their surprise, the two factions found themselves celebrating in the Duni cavern. With both of them giving birth on the same day, it was a sign. They couldn't help feeling their long night of despair was about to end. They wanted their old leaders to guide them again. Unfortunately, there was still intense disagreement about which one they wanted to lead them. Again, they took a vote. In light of Yasmine's advice to dig to the surface proving to be a wise decision, and the fact she was still the bearer of the deliverer's child, Yasmine's victory was even larger this time. The next morning, they sent Splatter to tell Yasmine they'd succeeded in digging a tunnel to the surface and to make a request: "We want you to lead a reconnaissance mission." Yasmine read it and sat motionless for a time. Lightning, who was always nearby since the beginning of their confinement, was also present at this meeting. Yasmine asked Lightning to get her a pen, paper, and an envelope. After writing a reply, she sealed it in the envelope and told Splatter to open and read it that night after dinner in the Duni cavern. Splatter did as he was requested.

In the next five days, finish digging to the surface. Secure a plate over the opening so it can bear the weight of a man and finish the ladder up to the opening. While the metal of the grid plate is no longer being electrically charged, it should still have magnetic properties. Take one of the E-Mag testers we got from the Topgrid transporter and measure the magnetic power that the ruins are still emitting. If it's strong enough to levitate a levi cycle carrying a rider, then jerry-rig a pulley system onto the ladder that will allow us to bring levi cycles to the surface. I want Dag to accompany me on the mission. Here's what we'll need: two levi cycles, two small levi-loaders to attach to the cycles, frybars, helmets, body armor, night-vision goggles, binoculars, walkie-talkies, three days of rations, and canteens. I want a fully amped E-Mag charger from the Seventy-Eighth garage in each of the Levi-loaders. Also, I'll need a wet nurse to come to the library and take care of Dan while we're away on this mission. I'll meet you at Fifty-Ninth in the IND tunnel at 0700 on the sixth morning from tonight. If the magnetic field being emitted isn't strong enough to lift the cycles, let me know, and I'll send you a different set of instructions.

In the silence that followed Splatter's recitation, they were certain of two things: that they'd picked the right person to proceed, and she was going to be a serious taskmaster. They'd have to work straight through the next five days to fulfill her requirements.

That same night, Yasmine went with Dan into Mayra's cavern. Mayra was nursing Sam. They looked at each other's babies and commiserated about labor and delivery. Finally, Yasmine dived in about their situation.

"Ma, I've been thinking about this a lot over these last few months. I know you believe the truth should always be told, but I'm not so sure anymore. I think sometimes the truth does need husbanding because sometimes the truth gets overwhelmed by the collective need of the moment. That's what happened to us. They needed to have a villain in order to release the fear erupting inside them, so they could find an escape from their desperation . . . There had to be a villain. You saw how quickly they turned on us. I remember the look in their eyes. They had to have someone to blame it on. It was the only way they could pull it together, could struggle on, so their hope didn't die.

"Look at the last Duni before Jack materialized. Their affections are upended by a breeze! An innuendo, a rumor, coming at just the right moment steals them from their supposed conviction. Just catch them off balance in their minds or their hearts, and everything you've shared together disappears. I know you've seen and dealt with it. Sometimes it works what you did then, confronting them, but when the situation turns seriously wrong, they've gotta have someone to blame. I'm sorry if I sound cynical because of what we've been through. I know it's not really them. It's some emotional by-product of trying to live as a community. It betrays them when disaster strikes, turns them into mindless pack animals. I don't hate them for it, but that doesn't mean I don't see it . . . and how wrong-headed it can end up making things."

She made herself look Mayra directly, in the eye. "You are the only villain now. Since the tunnel to the surface is almost finished, they've asked me to lead a recon mission six days from now." She saw the pain in Mayra's eyes and hurried on. "Listen . . . I'm pretty sure I've figured out the way we get to the *Protostar*. I think I'm seeing the sequence of events and the tasks that have to be executed in order to get us there. That's what I'm going to try to do with this mission they're sending me on. You need to be ready to lead them when I get back. Ma, you're the one who's guided us through close to thirty years of discovering who we are. You've channeled the visions that showed us our destiny.

"We are the ones meant to pilot that ship into space, and you are our leader. I want you to prepare to take back what's yours while I'm gone. I don't think it's going to take more than a couple days to find what I'm looking for. You need to prepare an evacuation plan so we can pack what we need and get out of here as quickly as possible. I know you'll want to take all the books. You need to figure out what else we'll need to take. We'll take along enough food supplies to get us through any learning curve, getting things up and running, but I'm sure *Protostar's* stocked with everything we need, so it's more about our history, our time here, when it comes to choosing what we take along. You need to identify those things for us and organize them all to evacuate in an efficient, orderly manner.

"We can deal with their fickle allegiances after I get back. I've got a good idea about how to handle that. I know you're hurt—because I'm hurt, and I'm angry! But honestly, you've taken their doubting shit in the past and risen above it. You need to do that now. I really believe I know how we can get the *Protostar*. But don't tell anybody I've talked to you. They don't know what I've got planned. Six days from now, we're going to start turning all this around."

Looking down at the newborn in her arms, Mayra smiled. "I don't know what to think anymore. Maybe they've finally made me a believer because, I have to be honest with you, what you're saying sounds totally crazy! But I guess it wouldn't hurt anything to fill the time with daydreaming about how to evacuate what's left of our home and be ready to move on . . . while I take care of my little angel. He's such a good baby."

On the morning of the sixth day, they lifted up the plate over the opening, and Yasmine cautiously emerged to take a look around. She was shocked to see a sky. She watched clouds slowly moving across the heavens and, despite standing on a mound of ruins, felt like she'd discovered paradise. She quickly ascertained that neither man or dog was anywhere in the immediate area. Their escape hatch was situated on the plateau of a mountain formed from white and gray rubble shot through with glittering shards of dome. Looking down, the topography was completely changed. There was no trace of their barricade buried somewhere below. The skyline was a range of sparkling monochromatic peaks in every direction with random forests of I-beams jutting through like tarnished steel trees. Dag followed her up onto the surface and, with Yasmine, was awestruck by the view.

"Wow . . . incredible."

Yasmine kneeled by the entrance and took a walkie-talkie from her flak vest. "All clear. Start winching up the cycles and the gear."

Looking around, waiting for the equipment to begin arriving, she was feeling more certain she'd figured it right. The last nine months, she'd been reading all of Danner's "printer manuals," going through the entire shelf they were kept on. She'd sketched out a sequence of certain events and considered the possibilities of them occurring so she could put her plan into action. First, she heard from Lightning that they'd taken her suggestion and were cutting up to the surface. Then she waited to see if the key event had come to pass. When he told her they heard nothing on the surface except occasional packs of dogs, she knew she was on the right track. Splatter came the next day and asked her to lead a recon mission. It was sweet serendipity and about damn time! She was off and running.

Once they had the cycles and the loaders hooked up (with the E-Mag chargers on board), they inventoried the packs on the back of each cycle. They'd checked them below, but it was part of their discipline. Satisfied they had everything, they checked the recharge rods of their frybars again and locked them in their thigh holsters. Mayra took the walkie-talkie from her vest.

"All right, we're all set. We're heading out. Send somebody up here at 2400, and we'll make contact then."

They switched on their cycles and the Levi-loaders. The machines floated up three feet above the rubble. It would be enough. Unfortunately, it meant they'd have to follow the terrain rather than take a straight line to their destination. Yasmine needed to have a talk with Dag before they started.

"Listen, I wanted you on this mission not only because you're an artist with a frybar. I know you're as loyal to Mayra as I am."

She had Dag's complete attention. "We're not going down to Fourteenth and look for the armory right away. We're going to look for other things first and hopefully make our comrades realize they need to put Ma back in charge. Are you okay with that?"

Dag's grin answered before he did. "Yeah! You bet. Where are we headed?"

"We're gonna try and find the remains of the Topgrid's spaceport."

"Great! Lead on, young dreamer."

Yasmine grinned, realizing he'd used Harrison's by-now-famous words to Splatter. They mounted their cycles, losing another six inches from their clearance, and headed south across the plateau. She heard him chuckling behind her.

"Oh, man! This is exciting."

They weaved a path through the valleys and ravines of their surreal landscape, trying to avoid going uphill as much as possible because it took them farther from the weak magnetic field in the remains of the grid plate. By midmorning, they knew they'd reached the southern end of Manhattan. The distinctive spire of the Freedom Tower, now an obelisk to constant conviction, rose above the grid girder's blackened "trees." Knowing its history from their library heartened Yasmine's conviction.

She needed the encouragement because now they were looking down on an even stranger landscape. A landscape in motion: water from the Atlantic Ocean, the Hudson, and East River all colliding in New York Harbor, swirling around metal islands formed out of chunks of grid plate while stirring mountains of white rubble in their cross currents. The chain of "islands" that appeared to provide the safest passage were on top of the crushed Brooklyn Bridge, pounded down to become the pilings on which pieces of grid plate rose up to create a miniature metallic range. But this ridge was broken in two places, and these gaps dropped down directly into the churning debris.

Nothing in Danner's manuals covered the effects of water on the magnetic fields being emitted by any submerged pieces of grid plate. These two major breaks in the chain could leave them with no magnetic field—dropping them into the water.

Unfortunately, the transporter that crashed into Cenpak only carried the civil-service Levi cycles known as Daytrippers and not the Sacker Windvipers. The Sacker cycles used C-power fusion drives for propulsion, but the Daytrippers were completely electric. If they were on Windvipers, they could shoot across the gaps on fusion drive alone.

She did know, vis-à-vis the Meissner effect, that the distance between the two like poles could be maintained, even if one of the poles grew weaker by boosting the power of the other pole. She'd brought along the E-Mag chargers for two reasons: the first was to recharge their cycles if they were unsuccessful finding what she was looking for. They could use them now to compensate for any change in the magnetic field and still have plenty of power left to perform their second purpose. But if there were no submerged pieces of grid plate in either of those two gaps, it wouldn't make any difference— they'd drop like stones. They faced the same problem, multiplied, if they ventured out in any other direction. Then the proverbial lightbulb lit up her brain! She realized if she used the E-Mag chargers full boost on the front E-Mags, it would make the front of the bike come up, like doing a "wheelie" in the twentieth back when cycles had wheels. She'd have to go as fast as she could along the precarious ridge leading up to the jump. Then the cycle would sail into the gap with the front end up, and just as it reached its highest point, she'd switch the boosted front E-Mags to a negative charge. Then the piece of grid plate she was headed for would reach out and grab her front end like a tractor beam pulling the cycle across the gap. It would be a hairy ride, and you'd have to switch the front E-Mags back to positive just before you hit. But it was the way to get across even with no magnetic field below. Yasmine explained her theory to Dag and asked if he thought he could do the maneuver.

"Piece of cake."

She couldn't help shaking her head at his easy male bravado. Dag was a positive fella. Yasmine decided they should plug the cable from the E-Mag charger into to their front E-Mags at low boost before they got started. This would bring their front ends up a little bit and help propel the cycle's diagonal ascent as they made the journey over the precarious ridges of broken grid plate.

They threaded their way carefully out onto the island chain, and she realized this was going to be even more difficult than she'd predicted. They had to stay right over the highest edge of each chunk or have their front end slip to either side, creating an unstable Meissner field, possibly flipping them down into the debris. By the time they reached the first gap, Yasmine was less confident about her brainstorm. But there was no turning back. She estimated it at thirty feet to the other side.

She went first, being sure to wait till the cycle's launch propelled it to its highest midair point before switching the front E-Mags to negative. When the cycle wrenched forward, she kept a fierce grip on the handlebars. Glancing briefly at the churning rubble, she focused on the front E-Mags to make sure they crossed the physical plane of her target before switching them back. While her landing was less than graceful, she had a sure control. Dag came next, getting some impressive height sailing across the gap to land like a ballerina on point. Well, he was leader of the cycle brigade, so she really shouldn't be surprised.

At the second gap, things got a little hairier. It was at least forty feet across. Her front E-Mags crossed the plane of the next chunk by barely an inch. It caused the cycle to recoil hard, upending the rear of the machine and bouncing it, rocking-horse style, for about twenty yards before she wrestled it down. She warned Dag to watch out for a rough landing, but it seemed to have no effect on his performance. His landing was as smooth as the first time around. They finished winding over the metal peaks and finally reached solid rubble on the Brooklyn side. This was where Yasmine planned to take a hard left, heading northeast into Queens, but their journey across the rubble swamp took a lot more time than she'd planned for. It was closing on sunset. She'd hoped, at least, to get into the outskirts of Queens, but they needed to scout out a defensible campsite before it got dark. They picked out a high mound with a small glen of steel beams surrounding its peak and unpacked their field rations. By the time they started to eat, the sun was setting in the distance over the New Jersey waste fill.

The surprise waiting for them when night truly fell was an ocean of glimmering stars. Over a landscape completely devoid of lights, their celestial brilliance overwhelms our aboveground visitors. Though they were both exhausted from the day's adventures, they lay on their backs, watching intently, trying to hang on to consciousness for as long as possible. Dag faded first into a purring snore, and Yasmine was about to follow when, suddenly, she saw an orange object streaking across the sky. She quickly roused herself, scrambling for the binoculars in her pack, adjusting the focus, until it was perfectly circular, trailing an orange tail across the Western Hemisphere. It was the second sign she was hoping for.

The next morning, they got up early, just after sunrise, packed, and headed out again. Here, on what had been the outer edge of the grid plate, there were far less steel beams protruding through the rubble, and most of the pieces of grid plate had dropped straight down with no scrapers upending them. The rubble itself was spread out more evenly too, with fewer hills or valleys. They made good time across the relatively flat chromatic plain. They were about to stop and dig into their field rations when Dag spotted several objects in the distance that jutted up in unusual shapes. They both got out their binoculars and took a closer look. It was what Yasmine hoped to see: a jumble of Satcruisers and other levi vehicles scattered across sections of a completely exposed grid plate. They'd found the Topgrid spaceport. Dag wanted to head for it immediately, but Yasmine checked his impulse.

"Let's break out the energy bars and watch it for a while . . . make sure nobody else is there."

Dag grabbed a couple bars from his pack and tossed one to Yasmine. "Exactly what are we looking for?"

She hesitated to tell him. She hadn't even told Mayra, but if she wanted his help, she had to tell Dag. "I'm hoping to find some Sackers' bodies in those ships. Harrison gave me half of a memory device and told me, if I wanted to use it, I had to find the other half in a Sacker's head."

Dag was suitably shocked by the information. "What's this device supposed to do?"

Yasmine locked eyes with him. "A lot of things . . . It contains everything Harrison knows. With it, we can fly the *Protostar*."

Now his jaw literally sagged, and his eyes kept getting bigger. "Holy shit!"

"It's called a thought recorder, and if I can find the receiver/ transmitter part that snaps together with the data part I already have, then I just make a superficial cut in my scalp above and behind my left temple and slip it in. It attaches to my skull. After that, all I have to do is touch it while thinking about any subject, and what Harrison knows about it starts streaming through my brain."

"Holy shit."

"Yeah."

"Then if we could find a way to get to the *Protostar* ..." Dag paused, overwhelmed by the possibility. "What about Harrison? Do you think maybe he's waiting there?"

"I don't know. I hope so. He would've had to deal with Han. Han wanted to take it for himself."

"Do you think that's what happened?"

"I don't know, but if I can find that piece, I can find out what happened. Harrison kept the transmission piece in his head. It kept sending information to the piece I have. If he stopped Han from stealing it, then the *Protostar* is still up there. I think he stopped Han. I saw something last night. I think it was one of their satellite cities. I think its orbit had degraded, and it was burning up in reentry. Something else happened after Big New fell."

"Oh man, holy shit!"

Yaz nodded toward the strange shapes in the distance. "If I find the other part of the thought recorder, we might even be able to fix one of those ships with what Harrison knows. That's the other reason I wanted you to come with me. Danner mentioned you watched him almost every day while he was assembling the *Firewalker*. I was hoping you paid attention."

Dag's grin was back. "I remember the basic concept of how a fusion drive works and the way C-power components connect into it . . . Yeah, I remember some of that."

Yasmine continued scanning the jumble of ships while they were talking. "Wait a second, we've got company."

Dag stuffed the last of his energy bar in his mouth and grabbed his binoculars. They both watched intently for a while. "Oh yeah, I got 'em. I count three . . . probably Yaks."

"Probably. I think there might be another one in that lean-to that's by that big ship on the far left."

"Wait a second ..." Dag was busy refining his focus. "Yeah, I got it . . . that's a Red Dragon flag next to that lean-to. They've made a claim on that ship, and they're guarding it . . . probably waiting for their techies."

They both lowered their binoculars and looked at each other. Finally, Dag broke the silence.

"How do you think we should take 'em?"

"Tonight. Late tonight. We can get closer on the cycles and then make our final approach on foot."

Suddenly Dag remembered they were supposed to contact Cenpak the night before.

"We forgot to call in last night."

"Yeah, I was never gonna do that. They'll have one guy up keeping guard. They probably all sleep in that lean-to. We'll take turns keeping an eye on them until we're ready to go."

"All right. I'll keep watch first. How come you didn't tell anybody about the thought-recorder?"

"It just seemed very dangerous. Everybody was dealing with our dire situation, going crazy, looking to blame . . . losing faith. It felt too dangerous to talk to anybody about it."

"Yeah, I can see that. Probably was a prudent move."

Yasmine put down her binoculars and surveyed the area right around them. About twenty-five yards in front of them and to their left was a pile of bricks sticking up above the rubble. She guessed it was the remains of a chimney. She tapped Dag's shoulder, and he lowered his binoculars, looking to her questioningly.

"Let's move down behind those bricks just in case they've got binoculars too."

They moved their cycles and Levi-loaders behind the brick pile. Then Yasmine removed her flak vest and spread it on the rubble in a small patch of shade the bricks provided. At a little past noon, the mid-September heat was becoming oppressive.

"I'm going to take a short nap. Wake me in an hour, and I'll spell you."

Dag nodded, the binoculars already back up to his face. Moments later, just as she was drifting off, he nudged her shoulder. "Yaz, our company has some more company."

She grabbed her pair, poking her head above the bricks to focus on the scene six hundred yards beyond them. She saw a vehicle like ones stored in the armory, a troop carrier raising a cloud of white dust behind it, barreling toward the jumble of Topgrid spacecraft.

"Probably those Yak techies they've been waiting for."

Following the vehicle, adjusting her focus as she did, she smiled. "Maybe they'll fix it for us. I count only two in the vehicle and what looks like a bunch of equipment in the back."

"Yeah, I see it. I think you're right. They're here to fix it."

"Let's hope they know their shit."

"What are we gonna do if they fix it quick and take off?"

"Lose. But half the day's already gone, and they've probably had a long ride coming from farther up Long Island. Even if they do fix it quick, which I doubt they will, they'll probably spend the night and take off in the morning." She put her binoculars down again and stretched out in the shade.

"Wake me in an hour."

They watched through the rest of the day, observing the two who'd arrived taking parts they brought on the troop carrier into the large ship at the far left in the grouping of damaged space vehicles. They decided it was probably a transporter, much like the one that crashed in Cenpak. When night fell, they switched to the night-vision binoculars attached to the front of their helmets. They weren't as powerful as their long-range binoculars, but the pit fire the Yaks had burning a few feet from their lean-to made it possible to see all six of them gathered around.

"So do we stick to the original plan?"

Yasmine handed a K-ration packet to Dag. "Yeah, I'm betting the techies will sleep in the back of their vehicle. The Yaks will be in the lean-to, except for the one on watch. Hopefully, he'll make it easy for us and stay by the fire. If we're really lucky, the techies brought some booz with them."

Dag tore open his packet and began munching on the contents. "If we pull this off, are you gonna drive that boat back to Cenpak?"

"If I can find the part I need for the thought recorder, that's exactly what I want to do. That's the other reason I brought the E-Mag chargers. If we place them at full-boost on either side of the ship and put our cycles on full boost at either end, with the residual magnetic charge in the grid plate, we should be able to get off the ground, then take off on fusion drive. At Cenpak, we've still got half a dozen E-Mag chargers to do it again when we take off for *Protostar*. But I need the other part of the thought recorder so I'll know how to fly that thing."

"Can I see it, the part you have?"

Yasmine reached across to her flak vest, unzipped one of its pouches, and pulled out the small black half-circle with its jagged silver edge, holding it up for Dag to inspect.

"Wow. It really is tiny. Harrison's whole mind is inside of that?"

"Yes, and once I get the transmitter part, if I ask about something and close my eyes, I can see it exactly the way he did."

"So you really could run the big ship—the *Protostar*."

"Yes, and I could teach everybody else how to run it too."

"That's how you're gonna get 'em to put Mayra back in charge."

"Yes, but that's not all I want."

Yasmine looked at the young warrior, thinking if she really wanted to reveal right now what she had in mind. She realized, she really did want to discuss it with someone. She'd been keeping her secrets for so long, and she knew Dag didn't have a conniving bone in his body.

"What else do you want?"

"Two things." She watched his eyes. "We're not dreaming anymore . . . he came! It's time to take a new name. My vision that night gave me the inspiration—*Riters*. R-i-t-e-r-s. Riters, as in 'rites of passage,' 'rites of man.' From now on, we call ourselves Riters."

Dag took a moment to reflect. "I like it . . . sounds like people on a cosmic quest. What's the other thing?"

"I want to make it something every house has to do: record their experience of this time in the tunnels, from when he came until we got on the *Protostar*." She grinned at Dag. "And I want them to do it the very old-fashion way, by using a pen and paper in an archives we'll create for future generations."

Dag grinned back. "Well, if you pull it off, your house will have the place of honor in it!"

"No, they won't. My house won't be in it for a hundred years. They have to agree to that too."

Dag was genuinely confused. "Why?"

"I have my reasons. Let's start figuring out how we're gonna hit them."

Dear student of history, wherever you are—squirreled away in our interstellar tin can or sitting out on your deck on some fabulous world a hundred years from now—I must confess, Yasmine's revenge is taking its toll. I'm running on empty here, so moving right along.

Dag and Yasmine attack that night. They kill the three Yaks and take the techies prisoner. They get them to explain the repairs they're doing. Yasmine offers them their lives if they get back on the job and finish the work that night. They agree, starting to head for the transporter, when Dag asks if they've taken any transmitters out of the dead Sackers' heads. One of them replies, "We've got a box of them in the truck." Dag oversees the techies as they work while Yasmine goes through the box, surprised there are several different models. She'll learn later on *Protostar*, the basic difference between a thought recorder and an Appro-recall implant is, with a thought recorder, you had data retention instead of the data being sent to a cloud, then selectively fed back to you (if it's considered appropriate for things running smoothly). Yaz finds the part that fits her piece, and after checking to make sure the repairs are proceeding smoothly, tells Dag to watch them closely. She's going to catch up on the news. Yaz goes out by the fire, just coals at this point, and snaps the transmitter/receiver into her piece, makes the cut just above and behind her left temple, and pushes the complete thought recorder into it. She can feel the tendrils deploying, tapping into her skull, and moving into her brain. What she didn't know at the time was, since the thought recorder's original connection was terminated, when she logged in, it downloaded Yasmine's short-term memory and began recording her thoughts. After watching the coals for some time, she finally touches the spot of her new incision, thinking, *What happened after Han took you?* Yasmine learns what you already know from my previous description.

This brings us to my favorite part since first hearing this account as a young girl. Han Larkill's famous last words: "All right, Jack, time to hop on your String and get the job done."

Han is dead. Darl is dead. Zim is dead. Tooco is dead. Sunsue will die with the passengers and crew when the Satcruiser crashes into

Appro-recall's satellite, which (because of its lower orbit) is a much easier target than Milsat. Han's body is flung from his Levi chair and bounces like a rag doll around the suite. The briefcase bomb is ripped from Han's chair cushion, disappearing in the "five."

The pilot is dead. The copilot is dead. Harrison merges with the Satcruiser guidance system, preparing to outmaneuver Appro-recall's automatic laser cannons. He resets the briefcase bomb, so it detonates on reentry into the third dimension. It is the end of Appro-recall and, within a matter of weeks, all the mindless souls in satellites and their enclaves on the planet. Maddened with no direction from the outside, or any experience or memory of direction from within, terror overwhelmed them.

The program that resulted in the creation of these beings, "Appropriate Recall," was designed by a human mind and, at least initially, installed by human hands. The machines never woke up, never staged a digital revolution. They just did what machines do: executed their programs. And they were programed by humans, relentlessly pursuing the ideal of ease and effortlessness.

So . . . riddle me this, dear students of history (yes, at some point, we all get bored enough to watch the ancient vids aboard *Protostar*), give me one other believable scenario whereby four hundred and twenty people escape from their rat hole to pilot the technological vanguard known as *Protostar*. Just one, give me *one*! Get this straight. Mayra sparked the Duni fires, and they lit the way, *the only way* to that miracle happening. Albeit, with the flame's penchant for surprise.

That's why Yasmine was true to Mayra because she knew Mayra was wise, even if, for a while at the end, Mayra, too lost heart. Mayra had already taught her with the example of her life when apparent justice and higher purpose lie smoking in the ruins, faith has to outstrip understanding for dreams to thrive . . . which brings us to the mystery of my great-grandmother and why she did what she did . . . chaining her progeny to four generations of silence, on the matter.

When Yasmine piloted the Sat transporter back to their escape hatch in the sea of white rubble, she left Dag on board with instructions to guard the ship until Outriders came up and relieved him. Then she climbed back down and went immediately to the Duni cavern. It was early morning, and most of the dreamers were having breakfast. She walked right into the Duni pit, stood in the ashes at its center, and told them to gather everyone there, except Mayra. She had something important to tell them. When she was certain everyone was present, this is what she said:

"At this moment, right outside, is waiting our deliverance to a new world. It's there because Harrison gave me a part of a tiny device called a thought recorder. He told me when I found the other piece, I could put it into my head, and I would have all the knowledge and experience he possessed at my command." Here, she lifted her hair to expose the incision she'd made. First, I asked for the access code to the auto-pilot on board Protostar. Then I used a Sat-transporter we found in the ruins of Big New to try to contact Protostar—It's up there waiting for us!

"And using the thought-recorder, I was able to fly that Sat-transporter, here. A ship that's as big as the one that crashed in Cenpak. It's here above us now! Dag is guarding it at the entrance to our escape tunnel." Looking around the crowd, she spotted Lightning and addressed him directly.

"It would probably be a good idea if some Outriders gave him a hand."

Lightning made a quick gesture to one lieutenant, and several Outriders made a sudden exit.

"Harrison is dead. He had to die to fulfill our destiny. It's the only way he could make it happen. That's why he had to leave. It's why I'm left here to tell you this. But I'm not going to tell you how he did it . . . although I know. And I'm not going to tell you whether Han was his friend or his foe, although I know that as well. You're going to need to figure that out for yourselves. You need to figure out everything for yourself. I am going to tell my child what happened when our deliverer materialized out of thin air, right here in this Duni cavern. He's going to know everything about Harrison and the decisions he made and why he made them, and he's going to tell his children about

494

the decisions that ultimately brought us to this moment, right now, with our deliverance at hand. But they're not going to tell you either. Not for a hundred years. Mark my words. They will keep my word for a hundred years. And if you want an explanation for that, here it is . . . *you pissed me off.*

"You came to believe because of our visions in the Duni, visions Mayra gave us, that you were the chosen ones, chosen to survive mankind's destruction of this planet and himself—because you embodied the true ideals of civilization! The truth is, we just happen to be the only ones left who barely aspired to keeping those ideals alive. If you doubt that, I invite you to examine your behavior over these past few months since permanent disaster *apparently* befell us. We have a very long journey ahead of us, and I promise you, I will give you all of Harrison's knowledge about how to run and maintain that great ship, which will, in time, take us to a new world where mankind can try it again. But in the meantime, you'd each better learn how to think for yourselves and teach your children how to do the same . . . because, otherwise, it's going to turn out the same way it did, this time with a bunch of self-serving pack animals calling the shots with the destiny of all mankind.

"And with that in mind, I want you to know, if you want me to fly that ship up to *Protostar*, you all have to agree to renounce the moniker 'dreamers of Cenpak.' This was given to me in the vision I was having when Harrison arrived that night. From now on, we are *Riters*—R-i-t-e-r-s—as in rites of passage, rites of man, and eventually, if we're really dedicated to discovering them, *rites of civilization.*

"Now I'm going to go up and ask Ma if she can find it in her heart to forgive us for forgetting everything she gave us and taught us because we all got scared again! And I'm going to beg her to lead me again. And hopefully, I can convince her to come down here and give you a chance to do the same. I'm going back to the ship now and wait for Ma's orders."

With that, Yasmine stepped from the ashes and went to see Mayra. She told her about the ship and addressing them all. She told Mayra, when their apologies satisfied her, she should put her evacuation plan into action. She said she'd be in the pilot's cabin, ready to fly them to *Protostar* on her command. Then she took her son, Dan, and a couple duffs of personal things up to the ship. Lightning came up from the Duni cavern and told Mayra, word for word, what Yasmine said. He told her everyone wanted to apologize. It took a while, but she did come down, after several emissaries (culminating with Splatter) made her realize she was still "Ma," and they needed her.

That dangerous night when everyone turned on them, Yasmine's faith in mankind's innate goodness was put to the test, and she lost a portion of it permanently. She would never again trust in the constancy of her fellow beings. While she did still love them, she no longer wanted their affection. It was from their scorn that she found the strength to pursue Harrison's mission. But she was tireless in sharing Harrison's knowledge with them, explaining eighteen hours a day to anyone and everyone who had a question. And there were a billion questions that needed answering and an education to be supplied, learning how to master the Topgrid's technology. Her son was the only one she shared her feelings with. And later, when he had a family of his own, she made them all swear to keep her secret before she let them hear everything that really happened. Eventually, listening to Harrison's personal account of his journey from beginning to end became an annual secret rite of their house.

After relentless petitioning by Mayra, Yasmine agreed for the sake of Harrison's legacy to let them know about the beginnings of his awakening, but she would only reveal that journey as far as Harrison getting sent to the mines. Now she got the second thing, she'd told Dag she wanted. She made it a condition for sharing this much of Harrison's account that Splatter must create the "Riters Archive" and have every family that lived through his coming pick one family member to record (in cursive), with pen and paper, their family's memories of their experience of it. Splatter asked her why the necessity to do it in such a tedious and archaic fashion, and Yasmine told him to consider it a rite to the effort made by all mankind from their very beginnings:

to communicate their experience to the generations who come after them . . . and because they pissed her off.

She kept her heart in the bosom of family and was an "impersonal fount" of Harrison's knowledge with everyone else until the day she died, when she charged them one last time to keep her word for a hundred years. And they had. A hundred years was up today, and though her hand was a swollen knot of agony, Dysan was honored to be the one who finally set the record straight and freed them from their burden. She understood Yasmine's purpose in withholding the information. She knew it would make them have to think for themselves about what happened, make them argue and conjecture. The pack animal she'd faced that night in the cavern, one malicious beast with eight hundred eyes—comrades she'd known all her life—suddenly turned into this alien monster. She wanted to make them incapable of ever turning into that again. Her hope was that the continued examination of themselves and their behavior would foster an awareness that inoculated them from their pack-animal madness.

But the reason she was so intransigent—turning her back on personal relations with any of them—went deeper. Yasmine, much more than they did, felt the terrible loss of their deliverer. Though it was incredibly brief, still she made a deep personal connection, and so did Harrison. They both felt the quickening of their souls in those brief hours together. She, much more than all the rest of them, was overwhelmed by his loss. Yet she didn't allow herself to focus on this or let the pain she was feeling consume her. No. Yasmine kept her mind focused on getting at the truth of what happened so the dreamers could find a way through this—so they could struggle to find a way to deal with this wrenching, horrific loss, a way to respond and even hope to overcome it. She was desperate to think of some way they could dig themselves out of this catastrophe!

And in the face of this remarkable selfless service, she was met with total rejection and murderous hatred. And the fact that not one of them ever stopped and thought about her loss, never offered any condolences . . . after that, she never again shared anything personal about Harrison with any of them.

And Dysan, even though she knew she was still "wet behind the ears," felt a kinship with her great-grandmother that gave her an intuitive insight into Yasmine's resolution. Yasmine was the real deal when it came to being a seeker. And those are the last people on Earth, or off it, whose hearts you should ever consider inconsequential. They will hold you accountable for that.

He was past initial defenses now, honing on his heart of darkness. Soon Harrison would start to rant. At their annual rite, her mother always cut it off here. She said it wouldn't reflect well on his legacy if Dysan included it now. But she suddenly remembered what she was going to face when she left this confessional—a heartache not unlike Yasmine's. Why not take a few more moments before stepping into that corridor and learning Shuta was gone? Let great-granddad rant. After everything he did for us, he deserves the consideration.

THE END

EPILOGUE

December 25, 2096

"COME AND GET ME, CAPPERS!

"YOU GOTTA BE FASTER THAN THAT! YOU GOTTA BE A LOT FASTER!"

"NEW BLOOD! What are you doing? GAME OVER, CLONIE!" "Weird coke—you can't lean on stars!"

"PRETTY COCKY SMILE, MOTHERDUFFER!"